THE DR

Peter F. Hamilton was born in Rutland in 1960, and still lives near Rutland Water. He began writing in 1987 and sold his first short story to *Fear* magazine in 1988. He has also been published in *Interzone* and the *In Dreams* and *New Worlds* anthologies, and in several small-press publications. His previous novels are the Greg Mandel series: *Mindstar Rising*, *A Quantum Murder* and *The Nano Flower*, and the bestselling Night's Dawn trilogy: *The Reality Dysfunction*, *The Neutronium Alchemist* and *The Naked God*. Also published by Macmillan (and Pan) are *A Second Chance at Eden*, a novella and six short stories set in the same brilliantly realized universe, and *The Confederation Handbook*, a vital guide to the Night's Dawn trilogy. His most recent novels are *Fallen Dragon*, *Misspent Youth*, *Pandora's Star* and *Judas Unchained*.

Also by Peter F. Hamilton

The Greg Mandel series

Mindstar Rising

A Quantum Murder

The Nano Flower

The Night's Dawn trilogy

The Reality Dysfunction

The Neutronium Alchemist

The Naked God

In the same timeline

A Second Chance at Eden

The Confederation Handbook
(a vital guide to the Night's Dawn trilogy)

Fallen Dragon

Misspent Youth

The Commonwealth Saga

Pandora's Star

Judas Unchained

Peter F. Hamilton

THE DREAMING VOID

PART ONE OF THE VOID TRILOGY

PAN BOOKS

First published 2007 by Macmillan

First published in paperback 2008 by Pan Books
an imprint of Pan Macmillan Ltd
Pan Macmillan, 20 New Wharf Road, London N1 9RR
Basingstoke and Oxford
Associated companies throughout the world
www.panmacmillan.com

ISBN 978-0-330-44302-9

9 8 7 6 5 4 3 2 1

A CIP catalogue record for this book is available from
the British Library.

Typeset by SetSystems Ltd, Saffron Walden, Essex
Printed and bound in the U K by
CPI Mackays, Chatham ME5 8TD

THE DREAMING VOID

Prologue

The starship *CNE Caragana* slipped down out of a night sky, its grey and scarlet hull illuminated by the pale iridescence of the massive ion storms which beset space for lightyears in every direction. Beneath the deep-space vessel, Centurion Station formed a twinkling crescent of light on the dusty rock surface of its never-named planet. Crew and passengers viewed the enclave of habitation with a shared sensation of relief. Even with the hyperdrive powering them along at fifteen lightyears an hour, it had taken eighty-three days to reach Centurion Station from the Greater Commonwealth. This was about as far as any human travelled in the mid-thirty-fourth century, certainly on a regular basis.

From his couch in the main lounge, Inigo studied the approaching alien landscape with a detached interest. What he was seeing was exactly as the briefing files projected months ago, a monotonous plain of ancient lava rippled with shallow gullies that led nowhere. The thin argon atmosphere stirred the sand in short-lived flurries, chasing wispy swirls from one dune to another. It was the station which claimed his real attention.

Now they were only twenty kilometres from the ground the lights began to resolve into distinct shapes. Inigo could easily pick out the big garden dome at the centre of the human section on the northernmost segment of the inhabited crescent. A lambent emerald circle, playing hub to a dozen black transport tubes that ran out to large accommodation blocks which could have been transplanted from any exotic environment resort in the Commonwealth. From those the tubes carried on across the lava to the cube-like observatory facilities and engineering support modules.

The pocked land to the south belonged to the alien habitats; shapes and structures of various geometries and sizes, most of them illuminated. Next to the humans were the silver bubbles of the hominoid Golant; followed by the enclosed grazing grounds where the Ticoth roamed amid their food herds; then came the mammoth interconnecting tanks of the Suline, an aquatic species. The featureless Ethox tower rose up ten kilometres past the end of the Suline's metal-encased lakes, dark in the visible spectrum but with a surface temperature of 180 degrees C. They were one of the species which didn't interact with their fellow observers on any level except for formal exchanges of data concerning the probes which orbited the Void. Equally taciturn were the Forleene, who occupied five big domes of murky crystal that glowed with a mild gentian light. And they were positively social compared to the Kandra, who lived in a simple metal cube thirty metres to a side. No Kandra ship had ever landed there since the humans joined the observation two hundred and eighty years ago; not even the exceptionally long-lived Jadradesh had seen one, and the Raiel had invited those boulder-like swamp-dwellers to join the project seven thousand years earlier.

A small smile flickered on Inigo's face as he took in all the diverse zones. It was impressive to see so many aliens physically gathered in one place, a collection which served to underline the importance of their mission. Though as his view strayed out to the shadows thrown by the station, he had to admit that the living were completely overshadowed by those who had passed on before them. Centurion Station's growth and age could be loosely measured in the same way as any humble terrestrial tree. It had developed in rings which had been added to over the centuries as new species had joined the project. The broad circle of land along the concave side of the crescent was studded with ruins, crumbling skeletons of habitats abandoned millennia ago as their sponsoring civilizations fell, or moved on, or evolved away from mere astrophysical concerns. Right at the centre the ancient structures had decayed to simple mounds of compacted metal and crystal flakes, beyond the ability of any archaeologist to decipher. Dating expeditions had established that this ancient heart of the station had been constructed over four-hundred-thousand years ago. Of course, as far as the timescale of the Raiel observation was concerned, that was still short.

A ring of green light was flashing on the lava field which served as a spaceport for the human section, calling down the *CNE Caragana*. Several starships were sitting on the drab rock beside the active landing zone; two hefty deep-space vessels of the same class as the *Caragana*, and some smaller starships used for placing and servicing the remote probes that constantly monitored the Void.

There was a slight judder as the starship settled, then the internal gravity field switched off. Inigo felt himself rise slightly on the couch's cushioning as the planet's seventy per cent gravity took over. It was silent in the lounge as the passengers took stock, then a happy murmur of conversation broke out to celebrate arrival. The chief steward asked everyone to make their way down to the main airlock, where they would suit up and walk over to the station. Inigo waited until his more eager colleagues had left before climbing cautiously to his feet and making his way out of the lounge. Strictly speaking, he didn't need a spacesuit, his Higher biononics could cocoon his body in perfect safety, protecting it from the thin malignant atmosphere, and even from the cosmic radiation that sleeted in from the massive stars of the Wall five hundred lightyears away. But . . . he'd travelled all this way partly to escape his unwanted heritage, now was not the time to show it off. He started suiting up along with the rest.

The handover party was a long tradition at Centurion Station. Every time a Navy ship arrived bringing new observers there was a short overlap before the previous group departed. It was celebrated in the garden dome as a sunset gala with the best buffet the culinary unit programs could produce. Tables were laid out under ancient oaks that glittered with hundreds of magic lanterns, and the dome overhead wore a halo of gold twilight. A solido projection of a string quartet played classical mood music on a little stage surrounded by a brook.

Inigo arrived quite early on, still adjusting the sleeves of his ultra-black formal evening suit. He didn't really like the jacket's long square-cut tails, they were a bit voguish for his taste, but had to admit the tailor back on Anagaska had done a superb job. Even today, if you wanted true quality clothes you needed a human in the style and fitting loop. He knew he looked good in it; in fact good enough that he didn't feel even remotely self-conscious.

The station's director was greeting all the arrivals personally. Inigo joined the end of the short line and waited his turn. He could see several aliens milling round the tables. The Golant, looking odd in clothes that approximated to the ones worn by humans. With their grey-blue skin and tall narrow heads, the polite attempt to blend in only made them appear even more out of place. There were a couple of Ticoth curled up together on the grass, both the size of ponies, though there any further resemblance ended. These were very obviously predator carnivores, with dark-green hide stretched tight over powerful muscle bands. Alarmingly big and sharp teeth appeared every time they growled at each other and the group of humans they were conversing with. Inigo instinctively checked his integral force-field function, then felt shameful for having done so. Several Suline were also present, floating about in big hemispherical glass tanks like giant champagne saucers that were held up by small regrav units. Their translators babbled away while they looked out at the humans, their bulbous bodies distorted and magnified by the curving glass.

'Inigo, I presume,' the director's overloud voice proclaimed. 'Glad to meet you; and you're bright and early for the party, as well, most commendable, laddy.'

Inigo smiled with professional deference as he shook the tall man's hand. 'Director Eyre,' he acknowledged. The briefing file's CV had told him very little about the director, other than claiming his age was over a thousand years.

Inigo suspected corrupted data, although the director's clothing was certainly historical enough; a short jacket and matching kilt with a very loud amethyst and black tartan.

'Oh please, call me Walker.'

'Walker?' Inigo queried.

'Short for LionWalker. Long story. Not to worry, laddy. Won't bore you with it tonight.'

'Ah. Right.' Inigo held his gaze level. The director had a thick stock of brown hair, but something glittered underneath it, as if his scalp was crawling with gold flecks. For the second time in five minutes Inigo held off using biononics; a field scan would have revealed what kind of technology the director was enriched with, it certainly wasn't one he recognized. He had to admit, the hair made LionWalker Eyre look youthful; just like the majority of the human race these days, no matter what branch – Higher, Advancer, Natural – vanity was pretty much uniform. But the thin grey goatee lent him an air of distinction, and cultivating that was very deliberate.

LionWalker waved his whisky tumbler across the darkened parkland, ice cubes chittering at the movement. 'So what brings you to our celebrated outpost, then, young Inigo? Thinking of the glory? The riches? Lots of sex? After all, there's not much else to do here.'

Inigo's smile tightened slightly as he realized just how drunk the director was. 'I just wanted to help. I think it's important.'

'Why?' The question was snapped out, accompanied by narrowed eyes.

'Okay. The Void is a mystery that is beyond even ANA to unravel. If we can ever figure it out we will have advanced our understanding of the universe by a significant factor.'

'Huh. Do yourself a favour, laddy, forget ANA. Bunch of decadent aristos who've been mentally taxidermied. Like they care what happens to physical humans. It's the Raiel we're helping, a people who are worth a bit of investment. And even those galumphing masterminds are stumped. You know what the Navy engineers found when they were excavating the foundations for this very garden dome?'

'No.'

'More ruins.' LionWalker took a comfortable gulp of whisky.

'I see.'

'No you don't. They were practically fossilized, nothing more than dust strata, over three quarters of a million years old. And from what I've picked up, looking at the early records the Raiel deign to make available, the observation has been going on a lot longer than that. A million years pecking away at a problem. Now that's dedication for you. We'd no be able to manage that, far too petty.'

'Speak for yourself.'

'Ah, I might have known, a believer.'

'In what?'

'Humanity.'

'That must be pretty common among the staff here, surely?' Inigo was wondering how to disengage himself, the director was starting to irritate him.

'Damn right, laddy. One of the few things that keeps me all cheered up out here all by my wee lonesome. Och ... here we go.' LionWalker tipped his head back, and stared out across the dome where the low layer of hazy light faded away. Overhead, the crystal was completely transparent, revealing the vast antagonistic nebulas that washed across the sky. Hundreds of stars shone through the glowing veil, spikes of light so intense they burned towards violet and into indigo. They multiplied towards the horizon as the planet spun slowly to face the Wall, that vast barrier of massive stars which formed the outermost skin of the galactic core.

'We can't see the Void from here, can we?' Inigo asked. He knew it was a stupid question. The Void was obscured on the other side of the Wall, right at the very heart of the galaxy. Centuries ago, before anyone had even ventured out of Earth's solar system, human astronomers had thought it was a massive black hole, they'd even detected X-ray emissions from the vast loop of superheated particles spinning round the event horizon, which helped confirm their theories. It wasn't until Wilson Kime captained the Commonwealth Navy ship *Endeavour* in the first successful human circumnavigation of the galaxy in 2560 that the truth was discovered. There was indeed an impenetrable event horizon at the core, but it didn't surround anything as natural and mundane as a superdense mass of dead stars. The Void was an artificial boundary guarding a legacy billions of years old. The Raiel claimed there was an entire universe inside, one that had been fashioned by a race that lived during the dawn of the galaxy. They had retreated into it to consummate their journey to the absolute pinnacle of evolution. In their wake, the Void was now slowly consuming the remaining stars in the galaxy. In that it was no different from the natural black holes found anchoring the centre of many galaxies; but while they employed gravity and entropy to pull in mass, the Void actively devoured stars. It was a process that was slowly yet inexorably accelerating. Unless it was stopped, the galaxy would die young, maybe three or four billion years before its allotted time. Far enough in the future that Sol would be a cold ember and the human race not even a memory. But the Raiel cared. This was the galaxy they were born in, and they believed it should be given the chance to live its full life.

LionWalker gave a little snort of amusement. 'No, of course you can't see it. Don't panic, laddy, there's no visible nightmare in our skies. DF7 is rising, that's all.' He pointed.

Inigo waited, and after a minute an azure crescent drifted up over the horizon. It was half the size of Earth's moon, with a strangely regular black mottling. He let out a soft breath of admiration.

There were fifteen of the planet-sized machines orbiting within the Centurion Station star system. Nests of concentric lattice spheres, each one possessing a different mass property and quantum field intersection, with the outer shell roughly the same diameter as Saturn. They were Raiel-built; a 'defence system' in case a Void devourment phase broke through the Wall. No one had ever seen them in action, not even the Jadradesh.

'Okay. That is impressive,' Inigo said. The DFs were in the files, of course. But a machine on that scale and head-on real was awesome.

'You'll fit in,' LionWalker declared happily. He slapped a hand on Inigo's shoulder. 'Go find yourself a drink. I made sure we had the very best culinary programs for alcohol synthesis. You can take that as a challenge.' He moved on to the next arrival.

Keeping one eye on DF7, Inigo made his way over to the bar. LionWalker wasn't kidding, the drinks were top quality, even the vodka that fountained up through the mermaid ice sculpture.

Inigo stayed at the party longer than he expected to. There was something about being thrown together with a bunch of like-minded devoted people that instinctively triggered his normally dormant social traits. By the time he finally got back to his apartment his biononics had been deflecting alcohol infiltration of his neurones for several hours. Even so, he permitted some to percolate through his artificial defences, enough to generate a mild inebriation and all the associated merits. He was going to have to live with these people for another year. No advantage in appearing aloof.

As he crawled into bed he ordered a complete de-saturation. That was one superb benefit of biononics: no hangover.

And so Inigo dreamed his first dream at Centurion Station. It wasn't his.

1

Aaron spent the whole day mingling with the faithful of the Living Dream movement in Golden Park's vast plaza, eavesdropping on their restless talk about the succession, drinking water from the mobile catering stalls, trying to find some shade from the searing sun as the heat and coastal humidity rose relentlessly. He thought he remembered arriving at daybreak; certainly the expanse of marble cobbles had been virtually empty as he walked across it. The tips of the splendid white metal pillars surrounding the area had all been crowned with rose-gold light as the local star rose above the horizon. He'd smiled round appreciatively at the outline of the replica city, matching up the topography surrounding Golden Park with the dreams he'd gathered from the gaiafield over the last ... well, for quite some time. Golden Park had started to fill up rapidly after that, with the faithful arriving from the other districts of Makkathran2 across the canal bridges and ferried in by a fleet of gondolas. By midday there must have been close to a hundred thousand of them. They all faced the Orchard Palace which sprawled possessively over the Anemone district on the other side of the Outer Circle Canal like a huddle of high dunes. And there they waited and waited with badly disguised impatience for the Cleric Council to come to a decision. Any sort of decision. The Council had been in conclave for three days now, how long could they possibly take to elect a new Conservator?

At one point in the morning he'd edged his way right up beside the Outer Circle Canal, close to the central wire and wood bridge that arched over to Anemone. It was closed, of course, as were the other two bridges on that section; while in ordinary times anyone from ultra-devout to curious tourist could cross over and wander round the vast Orchard Palace, today it had been sealed off by fit-looking junior Clerics who had undergone a lot of muscle enrichment. Camped out to one side of the temporarily forbidden bridge were hundreds of journalists from all over the Greater Commonwealth, most of them outraged by the stubborn refusal of Living Dream to leak information their way. They were easily identifiable by their chic modern clothes, and faces which were obviously maintained at peak gloss by a membrane of cosmetic scales; not even Advancer DNA produced complexions that good.

Behind them the bulk of the crowd buzzed about discussing their favourite candidate. If Aaron was judging the mood correctly, then just about ninety-five per cent of them were rooting for Ethan. They wanted him because they were done with waiting, with patience, with the status quo preached by all the other lacklustre caretakers since the Dreamer himself, Inigo, had slipped away from public life. They wanted someone who would bring their whole movement to that blissful moment of fulfilment they'd been promised from the moment they'd tasted Inigo's first dream.

Some time in the afternoon Aaron realized the woman

was watching him. Nothing obvious, she wasn't staring or following him about. Instinct smoothly clicked his awareness to her location – which was an interesting trait to know he had. From then on he was conscious of where she would casually wander in order to keep an easy distance between them, how she would never have her eyes in his direction when he glanced at her. She wore a simple short-sleeved rusty-orange top and knee-length blue trousers of some modern fabric. A little different from the faithful who tended to wear the more primitive rustic clothes of wool, cotton, and leather which were favoured by Makkathran's citizens, but not contemporary enough to be obvious. Nor did her looks make her stand out. She had a flattish face and a cute-ish button nose; some of the time her slim copper shades were across her eyes, while often she had them perched up in her short dark hair. Her age was unknowable, like everyone in the Greater Commonwealth her appearance was locked into biological mid-twenties. He was certain she was well past her first couple of centuries. Again, no tangible proof.

After they'd played the orbiting satellites game for forty minutes he walked over, keeping his smile pleasant. There were no pings coming off her that his macrocellular clusters could detect, no active links to the unisphere, nor any active sensor activity. Electronically, she was as Stone Age as the city.

'Hello,' he said.

She pushed her shades up with the tip of a finger and gave him a playful grin. 'Hello yourself. So what brings you here?'

'This is a historic event.'

'Quite.'

'Do I know you?' His instinct had been right, he saw; she was nothing like the placid faithful shuffling round them, her body language was all wrong; she could keep tight control of herself, enough to fool anyone without his training – *training?* – but he could sense the attitude coiled up inside.

'Should you know me?'

He hesitated. There was something familiar about her face, something he should know about her. He couldn't think what, for the simple reason that he didn't have any memories to pull up and examine. Not of anything, now he thought about it, certainly he didn't seem to have had a life prior to today. He knew that was all wrong, yet that didn't bother him either. 'I don't recall.'

'How curious. What's your name?'

'Aaron.'

Her laughter surprised him. 'What?' he asked.

'Number one, eh? How lovely.'

Aaron's answering grin was forced. 'I don't understand.'

'If you wanted to list terrestrial animals where would you start?'

'Now you've really lost me.'

'You'd start with the aardvark. Double A, it's top of the list.'

'Oh,' he mumbled. 'Yeah, I get it.'

'Aaron,' she chuckled. 'Someone had a sense of humour when they sent you here.'

'Nobody sent me.'

'Really?' She arched a thick eyebrow. 'So you just sort of found yourself at this historic event, did you?'

'That's about it, yes.'

She dropped the copper band back down over her eyes,

and shook her head in mock-dismay. 'There are several of us here, you know. I don't believe that's an accident, do you?'

'Us?'

Her hand gestured round at the crowd. 'You don't count yourself as one of these sheep, do you? A believer? Someone who thinks they can find a life at the end of these dreams Inigo so generously gifted to the Commonwealth?'

'I suppose not, no.'

'There's a lot of people watching what happens here. It's important, after all, and not just for the Greater Commonwealth. If there's a Pilgrimage into the Void some species claim it could trigger a devourment phase which will bring about the end of the galaxy. Would you want that to happen, Aaron?'

She was giving him a very intent stare. 'That would be a bad thing,' he temporized. 'Obviously.' In truth he had no opinion. It wasn't something he thought about.

'Obvious to some, an opportunity to others.'

'If you say so.'

'I do.' She licked her lips with mischievous amusement. 'So, are you going to try for my unisphere code? Ask me out for a drink?'

'Not today.'

She pouted fulsomely. 'How about unconditional sex, then, any way you like it?'

'I'll bank that one, too, thanks,' he laughed.

'You do that.' Her shoulders moved up in a slight shrug. 'Goodbye, Aaron.'

'Wait,' he said as she turned away. 'What's your name?'

'You don't want to know me,' she called out. 'I'm bad news.'

'Goodbye, Bad News.'

There was a genuine smile on her face as she looked back at him. A finger wagged. 'That's what I remember best,' she said, and was gone.

He smiled at the rear of her rapidly departing head. She vanished quickly enough amid the throng; after a minute even he couldn't spot her. He'd seen her originally because she wanted him to, he realized.

Us, she'd said, *there are several of us here.* That didn't make a lot of sense. But then she'd stirred up a lot of questions. *Why am I here?* he wondered. There was no solid answer in his mind other than it was the right place for him to be, he wanted to see who was elected. *And the memories, why don't I have any memories of anything else?* It ought to bother him, he knew, memories were the fundamental core of human identity, yet even that emotion was lacking. Strange. Humans were emotionally complex entities, yet he didn't appear to be; but he could live with it, something deep inside him was sure he'd solve the mystery of himself eventually. There was no hurry.

Towards late afternoon the crowd began to thin out as the announcement remained obstinately unforthcoming. Aaron could see disappointment on the faces moving past him on their way home, a sentiment echoed by the whispers of emotion within the local gaiafield. He opened his mind to the thoughts surrounding him, allowing them to wash in through the gateway which the gaiamotes had germinated inside his cerebellum. It was like walking through a fine mist of spectres, bestowing the plaza with flickers of unreal colour, images of times long gone yet remembered fondly; sounds muffled, as experienced through fog. His recollection of when he'd joined the gaiafield community was as hazy as the rest of his time before today, it didn't seem like the kind of thing he would do, too whimsical. Gaiafield was for adolescents who considered the multisharing of dreams and emotions to be deep and profound, or fanatics like Living Dream. But he was proficient enough with the concept of voluntarily shared thoughts and memories to grasp a coherent sensation from his exposure to the raw minds in the plaza. Of course, if it could be done anywhere it would be here in Makkathran2, which Living Dream had made the capital of the Greater Commonwealth's gaiafield – with all the contradictions that threw up. To the faithful, the gaiafield was almost identical to the genuine telepathy which the citizens of the real Makkathran possessed.

Aaron felt their sorrow first-hand as the day began to wind down, with several stronger undercurrents of anger directed at the Cleric Council. In a society where you shared thoughts and feelings, so the consensus went, an election really shouldn't be so difficult. He also perceived their subliminal wish slithering through the gaiafield: Pilgrimage. The one true hope of the whole movement.

Despite the regret now gusting around him, Aaron stayed where he was. He didn't have anything else to do. The sun had almost fallen to the horizon when there was some movement on the broad balcony along the front of the Orchard Palace. All across the plaza, people suddenly smiled and pointed. There was a gentle yet urgent movement towards the Outer Circle Canal. Security force fields along the side of the water expanded, cushioning those shoved up against the railings as the pressure of bodies increased behind them. Various news company camera pods zoomed through the air like glitter-black festival balloons, adding to the thrill. Within seconds the mood in the plaza had lifted to fiery anticipation; the gaiafield suddenly crackled with excitement, its intensity rising until Aaron had to withdraw slightly to avoid being deluged by the clashing storms of colour and ethereal shouts.

The Cleric Council marched solemnly out on to the balcony, fifteen figures wearing full length scarlet and black robes. And in their centre was a lone figure whose robe was a dazzling white, edged in gold, the hood pulled forward to obscure the face inside. The dying sun glowed against the soft cloth, creating a nimbus around him. A huge cheer went up from the crowd. Camera pods edged in as close to the balcony as their operators dared; Palace force fields rippled in warning, keeping them back. As one, the Cleric Council reached out into the gaiafield with their minds; unisphere access followed swiftly, making the grand announcement available right across the Greater Commonwealth to followers and nullifidians alike.

In the middle of the balcony, the white-robed figure reached up and slowly pushed back the hood. Ethan smiled beatifically out across the city and its adulating faithful. There was a kindness about his thin solemn face which suggested he was attuned to all their fears; he sympathized and understood. Everyone could see the dark bags under his eyes which could only come from the burden of accepting such a terrible high office, of carrying the expectations of every Dreamer. As his face was exposed to the rich sunlight so the cheering down in the plaza had increased. Now the other members of the Cleric Council turned towards the new Cleric Conservator, and applauded contentedly.

Without conscious intervention, the ancillary thought

routines operating inside Aaron's macrocellular clusters animated his ocular zoom. He scanned along the faces of the Cleric Council, designating each image with an integral code as the ancillary routines slotted them into macrocellular storage lacunas ready for instant recall. Later he would study them for any betraying emotion, an indicator of how they had argued and voted.

He hadn't known he had the zoom function, which piqued his curiosity. At his request the secondary thought routines ran a systems check through the macrocellular clusters enriching his nervous system. Exoimages and mental icons unfolded from neutral status to standby in his peripheral vision, lines of shifting iridescence bracketing his natural sight. The exoimages were all default symbols generated by his u-shadow, the personal interface with the unisphere which would instantly connect him to any of its massive data, communication, entertainment, and commerce functions. All standard stuff.

However, the mental icons he examined represented a great deal more than the standard physiological enrichments which Advancer DNA placed at the disposal of a human body; if he was reading their summaries correctly he was enriched with some extremely lethal biononic field function weaponry.

I know something else about me, he thought, *I have an Advancer heritage.* It was hardly a revelation, eighty per cent of Greater Commonwealth citizens had similar modifications sequenced into their DNA thanks to the old fanatic genetic visionaries on Far Away. But having biononics as well narrowed the scope fractionally, putting Aaron closer to his true origin.

Ethan raised his hands in an appeal for silence. The

plaza fell quiet as the faithful held their breath, even the babble from the media pack was stilled. A sensation of serenity coupled with steely resolution issued out of the new Cleric Conservator into the gaiafield. Ethan was a man who was sure of his purpose.

'I thank my fellow Councillors for this magnificent honour,' Ethan said. 'As I begin my tenure I will do what I believe our Dreamer wanted. He showed us the way – nobody can deny that. He showed us where life can be lived and changed until it is perfect however you chose to define that as an individual. I believe he showed us this for a reason. This city he built. The devotion he engendered. It was for one purpose. To *live the Dream*. That is what we will now do.'

There was cheering out on the plaza.

'The Second Dream has begun! We have known it in our hearts. You have known it. I have known it. We have been shown inside the Void again. We have soared with the Skylord.'

Aaron scanned the Council again. He no longer needed to review and analyse their faces for later. Five of them already looked deeply uncomfortable. Around him the cheering was building to an inevitable climax, as was the speech.

'The Skylord awaits us. It will guide us to our destiny. *We will Pilgrimage!*'

Cheering turned to a naked, violent roar of adulation. Inside the gaiafield, it was as though someone was setting off fireworks fuelled by pleasure narcotics. The burst of euphoria surging through the artificial neural universe was awesome in its brightness.

Ethan waved victoriously to the faithful, then gave a last smile and went back inside the Orchard Palace.

Aaron waited as the crowd wound down. So many cried with joy as they departed he had to shake his head in dismay at their simplicity. Happiness here was universal, obligatory. The sun crept down behind the horizon, revealing a city where every window glowed with warm tangerine light – just as they did in the real one. Songs drifted along the canals as the gondoliers gave voice to their delight in traditional fashion. Eventually even the reporters began to drift away, chattering among themselves; those with doubts were keeping their voices low. Out in the unisphere, news anchors and political commentators on hundreds of worlds were beginning their sombre doomsday predictions.

None of it bothered Aaron. He was still standing in the plaza as the civic bots emerged into the starlight and began clearing away the rubbish which the excitable crowd had left behind. He now knew what he had to do next; the certainty had struck him as soon as he heard Ethan speak. Find Inigo. That's why he was here.

Aaron smiled contentedly around the dark plaza, but there was no sign of the woman. 'Now who's bad news?' he asked, and walked back into the jubilant city.

*

Looking out from the balcony along the front of the Orchard Palace, Ethan watched the last rays of the sun slide over the crowd like a translucent gold veneer. Their cries of near-religious approval echoed off the thick walls of the Palace, he could even feel the vibration in the stone balustrade in front of him. Not that there had even been any inner doubts for him during his long difficult progress, but the response of the faithful was profoundly comforting. He knew he was right to push for his own vision, to haul the whole movement out of its slothful complacency. That was evolution's message: go forward or die. The reason for the Void's existence.

Ethan closed his mind to the gaiafield and strode off the balcony as the sun finally sank below the horizon. The others of the Council followed respectfully, their scarlet cloaks fluttering in agitation as they hurried to keep up.

His personal secretary, Chief Cleric Phelim, was waiting at the top of the broad ebony stairs which curved down to the cavernous Malfit Hall on the ground level. The man was in the grey and blue robes which indicated a rank just below that of a full Councillor – a status which Ethan was going to elevate in the next couple of days. His hood was hanging down his back, allowing the soft orange lighting to glimmer off the black skin of his shaven scalp. It gave him a formidable skeletal appearance unusual amid Living Dream members who followed the fashion of long hair that was prevalent in Makkathran. When he fell in beside Ethan he was almost a head taller. That height along with a face that could remain unnervingly impassive had been useful for unsettling a great many people; he could talk to anyone with his mind fully open to the gaiafield, and yet his emotional tone was completely beyond reach. Again, not something the politely passive community of Living Dream were accustomed to. To the Council hierarchy, Phelim and his mannerisms were an uncomfortable intruder. Privately, Ethan rather enjoyed the consternation his utterly loyal deputy generated.

The giant Malfit Hall was full of Clerics who began

applauding as soon as Ethan reached the bottom of the stairs. He took the time to bow at them as he made his way across the sheer black floor, smiling thanks and occasionally nodding in recognition. The images on the arching ceiling overhead mimicked the sky of Querencia; Malfit Hall was perpetually locked in dawn, producing a clear turquoise vault, with the ochre globe of the solid world Nikran circling gently around the edge, magnified to an extent where mountain ranges and a few scudding clouds were visible. Ethan's procession moved on into the Liliala Hall, where the ceiling hosted a perpetual storm, with its seething mantle of glowing clouds haloed in vivid purple lightning. Intermittent gaps allowed glimpses of the Mars Twins belonging to the Gicon's Bracelet formation, small featureless planets with a deep, dense red atmosphere that guarded whatever surface they might have from any enquiry. Senior Clerics were gathered beneath the flashing clouds. Ethan took longer here, muttering several words of thanks to those he knew, allowing his mind to radiate a gentle pride into the gaiafield.

At the arching door into the suite of rooms which the Mayor of Makkathran used to hold office, Ethan turned to the Councillors. 'I thank you once more for you confidence in me. Those who were reluctant in their endorsement, I promise to double my efforts to gain your support and trust in the years ahead.'

If any of them were vexed with their dismissal they shielded such thoughts from the openness of the gaiafield. He and Phelim alone passed into the private quarters. Inside, there were a series of grand interconnecting chambers. The heavy wooden doors were as intrusive here as they were in Makkathran; whatever species designed and built the original city clearly didn't have the psychology for enclosing themselves. Through the gaiafield, he could sense his own staff moving about within the reception rooms around him. His predecessor's team were withdrawing, their frail emotions of disgruntlement leaking into the gaiafield. Handover was normally a leisurely good-spirited affair. Not this time. Ethan wanted his authority stamped on the Orchard Palace within hours. Before the conclave began, he'd prepared an inner circle of loyalists to take charge of the main administrative posts of Living Dream. And as Ellezelin was a hierocracy, he was also faced with endorsing a new cabinet for the planet's civil government as well.

His predecessor, Jalen, had furnished the Mayor's sanctum in paoviool blocks, resembling chunks of stone that shaped itself as required, a state intuited from the gaiafield. Ethan settled into the seat that formed behind the long rectangular slab of desk. Dissatisfaction manifested itself in small emerald sparkles erupting like an optical rash on the paoviool surfaces around him.

'I want this modern rubbish out of here by tomorrow,' Ethan said.

'Of course,' Phelim said. 'Do you want Inigo's furnishings restored?'

'No. I want this as the Waterwalker showed us.'

Phelim actually smiled. 'Much better.'

Ethan glanced round the oval sanctum with its plain walls and high windows. Despite his familiarity with the chamber he felt as if he'd never seen it before. 'For Ozzie's sake, we did it!' he exclaimed, letting out a long breath of astonishment. 'I'm sweating. Actually sweating. Can you believe that?' When he brought his hand up to his brow, he realized he was trembling. For all the years he'd planned and worked and sacrificed for this moment, the reality of success had taken him completely by surprise. It had been a hundred and fifty years since he infused the gaiamotes in order to experience the gaiafield; and on his very first night of communion he'd witnessed Inigo's First Dream. A hundred and fifty years, and the reticent adolescent from the backwater External World of Oamaru had reached one of the most influential positions in the Greater Commonwealth still available to a simple Natural human.

'You were the one they all wanted,' Phelim said; he stood slightly to one side of the desk, ignoring the big cubes of paoviool where he could have sat.

'We did it together.'

'Let's not fool ourselves here. I would never be considered even for the Council.'

'Ordinarily, no.' Ethan looked round the sanctum again. The enormity was starting to sink in. He began to wonder what the Void would look like when he could see it with his own eyes. Once, decades ago, he had met Inigo. He hadn't been disappointed, exactly, but the Dreamer hadn't quite been what he'd expected. Not that he was sure what the Dreamer should have been like – more forceful and dynamic, perhaps.

'You want to begin?' Phelim asked.

'I think that's best. The Ellezelin cabinet are all faithful Living Dream members, so they can remain more or less as they are, with one exception. I want you as the Treasury Secretary.'

'Me?'

'We're going to build the starships for Pilgrimage. That isn't going to be cheap, we'll need the full financial resources of the whole Free Market Zone to fund construction. I need someone in the Treasury I can depend on.'

'I thought I was going to join the Council.'

'You are. I will elevate you tomorrow.'

'Two senior posts. That should be interesting when it comes to juggling schedules. And the empty seat on the Council I shall be filling?'

'I'm going to ask Corrie-Lyn to consider her position.'

Phelim's face betrayed a hint of censure. 'She's hardly your greatest supporter on the Council, admittedly, but I think she'd actually welcome Pilgrimage. Perhaps one of our less progressive colleagues . . . ?'

'It's to be Corrie-Lyn,' Ethan said firmly. 'The remaining Councillors who oppose Pilgrimage are in a minority, and we can deal with them at our leisure. Nobody will be challenging my mandate. The faithful wouldn't tolerate it.'

'Corrie-Lyn it is, then. Let's just hope Inigo doesn't come back before we launch the starships. You know they were lovers?'

'It's the only reason she's a Councillor.' Ethan narrowed his eyes. 'Are we still looking for Inigo?'

'Our friends are,' Phelim told him. 'We don't quite have those sort of resources. There's been no sign of him that they've reported. Realistically, if your succession to Conservator doesn't bring him back within the first month or so, I'd say we are in the clear.'

'Badly phrased. That makes it sound like we've done something wrong.'

'But we don't know why Inigo was reluctant to Pilgrimage.'

'Inigo is only human, he has flaws like the rest of us. Call it a failure of nerve at the last moment if you want to be charitable. My own belief is that he'll be watching events from somewhere, cheering us on.'

'I hope so.' Phelim paused as he reviewed the information accumulating in his exoimages, his u-shadow was balancing local data with a comprehensive overview of the election. 'Marius is here, requesting an audience.'

'That didn't take him long, did it?'

'No. There are a lot of formalities required of you tonight. The Greater Commonwealth President will be calling to congratulate you, as will the leaders of the Free Market planets, and dozens of our External World allies.'

'How is the unisphere coverage?'

'Early days.' Phelim checked the summaries his u-shadow was providing. 'Pretty much what we were expecting. Some hysterical anti-Pilgrimage hotheads saying you're going to kill all of us. Most of the serious anchors are trying to be balanced, and explain the difficulties involved. The majority seem to regard Pilgrimage as a politician's promise.'

'There are no difficulties in accomplishing Pilgrimage,' Ethan said in annoyance. 'I have seen the Skylord's dream. It is a noble creature, it will lead us inside the Void. We just have to locate the Second Dreamer. Any developments on that today?'

'None. Thousands are coming forward claiming to be dreaming the Skylord. They don't help our search.'

'You must find him.'

'Ethan ... it took our best Dream Masters months to assemble the existing fragments into the small dream we have. We believe in this case there is no firm link such as Inigo had with the Void. These fragments, they could be entering the gaiafield in a number of ways. Unaware

29

carriers. Directly from the Void? Perhaps it's Ozzie's galactic field. Then there's an overspill from the Silfen Motherholme or some other post-physical sentient having fun at our expense. Even Inigo himself.'

'It's not Inigo. I know that. I know the feel of his dreams, we all do. This is something different. I was the one who was drawn to those first few fragments, remember. I realized what they were. There is a Second Dreamer.'

'Well, now you are Conservator you can authorize a more detailed monitoring of the gaiafield's confluence nests, track down the origin that way.'

'Is that possible? I thought the gaiafield was beyond our direct influence.'

'The Dream Masters claim they can do this, yes. Certain modifications can be made to the nests. It won't be cheap.'

Ethan sighed. The conclave had been mentally exhausting, and that had just been the beginning. 'So many things. All at once.'

'I'll help you. You know that.'

'I do. And I thank you, my friend. One day we'll stand in the real Makkathran. One day we will make our lives perfect.'

'Soon.'

'For Ozzie's sake I hope so. Now, ask Marius in, please.' Ethan stood courteously to receive his guest. That it should be the ANA Faction representative he saw first was a telling point. He didn't relish the way he and Phelim had relied on Marius during his campaign to be elected Conservator. In an ideal universe they would have needed no outside aid, certainly not one with so many potentially worrying strings attached. Not that there was ever any suggestion of *quid pro quo* from Marius. None of the Factions inside the near-post-physical intelligence of Earth's Advanced Neural Activity system would ever be so blunt.

The representative smiled courteously as he was shown in. Of average height, he had a round face with sharp green eyes emphasized by wide irises; nose and mouth were narrow, and his ears were large but flattened back so severely they could have been ridges in the skull. His thick auburn hair was flecked with gold, no doubt the outcome of some Advancer ancestor vanity. There was nothing to indicate his Higher functions. Ethan was using his internal enrichments to run a passive scan, and if any of the representative's field functions were active they were too sophisticated to perceive. He wouldn't be surprised by that, Marius would be enriched with the most advanced biononics in existence. The representative's long black toga suit generated its own surface haze which flowed about him like a slim layer of mist, the faintest tendrils slithered behind him as he walked.

'Your Eminence,' Marius said, and bowed formally. 'My most sincere congratulations on your election.'

Ethan smiled. It was all he could do not to shudder. Every deep-honed primitive instinct he possessed had picked up on how dangerous the representative was. 'Thank you.'

'I'm here to assure you we will continue our support of your goals.'

'You don't consider Pilgrimage will trigger the end of the galaxy, then?' What he desperately wanted to ask was: who is *we*? But there were so many Factions inside ANA constantly making and breaking alliances it was virtually a null question. It was enough the Faction Marius represented wanted the Pilgrimage to go ahead. Ethan no longer cared that their reasons were probably the antithesis of his own, or if they regarded him as a simple political tool. Not that he would ever know. Pilgrimage was what mattered, delivering the faithful to their promised universe. All that mattered, in fact. He didn't care if he assisted someone else's political goal as long as it didn't interfere with his own.

'Of course not.' Marius grinned in such a way it was as if they were sharing some private joke about how stupid the rest of humanity was compared to themselves. 'If that was the case, then those already in the Void would have triggered that event.'

'People need to be educated. I would appreciate your help with that.'

'We will do what we can, of course. However, we are both working against a considerable amount of mental inertia, not to mention prejudice.'

'I am very conscious of that. The Pilgrimage will polarize opinion across the Greater Commonwealth.'

'Not just those of humans. There are a number of species who are showing an interest in this development.'

'The Ocisen Empire.' Ethan spat it out with as much contempt as possible.

'Not to be entirely underestimated,' Marius said. It wasn't quite chiding.

'The only ones I concern myself with are the Raiel. They have publicly stated their opposition to anyone trying to enter the Void.'

'Which is of course where our assistance will be most beneficial to you. Our original offer still stands, we will supply ultradrives for your Pilgrimage ships.'

Ethan, a scholar of ancient history, guessed this was

what the old religious icon Adam had felt when he was offered the apple. 'And in return?'

'The status quo which currently reigns in the Greater Commonwealth will be over.'

'And that benefits you, how?'

'Species survival. Evolution requires progression or extinction.'

'I thought you would be aiming for transcendence,' Phelim said flatly.

Marius didn't even look in his direction, his eyes remained fixed on Ethan. 'And that isn't evolution?'

'It's a very drastic evolution,' Ethan said.

'Not unlike your hopes of Pilgrimage.'

'So why not join us?'

Marius answered with a mirthless smile. 'Join us, Conservator.'

Ethan sighed. 'We've dreamed what awaits us.'

'Ah, so it boils down to the old human problem. Risk the unknown, or go with the comfortable.'

'I think the phrase you want is: better the devil you know.'

'Whatever. Your Eminence, we still offer you the ultra-drive.'

'Which no one has ever really seen. You just hint at it.'

'ANA tends to be somewhat protective towards its advanced technologies. However, I assure you it is real. Ultradrive is at least equal to the drive used by the Raiel, if not superior.'

Ethan tried not to smile at the arrogance.

'Oh, I assure you, Conservator,' Marius said. 'ANA does not make that boast lightly.'

'I'm sure it doesn't. So when can you supply them?'

'When your Pilgrimage ships are ready, the drives will be here.'

'And the rest of ANA, the Factions which don't agree with you, they'll just stand by and quietly let you hand over this supertechnology?'

'Effectively, yes. Do not concern yourself with our internal debates.'

'Very well, I accept your most generous offer. Please don't be offended, but we will also be building our own more mundane drive units for the ships – just in case.'

'We expected nothing else.' Marius bowed again, and left the room.

Phelim let out a soft whistle of relief. 'So that's it, we're just a trigger factor in their political wars.'

Ethan tried to sound blasé. 'If it gets us what we want, I can live with it.'

'I think you are wise not to rely on them exclusively. We must include our own drives in the construction program.'

'Yes. The design teams have worked on that premise from the beginning.' His secondary routines started to pull files from the storage lacunas in his macrocellular clusters. 'In the meantime, let us begin with some simple appointments, shall we?'

*

Aaron walked across the red marble bridge that arched over Sisterhood Canal, linking Golden Park with the Low Moat district. A strip of simple paddock land which had no city buildings, only stockades for commercial animals, and a couple of archaic markets. He strode along the meandering paths illuminated by small oil lanterns hanging from posts and on into the Ogden district. This was also grassland, but contained the majority of the city's wooden-built stables where the aristocracy kept their horses and carriages. It was where the main city gate had been cut into the wall.

The gates were open wide when he went through, mingling with little groups of stragglers heading back to the urban expanse outside. Makkathran2 was surrounded by a two-mile-wide strip of parkland separating it from the vast modern metropolis which had sprung up around it over the last two centuries. Greater Makkathran2 now sprawled over four hundred square miles, an urban grid that contained sixteen million people, ninety-nine per cent of whom were devout Living Dream followers. It was now the capital of Ellezelin, taking over from the original capital city of Riasi after the 3379 election returned a Living Dream majority to the planetary senate.

There was no powered transport across the park; no ground taxis or underground train, or even pedwalk strips. And, of course, no capsule was allowed into Makka-thran2's airspace. Inigo's thinking was simple enough: the faithful would never mind walking the distance; that was what everyone did on Querencia. He wanted authenticity to be the governing factor in his movement's citadel. Riding across the park, however, was permissible, after all, Querencia had horses. Aaron smiled at that notion as he set off past the gates. Then an elusive memory flickered like a dying hologram. There was a time when he had clung to the neck of some giant horse as they galloped across an undulating terrain. The movement was power-ful and rhythmic, yet strangely leisurely. It was as if the horse was gliding rather than galloping; bounding forward.

He knew exactly how to flow with it, grinning wildly as they raced onwards. Air blasting against his face, hair wild. Astonishingly deep sapphire sky bright and warm above. The horse had a small, tough-looking horn at the top of its forehead. Tipped with the traditional black metal spike.

Aaron grunted dismissively. It must have been some sensory immersion drama he'd accessed on the unisphere. Not real.

The midpoint of the park was a uniform ridge. When Aaron reached the crest it was as though he was stepping across a rift in time; behind him the quaintly archaic profile of Makkathran2 bathed in its alien orange glow; while in front were the modernistic block towers and neat district grids producing a multicoloured haze that stretched over the horizon. Regrav capsules slipped effortlessly through the air above it in strictly maintained traffic streams, long horizontal bands of fast motion winding up into cycloidal junctions that knitted the city together in a pulsing kinetic dance. In the south-eastern sky he could see the brighter lights of starships as they slipped in and out of the atmosphere directly above the spaceport. A never-ending procession of big cargo craft providing the city with economic bonds to planets outside the reach of the official Free Market Zone wormholes.

When he reached the outer rim of the park he told his u-shadow to call a taxi. A glossy jade-coloured regrav capsule dropped silently out of the traffic swarm above and dilated its door. Aaron settled on the front bench, where he had a good view through the one-way fuselage.

'Hotel Buckingham.'

He frowned as the capsule dived back up into the broad

stream circling round the dark expanse of park. Had that instruction come from him or his u-shadow?

At the first junction they whipped round and headed deeper into the urban grid. The tree-lined boulevards a regulation hundred metres below actually had a few ground cars driving along the concrete. People rode horses among them. Bicycles were popular. He shook his head in bemusement.

The Hotel Buckingham was a thirty-storey pentagon ribbed with balconies, and sending sharp pinnacles soaring up out of each corner. It glowed a lambent pearl-white, except for its hundreds of windows which were black recesses. The roof was a small strip of lush jungle. Tiny lights glimmered among the foliage as patrons dined and danced in the open air.

Aaron's taxi dropped him at the arrivals pad in the centre. He had a credit coin in his pocket, which activated to his DNA and paid for the ride. There was a credit code loaded in a macrocellular storage lacuna which he could have used, but the coin made the ride harder to trace. Not impossible by any means, just taking it out of reach of the ordinary citizen. As the taxi took off he glanced up at the tall monochromatic walls fencing him in, feeling unnervingly exposed.

'Am I registered here?' he asked his u-shadow.

'Yes. Room 3088. A penthouse suite.'

'I see.' He turned and looked directly at the penthouse's balcony. He'd known its location automatically. 'And can I afford that?'

'Yes. The penthouse costs 1500 Ellezelin pounds per night. Your credit coin has a limit of five million Ellezelin pounds a month.'

'A month?'

'Yes.'

'Paid by whom?'

'The coin is supported by a Central Augusta Bank account. The account details are secure.'

'And my personal credit code?'

'The same.'

Aaron walked into the lobby. 'Nice to be rich,' he told himself.

The penthouse was five rooms and a small private swimming pool. As soon as Aaron walked into the main lounge he checked himself out in the mirror. A face older than the norm, approaching thirty, possessing short black hair and (oddly) eyes with a hint of purple in their grey irises. Slightly oriental features, but with skin that was rough, and a dark stubble shadow.

Yep, that's me.

Which instinctive response was reassuring, but still didn't give any clues by way of identity.

He settled into a broad armchair which faced an external window, and turned up the opacity to stare out across the night-time city towards the invisible heart which Inigo had built. There was a lot of information in those mock-alien structures which would help him find his quarry. Not the kind of data stored in electronic files; if it was that easy Inigo would have been found by now. No, the information he needed was personal, which brought some unique access problems for someone like him, an unbeliever.

He ordered room service. The hotel was pretentious enough to employ human chefs. When the food arrived he could appreciate the subtleties of its preparation, there was a definite difference to culinary unit produce. He sat in the big chair, watching the city as he ate. Any route in to the senior Clerics and Councillors wouldn't be easy, he realized. But then, this Pilgrimage had presented him with a fairly unique opportunity. If they were going to fly into the Void, they'd need ships. It gave him an easy enough cover. That just left the problem of who to try and cultivate.

His u-shadow produced an extensive list of senior Clerics, providing him with gossip about who was allied with Ethan and who, post-election, was going to be scrubbing Council toilets for the next few decades.

It took him half the night, but the name was there. It was even featured on the city news web as Ethan began reorganizing Living Dream's hierarchy to suit his own policy. Not obvious, but it had a lot of potential: Corrie-Lyn.

*

The courier case arrived at Troblum's apartment an hour before he was due to make his presentation to the Navy review panel. He wrapped a cloak round himself and walked out to the glass lift in the lobby as the emerald fabric adjusted itself to his bulk. Ancient mechanical systems whirred and clanked as the lift slid smoothly downwards. They weren't totally original, of course, technically the whole building dated back over one thousand three hundred and fifty years. During that time there had been a lot of refurbishment and restoration work. Then five hundred years ago a stabilizer field generator was installed, which maintained the molecular bonds inside all the antique bricks, girders, and composite sheets comprising the main body of the building. Essentially, as long as there was power to the generator, entropy was held at arm's length.

Troblum had managed to acquire custodianship over a hundred years ago, following a somewhat obsessional twenty-seven-year campaign. Nobody owned property on Arevalo any more, it was a Higher world, part of the Central Commonwealth – back when the building had been put up they called it phase one space. Persuading the previous tenants to leave had taken up all his Energy and Mass Allocation for years, as well as his meagre social skills. He had used mediator councillors, lawyers, historical restitution experts, and even had to launch an appeal against Daroca City Council who managed the stabilizer generator. During the campaign he'd acquired an unexpected ally which had probably helped swing the whole thing in his favour. Whatever the means, the outcome was that he now had undisputed occupancy rights for the whole building. No one else lived in it, and very few had ever been invited in.

The lift stopped at the entrance hall. Troblum walked past the empty concierge desk to the tall door of stained glass. Outside, the courier case was hovering a metre and a half above the pavement, a dull metal box with transport certificates glowing pink on one end, and shielded against field scans. His u-shadow confirmed the contents and directed it into the hall, where it landed on his trolley. The base opened and deposited the package, a fat silvered cylinder half a metre long. Troblum kept the door open until the case departed, then closed it. Privacy shielding came up around the entrance hall and he walked back into the lift. The trolley followed obediently.

Originally, the building had been a factory, which gave each of the five floors very tall ceilings. Then, as was the way of things in those early days of the Commonwealth, the city expanded and prospered, pushing industry out of the old centre. The factory had been converted into high-class apartments. One of the two penthouse loft apartments which took up the entire fifth floor had been purchased by the Halgarth Dynasty as part of their massive property portfolio on Arevalo. The other apartments had all been restored to a reasonable approximation of their layout and décor in 2380, but Troblum had concentrated his formidable energies on the Halgarth one, where he now lived.

In order to get it as near perfect as possible he had extracted both architect and interior designer plans from the city's deep archive. Those had been complemented by some equally ancient visual recordings from the Michelangelo news show of that era. But his main source of detail had been the forensic scans from the Serious Crimes Directorate which he'd obtained direct from ANA. After combining the data, he had spent five years painstakingly recrafting the extravagant vintage décor; the end result of which gave him three *en suite* bedrooms and a large open-plan lounge which was separated from a kitchen section by a marble-topped breakfast bar. A window wall had a balcony on the other side, providing a grand view out across the Caspe River.

When the City Council's historical maintenance officer made her final review of the project she'd been delighted with the outcome, but the reason for Troblum's dedication completely eluded her. He'd expected nothing else, her field was the building itself. What had gone on inside at the time of the Starflyer War was his area of expertise. He would never use the word obsession, but that whole episode had become a lot more than just a hobby to him. One day he was determined he would publish the definitive history of the War.

The penthouse door opened for him. Solidos of the three girls were sitting on the blue-leather settee up by the window wall. Catriona Saleeb was dressed in a red and gold robe, its belt tied loosely so that her silk underwear was visible. Long curly black hair tumbled chaotically over her shoulders as she tossed her head. She was the smallest of the three, the solido's animation software holding her image as a bubbly twenty-one-year-old, carefree and eager. Leaning up against her, sipping tea from a big cup was Trisha Marina Halgarth. Her dark heart-shaped face had small dark-green butterfly wing OCtattoos flowing back from each hazel eye, the antique technology undulating slowly in response to each facial motion. Lastly, and sitting just apart from the other two, was Isabella Halgarth. She was a tall blonde, with long straight hair gathered into a single tail. The fluffy white sweater she wore was a great deal more tantalizing that it strictly ought to have been, riding high above her midriff, while her jeans were little more than an outer layer of blue skin running down long athletic legs. Her face had high cheekbones, giving her an aristocratic appearance that was backed up with an attitude of cool distain. While her two friends called out eager hellos to Troblum, she merely acknowledged him with a simple nod.

With a regretful sigh, Troblum told his u-shadow to isolate the girls. They'd been his companions for fifty years, he enjoyed their company a great deal more than any real human. And they helped anchor him in the era he so loved. Unfortunately, he couldn't afford distractions right now, however delightful. It had taken him decades to refine the animation programs and bestow valid I-sentient personalities to each solido. The three of them had shared the apartment during the Starflyer War, becoming involved in a famous disinformation sting by the Starflyer. Isabella herself had been one of the alien's most effective agents operating inside the Commonwealth, seducing high-ranking politicians and officials, and subtly manipulating them. For a while after the War, to be *Isabella-ed* was a Commonwealth-wide phrase meaning to be screwed over. But that infamy had faded eventually. Even among people who routinely lived for over five hundred years, events lost their potency and relevance. Today the Starflyer War was simply one of those formative incidents at the start of the Commonwealth, like Ozzie and Nigel, the Hive, the *Endeavour*'s circumnavigation, and cracking the Planters' nanotech. When he was younger, Troblum certainly hadn't been interested; then purely by chance he discovered he was descended from someone called Mark Vernon who apparently played a vital role in the War. He'd started to casually research his ancestor, wanting nothing more than a few details, to learn a little chunk of family background. That was a hundred and eighty years ago, and he was still as fascinated by the whole Starflyer War now as he had been when he opened those first files on the period.

The girls turned away from Troblum and the trolley that followed him in, chattering away brightly among themselves. He looked down at the cylinder as it turned transparent. Inside it contained a strut of metal a hundred and fifteen centimetres long; at one end there was a node of plastic where the frayed ends of fibre-optic cable stuck out like a straggly tail. The surface was tarnished and pocked, it was also kinked in the middle, as if something had struck it. Troblum unlocked the end of the cylinder, ignoring the hiss of gas as the protective argon spilled out. There was nothing he could do to stop his hands trembling as he slid the strut out; nor was there anything to be done about his throat muscles tightening. Then he was holding the strut up, actually witnessing the texture of its worn surface against his own skin. He smiled down on it the way a Natural man would regard his newborn child. Subcutaneous sensors enriching his fingers combined with his Higher field-scan function to run a detailed analysis. The strut was an aluminium-titanium alloy, with a specific hydrocarbon chain reinforcement; it was also two thousand four hundred years old. He was holding *in his own hands* a piece of the *Marie Celeste*, the Starflyer's ship.

After a long moment he put the strut back into the cylinder, and ran the atmospheric purge, sealing it back in argon. He would never physically hold it again, it was too precious for that. It would go into the other apartment where he kept his collection of memorabilia; a small specialist stabilizer field generator would maintain its molecular structure down the centuries. As was fitting.

Troblum acknowledged the authenticity of the strut and authorized his quasi-legal bank account on Wessex to pay the final instalment to the black-market supplier on Far Away who had acquired the item for him. It wasn't that having cash funds was illegal for a Higher, but Higher culture was based on the tenet of individuals being mature and intelligent enough to accept responsibility for themselves and acting within the agreed parameters of societal norm. *I am government*, was the culture's fundamental political kernel. However there was a lot of flexibility within those strictures. Quiet methods of converting a Higher citizen's Energy and Mass Allocation, the so-called Central Dollar, to actual hard cash acceptable on the External Worlds were well established for those who felt they needed such an option. EMA didn't qualify as money in the traditional sense, it was simply a way of regulating Higher citizen activity, preventing excessive or unreasonable demands being placed on communal resources, of whatever nature, by an individual.

As the trolley headed back out of the apartment, Troblum hurried to his bedroom. He barely had time to shower and put on a toga suit before he was due to leave. The glass lift took him down to the basement garage where his regrav capsule was parked. It was an old model, dating back two centuries, a worn chrome-purple in colour and longer than modern versions, with the forward bodywork stretching out like the nose-cone of some External World aircraft. He clambered in, taking up over half of the front bench which was designed to hold three people. The capsule glided out of the garage and tipped up to join the traffic stream overhead. Ageing internal compensators could barely cope with such a steep angle, so Troblum was pressed back into the cushioning as they ascended.

The centre of Daroca was a pleasing blend of modern structures with their smooth pinnacle geometries, pretty or substantial historical buildings like Troblum's, and the original ample mosaic of parkland which the founding council had laid out. Airborne traffic streams broadly followed the pattern of ancient thoroughfares. Troblum's capsule flew northward under the planet's bronze sunlight, heading out over the newer districts where the buildings were spaced further apart and big individual houses were in the majority.

Low in the western sky he could just make out the bright star that was Air. It was the project which had attracted him to Arevalo in the first place. An attempt to construct an artificial space habitat the size of a gas giant planet. After two centuries of effort the project governors had built nearly eighty per cent of the spherical geodesic lattice which would act as both the conductor and generator of a single encapsulating force field. Once it was powered up (siphoning energy directly from the star via a zero-width wormhole) the interior would be filled with a standard oxygen-nitrogen atmosphere, harvested from the system's outer moons and gas giants. After that, various biological components both animal and botanical would be introduced, floating around inside to establish a biosphere lifecycle. The end result, a zero-gee environment with a diameter greater than Saturn, would give people the ultimate freedom to fly free, adding an extraordinary new dimension to the whole human experience.

Critics, of which there were many, claimed it was a poor – and pointless – copy of the Silfen Motherholme which Ozzie had discovered, where an entire star was wrapped by a breathable atmosphere. Proponents argued that this was just a stepping stone, an important, inspiring testament that would expand the ability and outlook of Higher culture. Their rationale won them a hard-fought Central Worlds referendum to obtain the EMAs they needed to complete the project.

Troblum, who was first and foremost a physicist, had been attracted to Air by just that rationalization. He had spent a constructive seventy years working to translate theoretical concepts into physical reality, helping to build the force-field generators which studded the geodesic lattice. At which point his preoccupation with the Starflyer War had taken over, and he'd gained the attention of people running an altogether more interesting construction project. They made him an offer he couldn't refuse. It often comforted him how that section of his life mirrored that of his illustrious ancestor, Mark.

His capsule descended into the compound of the Commonwealth Navy office. It consisted of a spaceport field lined by two rows of big hangars and maintenance bays. Arevalo was primarily a base for the Navy exploration division. The starships sitting on the field were either long-range research vessels or more standard passenger craft; while the three matt-black towers looming along the northern perimeter housed the astrophysics laboratories and scientific-crew-training facilities. Troblum's capsule drifted through the splayed arches which the main tower stood on, and landed directly underneath it. He walked over to the base of the nearest arch column, toga suit surrounding him in a garish ultraviolet aurora. There weren't many people about, a few officers on their way to regrav capsules. His appearance drew glances; for a Higher to be so big was very unusual. Biononics usually kept a body trim and healthy, it was their primary function. There were a few cases where a slightly unusual biochemical makeup presented operational difficulties for biononics, but that was normally remedied by a small chromosome modification. Troblum refused to consider it. He was what he was, and didn't see the need to apologize for it to anyone in any fashion.

Even the short distance from the capsule to the column

made his heart race. He was sweating when he went into the empty vestibule at the base of the column. Deep sensors scanned him and he put his hand on a tester globe, allowing the security system to confirm his DNA. One of the lifts opened. It descended for an unnerving amount of time.

The heavily shielded conference room reserved for his presentation was unremarkable. An oval chamber with an oval rockwood table in the middle. Ten pearl-white shaper chairs with high backs were arranged round it. Troblum took the one opposite the door, and started running checks with the Navy office net to make sure all the files he needed were loaded properly.

Four Navy officers walked in, three of them in identical toga suits whose ebony surface effect rippled in subdued patterns. Their seniority was evidenced only in small red dots glowing on their shoulders. He recognized all of them without having to reference their u-shadows. Mykala, a third-level captain and the local ftl drive bureau director; Eoin, another captain who specialized in alien activities, and Yehudi, the Arevalo office commander. Accompanying them was First Admiral Kazimir Burnelli. Troblum hadn't been expecting him. The shock of seeing the commander of the Commonwealth Navy in person made him stand up quickly. It wasn't just his position that was fascinating, the Admiral was the child of two very important figures of the Starflyer War, and famous for his age: one-thousand-two-hundred-and-six years old, seven or eight centuries past the time most Highers downloaded themselves into ANA.

The Admiral wore a black uniform of old-fashioned cloth, stylishly cut. It suited him perfectly, emphasizing broad shoulders and a lean torso, the classic authority figure. He was tall with an olive skin and a handsome face; Troblum recognized some of his father's characteristics, the blunt jaw and jet black hair, but his mother's finer features were there also, a nose that was almost dainty and pale friendly eyes.

'Admiral!' Troblum exclaimed.

'Pleased to meet you,' Kazimir Burnelli extended a hand.

It took Troblum a moment before he realized what to do, and put out his own hand to shake – suddenly very pleased his toga suit had a cooling web and he was no longer sweating. The social formality file his u-shadow had pushed into his exovision was abruptly withdrawn.

'I'll be representing ANA:Governance for this presentation,' Kazimir said. Troblum had guessed as much. Kazimir Burnelli was the essential human link in the chain between ANA: Governance and the ships of the Navy deterrent fleet, a position of trust and responsibility he'd held for over eight hundred years. Something in the way he carried himself was indicative of all those centuries he'd lived, an aura of weariness that anyone in his presence couldn't help be aware of.

There were so many things Troblum was desperate to ask, starting with: *Have you stayed in your body so long because your father's life was so short?* And possibly: *Can you get me access to your grandfather?* But instead he meekly said, 'Thank you for coming, Admiral.' Another privacy shield came on around the chamber, and the net confirmed they were grade-one secure.

'So what have you got for us?' the Admiral asked.

'A theory on the Dyson Pair generators,' Troblum said.

He activated the chamber's web node so the others could share the data and projections in his files, and began to explain.

The Dyson Pair were stars three lightyears apart that were confined within giant force fields. The barriers had been established in AD1200 by the Anomine for good reason. The Prime aliens who had already spread from their homeworld around Alpha to Beta were pathologically hostile to all biological life except their own. The Starflyer was one of them that had escaped imprisonment, and it had manipulated the Commonwealth into opening the force field around Dyson Alpha, resulting in a war which had killed in excess of fifty million humans. Eventually, the force field had been reactivated by Ozzie and Mark Vernon, ending the War, but it had been a shockingly close call. The Navy had kept an unbroken watch on the stars ever since.

Centuries later, when the Raiel invited the Commonwealth to join the Void observation project at Centurion Station, human scientists had been startled by the similarity of the planet-sized defence systems deployed throughout the Wall stars and the generators that produced the Dyson Pair force fields.

Until now, Troblum said, everyone assumed the Anomine had a technology base equal to the Raiel. He disputed that. His analysis of the Dyson Pair generators showed they were almost identical in concept to the Centurion Station DF machines.

'Which proves the point, surely?' Yehudi said.

'Quite the opposite,' Troblum replied smoothly.

The Anomine homeworld had been visited several times by the Navy exploration division. As a species they had divided two millennia ago; with the most technologically advanced group elevating to post-physical sentience, while the remainder retroevolved to a simple pastoral culture. Although they had developed wormholes and sent exploration ships ranging across the galaxy, they had only ever settled a dozen or so nearby star systems, none of which had massive astroengineering facilities. The remaining pastoral societies had no knowledge of the Dyson Pair generators, and the post-physicals had long since withdrawn from contact with their distant cousins. An extensive search of the sector by successive Navy ships had failed to locate the assembly structure for the Dyson Pair generators. Until now, human astro-archaeologists had assumed the abandoned machinery had decayed away into the vacuum, or was simply lost.

Given the colossal scale involved, Troblum said, neither was truly believable. First off, however sophisticated they were, it would have taken the Anomine at least a century to build such a generator starting from scratch, let alone two of them – look how long it was taking Highers to construct Air, and that was with near unlimited EMAs. Secondly, the generators were needed quickly. The Prime aliens of Dyson Alpha were already building slower than light starships, which was why the Anomine sealed them in. If there had been a century gap while the Anomine beavered away at construction, the Primes would have expanded out to every star within a fifty-lightyear radius before the generators were finished.

'The obvious conclusion,' Troblum said, 'is that the Anomine simply appropriated existing Raiel systems from the Wall. All they would need for that would be a scaled-up wormhole generator to transport them to the Dyson Pair, and we know they already possessed the basic technology.

'What I would like is for the Navy to start a detailed search of interstellar space around the Dyson Pair. The Anomine wormhole drive or drives could conceivably still be there. Especially if it was a "one shot" device.' He gave the Admiral an expectant look.

Kazimir Burnelli paused as the last of Troblum's files closed. 'The Primes built the largest wormhole ever known in order to invade the Commonwealth across five hundred lightyears,' he said.

'It was called Hell's Gateway,' Troblum said automatically.

'You do know your history. Good. Then you should also know it was only a couple of kilometres in diameter. Hardly enough to transport the barrier generators.'

'Yes, but I'm talking about a completely new manifestation of wormhole-drive technology. A wormhole that doesn't need a correspondingly large generator: you simply project the exotic matter effect to the size required.'

'I've never heard of anything like that.'

'It can be achieved easily within our understanding of wormhole theory, Admiral.'

'Easily?' Kazimir Burnelli turned to Mykala. 'Captain?'

'I suppose it may be possible,' Mykala said. 'I'd need to re-examine exotic matter theory before I could say one way or another.'

'I'm already working on a method,' Troblum blurted.

'Any success?' Mykala queried.

Troblum suspected she was being derisive, but lacked the skill to interpret her tone. 'I'm progressing, yes. There's certainly no theoretical block to diameter. It's all down to the amount of energy available.'

'To ship a Dyson barrier generator halfway across the galaxy you'd need a nova,' Mykala said.

Now Troblum was sure she was mocking him. 'It needs nothing like that much energy,' he said. 'In any case, if they built the generators on or near their home star they would still have needed a transport system, wouldn't they? If they built them in situ, which is very doubtful, where is the construction site? We'd have found something that big by now. Those generators were moved from wherever the Raiel had originally installed them.'

'Unless it was produced by their post-physicals,' she said. 'Who knows what abilities they have or had.'

'Sorry, I'm going to have to go with Troblum on that one,' Eoin said. 'We know the Anomine didn't elevate to post-physical status until after the Dyson barriers were established, that's approximately a hundred and fifty years later.'

'Exactly,' Troblum said triumphantly. 'They had to be using a level of technology effectively equal to ours. Somewhere out there in interstellar space is an abandoned drive system capable of moving objects the size of planets. We need to find it, Admiral. I've already compiled a search methodology using current Navy exploration craft which I'd like—'

'Let me just stop you there,' Kazimir Burnelli said. 'Troblum, what you've given us so far is a very convincing hypothesis. So much so that I'm going to immediately forward your data to a senior department review committee. If they give me a positive verdict you and I will discuss the Navy's investigation options. And believe me, for this day and age, that's being fast-tracked, okay?'

'But you can sanction the exploration division to begin the search right away, you have that authority.'

'I do, yes; but it don't exercise it without good reason. What you've shown us is more than sufficient to start a serious appraisal. We will follow due process. Then if you're right—'

'Of course I'm fucking right,' Troblum snapped. He knew in a remote fashion he was acting inappropriately, but his goal was so close. He'd assumed the Admiral's unexpected appearance today meant the search could begin right away. 'I don't have the EMAs for that many starships myself, that's why the Navy has to be involved.'

'There would never be an opportunity for an individual to perform a search,' Kazimir replied lightly. 'Space around the Dyson Pair remains restricted. This is a Navy project.'

'Yes, Admiral,' Troblum mumbled. 'I understand.' Which he did. But that didn't quell the resentment at the bureaucracy involved.

'I notice you haven't included your results on this "one shot" wormhole drive idea,' Mykala said. 'That's a big hole in the proposal.'

'It's at an early stage,' Troblum said, which wasn't quite true. He'd held back on his project precisely because he was so near to success. It was going to be the clinching argument if the presentation hadn't gone well. Which in a way it hadn't. But ... 'I hope to be giving you some positive results soon.'

'That I will be very interested in,' Kazimir said, finally producing a smile that lifted centuries away from him. 'Thank you for bringing this to us. And I do genuinely appreciate the effort involved.'

'It's what I do,' Troblum said gruffly. He kept silent as

the shielding switched off, and the others left the chamber. What he wanted to shout after the Admiral was: *Your mother made her decisions without any committee to hold her hand, and as for what your grandfather would say about getting a consensus* ... Instead he let out a disgruntled breath as he sealed the files back into his storage lacuna. Meeting an idol was always such a risk, so few of them ever really matched up to their own legend.

*

The Delivery Man was woken by his youngest daughter just as a chilly dawn light was rising outside. Little Rosa had once again decided that five hours' sleep was quite sufficient for her, now she was sitting up in her cot wailing for attention. And milk. Beside him, Lizzie was just starting to stir out of a deep sleep. Before she could wake, he swung himself out of bed and hurried along the landing to the nursery. If he wasn't quick enough Tilly and Elsie would be woken up, then nobody would get any peace.

The paediatric housebot floated through the nursery door after him, a simple ovoid just over a metre high. It extruded Rosa's milk bulb through its neutral grey skin. Both he and his wife Lizzie hated the idea of a machine, even one as sophisticated as the housebot, caring for the child, so he settled her on his lap in the big chair at the side of the cot and started feeding her out of the bulb. Rosa smiled adoringly round the nozzle, and squirmed deeper into his embrace. The housebot extended a hose which attached to the outlet patch on her sleepsuit's nappy, and siphoned away the night's wee. Rosa waved contentedly at the housebot as it glided out of the nursery.

'Goobi,' she cooed, and resumed drinking.

'Goodbye,' the Delivery Man corrected. At seventeen months, Rosa's vocabulary was just starting to develop. The bionomic organelles in her cells were effectively inactive other than reproducing themselves to supplement her new cells as she grew. Extensive research had shown it was best for a Higher-born human to follow nature's original development schedule up until about puberty. After that the biononics could be used as intended; one function of which was to modify the body however the host wanted. He still wasn't sure that was such a good idea, handing teenagers unrestrained power over their own physiology frequently led to some serious self-inflicted blunders. He always remembered the time when he was fourteen and had a terrible crush on a seventeen-year-old girl. He'd tried to *improve* his genitals. It had taken five hugely embarrassing trips to a bionomic procedures doctor to sort out the painful abnormal growths.

When Rosa finished he carried her downstairs. He and Lizzie lived in a classic Georgian townhouse in London's Holland Park district. It had been restored three hundred years ago using modern techniques to preserve as much of the old fabric as possible without having to resort to stabilizer fields. Lizzie had overseen the interior when they moved in, blending a tasteful variety of furniture and utility systems that dated from the mid-twentieth century right up to the twenty-seventh, when ANA's replication facilities effectively halted human design on Earth. Two spacious sub-basements had been added, giving them an indoor swimming pool and a health spa, along with the tanks and ancillary systems that supplied the culinary cabinet and household replicator.

He took Rosa into the large iron-framed conservatory where her toys were stored in big wicker baskets. February had produced its usual icy morning outside, sending broad patterns of frost worming up the outside of the glass. For now, the only true splash of colour to enjoy in the garden came from the winter-flowering cherries on the curving bank behind the frozen fish pond.

When Lizzie came downstairs an hour later she found him and Rosa playing with glow blocks on the conservatory's heated flagstone floor. Tilly, who was seven, and Elsie their five-year-old, followed their mother in, and shouted happily at their younger sister, who ran over to them with outstretched arms, babbling away in her own incomprehensible yet excited language. The three girls started to build a tower out of the blocks, the higher they stacked the faster the colours swirled.

He gave Lizzie a quick kiss and ordered the culinary cabinet to produce some breakfast. Lizzie sat at the circular wooden table in their kitchen. An antiquities and culture specialist, she enjoyed the old-fashioned notion of a room specifically for cooking. Even though there was no need for it, she'd had a hefty iron range cooker installed when they moved in ten years ago. During winter its cosy warmth turned the kitchen into the house's engine room, they always gathered in here as a family. Sometimes she even used the range to cook things which she and the girls made out of ingredients produced by the culinary cabinet. Tilly's birthday cake had been the last.

'Swimming for Tilly this morning,' Lizzie said as she sipped at a big china cup of tea which a housebot delivered to her.

'Again?' he asked.

'She's getting a lot more confident. It's their new teacher. He's very good.'

'Good.' The Delivery Man picked up the croissant on his plate and started tearing it open. 'Girls,' he shouted. 'Come and sit down please. Bring Rosa.'

'She doesn't want to come,' Elsie shouted back immediately.

'Don't make me come and get you.' He avoided looking at Lizzie. 'I'm going to be away for a few days.'

'Anything interesting?'

'There've been allegations that some companies on Oronsay have got hold of level-three replicator tech,' he said. 'I'll need to run tests on their products.' His current vocation was to monitor the spread of Higher technology across the External Worlds. It was a process which the Externals got very sensitive about, with hardline Protectorate politicians citing it as the first act of cultural colonization, deserving retribution. However, industrialists on the External Worlds were constantly seeking to acquire ever-more sophisticated manufacturing systems to reduce their costs. Radical Highers were equally keen to supply it to them, seeing it precisely as that first important stage for a planet converting to Higher culture. What he had to do, on ANA:Governance's behalf, was to decide the intent behind supplying replicator systems. If Radical Highers were supporting the companies, then he would subtly disable the systems and collapse the operation. His main problem was making an objective decision; Higher technology inevitably crept out from the Central Worlds, in the same way that the External Worlds were always settling new planets around the edge of their domain. The boundary between Central and External was ambiguous to say the least, with some External Worlds openly welcoming the shift to Higher status. Location was always a huge factor in his decision. Oronsay was over a hundred lightyears out from the Central Worlds, which effectively negated the chance that this was simple technology seepage. If there were replicators there, it was either Radicals pushing them, or a very greedy company.

Lizzie's eyebrows lifted. 'Really? What sort of products?'

'Starship components.'

'Well, that should come in handy out there right now, very profitable I imagine.'

He appreciated her guarded amusement. The last few days had seen a rush of starship company officials to Ellezelin, eager to do deals with the new Cleric Conservator.

The girls scuttled in and settled at the table; Rosa clambered on to the twenty-fifth-century suede mushroom that was her tiny-tot seat. It morphed around her, gripping firmly enough to prevent her from falling out, and expanded upwards to bring her level with the table top. She clapped her hands delightedly to be up with her family. Elsie solemnly slid a bowl of honey pops across, which Rosa grabbed. 'Don't spill it today,' Elsie ordered imperiously.

Rosa just gurgled happily at her sister.

'Daddy, will you teleport us to school?' Tilly asked, her voice high and pleading.

'You know I'm not going to,' he told her. 'Don't ask.'

'Oh please, Daddy, *please*.'

'Yes, Daddy,' Elsie chipped in. 'Please t-port. I like it. Lots and lots.'

'I'm sure you do, but you're getting on the bus. Teleport is a serious business.'

'School is serious,' Tilly claimed immediately. 'You always say so.'

Lizzie was laughing quietly.

'That's diff—' he began. 'All right, I'll tell you what I'll do. If you behave yourselves while I'm gone, *and only if*, then I'll teleport you to school on Thursday.'

'Yes yes!' Tilly exclaimed. She was bouncing up and down on her chair.

'But you have to be exceptionally good. And I will find out, your mother will tell me.'

Both girls immediately directed huge smiles at Lizzie.

After breakfast the girls washed and brushed their hair in the bathroom; with Elsie having long red hair it always took her an age to untangle it. Parents checked homework files to make sure it had all been done. Housebots prepared school uniforms.

Half an hour later the bus slipped down out of the sky, a long turquoise regrav capsule that hovered just above the greenway outside the house where the road used to be centuries before. The Delivery Man walked his daughters out to it, both of them wearing cloaks over their red blazers, the protective grey shimmer warding off the cold damp air. He checked one last time that Tilly had her swimwear, kissed them both goodbye, and stood waving as the bus rose quickly. The whole idea of riding to school together was to enhance the children's sense of community, an extension of the school itself, which was little more than an organized play and activities centre. Their real education wouldn't begin until their biononics became active. But it still gave him an emotional jolt to see them vanishing into the gloomy horizon. There was only one school in London these days, south of the Thames in Dulwich Park. With a total population of barely a hundred and fifty thousand the city didn't need another. Even for Highers the number of children was low; but then Earth's natives were notoriously reserved. The first planet to become truly Higher, it had been steadily reducing its population ever since. Right at the beginning of Higher culture, when biononics became available and ANA went on line, the average citizen's age was already the highest in the Commonwealth. The elderly downloaded, while the younger ones who weren't ready for migration to a post-physical state emigrated out to the Central Worlds until they chose to conclude their biological life. The result was a small residual population with an exceptionally low birth-rate.

The Delivery Man and Lizzie were a notable exception in having three kids. But then they'd registered a marriage as well, and had a ceremony in an old church with their friends witnessing the event – a Christian priest had been brought in from an External World that still had a working religion. It was what Lizzie had wanted, she adored the old traditions and rituals. Not enough to actually get pregnant, of course, the girls had all been gestated in a womb vat.

'You be careful on Oronsay,' she told him as he examined his face in the bathroom mirror. It was, he acknowledged, rather flat with a broad jaw, and eyes that crinkled whenever he smiled or frowned no matter how many anti-ageing techniques were applied to the surrounding skin areas, Advancer or Higher. His Advancer genes had given his wiry muddy-red hair a luxuriant growth-rate which Elsie had inherited. He'd modified his facial follicles with biononics so that he no longer had to apply shaving gel twice a day; but the process wasn't perfect, every week he had to check his chin and dab gel on recalcitrant patches of five o'clock shadow. More like five o'clock puddles, Lizzie claimed.

'I always am,' he assured her. He pulled on a new toga suit and waited until it had wrapped around him. Its surface haze emerged, a dark emerald shot though with silver sparkles. Rather stylish, he felt.

Lizzie, who never wore any clothes designed later than the twenty-second century, produced a mildly disapproving look. 'If it's that far from the Central Worlds it's going to be deliberate.'

'I know. I will watch out, I promise.' He kissed Lizzie in reassurance, trying to ignore the guilt that was staining his thoughts like some slow poison. She studied his face, apparently satisfied with his sincerity, which only made the lie even worse. He hated these times when he couldn't tell her what he actually did.

'Missed a bit,' she announced spryly, and tapped her forefinger on the left side of his jaw.

He peered into the mirror and grunted in dismay. She was right, as always.

When he was ready, the Delivery Man stood in the lounge facing Lizzie, who held a squirming Rosa in her arms. He held a hand up to wave as he activated his field interface function. It immediately meshed with Earth's T-sphere, and he designated his exit coordinate. His integral force field sprang up to shield his skin. The awesome, intimidating emptiness of the translation continuum engulfed him, nullifying every sense. It was this infinite microsecond he despised. All his biononic enrichments told him he was surrounded by nothing, not even the residual quantum signature of his own universe. With his mind starved of any sensory input, time expanded excruciatingly.

Eagles Harbour flickered into reality around him. The giant station hung seventy kilometres above southern England; one of a hundred and fifty identical stations which between them generated the planetary T-sphere. ANA: Governance had fabricated them in the shape of mythological flying saucers three kilometres in diameter, a whimsy it wasn't usually associated with.

He'd emerged into a cavernous reception centre on the station's outer rim. There were only a couple of other people using it, and they paid him no attention. In front of him, a vast transparent hull section rose from the floor to curve away above, allowing him to look down on the entire southern half of the country. London was almost directly underneath, clad in slow-moving pockets of fog that oozed around rolling high ground like a white slick. The last time he and Lizzie had brought the kids up here was a clear sunny day, when they'd all pressed up against the hull while Lizzie pointed out historical areas, and narrated the events that made them important. She'd explained that the ancient city was now back down to the same physical size it'd been in the mid-eighteenth century. With the planet's population shrinking, ANA:Governance had ruled there were simply too many buildings left to maintain. Just because they were old didn't necessarily make them relevant. The ancient public buildings in London's centre were preserved, along with others deemed architecturally or culturally significant. But as for the sprawl of suburb housing . . . there were hundreds of thousands of examples of every kind from every era. Most of them were donated or sold off to various individuals and institutions across the Greater Commonwealth, while those that were left were simply erased.

The Delivery Man took a last wistful look down at the mist-draped city, feeling guilt swell to a near-painful level. But he could never tell Lizzie what he actually did; she wanted stability for their gorgeous little family. Rightly so.

Not that there was any risk involved, he told himself as each assignment began. Really. At least: not much. And if anything ever did go wrong his Faction could probably re-life him in a new body and return him home before she grew suspicious.

He turned away from London and made his way across the reception centre's deserted floor to one of the transit tubes opposite. It sucked him in like an old vacuum hose, propelling him towards the centre of Eagles Haven where the interstellar wormhole terminus was located. The scarcity of travellers surprised him, there were no more passengers than normal using the station. He'd expected to find more Highers on their inward migration to ANA. Living Dream was certainly stirring things up politically among the External Worlds. The Central Worlds regarded the whole Pilgrimage affair with their usual disdain. Even so, their political councils were worried, as demonstrated by the number of people joining them to offer their opinion.

It was a fact that with Ethan's ascension to Cleric Conservator, the ANA Factions were going to be manoeuvring frantically for advantage, trying to shape the Greater Commonwealth to their own vision. He couldn't work out which of them was going to benefit most from the recent election; there were so many, and their internal allegiances were all so fluid anyway, not to mention deceitful. It was an old saying that there were as many Factions as there were ex-physical humans inside ANA; and he'd never encountered any convincing evidence to the contrary. It resulted in groupings that ranged from those who wanted to isolate and ignore the physical humans (some anti-animal extremists wanted them exterminated altogether) to those who sought to elevate every human, ANA or physical, to a transcendent state.

The Delivery Man took his assignments from a broad alliance that was fundamentally conservative, following a philosophy that was keen to see things keep running along as they were – although opinions on how that should be achieved were subject to a constant and vigorous internal debate. He did it because it was a view he shared. When he eventually downloaded, in another couple of centuries or so, that would be the Faction he would associate himself with. In the meantime he was one of their unofficial representatives to the physical Commonwealth.

The station terminus was a simple spherical chamber containing a globe fifty metres in diameter whose surface glowed with the lambent violet of Cherenkov radiation, emanating from the exotic matter used to maintain the wormhole's stability. He slipped through the bland sheet of photons, and was immediately emerging from the exterior of a corresponding globe on St Lincoln. The old industrial planet was still a major manufacturing base for the Central Worlds, and had maintained its status as a hub for the local wormhole network. He took a transit tube to the wormhole for Lytham, which was one of the furthest Central Worlds from Earth; its wormhole terminus was secured at the main starport. Only the Central Worlds were linked together by a long-established wormhole network. The External Worlds valued their cultural and economic independence too much to be connected to the Central Worlds in such a direct fashion. With just a few exceptions travel between them was by starship.

A two-seater capsule ferried the Delivery Man out to the craft he'd been assigned. He glided between two long rows of pads where starships were parked. They ranged in size from sleek needle-like pleasure cruisers, up to hundred-metre passenger liners capable of flying commercial routes up to a hundred lightyears. The majority were fitted with hyperdrives; though some of the larger mercantile vessels used continuous wormhole generators, which were slower but more economic for short-range flights to neighbouring stars. There were no cargo ships anywhere on the field; Lytham was a Higher planet, it didn't manufacture or import consumer items.

The *Artful Dodger* was parked towards the end of the row. A surprisingly squat chrome-purple ovoid, twenty-five metres high, standing on five tumour-like bulbs which held its wide base three metres off the concrete. The fuselage surface was smooth and featureless, with no hint of what lay underneath. It looked like a typical private hyperdrive ship, belonging to some wealthy External World individual or company; or a Higher Council with diplomatic prerogative. An ungainly metal umbilical tower stood at the rear of the pad, with two slim hoses plugged into the ship's utility port, filling the synthesis tanks with baseline chemicals.

The Delivery Man sent the capsule back to the rank in the reception building and walked underneath the starship. His u-shadow called the ship's smartcore, and confirmed his identity, a complex process of code and DNA verification before the smartcore finally acknowledged he had the authority to take command. An airlock opened at the centre of the ship's base, a dint that distended upwards into a tunnel of darkness. Gravity eased off around him, then slowly inverted, pulling him up inside. He emerged into the single midsection cabin. Inert, it was a low hemisphere of dark fabric which felt spongy to the touch. Slim ribs on the upper surface glowed a dull blue, allowing him to see round. The airlock sealed up below his feet. He smiled round at the blank cabin, sensing the power contained behind the bulkheads. The starship plugged into him at some animal level, circumventing all the wisdom and cool of Higher behaviour. He relished the power that was available, the freedom to fly across the galaxy. This was liberation in the extreme.

How the girls would love to ride in this.

'Give me something to sit on,' he told the smartcore, 'turn the lights up, and activate flight control functions.'

An acceleration couch bloomed up out of the floor as the ribs brightened, revealing a complex pattern of black lines etched on the cabin walls. The Delivery Man sat down. Exoimages flipped up, showing him the ship's status. His u-shadow cleared him for flight with the spaceport governor, and he designated a flight path to Ellezelin, two hundred and fifteen lightyears away. The umbilical cables withdrew back into their tower.

'Let's go,' he told the smartcore.

Compensator generators maintained a level gravity inside the cabin as the *Artful Dodger* rose on regrav. At fifty kilometres altitude, the limit of regrav, the smartcore switched to ingrav, and the starship continued to accelerate away from the planet. The Delivery Man began to experiment with the internal layout, expanding walls and furniture out of the cabin bulkheads. The dark lines flowed and bloomed into a great variety of combinations, allowing up to six passengers to have tiny independent sleeping quarters which included a bathroom formation; but for all its malleability, the cabin was basically variations on a lounge. If you were travelling with anyone, he decided, let alone five others, you'd need to be very good friends.

A thousand kilometres above the spaceport, the *Artful Dodger* went ftl, vanishing inside a quantum field interstice with a photonic implosion that pulled in all the stray electromagnetic radiation within a kilometre of its fuselage. There were no differences perceptible to ordinary human senses, he might have been in an underground chamber for all he knew, and the gravity remained perfectly stable. Sensors provided him with a simplified image of their course as it related to large masses back in spacetime, plotting stars and planets by the way their quantum signature affected the intersecting fields through which they were flying. Their initial speed was a smooth fifteen lightyears per hour, near the limit for a hyperdrive, which the sophisticated Lytham planetary spacewatch network could track out to a couple of lightyears.

The Delivery Man waited until they were three lightyears beyond the network, and told the smartcore to accelerate again. The *Artful Dodger*'s ultradrive pushed them up to a phenomenal fifty-five lightyears per hour. It was enough to make the Delivery Man flinch. He had only been on an ultradrive ship twice before; there weren't many of them; ANA had never released the technology to the Central

Worlds. Exactly how the Conservative Faction had got hold of it was something he studiously avoided asking.

Two hours later he reduced speed back down to fifteen lightyears an hour, and allowed the Ellezelin traffic network to pick up their hyperspacial approach. He used a TD channel to the planetary datasphere and requested landing permission for Riasi spaceport.

Ellezelin's original capital was situated on the northern coast of Sinkang, with the Camoa River running through it. He looked down on the city as the *Artful Dodger* sank down towards the main spaceport. It had been laid out in a spiderweb grid, with the planetary Parliament at the heart. The building was still there, a grandiose structure of towers and buttresses made from an attractive mixture of ancient and modern materials. But the planet's government was now centred in Makkathran2. The senior bureaucrats and their departments had moved with it, leading a migration of commerce and industry. Only the transport sector remained strong in Riasi now. The wormholes which linked the planets of the Ellezelin Free Trade Zone together were all located here, incorporated into the spaceport, making it the most important commercial hub in the sector.

The *Artful Dodger* landed on a pad little different to the one it had departed barely three hours before. The Delivery Man paid a parking fee for a month in advance with an untraceable credit coin, and declined an umbilical connection. His u-shadow called a taxi capsule to the pad. While he was waiting for it, the Conservative Faction called him.

'Marius has been seen on Ellezelin.'

It was the second time that day the Delivery Man

flinched. 'I suppose that was inevitable. Do you know why he's here?'

'To support the Cleric Conservator. But as to the exact nature of that support, we remain uncertain.'

'I see. Is he here in the spaceport?' he asked reluctantly. He wasn't a front-line agent, but his biononics had very advanced field functions in case he ever stumbled into an aggressive situation. They ought to be a match for anything Marius could produce. Although any aggression would be most unusual. Faction agents simply didn't settle their scores physically. It wasn't done.

'We don't believe so. He visited the Cleric Conservator within an hour of the election. After that he dropped out of sight. We are telling you simply so that you can be careful. It would not do for the Accelerators to know our business any more than they want us to know theirs. Leave as quickly as possible.'

'Understood.'

The taxi capsule took him over to the spaceport's massive passenger terminal. He checked in for the next United Commonwealth Starlines flight back to Akimiski, the closest Central World. All the time he waited in the departure lounge overlooking the huge central concourse he kept his scan functions running, checking to see if Marius was in the terminal. When the passengers boarded forty minutes later, there had been no sign of him, nor any other Higher agent.

The Delivery Man settled into his first-class compartment on the passenger ship with a considerable sense of relief. It was a hyperdrive ship, which would take fifteen hours to get to Akimiski. From there he'd make a quick trip to Oronsay to maintain his cover. With any luck he'd be back on Earth in less than two days. It would be the weekend, and they'd be able to take the girls to the southern sanctuary park in New Zealand. They'd enjoy that.

*

The Rakas bar occupied the whole third floor of a round tower in Makkathran2's Abad district. Inevitably, the same building back in Makkathran also had a bar on the third floor. From what he'd seen in Inigo's dreams, Aaron suspected the furniture here was better, as was the lighting, not to mention the lack of general dirt which seemed so pervasive within the original city. It was used by a lot of visiting faithful who were perhaps a little disappointed by how small the nucleus of their movement actually was in comparison to the prodigious metropolises of the Greater Commonwealth. There was also a much better selection of drinks than the archetype boasted.

Aaron presumed that was the reason why ex-Councillor the Honourable Corrie-Lyn kept returning here. This was the third night he'd sat at a small corner table and watched her up at the counter knocking back an impressive amount of alcohol. She wasn't a large woman, though at first glance her slender figure made her seem taller than she was. Ivory skin was stippled by a mass of freckles whose highest density was in a broad swathe across her eyes. Her hair was the darkest red he'd ever seen. Depending on how the light caught her, it varied from shiny ebony to gold-flecked maroon. It was cut short which, given how thick it was, made it curl heavily; the way it framed her dainty features made her appear like a particularly diabolic teenager. In reality she was three hundred and seventy. He knew she wasn't Higher, so she must have a superb Advancer metabolism; which presumably was how she could drink any badboy under the table.

For the fourth time that evening, one of the faithful but not terribly devout went over to try his luck. After all, the good citizens of Makkathran had very healthy active sex lives. Inigo showed that. The group of blokes he was with, sitting at the big window seat, watched with sly grins and minimal sniggering as their friend claimed the empty stool beside her. Corrie-Lyn wasn't wearing her Cleric robes, otherwise he would never have dared to go within ten metres. A simple dark purple dress, slit under each arm to reveal alluring amounts of skin wound up the lad's courage. She listened without comment to his opening lines, nodded reasonably when he offered to buy a drink, and beckoned the barkeeper over.

Aaron wished he could go over and draw the lad away. It was painful to watch, he'd seen this exact scene play out many times over the last few nights. The barkeeper came over with two heavy shot glasses and a frosted bottle of golden Adlier 88Vodka. Brewed on Vitchan, it bore no real relation to original Earth vodka, except for the kick. This was refined from a seasonal vine, Adlier, producing a liqueur that was eighty per cent alcohol and eight per cent tricetholyn, a powerful narcotic. The barkeeper filled both glasses and left the bottle.

Corrie-Lyn lifted hers in salute, and downed it in one. The hopeful lad followed suit. As he winced a smile against the burn of the icy liquid Corrie-Lyn filled both glasses again. She lifted hers. Somewhat apprehensively, the lad did the same. She tossed it down straight away.

There was laughter coming from the group at the

window now. Their friend slugged back the drink. There were tears in his eyes; an involuntary shudder ran along his chest as if he was suppressing a cough. Corrie-Lyn poured them both a third shot with mechanical precision. She downed hers in a single gulp. The lad gave a disgusted wave with one hand and backed away to jeering from his erstwhile pals. Aaron wasn't impressed; last night one of the would-be suitors had kept up for five shots before retreating, hurt and confused.

Corrie-Lyn slid the bottle back along the counter top, where the barkeeper caught it with an easy twist of his wrist and deposited it back on the shelf. She turned back to the tall beer she'd been drinking before the interruption, resting her elbows on either side of the glass, and resumed staring at nothing.

Watching her, Aaron acknowledged that cultivating Corrie-Lyn was never going to be a subtle play of seduction. There was only going to be one chance, and if he blew that he'd have to waste days finding another angle. He got to his feet and walked over. As he approached he could sense her gaiafield emission, which was reduced to a minimum. It was like a breath of polar air, cold enough to make him shiver; her silhouette within the ethereal field was black, a rift into interstellar space. Most people would have hesitated at that alone, never mind the Adlier 88 humiliation. He sat on the stool which the lad had just vacated. She turned to give him a dismissive look, eyes running over his cheap suit with insulting apathy.

Aaron called the barkeeper over and asked for a beer. 'You'll excuse me if I don't go through the ritual degradation,' he said. 'I'm not actually here to get inside your panties.'

'Thong.' She took a long drink of her beer, not looking at him.

'I ... what?' That wasn't quite the answer he was prepared for.

'Inside my thong.'

'I suddenly feel an urge to get ordained into your religion.'

She grinned to herself and swirled the remains of her beer round. 'You've had enough time, you've been hanging round here for a few days now.'

His beer arrived and Corrie-Lyn silently swapped it for her own.

Aaron raised his finger to the barkeeper. 'Another. Make that two.'

'And it's not a religion,' she said.

'Of course not, how silly of me. Priest robes. Worshipping a lost prophet. The promise of salvation. Giving money to the city temple. Going on Pilgrimage. I apologize, easy mistake to make.'

'Keep talking like that offworlder, you'll wind up head first in a canal before dawn.'

'Head first or head-less?'

Corrie-Lyn finally turned and gave him her full attention; her smile matched up to her impish allure. 'What in Ozzie's Great Universe do you want?'

'To make you very rich indeed.'

'Why would you want to do that?'

'So I can make myself even richer.'

'I'm not very good at bank heists.'

'Yeah, guess it doesn't come up much at Priest school.'

'Priests ask you to have faith. We can take you straight

to heaven, we even give you a sneak preview so you know what you're getting.'

'And that's where we come in.'

'We?'

'FarFlight Charters. I believe your not-religion is currently in need of starships, Councillor Emeritus.'

Corrie-Lyn laughed. 'Oh, you are dangerous, aren't you?'

'No danger, just an aching to be rich.'

'But I'm on my way to our heaven in the Void. What do I need with Commonwealth money?'

'Even the Waterwalker used money. But I'm not going to argue that case with you; or any other for that matter. I'm just here to make the proposition. You have contacts I need, and it is my belief you're none too happy with your old friends on the Cleric Council right now. Might be willing to bend a few ethics here and there – especially here. Am I speaking the right of things, Councillor Emeritus?'

'Why use the formal mode of address? Be bold, go the whole way, call me shitlisted. Everyone else does.'

'The unisphere news clowns have many labels for all of us. That doesn't mean you haven't got the names I need up here.' He tapped the side of his head. 'And I suspect there's enough residual respect for you in the Orchard Palace to open a few doors for me. Isn't that the way of it?'

'Could be. So what's your name?'

'Aaron.'

Corrie-Lyn smiled into her beer. 'Top of the list, huh?'

'Number one, Councillor Emeritus. So how about I buy you dinner? And you either have fun stringing me along, or give me your private bank account code so I can fill it up. Take your time to decide.'

'I will.'

FarFlight Charters was a legitimately registered company on Falnox. Anyone searching its datacore would have found it brokered for several spacelines and cargo couriers on seven External planets, not a huge operation but profitable enough to employ thirty personnel. Luckily for Aaron it was a simple front which had been put in place should he need it. He didn't know by whom. Didn't care. But if it had been real, then his expenses would have had serious implications for this year's profitability. This was the third night he'd wined and dined Corrie-Lyn, with much emphasis on the wine. The meals had all been five-star gourmet, as well. She liked Bertrand's in Greater Makkathran; a restaurant which made the Hotel Buckingham look like a flophouse for yokels. He didn't know if she was testing his resolve or not. Given the state she was in most nights she probably didn't know herself.

She did dress well, though. Tonight she wore a simple little black cocktail dress whose short skirt produced a seductive hem of mist that swirled provocatively every time she crossed or uncrossed her legs. Their table was in a perfectly transparent overhanging alcove on the seventy-second floor, providing an unenhanced view out across the huge night-time city. Directly below Aaron's feet, capsules slid along their designated traffic routes in a thick glare of navigation strobes. Once he'd recovered from the creepy feeling of vertigo needling his legs the view was actually quite invigorating. The seven-course meal they were eating was a sensory delight. Each dish accompanied by a wine the chef had selected to complement it. The waiter had given up offering a single glass to Corrie-Lyn, now he just left the bottle each time.

'He was a remarkable man,' Corrie-Lyn said when she finished her gilcherry leaf chocolate torte. She was talking about her favourite topic again. It wasn't difficult to get her started on Inigo.

'Anyone who can create a movement like Living Dream in just a couple of centuries is bound to be out-of-the-ordinary.'

'No no,' Corrie-Lyn waved her glass dismissively. 'That's not the point. If you or I had been given those dreams, there would still be Living Dream. They inspire people. Everyone can see for themselves what a beautiful simple life can be lived in the Void, one you can perfect no matter how screwed up or stupid you are, no matter how long it takes. You can only do that inside the Void, so if you promise to make that ability available to everyone you can't *not* gather a whole load of followers, now can you? It's inevitable. What I'm talking about is the man himself. Mister Incorruptible. That's rare. Give most people that much power and they'll abuse it. I would. Ethan certainly fucking does.' She poured the last of a two-and-a-half-century-old Mithan port into an equally ancient crystal glass.

Aaron smiled tightly. The alcove was open to the main restaurant floor, and Corrie-Lyn had downed her usual amount.

'That's why Inigo set up the movement hierarchy like an order of monks. Not that you couldn't have lots of sex,' she sniggered. 'You just weren't supposed to take advantage of the desperate faithful; you just screw around among your own level.'

'So far, so pretty standard.'

'Course, I wasn't very pure. We had quite a thing going, me and Inigo. Did you know that?'

'I do believe you mentioned it once or twice.'

'Course you did, that's why you hit on me.'

'This isn't hitting on you, Corrie-Lyn.'

'Slim and fit.' She licked her lips. 'That's what I am, wouldn't you agree?'

'Very much so.' Actually, he didn't want to admit how physically attractive she was. It helped that any sexual impulse he might have felt was effectively neutralized by her drinking. After the first hour of any evening, she wasn't a pleasant person to be around.

Corrie-Lyn smiled down at her dress. 'Yeah, that's me all right. So . . . we had this thing, this fling. I mean, sure, he saw other women. For Ozzie's sake, the poor shit had a billion females willing and eager to rip their clothes off for him and have his babies. And I enjoyed it too, I mean, hell, Aaron, some of them made me look like I'd been hit hard by the ugly stick.'

'I thought you said he was incorruptible.'

'He was. He didn't take advantage is what I'm saying. But he's human. So am I. There were distractions, that's all. The cause. The vision. He stayed true to that, he gave us the dreams of the Void. He believed, Aaron, he believed utterly in what he was shown. The Void really is a better place for all of us. He made me believe, too. I'd always been a loyal follower. I had *faith*. Then I actually met him,

I saw his belief, his devotion, and through that I became a true apostle.' She finished the port and slumped back in her chair. 'I'm a zealot, Aaron. A true zealot. That's why Ethan kicked me off the Council. He doesn't like the old guard, those of us who remain true. So you, mister, you just keep your snide patronizing bollocks to yourself, you bastard, I don't fucking care what you think, I hate your smartarse weasel words. You don't believe and that makes you evil. I bet you haven't even experienced one of the dreams. That's your mistake, because they're real. For humans the Void is heaven.'

'It could be heaven. You don't know for sure.'

'See!' She wagged a finger in his direction, barely able to focus. 'You do it every time. Smartarse words. Not stupid enough to agree with me, oh no, but enough to make me have a go at preaching to you. Setting it up so I can save you.'

'You're wrong. This is all about the money.'

'Ha!' She held up the empty bottle of port, and scowled at it.

Aaron hesitated, he could never quite tell how much control she had. He took a risk and pushed. 'Anyway, if the Void is salvation, why did he leave?'

The result wasn't quite what he'd expected. Corrie-Lyn started sobbing.

'I don't know!' she wailed. 'He left us. Left all of us. Oh where are you, Inigo? Where did you go? I loved you so much.'

Aaron groaned in dismay. Their quiet meal was now a full-blown public spectacle. Her sobs were increasing in volume. He hurriedly called the waiter and shuffled round the seats to sit next to Corrie-Lyn, putting himself between her and the other curious patrons. 'Come on,' he murmured. 'Let's go.'

There was a landing platform on the thirtieth floor, but he wanted her to get some fresh air, so they took a lift straight down to the skyscraper's lobby. The boulevard outside was almost deserted. A slim road running down the middle was partially hidden behind a long row of tall bushy evergreen trees. The footpath alongside was illuminated by slender glowing arches.

'Do you think I'm attractive?' Corrie-Lyn slurred as he encouraged her to walk. Past the skyscraper there were a couple of blocks of apartments, all surrounded by raised gardens. Local nightbirds swooped and flittered silently through the arches. It was a warm air, with the smell of sea ozone accompanying the humid gusts coming in from the coast.

'Very attractive,' Aaron assured her. He wondered if he should insist she take the detox aerosol he'd brought along for this very eventuality. The trouble with drinkers of this stature was that they didn't want to sober up that quickly, especially not when they were burdened with as much grief as Corrie-Lyn.

'Then how come you don't try it on? Is it the drink? Do you not like me drinking?' She broke away to look at him, swaying slightly, her eyes blurred from tears, hauntingly miserable. With her light coat undone to show off the exclusive cocktail dress, she presented a profoundly unappealing sight.

'Business before pleasure,' Aaron said, hoping she'd accept that and just shut the hell up. He should have caught a taxi from the skyscraper's platform. As if she was finally picking up on his exasperation, she turned fast and started walking.

Someone appeared on the path barely five metres in front of them, a man in a one-piece suit that still had the remnants of its black stealth envelope swirling away like water in low gravity. Aaron scanned round with his full field functions. Two more people were shedding their envelopes as they walked up behind him. His combat routines moved smoothly to active status, accessing the situation. The first of the group to confront them was designated One. Eighty per cent probability he was the commander. The subordinates were tagged Two and Three. His close-range situation exoimage showed all three of them glowing with enrichments. He actually relaxed: by confronting him they'd taken away all choice. With that accepted, there would only be one outcome now. He simply waited for them to present him with the maximum target opportunity.

Corrie-Lyn blinked in mild bewilderment, peering forward at the first man as she clutched her small scarlet bag to her belly. 'I didn't see you. Where were you?'

'You don't look too good, Your Honour,' One replied. 'Why don't you come along with us?'

Corrie-Lyn pressed back into Aaron's side, degrading his strike ability by a third. 'No,' she moaned. 'No, I don't want to.'

'You're bringing the Living Dream into disrepute, Your Honour,' One said. 'Is that what Inigo would have wanted?'

'I know you,' she said wretchedly. 'I'm not going with you. Aaron, don't leave me. Please.'

'Nobody is going anywhere they don't want to.'

One didn't even look at him. 'You. Fuck off. If you ever want a sales meeting with a Councillor, be smart now.'

'Ah, well now, here's the thing,' Aaron said affably. 'I'm so stupid I can't afford an IQ boost come regeneration time. So I just stay this way for ever.' Behind him, Two and Three were standing very close now. They both drew small pistols. Aaron's routines identified their hardware as jelly guns. Developed a century and a half ago as a lethal short-range weapon, they did exactly as specified on human flesh. He could feel accelerants slipping through his neurones, quickening his mental reaction time. Biononic energy currents synchronized with them, upgrading his physical responses to match. The effect dragged out spoken words, so much so he could easily predict what was going to be said long before One finished his sentence.

'Then I'm sorry for you.' One sent a fast message to subordinates, which Aaron intercepted, it was nothing more than a simple code. He didn't even need to decrypt it. Both of them raised their weapons. Aaron's combat routines were already moving him smoothly. He twisted Corrie-Lyn out of the way as he bent down. The first shot from Two's jelly gun seared through the air where Aaron's head had been less than a second before. The beam struck the wall, producing a squirt of concrete dust. Aaron's foot came up fast, smashing into the knee of Three. Their force fields clashed with a screech, electrons flaring in a rosette of blue-white light. The velocity and power behind Aaron's kick was enough to distort his opponent's protection. Three's leg shattered as it was punched backwards, throwing the whole body sideways. Aaron's energy currents formatted a distortion pulse which slammed into One. He was flung back six metres into the garden wall, hitting it with a dull thud. His straining force field pushed out a dangerous bruised-purple nimbus as another of Aaron's distorter pulses pummelled him, trying to shove him clean through the wall. His back arched at the impact, force field close to outright failure.

Two was trying to swing his pistol round, tracking a target that was moving with inhuman speed. All his enriched senses revealed was a blurred shape as Aaron danced across the path. He never got a lock, Aaron's hand materialized out of a dim streak to chop across his throat, overloading the force field. His neck snapped instantly, and the corpse flew through the air. Aaron snatched the jelly gun from Two's hand at the same time, wrenching the fingers off with a liquid crunching sound. It took Aaron a fraction of a second to spin round again. His force field expanded into the ground, an anchor snatching away inertia, allowing him to stop instantly, the pistol aligned on One as the dazed man was clambering unsteadily to his feet. Blood from the severed fingers dripped down on to the path. One froze, sucking down air as he stared at the nozzle of the jelly gun. Aaron opened his grip, allowing the fingers to slither away. 'Who are they?' he yelled at Corrie-Lyn, who was lying on the sodden grass where she'd landed. She was giving One a bewildered look. 'Who?' Aaron demanded.

'The ... the police. That's Captain Manby, special protection division.'

'That's right,' Manby wheezed as he flinched against the pain. 'So you just put that fucking gun down. You're already drowning in shit so deep you'll never see the universe again.'

'Join me at the bottom.' Aaron pressed the trigger on the jelly gun, holding it down on continuous fire mode. He added his own distortion pulse to the barrage. Manby's force field held out for almost two seconds before collapsing. The jelly gun pulses struck the exposed body. Aaron turned and fired again, overloading Three's force field.

Corrie-Lyn threw up as waves of bloody sludge from both ruined corpses cascaded across the ground. She was wailing like a wounded kitten when Aaron hauled her to her feet. 'We have to go,' he shouted at her. She shrank back from his hold. 'Come on, now! Move!' His u-shadow was already calling down a taxi.

'No,' she whimpered. 'No, no. They didn't . . . you just killed them. You killed them.'

'Do you understand what this is?' he growled at her, his voice loud, aggressive; using belligerence to keep her off balance. 'Do you understand what just happened? Do you? They're an assassination squad. Ethan wants you dead. Permanently dead. You can't stay here. They'll keep coming after you. Corrie-Lyn! I can protect you.'

'Me?' she sobbed. 'They wanted me?'

'Yes. Now come on, we're not safe here.'

'Oh sweet Ozzie.'

He shook her. 'Do you understand?'

'Yes,' she whispered. By the way she was shaking Aaron thought she was going into mild shock. 'Good,' he started to walk towards the descending taxi, hauling her along, heedless of the way she stumbled to keep up. It was hard not to smile. He couldn't have delivered a better result to the evening if he'd planned it.

Inigo's first dream

When Edeard woke, his dream was already a confused fading memory. The same thing happened every morning. No matter how hard he tried he could never hold on to the images and sounds afflicting him every night. Akeem said not to worry; that his dreams were made up from the gentle spillage of other sleeping minds around him. Edeard didn't believe the things he dreamed of came from anywhere like their village, the fragments he occasionally did manage to cling to were too strange and fascinating for that.

Cool pre-dawn light was showing up the cracks in the window's wooden shutters. Edeard lay still for a while, cosy under the pile of blankets that covered his cot. It was a big room, with whitewashed plaster walls and bare floorboards. The rafters of the hammer-beam roof above were ancient martoz wood that had blackened and hardened over the decades until they resembled iron. There wasn't much by way of furniture, two thirds of the floor space was completely empty. Edeard had shoved what was left down to the end which had a broad window. At the foot of the cot was a crude chest where he kept his meagre collection of clothes; there was a long table covered in his enthusiastic sketches of possible genistar animals; several chairs; a dresser with a plain white bowl and pitcher of water. Over in the corner opposite the cot, the fire had burnt out sometime in the night, with a few embers left glimmering in the grate. It was difficult to heat such a large volume, especially in winter, and Edeard could see his breath as a fine white mist. Technically, he lived in the apprentice dormitory of Ashwell village's Eggshaper Guild, but he was the only occupant. He'd lived there for the past six years, ever since his parents died when he was eight years old. Master Akeem, the village's sole remaining shaper, had taken him in after the caravan they had joined in order to travel through the hills to the east was attacked by bandits.

Edeard wrapped a blanket round his shoulders and hurried over the cold floor to the small brick-arch fire-place. The embers were still giving off a little heat, warming the clothes he'd left on the back of a chair. He dressed hurriedly, pulling up badly worn leather trousers and tucking an equally worn shirt into the waist before struggling into a thick green sweater. As always the fabric smelled of the stables and their varied occupants, a melange of fur and food and cages; but after six years at the Guild he was so used to it he hardly noticed. He sat back on the cot to pull his boots on; they really were too small for him now. With the last eighteen months seeing more genistars in the stables and Edeard taking on official commission duties, their little branch of the Eggshaper Guild had seen a lot more money coming it. Hardly a fortune, but sufficient to pay for new clothes and boots, it was just that he never had time to visit the cobbler. He winced slightly as he stood up, trying to wriggle his toes which were squashed together. It was no good, he was definitely going to take an hour out of his busy day to visit the cobbler. He grinned. *But not today.*

Today was when the village's new well was finished. It was a project in which the Eggshaper Guild was playing an unusually large part. Better than that, for him, it was an innovative part. Edeard knew how many doubters there were in the village: basically everybody. But Master Akeem had quietly persuaded the elder council to give his young apprentice a chance. They said yes only because they had nothing to lose.

He made his way downstairs, then hurried across the narrow rear yard to the warmth of the Guild dining hall. Like the dormitory, it was a sharp reminder that the Eggshaper Guild had known better times. A lot better. There were still two rows of long bench tables in the big hall, enough to seat fifty shapers and their guests on feast nights. At the far end the huge fireplace had iron baking ovens built in to the stonework on either side, and the roasting spit was large enough to handle a whole pig. This morning, the fire was just a small blaze tended by a couple of ge-monkeys. Normally, people didn't let the genistars get anywhere near naked flames, they were as skittish as any terrestrial animal, but Edeard's orders were lucid and embedded deeply enough that the ge-monkeys could manage the routine without panicking.

Edeard sat at the table closest to the fire. His mind directed a batch of instructions to the ge-monkeys using simple telepathic longtalk. He used a pidgin version of Querencia's mental language, visualizing the sequence of events he wanted in conjunction with simple command phrases, making sure the emotional content was zero (so many people forgot that, and then couldn't understand why the genistars didn't obey properly). The ge-monkeys started scurrying round; they were big creatures, easily the weight of a full-grown human male, with six long legs along the lower half of their body, and six even longer arms on top, the first two pairs so close together they seemed to be sharing a shoulder joint, while the third pair were set further back along a very flexible spine. Their bodies were covered in a wiry white fur, with patches worn away on joints and palms to reveal a leathery cinder-coloured hide. The head profile was the same as all the genistar variants, a plain globe with a snout very close to a terrestrial dog; the ears were situated on the lower part of the head back towards the stumpy neck, each one sprouting three petals of long creased skin thin enough to be translucent.

A big mug of tea was placed in front of Edeard, swiftly followed by thick slices of toast, a bowl of fruit and a plate of scrambled eggs. He tucked in heartily enough, already running through the critical part of the day's operation at the bottom of the well. His farsight picked up Akeem when the old man was still in the lodge, the residence for senior shapers annexed to the hall. Edeard could already perceive through a couple of stone walls, sensing physical structures as if they were shadows, while minds buzzed with an iridescent glow. That vision was of a calibre which eluded a lot of adults; it made Akeem inordinately proud of his apprentice's ability, claiming his own training was the true key to developing Edeard's potential.

The old shaper came into the hall to find the ge-monkeys ready with his breakfast. He grunted favourably as he gave Edeard's shoulder a paternal squeeze. 'Did you sense me getting up in my bedroom, boy?' he asked, gesturing at his waiting plate of sausage and tomato.

'No sir,' Edeard said happily. 'Can't manage to get through four walls yet.'

'Won't be long,' Akeem said as he lifted up his tea. 'The way you're developing I'll be sleeping outside the village walls by midsummer. Everyone's entitled to some privacy.'

'I would never intrude,' Edeard protested. He mellowed and grinned sheepishly as he caught the amusement in the old shaper's mind. Master Akeem had passed his hundred and eightieth birthday several years back, so he claimed, though he was always vague about the precise year that happened. Life expectancy on Querencia was supposed to be around two hundred years, though Edeard didn't know of anyone in Ashwell or the surrounding villages who'd actually managed to live that long. However, Akeem's undeniable age had given him a rounded face with at least three chins rolling back into a thick neck, and a lacework of red and purple capillaries decorated the pale skin of his cheeks and nose, producing a terribly wan appearance. A thin stubble left behind after his perfunctory daily shave was now mostly grey, which didn't help the careworn impression everyone received when they saw him for the first time. Once a week the old man used the same razor on what was left of his silver hair.

Despite his declining years, he always insisted on dressing smartly. His personal ge-monkeys were well versed in laundry work. Today his tailored leather trousers were clean, boots polished; a pale yellow shirt washed and pressed. He wore a jacket woven from magenta and jade yarn, with the egg-in-a-twisted-circle crest of the Eggshaper

Guild on the lapel. The jacket might not be as impressive as the robes worn by Guild members in Makkathran, but in Ashwell it was a symbol of prestige, earning him respect. None of the other village elders dressed as well.

Edeard sheepishly realized he was fingering his own junior apprentice badge, a simple metal button on his collar; the emblem similar to Akeem's, but with only a quarter circle. Half the time he forgot to pin it on in the morning. After all, nobody showed him any respect, ever. But if all went well today he'd be entitled to a badge with half a circle. Akeem said he could never remember anyone attempting a shaping so sophisticated for their senior apprentice assessment.

'Nervous?' the old man asked.

'No,' Edeard said immediately. Then he ducked his head. 'They work in the tank, anyway.'

'Of course they do. They always do. Our true skill comes in determining what works in real life. From what I've seen, I don't believe there will be a problem. That's not a guarantee, mind. Nothing in life is certain.'

'What did you shape for your senior apprentice assessment?' Edeard asked.

'Ah, now well, that was a long time ago. Things were different back then, more formal. They always are in the capital. I suspect they haven't changed much.'

'Akeem!' Edeard pleaded; he loved the old man dearly, but oh how his mind wandered these days.

'Yes yes. As I recall, the assessment required four ge-spiders; functional ones, mind. They had to spin drosilk at the Grand Master's presentation, so everyone wound up shaping at least six or seven to be safe. We also had to shape a wolf, a chimp, and an eagle. Ah,' he sighed. 'They were hard days. I remember my Master used to beat me continually. And the larks we used to get up to in the dormitory at night.'

Edeard was slightly disappointed. 'But I can do ge-spiders and all the rest.'

'I know,' Akeem said proudly, and patted the boy's hand. 'But we both know how gifted you are. A junior apprentice is normally seventeen before taking the kind of assessment you're getting today, and even then a lot of them fail the first time. This is why I've made your task all the harder. A reshaped form that works is the standard graduation from apprenticehood to practitioner.'

'It is?'

'Oh yes. Of course I've been dreadfully remiss in the rest of the Guild teachings. It was hard enough to make you sit down long enough to learn your letters. And you're really not old enough to take in the Guild ethics and all that boring old theory, no matter how precise they are when I gift them to you. Though you seem to grasp things at an instinctive level. That's why you're still only going to be an apprentice after this.'

Edeard frowned. 'What kind of ethics could be involved in shaping?'

'Can't you think?'

'No, not really. Genistars are such a boon. They help everyone. Now I'm helping you sculpt, we can produce more standard genera than before, the village will grow strong and rich again.'

'Well I suppose as you're due to become a senior apprentice we should start to consider these notions. We'd need more apprentices if that were to truly come about.'

'There's Sancia, and little Evox has a powerful longtalk.'

'We'll see. Who knows? We might prove a little more acceptable after today. Families are reluctant to offer their children for us to train. And your friend Obron doesn't help matters.'

Edeard blushed. Obron was the village's chief bully, a boy a couple of years older than him, who delighted in making Edeard's life a misery outside the walls of the Guild compound. He hadn't realized Akeem had known about that. 'I should sort him out properly.'

'The Lady knows you've had enough provocation of late. I'm proud you haven't struck back. Eggshapers are always naturally strong telepaths, but part of that ethics course you're missing is how we shouldn't abuse our advantage.'

'I just haven't because . . .' He shrugged.

'It's not the right thing to do, and you know that,' Akeem concluded. 'You're a good boy, Edeard.' The old man looked at him, his thoughts a powerful mixture of pride and sadness.

Proximity to the emotional turmoil made Edeard blink away the water now unexpectedly springing into his eyes. He shook his head, as if to disentangle himself from the old man's mind. 'Did you ever have someone like Obron ragging you when you were an apprentice?'

'Let's just say one of the reasons I came to stay in Ashwell was because my interpretation of our Guild ethics differed from the Masters of the Blue Tower. And please remember, although I am your Master and tutor, I also require Guild standards to be fulfilled. If I judge you lacking you will not get your senior apprentice badge today. That includes taking care of your ordinary duties.'

Edeard pushed his empty plate away and downed the last of his tea. 'I'd better get to it, then, Master.'

'I also fail anyone who shows disrespect.'

Edeard pulled a woolly hat on against the chill air, and went out into the Guild compound's main courtyard. It was unusual in that it had nine sides. Seven were made up from stable blocks, then there was a large barn, and the hatchery. None of them were the same size or height. When he first moved in, Edeard had been impressed. The Eggshaper Guild compound was the largest collection of buildings in the village; to someone who'd been brought up in a small cottage with a leaky thatch roof it was a palatial castle. Back then he'd never noticed the deep cloak of kimoss staining every roof a vivid purple; nor how pervasive and tangled the gurkvine was, covering the dark stone walls of the courtyard with its ragged pale-yellow leaves, while its roots wormed their way into the mortar between the blocks, weakening the structure. This morning he just sighed at the sight, wondering if he'd ever get round to directing the ge-monkeys on a clean-up mission. Now would be a good time. The gurkvine leaves had all fallen to gather in the corners of the courtyard in great mouldering piles, while the moss was soaking up the season's moisture, turning into great spongy mats which would be easy to peel off. Like everything else in his life, it would have to wait. *If only Akeem could find another apprentice*, he thought wistfully. *We spend our whole lives running to catch up, just one extra person in the Guild would make so much difference.*

It would take a miracle granted by the Lady, he acknowledged grudgingly. The village families were reluctant to allow their children to train at the Eggshaper Guild. They appreciated how dependent they were on genistars, but even so they couldn't afford to lose able hands. The Guild was just like the rest of Ashwell, struggling to keep going.

Edeard hurried across the courtyard to the tanks where his new reshaped cats were kept, silently asking the Lady why he bothered to stay in this backward place on the edge of the wilds. To his right were the largest stables, where the defaults shuffled round their stalls. They were simple beasts, unshaped egg-laying genistars, the same size as terrestrial ponies, with six legs supporting a bulbous body. The six upper limbs were vestigial, producing bumps along the creature's back, while in the female over thirty per cent of the internal organs were ovaries, producing an egg every fifteen days. Males, of which there were three, lumbered round in a big pen at one end, while the females were kept in a row of fifteen separate stalls. For the first time since Akeem had taken him in, the stalls were all occupied; a source of considerable satisfaction to Edeard. Not even a Master as accomplished as Akeem, and despite his age he was a singular talent, could manage fifteen defaults by himself. Shaping an egg took a long time, and Edeard had as many grotesque failures as he had successes. First of all, the timing had to be right. An egg needed to be shaped no earlier than ten hours after fertilization, and no later than twenty-five. How long it took depended on the nature of the genus required.

Edeard had often spent half the night sitting in a stall's deep-cushioned shaper chair with his mind focused on the egg. Eggshaping, as Akeem had so often described it, was like sculpting intangible clay with invisible hands. The ability was a gentle combination of farsight and telekinesis. His mind could see inside the egg, and only those who could do that with perfect clarity could become shapers. Not that he liked to boast, but Edeard's mental vision was the most acute in the village. What he saw within the shell was like a small exemplar of a default genistar made out of grey shadow substance. His telekinesis would reach out and begin to shape it into the form he wanted – but slowly, so frustratingly slowly. There were limits. He couldn't give a genistar anything extra: seven arms, two heads ... What the process did was activate the nascent structures inherent within the default physiology. He could also define size, though that was partially determined by what type of genus he was shaping. Then there were sub-families within each standard genus, chimps as well as monkeys, a multitude of horse types – big, small, powerful, fast, slow. A long list which had to be memorized perfectly. Shaping was inordinately difficult, requiring immense concentration. A shaper had to have a lot more than eldritch vision and manipulation; he or she had to have the *feel* of what they were doing, to know instinctively if what they were doing was right, to see potential within the embryonic genistar. In the smaller creatures there would be no room for reproductive organs, so they had to be disengaged, other organs too had to be selected where appropriate. But which ones? Small wonder even a Grand Master produced a large percentage of invalid eggs.

Edeard walked past the default stables, his farsight flashing through the building, checking that the ge-monkeys were getting on with their jobs of mucking out and feeding. Several were becoming negligent and disorderly, so he refreshed their instructions with a quick longtalk message. A slightly deeper scan with his farsight showed him the state of the gestating eggs inside the defaults. Of the eleven that had been shaped, three were showing signs that indicated problems were developing. He gave a resigned sigh. Two of them were his.

After the defaults came the horse stables. There were nine foals currently accommodated, seven of which were growing up into the large sturdy brutes which would pull ploughs and carts out on the surrounding farms. Most of the commissions placed on Ashwell's Eggshaper Guild were for genistars which could be used in agriculture. The custom of domestic ge-monkeys and chimps was in decline, which Edeard knew was just because people didn't take the time to learn how to instruct them properly. Not that they were going to come here and take lessons from a fourteen-year-old boy. It annoyed him immensely; he was certain the village economy could be improved fourfold at least if they just listened to him.

'Patience,' Akeem always counselled, when he raged against the short-sighted fools who made up their neighbours. 'Often to do what's right you first have to do what's wrong. There will come a time when your words will be heeded.'

Edeard didn't know when that would be. Even if today was successful he didn't expect a rush of people to congratulate him and seek out his advice. He was sure he was destined to forever remain the freaky boy who lived alone with batty old Akeem. A well matched pair, everyone said when they thought he couldn't farsight them.

The monkey and chimp pen was on the other side of the horses. It only had a couple of infant monkeys inside, curled up in their nest. The rest were all out and about, performing their duties around the Guild compound. They didn't have any commissions for ge-monkeys on their books; even the smithy who worked five didn't want any extras. *Perhaps I should bring people round the Guild buildings*, Edeard thought, *show them what the ge-monkeys can do if they're ordered correctly. Or Akeem could show them, at least. Just something that would break the cycle, make people more adventurous.* The freaky boy's daydream.

After the monkey pen came the kennels. Ge-dogs remained in high demand, especially the kind used for herding cattle and sheep. Eight pups were nursing from the two milk-bitches which he'd shaped himself. They allowed the defaults to go straight back to egg production without an extended nursing period. It had taken twelve invalid eggs before he'd succeeded in shaping the first. The innovation was one he'd introduced after reading about the milk-bitch in an ancient Guild text, now he was keen to try and extend it across all the genistar types. Akeem had been supportive when the first had hatched, impressed as much by Edeard's tenacity as his shaping skill.

The compound's main gateway was wedged in between the dog kennels and the wolf kennels. There were six of the fierce creatures maturing. Always useful outside the village walls, the wolves were deployed as guards for Ashwell and all its outlying farmhouses; they were also taken on hunts through the forests, helping to clear out Querencia's native predators as well as the occasional bandit group. Edeard stopped and looked in. The ge-wolves were lean creatures with dark-grey fur that blended in with most landscapes, their long snouts equipped with sharp fangs which could bite clean through a medium-sized branch, let alone a limb of meat and bone. The large pups mewled excitedly as he hung over the door and patted at them. His hand was licked by hot serpentine tongues. Two of them had a pair of arms, another of his innovations. He wanted to see if they could carry knives or clubs. Something else he'd found in an old text. Another idea the villagers had shaken their heads in despair at.

Out of the whole courtyard, he liked the aviary best. A squat circular cote with arched openings twenty feet above the ground, just below the eaves. There was a single doorway at the base. Inside, the open space was criss-crossed by broad martoz beams. Over the years the wood had been heavily scarred by talons, so much so that the original square cut was now rounded on top. There was only a single ge-eagle left, as big as Edeard's torso. The bird had a double wing arrangement, with two limbs supporting the large front wing and giving it remarkable flexibility, while the rear wing was a simple triangle for stability. Its gold and emerald feathers cloaked a streamlined body, with a long slender jaw where the teeth had merged into a single serrated edge very similar to a beak.

Trisegment eyes blinked down at Edeard as he smiled up. He so envied the ge-eagle, how it could soar free and clear of the village with all its earthbound drudgery and irrelevance. It had an unusually strong telepathic ability, allowing Edeard to experience wings spread wide and the wind slipping past. Often, whole afternoons would pass with an enthralled Edeard twinned with the ge-eagle's mind as it swooped and glided over the forests and valleys outside, providing an intoxicating taste of the freedom that existed beyond the village.

It rustled its wings, enthused by Edeard's appearance and the prospect of flight. *Not yet*, Edeard had to tell it reluctantly. Its beak was shaken in disgust and the eyes shut, returning it to an aloof posture.

The hatchery came between the aviary and the cattery. It was a low circular building, like a half-size aviary. Its broad iron-bound wooden door was closed and bolted. The one place in the compound that ge-monkeys weren't permitted to go. Edeard had the task of keeping it clean and tidy. A sheltered stone shelf to the right of the door had nine thick candles alight, traditionally one for each egg inside. He swept his farsight across them all, happy to confirm the embryos were growing satisfactorily. After they'd been laid, the eggs took about ten days to hatch, cosseted in cradles that in winter months were warmed by slow-smouldering charcoal in a massive iron stove. He'd need to rake out the ashes and add some more lumps before midday. One of the eggs was due to hatch tomorrow, he judged, another horse.

Finally, he went into the cattery, the smallest of the buildings walling the courtyard. Standard genistar cats were small semi-aquatic creatures, with dark oily fur and broad webbed feet, devoid of upper limbs. Guild convention had them as one of the seven standard genera, though nobody outside the capital Makkathran ever found much use for them. It was the gondoliers who kept a couple on each boat, using them to keep the city's canals clean of weed and rodents.

The cattery was a rectangular room taken up by big knee-high stone tables. Light came in through windows set into the roof. As a testament to how prolific the kimoss had become, Edeard now always supplemented his ordinary sight with farsight as he shuffled along the narrow aisles between the tables. From inside, the windows had been reduced to narrow slits that provided a meagre amethyst radiance.

Glass tanks sat along the tables. They were ancient, basins the size of bulky coffins, dating back to when the whole compound had been built. Half of them had cracked sides, and dried and dead algae stained the glass, while the bottoms were filled with gravel and desiccated flakes of mud. Edeard had refurbished five to hold his reshaped cats, with another three modified to act as crude reservoirs. The pipes he used to test their ability were strewn across the floor in a tangled mess. All five reshaped cats lay on the gravel bed of the tanks, with just a few inches of water rippling sluggishly round them. They resembled fat lozenges of glistening ebony flesh, half the size of a human. There were no limbs of any kind, just a row of six circular gills along their flanks dangling loose tubes of thick skin. The head was so small it looked completely undeveloped to the point of being misshapen; there were no eyes or ears. It was all Edeard's farsight could do to detect any sparkle of thought at all within the tiny brain.

He grinned down cheerily at the unmoving lumps, searching through them for any sign of malady. When he was satisfied their health was as good as possible, he stood perfectly still, taking calm measured breaths the way Akeem had taught him, and focused his telekinesis on the first cat, the third hand as most villagers called it. He could feel the black flesh within his incorporeal grip, and lifted it off the bed of mucky gravel.

Half an hour later, when Barakka the village cartwright drove his wagon into the courtyard he found Edeard and Akeem standing beside five tarpaulins with the reshaped cats lying on them. He wrinkled his face up in disgust at the bizarre creatures, and shot the old Guild Master a questioning look.

'Are you sure about this?' he asked as he swung himself off the bench. The cartwright was a squat man, made even broader by eight decades of hard physical labour. He had a thick, unruly ginger beard that served to make his grey eyes seem even more sunken. His hand scratched at his buried chin as he surveyed the ge-cats, doubt swirling openly in his mind, free for Edeard to see. Barakka didn't care much for the feelings of young apprentices.

'If they work they will bring a large benefit to Ashwell,' Akeem said smoothly. 'Surely it's worth a try?'

'Whatever you say,' Barakka conceded. He gave Edeard a sly grin. 'Are you aiming to be our Mayor, boy? If this works you'll get my blessing. I've been washing in horse muck these last three months. Course, old Geepalt will have his nose right out of joint.'

Geepalt, the village carpenter, was in charge of the existing well's pump, and by rights should have built a new pump for the freshly dug well. He was chief naysayer on allowing Edeard to try his innovation – it didn't help that Obron was his apprentice.

'There are worse things in life than an annoyed Geepalt,' Akeem said. 'Besides, when this works he'll have more time for profitable commissions.'

Barakka laughed. 'You old rogue! It is your tongue not your mind which shapes words against their true meaning.'

Akeem gave a small, pleased bow. 'Thank you. Shall we begin loading?'

'If Melzar's team is ready,' Barakka said.

Edeard's farsight flashed out, surveying the new well, with the crowd gathering around it. 'They are. Wedard has called the ge-monkey digging team out.'

Barakka gave him a calculating stare. The new well was

being dug on the other side of the village from the Eggshaper Guild compound. His own farsight couldn't reach that far. 'Very well, we'll put them on the wagon. Can you manage a third of the weight, boy?'

Edeard was very pleased that he managed to stop any irony from showing amid his surface thoughts. 'I think so, sir.' He caught Akeem's small private smile; the Master's mind remained calm and demure.

Barakka gave the reshaped cats another doubting look, and scratched his beard once more. 'All right then. On my call. Three. Two. One.'

Edeard exerted his third hand, careful not to boost more than he was supposed to. With the three of them lifting, the reshaped cat rose smoothly into the air and floated into the back of the open wagon.

'They're not small, are they?' Barakka said. His smile was somewhat forced. 'Good job you're helping, Akeem.'

Edeard didn't know if he should protest or laugh.

'We all play our part,' Akeem said. He was giving Edeard a warning stare.

'Second one, then,' Barakka said.

Ten minutes later they were rolling through the village, Barakka and Akeem sitting on the wagon's bench, while Edeard made do with the rear, one arm resting protectively over a cat. Ashwell was a clutter of buildings in the lee of a modest stone cliff that had sheered out of the side of a gentle slope. Almost impossible to climb, the cliff formed a good defence, with a semicircular walled rampart of earth and stone completing their protection from any malign forces that might ride in from the wild lands to the north-east. Most of the buildings were simple stone cottages with thatch roofs and slatted shutters. Some larger buildings had windows with glass panes that had been brought in from the western towns. Only the broad main street running parallel to the cliff was cobbled, the lanes running off it were little more than muddy ruts worn down to the stone by wheels and feet. Although the Eggshaper compound was the biggest collection of buildings, the tallest was the church of the Empyrean Lady, with its conical spire rising out of the north side of the low dome. Once upon a time the stone church had been a uniform white, but many seasons of neglect had seen the lightest sections moulder down to a drab grey, with kimoss pullulating in the slim gaps between the big blocks.

The road down to the village gate branched off midway along main street. Edeard looked along it, seeing the short brick-lined tunnel which cut through the sloping rampart; at the far end the massive doors were open to the outside world. On the top of the wall, twin watchtowers stood on either side of the door, with big iron bells on top. They would be rung by the guards at any sign of trouble approaching. Edeard had never heard them. Some of the older villagers claimed to remember their sound when bandit gangs had been spotted crossing the farmlands bordering the village.

As Edeard looked at the top of the rampart wall with its uneven line and many different materials he wondered how hard it actually would be to overcome their fortifications. There were places where crumbling gaps had been plugged by thick timbers, which themselves were now rotting beneath swathes of kimoss; and even if every man and woman in the village carried arms they couldn't stretch along more than a third of the length. In reality, then, their safety depended on the illusion of strength.

A sharp prick of pain on his left shin made him wince. It was a telekinetic pinch, which he warded off with a strong shield over his flesh. Obron and two of his cronies were flanking the wagon, mingling with the other villagers who were heading up to the new well. There was a sense of carnival in the air as the wagon made its slow procession through Ashwell, with people abandoning their normal work to tag along and see the innovation.

Now Edeard had been jerked away from his mild daydreaming he picked up on the bustle of amusement and interest filling the aether through the village. Very few people were expecting his reshaped cats to work, but they were looking forward to witnessing the failure. *Typical,* he thought. *This village always expects the worst. It's exactly the attitude that's responsible for our decline; not everything can be blamed on bad weather, poor crops, and more bandits.*

'Hey, Egg-boy,' Obron jeered. 'What are those abortions? And where are your pump genistars?' He laughed derisively, a cackling that was quickly duplicated by his friends.

'These are—' Edeard began crossly. He stopped as their laughter rose, wishing the wagon could travel a lot faster. There were smiles on the faces of the adults walking alongside as they witnessed typical apprentice rivalry – remembering what it had been like when they were young. Obron's thoughts were vivid and mocking. Edeard managed to keep his own temper. Revenge would come as soon as the cats were in place. There would be respect for the Eggshaper Guild, with a corresponding loss of status for the carpenters.

He was still clinging smugly to that knowledge when the wagon rolled up beside the new well. It was four months ago when the village's old well had partially collapsed. Rubble and silt had been sucked up into the pump, a large contraption assembled by the Carpentry Guild, with big cogwheels and leather bladders that were compressed and expanded by three ge-horses harnessed to a broad axle wheel. They walked round and round in a circle all day long, producing gulps of water that slopped out of the pipe into a reservoir trough for everyone to use. As no one had noticed the sludge at first, the ge-horses just kept on walking until the pump started to creak and shudder. It had been badly damaged.

Once the extent of the damage to the well had been assessed, the elder council had decreed a new well should be dug. This time, it was at the top of the village, close to the cliff where the water percolating down from the slopes above should be plentiful enough. There were also ideas that a simple network of pipes could carry fresh water into each house. That would have required an even larger pump to be built. At which point Akeem had brought his apprentice's idea to the council.

The crowd which had gathered round the head of the new well was good-natured enough when the wagon stopped. Melzar, who listed Water Master among many other village titles, was standing beside the open hole, talking to Wedard, the stonemason who had overseen the team of ge-monkeys that performed the actual digging. They both gave the reshaped cats an intrigued look. Edeard wasn't really aware of them, he could hear a lot of sniggering. It mostly came from the gang of apprentices centred around Obron. His cheeks flushed red as he struggled to hold the anger from showing in his surface thoughts.

'Have faith in yourself,' someone whispered into his

mind, a skilfully directed longtalk voice directed at him alone. The sentiment was threaded with a rosy glow of approval.

He looked round to see Salrana smiling warmly at him. She was only twelve, dressed in the blue and white robe of a Lady's novice. A sweet, good-natured child she had never wanted to do anything other than join the Church. The Lady's Mother of Ashwell, Lorellan, had been happy to start her instructions. Attendance was never high in the village church apart from the usual festival services. Like Edeard, Salrana never quite fitted into the mainstream of village life. It made them feel kindred. She was like a younger sister. He grinned back at her as he clambered down off the wagon. Lorellan, who was standing protectively to one side of her, gave him a bland smile.

Melzar came over to the back of the wagon. 'This should be interesting.'

'Why, thank you,' Akeem said. The cold air was turning the blood vessels on his nose and cheeks an even darker shade than normal.

Melzar inclined his head surreptitiously towards the surrounding crowd. Edeard didn't turn round, his farsight revealed Geepalt standing in the front row, feet apart and arms folded, a glower on his thin features. Contempt scudded across his surface thoughts, plain for everyone to sense. Edeard was adept enough to detect the currents of concern underneath.

'What's the water like?' Barakka asked.

'Cold, but very clear,' Melzar said contentedly. 'Digging the well this close to the cliff is a boon. There is a lot of water filtering through the rock from above us, and it's wonderfully pure. No need to boil it before we make beer, eh? Got to be good news.'

Edeard shuffled closer to the hole, half expecting Obron's third hand to shove at him. His feet squelched on the semi-frozen mud around the flagstones, and he peered over the rim. Wedard had done a good job of lining the circular shaft, the stones were perfectly cut, and fixed better than a lot of cottage walls. This well wouldn't crumble and collapse like the last one. Darkness lurked ten feet below the rim like an impenetrable mist. His farsight probed down, reaching the water over thirty feet below ground level.

'Are you ready?' Melzar asked. The voice was sympathetic. Without the Water Master's support, the council would never have allowed Edeard to try the cats.

'Yes, sir.'

Edeard, Akeem, Melzar, Barakka, and Wedard extended their third hands to lift the first cat off the wagon. Everyone in the crowd used their farsight to follow it into the gloomy shaft. Just as it reached the water, Edeard tensed. *Suppose it sinks?*

'And release,' Akeem said so smoothly and confidently that Edeard had no alternative but to let go. The cat bobbed about, completely unperturbed. Edeard realized he'd been holding his breath, anxiety scribbled right across his mind for everyone to sense, especially Obron. His relief was equally discernible to the villagers.

It wasn't long before all five cats were floating on the water. Melzar himself lowered the thick rubber hose, unwinding it slowly from the cylinder it was spooled round. The end was remarkably complicated, branching many times as if it had sprouted roots. Edeard lay flat on the flagstones around the rim, heedless of the freezing mud soaking into his sweater. Warm air gusted up from the shaft to tickle his face. He closed his eyes, allowing himself to concentrate solely on his third hand as it connected the hose ends to the cat gills. Simple muscle lips closed round the rubber tubes on his command, forming a tight seal. A standard genistar cat had three big flotation bladders, giving them complete control over their own buoyancy as they swam, allowing them to float peacefully or dive down several yards. It was these bladders which Edeard had shaped the new cats around, expanding them to occupy eighty per cent of the total body volume, surrounding them with muscle so that they were crude pumps, like a heart for water. His longtalk ordered them to start the muscle squeeze sequence, building up an elementary rhythm.

Everyone fell silent as he stood up. Eyes and farsight were focused on the giant stone trough which had been set up next to the well. The hose end curved over it. For an achingly long minute nothing happened, then it emitted a gurgling sound. Droplets of water spat out, prelude to a foaming torrent that poured into the trough. It began to fill up remarkably quickly.

Edeard remembered the flow of water from the old well pump: this had several times the pressure. Melzar dipped a cup into the water and tasted it. 'Fresh and pure,' he announced in a loud voice. 'And better than that: abundant.' He stood in front of Edeard, and started clapping, his eyes ranging round the crowd, encouraging. Others joined in. Soon Edeard was at the centre of a storm of applause. His cheeks were burning again, but this time he didn't care. Akeem's arm went round his shoulder, mind aglow with pride. Even Geepalt was acknowledging the success, albeit grudgingly. Of Obron and his cronies there was no sign.

There was the tidying up, of course. Sacs of the oily vegetable mush which the cats digested were filled and positioned beside the well; valves adjusted so they dripped a steady supply down slender tubes. Edeard connected the far end of each tube to the mouth of a cat, instructing them to suckle slowly. Wedard and his apprentices fastened the hose to the side of the well. The ground was cleared. Finally, the huge stone capping slab was moved over the shaft, sealing the cats into their agreeable new milieu. By that time apprentices and household ge-monkeys were already queuing at the trough with large pitchers.

'You have a rare talent, my boy,' Melzar said as he watched the water lapping close to the top of the trough, 'I see we're going to have to dig a drain to cope with the overspill. Then no doubt the council will soon be demanding that mad pipe scheme to supply the houses. Quite a revolution, you've started. Akeem, I'd be honoured if you and your apprentice would join us for our evening meal.'

'I will be happy to liberate some of the wine you hold prisoner,' Akeem said. 'I've heard there are whole dungeons full under your Guild hall.'

'Ha!' Melzar turned to Edeard. 'Do you like wine, my boy?'

Edeard realized that the question was actually genuine, for once he wasn't simply being humoured. 'I'm not sure, sir.'

'Best find out, then.'

The crowd had departed, creating a rare atmosphere of satisfaction pervading the village. It was a good way to start the new spring season, ran the feeling, a good omen that times were getting better. Edeard stayed close to the trough as the apprentices filled their pitchers. He wasn't sure if he was imagining it, but they seemed to be treating him with a tad more approbation than before. Several even congratulated him.

'Haunting the site of your victory?'

It was Salrana. He grinned at her. 'Actually, just making sure the cats don't keel over from exhaustion, or the hoses don't tear free. Stuff like that. There's a lot that can go wrong yet.'

'Poor, Edeard, always the pessimist.'

'Not today. Today was . . .'

'Glorious.'

He eyed the low clouds that were blocking the sun from view. 'Helpful. For me and the village.'

'I'm really pleased for you,' she exclaimed. 'It takes so much courage to stand up for your own convictions, especially in a place like this. Melzar was right; this is a revolution.'

'You were eavesdropping! What would the Lady say?'

'She would say, Well done, young man. This will make everyone's life a little better. Ashwell has one thing less to worry about, now. The people need that. Life is so hard, here. From small foundations of hope, empires can be built.'

'That has to be a quote,' he teased.

'If you attended church, you'd know.'

'I'm sorry. I don't get much time.'

'The Lady knows and understands.'

'You're such a good person, Salrana. One day you'll be the Pythia.'

'And you'll be Mayor of Makkathran. What a grand time we'll have together, making all of Querencia a happy place.'

'No more bandits. No more drudgery – especially not for apprentices.'

'Or novices.'

'They'll talk about our reign until the Skylords return to carry us all into the heart.'

'Oh look,' she squealed and pointed excitedly at the trough. 'It's overflowing! You've given us too much water, Edeard.'

He watched as the water began to spill over the lip of the trough. Within seconds it had become a small stream frothing across the mud towards their feet. They both ran aside, laughing.

2

Justine Burnelli examined her body closely before she put it on again. After all, it had been over two centuries since the last time she'd worn it. During the intervening years it had been stored in an exotic matter cage that generated a temporal suspension zone so that barely half a second had passed inside.

The cage looked like a simple sphere of violet light in ANA's New York reception facility, a building that extended for a hundred and fifty storeys below Manhattan's streets. Her cage was housed on the ninety-fifth floor, along with several thousand identical radiant bubbles. ANA normally maintained a body for five years after the personality downloaded out of it, just in case there were compatibility problems. Such an issue was unusual, the average was one in eleven million who rejected a life inside ANA and returned to the physical realm. Once those five years were up, the body was discontinued. After all, if a personality *really* wanted to leave ANA after that, a simple clone could be grown – a process not dissimilar to the old-fashioned re-life procedure that was still available out among the External Worlds.

However, ANA:Governance considered it useful to have

physical representatives walking the Greater Commonwealth in certain circumstances. Justine was one of them. It was partly her own fault. She'd been over eight hundred years old when Earth built its repository for Advanced Neural Activity, the ultimate virtual universe where everyone was supposedly equal in the end. After so much life she was very reluctant to see her body 'discontinued', in much the same way she'd never quite acknowledged that re-life was true continuation. For her, clones force-fed on a dead person's memories were not the same person, no matter that there was no discernible difference. That early-twenty-first century upbringing of hers was just too hard to shake off, even for someone as mature and controlled as she had become.

The violet haze faded away to reveal a blonde girl in her biological mid-twenties. Rather attractive, Justine noted with a little tweak of pride, and very little of that had come from genetic manipulation down the centuries. The face she was looking at was still recognizable as the brattish party *it* girl of the early twenty-first century who'd spent a decade on the gossip channels as she dated her way through East Coast society and soap actors. Her nose had been reduced, admittedly, and pointed slightly. Which, now she regarded it critically, was possibly a little too cutesy, especially with cheekbones that looked like they were made from avian bone they were so sharp yet delicate. Her eyes had been modified to a pale blue, matching Nordic white skin that tanned to honey gold, and hair that was thick white-blonde, falling down below her shoulders. Her height was greater than her friends from the twenty-first century would have remembered; she'd surreptitiously added four inches during various rejuvenation treatments; despite the temptation she hadn't gained all that length in her legs, she'd made sure her torso was in proportion with a nicely flat abdomen which was easy to maintain thanks to a slightly accelerated digestive tract. Happily she'd never gone for ridiculous boobs – well, except that one time when she was rejuving for her two hundredth birthday and did it just to find out what it was like having a Grand Canyon cleavage. And yes men did gape and come out with even more stupid opening lines, but as she could always have whoever she wanted anyway there was no real advantage and it wasn't really her so she'd got rid of them at the next rejuvenation session.

So there she was, in the flesh, and still in good shape, just lacking a mind. With the monitor program confirming her visual review she poured her consciousness back into her brain. The memory reduction was phenomenal, as was the loss of all the advanced thought routines which comprised her true personality these days. Her old biological neurone structure simply didn't have the capacity to hold what she had become in ANA. It was like being lobotomized, actually feeling your mind wither away to some primitive insect faculty. *But only temporary*, she told herself – so sluggishly!

Justine drew her first breath in two hundred years, chest jerking down air as if she was waking from a nightmare. Her heart started racing away. For a moment she did nothing – not actually remembering what to do – then the reliable old automatic reflexes kicked in. She drew another breath, getting a grip on her panic, overriding the old Neanderthal instincts with pure rationality. Another regular breath. Calming her heart. Exoimages flickered into her peripheral vision, bringing up rows of default symbols from her enrichments. She opened her eyes. Long ranks of violet bubbles stretched out in all directions around her like some bizarre artwork sculpture. Somehow her meat-based mind was convinced she could see the shapes of people inside. That was preposterous. Inside ANA she'd obviously allowed herself to discard the memory of how fallible and hormone susceptible a human brain was.

A slow smile revealed perfect white teeth. *At least I'll get to have some real sex before I download again.*

Justine teleported out of the New York reception facility right into the centre of the Tulip Mansion. Stabilizer fields had maintained the ancient Burnelli family home through the centuries, keeping the building's fabric in pristine condition. She gave a happy grin when she saw it again with her own eyes. If she was honest with herself it was a bit of a monstrosity; a mansion laid out in four 'petals' whose scarlet and black roofs curved up to a central tower 'stamen' which had an apex 'anther' made from a crown of carved stone coated in gold foil. It was as gaudy as it was striking, falling in and out of fashion over the decades. Justine's father, Gore Burnelli, had bought the estate in Rye county just outside New York, establishing it as a base for the family's vast commercial and financial activities in the middle of the twenty-first century. It had remained a centre for them while the Commonwealth was established and expanded outwards until finally its social and economic uniformity was shattered by biononics, ANA, and the separation of Higher and Advancer cultures. Today the family still had a prodigious business empire spread across the External Worlds, but it was managed in a corporate structure by thousands of Burnellis, none of whom was over three hundred years old. Gore, along with his original clique of close relatives (including Justine) who used to orchestrate it all, had long since downloaded into ANA. Though Gore had never formally and legally handed over ownership to his impatient descendants. It was, he assured them, purely a quirk for their own benefit, ensuring the whole enterprise could never be broken up, thus giving the family a cohesion that so many others lacked. Except Justine knew damn well that even in his enlightened, expanded, semi-omnipotent state within ANA, Gore wasn't about to hand anything over he'd spent centuries building up. *Quirk, my ass.*

She'd materialized in the middle of the mansion's ballroom. Her bare feet pressed down on a polished oak floor that was nearly as shiny as the huge gilt-edged mirrors on the wall. A hundred reflections of her naked body grinned sheepishly back at her. Deep-purple velvet drapes curved around the tall window doors which opened out on a veranda dripping with white wisteria. Outside, a bright low February sun shone across the extensive wooded grounds with their massive swathes of rhododendrons. There had been some fabulous parties held in here, she recalled. Fame, wealth, glamour, power, notoriety, and beauty mingling in a fashion that would have made Jane Austen green with envy.

The doors were open, leading out into the broad corridor. Justine walked through, taking in all the semi-familiar sights, welcoming the warm rush of recognition. Alcoves were filled with furniture that had been antique even before Ozzie and Nigel built their first wormhole generator; and as for the artwork, you could buy a small continent on an External World with just one of the paintings.

She padded up the staircase which curved its way through the entrance hall, and made her way down the north petal to her old bedroom. Everything was as she'd left it, maintained for centuries by the stabilizer fields and maidbots; a comforting illusion that she or any other Burnelli could walk in at any time and be given a perfect greeting in their ancestral home. The bed was freshly made, with linen taken out of the stabilizer field and freshened as soon as she and ANA had agreed to the reception. Several clothes were laid out. She ignored the modern toga suit, and went for a classical Indian-themed emerald dress with black boots.

'Very neutral.'

Justine jumped at the voice. Irritation quickly supplanted perturbation. She turned and glared at the solido standing in the doorway. 'Dad, I don't care how far past the physical you claim to be, you DO NOT come into a girl's bedroom without knocking. Especially mine.'

Gore Burnelli's image didn't show much contrition. He simply watched with interest as she sat on the bed and laced her boots up. He'd chosen the representation of his twenty-fourth-century self, which was undoubtedly the image for which he was most renowned: a body whose skin had been turned to gold. Over that he wore a black V-neck sweater and black trousers. The perfect reflective surface made it difficult to determine his features. Without the gold sheen he would have been a handsome twenty-five-year-old with short-cropped fair hair. His face, which at the time he had it done was nothing more than merged organic circuitry tattoos, was all the more disconcerting thanks to the perfectly ordinary grey eyes peering out of the gloss. That Gore looked out on the world from behind a mask of improvements was something of a metaphor. He was a pioneer of enhanced mental routines, and had been one of the founders of ANA.

'Like it matters,' he grunted.

'Politeness is always relevant,' she snapped back. Her temper wasn't improved by the way her fingers seemed to lack any real dexterity. She was having trouble tying the boot laces.

'You were a good choice to receive the Ambassador.'

She finally managed to finish the bow, and lifted a quizzical eyebrow. 'Are you jealous, Dad?'

'Of becoming some kind of turbo-version of a monkey again? Yeah, right. Thinking down at this level and this speed gives me a headache.'

'Turbo-monkey! You nearly said animal, didn't you?'

'Flesh and blood is animal.'

'Just how many Factions do you support?'

'I'm a Conservative, everyone knows that. Maybe a few campaign contributions to the Outwards.'

'Humm.' She gave him a suspicious look. Even in a body, she knew the rumours that ANA gave special dispensation to some of its internal personalities. ANA: Governance denied it, of course; but if anyone could manage to be more equal than others it would be Gore, who'd been in there right at the start as one of the founding fathers.

'The Ambassador is nearly here,' Gore said.

Justine checked her exoimages, and started to re-order her secondary thought routines. Her body's macrocellular clusters and biononics were centuries out of date, but still perfectly adequate for the simple tasks today would require. She called her son, Kazimir. 'I'm ready,' she told him.

As she walked out of her bedroom she experienced a brief chill that made her glance back over her shoulder. *That's the bed where we made love. The last time I saw him alive.* Kazimir McFoster was one memory she had never put into storage, never allowed to weaken. There had been others since, many others, both in the flesh and in ANA, wonderful, intense relationships, but none ever had the poignancy of dear Kazimir whose death was her responsibility.

Gore said nothing as his solido followed her down the grand staircase to the entrance hall. She suspected that he suspected.

Kazimir teleported into the marbled entrance hall; appearing dead centre on the big Burnelli crest. He was dressed in his Admiral's tunic. Justine had never seen him wear anything else in six hundred years. He smiled in genuine welcome and gave her a gentle embrace, his lips brushing her cheek.

'Mother. You look wonderful as always.'

She sighed. He did look *so* like his father. 'Thank you, darling.'

'Grandfather.' He gave Gore a shallow bow.

'Still holding up in that old receptacle, then,' Gore said. 'When are you going to join us here in civilization?'

'Not today, thank you, Grandfather.'

'Dad, pack it in,' Justine warned.

'It's goddamn creepy if you ask me,' Gore grumbled. 'No one stays in a body for a thousand years. What's left for you out there?'

'Life. People. Friends. True responsibility. A sense of wonder.'

'We got a ton of that in here.'

'And while you look inwards, the universe carries on around you.'

'Hey, we're very aware of extrinsic events.'

'Which is why we're having this happy family reunion today.' Kazimir gave a small victory smile.

Justine wasn't even listening to them any more, they always ran through this argument as if it was a greeting ritual. 'Shall we go, boys?'

The doors of the mansion swung open and she walked out on to the broad portico without waiting for the others. It was a cold air outside; frost was still cloaking the deeper hollows in the lawn where the long shadows prevailed. A few clouds scudded across the fresh blue sky. Pushing its way through them was the Ocisen Empire ship sliding in from the south-east. Roughly triangular, it measured nearly two hundred metres long. There was nothing remotely aerodynamic about it. The fuselage was a dark metal, mottled with aquamarine patches that resembled lichen. Its crinkled surface was cratered with indentations that sprouted black spindles at the centre, whilst long boxes looked as though they'd been welded on at random. A cluster of sharp radiator fins emerged from the rear section, glowing bright red.

Gore gave a derisive chuckle. 'What a monstrosity. You'd think they could do better now we've given them regrav.'

'We took five hundred years to get from the Wright brothers at Kitty Hawk to the *Second Chance*,' Justine pointed out.

Gore looked up as the alien starship slowed to a halt above the mansion's grounds. 'Do you think it'll have jets of dry ice gushing out when it lands, or maybe they've mounted a giant laser gun that'll blast the White House to smithereens?'

'Dad, be quiet.'

The ship descended. Two rows of hatches along its belly swung open.

'For fuck's sake, haven't they even heard of malmetal?' Gore complained.

Long fat landing legs telescoped out. The movement was accompanied by a sharp hissing sound as high-pressure gas vented through grilles in the undercarriage bays.

Justine had to suck her lower lip in to stop herself giggling. The starship was ridiculous, the kind of contraption Isambard Kingdom Brunel would have built for Queen Victoria.

It touched down on the lawn, its landing pads sinking deep into the grass and soft soil. Several radiator fins sliced down into silver birch trees, their heat igniting the wood. Burning branches dropped to the ground.

'Wow, the damage it causes. How will our world survive? Quick, you kids flee to the woods, I'll hold them off with a shotgun.'

'Dad! And cancel your solido, you know what the Empire thinks of ANA personalities.'

'Stupid *and* superstitious.'

His solido vanished. Justine watched his icon appear in her exoimage. 'Now behave,' she told him.

'That ship is leaking radiation all over the place,' Gore commented. 'They haven't even shielded their fusion reactor properly. And who uses deuterium anyway?'

Justine reviewed the sensor data, scanning the ship's hotspots. 'It's hardly a harmful emission level.'

'The Ocisens aren't as susceptible to radioactivity as

humans are,' Kazimir said. 'It's one reason they were able to industrialize space in their home system with what equates to our mid-twenty-first-century technology. They simply didn't require the shielding mass we would have needed.'

Halfway down the starship's fuselage a multi-segment airlock door unwound. The Ambassador for the Ocisen Empire floated out, sitting on top of a hemispherical regrav sled. Physically, the alien wasn't impressive; a small barrel-shaped torso wrapped in layers of flaccid flesh that formed overlapping folds. Its four eyes were on serpent stalks curving out from the crest, while four limbs were folded up against the lower half of its body. They were encrusted in cybernetic systems, amplifying its strength and providing a number of manipulator attachments ranging from delicate pliers up to a big hydraulic crab pincer. Further support braces ran up its body, resembling a cage of chrome vertebrae that ended in a collar arrangement just below the base of the eye stalks. Patches of what looked like copper moss were growing across various sections of its flesh; they sprouted small rubbery stalks covered in minute sapphire flowers.

Justine bowed formally as the sled stopped in front of her, floating half a metre off the ground, which put the Ambassador's eye stalks above her. Even with the regrav unit and the physical support it was obvious the Ambassador had come from a low-gravity world. It sagged against the metal and composite structures holding it up. Two of the eye stalks bent round so they were aligned on her.

'Ambassador, thank you for visiting us,' Justine said.

'We are pleased to visit,' the Ambassador answered, its voice a whispery burble coming from a slender vocalizer gill between his eye stalks. Translated into English by the sled processors, a speaker on the rim boomed the reply to Justine.

'My home welcomes you,' she said, remembering the formality.

Another of the Ambassador's eye stalks curved round to stare at Kazimir. 'You are the human Navy commander.'

'That is correct,' Kazimir said. 'I am here as you requested.'

'Many of my nest ancestor cousins fought in the Fandola assault.' Thin droplets of spittle ran out of the Ambassador's gill, to be absorbed by drain holes in its support collar.

'I am sure they fought with honour.'

'Honour be damned. We would have enjoyed victory over the Hancher vermin if you had not intervened that day.'

'We are friends with the Hancher. Your attack was ill-advised; I warned you we would not abandon our friends. That is not our way.'

The fourth eye stalk turned on Kazimir. 'You in person warned the Empire, Navy commander?'

'That is correct.'

'You live so long. You are no longer natural.'

'Is this why you are here, Ambassador, to insult me?'

'You overreact. I state the obvious.'

'We do not hide from the obvious,' Justine said. 'But we are not here today to dwell upon what was. Please come in, Ambassador.'

'You are kind.'

Justine walked into the entrance hall with the Ambassador's sled gliding along behind her. Somehow it managed to keep a distance that wasn't too close as to be blatantly rude, but still close enough to be disconcerting.

Kazimir's icon blinked up beside Gore's in her peripheral vision. 'You know,' he said, 'the Ocisens only started painting their sleds black after they found out humans are unsettled by darkness.'

'If that's the best they can come up with it's a wonder their species ever survived the fission age,' she replied.

'We shouldn't be in too much of a hurry to mock them,' Gore replied. 'However much we sneer, they do have an empire, and they would have obliterated the Hancher if we hadn't stepped in.'

'I'd hardly consider that to be an indicator of their superiority,' Justine told them. 'And they're certainly not a threat to us. Their technology level is orders of magnitude below Higher culture, let alone ANA.'

'Yes, but right now they only have one policy, to acquire better technology, especially weapons technology. A sizeable percentage of the Emperor's expansion budget is diverted to building long-range exploration ships in the hope they'll come across a world whose inhabitants have gone post-physical, and they can help themselves to whatever's left behind.'

'Let's hope they never encounter a Prime immotile.'

'They've made seventeen attempts to reach the Dyson Pair,' Kazimir told her. 'And they currently have forty-two ships searching for an immotile civilization beyond the region of space we Firewalled.'

'I didn't know that. Is there any danger they'll find a rogue Prime planet?'

'If we can't find one, they certainly won't be able to.'

Justine led their little party into the McLeod room, and

sat at the head of the large oak table running down the middle. Kazimir took the chair at his mother's side, while the Ambassador hovered at the other end. Its eye stalks bent round slowly, as if it was having trouble with what it saw as it scanned the walls. The room's décor was Scottish themed, which surrounded the alien with tartan drapes, ancient Celtic ceremonial swords, and solemn marble mannequins dressed in clan kilts. Several sets of bagpipes were displayed in glass cases. A fabulous pair of stag antlers hung above the stone mantelplace that had been imported from a Highland castle.

'Ambassador,' Justine said formally, 'I represent the human government of Earth. I am physical, as you asked, and I am empowered to negotiate on the government's behalf with the Ocisen Empire. What do you wish to discuss?'

Three of the Ambassador's eyes curved round to stare at her. 'Although we disapprove of living creatures placing themselves subordinate to the mechanical, we consider your planetary computer is the true ruler of the Commonwealth. That is why I required this direct meeting, rather than with the Senate as usual.'

Justine wasn't about to start arguing about political structures with an alien who saw everything in terms of black and white. 'ANA has considerable influence beyond this planet. That is so.'

'Then you must work with the Empire to avert a very real danger.'

'What danger is that, Ambassador?' *As if none of us know.*

'A human organization is threatening to send ships into the Void.'

'Yes, our Living Dream movement wants to send its followers on a Pilgrimage there.'

'I am familiar with human emotional states after being exposed to your kind for so long, so I am curious why you do not react to this event with any sense of distress or concern. It is through humans that we know of the Void, therefore you know what effect your Living Dream is proposing to trigger.'

'They do not propose anything, they simply wish to live the life of their idol.'

'You are deliberately denying the implication. Their entry to the Void will provoke a massive devourment phase. The galaxy will be ruined. Our Empire will be consumed. You will kill us and countless others.'

'That will not happen,' Justine said.

'We are reassured that you intend to stop the Living Dream.'

'That's not what I said. It is not our belief that their Pilgrimage will cause a devourment phase of any size. They simply do not possess the ability to pass through the event horizon which guards the Void. Even the Raiel have trouble doing that, and Living Dream does not have access to a Raiel ship.'

'Then why are they launching this Pilgrimage?'

'It is a simple political gesture, nothing more. The Ocisen Empire, nor any other species in the galaxy, does not have anything to worry about.'

'Do you guarantee that your Living Dream group cannot get through the event horizon? Other humans have crossed over into the Void. They are the cause of this desire to Pilgrimage, are they not?'

'Nothing is certain, Ambassador, you know that. But the likelihood—'

'If you cannot guarantee it, then you must prevent the ships from flying.'

'The Greater Commonwealth is a democratic institution, complicated in this case by Living Dream being both trans-stellar and the legitimate government of Ellezelin. The Commonwealth constitution is specifically designed to protect every member's right to self-determination on an individual and governmental level. In other words we don't actually have the legal right to prevent them from embarking on their Pilgrimage.'

'I am familiar with human lawyers; everything can be undone, nothing is final. You play with words, not reality. The Empire recognizes only power and ability. Your computer government has the physical power to prevent this Pilgrimage, am I not correct?'

'Ability does not automatically imply intent,' Justine said. 'ANA:Governance has the ability to do many things. We do not do them because of the laws which govern us, both legal and moral.'

'It is not part of your morality to destroy this galaxy. You can prevent this.'

'We can argue strongly against it,' she said, wishing she didn't agree quite so much with the Ocisen.

'The Empire requires a tangible commitment. The Pilgrimage ships must be neutralized.'

'Out of the question,' Justine said. 'We cannot interfere with the lawful activities of another sovereign state, it goes against everything we are.'

'If you do not prevent the launch of this atrocity, then

127

the Empire will. Even your lawyers will agree we have the right to species self-preservation.'

'Is that a threat, Ambassador?' Kazimir asked quietly.

'It is the course of action you have forced upon us. Why do you not see this? Are you afraid of your primitive cousins? What can they threaten you with?'

'They do not threaten us, we respect each other. Can you make the leap to understand that?'

Justine tried to read the Ambassador's reaction to the jibe, but it seemed unperturbed. Spittle continued to dribble from its vocalizer gill, while its arms flopped round like landed fish inside their cybernetic casings. 'Your laws and their hypocrisy will always elude us,' the Ambassador said. 'The Empire knows you always include extraordinary powers within your constitutions to impose solutions in times of crisis. We require you to invoke them now.'

'ANA:Governance will be happy to introduce a motion in the Senate,' Justine said. 'We will ask that Living Dream desists from reckless action.'

'Will you back this by force if they refuse?'

'Unlikely,' Kazimir said. 'Our Navy exists to protect us from external enemies.'

'What is the Void devourment, if not an enemy? Ultimately it is everyone's enemy. The Raiel acknowledge this.'

'We do understand your unease, Ambassador,' Justine said. 'I would like to reassure you we will work wholly to prevent any catastrophe from engulfing the galaxy.'

'The Raiel could not prevent devourment. Are you greater than the Raiel?'

'Probably not,' she muttered. Did it understand sarcasm?

'Then we will prevent your ships from flying.'

'Ambassador, I have to advise the Ocisen Empire against such a course of action,' Kazimir said. 'The Navy will not permit you to attack humans.'

'Do not think you can intimidate us, Admiral Kazimir. We are not the helpless species you attacked at Fandola. We have allies now. I represent many powerful species who will not allow the Void to begin its final devourment phase. We do not stand alone. Do you think your Navy can defeat the whole galaxy?'

Kazimir seemed unperturbed. 'The Navy acts only in defence. I urge you to allow the Commonwealth to solve an internal problem in our own way. Humans will not trigger a large-scale devourment.'

'We will watch you,' the Ambassador boomed. 'If you do not prevent these Pilgrimage ships from being built and launched, then we and our new, powerful, allies will act in self-defence.'

'I do understand your concern,' Justine said. 'But I would ask you to trust us.'

'You have never given us a reason to,' the Ambassador said. 'I thank you for your time. I will return to my ship, I find your environment unpleasant.'

Which was quite subtle for an Ocisen, Justine thought. She stood and accompanied the Ambassador back out to its ship. Gore materialized beside her as the hulking machine rose into the sky.

'Allies, huh? You know anything about that?' he asked Kazimir.

'Not a thing,' Kazimir said. 'They could be bluffing. Then again, if they are serious about stopping the Pilgrimage, they will need allies. They certainly can't do it alone.'

'Could it be the Raiel?' Justine asked in surprise.

Kazimir shrugged. 'I doubt it. The Raiel don't go sneaking round doing deals to pitch one species against another. If the Empire had approached them, I feel confident they would have told us.'

'A post-physical, then?'

'Not impossible,' Gore conceded. 'Most of them regard us as vulgar little newcomers to an exclusive club. Those that talk to us, anyway. Most can't even be arsed to do that. But I'd be very surprised if one had. They'd probably be quite interested in observing the final devourment phase.'

'How about you?' Justine enquired lightly.

Gore smiled, snow-white teeth shining coldly between gold lips. 'I admit, it would be a hell of a sight. From a distance. A very large distance.'

'So what do you recommend?' Justine asked.

'We certainly need to start the motion in the Senate,' Kazimir said. 'The Ambassador was quite right. I don't think we can allow the Pilgrimage to launch.'

'Can't stop 'em,' Gore said with indecent cheerfulness. 'It's in the constitution.'

'We do have to find a solution,' Justine said. 'A political one. And quickly.'

'That's my girl. Are you going to address the Senate yourself? You carry a lot of weight out there: history in the flesh.'

'And it would be helpful to get confirmation from the Raiel,' Kazimir said. 'You do have the personal connection.'

'What?' Justine's shoulders slumped. 'Oh hellfire. I wasn't planning on leaving Earth.'

'I expect the Hancher Ambassador would like some reassurance, as well,' Gore added maliciously.

Justine turned to give her father a level stare. 'Yes, there's a lot of people and Factions we need to keep an eye on.'

'I'm sure Governance knows what it's doing. After all, you were its first choice. Can't beat that.'

'Actually, I was second.'

'Who was first?' Kazimir asked curiously.

'Toniea Gall.'

'That bitch!' Gore spat. 'She couldn't get laid in a Silent World house the day after she rejuved. Everyone hates her.'

'Now Dad, history decided the resettlement period was a minor golden age.'

'Fucking minuscule, more like.'

Justine and Kazimir smiled at each other. 'She was a good President as I recall,' Kazimir said.

'Bullshit.'

'I'll go and visit the Hancher Embassy on my way to the Senate,' Justine said. 'It would be nice to know about the Empire's military movements.'

'I'll start reassigning our observation systems inside the Empire to see if we can get a clearer picture of what's going on,' Kazimir said.

As Justine's body teleported out of Tulip Mansion, Gore's primary consciousness retreated to his secure environment within the vastness of ANA. As perceptual reality locations went, it was modest. Some people had created entire universes for their own private playground, setting up self-governing parameters to maintain the configuration. The bodies, or cores, or focal points they occupied within their concepts were equally varied, with abilities defined purely by the individual milieu. Quite where such domains extended to was no longer apparent. ANA had ceased to be limited to the physical machinery which had birthed it. The operational medium was now tunnelled into the quantum structure of spacetime around Earth, fashioning a unique province in which its manifold post-human intelligences could function. The multiple interstices propagated through quantum fields with the tenacity and fragile beauty of a nebula, an edifice forever shifting in tandem with the whims of its creators. It was no longer machine, or even artificial life. It had become alive. What it might evolve into was the subject of considerable and obsessive internal debate.

The Factions were not openly at war over ANA's ultimate configuration, but it was a vicious battle of ideas. Gore hadn't been entirely truthful when he claimed to be a Conservative. He did support the idea of maintaining the status quo, but only because he felt the other more extreme factions were being far too hasty in offering their solutions. Apart from the Dividers, of course, who wanted ANA to fission into as many parts as there were Factions, allowing each to go their own way. He didn't agree with them either; what he wanted was more time and more information, that way he believed the direction they should take would become a lot more evident.

He appeared on a long beach, with a rocky headland a few hundred metres ahead of him. Perched on top was an old stone tower with crumbling walls and a white pavilion structure attached to the rear. The sun was hot on his head and hands; he was wearing a loose short-sleeve shirt and knee-length trousers. His skin was ordinary, without any enrichments. The self-image and surroundings were taken from the early twenty-first century, back when life was easier even without sentient machines. This was Hawks-bill Bay, Antigua, where he used to come with his yacht, *Moonlight Madison*. There had been a resort clustered along the shore in those days, but in this representation the land behind the beach was nothing more than a tangle of palm trees and lush grass, with brightly coloured parrots zipping between the branches. It didn't have the wind that blew constantly through the real Caribbean, either; although the sea was an astonishingly clear turquoise where fish swam close to shore.

There was a simple dirt path up the headland, leading to the tower. The pavilion with its fabric roof covered a broad wooden deck and a small swimming pool. There was a big oval table at one end, with five heavily cushioned chairs around it. Nelson Sheldon was already sitting there, a tall drink resting on the table in front of him.

In the days before ANA, Nelson had been the security chief for the Sheldon Dynasty, the largest and most power-ful economic empire that had ever existed. When the original Commonwealth society and economy split apart and reconfigured as the Greater Commonwealth, the Dynasty retained a great deal of its wealth and power, but things weren't the same. After Nigel Sheldon left, it lost cohesion and dispersed out among the External Worlds; still a force to be reckoned with, politically and economi-cally, but lacking the true clout of before.

Over two centuries spent looking after the Dynasty's welfare had turned Nelson into a pragmatist of the first order. It meant he and Gore saw the whole ANA evolution outcome in more or less the same terms.

Gore sat at the table and poured himself an iced tea from the pitcher. 'You accessed all that?'

'Yeah. I'm interested who the Empire has as an ally, or even allies.'

'Probably just a bluff.'

'You're overestimating the Ocisens, they lack the imagination for a bluff. I'd say they've managed to dig up some ancient reactionary race with a hard-on for the good old days and a backyard full of obsolete weapons.'

'ANA:Governance is going to have to give that one some serious attention,' Gore said. 'We can't have alien warships invading the Commonwealth. Been there, done that. Ain't going to let it happen twice. It was one of the reasons we started building ANA, so that humanity is never at a technological disadvantage again. There's a lot of very nasty hardware lying round this galaxy.'

'Amongst other things,' Nelson agreed sagely. 'We are going to have to give the Void some serious attention soon – just as the Accelerators wanted.'

'I want us to give the Void serious attention,' Gore said. 'We can hardly claim to be masters of cosmological theory if we can't even figure it out. It's only the analysis timescale which everyone disagrees on.'

'And the method of analysis, but yes I'll grant you we do need to know how the damn thing is generated. It's one of the reasons I'm with you on our little conspiracy.'

'Think of us as a very small Faction.'

'Whatever. I stopped screwing round with semantics a long time ago. Purpose is absolute, and if you can't define it: tough. And our purpose is to undo the damage the Accelerators have caused.'

'To a degree, yes. The Conservatives will be most active on that front, we can trust them to do a decent job. I want to try and think a couple of steps ahead. After all we're not animal any more, we don't just react to a situation. We're supposed to be able to see it coming. Ultimately something has to be done about the Void problem. Understanding its internal mechanism is all very well, but it cannot be allowed to carry on threatening the galaxy.'

Nelson raised a glass to his lips, and smiled in salute. 'Way to go, tough guy. Where the Raiel failed . . .'

'Where the Raiel tell us they failed. We have no independent confirmation.'

'Nothing lasts long enough, apart from the Raiel themselves.'

'Bullshit. Half the post-physicals in the galaxy have been around for a lot longer.'

'Yeah, and those that were don't bother to communicate any more. They're all quiet, or dead, or transcended, or retroevolved. So unless you want to go around and poke them with a big stick, the Raiel are our source. Face it, ANA is good, great even, we're damn nearly proto-gods, but in terms of development we are still lagging behind the Raiel, and they plateaued millions of years ago. The Void defeated them. They converted entire star systems into defence machines, they *invaded* the fucking place with an armada, and they still couldn't switch it off, or kill it or blow it to hell.'

'They went at it the wrong way.'

Nelson laughed. 'And you know the right way?'

'We have an advantage they never did. We have insider knowledge, a mole.'

'The Waterwalker? In Ozzie's name, tell me you're joking.'

'You know who paid the most attention to Inigo's dreams right at the start? The Raiel. They didn't know what was inside. They built ships which could theoretically withstand any quantum environment, yet not one of them ever returned. We're the ones who showed them what's in there.'

'It's a very small glimpse, a single city on a standard H-congruous planet.'

'You're missing the point.' His arm swept round Hawksbill to point at the thick pillar of black rock protruding from the water several hundred metres out to sea. Small waves broke apart on it, churning up a ruck of spume. 'You bring any human prior to the twenty-fifth century into here, and they'd think they were in a physical reality. But if you or I were to observe the environment through them, we'd soon realize there were artificial factors involved. The Waterwalker gives us the same opportunity. His telepathic abilities have provided a very informative glimpse into the nature of the universe hiding inside that bastard event horizon. For all it looks like our universe with planets and stars, it most definitely is not. This Skylord of the Second Dream confirms that. The Void has a Heart which is most distinctive, even though we haven't been shown it yet.'

'Knowing it's different in there doesn't give us any real advantage.'

'Wrong. We know nothing can be achieved on a physical level; you can't use quantumbusters against it, you can't send an army in to wipe out the chief villain's control room. The Void is the ultimate post-physical in the galaxy, and probably all the other galaxies we can see. What we have to do is communicate with it if we ever want to achieve any resolution to the problem it presents to our stars. I don't believe the Firstlife ever intended it to be dangerous; they didn't know there was anything left out-side it could ever threaten. That's our window. We know humans can get inside, even though we're not sure how they did it that first time. We know there are humans in there who are attuned to its fabric. Through them we may be able to affect change.'

'The Waterwalker is dead. He has been for millennia of internal time.'

'Even if he were unique, which I don't believe for a minute, time is not a problem, not in there. We all know that. What we have to do is get inside and forge that tenuous little link to the Heart. That's the key to this.'

'You want to visit the Void? To fly through the event horizon?'

'Not me. Much as my ego would love being the union point, there's no empirical evidence that I would have the telepathic ability inside. Even if we took ANA inside there's no certainty it could become the conduit. No. We have to employ a method that has a greater chance of success.'

Nelson shook his head in dismay and not a bit of disappointment. 'Which is?'

'I'm working on it.'

*

It wasn't an auspicious start to the day. Araminta hadn't overslept. Not exactly. She had an Advancer heritage which gave her a complete set of macrocellular clusters, all func-tioning efficiently; she could order her secondary thought routines competently. So naturally she'd woken up on time with a phantom bleeping in her ears and synchronized blue light flashing along her optic nerve. It was just after that wake-up spike she always had difficulty. Her flat only had two rooms, a bathroom cubicle and a combi main room; that was all she could afford on her waitress pay. For all that it was cheap, the expanded bed with its a-foam mattress was very comfortable. After the spike she lay curled up in her cotton pyjamas, cosy as a nesting frangle. Hazy morning sunlight stole round the curtains, not bright enough to be disturbing, the room maintained itself at a comfortable warmth. If she bothered to check the flat's management programs everything was ready and waiting; the day's clothes washed and aired, a quick light breakfast in the cuisine cabinet.

So I can afford to laze for a bit.

The second alarm spike jerked her awake again, vanquishing the weird dream. This spike was harsher than the first, deliberately so, as it was an urgent order to get the hell up – one she never needed. When she cancelled the noise and light she assumed she'd messed up the secondary routines, somehow switching the order of the spikes. Then she focused on the timer in her exoimages.

'Shit!'

So it became a struggle to pull on her clothes whilst drinking the Assam tea and chewing some toast. A leisurely shower was replaced by spraying on some travel-clean, which never worked like the ads promised, leaving busy glamorous people fresh and cleansed as they zipped between meetings and clubs. Instead she hurried out of the flat with her mouse-brown hair badly brushed, her eyes red-rimmed and stinging slightly from the travel-clean, and her skin smelling of pine bleach.

Great. That should earn me some big tips, she thought grouchily as she hurried down to the big building's underground garage. Her trike pod purred its way out into

Colwyn City's crowded streets and joined the morning rush of commuters. In theory the traffic should have been light, most people these days used regrav capsules, floating in serene comfort above the wheeled vehicles except when they touched down on dedicated parking slots along the side of the roads or rooftop pads. But at this early hour the city's not-so-well-off were all on their way to work, filling the concrete grid close to capacity with pods, cars, and bikes; and jamming the public rail cabs.

Araminta was half an hour late when her pod pulled up at the back of Nik's. She rushed in through the kitchen door, and got filthy looks from the rest of the staff. 'Sorry!' The restaurant was already full of the breakfast crowd, mid-level executives who liked their food natural, prepared by chefs rather than cuisine units, and served by humans not bots.

Tandra managed to lean in close as Araminta fastened her apron. She sniffed suspiciously and winked. 'Travel-clean, huh. I guess you didn't get home last night?'

Araminta hung her head, wishing she did have an excuse like that. 'I was up late last night, another design course.'

'Honey, you've got to start burning the candle at both ends. You're real young and a looker, get yourself out there again.'

'I know. I will.' Araminta took a deep breath. Went over to Matthew who was so disgusted he didn't even rebuke her. She lifted three plates from the ready counter, checked the table number, cranked her mouth open to a smile, and pushed through the doors.

The breakfast session at Nik's usually lasted for about ninety minutes. There wasn't a time limit, but by quarter to nine the last customers were heading for the office or store. Occasionally, a tourist or two would linger, or a business meeting would run over time. Today there weren't many lagging behind. Araminta did her penance by supervising the cleaning bots as the tables were changed ready to serve morning coffee to shoppers and visitors. Nik's had a good position in the commercial district, five blocks from the docks down on the river.

Tables started to fill up again after ten o'clock. The restaurant had a curving front wall, with a slim terrace running around it. Araminta went along the outside tables, adjusting the flowers in the small vases and taking orders for chocolettos and cappuccinos. It kept her out of Matthew's way. He still hadn't said anything to her, a bad sign.

Some time after eleven the woman appeared and started moving along the tables, talking to the customers. Araminta could see several of them were annoyed, waving her away. Since Ethan declared Pilgrimage ten days ago, Living Dream disciples from the local fane had been coming in and pestering people. It was starting to be a problem.

'Can I help you?' Araminta asked, keeping the tone sharp; this was a chance to earn more redemption points with Matthew. The woman was dressed in a charcoal-grey cashmere suit, old-fashioned but expensive with a long flowing skirt, the kind of thing Araminta might have worn before the separation, back in the days when she had money. 'We have several tables available.'

'I'm collecting signature certificates,' the woman said. She had a very determined look on her face. 'We're trying to get the council to stop ingrav capsule use above Colwyn City.'

'Why?' It came out before Araminta really thought about it.

The woman narrowed her eyes. 'Regrav is bad enough, but at least they're speed and altitude limited inside the city boundary. Have you ever thought what would happen if an ingrav drive failed? They fly semi-ballistic parabolas, that means they'd *plummet* down at half-orbital velocity.'

'Ah, yes, I see.' She could also see Matthew giving them a wary look.

'Suppose one crashed on to a school at that speed? Or a hospital? There's just no need for them. It's blatant consumerism without any form of responsibility. People are only buying them to show off. And there are studies that suggest the ingrav effect puts a strain on deep geological faults. We could have an earthquake.'

Araminta was proud she didn't laugh out loud. 'I see.'

'The city traffic network wasn't designed with those sort of speeds in mind, either. The number of near-miss incidents logged is rising steadily. Will you add your certificate? Help us keep our lives safe.'

A file was presented to Araminta's u-shadow. 'Yes, of course. But you'll have to order a tea or coffee, my boss is already cross with me this morning.' She flicked her gaze towards Matthew as she added her signature certificate to the petition, confirming she was a Colwyn City resident.

'Typical,' the woman grunted. 'They never think of anything but themselves and their profit.' But she sat down and ordered a peppermint tea.

'What's her problem?' Matthew asked as Araminta collected the tea.

'The universe is a bad place, she just needs to unwind a

little.' She gave him a sunny smile. 'Which is why we're here.'

Before he could say anything else she skipped back to the terrace.

At half past eleven Araminta's u-shadow collated the morning's property search it had run through the city's estate agencies, and shunted the results into one of her storage lacunas. She was on her break in the little staff lounge beside the kitchen. It didn't take her long to review them all; she was looking for a suitable flat or even a small house somewhere in the city. There weren't many that fitted her criteria: cheap, in need of renovation, near the centre. She tagged three agency files as possibles, and checked on how yesterday's possibles were doing. Half of them had already been snapped up. You really had to be quick in today's market, she reflected wistfully. *And have money, or at least some decent credit.* A renovation was her dream project; buying a small property and refurbishing it in order to sell on at a profit. She knew she could be good at it. She'd taken five development and design courses in the last eight months since separating from Laril, as well as studying every interior decorating text her u-shadow could pull out of the unisphere. Property development was a risky proposition, but every case she'd accessed showed her that the true key was dedication and hard work, as well as a lot of market research. And from her point of view she could do it by herself. She wouldn't depend on anyone. But first, she needed money . . .

Araminta was back in the restaurant at twelve, getting the table settings changed ready for lunch, learning the specials the chef was working on. The anti-ingrav crusader had gone, leaving a three-Viotia-pound tip; and Matthew was treating her humanely again. Cressida walked in at ten past twelve. She was Araminta's cousin on her mother's side of the family, partner in a mid-sized law firm, a hundred and twenty-three years old, and spectacularly beautiful with flaming red hair and skin maintained to silky perfection by expensive cosmetic scales. She was wearing a two-thousand-Vpound emerald and platinum toga suit. Just by walking into Nik's she was raising the whole tone of the place. She was also Araminta's lawyer.

'Darling.' Cressida waved and came over for a big hug; air-kissing had never been part of her style. 'Well, have I got news for you,' she said breathlessly. 'Your boss won't mind if I steal you for a second, will he?' Without bothering to check she grabbed Araminta's hand and pulled her over to a corner table.

Araminta winced as she imagined Matthew's stare drilling laser holes in her back. 'What's happened?'

Cressida's grinned broadly, her liquid scarlet lip gloss flowing to accommodate the big stretch. 'Dear old Laril has skipped planet.'

'*What?*' Araminta couldn't quite believe that. Laril was her ex-husband. A marriage which had lasted eighteen utterly miserable months. Everyone in her immediate family had objected to Laril from the moment she met him. They had cause. She could admit that now; she'd been twenty-one while he was three hundred and seven. At the time she'd thought him suave, sophisticated, rich, and her ticket out of boring, small (minded), agricultural Langham, a town over on the Suvorov continent, seven thousand miles away. They thought he was just another filthy Punk Skunk; there were enough of them kicking around the Commonwealth especially on the relatively unsophisticated planets that made up the outer fringes of the External Worlds. Jaded old folks who had the money to look flawlessly adolescent, but still envied the genuinely youthful for their spirit and exuberance. Every partner they snagged was centuries younger in a futile hope that their brio would magically transfer over. That wasn't quite the case with Laril. Close, though.

Her branch of the family on her father's side had a business supplying and maintaining agricultural cybernetics, an enterprise which was the largest in the county, and one in which Araminta was expected to work in for at least the first fifty years of her life. After that apprenticeship, family members were then considered adult and wealthy enough to take off for pastures new (a depressing number set up subsidiaries of the main business across Suvorov), leaving gaps for the latest batch of youngsters to fill, turning the cycle. It was a prospect which Araminta considered so soul-crushing she would have hired out as a love slave to a Prime motile in order to escape. By contrast, Laril, an independent businessman with an Andribot franchise among other successful commercial concerns, was like being discovered by Prince Charming. And given that these days an individual's age wasn't a physical quantity, her family objection to the three-century difference was *so* bourgeois. It certainly guaranteed the outcome of the affair.

The fact that they'd been more or less right about him using her only made her post-separation life even worse. She could never go back to Langham now. Fortunately, Cressida wasn't judgemental, considering Araminta's colossal mistake as part of life's rich experience. 'If you don't screw up,' she'd told a weeping Araminta at their first meeting, 'you haven't got a base to launch your improvement from. Now what does the separation clause in the marriage contract entitle you to?'

Araminta, who had overcome a mountain of shame even to go to a family member (however distant) for legal help at the start of the divorce had to admit theirs had been an old-fashioned wedding, of the till-death-do-us-part variety. They'd even sworn that to the licensed priest in Langham chapel. It was all very romantic at the time.

'No contract?' an amazed and horrified Cressida had asked. 'Gosh, darling, you are headed for a Mount Herculaneum of improvement aren't you?'

It was a mountain which Laril's lawyers were doing their very best to prevent her ever setting foot on; their counter-suit had frozen Araminta's own assets, all seven hundred and thirty-two pounds she had in her savings account. Even Cressida with all her firm's resources was finding it hard to break through Laril's legal protection, and as for his commercial activities, they had proved even more elusive to pin down. All his early talk of being the centre of a Dynasty-like network of profitable companies was either a lie or a cover-up for some astonishing financial irregularities. Intriguingly, Viotia's National Revenue Service had no record of him paying tax at any time in the last hundred years, and were now showing a healthy interest in his activities.

'Skipped. Departed. Left this world. Gone vertical. Uprooted.' Cressida grasped Araminta's hands and gave them a near-painful squeeze. 'He didn't even pay his lawyers.' And her happiness at that eventuality was indecent. 'And now they're just another name on the list of fifty creditors after his arse.'

Araminta's brief moment of delight suddenly darkened. 'So I get nothing?'

'On the contrary. His remaining solid assets, that's his townhouse, and the stadium food franchise, which we did manage to freeze right at the start are rightfully yours. Admittedly, they don't quite add up to the kind of assets that bragging about will sway a naive young girl's head.'

Araminta blushed furiously.

'But not to be sneered at. Unfortunately, there is the question of back taxes. Which I'm afraid amounts to three hundred and thirty-seven thousand Viotia pounds. And if the NRS could ever prove half of Laril's ventures that you told me about, they'd claim the rest too. Bloodsucking fiends. However, they can't prove a damn thing thanks to the excellent encryption and strange lack of records your slippery ex has muddled his life with. Then there's my fee, which is ten per cent seeing as how you're family and I admire your late-found pride. So, the rest is yours, clear and free.'

'How much?'

'Eighty-three thousand.'

Araminta couldn't speak. It was a fortune. Agreed, nothing like the corporate megastructure Laril had claimed he owned and controlled, but still more than she'd expected and asked for in the divorce petition. Ever since she walked into Cressida's office she'd allowed herself to dream she might, just might, come out of this with thirty or forty thousand, that Laril would pay just to be rid of her. 'Oh, great Ozzie, you are kidding,' she whispered.

'Not a bit of it. A judge friend of mine has allowed us to expedite matters, on account of the circumstances of truly tragic hardship I claimed you're suffering. Your savings are now unfrozen, and we'll transfer Laril's money into your account at four o'clock this afternoon. Congratulations. You're a free and single woman again.'

Araminta was horrified that she was crying, her hands seemed to flap about in front of her face of their own volition.

'Wow!' Cressida put her arm around Araminta's shoulder, rocking her playfully. 'How do you take bad news?'

'It's over? Really over?'

'Yep. Really. So what say you and I go celebrate. Tell your manager where to stick his menu, go pour soup over a customer's head, then we'll hit the coolest clubs in town and ruin half the male population. How about it?'

'Oh.' Araminta looked up, wiping tears with the back of her hand; the mention of Matthew made her realize she was supposed to be serving. 'I need to get back. Lunch is really busy. They rely on me.'

'Hey, calm down, take a minute. Think of what's happened here.'

Araminta nodded her head sheepishly, glancing round the restaurant. Her co-workers were all trying not to glance in her direction; Matthew was annoyed again. 'I know. I'm sorry. It's going to take a while to sink in. I can't believe it's all over. I've got to ... Oh, Ozzie, there are so many things I want to do.'

'Great! Let's get you out of here and bring on the serious partying. We'll start with a decent meal.'

'No.' Araminta could see Tandra staring anxiously, and gave her a weak thumbs up in return. 'I can't just walk out, that's not fair on everyone else here. They'll need to get a replacement. I'll hand in my notice properly, and work the rest of the week for them.'

'Dammit, you are horrendously sweet. No wonder your filthy ex could take advantage so easily.'

'It won't happen again.'

'Too bloody true it won't.' Cressida stood up, smiling proudly. 'From now on I'm vetting anyone you date. At least come out for a drink tonight.'

'Um, I really do need to go home after this and work things out.'

'Friday night, then. Come on! Everyone goes out Friday night.'

Araminta couldn't help the grin on her face. 'All right. Friday night.'

'Thank Ozzie for that. And get yourself some serious bad-girl clothes first. We're going to do this properly.'

'Okay. Yeah, okay, I will.' She could actually feel her mood changing, like some warm liquid invading her arteries. 'Uh, where do I go for clothes like that?'

'Oh, I'll show you, darling, don't you worry.'

Araminta did work the lunch shift, then told Matthew she was quitting, but was happy to stay on as long as he needed her. He completely surprised her by giving her a kiss and congratulating her on finally breaking free of Laril. Tandra got all teary and affectionate while the others gathered round to hear the news and cheer.

By half past three in the afternoon she'd put on a light coat and walked out. The cool late spring air outside sobered her up, allowing her to think clearly again. Even so, she walked the route she so often walked in the afternoon. Along Ware Street, take a left at the major junction and head down the slope along Daryad Avenue. The buildings on either side were five or six storeys tall, a typical mix of commercial properties. Regrav capsules slid silently overhead, while the metro track running down the centre of the avenue hummed with public cabs. Right now the roads had few vehicles, yet Araminta still waited at the crossings for the traffic solidos to change shape and colour. She barely noticed her fellow pedestrians.

The Glayfield was a bar and restaurant at the bottom of the slope, occupying two storeys of an old wood and composite building, part of the original planet landing camp. She made her way through the dark deserted bar to the stairs at the back, and went up to the restaurant. That too was virtually empty. Up at the front it boasted a sheltered balcony where in her opinion the tables were too close; waitresses would have trouble squeezing between them when they were full. She sat at one next to the rail which gave her an excellent view along Daryad Avenue. This was where she came most afternoons to wind down after her shift at Nik's, sitting with a hot orange chocolate watching the people and the ships. Over to her right the Avenue curved upwards into the bulk of the city, producing a wall of tall buildings expressing the many construction phases and styles that had come and gone in Colwyn's hundred-and-seventy-year history. While to her left the River Cairns cut through the land in a gentle northward curve as it flowed out to the Great Cloud Ocean twenty miles away. The river was half a mile wide in the city, the top of a deep estuary which made an excellent natural harbour. Several marinas had been built on both sides, providing anchorage to thousands of private yachts, ranging from little sailing dinghies up to regrav-assisted pleasure cruisers. Two giant bridges spanned the water, one a single unsupported arch of nanotube carbon, the other a more traditional suspension bridge with pure white pillars a flamboyant three hundred metres tall. Capsules slid along beside them, but the ground traffic was almost nonexistent these days. They were mainly used by pedestrians. They led over to the exclusive districts on the south bank, where the city's wealthier residents flocked amid long green boulevards and extensive parks.

On the northern shore, barely half a mile from the Glayfield, the docks were built into the bank and out into the mudflats; two square miles of cargo-handling machinery and warehouses and quays and landing pads and caravan platforms. It was the hub from which the Izyum continent had been developed, the second starport on the planet. There was no heavy industry on Viotia; major engineering systems and advanced technology were all imported. With Ellezelin only seventy-five lightyears away, Viotia was on the fringe of the Free Trade Zone. A market which the local population grumbled was free for Ellezelin companies all right, but disadvantaged everyone else caught in their commercial web. There wasn't a wormhole linking Viotia to Ellezelin. Yet. But talk was that in another hundred years when Viotia's internal market had grown sufficiently, one would be opened allowing the full range of cheap Ellezelin products to flood through, turning them into an economic colony. In the meantime, starships from External Worlds came and went. She watched them as she sipped her orange chocolate; a line of huge freighters, their metal hulls as dull as lead, heavy and ungainly, drifting down vertically out of the sky. Behind them, the departing ships rose away from the planet, brushing through Viotia's legendary pink clouds, accelerating fast once they reached the stratosphere. Araminta gave them a mild grin, thinking of the anti-ingrav woman. If she was right what would the starships' field effect be doing to the geology beneath the city? Maybe a simple wormhole would be the answer; she rather liked the idea, a throwback to the First Commonwealth era of genteel and elegant train travel between star systems. It was a shame that the External Worlds rejected such links out of hand, but they valued their political freedom too much to risk a return to a monoculture, especially with the threat of Higher culture overwhelming their hard-won independence.

Araminta stayed at the table long after she usually packed up and went home. The sun began to fall, turning the clouds a genuine gold-pink as the planet's hazy mesosphere diffused the dying rays of the K-class star. Transocean barges shone brightly out on the Cairns, regrav engines keeping their flat hulls just above the slow rippling water as they nosed out of the dock and headed for the open sea and the islands beyond. She was always soothed by the sight of the city like this, a huge edifice of human activity buzzing along efficiently; a reassurance that civilization did actually work, that nothing could kick the basics out from under her. And now, finally, she could begin to take an active part, to carve out a life for herself. The files from the property agencies floated gently through her exoimage display, allowing her to plan what she might do to them in more detail than she ever bothered before. Without money such reviews had been pointless daydreams, but this evening they took on a comfortable solidity. Part of her was scared by the notion. If she made a mistake now, she'd be back waitressing tables for the next few decades. She only had one shot. Eighty-three thousand was a tidy sum, but it had to be made to work for her. Despite the trepidation, she was looking forward to the challenge. It marked her life truly beginning.

The sun set amid a warm scarlet glow. It seemed to match Araminta's mood. By then, the first customers of the evening were starting to fill up the restaurant. She left a big tip, and went downstairs. Her usual routine had her walking back to Nik's, maybe do some shopping on the way, and taking the trike pod home. But there was nothing usual about today. There was music blasting through the bar. People were leaning on the counter, ordering drinks and aerosols. Araminta glanced down at her clothes. She was wearing a sensible skirt, navy blue, that came down below her knees, a white top with short sleeves was made from a fabric that was specifically wipe-clean so she could cope with spills. Around her, people had made an effort to smarten up for the evening and she felt slightly downmarket by comparison.

But then who are they to judge me?

It was a liberating thought, of the kind she hadn't entertained since leaving Langham. Back when the future was full of opportunity, at least in her imagination.

Araminta sidled her way up to the bar and studied the bottles and beer taps. 'Green Fog, please,' she told the barman. It earned her a slightly bemused smile, but he mixed it perfectly anyway. She drank it slowly, trying not to let the smouldering mist get up her nose. Sneezing would really blow away any remaining credibility.

'Haven't seen anybody drink one of those for a while,' a man's voice said.

She turned and looked at him. He was handsome in that precise way everyone was these days, with features aligned perfectly, which she guessed meant he'd been through at least a couple of rejuve treatments. Like the rest of the bar's clientele, he'd dressed up, a simple grey and purple toga jacket that cloaked him in a gentle shimmer.

And he's not Laril.

'Been a while since I was let out,' she retorted. Then smirked at her own answer, the fact she was bold enough to say it.

'Can I get you another? I'm Jaful, by the way.'

'Araminta. And no, not a Green Fog, that's a nostalgia thing for me. What's current?'

'They say Adlier 88Vodka is going down in all the wrong places.'

She finished her Green Fog in a single gulp. Tried not to grimace too hard. And pushed the empty glass across the bar. 'Best start there, then.'

'Are you awake?'

Araminta stirred when she heard the question. She wasn't awake exactly, more like dozing pleasantly, content in the afterglow of a night spent in busy lovemaking. Her mind was full of a strange vision, as if she was being chased through the dark sky by an angel. Her slight movement was enough for Jaful. His hands slid up her belly to cup her breasts. 'Uh,' she murmured, still drowsy as the angel dwindled. Jaful rolled her on to her front, which was confusing. Then his cock was sliding up inside her again, hard and insistent. It wasn't a comfortable position. Each thrust pushed her face down into the soft mattress. She wriggled to try and get into a more acceptable

153

stance, which he interpreted as full acceptance. Heated panting became shouts of joy. Araminta cooperated as best she could but the pleasure was minimal at best. *Out of practice*, she thought, and tried not to laugh. He wouldn't understand if she did. At least she was doing her best to make up for lost time, though. They'd coupled three or four times after they got back to his place.

Jaful climaxed with a happy yell. Araminta matched him. *Yep, remember how to do that bit as well.* Eighteen months with Laril had made faking orgasms automatic.

Jaful flopped on to his back, and let out a long breath. He grinned at her. 'Fantastic. I haven't had a night like that for a long time, if ever.'

She dropped her voice a couple of octaves. 'You were good.' It was so funny, like they were reading from a script.

Picked up in a bar. Back to his place for a one night stand. Compliment each other. Both of them playing their part of the ritual to perfection.

But it has been fun.

'I'm going to grab a shower,' he said. 'Tell the culinary unit what you want. It's got some good synthesis routines.'

'I'll do that.' She watched him stroll across the room and into the en suite. Only then did she stare round in curiosity. It was chic city bachelor pad, that much was evident by the plain yet expensive furniture and contemporary art. The wall opposite the bed was a single window, covered with snow-white curtains.

Araminta started hunting round for her clothes as the spore shower came on. Underwear (practical rather than sexy, she acknowledged with a sigh) close to the bed. Skirt halfway between bed and door. Her white top in the lounge. She pulled it on, then looked back at the bedroom.

The shower was still on. Did he always take so long, or was he sticking with the part of the script that gave her a polite opportunity to exit. She shrugged, and let herself out.

There wasn't anything wrong with Jaful. She'd certainly enjoyed herself in his bed for most of the time. It was just that she couldn't think what they could say to each other over breakfast. It would have been awkward. This way she kept the memory agreeable. 'More practice,' she told herself, and smiled wickedly. *And why not? This is real life again.*

The building had a big lobby. When she walked out into the street she blinked against the bright pink light, it was twelve minutes until she was supposed to start the morning shift at Nik's. Her u-shadow told her she was in the Spalding district, which was halfway across the city. So she called a taxi down. It took about thirty seconds until the yellow and purple capsule was resting a couple of centimetres above the concrete, three metres in front of her. She watched in bemusement as the door opened. In all her life she'd never called a taxi herself; it had always been Laril who ordered them. After the separation, of course, she couldn't afford them. *Another blow for freedom.*

As soon as she arrived at Nik's she rushed into the staff toilets.

Tandra gave her a leery look when she came out, tying her apron on. 'You know, those look like the very same clothes you wore when you left yesterday.' She sniffed elaborately. 'Yep, travel-clean again. Did something happen to your plumbing last night?'

'You know. I'm really going to miss you when I leave,' Araminta replied, trying not to laugh.

'What's his name? How long have you been dating?'

'Nobody. I'm not dating, you know that.'

'Oh, come on!'

'I need coffee.'

'Not much sleep, huh?'

'I was reviewing property files, that's all.'

Tandra gave her a malicious sneer. 'Sweetie, I ain't never heard it called that before.'

After the breakfast shift was over, Araminta ran her usual review. This time was different. This time her u-shadow contacted the agencies who gave her virtual tours of the five most promising properties using a full-sense relay bot. On that basis, she made an appointment to visit one that afternoon.

As soon as she walked through the door, she knew it was right for her. The flat was the second floor of a converted three-storey house in the Philburgh district. A mile and a half north of the dock and three blocks back from the river, with two bedrooms it was perfect for someone working in the city centre on a modest salary. There was even a balcony which you could just see the Cairns from, if you really leaned out over the railing.

She went through the official survey scan with the modern analysis programs recommended by half a dozen professional property development companies. It needed redecorating, the current vendor had lived there for thirty years and hadn't done much to it. The plumbing needed replacing, it would require new domestic units. But the structure was perfectly sound.

'I'll take it,' she told the agent.

An hour negotiating with the vendor gave her a price of fifty-eight thousand. More than she would have liked, but it did leave her with enough of a budget to give the place a decent refurbishment. There wouldn't be much left over to live on, but if she completed the work within three or four months she wouldn't need a bank loan. It would be tough, just looking round the lounge with its broken dust capillary flooring and ageing lightfabric walling, she could see the amount of work involved. That was when she experienced a little moment of doubt. *Come on*, she told herself, *you can do this. This is what you've waited for, this is what you've earned.*

She took a breath, and left the flat. She needed to get back to her place and grab a shower. Travel-clean could only cope for so long. Then, she might just get changed and go out again. There were a lot of bars in Colwyn City she'd heard about and never visited.

*

Troblum double woke in two of the penthouse's bedrooms. His actual self lay on a bed made from a special foam that supported his large body comfortably, providing him with a decent night's sleep. It had been Catriona's room, decorated in excessively pink fabrics and ornaments; a lot of the surfaces were fluffy, a very girly girl's room which he was now quite used to. His parallel sensorium was coming from a twinning link to the solido of Howard Liang, a Starflyer agent who had been part of the disinformation mission. Howard was in the penthouse's main bedroom, sharing a huge circular bed with the three girls. It was another aspect of the solidos which Troblum had spent years refining. Now, whenever he wanted sex the four characters would launch themselves eagerly into a mini-orgy. The permutations their supple young bodies could combine into were almost endless, and they could keep going for as long as Troblum wanted. He immersed himself for hours, his own body drinking down the pleasure which Howard's carefully formatted neural pathways experienced, as much the puppet as the puppeteer. The four of them together wasn't strictly speaking a historical reality. At least he'd never found any evidence for it. But it wasn't impossible, which sort of legitimized the extrapolation.

The image and feeling of the beautiful naked bodies draped across him faded away as his actual body reasserted itself, cancelling the twinning with Howard. After the shower had squirted dermal fresher spores over him, he walked through into the vast lounge, bronze sunlight washing warmly across his tingling skin. His u-shadow reported there was still no message from Admiral Kazimir, which he chose to interpret as good news. The delay at least meant it was still being considered. Knowing the Navy bureaucracy, he suspected that the review committee still hadn't formally met. His theory was struggling against a lot of conventional beliefs. Briefly, he considered calling the Admiral direct in order to urge him along, but his personal protocol routines advised against.

He wrapped one of his cloaks round himself, then took the lift down to the lobby. It was only a short walk down to the Caspe River where his favourite café was situated on the edge of the quiet water. The building was made from white wood, and sculpted to resemble a Folgail, a bird even more sedate than a terrestrial swan. His usual table underneath a wing arch was free and he sat himself down. He gave his order to the café network, and waited while a servicebot brought him a freshly squeezed apple and gonberry juice. The chef, Rowury, spent several days every week in the café, cooking for his enthusiastic clientele of foodies. For a culture which prided itself on its egalitarian ethos, Highers could be real snobs about some traditions and crafts, and 'proper' food was well up on the list. There were several restaurants and cafés in Daroca set up as showcases for their gastronomic patrons.

The first dish to arrive was a shredded cereal with fruit and yogurt, all grown naturally (by agriculture enthusiasts), and brought in from five different planets. Troblum started spooning it up. Rowury had come up with a delicious combination, the taste was subtle yet distinctive. It was a shame he couldn't have a second dish, but apart from the delbread toast the quantities here were fixed. If you wanted repeats, seconds or giant portions then you visited a fully automated eatery.

Troblum had finished the cereal and started on his tea when someone sat down in front of him. He looked up in annoyance. The café was full – inevitably, but that was no excuse for rudeness. The rebuke never made it out of his lips.

'Hope you don't mind,' Marius said as he settled in the chair, his black toga suit trailing thin wisps of darkness behind him as if he was time-lapsed. 'I've heard good reports about this place.'

'Help yourself,' Troblum said grouchily. He knew he shouldn't show too much resentment at Marius's appearance, after all the Faction representative had channelled the kind of EMA funds to Troblum's private projects which were normally only available to huge public enterprises. It was the demands placed on him in return which he found annoying, not the challenges themselves, they were intriguing, but they always took so much time. 'Oh you already have.'

The servicebot delivered a second china cup for Marius. 'How are you keeping, Troblum?'

'Fine. As you know.' His field functions detected a subtle shielding unfurling round the table, originating from Marius. Not obvious, but enough to prevent anyone from hearing or scanning what they were saying. He'd never liked the representative, and it was unusual to meet in person. An unarranged meeting was unheard of, it made Troblum worry about the reason. *Something they consider very important.*

Marius sipped the tea. 'Excellent. Assam?'

'Something like that.'

'Those left on Earth do take a lot of pride in maintaining their ancient heritages. I doubt they actually go out and pick the leaves themselves, though. What do you think?'

'I couldn't give a fuck.'

'There are a lot of things that elude you, aren't there, my friend?'

'What do you want?'

Marius fixed his green eyes on Troblum, the faintest shiver of distaste manifesting in his expression. 'Of course, bluntness to the fore. Very well. The briefing you gave to the Navy concerning the Dyson Pair.'

'What about it?'

'It's an interesting theory.'

'It's not a theory,' Troblum said in irritation. 'That has to be the explanation for the origin of the Dark Fortress.'

'The what?'

'Dark Fortress. It's what the Dyson Alpha generator was

originally called. I think it was Jean Douvoir who named it that first, he was on the original *Second Chance* exploration mission, you know. It was meant ironically, but after the War it fell out of fashion, especially with the Firewall campaign, people just didn't—'

'Troblum.'

'Yeah?'

'I couldn't give a fuck.'

'I've got the unabridged logs from the *Second Chance* stored in my personal secure kube if you'd like to check.'

'No. But I believe your theory.'

'Oh for Ozz—'

'Listen,' Marius snapped. 'Seriously, I believe you. It was excellently argued. Admiral Kazimir thought well enough of your presentation to order a full review, and he is not easily won over. They are taking you seriously.'

'Well, that's good then. Isn't it?'

'In the greater scheme of things, I'm sure it is. However, you might like to consider where your comprehensive knowledge of the Dark Fortress came from.'

'Oh.' Now Troblum was really worried. 'I never mentioned I was there.'

'I know that. The point is, that we really don't want ANA:Governance to be aware of the detailed examination you and your team made of the Dark Fortress. Not right now. Understand?'

'Yes.' Troblum actually ducked his head, which was ridiculous, but he did feel contrite; maybe he should have realized his presentation would draw a little too much attention to him. 'Do you think the Navy will review my background?'

'No. They have no reason to right now. You're just a

physicist petitioning for EMA funds. It happens all the time. And that's the way we'd like it to remain.'

'Yeah, I get it.'

'Good. So if the review committee advises the Admiral that no further action should be taken, we'd prefer you not to kick up a fuss.'

'But what if they favour a proper search?'

'We're confident they won't.'

Troblum sat back, trying to work out the politics. It was difficult for him to appreciate the motivation and psychology of other people. 'But if you have that much influence on the Navy, why worry?'

'We can't affect the Navy directly, not with Kazimir as the safeguard. But your advisory review committee is mostly external, some of them are sympathetic to us, as you are.'

'Right.' Troblum could feel despair starting to cloud his mind. 'Will I be able to put it forward again after the Pilgrimage?'

'We'll see. Probably, yes.'

It wasn't exactly good news but it was better than a flat refusal. 'And my drive project?'

'That can continue, providing you don't publicize what you're doing.' Marius smiled reassurance. It didn't belong on his face. 'We do appreciate your help, Troblum, and we want to keep our relationship mutually beneficial. It's just that events are entering a critical stage right now.'

'I know.'

'Thank you. I'll leave you alone to enjoy your food now.'

With suspicious timing, the servicebot arrived as Marius departed. Troblum stared at the plate it deposited in front of him, a tower of thick buttered pancakes was layered with bacon, yokcheese, scrambled garfoul eggs, black pudding, and topped with strawberries. Maple syrup and afton sauce ran down the sides like a volcanic eruption. The edges of the plate were artistically garnished with miniature hash browns, baked vine salfuds and roasted golden tomatoes.

For the first time in years, Troblum didn't feel remotely hungry.

Inigo's second dream

Edeard had been looking forward to the trip for months. Every year in late summer the village elders organized a caravan to trek over to Witham, the closest medium-sized town in Rulan province, to trade. By tradition, all the senior apprentices went with it. This was part of their landcraft training, of which they had to have a basic knowledge before they could qualify as practitioners. They were taught how to hunt small animals, to clear farmland ditches, which fruit to pick, how to handle a plough, what berries and roots were poisonous, along with the basics of how to make camp in the wild.

Even the fact that Obron would be a travelling companion for three weeks hadn't dented Edeard's enthusiasm. He was finally going to get out of Ashwell. Sure he'd been to all the local farms, but never further than half a day's travel away. The caravan meant he would see a lot more of Querencia, the mountains, people other than the villagers he'd lived among for fifteen years, forests. A chance to see how others did things, explore new ideas. There was so much waiting for him out there. He was convinced it was going to be fantastic.

The reality almost lived up to his expectations. Yes,

Obron was a pain, but not too much. Ever since Edeard's success with the ge-cats, the constant hassle hadn't ended but it had certainly eased off. They didn't speak as friends, but on the journey out Obron had been almost civil. Edeard suspected that was partially down to Melzar, who was caravan master, and who had made it very clear before they left that he would not tolerate any trouble.

'It might seem like this is some kind of holiday,' Melzar told the assembled apprentices in the village hall the night before they departed. 'But remember this is part of your formal education. I expect you to work hard and learn. If any of you cause me *any* problems, you will be sent back to Ashwell right away. If any of you slack off or do not reach what I consider a satisfactory level of landcraft, I will inform your Master and you will be dropped back a year from qualification. Understood?'

'Yes, sir,' the apprentices muttered grudgingly. There were a lot of smirks hidden from Melzar as they filed out.

They had taken five days to reach Witham. There were seventeen apprentices and eight adults in the caravan. Three big carts carried goods and food; over thirty farm beasts were driven along with them. Everyone rode ge-horses; for some apprentices it was the first time they'd ever been up on the animals. Melzar quickly assigned Edeard to help tutor them. It allowed him to open up conversations with lads who'd ignored him before, after all he was the youngest senior apprentice in Ashwell. But out here on the road they began to accept him as an equal rather than the freaky boy Obron always complained about. Melzar also entrusted him with controlling the ge-wolves they used to keep guard.

'You're better than all of us at guiding those brutes, lad,' he'd said as they made camp that first night. 'Make sure they do their job properly. Keep three of them with us, and I want the other four patrolling round outside.'

'Yes, sir, I can do that.' It wasn't even a brag, those were simple orders.

Talk that night among the apprentices was of bandits and wild tribes, each of them doing their best to tell the most horrific stories. Alcie and Genril came top with the cannibal tribe that supposedly lived in the Talman Mountains. Edeard didn't mention that his own parents had been killed while on a caravan, but everyone knew that anyway. He was thrown a few glances to check out how he was reacting. His nonchalance earned him quiet approval. Then Melzar came over and told them all not to be so gruesome, that bandits weren't half as bad as legend. 'They're basically nomad families, nothing more. They're not organized into gangs. How could they be? If they were a real threat we'd call the militia from the city, and go after them. It's just a few bad 'uns that give the rest a lousy rep. No different from us.'

Edeard wasn't so sure. He suspected Melzar was just trying to reassure them. But the conversation moved on, quietening down as they gossiped about their Guild Masters. Judging by their talk, Edeard was convinced he'd got a saint in Akeem. Obron even claimed Geepalt would beat the carpentry apprentices if they messed up.

Witham might have been five times the size of Ashwell, but it shared the same air of stagnation. It was set in rolling, heavily cultivated farmland, with a river running through the middle; unusually it had two churches for the Lady. Edeard bit back on any disappointment as they rode through the big gates. The buildings were stone or had thick timber frames supporting some kind of plaster panelling. Most of the windows were glass rather than the shutters used in Ashwell. And the streets were all stone cobble. He found out later that water was delivered into houses through buried clay pipes, and the drains worked.

They spent two days in the central market square, negotiating with merchants and locals, then stocking up with supplies (like glass) that weren't made in Ashwell. The apprentices had been allowed to bring examples of their own work to sell or trade. Edeard was surprised when Obron brought out a beautifully carved box made from martoz wood, polished to a ebony lustre. Who would have thought an arse like him could create something so charming? Yet a merchant gave him four pounds for it.

For himself, Edeard had brought along six ge-spiders. Always the trickiest of the standard genera to sculpt, they were highly valued for the drosilk they spun. And these had only just hatched, they'd live for another eight or nine months; during that time they would spin enough silk to make several garments, or armour jackets. Three ladies from the Weaver's Guild bid against each other for them. For the first time in his life Edeard's farsight couldn't quite discern how eager they were when they haggled with him; they covered their emotions with steely calm, the surface of their minds as smooth as a genistar egg. He just hoped he was doing the same when he agreed to sell for five pounds each. Surely they could sense his elation? It was more money than he'd seen in his life, let alone held in his hands. Somehow he didn't manage to hang on to it for very long. The market was huge, with so many fabulous items, as well as clothes of a quality rarely found in Ashwell. He felt almost disloyal buying there, but he did so need a decent full-length oilskin coat for the coming winter, and found one with a quilted lining. Further on there was a stall selling knee-high boots with sturdy silkresin soles that would surely last for years – a good investment, then. They also sold wide-brimmed leather hats. To keep the sun off in summer, and the rain in winter, the leatherworker apprentice explained. She was a lovely girl and seemed genuinely eager for him to have the right hat. He dragged out the haggling as long as he dared.

His fellow apprentices laughed when he returned dressed in his new finery. But they had spent their own money, too. And few had been as practical as him.

That evening Melzar allowed them to visit the town's taverns unchaperoned, threatening horrifying punishments if anyone caused trouble. Edeard joined up with Alcie, Genril, Janene and Fahin. He spent the evening hoping to catch sight of the leatherworker apprentice, but by the time they reached the third tavern the town's unfamiliar ales had rendered them incapable of just about anything other than drinking more ale. And singing. The rest of the evening was forever beyond recollection.

When he woke up, slumped under one of the Ashwell carts, Edeard knew he was dying. He'd obviously been poisoned then robbed. Too much of his remaining money was missing, he could barely stand, he couldn't eat, he stank worse than the stables. It was also the first night he couldn't remember being troubled by his strange dreams. Then he found out it was a mass poisoning. All the apprentices were in the same state. And all of the adults found it hilarious.

'Another lesson learned,' Melzar boomed. 'Well done. You lot should graduate in record time at this rate.'

'What a swine,' Fahin grunted as Melzar walked away.

He was a tall boy, so thin he looked skeletal. As a doctor's apprentice he'd managed to get one of the few pairs of glasses in Ashwell to help his poor vision. They weren't quite right for him, magnifying his eyes to a quite disturbing degree for anyone standing in front of him. At sometime during the night he'd lost his jacket, now he was shivering, and not entirely from the cold morning air. Edeard had never seen him looking so pale before.

Fahin was searching through the leather physick satchel that he always carried. It was full of packets of dried herbs, small phials, and some rolled linen bandages. The satchel made him the butt of many jokes in the taverns all last night, yet he refused to abandon it.

'Do you think they'll let us ride in the carts?' Janene asked mournfully as she looked at the adults, who were huddled together chortling. 'I don't think I can take riding on a ge-horse this morning.'

'Not a chance,' Edeard said.

'How much money have you got left?' Fahin asked. 'All of you.'

The apprentices began a reluctant search through their pockets. Fahin managed to gather up two pounds in change, and hurried off to the herbalist stall. When he came back he started brewing up tea, emptying in several packets of dried leaves and adding the contents of a phial from the satchel.

'What is that?' Alcie asked as he sniffed the kettle and stepped back, his eyes watering. Edeard could smell it too, something like sweet tar.

'Growane, flon seed, duldul bird eyes, nanamint.' Fahin squeezed some limes into the boiling water, and started stirring.

'That's disgusting!' Obron exclaimed.

'It'll cure us, I promise on the Lady.'

'Please tell us you rub it on,' Edeard said.

Fahin wiped the condensation from his glasses, and poured himself a cup. 'Gulp it down in one, that's best.' He swallowed. His cheeks bulged as he grimaced. Edeard thought he was going to spew it up again.

The other apprentices gave the kettle a dubious look. Fahin poured the cup full again. Edeard could sense the doubt in their minds; he felt for Fahin who was trying to do his best to help and be accepted. He put his hand out and took the cup. 'One gulp?'

'Yes,' Fahin nodded.

'You're not going to . . .' Janene squealed.

Edeard tossed it back. A second later the taste registered, kind of what he imagined eating manure would be like. 'Oh Lady! That is . . . Urrgh.' His stomach muscles squeezed up, and he bent over, thinking he was going to be sick. A weird numbness was washing through him. He sat down as if to catch his breath after a winding blow.

'What's it like?' Genril asked.

Edeard was about to slag Fahin off something rotten. 'Actually, I can't feel anything. Still got a headache, though.'

'That takes longer,' Fahin wheezed. 'Give it fifteen minutes. The flon seed needs to get into your blood and circulate. And you need to drink about a pint of water to help.'

'So what was the lime for?'

'It helps mask the taste.'

Edeard started laughing.

'It actually works?' an incredulous Alcie asked.

Edeard gave him a shrug. Fahin poured another cup.

It turned into a ritual. Each of the apprentices gulped down the vile brew. They pulled faces and jeered and cheered each other. Edeard quietly went and fetched himself a bottle of water from the market's pump. Fahin was right, it did help clear his head. After about quarter of an hour he was feeling okay again. Not a hundred per cent, but the brew had definitely alleviated the worst symptoms. He could even consider some kind of breakfast.

'Thanks,' he told Fahin. The tall lad smiled in appreciation.

Afterwards, when they packed the carts and got the ge-horses ready, the apprentices were all a lot easier around each other, the joshing and pranks weren't so hard-edged as before. Edeard imagined that this was what it would be like from now on. They'd shared together, made connections. He often envied the casual friendships between the older people in the village, the way they got on with each other. It was outings like this that saw such seeds rooting. In a hundred years' time, maybe it would be he and Genril laughing at hung-over apprentices. Of course, that would be a much bigger caravan, and Ashwell would be the same size as Witham by then.

Melzar led the caravan on a slightly different route back, curving westward to take in the foothills of the Sardok mountain range. It was an area of low valleys with wide floors, mostly wooded, and home to a huge variety of native creatures. There were few paths other than those carved out by the herds of chamalans who grazed on the pastures between the forests. Farsight and the ge-wolves also sniffed out drakken pit traps which would have swallowed up a ge-horse and rider. The drakken were burrowing animals the size of cats, with five legs in the usual Querencia arrangement of two on each side and a thick highly flexible limb at the rear which helped them make their loping run. The front two limbs had evolved into ferociously sharp claws which could dig through soil at a phenomenal rate. They were hive animals, digging their vast warrens underground, with populations over a hundred strong. Singularly they were harmless, but they attacked in swarms which even a well-armed human had trouble fighting off. Their ability to excavate big caverns just below the surface provided them with the means to trap their prey; even the largest of native creatures were susceptible to the pit traps.

A bi-annual hunt had eliminated the drakken from the lands around Ashwell, but here in the wild they were prevalent. Watching for them heightened Edeard's senses as they passed through the endless undulating countryside. On the third day out of Witham they reached the fringes of the foothills and entered one of the massive forests there, parts of which reached across to the base of the Sardoks themselves.

Edeard had never been in a forest this size before; according to Melzar it predated the arrival of humans on Querencia two thousand years ago. The sheer size of the trees seemed to back up his claim, tall and tightly clustered, their trunks dark and lifeless for the first fifty feet until they burst into a thick interlaced canopy where branches and leaves struggled against each other for light. Little grew on the floor beneath, and in summer when the leaves were in full bloom not much rain dripped through either. A huge blanket of dead, crisped leaves covered the ground, hiding hollows from sight, requiring the humans to use their farsight in order to guide the ge-horses safely round crevices and snags.

It was quiet in the gloom underneath the verdant living awning, the still air amplifying their mildest whisper to a shout that reverberated the length of the plodding caravan. The apprentices slowly abandoned their banter, becoming silent and nervy.

'We'll make camp in a valley I know,' Melzar announced after midday. 'It's an hour away, and the forest isn't as wretched as it is here. There's a river as well. We're well past the trilan egg season so we can swim.'

'We're stopping there?' Genril asked. 'Isn't that early?'

'Don't get your hopes up, my lad. This afternoon you're going galby hunting.'

The apprentices immediately brightened. They'd been promised hunting experience, but hadn't expected it to be galbys, which were large canine equivalents. Edeard had often heard experienced adults tell of how they thought they'd got a galby cornered only to have it jump to freedom. Their hind limb was oversized and extremely powerful, sometimes propelling them as much as fifteen feet in the air.

True to Melzar's word, the forest began to change as they reached a gentle downhill slope. The trees were spread out, and shorter, allowing pillars of sunlight to swarm down. Grass grew again, swiftly becoming an unbroken stratum. Bushes grew in the long gaps between trees, their leaves ranging from vivid green to a dark amethyst. Edeard couldn't name more than a handful of the berries he could see, there must have been dozens of varieties.

As the light and humidity increased, so the yiflies and bitewings began to appear; soon they were swirling overhead in huge clumps before zooming down to nip all the available human skin. Edeard was constantly using his third hand to ward them off.

They stopped the carts by a small river, and corralled the genistars. That was when Melzar finally distributed the five revolvers and two rifles he'd been carrying. The majority belonged to the village, though Genril had his own revolver, which he said had been in his family since the arrival. Its barrel was longer than the others, and made out of a whitish metal that was a lot lighter than the sturdy gun-grade steel produced by the Weapons Guild in Makkathran.

'Carved from the ship itself,' Genril said proudly as he checked the mechanism. Even that snicked and whirred with a smoothness which the city-made pistols lacked. 'My first ancestor salvaged some of the hull before the tides took the ship down into the belly of the sea. It's been in our family ever since.'

'Crap,' Obron snorted. 'That would mean it's over two thousand years old.'

'So?' Genril challenged as he squeezed some oil out of a small can, rubbing it on to the components with a soft linen cloth. 'The ship builders knew how to make really strong metal. Think about it, you morons, they *had* to have strong metal, the ship fell out of the sky and still survived, and in the universe they came from ships flew between planets.'

Edeard didn't say anything. He'd always been sceptical about the whole ship legend. Though he had to admit, it was a *great* legend.

Melzar slung one of the rifles over his shoulder and came round with a box of ammunition. He handed out six of the brass bullets to each of the apprentices who had been given a revolver. 'That's quite enough,' he told them when there were complaints about needing more. 'If you can't hit a galby after six shots, it's either jumped back out of range or it's happily eating your liver. Either way, that's all you get.'

Only five apprentices had been given a gun (including Genril). Edeard wasn't one of them. He looked on rather enviously as they slid the bullets into the revolving chamber.

Melzar crouched down, and began to draw lines in the earth. 'Gather round,' he told them. 'We're going to split into two groups. The shooters will be lined up along the ridge back there.' His hand waved into the forest where the land rose sharply. 'The rest of us will act as the flushers. We form a long line with one end *there*, which will move forward in a big curve until we're level with the first shooter. That should force anything bigger than a drakken out in front of us, and hopefully into the firing line. *Under no circumstances* does anyone go past the first shooter. I don't care if you're best friends and using longtalk, you do not walk in front of the guns. Understood?'

'Yes, sir,' they all chorused.

'Okay then, after the first sweep we'll change over the guns and move to a new location.' He glanced up at the sky which was now starting to cloud over. 'There'll be enough light to do this three times this afternoon, which will give everyone a chance to use a pistol.'

'Sir, my father said only I can use our pistol,' Genril said.

'I know,' Melzar said. 'You get to hang on to it but not the ammunition when you're in the flusher line. Now: if you're a part of the flusher line, you must keep within farsight perception of the people on either side. So in reality that means I want you spaced no more than seventy yards apart. Orders to start, stop, and group together will be issued vocally and in longtalk. You will relay both along the line. You will obey them at all times. The flusher line will use three ge-wolves to help encourage the galbys to run. This time, Edeard and Alcie will control one each, I will take the third. No one else is to order them, I don't want them confused. Any questions? No. Good. Let's go, and the Lady smile on us.'

Edeard called one of the ge-wolves over, and set off in the group following Melzar. Toran, one of the farmers, led the pistol carriers up towards the stony ridge.

'I don't see the point of this,' Fahin complained grimly as he hiked along beside Edeard. 'We've all done pistol shooting at the targets outside the walls, and galbys aren't eatable.'

'Don't you listen to anything?' Janene said. 'This is all about experience. There's a world of difference between firing at a target and being out here in the woods with dangerous animals charging round. The elder council needs to know they can rely on us to defend the village in an emergency.'

Except Melzar told us the nomad families aren't threatening, Edeard thought. *So what is the village wall actually for? I must ask Akeem when I get back.*

'So what if the galbys don't go towards the shooting line?' Fahin asked. 'What if they come at us?' He gripped his satchel tighter, as if it could shield him from the forest's animals.

'They won't,' Edeard said. 'They'll try and avoid us, because we're a group.'

'Yeah, in theory,' Fahin grumbled.

'Quit whinging, for the Lady's sake,' Obron said. 'Melzar knows what he's doing; he's done this with every caravan for the last fifty years. Besides, galbys aren't all that dangerous. They just look bad. If one comes at you, use your third hand to shield yourself.'

'What if we flush out a fastfox?'

The apprentices groaned.

'Fastfoxes live down on the plains,' an exasperated Alcie said. 'They're not mountain animals. You're more likely to get one in Ashwell than here.'

Fahin pulled a face, not convinced.

As they approached the edge of the forest again, Melzar used his longtalk to tell them, 'Start to spread out. Remember, keep the people on both sides within your farsight. If you lose contact, longtalk them.'

Edeard had Obron on one side and Fahin on the other. He wasn't too happy about that. If anyone was going to screw up it would be Fahin. The lanky boy really wasn't an outdoors type; and Obron wasn't likely to help either of them. *But the worst thing Fahin can do is fall behind. It's not like he's got a pistol. And he'll yell hard enough if he can't see us.* He sent the ge-wolf ranging from side to side. The mood of excitement was filling his farsight, the minds of everyone in the flusher line twinkling with anticipation.

They moved forwards, slowly spreading out as Melzar directed until they had formed the line. The trees were growing tall again, their dark-green canopy insulating the apprentices from the cloudy sky.

'Move forwards,' Obron ordered. Edeard smiled and repeated the instruction to Fahin, who grimaced.

Edeard was pleased he'd kept his new boots on. The forest floor here was littered with sticks among manky clumps of grass, uneven ground with plenty of sharp stones. His ankles were sore where the new leather pinched, yet they protected his feet well enough.

With his farsight scouring the land ahead he kept a slow pace, making sure the line stayed straight. Melzar told them to start making a racket. Obron was shouting loudly, while Fahin let out piercing whistles. For himself, Edeard picked up a thick stick and thwacked it against the tree trunks as he passed by.

There were more bushes in this part of the forest. Big zebrathorns with their monochrome patterned leaves and oozing (highly poisonous) white berries, coaleafs that were like impenetrable black clouds squatting on the earth. Small creatures were exposed to his farsight, zipping out of the way of the humans. Nothing big enough to be a drakken, let alone a galby. The ground became soft under his feet, wet loam that leaked water from every footprint. The scent of mouldering leaf was strong in his nose. He was sure he could smell fungus spores.

Obron was out of eyesight now, somewhere behind the bushes. Edeard's farsight picked him up on the other side of dense trunks.

'Close up a little,' he longtalked.

'Sure sure,' Obron replied casually.

A ripple of excitement went down the line. Somewhere up towards Melzar's end a galby sped away, not quite in the direction of the shooting line. Edeard's heart started to beat quickly. He knew he was smiling and didn't care. This was the kind of thing he'd wanted ever since he learned he was going on the caravan. There were galbys here! He would get a chance to flush one, and if he was really lucky maybe take a shot later on.

Something squawked above him. Edeard flicked his farsight focus upwards in time to see a couple of birds dart up through the canopy. There was a thicket up ahead, a dense patch of zebrathorn, just the kind of place for a galby to nest in. His farsight swept through it, but there were dark zones and steep little gullies he couldn't be sure about. He sent the ge-wolf slinking in through the bushes as he skirted round the outside. Now he couldn't see Fahin either, but his farsight registered the boy's mind.

Apprehension hit him like a solid force, the mental equivalent of being doused in icy water. Suddenly all his delight deserted him. His fingers actually lost their grip on the stick as his legs seized up. Something *terrible* was happening. He knew it.

'What?' he gasped. He was frightened, and worse, frightened that he was frightened. *This makes no sense.*

In the middle of the thicket, the ge-wolf he was casually directing lifted its head and snarled, responding to the turmoil bubbling along his tenuous longtalk contact.

'Edeard?' Fahin called. 'What's wrong.'

'I don't . . .' Edeard pulled his arms in by his side as his knees bent, lowering him to a crouch. He instinctively closed his third hand around himself to form the strongest shield he was capable of. *Lady, what's the matter with me?* He pushed his farsight out as far as he could, and swept round as if it was some kind of illuminating beam. The tree trunks were too dense to get any kind of decent picture of anything beyond his immediate vicinity.

'What is the matter with you?' Obron asked. His mental tone was scathing.

Edeard could sense both apprentices hesitating. The ge-wolf was wriggling round, trying to get out of the thicket and back to him. Dry leaves rustled, and he whirled round, raising the stick protectively. 'I think someone's here.' He directed his farsight where he thought the sound had come from, pushing its focus as hard as he could. There were a few tiny rodent creatures scuttling along the forest floor. They could have made the noise—

'What do you mean: someone?' Fahin demanded. 'Who?'

Edeard was gritting his teeth with the effort of extending his farsight to the limit. 'I don't know, I can't sense them.'

'Hey, we're falling behind,' Obron longtalked impatiently. 'Come on, get moving.'

Edeard stared back into the forest. *This is stupid.* But he couldn't get rid of his dread. He took a last look at the forest behind, then turned. The arrow came out of the empty trees on his left, moving so fast he never saw it, only his farsight caught the slightest ripple of motion. His shield tightened up as he gasped, his mind clamouring its shock.

The arrow hit his left pectoral muscle. His telekinetic shield held. The force of impact was sufficient to knock him backwards. He landed on his arse. The arrow tumbled down in the loam and weeds beside him; a long blackened shaft with dark-green needlehawk feathers and a wicked barbed metal tip dripping some thick violet liquid. Edeard stared at it in horror.

'Edeard?'

His mind was swamped by the telepathic voices. It

seemed as if the entire flusher line was mentally shouting at him, demanding an answer.

'Arrow!' he broadcast back at them as forcefully as he could. His eyes didn't move from the arrow lying beside him, showing everyone. 'Poison arrow!'

A mind materialized thirty yards away, sparkling vivid sapphire amid the cluttered grey shadows which comprised Edeard's ethereal vision of the forest.

'Huh?' Edeard jerked his head round. A man stepped out from behind a tree, dressed in a kind of ragged cloak that was almost the same colour as the forest's trunks. His hair was wild, long and braided, filthy with dark-red mud. More mud was smeared across his face and caked his beard. He was snarling, anger and puzzlement leaking out of his mind. One hand reached over his shoulder and pulled another arrow from his quiver. He notched it smoothly into the biggest bow Edeard had ever seen, levelling it as his arm pulled back.

Edeard screamed with voice and mind, a sound he could hear replicated along the flusher line. Even his assailant winced as he let fly.

Edeard thrust his hands out, a motion he followed with his third hand using his full strength. The arrow burst into splinters before it had covered half of the distance between them.

This time it was the forest man who radiated shock into the aether.

'Bandits.' Melzar's call echoed faintly round Edeard, spoken and telepathic. 'It's an ambush. Group together everyone, combine your strength. Shield yourselves. Toran, help us!'

Edeard was scrambling to his feet, vaguely aware of other shouts and adrenaline-boosted emotional pulses reverberating across the forest. More bandits were emerging from their concealment. Arrows were being fired. His mind reached for the ge-wolf, directing it with frenzied urgency. There wasn't going to be time. The forest man had slung his bow to the ground, and was charging. A knife glinted in his hand.

A telekinetic shove nearly knocked Edeard back to the ground. He countered it easily, feeling the force slither over his skin like icy fingers. The bandit was trying for a heartsqueeze, an attack method which apprentices talked about in nervous awe when they gathered together back in Ashwell. Using telekinesis inside someone else's body was the ultimate taboo. Anyone found to have committed the act was exiled. For ever.

Now a bandit was thundering towards Edeard. Knife ready. Death lust fevering his mind. Third hand scrabbling to assail vulnerable organs.

His earlier fear had left Edeard. He wasn't even thinking about the others. A maniac was seriously trying to kill him. That was the whole universe. And as Akeem had explained during their all-too-brief sessions on defensive telekinetic techniques, there is no such thing as a disabling blow.

Edeard stood up and let his arms drop to his side, closing his eyes. He shaped his third hand. Waiting. The pounding of the bandit's bare feet on the forest floor reached his ears. *Waiting.* The man's berserker cry began. The knife rose up, gripped by white knuckles. *Wait . . . judge the moment.* Edeard's farsight revealed the man in perfect profile, he even perceived the leg muscles exerting themselves to the limit as they began the leap. *Any second—*

The attempted heartsqueeze ended, telekinesis was channelled to assist the attack leap, to strengthen the knife thrust.

—*now.*

The bandit left the ground. Edeard pushed his third hand underneath the airborne figure and shoved, effort forcing a wild roar from his throat. He'd never exerted himself so much before, not even when Obron's torment was at its worst.

In an instant the bandit's semi-triumphant scream turned to pure horror. Edeard opened his eyes to see a pair of mud-encrusted feet sail over his head. 'FUCK YOU!' he bellowed, and added the slightest corrective sideways shove to the trajectory. The bandit's head smashed into a bulky tree four yards above the ground. It made a horrible *thud*. Edeard withdrew his third hand. The man dropped like a small boulder, emitting a slight moan as he struck the ground. The ge-wolf pounced.

Edeard turned away. All his emotions returned with tidal-wave power as the ge-wolf began tearing and clawing at the inert flesh. He'd forgotten just how fierce the creatures were. His legs were threatening to collapse under him they were shaking so bad, while his stomach heaved.

The loud crack of shots ripped across the forest. They made Edeard spin round in alarm. *That has to be us. Right?*

There were shouts and cries all around. Edeard didn't know what to do. One of the cries was high pitched: Janene.

'Lady please!' Obron wailed. His mind was pouring out dread like a small nova.

Edeard's farsight flashed out. Two fastfoxes were racing straight at the weeping apprentice. He'd never seen one before, but knew instantly what they were. Only just smaller than a ge-wolf, but faster, especially on the sprint, a streamlined predator with a short ebony fur stiff enough to act like armour. Head that was either fangs or horns, and way too many of both. Its hindlimb was thick and strong, allowing it a long sprint-jump motion as the ultimate lunge on its prey.

They had collars on.

Edeard started running towards them and reached out with his third hand. They were forty yards away, yet he still felt their metal-hard muscles flexing in furious rhythm. He didn't even know if they had hearts like humans and terrestrial beasts, let alone where they were. *So forget a heartsqueeze.* His telekinesis penetrated the brain of the leading one and simply *shredded* all the tissue he found there. It dropped in mid-bound; flaccid body ploughing a furrow through the carpet of dry leaves. The remaining fastfox lurched aside, its demon head swinging around to try and find the threat. It stopped, growling viciously as Edeard trotted up. Limbs bent as it readied itself to pounce.

'What are you doing?' Obron bawled.

Edeard knew he was acting crazy. Didn't care. Adrenaline was powering him on recklessly. He snarled back at the fastfox, almost laughing at it. Then before the creature could move he closed his third hand round it, and lifted it clean of the ground. The fastfox screeched in fury. Its limbs ran against nothing, pumping so fast they were a blur.

'Are you doing that?' an incredulous Obron asked.

'Yeah,' Edeard grinned.

'Oh crap. *Look out!*'

Three bandits were running towards them. They were dressed the same as the one who attacked Edeard, simple ragged camouflage cloaks, belts with several dagger sheaths. One of them carried a bow.

Edeard sent out a single longtalk command, summoning the ge-wolf.

The bandits were slowing. Consternation began to glimmer in their minds as they saw the furious fastfox scrabbling uselessly in mid-air. More gunshots rang through the forest.

'Protect yourself,' Edeard ordered sharply as the bandit with a bow notched an arrow. Obron's shield hardened.

The three bandits came to a halt, still staring disbelievingly at the writhing fastfox. Edeard rotated the predator slowly and deliberately until it was pointing directly at them. He was studying the animal's thoughts, noting the simple motivational currents. It was similar to a genistar mind, although the strongest impulses seemed to be fear-derived. *Some kind of punishment/reward training, probably.* The bandit with the bow shot his arrow. Obron yipped as Edeard confidently swiped it aside.

There was another pause as the bandits watched it clatter against a tree. Telekinetic fingers skittered across Edeard's skin, easily warded off. All three bandits drew short swords. Edeard slammed an order into the fastfox's mind, sensing its original compulsions changing. It stopped trying to run and snarled at the bandits. One of them gave it a startled look. Edeard dropped it lightly on the ground.

'Kill,' he purred.

The fastfox moved with incredible speed. Then its hindlimb slapped the earth and powered it forward in a low arc. Telekinetic shields hardened round the bandits. Against one demented predator they might have stood a chance. The ge-wolf hit them from the side.

'Oh, Lady,' Obron shuddered as the screaming began. He paled at the carnage, yet couldn't pull his gaze away.

'Come on,' Edeard caught his arm. 'We have to find Fahin. Melzar said to join up.'

Obron stumbled forward. A burst of pistol fire reverberated through the trees. It must be from the shooting line, Edeard thought, they've come to help. The turbulent shouting was turning into distinct calls. Edeard heard several apprentice names yelled. Longtalk was hysterical snatches of thought mostly overwhelmed with emotional outpourings, a few raw visions threatened to overwhelm him. Pain, twinned with blood pumping out from a long gash in Alcie's thigh. Arrow sticking out of a tunic, numbness from its entry point spreading quickly. Mud-caked faces bobbing as punches were thrown. Impact pain. Camouflaged bandit sprinting between trees as the rifle barrel tracked. Fastfox a streak of grey-black. Blood forming a huge puddle around a torn corpse.

Edeard ran round the side of the zebrathorn thicket. 'Fahin! Fahin, it's us. Where are you?' He couldn't see anyone. There was no revealing glimmer of thought in his farsight. 'Fahin!'

'He's gone,' Obron panted. 'Did they get him? Oh, Lady!'

'Is there any blood?' Edeard was scanning the leaves and soil.

'Nothing. Oh—'

Edeard followed Obron's gaze and caught sight of a bandit running through the woods. The man had a sword in his hand, dripping with blood. Anger surged through Edeard, and he reached out with his third hand, yanking at the man's ankle, then pushing him down hard. As the bandit fell, Edeard twisted the sword, bringing the blade vertical. The agonized bellow as he was impaled made Edeard recoil in shock. The bandit's dying mind wept with frustration and anguish. Then the glimmer of thoughts were extinguished.

'He was fifty yards away,' Obron whispered in astonishment and no small measure of apprehension.

'Fahin,' Edeard called. 'Fahin, can you hear me?' His farsight picked out a tiny iridescent glow that suddenly appeared inside the thicket. 'Fahin?'

'Edeard?' the lanky boy's longtalk asked fearfully.

'Yes! Yes, it's me and Obron. Come on, come out. It's safe. I think.'

They both watched as Fahin crawled out of the bushes. His face and hands had been scratched mercilessly, his loose woollen sweater was missing completely. Tacky berry juice was smeared into his hair and over his glasses, which hung from one ear. Amazingly, he was still clutching his physick satchel. Obron helped him up, and abruptly found himself being hugged. 'I was so frightened,' Fahin mumbled piteously. 'I fled. I'm sorry. I should have helped.'

'It's okay,' Obron said. 'I wasn't much use either.' He turned and gave Edeard a long thoughtful look, his mind tightening up pensively. 'Edeard saved me. He's killed a score of them.'

'No,' Edeard protested. 'Nothing like that—' then trailed off as he realized he really had killed people today. His guilty glance stole back to the bandit impaled on his own sword. A man was dead, and he'd done it. But the sword had been slick with blood. And the other bandits . . . they would have killed us. *I didn't have a choice.*

Sometimes you have to do what's wrong in order to do what's right.

'Can anyone still see or sense bandits?'

Edeard's head came up as he received Melzar's weak longtalk. Obron and Fahin were also looking round.

'Anyone?' Melzar asked. 'Okay, then please make your way towards me. If anyone is injured, please help bring them along. Fahin, are you here?'

Somehow, Melzar being alive made the world a little less intimidating for Edeard. He even managed a small grin. Obron let out a whistle of relief.

'Yes, sir, I'm here,' Fahin replied.

'Good lad, hurry up please, we have injured.'

'Oh, Lady,' Fahin groaned. 'I'm just an apprentice. The doctor won't even let me prepare some of her leaves.'

'Just do the best you can,' Edeard said.

'But—'

'You cured our hangovers,' Edeard said. 'Nobody will start mouthing off at you for helping the injured. We're not expecting you to be as good as old Doc Seneo. But Fahin, you have to do something. You can't turn your back on wounded people. You just can't. They need you.'

'He's right,' Obron said. 'I think I heard Janene scream. What would her parents say if you walked away?'

'Right, yes,' Fahin said. 'You're right, of course. Oh Lady, where are my glasses? I can't do everything by farsight.' He turned back to the thicket.

'They're here,' Edeard said. His third hand lifted them gently into place, at the same time wiping the berry goop from them.

'Thank you,' Fahin said.

They hurried through the forest towards Melzar. Other

figures were moving with them in the same direction. Several apprentices sent panicky hellos via longtalk. Edeard remembered an image of Alcie, the wound in his thigh. It had looked bad.

Toran and the apprentices with pistols had gathered into a defensive group with Melzar. Edeard exchanged a relieved greeting with Genril, who was all jitters. He said he had one bullet left in his revolver, and he was sure he'd hit at least one bandit. 'I got really scared when the fastfoxes charged us. Toran killed one with his rifle. Lady! He's a good shot.'

'You should see what Edeard did,' Obron said flatly. 'He doesn't need guns.'

'What?' Genril asked. 'What did you do?'

'Nothing,' Edeard said. 'I know how to deal with animals, that's all. You know that.'

'Just how strong are you?' Obron asked.

'Yeah,' Genril said. 'We heard your longtalk right over on the ridge, it was like you were next to me screaming into my skull. Lady, I almost ducked when that arrow came at you.'

'Does it matter?' Edeard asked. He was looking round, wondering where the others were. Out of the twelve apprentices and four adults in the flusher line, only five had made it so far, including the three of them. Then Canan the carpenter arrived carrying an unconscious Alcie. Fahin gave his friend a worried look, seeing the crudely wrapped wound already soaked in blood. His mind started to get agitated.

'Go,' Edeard directed with a quiet longtalk. 'Do as much as you can.'

'P-p-put him down,' Fahin said. He knelt beside Alcie and started rummaging through his satchel.

Edeard turned back to the forest, sending his farsight ranging out. *Where are the others?* His heart quickened as he detected some movement. A couple of apprentices came running through the trees.

'It's all right,' Melzar said soothingly. 'You're safe now.'

'We left Janene,' one of them wailed. 'We tried to save her, but she took an arrow. I ran—' He collapsed on the ground, sobbing.

'Nine,' Edeard whispered as he kept his vigil. 'Nine out of twelve.'

Melzar's hand came down on his shoulder. 'It would have been none without you,' he said quietly. 'Your warning saved us. Saved me, in fact. I owe you my life, Edeard. We all do.'

'No,' Edeard shook his head sadly. 'I didn't warn you. I was terrified. That was all. You heard my fear.'

'I know. It was – powerful. What happened? What tipped you off?'

'I . . .' He frowned, remembering the sensation of fear that had gripped him. There was no reason for it. 'I heard something,' he said lamely.

'Whatever, I'm glad.'

'Why couldn't we sense them? I thought I had good farsight. They were closer to me than Obron and Fahin and I never knew.'

'There are ways you can eclipse your thoughts, bend them away from farsight. It's not a technique we're very familiar with in Ashwell, and I've never seen it practised so well as today. The Lady knows where they learned it from. And they tamed fastfoxes, too. That's astonishing. We'll have to send messengers out to the other towns and warn them of this new development.'

'Do you think there are more of them out there?' Edeard could imagine whole armies of bandits converging on their little caravan.

'No. We put them to flight today. And even if there were others lurking about, they have pause for thought now. Their ambush failed. Thanks to you.'

'I bet Janene and the others don't think it failed,' Edeard said bitterly. He didn't care that he was being rude to Melzar. After this, nothing much seemed to matter.

'There's no answer I can give you to that, lad. I'm sorry.'

'Why do they do this?' Edeard asked. 'Why do these people live out here hurting others? Why don't they live in the villages, in a house? They're just savages.'

'I know, lad. But this is all they know. They're brought up in the wilds and they'll bring their children up the same way. It's not a cycle we can break. There are always going to be people living out beyond civilization.'

'I hate them. They killed my parents. Now they've killed my friends. We should wipe them out. All of them. It's the only way we'll ever be allowed to live in peace.'

'That's anger talking.'

'I don't care, that's what I feel. That's what I'll always feel.'

'It probably is. Right now I almost agree with you. But it's my job to get everyone home safely.' Melzar leaned in close, studying Edeard's expression and thoughts. 'Are you going to help me with that?'

'Yes, sir. I will.'

'Okay, now call back our ge-wolves.'

'Right. What about the fastfox?' Edeard was still aware of the animal prowling round at the limit of his farsight. It was confused, missing its original master.

'The fastfox?'

'Edeard tamed it,' Obron said. 'His third hand scooped it up, and he made it attack the bandits.'

The other apprentices turned to look at Edeard. Despite the exhaustion and apprehension dominating their thoughts a lot of them were registering surprise, and even some concern.

'I told you,' Edeard said sullenly. 'I know how to deal with animals. It's what my whole Guild does.'

'Nobody's ever tamed a fastfox,' Toran said. Melzar flashed him an annoyed glance.

'The bandits did,' Genril said. 'I saw the collars on them.'

'They'd already learned to obey,' Edeard explained. 'My orders were stronger, that's all.'

'All right,' Melzar said. 'Call the fastfox in. If you can control it, we'll use it to guard the caravan. If not, well . . .' He patted his rifle. 'But I'll warn you now, lad, the village elders won't allow you to keep it.'

3

In Aaron's opinion, Riasi had benefited from being stripped of its capital city status. It retained the grand structures intrinsic to any capital, as well as the expansive public parks, a well-financed transport grid, and excellent leisure facilities, yet with the ministries and their bureaucrats decamped across the ocean to Makkathran2 the stress and hassle had been purged from everyday life. So too had exorbitant housing costs. What was left was a rich city with every possible amenity; consequently, its population were kicking back and enjoying themselves.

It made things a lot easier for Aaron. The taxi flight from Makkathran2 had taken nine hours; they'd landed at the spaceport, one of hundreds of identical arrivals. Mercifully, Corrie-Lyn had spent most of the journey asleep. When she did wake she placidly did whatever he told her. So they moved through the vast passenger terminus on the ped walks, visiting just about every lounge there was. Only then did he go back out to the taxi rank and take a trip to the old Parliament building at the centre of the city. It was late morning by then, with a lot of activity in the surrounding district. They swapped taxis again. Then again. Three taxis later they finally touched down in a residential zone on the east bank of the Camoa River.

During the flight from Makkathran2, Aaron had rented a ground-floor apartment in a fifteen-storey tower. It was anonymous enough, a safe house he called it. To Corrie-Lyn it probably seemed secure. Aaron knew his multiple taxi journeys and untraceable coin payment for the apartment were strictly amateur stuff. Any half-decent police officer could track them down within a day.

For two days he did nothing. It took Corrie-Lyn the entire first day just to sober up. He allowed her to order anything she wanted by way of clothes and food, but forbade any alcohol or aerosols. For the second day she just sulked, a state exacerbated by a monster hangover. He knew there was plenty of trauma involved too as she reconciled what had happened with Captain Manby's squad. That night he heard her crying in her room.

Aaron decided to go all out with breakfast the next morning to try and reach through her mood. He combined the culinary unit's most sophisticated synthesis with items delivered fresh from a local delicatessen. The meal started with Olberon bluefruit, followed by French toast with caramelized banana; their main course was buckwheat crepes with fried duck eggs, grilled Uban mushroom, and smoked Ayrshire bacon, topped by a delicate omelette aux caviar. The tea was genuine Assam, which was all he could ever drink in the morning – it wasn't his best time of day.

'Wowie,' Corrie-Lyn said in admiration. She'd wandered in from her bedroom all bleary eyed, dressed in a fluffy blue towelling robe. When she saw what was being laid out she perked up immediately.

'There's sugar for the bluefruit,' he told her. 'It's refined from Dranscome tubers, best in the galaxy.'

Corrie-Lyn sprinkled some of the silvery powder over the bluefruit, and tried a segment. 'Umm, that is good.' She spooned out some more.

Aaron sat opposite her and took his first sip of tea. Their table was next to a window wall, giving them a view out across the river. Several big ocean-going barges were already coasting along just above the rippling water; smaller river traffic curved round them. He didn't see them, his eyes were on the loose front of her robe which revealed the slope of her breasts. Firm and excellently shaped, he admired cheerfully; she certainly had a great body, his gaze tracking down to her legs to confirm. There were no mental directives either way on having sex with her. So he suspected the hormonal admiration was all his own. It made him grin. *Normal after all.*

'You're not a starship-leasing agent,' Corrie-Lyn said abruptly, her face pulled up in a peeved expression.

He realized he was allowing some of his feelings to ooze out into the gaiafield. 'No.'

'So what are you?'

'Some kind of secret agent, I guess.'

'You *guess*?'

'Yeah.'

'Don't you know?'

'Not really.'

'What do you mean?'

'Simple enough. If I don't know anything I can't reveal anything. I just have things I know I have to do.'

'You mean you haven't got any memories of who you are?'

'Not really, no.'

'Do you know who you're working for?'

'No.'

'So how do you know you should be working for them?'

'Excuse me?'

'How do you know you're not working for the Ocisen Empire, that you're helping bring down the Greater Commonwealth? Or what if you're a left-over Starflyer agent? They say Paula Myo never did catch all of them.'

'Unlikely, but admittedly I don't know.'

'Then how can you live with yourself?'

'I think it's improbable that I'm doing something like that. If you asked me to do it now, I wouldn't. So I wouldn't have agreed to do it before my full memory was removed.'

'Your full memory.' Corrie-Lyn tasted the idea with the same care as she'd sampled the bluefruit. 'Anyone who agrees to have their memory taken out just to get an illegal contract has got to be pretty extreme. And you kill people, too. You're good at it.'

'My combat software was superior to theirs. And they'll be re-lifed. Your friend Captain Manby is probably already walking around looking for us. Think how much improved his motivation is now, thanks to me.'

'Without your memories you can't know what your true personality is.'

Aaron reached for his French toast. 'And your point is?'

'For Ozzie's sake, doesn't that trouble you?'

'No.'

She shook her head in amazement. 'That's got to be an artificial feeling.'

'Again, so what? It makes me efficient at what I do.

Personality trait realignment is a useful procedure at re-life. If you want to be a management type, then have your neural structure altered to give yourself confidence and aggression.'

'Choose a vocation and mould yourself to fit. Great, that's so human.'

'Now then what's your definition of human these days? Higher? Advancer? Originals? How about the Hive? Huxley's Haven has kept a regulated society functioning for close to one and a half thousand years; every one of them proscribed by genetic determination, and they're still going strong, with a population that's healthy and happy. Now you go and tell me plain and clear: which of us won the human race?'

'I'm not arguing evolution with you. Besides it's just a distraction to what you are.'

'I thought we'd gone and agreed that neither of us knows what I am. Is that what fascinates you about me?'

'In your pervert dreams!'

Aaron grinned and crunched down on some toast.

'So what's your mission?' Corrie-Lyn asked. 'What do you *have to do*, kidnap Living Dream Councillors?'

'Ex-Councillors. But no, that's not the way of it.'

'So what do you want with me?'

'I need to find Inigo. I believe you can help.'

Corrie-Lyn dropped her spoon and stared at him in disbelief. 'You've got to be kidding.'

'No.'

'You expect me to help you? After what you've just said?'

'Yes. Why not?'

'But . . .' she spluttered.

'Living Dream is trying to kill you. Understand this: they're not going to stop. If anything, the other night will only make them more determined. The only person left in the galaxy who can put the brakes on your dear new Cleric Conservator is Inigo himself.'

'So that's who you're working for, the anti-Pilgrimage lobby.'

'There's no guarantee that Inigo will stop the Pilgrimage if he comes back. You know him better than anybody. Do I speak the right in that?'

She nodded forlornly. 'Yeah. I think you might.'

'So help me find him.'

'I can't do that,' she said in a low voice. 'How can you ask when even you don't know what you'll do to him if we find him.'

'Anyone who has hidden himself this well is never going to be taken by surprise even if we do manage to track him down. He knows there are a lot of serious people looking for him. Besides, if I wanted to kill him, why would I take the trouble of hunting him down. If he's off the stage he can't direct any of the actors, now can he? So if I want him back, I must want him back intact.'

'I don't know,' she said weakly.

'I saved your life.'

Corrie-Lyn gave him a sly smile. 'The software running you saved my life. It did it because you needed me. I'm your best hope, remember.'

'You're my number one choice.'

'Better get ready to schmooze number two.'

'Not even my liver could take another night in Rakas. I *do* need you, Corrie-Lyn. And what about you? What do you need? Don't you want to find him? Don't you want to hear why he upped and left you and all the billions who believed in him? Did he lose faith? Was Living Dream just that all along, nothing more than a dream?'

'Low blow.'

'You can't do nothing. You're not that kind of person. You know Inigo must be found before the Pilgrimage leaves. Somebody *will* find him. Nobody can stay hidden for ever, not in this universe. Politics simply won't allow it. Who do you want to find him?'

'I . . . I can't,' Corrie-Lyn said.

'I understand. I can wait, at least for a little while longer.'

'Thanks.' She put her head down and started to eat her French toast, almost as if she was ashamed by the decision.

Aaron didn't see her for nearly three hours after breakfast. She went back into her bedroom and stayed there. His u-shadow monitored a small amount of unisphere use; she was running through standard information files from the Living Dream fanes in the city. He had a shrewd idea what she was looking for, a friend she could trust, which meant things could well be swinging his way. If they set foot outside it wouldn't be long before Manby or his replacement were racing up behind them, guns flaring.

When she came out she was wearing a loose-neck red sweater and tight black trousers; a silver necklace made a couple of long loops round her neck before wrapping round her hips. She'd fluffed her dark hair neatly, and infused it with purple and green sparks that glimmered on a long cycle. He gave her an appreciative smile. Which she ignored.

'I need to talk to someone,' she announced.

Aaron tried not to make his smirk too obvious. 'Sure thing. I hope you're not going to insist on going alone. There are bad people out there.'

'You can come with me, but the conversation is private.'

'Okay. Can I ask if you've already set up a meeting?'

'No.'

'Good. Don't call anyone. The Ellezelin cybersphere has government monitors in its nodes. Manby's team will fall on you like a planet-killer asteroid.'

Her expression flickered with worry. 'I already accessed the unisphere.'

'That's okay. They probably can't trace your u-shadow access,' he lied. 'Do you know where this person is likely to be?'

'The Daeas fane, that's over on the south side of the city.'

'Right then, we'll take a taxi to that district and land a couple of blocks away. Once we're at the fane we'll try and get a visual on your friend.'

'He's not a friend,' she said automatically.

Aaron shrugged. 'Whoever the person is. If we find him then you can have your chat in private, okay. Calling him is our last resort; and please let me do that. My u-shadow has fixes available that should circumvent the monitor systems.'

She nodded agreement, picked up her scarlet bag and wrapped a long fawn-coloured scarf round her shoulders. 'Let's go.'

Aaron was perfectly relaxed in the taxi flight over the city. He spent it looking down on the buildings, enjoying the vertical perspective as the towers flipped past underneath. The inhabitants certainly enjoyed their roof gardens, nearly half of them had some kind of terrace fenced in by greenery; swimming pools were everywhere.

He didn't know what the outcome of Corrie-Lyn's meeting would be. Nor did he really care. His only certainty was that he'd know exactly what to do when the time came. There was, he reflected, a lot of comfort to be had in his unique level of ignorance.

They landed on an intersection at the edge of the Daeas district. It was a commercial area dominated by the mono-lithic buildings that had been the Ellezelin Offworld Office, the ministry which had masterminded the Free Market Zone and Ellezelin's subsequent commercial and diplo-matic domination of neighbouring star systems. Now the structures were given over to hotels, casinos, and exclusive malls. They walked along the ornate stone facades towards the fane, with Aaron making sure they didn't take a direct route. He wanted time to scan round and check for possible – make that probable – hostiles.

'Did you know he was leaving before he actually went?' Aaron asked.

Corrie-Lyn gave him an unsettled glance. 'No,' she sighed. 'But we'd cooled off quite a while back. I hadn't been excluded, exactly, but I wasn't in the inner circle any more.'

'Who was?'

'That's the thing. No one, really. Inigo had been getting more and more withdrawn for a long time. Years. Because we were so close, it took a time for me to notice how distant he was growing. You know what it's like.'

'I can imagine,' he said, which earned him a frown. 'So there was no one event, then?'

'Ah, you're talking about the fabled Last Dream, aren't

you? No, not that I was aware. But then that rumour had to come from somewhere.'

Even before they won a majority in Parliament, the Living Dream's Chief Councillor of Riasi boasted that you could never travel more than two kilometres in the city without encountering a fane. The buildings didn't have a specific layout: anything which had a hall large enough to accommodate the faithful, along with office space and living quarters, would do. Given the inherent wealth of the Daeas district it was inevitable that the local fane should be impressive; a contemporary Berzaz cube, with horizontal stripes twisted at fifteen degrees to each other, their fluid-luminal surfaces shining with an intensity that automatically matched the sunlight, delineating each floor in a spectromatic waterfall. The overall effect was a city block that was trying to screw itself into the ground. It was surrounded by a broad plaza with a fountain at each point. Tall jets squirted out from the centre of inclined rings that were ticked out with ingrav to make the water flow upslope.

Aaron scanned round the bustling plaza, performing a meticulous assessment of the locale, allowing his combat software to plot escape routes. His u-shadow was busy extracting the civic plans for the neighbouring buildings, along with utility tunnels and traffic routes. Directly opposite the fane's main entrance was an arcade with a curving crystal roof sheltering fifty high-class shops and boutiques on three levels; it had multiple entrances on to three streets and five underground cargo depots, as well as seven cab platforms and ten rooftop landing pads. That would be difficult to cover even for a large surveillance team. Next to it was a staid old ministry building that now housed several financial institutions and a couple of export merchants. There weren't so many ways in and out, but it did have a large subterranean garage full of expensive regrav capsules. The boulevard running alongside was lined with shops and entertainment salons mixed in with bars and restaurants; tables outside played host to a vibrant café culture. Aaron's u-shadow called down three taxis and parked them on public pads nearby, paying for them to wait with three independent and genuinely untraceable coin accounts.

'Do you want me to go in and try and find him?' Corrie-Lyn asked.

Aaron studied the fane's main entrance, a truncated archway which the fluid-luminal flowed round on either side, presenting it as a dark passageway. Plenty of people were coming and going, the majority dressed in the kind of clothes found on Querencia. Brightly coloured Cleric robes were easy to spot.

'I'm assuming this somebody is a Living Dream Cleric, quite a senior one given your own rank.'

She gave him a short nod. 'Yves. He's still the deputy here. I've known him for fifty years. Completely devoted to Inigo's vision.'

'Old guard, then.'

'Yes.'

'Okay, not likely to bump into him running errands round the place then. He's going to stay put in his office.'

'That's on the fourth floor. I can probably get up there, I do have some clearance. I'm not sure I can take you with me.'

'Any clearance you had will be revoked by now. And if you interface with a Living Dream network it'll send up an alert they can see back on Old Earth.'

'So what do you want to do, then?'

'If honesty doesn't pay ... I have a few tricks that should be able to get us up to his office without drawing attention to ourselves. All you have to do is pray he doesn't turn us in the minute we say "hello".'

'I say hello,' she emphasized.

'Whatever.' His software had now identified three probable hostiles amid the bustle of pedestrians across the plaza. Looking at the shimmering building he got the distinct sensation of a trap waiting to snap shut. His trouble was that pointing out the three suspects wouldn't be anything like enough to convince Corrie-Lyn that she should be doing her utmost to help him. That would require a genuine scare on the same scale as Captain Manby had provided back in Greater Makkathran. The difference being this time she would be awake, sober, and clean. She had to realize Living Dream was her enemy on every level.

'We'll go in by the front door,' he said. 'No sense drawing attention to ourselves trying to sneak in round the back.'

'Each side of the fane has an entrance which leads to the main reception hall. They're all open, we welcome everyone.'

'I was speaking metaphorically,' he said. 'Come on.' His u-shadow told him the Riasi metropolitan police had just received an alert that two political activists known to be aggressive had been seen in the city. 'Ladies and Gentlemen, Elvis is well and truly back in the building,' he muttered without really knowing why.

Corrie-Lyn let out a hiss of exasperation at his nonsense, and headed off towards the fane's entrance. Aaron followed behind, smiling at her attitude. The thoughts within the plaza's gaiafield were pleasurable and enticing, a melange of sensations that made the hair along his spine stand up. It was almost as if the inside of his skull was being caressed. Something wonderful resided inside the fane the gaiafield promised him. He just had to step inside . . .

Aaron grinned at the crudity of the allure, it was the mental equivalent of fresh baked bread on a winter's morning. He imagined it would be quite an attraction to any casual passer-by; the problem he had with that was the lack of any such specimen, the majority of Ellezelin's population were all Living Dream devotees. But this fane like all the others in the Greater Commonwealth housed a gaiafield confluence nest, it was inevitable the lure effect would be at its peak in the plaza.

No one even looked at them as they walked into the archway with its moiré curtain of luminescence. Aaron's level-one field scan showed him the three suspects outside had started to move towards the fane. Hopefully they couldn't detect such a low-power scan, they certainly didn't appear to be enriched with biononics.

There were sensors built into the entrance, standard systems recording their faces and signatures, making sure they had no concealed weapons. The kind every public building was equipped with. Aaron's biononics deflected them easily enough.

Inside, the siren call within the gaiafield slackened off to be replaced by a single note of harmony. Décor and aether blended to give a sense of peaceful refuge, even the air temperature was pleasantly cool. The reception hall was a replica of the main audience chamber in the Orchard Palace where the Mayor greeted honoured citizens. Here, Clerics talked quietly to small groups of people. Aaron and

Corrie-Lyn walked through the hall and into the cloister which let to the eastern entrance. A corridor on the right had no visible barrier. Aaron's biononic fields manipulated the electronics guarding it, and the force field disengaged. He paused, checking the building network, but there was no alarm.

'In we go,' he told her quietly.

A lift took them up to the fourth floor, opening into a windowless corridor narrower than the one downstairs. As they stepped out, his u-shadow informed him that the three waiting taxis had all just had their management programs examined. Aaron was undecided at what point to tell her that they were being targeted again. The longer he left it, the more difficult it would be to extricate them from the fane. He needed her just rattled enough to sign up for his mission, but not too scared she lost all sense.

With activity in the fane still at a minimum he walked with her along several corridors until they reached Yves' office. The room had an active screen, but Aaron's field scan could cut right through it. There was just one person inside, no enrichments showing.

Corrie-Lyn put a hand lightly on Aaron's chest. 'Just me,' she said. Her voice had dropped to a husky tone. He couldn't tell if she was being playful or insistent. Either way, there didn't seem to be a threat in the office, so he smiled gracefully and gestured at the door.

Once she was inside, he walked down the rest of the corridor, checking the other rooms. A woman in plain brown and blue Cleric robes came out of one after he'd passed. She frowned and said: 'Can I help—'

Aaron shot her with a low-power stun pulse from the weapons enrichment in his left forearm. His scrambler field severed her connection with the unisphere as she crumpled on to the floor, blocking the automatic call for help to the police and city medical service emitted by her multicellular clusters. He didn't even bother scooping her up and shoving her inside an empty room. That simply wasn't the kind of timescale he was looking at.

When he started back to Yves' office, all the lifts began to descend to the ground floor. By expanding his level-one field scan to its limit he could just detect weapons powering up down there. He walked straight into Yves' office. 'We have to go—' he began, then cursed silently.

Corrie-Lyn was sitting on the edge of a long leather couch, with Yves slumped at the other end. Her red bag was open, an aerosol in her fist, moving hurriedly, guiltily, from her face. A blissful expression weighed down her eyelids and mouth. Aaron couldn't believe he hadn't checked her bag while she'd been sleeping. It was completely unprofessional.

'Oh hi,' she slurred. 'Yves, this is the guy I was telling you about, my saviour. Aaron, this is Yves, we were just catching up.'

Yves waved his hand at Aaron, producing a dreamy smile. 'Cool.'

'Fuck!' Aaron shot the man with a stun pulse. He was shifting the weapon on Corrie-Lyn when his tactical programs interrupted the action. In her current state it would be a lot easier for him to evacuate her if she was unconscious and inert, however she had to be aware of the danger she was in to make the right choice and confide in him.

Yves tumbled backwards over the end of the couch and landed on the floor with a soft thud. His legs were propped up by the end of the couch, shoes pointing at the ceiling. Corrie-Lyn stared at her old friend as his feet slowly slithered sideways.

'What are you *doing*?' she wailed.

'Putting my arse on the line to save yours. Can you walk?'

Corrie-Lyn hauled herself along the couch to peer down at the crumpled body. 'You killed him! Yves! Oh, Ozzie, what are you, you bastard?'

'He's stunned. Which gives him the perfect alibi. Now can you walk?'

She turned her head to peer at Aaron, which was clearly an action that required a lot of effort. 'He's all right?'

'Oh sod it!' He didn't have time to waste being her shrink. 'Yep, he's fine. Forget him, we have to get out of here right now.' He pulled her off the couch and slung her over his shoulder.

Corrie-Lyn wailed again. 'Put me down.'

'You can't even stand up, let alone walk. And we need to run.' The field medic sac in his thigh opened and ejected a drug pellet. Aaron slapped it against Corrie-Lyn's neck, above the carotid. 'That should straighten you out in a minute.'

'No no no,' she protested. 'Leave me alone.'

Aaron ignored her and went out into the corridor. She was hanging over his shoulder, arms beating ineffectually at his buttocks as she cursed him loudly. Several Clerics opened their doors to see what the commotion was. Aaron stunned each one as they appeared.

'What's happening?' Corrie-Lyn slurred.

'Getting out of here. Your old friends have found us.'

Her arms stopped flailing and she started to weep.

Aaron shook his head in dismay; he'd thought she was more capable than this. He reached the lift and his bionics produced a small disruptor effect. The lift doors cracked, their glossy surface darkening as if he was watching them age centuries in every second. They crumbled away into dust and flakes, pouring away down the shaft where they pattered on to the top of the lift as it stood waiting on the ground floor. Aaron tightened his grip on Corrie-Lyn and jumped down the shaft. She screamed as the darkness rushed past her, a genuine terrified-for-her-life bellow of fear.

His integral force field expanded, cushioning their landing. Another disruptor pulse flashed out from his bionics and the top of the lift disintegrated beneath his feet. Two very startled police officers were looking up as he fell through on top of them. Both of them had force field webbing, which protected them from the impact. The weapons enrichment in Aaron's forearm had to increase its power level by two orders of magnitude to puncture the webbing with a stun pulse. He walked out, still carrying a now-silent Corrie-Lyn. There were several police officers in the corridor between the lift and the welcome hall. They shouted at him to stop, which he ignored. A barrage of energy shots smacked across his force field, encasing him and Corrie-Lyn in a screeching purple nimbus. It didn't even slow him down. He emerged into the welcome hall to see Clerics and visitors running for cover, yelling for help vocally and digitally. Police were taking cover in the archways to three corridors, their weapons peppering him with shots. He fired several low-power disruptor pulses at the hall's ceiling. Thick clouds of composite fragments plummeted down, filling the air with cloying particles; steel and carbon girders sagged, emitting dangerous groans. Police officers flinched, retreating away from the collapsing hall. Aaron walked on towards the main entrance while Corrie-Lyn gasped and moaned in martyred dismay at the chaos raging around them.

Outside, the city cybersphere was broadcasting distress and warning messages to anyone within two blocks of the fane. People were scurrying out of the plaza, an exodus which Aaron's tactical programs decided worked against him. Sentient police software was downloading into the district's cybersphere nodes, taking charge, safeguarding the local network from any subversion he might try and activate, suspending capsule and ground traffic, monitoring sensors, sealing him in.

Aaron's u-shadow went for the unguarded systems managing the plaza's fountains, changing the direction of the ingrav effect on the angled rings. The tall jets began to waver, then suddenly swung down until they were horizontal. They slashed from side to side, hosing everyone in the plaza like giant water cannon. People went tumbling across the stone floor, buffeted by thick waves of spray. Aaron reached the fane's entrance and began sprinting across the plaza, partially obscured from the police by the seething spume clouds. His bionomics strengthened his leg muscles, the field effect amplifying and quickening every movement. He covered the first hundred metres in seven seconds. Flailing bodies washed past him as the jets continued to play back and forth. Police officers were singled out for merciless drubbing. Their force fields did little to protect them from the powerful deluge, and they toppled easily from the soaking punches. Those that did fire energy shots into the furious spray simply created crackling vortices of ions that spat out curlicues of scalding steam. Victims on the ground scrabbled desperately out of the way as the dangerous vapour stabbed out, screaming at them to stop shooting.

The fountains began to run out of water when Aaron was two thirds of the way across the plaza. Two energy shots hit his force field, throwing off a plume of sparks. The strike made him skid on the wet stone.

'Slow down,' Corrie-Lyn yelped as he regained his footing. 'Oh, Ozzie, NO!'

Aaron's sensory field scanned round. The fane was starting to collapse, folding in on itself and twisting gently, as if in mimicry of the pattern of its fluid-luminary surfaces. 'I must have damaged more than I realized,' he grunted. Dust and smoke were flaring out of the entrances like antique rocket engine plumes, billowing over the plaza.

He reached the entrance to the arcade. People had been crowded round, watching the spectacle in the plaza. When Aaron appeared out of the chaos and started charging towards them they'd backed away fast. Now they scattered like frightened birds; no one in the Commonwealth was accustomed to civil trouble, let alone Riasi's residents. As he paused on the threshold, at least five police officers were given a clear line of sight. Energy slammed into his force field, producing a fearsome starblast of photons, its screeching loud enough to overwhelm Corrie-Lyn's howls. Unprotected surfaces around him started to blister and smoulder. He fired three bolts of his own, hidden in the mêlée, targeting structural girders around the archway. The crystal ceiling began to sag, huge cracks ripped through the thick material. Behind them, the fane finally crumpled, the process accelerating. Chunks of debris went scything across the plaza to impact the surrounding buildings. Tens of thousands of glass fragments created a lethal shrapnel cloud racing outwards. The police officers stopped shooting as they sought cover.

Corrie-Lyn was sobbing hysterically at the sight, then the arcade's archway started to disintegrate. She froze as giant daggers of the crystal roof plunged down around them. Fire alarms were yammering, and bright-blue suppressor foam started to pour down from the remaining nozzles overhead. Aaron dived into the third store, which sold hand-made lingerie. A slush of foam rippled out across the floor as it slid off his force field. Two remaining assistants saw him and sprinted for a fire exit.

'Can you walk?' he asked Corrie-Lyn. His u-shadow was attacking the police programs in the arcade's nodes, interfering with the building's internal sensors, and trying to cut power lines directly. It sent out a call to one of the parked taxis, directing it to land at the back of the arcade.

When he pulled Corrie-Lyn off his shoulder all she could do was cross her arms and hug her chest. Her legs were trembling, unable to hold her weight.

'Shit!' He shunted her up over his shoulder again, and went into the back of the store. There was a door at the top of the stairs which led down into the basement stockroom, which he descended quickly. His field scan showed him a whole flock of police regrav capsules swooping low over the plaza, while a couple of hardy officers were making their way over the tangle of archway girders. They seemed to be carrying some very high-powered weaponry.

It was cooler in the stockroom, the air dry and still. Overhead lights came on to reveal a rectangular room with smooth concrete walls, filled with ranks of metal shelving. The far end was piled up with old advertising displays. His u-shadow reported that it was having some success in blocking the police software from nearby electronics. They would know he was there, but not what he was doing.

The big malmetal door to the loading bay furled aside, and he went out into the narrow underground delivery road which served all the stores. It was empty, the police prohibition on all traffic was preventing any cargo capsules from using it. Ten metres away on the other side was a hatchway into a utility tunnel. His u-shadow popped the lock and it swung open. He sprinted across the delivery road and clambered inside pushing an unresisting Corrie-Lyn ahead of him. The hatch snapped shut.

Aaron scanned round. There was no light in the tunnel other than a yellow circle glowing round the hatch's emergency handle. It wasn't high enough for him to walk along, he'd have to stoop. Corrie-Lyn was sitting slumped against the wall just beside the hatch.

'There are no visual sensors inside the tunnel,' his u-shadow reported. 'Only fire and water alarms.'

'Water?'

'In case of flooding. It is a city regulation.'

'Typical bureaucratic overkill,' he muttered. 'Corrie-Lyn we have to keep going.'

She didn't acknowledge. Her limbs were still trembling uncontrollably. But she moved when he pushed at her. Together they shuffled along the tunnel, hunched over like monkeys. There were hatches every fifty metres. He stopped at the sixth one and let his field scan function review the immediate vicinity outside. It didn't detect anyone nearby. His u-shadow unlocked it, and they crawled out into the base of a stairwell illuminated by blue-tinged polyphoto strips on the wall.

'The building network is functioning normally,' his u-shadow said. 'The police sentients are currently concentrating their monitor routines on the fane and the arcade.'

'That won't last,' he said, 'they'll expand outward soon enough. Crack one of the private capsules for me.'

He pulled Corrie-Lyn to her feet. With one arm under her shoulder, supporting her, they went up a flight of stairs. The door opened into the underground car park of the old ministry building. His u-shadow had infiltrated the control net of a luxury capsule, and brought it right over to the stairwell.

The capsule slid up out of the park's chuteway at the back of the building, and zipped up into the nearby traffic stream. Police sentients queried it, and Aaron's u-shadow provided them with a genuine owner certificate code. Corrie-Lyn stared down at the sluggish mass of boiling dust behind them. Her limbs had stopped trembling. He wasn't sure if that was the mild suppressor drug he'd given her finally flushing the aerosol out of her system, or if a deeper level of shock was setting in.

A small fleet of civic emergency capsules and ambulances was heading in to the fane.

'They just shot at us,' she said. 'They didn't warn us or tell us to stop first. They just opened fire.'

'I had jumped down a lift shaft to try and get out,' he pointed out. 'That's a reasonable admission of guilt.'

'For Ozzie's sake! If you didn't have a force-field web we'd be dead. That's not how the police are supposed to act. They were police, weren't they?'

'Yeah. They're the city police, all right.'

'But we did get out,' she sounded puzzled. 'There were how many . . . ten of them? Twenty?'

'Something like that, yeah.'

'You just walked out like nothing could stop you. It didn't matter what they did.'

'That's Higher biononics for you. The only way standard weaponry can gain an advantage is overwhelming firepower. They weren't carrying that much hardware.'

'You're Higher?'

'I have weapons-grade biononics. I'm not sure about the culture part of it. That way of life seems slightly pointless to me, sort of like the pre-Commonwealth aristocracy.'

'What's that?'

'Very rich people living a life of considerable ease and decadence while the common people slaved away into an early grave, with all their labour going to support the aristocrats and their way of life.'

'Oh. Right.' She didn't sound interested. 'Inigo was Higher.'

'No he wasn't.' Aaron said it automatically.

'Actually, he was. But he kept that extremely quiet. Only a couple of us ever knew. I don't think our new Cleric Conservator is aware of his idol's true nature.'

'Are you—'

'Sure? Yes, I'm sure.'

'That's remarkable. There's no record of it; that's a hell of an achievement these days.'

'Like I said, he kept it quiet. No one would have paid any attention to a Higher showing them his dreams, not out here on the External Worlds. He needed to appear as ordinary as possible. To be accepted as one of us.'

Aaron gave an amused grunt. 'Highers are people, too.'

'Some of them.' She gave him a meaningful glance.

'Was Yves the other Cleric who knew about Inigo?'

'No.' She drew a short gasp, and glanced back. 'Oh, Ozzie, Yves! He was unconscious when the fane collapsed.'

'He'll be all right.'

'All right?' she yelled, finally becoming animated. 'All right? He's dead!'

'Well, he'll probably need re-lifing, yeah. But that's only a couple of months' downtime these days.'

She gave him an incredulous snort, and leant against the capsule's transparent fuselage to gaze down on the city.

Shock, anger, and fright, he decided. Mostly fright. 'You need to decide what to do next,' he told her as sympathetically as he could. 'Team up with me, or . . .' He shrugged. 'I can give you some untraceable funds, that should help keep you hidden.'

'Bastard.' She wiped at her eyes, then looked down at herself. Her red sweater had large damp patches, and the lower half of her trousers were caked in blue foam. Her knees were grazed and filthy from the inside of the utility tunnel. Her shoulders slumped in resignation. 'He used to go somewhere,' she said in a quiet emotionless voice.

'Inigo?'

'Yes. This isn't the first time he took off on a sabbatical and left Living Dream covering up for his absence. But none of the other times were for so long. A year at most.'

'I see. Where did he go?'

'Anagaska.'

'That's his birthworld.'

'Yes.'

'An External World. One of the first. Advancer through and through,' he said significantly.

'I'm not arguing with you.'

'Did he ever take you?'

'No. He said he was visiting family. I don't know how true that was.'

Aaron reviewed the files on Inigo's family. There was very little information; they didn't seek publicity, especially after he founded Living Dream. 'His mother migrated inwards a long time ago. She downloaded into ANA in 3440, after first becoming . . .'

'Higher, yes I know.'

He didn't follow the point; but for someone to convert to Higher without leaving any record was essentially impossible. Corrie-Lyn must have been mistaken. 'There's no record of any brothers or sisters,' he said.

Corrie-Lyn closed her eyes and let out a long breath. 'His mother had a sister, a twin. There was something . . . I don't know what, but some incident long ago. Inigo hinted at it; the sisters went through this big trauma together. Whatever it was drove them apart, they never really reconciled.'

'There's nothing in the records about that, I didn't even know he had an aunt.'

'Well now you do. So what next?'

'Go to Anagaska. Try and find the aunt or her children.'

'How do we get there? I imagine the police will be watching the spaceports and wormholes.'

'They will eventually. But I have my own starship.' He stopped in surprise as knowledge of the starship emerged into his mind from some deep memory.

Corrie-Lyn's eyes opened in curiosity. 'You do?'

'I think so.'

'Sweet Ozzie, you are so strange.'

Seventeen minutes later the capsule slid down to land beside a pad in Riasi's spaceport. Aaron and Corrie-Lyn climbed out and looked up at the chrome-purple ovoid that stood on five bulbous legs.

She whistled in admiration. 'That looks deliciously expensive. Is it really yours?'

'Yeah.'

'Odd name,' she said as she walked under the curving underbelly of the fuselage. 'What's the reference?'

'I've no idea.' His u-shadow opened a link to the *Artful Dodger*'s smartcore, confirming his identity with a DNA verification along with a code he abruptly remembered. The smartcore acknowledged his command authority.

'Hang on,' Aaron told Corrie-Lyn, and grabbed her hand. The base of the starship bulged inwards, stretching into a dark tube. Gravity altered around them and they slid up inside the opening.

*

Sholapur was one of those Commonwealth planets that didn't quite work. All the ingredients for success and normality were there: a standard H-congruous biosphere, G-type star, oceans, big continents with great landscapes of deserts, mountains, plains, jungles, and vast deciduous forests, handsome coastlines and long meandering archipelagos. The local flora had several plants humans could eat; while the wildlife wasn't wild enough to pose much of a threat. Tectonically it was benign. The twin moons were small, orbiting seven hundred thousand kilometres out to produce the kind of tides and waves that satisfied every kind of marine sports enthusiast.

So physically, there was nothing wrong with it. That just left the people.

Settlement began in 3120, the year ANA officially became Earth's government. It was the kind of incentive which flushed a lot of the remaining political, cultural, and religious malcontents out of the Central Worlds. The greatest machine ever built was obviously taking over, and Higher culture was now so dominant it could never be revoked. They left in their millions to settle the then furthest External Worlds. At 470 lightyears from Earth, Sholapur was an attractive proposition for anyone looking for a distant haven. To begin with, everything went smoothly. There was commercial investment, the immigrants were experienced professionals; cities and industrial parks sprang up, farms were established. But the groups who arrived from the Central Worlds weren't just dissatisfied with Higher culture, they tended to be insular, intolerant of other ideologies and lifestyles. Petty local disputes had a way of swelling to encompass entire ethnic or ideological communities. Internal migration accelerated, transforming urban areas into miniature city states; all with massively different laws and creeds. Cooperation between them was minimal. The planetary parliament was 'suspended' in 3180, after yet another debate ended in personal violence between Senators. And that more or less marked the end of Sholapur's economic and cultural development. It was regarded as hermitic by the rest of the Commonwealth. Even the External Worlds with all their attitude of forthright independence viewed it like a kind of embarrassing drop-out cousin. The nearest settled worlds called it

Planet of the Hotheads, and had little contact. Despite that, a great many starships continued to visit. Some of the micro-nations had laws (or a lack of laws) which could be advantageous to certain types of merchant.

Five thousand kilometres above the planetary surface, the starship *Mellanie's Redemption* fell out of hyperspace amid a collapsing bubble of violet Cherenkov radiation. There was no single planetary traffic control Troblum could contact; instead he filed an approach request with Ikeo City, and received permission to land.

The *Mellanie's Redemption* measured thirty metres long, a sleek flared cone shape, with forward-curving tailfins that looked functionally aerodynamic. In fact they were thermal radiators added to handle the extensively customized power system. The cabin layout was a central circular lounge ringed by ten sleeping cubicles and a washroom. Hyper-drive ships didn't come much bigger, they simply weren't cost effective to build. Starline companies used them almost exclusively for passengers wealthy enough to pay for fast transport. Most starships used a continuous wormhole drive; they were slower but could be built to any size required, and carried the bulk of interstellar trade around the External Worlds. Originally, *Mellanie's Redemption* had been a specialist craft, built to carry priority cargo or passengers between the External Worlds. A risky prop-osition at the best of times. The company who com-missioned her had lurched from one financial crisis to another until Troblum made them an offer for their superfast lame duck. He claimed she would be refitted as a big personal yacht, which was a white lie. It was her three large cargo holds which made her perfect for him; their volume was ideal for carrying the equipment he was working on to recreate the Anomine 'one shot' wormhole. Marius had agreed to the acquisition, and the additional EMAs materialized in Troblum's account. Although the ship was supposed to remain on Arevalo until Troblum was ready to move the project to its test stage he found it indispensable for some of the transactions he was involved in. The addition of a Navy-grade stealth field was especially beneficial when it came to slipping away from Arevalo without Marius being aware of anything untoward.

City was a somewhat overzealous description for Ikeo which comprised a fifty-kilometre stretch of rugged sub-tropical coastline with a small town in the middle and a lot of mansions spread along the cliff tops on either side. The province's ideology could best be described as a free trade area, with several individuals specializing in artefact salvage. It did have a resident-funded police force, which its poorer neighbouring states referred to as a strategic defence system.

Mellanie's Redemption descended at the focal point of several ground-based tracking sensors. She landed on pad 23 at the city's spaceport, a two-kilometre circle of mown grass with twenty-four concrete pads, a couple of black dome-shaped maintenance hangars, and a warehouse owned by an Intersolar service supply company. There were no arrival formalities. A capsule drew up beside the starship as Troblum walked down the short airstair, puffing heavily from the rush of heat and humidity that hit him as soon as the airlock opened.

The capsule took him several kilometres out of town to a Romanesque villa atop a low cliff. Three sides of the single-storey building surrounded an elaborate pool and patio area festooned with colourful plants. Several waterfalls spilled down large strategically positioned boulders to splash into the pool. The view down on to the white beach was spectacular, with a needle-profile glide-boat anchored just offshore.

Stubsy Florac was waiting for him by the bar at the side of the pool. Not that anyone called him 'Stubsy' to his face; Florac was sensitive about his height. Sensitive to a degree that he didn't get it changed during rejuvenation therapy because to do that would be to admit that he was a head shorter than most adults and that it bothered him enough to do something about it. He wore knee-length sports trousers and a simple pale-blue shirt open to the waist to reveal a chest covered in hair and a stomach that was starting to bulge. When Troblum appeared he smiled broadly and pushed his oversize sunglasses on to his forehead. His hairline was a lot higher and thinner than Troblum was used to seeing even on External World citizens.

'Hey! My man,' Florac exclaimed loudly. He held his arms out and shifted his hips from side to side. 'You been dieting, or what?' He laughed loudly again at his own joke. All his companions smiled.

There were seven of them visible in the pool area, either lying on sunloungers, or sitting at the table in the shallow end of the pool sipping drinks that were mostly fruit and ice. Troblum was always slightly uncomfortable about the girls Stubsy kept at the villa. Not quite clones, but there were standard requirements. For a start they were all a lot taller than their boss, two were even taller than Troblum; naturally they were beautiful, with long silken hair, bodies toned as if they were part of some ancient Olympic athlete squad, and wearing tight bikinis – dressing for dinner here was putting on a pair of shorts and sandals. A low-level field scan revealed them to be enriched with several advanced weapons systems; half of the muscle ridges etched beneath their taut skin was actually force-field webbing. If they ganged up on Troblum they could probably overwhelm his biononic defences. They acted like a hybrid of floozies and executive assistants. Troblum knew the image which the whole stable arrangement was supposed to convey, but just didn't understand why. Stubsy must have a lot more insecurities than just his height.

Troblum's worn old toga suit rippled round his vast body as he raised his arms. 'Do I look smaller?'

'Hey, come on, I'm just fucking with you. What I got, it entitles me.'

'What you claim you've got.'

'Man, just shove that stake in a little further, I don't think it went right through my heart. How are you, man? It's been a while.' Stubsy gave Troblum a hug, arms reaching almost a third of the way round. Squeezing like he was being reunited with a parent.

'Too long,' Troblum suggested.

'Still got your ship. Sweet ship. You Higher guys, you live the life all right.'

Troblum looked down on Stubsy's head. 'So come and join us.'

'Wowa there! Not quite ready for that. Okay? Man, don't even joke about. I'd need to spend a decade wiping all my bad memories before they'd let me set foot on the Central Worlds. Hey, you want a drink. Couple of sandwiches, maybe. Alcinda, she knows how to boss a culinary unit around.' He lowered his voice and winked. 'Not the only thing she knows her way around, huh.'

Troblum tried not to grimace in dismay. 'Some beer maybe.'

'Sure sure.' Florac gestured to some chairs beside a table. They sat down while one of the girls brought a large mug of light beer over. 'Hey, Somonie, bring it out for my man, will you?'

A girl in a vivid-pink bikini gave a short nod and went inside.

'Where did you find it?' Troblum asked.

'A contact of mine. Hey, have I been retrofitted without a brain and somebody not tell me? If I tell you about my people what's left for me in this universe?'

'Quite.'

'You know I've got a network pumping away down there in the civilized Commonwealth. This week it's some guy, next it's another. Who knows where shit is going to appear? You want to stab me in the back, first you got to build yourself your own network.'

'I already have.'

Florac blinked, his best-friends smile fading. 'You have?'

'Sure. Hundreds of guys like you.'

'You kill me, you know that?' He laughed, too loud, and raised his glass. 'People like me. Ho man!'

'I meant, what planet was it recovered from? My record search confirmed Vic Russell handed it back in to the Serious Crimes Directorate when he returned from the Boongate relocation. It was obsolete by then. The SCD would have disposed of it.'

'Beats me,' Florac said with a shrug. 'Guess there were people like you and me around even back in those days.'

Troblum said nothing. The salvager could be right. For all his personality faults and distasteful lifestyle, he had always provided bona fide items. A large number of arte-facts in Troblum's museum had come from Florac.

Somonie returned from the villa carrying a long stable-environment case. It was heavy, her arm muscles were standing proud. She put it on the table in front of Troblum and Stubsy.

'Before we go any further,' Troblum said. 'I have the SCD serial code. The genuine one. So. Do you still want to open the case?'

'I don't give a shit what fucking number you think you got, man, this is for real. And *hey* guess what, you aren't the only asshole in the Commonwealth that creams himself over this shit. I come to you first because I figure we got a friendship going by now. You want to call me out, you want to crap all over my reputation, and you know what, fatboy, you can roll all the way back to your ship and fuck the hell off this world. My fucking world.'

'We'd better look at it then,' Troblum said. 'I'd hate to lose your friendship.' He didn't care about Stubsy Florac, there were dozens of scavengers just like him. But it was an interesting claim; he'd never really thought there were other collectors outside museums. He wondered idly if they could be persuaded to sell. Perhaps Florac could enquire . . .

Florac's u-shadow gave the case a key, and the top unfurled to reveal an antique ion rifle. A protective shield shimmered faintly around it, but Troblum could clearly see the metre-long barrel which ended in a stubby black metal handle that had several attachment points and an open induction socket on the bottom.

'Yeah well,' Stubsy said with a modest grimace, which could almost have been embarrassment. 'The other bit is missing. Obviously. But what the fuck, this is the business end, right? That's what counts.'

'There is no "other bit",' Troblum said. 'This is designed to be used by someone in an armour suit; it clips on to the lower arm.'

'No shit?'

It was an effort for Troblum to speak calmly. The weapon certainly looked genuine. 'Would you turn off the field, please.'

The shimmer vanished. Troblum's field function swept across the antique rifle. Deep in the barrel's casing were long chains of specifically arranged molecules, spelling out a unique code. He licked the sweat from his upper lip. 'It's real,' he whispered hoarsely.

'Yo!' Stubsy slapped his hands together in victory. 'Do I ever let you down?'

Troblum couldn't stop staring at the weapon. 'Only in the flesh. Would you like payment now?'

'Man, this is why I love you. Yes. Yes please. I would very much like payment now, please.'

Troblum told his u-shadow to transfer the funds.

'You want to stay for dinner?' Stubsy asked. 'Maybe party with some of the girls?'

'Put the protective field back on, please. This humidity is inimical.'

'Sure thing. So, which one do you like?'

'You don't have any idea how important this artefact is, do you?'

'I know it's value, man, that's what counts. The fact some policeman shot an alien with it a thousand years ago doesn't exactly ding my bell.'

'Vic Russell worked with Paula Myo. And I know you've heard of her.'

'Sure man, this planet's living nightmare. Didn't know she was around in those days, too.'

'Oh yes, she was around even before the Starflyer War. And it wasn't an alien Vic shot, it was Tarlo, a Directorate colleague who had been corrupted by the Starflyer, and betrayed Vic and his wife. Arguably, Tarlo is one of the most important Starflyer agents there was.'

'Ozzie, now I get it: this was the gun that killed him. That connects you.'

'Something like that.'

'So are you interested in genuine alien stuff as well?'

'Anything that is part of the Starflyer's legacy. Why, have you located another section of its ship?'

Stubsy shook his head. 'Fraid not, man. But one of my neighbours, she specializes in weird alien technology and other interesting little chunks. You know, the odd sample that crews on pathfinder missions pick up, stuff you never get to hear about in the unisphere, stuff ANA and the Navy like to keep quiet. You want I should put you in touch, I got a unisphere code, she's very discreet. I'll vouch for her.'

'Tell her if she ever comes across any Anomine relics I'll be happy to talk,' he said, knowing she wouldn't. 'Apart from that, I'm not interested.'

'Okay, just thought I'd ask.'

Troblum raised himself to his feet, quietly pleased he didn't need his bononics to generate a muscle reinforcement field; but then this world had a point-eight standard gravity. 'Could you call your capsule for me, please?'

'Money's in, so sure. This is another reason I like you, man, we don't have to screw around making up small talk.'

'Exactly.' Troblum picked up the stable-environment case. It was heavy; he could feel a mild sweat break out on his forehead and across his shoulders as he lifted it into the crook of his arm. Hadn't Stubsy ever heard of regrav?

'Hey, man, you're the only Higher I know, so I've got to like ask you this. What's ANA's take on this whole Pilgrimage thing? Is it a bunch of crap, or are we all going to get cluster fucked by the Void?'

'ANA:Governance put out a clear statement on the unisphere. The Pilgrimage is regrettable, but it does not believe the actions of Living Dream pose any direct physical threat to the Greater Commonwealth.'

'I accessed that, sure. Usual government bullshit then, huh. But . . . what do you think, man? Should I be stocking up my starship and heading out?'

'Out where, exactly? If the anti-Pilgrimage faction is right, the whole galaxy is doomed.'

'You are just one giant lump of fun, aren't you? Come on, man, give it to me straight. Are we in the shit?'

'The contacts I have inside ANA aren't worried, so neither am I.'

Stubsy considered that seriously for a moment before reverting to his usual annoyingly breezy self. 'Thanks, man, I owe you one.'

'Not really. But if I find a way to collect, I'll let you know.'

Troblum puzzled over Stubsy's question in the capsule back to his ship. Perhaps he'd been unwise to admit to contacts inside ANA, but it was a very general reference. Besides, he didn't really consider Stubsy to be some kind of agent working for Marius's opponents – of which there were admittedly many. Of course the Starflyer had procured agents a lot more unlikely than Stubsy. But if Stubsy was an agent for some ANA Faction they were playing a long game, and from what Troblum understood, the Pilgrimage situation would be resolved sooner rather than later. Troblum shook his head and shifted the case slightly. It was an interesting theory, but he suspected he was overanalysing events. Paranoia was healthy, but he wouldn't like to report that particular suspicion to Marius. More likely it was a genuine concern on Stubsy's part, one born of ignorance and popular prejudice. That was a lot easier to believe.

The capsule arrived back at *Mellanie's Redemption* and Troblum carefully carried the stable-environment case into the starship. He resisted the impulse to open it for one last check, but did stow it in his own sleeping cabin for the flight back to Arevalo.

*

The first thing Araminta knew about the failure was when a shower of sparks sizzled out of the bot's power arm, just above the wrist multi-socket where tools plugged in. At the time she was on her knees beside the Juliet balcony door, trying to dismantle its seized-up actuator. The unit hadn't been serviced for a decade at least. When she got the casing open every part of it was covered in grime. She wrinkled her nose up in dismay, and reached for the small all-function electrical toolkit she'd bought from Askahar's Infinite Systems, a company that specialized in recycled equipment for the construction trade. Her u-shadow grabbed the user instructions from the kit's memory and filtered them up through her macrocellular clusters into her brain; supposedly they gave her an instinctive ability to apply the little gizmos. She couldn't even work out which one would stand a chance of cleaning away so much gunk. The cleanser utensils were intended for delicate systems with a light coating of dust. Not this compost heap.

Then as she peered closer at the actuator components bright light flashed across them. She turned just in time to see the last cascade of sparks drizzle down on the pile of sealant sheets stacked up in the corner of the flat's lounge. Wisps of smoke began to wind upwards. The bot juddered to a halt, as the whole lower segment of its power arm darkened. As she watched, its pocked silvery casing tarnished rapidly from the heat inside.

'Ozzie's mother!' she yelped, and quickly started stamping on the sheets, trying to extinguish the glowing points which the sparks had kindled. Her u-shadow couldn't get any access to the bot at all, it was completely dead, and now there was a definite hot-oil smell in the air. Another bot slid away and retrieved an extinguisher bulb from the kitchen. It returned and sprayed blue foam on the defunct bot's arm. Araminta groaned in dismay as the bubbling fluid scabbed over and dripped on to the floorboards, soaking in. The whole wood-look was coming back in vogue, which was why she'd ordered the bot to abrade the original old floorboards down to the grain. As soon as they were done she was going to spread the sealant sheets down while the rest of the room was decorated and fitted, then she'd finish the boards with a veneer polish to bring out the wavy gold and rouge pattern of the native antwood.

Araminta scratched at the damp stain with her fingernail, but it didn't seem too bad. She'd just have to get another bot to abrade the wood down still further. There were five of the versatile machines performing various tasks in the flat, all second or third hand; again bought from Askahar's Infinite Systems.

Now the immediate danger of fire was over her u-shadow called Burt Renik, proprietor of Askahar's Infinite Systems.

'Well there's nothing I can do,' he explained after she'd told him what had happened.

'I only bought it from you two days ago!'

'Yes, but why did you buy it?'

'Excuse me! You recommended it.'

'Yes, the Candel 8038; it's got the kind of power level you wanted for heavy duty attachments. But you came to me rather than a licensed dealer.'

'What are you talking about? I couldn't afford a new model. The unisphere evaluation library said it was dependable.'

'Exactly. And I sell a lot of refurbished units because of that. But the one you bought had a manufacturer's decade-warranty that expired over a decade ago. Now with all the goodwill in Ozzie's universe, I have to tell you: you get what you pay for. I have some newer models in stock if you need a replacement.'

Araminta wished she had the ability to trojan a sensorium package past his u-shadow filters, one that would produce the painburst he'd get from a good smack on the nose. 'Will you take part exchange?'

'I could make you an offer on any components I can salvage, but I'd have to bring the bot in to the workshop to analyse what's left. I can come out, oh ... middle of next week, and there would have to be a collection charge.'

'For Ozzie's sake, you sold me a dud.'

'I sold you what you wanted. Look, I'm only offering to salvage parts as a goodwill gesture. I'm running a business, I want return customers.'

'Well you've lost this one.' She ended the call and told her u-shadow never to accept a call from Burt Renik again. 'Bloody hell!' Her u-shadow quickly revised her refurbishment schedule, adding on an extra three days to her expected completion date. That assumed she wouldn't buy a replacement for the 8038. It was a correct assumption. The budget wasn't working out like she'd originally planned. Not that she was overspending, but the time involved in stripping out all the old fittings and démodé decorations was taking a lot longer than her first estimate.

Araminta sat back on the floor and glared at the ruined bot. *I'm not going to cry. I'm not that pathetic.*

The loss of the 8038 was a blow, though. She'd just have to trust the remaining bots would hold out. Her u-shadow began to run diagnostic checks on them while she tried to detach the abrader mat from the 8038's foam-clogged multi-socket. The attachment was expensive and, unlike the bot, brand new. Her mood wasn't helped by the current state of the flat. She had been working on it for five days solid now, stripping it down to bare walls, and gutting the ancient domestic equipment. The whole place looked just terrible. Every surface was covered in fine particles, with sawdust enhancing the whole dilapidated appearance; also not helped by the way any sound echoed round the blank rooms. After tidying things up today, she could start the refurbishment stage. She was sure that would re-fire her enthusiasm. There had been times over the last week when she'd had moments of pure panic, wondering how she could have been so stupid to have gambled everything on this ancient cruddy flat.

The abrader attachment came free and she pulled it out. With her u-shadow controlling them directly, two of the remaining bots hauled their broken sibling out of the flat and dumped it in the commercial refuse casket parked outside. She winced every time it bumped on the stairs, but the other occupants were out, they'd never know how the dints got there.

With the abrader plugged in to another bot, a Braklef 34B – only eight years old – she turned her attention back to the balcony door actuator. She knew if she started moping over the broken bot she'd just wind up feeling sorry for herself and never get anything done. She simply couldn't afford that.

The simplest thing, she decided, was to break the actuator down and clean the grime off manually; after that she could use the specialist tools to get the systems up to required standard. Her other toolbox, the larger one, had a set of power keys. She set to with more determination than she had any right to without resorting to aerosols.

As she worked, her u-shadow skimmed the news, local and Intersolar, and summarized topics she was interested in, feeding it to her in a quiet neural drizzle. Now she'd bought the flat, she'd cancelled the daily review of city property. It would be too distracting, especially if something really good appeared on the market. So instead she chortled quietly at the images in her peripheral vision as a city councillor's son was indicted on charges of land fraud. The investigators were rumoured to be closing in on Daddy, who sat on the city board for zoning management. Last night, Debbina, the first-born daughter of billionaire

Sheldonite Likan had been arrested once again for lewd conduct in a public place. The image of her coming out of Colwyn Central police station flanked by her lawyers this morning showed her still wearing a black spray dress from the previous evening, and her blonde hair in disarray. Hansel Industries, one of Ellezelin's top 100 companies, was discussing opening a manufacturing district just outside Colwyn; the details were accompanied by economic projections. She couldn't help scan the effect on property prices.

As far as Intersolar political news was concerned the only item was the new Senate motion introduced by Marian Kantil, Earth's Senator, that Living Dream desist from reckless action in respect to its Pilgrimage. Ellezelin's Senator responded to the motion by walking out. He was followed by the Senators from Tari, Idlib, Lirno, Quhood and Agra – the Free Trade Zone planets. Araminta wasn't surprised to find Viotia's Senator had abstained from the vote, as had seven other External Worlds, all on the fringe of the Zone, and all with a large percentage of Living Dream followers in their population. The report went on to show the huge manufacturing yard on the edge of Greater Makkathran, where the Pilgrimage ships would be assembled. Araminta stopped cleaning the actuator to watch. An armada of civic construction machinery was laying down the field, flattening fifteen square miles of countryside ready for its cladding of concrete. The first echelon of machines swept the ground with dispersant beams, chewing into the side of hillocks and escarpments; loosening any material that stood above the required level. All the resulting scree slides of pulverized soil and sand were elevated by regrav modules then channelled by force fields into thick solid streams that curved through the air and stretched back to the holds of vast ore barges hovering at the side of the estuary which made up one side of the yard. Following the levelling operation was a line of more basic machinery which drove deep support piles into the bedrock to support the weight of the starship cradles. The Pilgrimage fleet was to be made up of twelve cylindrical vessels, each a mile long, and capable of carrying two million pilgrims in suspension. Already Living Dream was talking about them being merely the 'first wave'.

Araminta shook her head in mild disbelief that so many people could be so stupid, and switched to local reports of business and celebrities.

Two hours later, Cressida arrived. She frowned down at the prints her shiny leather pumps with their diamond-encrusted straps made in the thick layer of dirt coating the hall floor. Her cashmere fur dress contracted around her to save her skin from exposure to the dusty air. One hand was raised to cover her mouth, gold and purple nailprint friezes flowing in slow motion.

Araminta smiled up uncertainly at her cousin. She was suddenly very self-conscious standing there in her filthy overalls, hair wound up and tucked into a cap, hands streaked with black grease.

'There's a dead bot in your casket,' Cressida said. She sounded annoyed by it.

'I know,' Araminta sighed. 'Price of buying cheap.'

'It's one of yours?' Cressida's eyebrows lifted. 'Do you want me to call the supplier and have it replaced?'

'Tempting. Ozzie knows it wasn't actually that cheap relative to my budget, but no I'll fight my own battles from now on.'

'That's my family. Stupidly stubborn to the last.'

'Thanks.'

'I'm here for two reasons. One to look round. Okay, done that. Came a month too early, obviously. Two, I want all the frightful details of Thursday night. You and that rather attractive boy Keetch left very early together. And darling I do mean *all* the details.'

'Keetch is hardly a boy.'

'Pha! Younger than me by almost a century. So tell your best cousin. What happened?'

Araminta smiled bashfully. 'You know very well. We went back to his place.' She proffered a limp gesture at the dilapidated hallway. 'I could hardly bring him here.'

'Excellent. And?'

'And what?'

'What does he do? Is he single? What's he like in bed? How many times has he called? Is he yearning and desperate yet? Has he sent flowers or jewellery or is he all pathetic and gone the chocolates route? Which resort bedroom are you spending the weekend in?'

'Wow, just stop there.' Araminta's smile turned sour. In truth Keetch had been more than adequate in bed and he had even tried to call her several times since Thursday. Calls she had no intention of returning. The thrill of liberation, of playing the field, of experimenting, of answering to no one, of making and taking her own choices, of just plain having fun; it was all she wanted right now. A simple life without commitments or attachments. *Right now* was what she should have been doing instead of being married. 'Keetch was very nice, but I'm not seeing him again. I'm too busy here.'

'Now I am impressed. Hump 'em and dump 'em.

There's quite a core of raw steel hidden inside that ingénue facade, isn't there?'

Araminta shrugged. 'Whatever.'

'If you ever want a career in law, I'll be happy to sponsor you. You'll probably make partner in under seventy years.'

'Gosh, now there's an enticement.'

Cressida dropped her hand long enough to laugh. 'Ah well, I tried. So are we on for Wednesday?'

'Yes, of course.' Araminta enjoyed their girls' nights out. Cressida seemed to know every exclusive club in Colwyn City, and she was on all their guest lists. 'So what happened to you after I left? Did you catch anyone?'

'At my age? I was safely tucked up in bed by midnight.'

'Who with?'

'I forget their names. You know you really must go up a level and join an orgy. They can be fantastic, especially if you have partners who know *exactly* what they're doing.'

Araminta giggled. 'No thanks. Don't think I'm quite ready for that yet. What I'm doing is pretty adventurous for me.'

'Well when you're ready . . .'

'I'll let you know.'

Cressida inhaled a breath of dust and started coughing. 'Ozzie, this place is bringing back too many memories of my early years. Look, I'll call later. Sorry I'm not much practical help, but truthfully, I'm crap with design programs.'

'I want to do this by myself. I'm *going* to do this by myself.'

'Hell, make that partner in fifty years. You've got what it takes.'

'Remind you of you?' Araminta asked sweetly.

'No. I think you're sharper, unfortunately. Bye, darling.'

Lunch was a sandwich in her carry capsule as she flew across the city to the first of three suppliers on her list. The carry capsule, like her bots, had seen better days; according to the log she was the fifth owner in thirty years. Perfectly serviceable, the sales manager had assured her. It didn't have the speed of a new model, and if the big rear cargo compartment was filled to the rated load then it wouldn't quite reach its maximum flight ceiling. But she had a lot more confidence in the capsule than the 8038 bot; because of its age it had to pass a strict Viotia Transport Agency flightworthiness test every year, and the last one had been two months before she bought it.

The capsule settled on the lot of Bovey's Bathing and Culinaryware, one of eight macrostores that made up a small touchdown mall in the Groby district. She walked into the store, looking round the open display rooms that lined a broad aisle with many branches. Bathrooms and kitchens alternated, promoting a big range of size, styles, and price, though the ones by the door tended to be elaborate. She looked enviously at the larger luxury units, thinking about the kind of apartment she'd develop one day in which such extravagance was a necessity.

'Can I help you?'

Araminta turned round to see a man dressed in the store's blue and maroon uniform. He was quite tall with his biological age locked in around his late twenties, dark skin offset by sandy-blond hair. Nice regular features, she thought, without being too handsome. His eyes were light grey, revealing a lot of humour. If they were meeting in a club she'd definitely let him buy her a drink – she might even offer to buy him one first.

'I'm looking for a kitchen and a bathroom. Both have to look and feel high grade, yet cost practically nothing.'

'Ah, now that I can understand, and provide for. I'm Mr Bovey, by the way.'

She was quite flattered the owner himself would come down on the floor and single her out to help. 'Pleased to meet you. I'm Araminta.'

He shook her hand politely. She thought he was debating with himself if he should try for a platonic greeting kiss. It was one of those times when she wished she had a connection to the gaiafield, which would enable her to gauge his emotions, assuming he'd broadcast them. Which as the owner of the store and therefore a professional he wouldn't. *Damn. Come on girl, focus.*

'What sort of dimensions can you give me to play with?' he asked.

Araminta gave him a slightly cheeky grin, then stopped. Perhaps it wasn't a double-entendre. Certainly sounded like one, though. 'Here you go,' she told him as her u-shadow produced the blueprint file. 'I would appreciate some help on price. This is my first renovation project, I don't want it to be my last.'

'Ah.' His eyes strayed to her hands, which still had lines of grime etched on the skin. 'Boss and workforce, I can relate to that.'

'Depleted workforce today, I'm afraid. One of my bots blew up. I can't afford any more expensive mistakes.'

'I understand.' He hesitated. 'You didn't get it from Burt Renik, did you?'

'Yes,' she said cautiously. 'Why?'

'Okay, well for future reference – and I didn't tell you this – he's not the most reliable of suppliers.'

'I know he's not the gold standard, but I checked on the evaluation library for that model. It was okay.'

This time he did wince. 'Next time you buy something in the trade, including anything from me, I'd recommend some research on Dave's Coding.' His u-shadow handed over the address. 'The evaluation library is fine, all those "independent" reports on how the product worked – well, the library is financed and managed by corporations, that's why there's never really a bad review. Dave's Coding is truly autonomous.'

'Thank you,' she said meekly as she filed the address in one of her storage lacunas. 'I'll take an access sometime.'

'Glad to help. In the meantime, try aisle seven for a kitchen. I think we can supply your order from there.'

'Thanks.' She walked off to aisle seven, more than a little disappointed he didn't accompany her. Perhaps he had a policy of not flirting with customers. *Shame.*

The man waiting in aisle seven had on an identical blue and maroon uniform. He was perhaps five years older than Mr Bovey, but even taller, with a slender marathon runner frame. His skin was Nordic pale with ginger hair cut short except for a slender ridge right at the crest of his skull. Strangely, his green eyes registered the same kind of general amusement at the world as Mr Bovey.

'I'd recommend these two kitchen styles,' he said in greeting, and gestured at a small display area. 'They're a good fit to your dimensions, and this one is an end-of-the-line model. I've got two left in the warehouse, so I can give you a sweet deal.'

Araminta was slightly nonplussed. Mr Bovey had obviously passed on her file to this employee; but that was no reason for him to start off as if they were already on familiar terms. 'Let's take a look,' she said, lowering the temperature of her voice.

It turned out the end-of-the-line model was quite satisfactory, and it was a good deal. As well as a mid-range culinary unit with a range of multichem storage tanks she got a breakfast bar and stools, ancillaries like a fridge, food prepper, maidbot, shelving and cupboards. The style was chaste white, with black and gold trim. 'If you throw in delivery, I'll take it,' she told him.

'Any time you want it, I'll get it to you.'

She ignored the flirty overture, and told her u-shadow to pay the deposit.

'Bathrooms: aisle eleven,' he told her with unabashed enthusiasm.

The salesman waiting for her in aisle eleven had allowed himself to age into his biological fifties, which was unusual even for Viotia. His ebony skin was just starting to crinkle, with his hair greying and thinning. 'I've got four that I think will suit your aesthetics,' was his opening gambit.

'Hello,' she snapped at him.

'Ah . . . yes?'

'I'm Araminta, pleased to meet you. And I'm looking for a bathroom for my flat. Can you help me?'

'What . . .?'

'This whole relay thing you've got going here really isn't polite. You could at least say hi to me first before you access the file you're all shooting around here. I am a person, you know.'

'I think . . . ah.' His surprised expression softened.

Araminta found it a lot more disconcerting than his initial smug chumminess.

'You do know what I am, don't you?' he asked.

'What do you mean?'

'I am Mr Bovey. We are all Mr Bovey in this store. I am a multiple human.'

Araminta was certain she'd be turning bright red with embarrassment. She knew what a multiple was, of course; one personality shared between several bodies through an adaptation of the gaiafield technology. This way, its practitioners claimed, was the true evolutionary leap for humanity that everyone else was pursuing down futile dead ends. A multiple human could never die unless every body was killed, which was unlikely in the extreme. In a quiet non-evangelical way they believed that everyone would one day become multiple. Perhaps after that the personalities would start fusing, leaving one consciousness with a trillion bodies – a much better outcome than downloading into the artificial sanctity of ANA.

It was a human heresy, their detractors claimed, a long-term conspiracy to imitate the Prime aliens of Dyson Alpha. More vocal opponents accused the multiple life-style of being started by left-over Starflyer agents trying to continue their dead master's corrupting ideology.

'I'm sorry,' she said, shamefaced. 'I didn't know.'

'That's okay. Partly my fault in assuming you did. Most people in the trade know.'

Araminta gave a wry grin. 'I guess continuity of service is a big plus.'

'I've got to be better than Burt Renik.'

'Definitely!'

'All right then. So are you and I good to go and look at bathrooms?'

'Of course we are.'

Araminta wound up buying the third suite the older Mr Bovey showed her. It wasn't out of guilt, he was genuinely offering a good deal, and the plain gold and green style was perfect for the flat. And once she'd let her awkwardness subside, he was fun to talk to. She couldn't quite throw off the weird little feeling of disconnection talking to his older body and knowing he was exactly the same person who'd greeted her, and that body was probably smiling privately at her while dealing with another customer.

'Just let us know when you want it delivered,' he said when her u-shadow handed over the deposit.

'Do you ... that is: some of you. Ones of you. Handle delivery as well?'

'Don't worry, tense hasn't caught up with us multiples yet. And yes, I'll be the one in the carry capsule and helping the bots when they get stuck on the stairs. Not necessarily this body given its age, but me.'

'I'll look forward to seeing the rest of you.'

'There's a couple of mes who are young and handsome. Call it vanity if you like, I'm not immune to all the usual human flaws. I'll try and schedule thems for the delivery.'

'As handsome as you?'

'Hey, there's no more discount. You've squeezed me dry already.'

She laughed. 'I'd better get back to work then.'

Araminta smiled the whole flight back to the flat. Mr Bovey really had been charming. All his versions. She suspected it was more than good client relations. And was he joking about the young and handsome bodies? Actually, even the last one she'd seen, the older one, was quite distinguished. And what if he did ask her out for a date? Would it be just her and twenty of him sitting at a table?

If he asks.

And if he did, what am I going to answer?

The whole idea was unusual, which made it very interesting.

And what if the evening went well? Do I ask twenty of him back to my place?

Oh stop it!

She was still smiling when she walked back up the stairs and opened the front door. Then her mood came down at the sight of the flat. The bots had made some progress cleaning up; but one with a vacuum attachment was all clogged up. None of the bots had self-maintenance capacity, so she'd have to clear that out manually. And she'd still not put the balcony door actuator back together. It could well be quite a while before Mr Bovey delivered her new kitchen and bathroom and she got round to finding out how well she'd read their encounter.

Late in the afternoon when the place was finally getting straightened out she'd started spreading the sealant sheets over the lounge's floorboards. That was when her u-shadow told her there was a call from Laril. 'Are you sure?' she asked it.

'Yes.'

She debated with herself if she should call Cressida, maybe the Revenue Service would pay a reward. 'Where's he calling from?'

'The routing identity originates on Oaktier.' A summary slid into her peripheral vision.

'A Central Commonwealth World,' she read. 'What's he doing there?'

'I do not know.'

'Right,' she sat on the cube that was her portable bed and took her gloves off. Wiped her forehead. Took a breath. 'Okay, accept the call.' His image appeared in her exovision's primary perspective, making it seem as if he was standing right in front of her. If he was providing a real representation he hadn't changed much. Thin brown hair cut short, round face with a chubby jaw and a wide neck, as always thick dark stubble longer than she liked. It was scratchy, she remembered. He never gelled it down smooth no matter how many times she asked.

'Thanks for taking the call,' he said. 'I wasn't sure you would.'

'Neither was I.'

'I hear you're doing okay; you got the money.'

'I was awarded the money by the court. Laril, what are you doing? Why are you on Oaktier?'

'Isn't it obvious?'

That took a few seconds to register, and even longer to accept. It must be some stunt, some scam. 'You're migrating inwards?' she asked, incredulous.

He smiled the same carefree smile he'd used when they first met. It was very appealing, warm and confident. She hadn't seen it much after they married.

'Happens to all of us in the end,' he said.

'No! I don't believe it. You are going Higher? You?'

'My first batch of biononics have been in a week. They're starting to integrate some basic fields. It's quite an experience.'

'But . . .' she spluttered. 'For Ozzie's sake. Higher culture would never take you. What did you do, erase half your memories?'

'That's a pretty common myth. Higher culture isn't the old Catholic Church, you know; you don't have to confess and recant your past sins. It's current attitude which counts.'

'I know they don't take criminals. There was that case centuries ago – Jollian thought that he could escape what he'd done with a memory wipe and a migration to the Inner Worlds. Paula Myo caught up with him and had his bionomics removed so he could face trial on the External Worlds as the type of human he was when he committed his crime. I think he got a couple of hundred years' suspension.'

'That's what you think of me, that I qualify for the Jollian precedent? Well thanks a whole lot, Araminta. A couple of things you might want to consider. One, Paula Myo isn't after me. And she isn't after me because I haven't committed any crime.'

'Have you told the Viotia Revenue Service that?'

'My business economics were a mess, sure. I'm not hiding from that. I even told my Higher initiator about my finances. You know what she said?'

'Go on.'

'Higher culture is about rejecting the evil of money.'

'How very convenient for you.'

'Look, I just wanted to call and apologize. I'm not asking for anything. And I wanted to make sure you're all right.'

'A bit late for that, isn't it?' she bridled. 'I'm not part of some therapy session you have to complete before they'll take you.'

'You're misunderstanding this, perhaps with anger leading you away from what I'm actually saying.'

'Ozzie! This *is* your therapy session.'

'We don't need therapy to become Higher, it is inevitable. Even you will migrate eventually.'

'Never.'

His image produced a fond lopsided smile. 'I remember thinking that once. Probably when I was in my twenties. I know it probably doesn't make a lot of sense to someone your age when every day is fresh, but after a few centuries living on the External Worlds you begin to get bored and frustrated. Every day becomes this constant battle; politicians are corrupt and crap, projects never get finished on time or in budget, bureaucrats delight in thwarting you, and then there's the eternal fight for money.'

'Which you lost.'

'I fed myself and my families for over three centuries thank you very much. Even you came out ahead with the residue of that work. But face it, I didn't achieve much now did I? A few tens of thousands of dollars to show for three and a half centuries. That's not exactly leaving your mark on the universe, is it? And it's not just me, there are billions of humans that are the same. The External Worlds are fun and exciting with their market economy and clashing ideologies and outward urge. Youth thrives on that kind of environment. Then there comes a day when you have to look back and take stock. You did that for me.'

'Oh come on! You're blaming me for the dog's dinner you made of your affairs?'

'No. I'm not blaming you. Don't you get it? I'm thanking you. I was old, it took you to reveal that to me. The contrast between us was so great even I couldn't close my eyes to it for ever. There really is no fool like an old fool, and part of that foolishness came from deluding myself. I was tired of that life and didn't want to admit it. Turning Punk Skunk and taking a young wife was just another way of trying to ignore what I'd become. Even that didn't work, did it? I was making both of us miserable.'

'That's putting it mildly,' she muttered. In a way though, it was gratifying hearing him admit it was all his fault. 'I left my whole family behind because of you.'

He showed her a sly smile. 'And that was a bad thing?'

'Yeah, all right,' she grinned puckishly. 'You did me a favour there. I'm not really cut out for two centuries of selling agricultural cybernetics.'

'I knew that the minute I set eyes on you. So how's the world of property development coming on?'

'Harder than I thought,' she admitted. 'There are so many stupid little things that bug me.'

'I know. Well imagine today's frustration multiplied by three hundred years, that's how I wound up feeling.'

'And now you don't?'

'No.'

'I don't believe Higher culture is free of bureaucracy, or corruption, or idiots, or useless politicians. They might not be so blatant, but they're there.'

'No, they're not. Well . . . okay, but nothing like as bad as they are in the External Worlds. You see, there's no need for any of that. So many of the social problems the External Worlds suffer from are born out of markets, capital and materialism; that's what old-style economics produces, in fact trouble just is about all it produces. The cybernated manufacturing and resource allocation procedure which

Higher culture is based on takes all those difficulties out of the equation. That and taking a mature sensible perspective. We don't struggle for the little things any more, we can afford to take the longer, intellectual view.'

'You talk like you're one of them already.'

'*Them.* That's perspective for you. Higher culture is mainly a state of mind, but backed up by physical affluence.'

'You are what the External Worlds strive to be: everyone's a millionaire.'

'No. Everyone has equal access to resources, that's what you lack. Though I'd point out that External Worlds always convert to Higher culture in the end. We are the apex of human social and technological achievement. In other words, this is what the human race has been aiming for since proto-humans picked up a club to give us an advantage against all the other predators competing for food out on the African plains. We improve ourselves at every opportunity.'

'So why didn't you go straight to ANA and download? That's how Highers improve themselves, isn't it?'

'Ultimately, I will, I suppose. But Higher is the next stage for me. I want a time in my body which isn't such an effort. A couple of centuries where I can just relax and learn. There are so many things I want to do and see which I never could before. The opportunities here are just astounding.'

Araminta laughed silently; that at least sounded like the old Laril. 'Then I suppose I wish you good luck.'

'Thank you. I really didn't want to leave things the way they were between us. If there's anything you ever need, please call, even if it's just a shoulder to cry on.'

'Sure. I'll do that,' she lied, knowing she never would. She felt indecently content when he ended the call. Closure obviously worked both ways.

*

The people had no faces. At least none that he was aware of. There were dozens of them, men, women, even children. They were in front of him. Running. Fleeing like cattle panicked by a carnivore. Their screams threatened to split his eardrums. Words rose struggling out of the soundwall. Mostly they were pleas for help, for pity, for sanctuary, for their lives. However hard they ran he kept up with them.

The bizarre mêlée was taking place in some kind of elaborate hall with crystal grooves running across its domed ceiling. Rows of curving chairs hindered the frantic crowd as they raced for the exit doors. He wouldn't or couldn't turn round. He didn't know what they were trying to escape from. Energy weapons screeched, and the people flung themselves down. For himself, he remained standing, looking down at their prone bodies. Somehow he was remote from the horror. He didn't know how that could be. He was there with them, he was a part of whatever terror was happening here. Then some kind of shadow slid across the floor like demon wings unfolding.

Aaron sat up in bed with a shocked gasp. His skin was cold, damp with sweat. Heart pounding. It took a moment for him to recognize where he was. The lights in the sleeping cabin were brightening, showing him the curving bulkhead walls. He blinked at them as the dream faded.

Somehow he knew the strange images were more than a

dream. They must be some memory of his previous life, an event strong enough to cling on inside his neurones while the rest of his identity was wiped. He was curious and daunted at the same time.

What the hell did I get myself mixed up in?

Thinking about it, whatever the affray was, it didn't look any worse than anything this mission had generated so far. His heart had calmed without any help from his biononics. He took a deep breath and climbed off the cot.

'Where are we?' he asked the *Artful Dodger*'s smartcore.

'Six hours out from Anagaska.'

'Good.' He stretched and rolled his shoulders. 'Give me a shower,' he told the smartcore. 'Start with water; shift to spores when I tell you.'

The cabin began to change, cot flowing back into the bulkhead, the floor hardening to a black and white marble finish. Gold nozzles extruded from each corner, and warm water gushed out.

Even given the ship's obvious Higher origin, it had come as a wondrous surprise to discover it was equipped with an ultradrive. Aaron had thought such a thing to be nothing more than rumour. That was when he realized he had to be working for some ANA Faction. It was an idea he found more intriguing than the drive. It also meant the Pilgrimage was being taken a lot more seriously than people generally realized.

After the spores cleaned and dried his skin he dressed in a simple dark purple one-piece suit and went out into the main lounge. His small cabin withdrew into the bulkhead, providing a larger floorspace. Corrie-Lyn's cabin was still engaged, a simple blister shape protruding into the hemispherical lounge. His suggestion yesterday that they share a bunk had been met by a cold stare and an instant: 'Good night.'

She probably wouldn't come out again until they touched down.

The culinary unit provided an excellent breakfast of fried benjiit eggs and Wiltshire drycure bacon, with toast and thick-cut English marmalade. Aaron was nothing if not a traditionalist. *So it would seem*, he mused.

Corrie-Lyn emerged from her cabin while he was munching away on his third slice of toast. She'd dressed in a demure (for her) turquoise and emerald knee-length cashmere sweater dress which the ship's synthesizer had produced. Her cabin sank back into the bulkhead, and she collected a large cup of tea from the culinary unit before sitting down opposite Aaron.

Recognizing a person's emotional state was an important part of Aaron's assessment routine. But this morning Corrie-Lyn was as unreadable as a muted solido.

She stared at him for a while as she sipped her tea, apparently unperturbed by the awkwardness of the situation.

'Something on your mind?' he asked mildly, breaking the silence. That he was the one who broke it was a telling point. There weren't many people who could make him socially uncomfortable.

'Not *my* mind,' she said, a little too earnestly.

'Meaning? Oh come on, you're an attractive woman. I was bound to ask. You'd probably be more insulted if I didn't.'

'Not what I'm talking about.' She waved her hand dismissively. 'That was some dream you had.'

'I . . . Dream?'

'Did you forget? I didn't become a Living Dream Councillor just because I've got a great arse. I immerse myself in people's dreams, I explore their emotional state and try to help them come to terms with what they are. Dreams are very revealing.'

'Oh shit! I leaked that into the gaiafield.'

'You certainly did. I'd like to tell you that you are one very disturbed individual. But that would hardly be a revelation, now would it?'

'I've seen my fair share of combat. Hardly surprising my subconscious throws up crap like that.'

She gave a small victory smile. 'But you don't remember any combat, do you? Not previous to this particular incarnation. That means whatever event you participated in was truly epochal for it to have survived in your subconscious. Wipe techniques are generally pretty good these days, and I suspect you had access to the very best.'

'Come off it. That was too weird to be a memory.'

'Most dreams are engendered by memory, except Inigo's of course. They have their roots in reality, in experience. What you see is the event as your real personality recognizes it. Dreams are very truthful things, Aaron, they're not something you can ignore, or take an aerosol to ward off. Unless you face that which you dream you will never truly be at peace with yourself.'

'Do I cross your palm with silver now?'

'Sarcasm is a very pitiful social defence mechanism, especially in these circumstances. Both of us know how disturbed you were. You cannot shield yourself and your emotions from someone as experienced as myself. The gaiafield will show you for what you are.'

Aaron made very sure the gaiamotes were completely closed up, allowing nothing to escape from inside his skull. 'Okay then,' he grumbled. 'What was I dreaming?'

'Something in your past.'

'Hey wow. Surely I am in the presence of a truly galactic master of the art.'

Unperturbed Corrie-Lyn took another drink of tea. 'More relevantly: a darkness from your past. In order to have survived erasure and to manifest so strongly, I would evaluate it as a crux in your psychological development. Those people were very frightened; terrified even. For so many to be running so fearfully the threat must have been lethal. That is rare in the Commonwealth today, even among the outermost External Worlds.'

'So I was running an evacuation mission out of some disaster. Rare but not unfeasible. There's a lot goes on among the External Worlds that the more developed planets turn a blind eye to.'

Corrie-Lyn gave him a sad smile. 'You were above them, Aaron. Remember? Not running with them. You were what they feared. You and what you represented.'

'That's bullshit.'

'Men. Women. Children. All fleeing you. All hysterical and horror-struck. What were you going to do to them, I wonder. We established back at the fane that you have no conscience.'

'Very clever,' he sneered. 'I pissed you off, and now you come gunning for a little psychological payback. Lady, I have to tell you, it takes a great deal more than anything you've got to spook me out, and that's Ozzie's honest truth.'

'I'm not trying to spook you anywhere, Aaron,' she said

with quiet earnest. 'That's not what Living Dream, the true Living Dream, is about. We exist to guide human life to its fulfilment. The promise of the Void is a huge part of that, yes; but it is not the only component to understanding what you are, your basic nature. I want to liberate the potential inside you. There is more than senseless violence lurking inside your mind, I can sense that. You can be so much more than what you are today, if you'd just let me help. We can explore your dreams together.'

'Call me old fashioned, but my dreams are my own.'

'The darkness you witnessed at the end interests me.'

'That shadow?' Despite himself, Aaron was curious she'd picked up on it.

'A *winged* shadow – which has a strong resonance for most humans no matter which cultural stream they come from. But it was more than a simple shadow. It held significant meaning to you. A representation of your subconscious, I think. After all, it didn't surprise you. If anything you felt almost comfortable with it.'

'Whatever. We have more important things to concentrate on right now. Touchdown is in five and a half hours.' Something in his mind was telling him to close this conversation down now. She was trying to distract him, to throw him off guard. He couldn't allow that, he had to remain completely focused on his mission to locate Inigo.

Corrie-Lyn raised an eyebrow. 'Are you seriously saying you're not interested? This is the real you we're talking about.'

'I keep telling you, I'm happy with what I am. Now, you said Inigo came to Anagaska to visit his family.'

She gave him a disheartened gaze. 'I said he visited his homeworld on occasion, when everything got too much for him. All I know was that he had family. Any further inference is all your own.'

'His mother migrated inwards then downloaded into ANA. What about the aunt?'

'I don't know.'

'Did the aunt have children? Cousins he would have grown up with?'

'I don't know.'

'Was there a family estate? A refuge he felt secure in?'

'I don't know.'

He sat back, and just about resisted glaring at her. 'His official biography says he grew up in Kuhmo. Please tell me that isn't a lie?'

'I'd assume it was correct. That is, I have no reason to doubt it. It's where Living Dream built his library.'

'Central worship point for your living god, huh?'

'I'm not surprised you don't want to know yourself. You're a real shit, you know that.'

The good ship *Artful Dodger* slipped back into real space a thousand kilometres above Anagaska. Aaron told the smartcore to register with the local spacewatch network and request landing permission at Kuhmo spaceport. The request was granted immediately, and the starship began its descent into the middle of the cloud-smeared eastern continent.

When it was first confirmed as H-congruous and assigned for settlement by CST back in 2375, Anagaska was an unremarkable world in what was then called phase three space, destined for a long slow development. Then the Starflyer plunged the Commonwealth into war against the Prime aliens and its future changed radically.

Hanko was one of the forty-seven planets wrecked during the Prime's last great assault against the Commonwealth, its sun pummelled by flare bombs and quantum-busters, saturating the defenceless planet's climate and biosphere with a torrent of lethal radiation for weeks on end. Its hundred and fifty million strong population was trapped under city force fields on a dying world whose very air was now deadly poison. Evacuation was the only possible option. And thanks to Nigel Sheldon and the CST company operating Hanko's wormhole link, its citizens were shunted across forty-two lightyears to Anagaska.

Unfortunately, Anagaska at the time was nothing more than wild forest, native prairie, and hostile jungle; with a grand total of five pre-settlement research stations housing a few hundred scientists. Nigel even had a solution to that. The interior of the wormhole transporting Hanko's population to their new home was given a different, very slow, temporal flow rate relative to the outside universe. With the War over, trillions of dollars were poured into creating an infrastructure on Anagaska and the other forty-six refuge worlds. It took over a century to complete the basic civic amenities and housing, producing cities and towns that were near-Stalinist in their layout and architecture. But when the wormhole from Hanko finally opened on Anagaska, everyone who came through was provided with a roof over their head and enough food to sustain them while they built up their new home's agriculture and industry.

It was perhaps inevitable that after such a trauma, the refuge worlds were slow to develop economically. Their major cities progressed sluggishly in an era when the rest of the Commonwealth was undergoing profound change.

As to the outlying towns, they became near-stagnant back-waters. Nobody starved, nobody was particularly poor, but they lacked the dynamism that was sweeping the rest of humanity as biononics became available, ANA came online, and new political and cultural blocs were formed.

Kuhmo was such a town. Little had changed in the seven centuries between the day its new residents arrived, stumbling out of giant government transporters, and the time Inigo was born. When he was a child, the massive hexagonal arcology built to house his ancestors still dominated the centre of the civic zone, its uninhabited upper levels decaying alarmingly while its lower floors offered cheap accommodation to underprivileged families and third-rate businesses. In fact it was still there sixty years later when he left, a monstrous civic embarrassment to a town that didn't have the money to either refurbish or demolish it.

A hundred years later, the arcology's upper third had finally been dismantled with funds from Anagaska's federal government made available on public safety grounds. Then Living Dream made the town council a financial offer they couldn't really refuse. The arcology was finally razed, its denizens rehoused in plush new purpose-built suburbs. Where it had stood, a new building emerged, nothing like as big, but far more important. Living Dream was constructing what was to be Anagaska's primary fane, with a substantial library and free college attached. It attracted the devout from across the planet and a good many nearby star systems, many of them staying, changing the nature of Kuhmo for ever.

Aaron stood under the tall novik trees that dominated

the fane's encircling park, and looked up at the tapering turrets with their bristling bracelets of stone sculptures, his nose wrinkling in dismay. 'The arcology couldn't have been worse than this,' he declared. 'This is your leader's ultimate temple, his statement to his birthplace that he's moved onwards and upwards? Damn! He must have really hated his old town to do this to it. All this says to me is beware of Kuhmoians bearing gifts.'

Corrie-Lyn sighed and shook her head. 'Ozzie, but you are such a philistine.'

'Know what I like, though. And, lady, this ain't it. Even the old Big15 worlds had better architecture than this.'

'So what are you going to do, hit it with a disruptor pulse?'

'Tempting, I have to admit. But no. We'll indulge in a little data mining first.'

The Inigo museum, in reality a shrine, was every bit as bad as Aaron expected it to be. For a start they couldn't just wander round. They had to join the queue of devout outside the main entrance and were assigned a 'guide'. The tour was official and structured. Each item was accompanied by a full sense recording and corresponding emotional content radiating out into the gaiafield.

So he gritted his teeth and put on a passive smile as they were led round Inigo's childhood home, diligently uprooted from its original location two kilometres away and lovingly restored using era-authentic methods and materials. Each room contained a boring yet worshipful account of childhood days. There were solidos of his mother, Sabine. Cute dramas of his grandparents whose house it was. A sad section devoted to his father, Erik Horovi, who left Sabine a few short months after the birth. Cue reconstruction of the local hospital maternity ward.

Aaron gave the solido of Erik a thoughtful stare, and sent his u-shadow into its public datastore to extract useful information. Erik had been eighteen years old when Inigo was born. When Aaron checked back, Sabine was a month short of her eighteenth birthday when she gave birth.

'Didn't they have a contraception program here in those days?' he asked the guide abruptly.

Corrie-Lyn groaned and flushed a mild pink. The guide's pleasant smile flickered slightly, returning in a somewhat harder manifestation. 'Excuse me?'

'Contraception? It's pretty standard for teenagers no matter what cultural stream you grow up in.' He paused, reviewing the essentially nonexistent information on Sabine's parents. 'Unless the family was old-style Catholics or initiated Taliban or Evangelical Orthodox. Were they?'

'They were not,' the guide said stiffly. 'Inigo was proud that he did not derive from any of Earth's appalling medieval religious sects. It means his goals remain untainted.'

'I see. So his birth was planned, then?'

'His birth was a blessing to humanity. He is the one chosen by the Waterwalker to show us what lies within the Void. Why do you ask? Are you some kind of unisphere journalist?'

'Certainly not. I'm a cultural anthropologist. Naturally I'm interested in procreation rituals.'

The guide gave him a suspicious stare, but let it pass. Aaron's u-shadow had been ready to block any query the man shot into the local net. They'd managed to get through the museum's entrance without any alarm, which meant

Living Dream hadn't yet issued a Commonwealth-wide alert. But they'd certainly respond swiftly enough to any identity file matching himself and Corrie-Lyn, no matter what planet it originated from. And the fact it came from Anagaska barely two days after the Riasi incident would reveal exactly what type of starship they were using. He couldn't allow that.

'Hardly a ritual,' the guide sniffed.

'Anthropologists think everything we do is summed up in terms of rituals,' Corrie-Lyn said smoothly. 'Now tell me, is this really Inigo's university dorm?' She waved her hand eagerly at the drab holographic room in front of them. Various shabby and decayed pieces of furniture that resembled those shown in full 3Dcolour were on display in transparent stasis chambers.

'Yes,' the guide said, returning to equilibrium. 'Yes it is. This is where he began his training as an astrophysicist; the first step on the path that took him to Centurion Station. As an environment, its significance cannot be overstated.'

'Gosh,' Corrie-Lyn cooed.

Aaron was impressed that she kept a straight face.

'What was that all about?' Corrie-Lyn asked when they were in a taxi capsule and heading back for the spaceport hotel.

'You didn't think it was odd?'

'So two horny teenagers decided to have a kid. It's not unheard of.'

'Yes it is. They were both still at school. Then Erik vanishes a few months after the birth. Plus you tell me Inigo had an aunt, who has been very effectively written out of his family. And you claim Inigo is Higher, which must have happened either at birth or early in his life; that is, prior to his Centurion mission.'

'What makes you say that?'

'Because, as you said, he took extreme care to hide it from his followers; it's not logical to assume he'd acquire biononics after he began Living Dream.'

'Granted, but where does all this theorizing get you?'

'It tells me just what a load of bullshit his official past is,' Aaron said, waving a hand back at the shrinking museum. 'That farce is a perfect way of covering up his true history, it provides a flawless alternative version with just enough true points touching verifiable reality as to go unquestioned. Unless of course you're like us and happen to know some awkward facts which don't fit. If he was born Higher, then one of his parents had to be Higher. Sabine almost certainly wasn't; and Erik conveniently walks out on his child a few months after the birth.'

'It was too much for the boy, that's all. If Inigo's birth was an accident like you think, that's hardly surprising.'

'No. That's not it. I don't think it was an accident. Quite the opposite.' He told his u-shadow to review local events for the year prior to Inigo's birth, using non-Living Dream archives. They'd almost reached the hotel when the answer came back. 'Ah ha, this is it.' He shared the file with her. 'Local news company archive. They were bought out by an Intersolar two hundred years ago and the town office downgraded to closure which is why the files were deep cached. The art block in Kuhmo's college burned down eight and a half months before Inigo was born.'

'It says the block was the centre of a gang fight,' Corrie-Lyn said as she speed-reviewed. 'A bunch of hothead kids duking out a turf war.'

'Yeah right. Now launch a search for Kuhmo gang-culture. Specifically for incidents with weapons usage. Go ahead. I'll give you thousand to one odds there aren't any other files, not for fifty years either side of that date. Look at the history of this place before Inigo built his monstrosity. There was nothing here *worth* fighting over; not even for kids on the bottom of the pile. The Council switched between three parties, and they were all virtually indistinguishable, their policies were certainly the same: low taxes, cut back on official wastage, attract business investment, and make sure the parks look pretty. Hell, they didn't even manage to get rid of the arcology by themselves. That thing stood there for nearly nine hundred years. Nine *hundred*, for Ozzie's sake! And they couldn't get their act together for all that time. Kuhmo is the ultimate middle-class dead-end, drifting along in the same rut for a thousand years. Bad boys don't want a part of that purgatory, it's like a suspension sentence but with sensory torture thrown in; they just want to leave.'

'All right, *all right*, I submit. Inigo has a dodgy family history. What's your point?'

'My theory is a radical infiltration; it's about the right time period. And that certainly won't be on any news file, deep cached or otherwise.'

'So how do we find out what really happened?'

'Only one way. We have to ask the Protectorate.'

Corrie-Lyn groaned in dismay, dropping her head into her hands.

*

The maintenance hangar was on the edge of Daroca's spaceport. One of twenty-three identical black-sheen cubes in a row; the last row in a block of ten. There were eighteen blocks in total. It was a big spaceport, much larger than the Navy compound on the other side of the city. Daroca's residents were a heavily starfaring folk, and the Air project had added considerably to the numbers of spaceships in recent centuries. Without any connection to the unisphere's guidance function a person could wander round the area all day and not be able to distinguish between any of the hangars. A subtle modification to the spaceport net management software provided a near identical disorientation function to any uninvited person who was using electronic navigation to find Troblum's hangar. While the other structures were always opening their doors to receive or disgorge starships, Troblum's was kept resolutely shut except for his very rare flights. When the doors did iris back, a security shield prevented any visual or electronic observation of the interior. Even the small workforce who loyally turned up day after day parked their capsules outside and used a little side door to enter. They then had to pass through another three shielded doors to enter the hangar's central section. Nearly two thirds of the big building was taken up by extremely sophisticated synthesis and fabrication machinery. All of the systems were custom-built; the current layout had taken Troblum over fifteen years to refine. That was why he needed other people to help him. Neumann cybernetics and biononic extrusion were magnificent systems for everyday life, but for anything beyond the ordinary you first had to design the machinery to build the machines which fabricated the device.

Troblum had no trouble producing the modified exotic matter theory behind an Anomine planet-shifting ftl engine, and even describing the basic generator technology he wanted. But turning those abstracts into physical reality was tough. For a start he needed information on novabomb technology, and even after nearly 1,200 years the Navy kept details of that horrendously powerful weapon classified. Which was where Emily Alm came in.

It was Marius who had put the two of them in touch. Emily used to work for the Navy weapons division on Augusta. After three hundred years she had simply grown bored.

'There's no point to it any more,' she told Troblum at their first meeting. 'We haven't made any truly new weapons for centuries. All the lab does is refine the systems we have. Any remotely new concept we come up with is closed down almost immediately by the top brass.'

'You mean ANA:Governance?' he'd asked.

'Who knows where the orders originate from? All I know is that they come down from Admiral Kazimir's office and we jump fast and high every time. It's crazy. I don't know why we bother having a weapons research division. As far as I know the deterrence fleet hasn't changed ships or armaments for five hundred years.'

The problem he'd outlined to her was interesting enough for her to postpone downloading into ANA. After Emily, others had slowly joined his motley team; Dan Massell whose expertise in functional molecular configuration was unrivalled, Ami Cowee to help with exotic matter formatting. Several technicians had come and gone over the years, contributing to the Neumann cybernetics array, then leaving as their appliance constructed its required successor. But those three had stuck with him since the early years. Their age and Higher-derived patience meant they were probably the only ones who could tolerate him for so long. That and their shared intrigue in the nature of the project.

When Troblum's ageing capsule landed on the pad outside the hangar he was puzzled to see just Emily's and Massell's capsules sitting on the concrete beside the glossy black wall. He'd been expecting Ami as well.

Then as soon as he was through the second little office he knew something was wrong. There was no quiet vibration of machinery. As soon as the shield over the third door cut off, his low-level field could detect no electronic activity beyond. The hangar had been divided in half, with *Mellanie's Redemption* parked at one end, a dark bulky presence very much in the shade of the assembly section. Troblum stood under the prow of the ship, and looked round uncomprehendingly. The Neumann cybernetic modules in front of him were bigger than a house; joined into a lattice cube of what looked like translucent glass slabs the size of commercial capsules, each one glowing with its individual primary light. It was as if a rainbow had shattered only to be scooped up and shoved into a transparent box. At the centre, three metres above Troblum's head, was a scarlet and black cone, the ejector mechanism of the terminal extruder. It should have been wrapped in a fiercely complex web of quantum fields, intersecting feeder pressors, electron positioners, and molecular lock injectors. He couldn't detect a glimmer of power. If all had gone well over the last few days the planet-shift engine should have been two-thirds complete, assembled atom by atom in a stable matrix of superdense matter held together by its own integral coherent bonding field. By now the cylinder would be visible within the extruder, glimmering from realigned exotic radiation as if it contained its own galaxy.

Instead, Emily and Massell were sitting on a box-like atomic D-K phase junction casing at the base of the cybernetics, drinking tea. Both silent with mournful faces, they flashed him a guilty glance as he came in.

'What happened?' he demanded.

'Some kind of instability,' Emily said. 'I'm sorry, Troblum. The bonding field format wasn't right. Ami had to shut it down.'

'And she didn't tell me!'

'Couldn't face you,' Massell said. 'She knew how disappointed you'd be. Said she didn't want to be responsible for breaking your heart.'

'That's not— Arrrgh,' he groaned. Biononics released a flood of neural inhibitors as they detected his thoughts growing more and more agitated. He shivered as if he'd been caught by a blast of arctic air. But his focus was perfectly clear. A list of social priorities flipped up into his exovision. 'Thank you for waiting to tell me in person,' he said. 'I'll call Ami and tell her it wasn't her fault.'

Emily and Massell exchanged a blank look. 'That's kind of you,' she said.

'How big an instability?'

Massell winced. 'Not good. We need to re-examine the whole effect, I think.'

'Can we just strengthen it?'

'I hope so, but even that will be a domino on the internal structure.'

'Maybe not,' Emily said with a weak confidence. 'We included some big operating margins. There's a lot of flexibility within the basic parameters.'

Troblum fell silent with a dismay which even the inhibitors couldn't overcome. If Emily was wrong, if they needed a complete redesign, then the Neumann cybernetics would need to be rebuilt. It would take years. Again. And this drive generator had been his true hope, he'd genuinely thought he would have a functional device by the end of the week. It was the only way to get people to agree with his theory. Marius would see the Navy never backed a search, he was sure of that. This was all that was left to him, his remaining shred of proof.

'You can get the resource allocation, can't you?' Massell said in an encouraging voice. 'I mean, you've managed to push your theory to this level.' His gesture took in the silent hulk of Neumann cybernetics. 'You've got to have some powerful political allies on the committees. And this wasn't a setback as such; only one thing was out of alignment.'

Troblum deliberately avoided looking in Emily's direction. Massell hadn't been one of Marius's candidates. 'Yes, I can probably get the EMA for a rebuild.'

'Okay then! Do you want to get on it right away, or leave it a few days?'

'Give it a few days,' Troblum said, reading from his social priority list. 'We'll all need a while to recharge after this. I'll start going over the telemetry and give you a call when I think I know what the new bonding field format should be.'

'Okay.' Massell gave him an encouraging smile as he slid off the casing. 'There's a certain Air technician I've been promising a resort time-out with. I'll let her know I'm free.' He gave Emily a blank gaze, then left.

'Will there be the resources to carry on?' she asked.

'I don't know. Maybe not from our mutual friend.' At the back of his mind was a nasty little thought that this had been the result which benefited Marius best. Just how far would the Accelerator Faction representative go to achieve that? 'But I'll carry it on one way or another. I still have some personal EMA left.'

Her expression grew sceptical as she looked round the huge assemblage of ultra-sophisticated equipment. 'All right. If you need any help reviewing the data, let me know.'

'Thanks,' he said.

Troblum's office wasn't much. A corner in one of the annexe rooms big enough for a large wingback chair in the middle of a high-capacity solido projection array. He slumped down into the worn cushioning and stared through the narrow window into the hangar's assembly section. Now he was alone and the neural chemicals were wearing off, he didn't have the heart to begin a diagnostic review. The drive engine should have slid smoothly out of the extruder and into the modified forward cargo hold of *Mellanie's Redemption*. He would have been ready to show the Commonwealth he was right by the end of the week, to open up a whole new chapter in galactic history. Highers weren't supposed to become frustrated but right now he wanted to kick the shit out of the Neumann cybernetics.

Some time later that afternoon the hangar security net informed Troblum a capsule had landed on the pad outside. Frowning, he flipped the sensor image out of his peripheral vision, and watched as the capsule's door flowed open. Marius stepped out.

Troblum actually feared for his life. The warning at the restaurant had been awful enough. But Troblum had been so sure the design for the drive engine was valid he couldn't stop thinking that the whole manufacturing process had somehow been deliberately knocked out of kilter – sabotaged, in other words. There was only one person who could have that done. He gave the *Mellanie's Redemption* a calculating glance. Even with his Faction-supplied biononics, Marius wouldn't be able to shoot through the ship's force field.

It wasn't going to happen. Troblum didn't have anywhere to run to; he certainly didn't have a friend – not one, not anywhere. And if Marius was here to eliminate him, it was on orders from the Accelerators. Hiding inside the starship would only postpone the inevitable.

I must start thinking about this, about a way out.

Reluctantly, he ordered the hangar net to open the side door.

Marius came into the office, gliding along in his usual smooth imperturbable fashion. He glanced round, not bothering to hide his distaste. 'So this is where you spend your days.'

'Something wrong with that?'

'Not at all.' Marius gave a thin smile. 'Everyone should have a hobby.'

'Do you?'

'None you'd appreciate.'

'So what are you here for? I did as you asked, I haven't pressed the Navy.'

'I know. And that hasn't gone un-noted.' He studied the huge stack of Neumann cybernetics through the office window. 'My commiserations. You put a lot of effort into today.'

'How did you know . . .'

The representative's eerie green eyes turned back to stare at Troblum. 'Don't be childish. Now, I'm here because you need more funds and we have another little project which might interest you.'

'A project?' Since he didn't seem in danger of immediate slaughter, Troblum couldn't help the tweak of interest.

'One you'll find difficult to refuse once you know the details. Its an ftl drive which we're putting into production. Who knows? Perhaps there will be some overspill into this which you can take advantage of.'

Troblum really couldn't think what type of drive the ANA Faction might want, especially after the last ultra-classified project he'd worked on for Marius. 'And you'll help me acquire extra EMAs for a rebuild here?'

'Budgets are tight in these uncertain times, but a swift and successful conclusion to our drive programme would probably result in some unused allocation we can divert your way. However, we also have something else you might be interested in, a bonus if you like.'

'What's that?'

'Bradley Johansson's genome.'

'What? Impossible. There was nothing left of him.'

'Not quite. He rejuvenated several times at a clinic on an Isolated world. We had an access opportunity several centuries ago.'

'Are you serious?'

Marius simply raised an eyebrow.

'That sounds good,' Troblum said. 'Really good. I almost don't have to think about it.'

'I need an answer now.'

Once again Troblum was uncertain what would happen if he said no. He couldn't detect any active embedded weapons in the representative, but that didn't mean death wouldn't be sudden and irrevocable. Talk about carrot and stick. 'All right. But first I have to spend a couple of days analysing what happened here.'

'We would like you to fly to our assembly station immediately.'

'If I can't settle this problem to my own satisfaction I won't be any good to you. I think you know that.'

Marius hardened his stare, his eyes darkening from emerald to near-black. 'Very well, you can have forty-eight hours. No more. I expect you to be on your way by then.' He transferred a flightplan file over to Troblum's u-shadow.

'I will be.' It took a lot of biononic intervention to prevent Troblum from shaking as the representative left the office. There wasn't anything he could do to stop the sweat staining his suit right along his spine. When the sensors showed him the representative's capsule lifting off the pad, he turned to gaze back into the assembly section. It was all far too neat. The problem on the verge of success. The generous offer to help pay for a solution, plus the unbelievable promise of being able to clone Bradley Johansson. Troblum let his biononic field sweep out to flow through the inert cybernetics. 'What did that bastard do?' he murmured. Around him the solido projectors snapped on, filling the air with a multicoloured blizzard of fine equations, sparkling as they interacted. Somewhere there had to be a flaw in the blueprint that had taken him fifteen painstaking years to devise, a deliberate glitch. The only person who could put it there was Emily. He called up the sections she was directly involved with. There was an emotion tugging at him as he started to review the data. It took a while, but he eventually realized it was sadness.

*

From the office he was visiting in the hangar five down from Troblum's, the Delivery Man could just see Marius's capsule as it took to the air again. All he used was his eyes, there was no way the Accelerator representative could know he was under direct observation. 'He's gone,' he reported. 'And that hangar has distorted the spaceport's basic guidance protocols – you can't get there unless you're invited. It's definitely a nest for some bad-boy activity. Do you want me to infiltrate?'

'No thank you,' the Conservative Faction replied. 'We'll use passive observation for the moment.'

'What about this Troblum character it's registered to?'

'Records indicate he's some kind of Starflyer War enthusiast. His starship flightplan logs are interesting, he visits some out of the way places.'

'Do you think he's another representative?'

'No. He's a physicist, with some high-level Navy contacts.'

'He's involved with the Navy?'

'Yes.'

'In what regard?'

'Left-over artefacts and actions from the Starflyer War. His interest verges on the fanatical.'

'So why would Marius pay him a personal visit?'

'Good question. We will research him further.'

'I can go home now?'

'Yes.'

'Excellent.' If he got to Arevalo's interstellar wormhole terminus in the next ten minutes, he could be back home in time for tea with the girls.

It was a glorious summer evening, the bright sun tinting to copper over the Eggshaper Guild compound while Edeard walked across the main nine-sided courtyard. He took a contented breath as he watched the team of five ge-chimps cleaning the last patch of kimoss off the kennel roof. Their strong little claw hands were tearing up long dusty strips of the thick purple vegetation, exposing the pale slate. The kennels were the last of the courtyard buildings to be spruced up. Roofs and gutterings all around the other sides were clean and repaired. There were no more leaks down on to the young genistars, no more drains overflowing every time it rained. The walls had also benefited from the new chimp team renovating the Guild compound. The mass of gurkvine had been pruned back to neat fluttering yellow rectangles between doors and windows, allowing the apprentice stonemasons to restore the mortar joints in the walls. An additional benefit of the long-neglected pruning was a bumper crop of fruit this year, with dangling clusters of succulent claret-coloured berries hanging almost to the ground.

Edeard stopped to allow Gonat and Evox herd the ge-horse foals into the stables for the night. 'All brushed down and ready?' he asked the two young apprentices. He cast his farsight over the animals, checking their short, rough fur for smears of dirt.

'Of course they are,' Evox exclaimed indignantly. 'I do know how to instruct a ge-monkey, Edeard.'

Edeard grinned good-naturedly, struck by the way he now sounded like Akeem in the way he presided over the Guild's three new apprentices. He could sense Sancia in a stall over in the default stables, sitting quietly in a chair as her third hand flowed around an egg, subtly sculpting the nature of the embryonic genistar. The youngsters were talented. Impatient, naturally, but eager to learn. Two of the new ge-horses had been sculpted by Evox, who was inordinately proud of the foals.

Taking on the apprentices had been a real turning point for Akeem and Edeard. Evox had joined them barely a week after the fateful Witham caravan last year. Sancia and Gonat had moved into the apprentice dormitory before winter set in; and now two more farmers were already discussing sending children to the Guild, at least for the coming winter months. After a hectic six months of initiation and adjustment, things had settled down in the compound. Edeard even found he had some of that most luxurious commodity: spare time. And that was on top of having the compound's ge-chimp team to start the desperately needed renovation. With the apprentices honing their instructional skills, the chimps had performed some internal restoration, whitewashing walls, cleaning floors and even preserving food in jars and casks. This coming winter season wouldn't be anything like as bleak as those of the past.

'How are the cats?' Gonat asked.

'Just going to inspect them,' Edeard said. So successful had the ge-cats been at extracting water, that the council had commissioned a second well to be dug at the other end of the cliff face behind the village. As well as producing replacements for the existing well, Edeard now had to supervise a whole new nest. In truth they didn't last as long as he'd hoped, barely two years. And they were still inordinately difficult to sculpt. 'Don't forget we have a delivery from Doddit farm in the morning. Make sure there's enough room in the stores.'

'Yes,' Gonat and Evox groaned. They mentally pushed and goaded the frisky foals into their stable before Edeard could heap any more tasks on them. The whole courtyard resonated to the hoots, snarls, bleating, and barks of various genera. With the apprentices now capable of basic sculpting, the Guild had suddenly doubled hatching rates. There were a full twenty defaults in the stables; Akeem had consulted with Wedard on building more. The majority of the animals still went out to the farms, but most houses in the village had cleaned out their disused nests and asked for a ge-chimp or a monkey. The demand for ge-wolves since the Witham caravan had increased dramatically. It was all kind of what Edeard had wanted, but he was still disheartened by the way the older villagers refused to let him give them a simple refresher course in instruction, gruffly informing him they'd been ordering genistars round since before his parents were born. True enough; but if you'd been doing it wrong since then nothing was going to change, and they'd wind up with a lot of badly behaved genistars cavorting round Ashwell annoying everyone. So Edeard surreptitiously tried to make sure that the village children had a decent grounding in the ability. The Lady's

Mother, Lorellan, helped in her own quiet way by allowing Edeard to sit in on her own instructions to the village youth. Nobody dared protest about that.

Edeard reached the main hall, and sped up the stairs, pleased to be away from the courtyard. One further side effect of their Guild's rising fortune and greater genistar numbers was the stronger smell seeping out from the stables. He'd moved out of the apprentice dormitory the week Evox arrived, taking over a journeyman's room. 'I can't confirm you as a Master yet,' Akeem had said gravely, 'no matter what you did beyond these walls, or how proficient you are. Guild procedures must be followed. To be a Master you must have served at least five years as a journeyman.'

'I understand,' Edeard had replied, secretly laughing at the formality. *Lady help us from the way old people try to keep the world in order . . .*

'And I'll thank you to take the Guild a little more seriously, please,' Akeem had snapped.

Edeard rapidly wound down his amusement. Akeem seemed able to sense any emotion, however well-hidden.

His new room actually had some furniture in it. A decent desk he'd commissioned himself from the Carpentry Guild; a cupboard and a chest of drawers – needed to store his growing new wardrobe. His cot had a soft mattress of goose down. After some gruesome disasters, he'd eventually got the finer points of laundry ritual over to his personal ge-monkey; so once a week he had fresh sheets, scented with lavender from the herb bed in the compound's small kitchen garden – also now properly maintained.

He washed quickly, using the big china jug of water. The Guild compound wasn't yet connected up to the village's rudimentary water-pipe network, but Melzar had promised it would be done by the end of the month. Both he and the smithy were trying to design a domestic stove which would heat water for individual cottages, producing various ungainly contraptions with pipes coiled round them. So far the pipes had all burst or leaked, but they were making progress.

Edeard scraped Akeem's ancient spare razor over his straggly chin hairs, wincing at the little cuts the jagged blade made. A new razor was next on his list of commissions – and a decent mirror. The ge-chimps had left a pile of newly washed clothes from which he chose a loose white cotton shirt, wearing it with his smart drosilk trousers. He'd found several weaver women in the village who would willingly make clothes for him in return for ge-spiders. Akeem called the unregistered trade enterprising, cautioning that it must not interfere with their official commissions. He still had the boots he'd bought in Witham. A little worn now after a year, but they remained comfortable and intact; the only problem was how tight they were becoming. He'd put on nearly two inches of height in the last year, not that he'd bulked out at all. His horror was that he'd wind up looking like Fahin as he put on more height without the corresponding girth.

He opened the top of the small stone barrel in the corner opposite the fire and removed the leather shoulder bag. It was one place relatively immune from casual farsight. He checked the bag's contents hadn't been discovered by the other apprentices, and slung its strap over his arm.

'Very dapper,' Akeem observed.

Edeard jumped, clutching the bag in an obviously guilty fashion. He hadn't noticed the old Master sitting in the main hall. Everyone had been trying to duplicate the way the bandits had shielded themselves, with varying degrees of success. Edeard wasn't sure how much mental effort Akeem put into the effect. He'd always had the ability to just sit quietly and blend naturally into the background.

'Thank you,' Edeard replied. He self-consciously tugged at the bottom of his shirt.

'Off out, are you?' Akeem asked with sly amusement, he gestured at the long table set for five. He'd made nothing of the bag.

'Er, yes. My tasks are complete. I'll start sculpting the new horses and dogs for Jibit's farm tomorrow. Three of the defaults are ovulating; the males are in their pens.'

'Some things are definitely easier for other species,' Akeem observed, and gave Edeard's clothes another meaningful look. 'So which of our town's fine establishments are you gracing tonight?'

'Um, I can't afford the tavern. It's just me and some of the other apprentices getting together, that's all.'

'How lovely. Are any of your fellow apprentices female by any chance?'

Edeard clamped down hard on his thoughts, but there was nothing he could do about his burning cheeks. 'I guess Zehar will be there. Possibly Calindy.' He shrugged his innocence in such matters.

For once Akeem appeared awkward, though he'd put a strong shield around his own thoughts. 'Lad . . . perhaps sometime we should talk about such things.'

'Things?' Edeard muttered in alarm.

'Girls, Edeard. After all, you are sixteen now. I'm sure you notice them these days. You do know what to ask Doc Seneo for if uh . . . *circumstances* become favourable.'

Edeard's expression was frozen into place as he prayed to the Lady for this horror to end. 'I ... er, yes. Yes I do. Thank you.' *Go to Doc Seneo and ask for a phial of vinak juice? Oh dear Lady, I'd rather chop it off altogether.*

Akeem sat back in his chair and let his gaze rise to the ceiling. 'Ah, I remember my own youthful amorous adventures back in Makkathran. Oh those city girls in all their finery; the ones of good family would do nothing else all day long but pamper and groom themselves for the parties and balls that were thrown at night. Edeard I so wish you could see them. There isn't one you wouldn't fall in love with at first sight. Of course, they all had the devil in them when you got their bodice off, but what a vision they were.'

'I *have* to go or I'll be late,' Edeard blurted. Someone of Akeem's age shouldn't be allowed to use words like amorous and bodice.

'Of course,' the old Master seemed amused by something. 'I have been selfish keeping you here.'

'I'm not that late.'

'And I don't mean tonight.'

'Uh ...'

'I'm not up to instructing you any more, Edeard. You have almost outgrown your Master. I think you should go to Makkathran to study at the Guild in their Blue Tower. My name may still be remembered. At the very least my title demands some prerogatives; I can write you a letter of sponsorship.'

'I ... No. No, I can't possibly go.'

'Why not?' Akeem asked mildly.

'To Makkathran? Me? It's, no. Anyway, it's ... it's so far away I don't even know how far. How would I get there?'

'Same way everyone does, my boy, you travel in one of

the caravans. This is not impossible or remote, Edeard. You must learn to lift your eyes above the horizon, especially in this province. I would not see you stifled by Ashwell. For that is what surely will happen if you remain. I do not want your talent wasted. There is more to this world, this life, than a single village alone on the edge of the wilderness. Why, just travelling to Makkathran will show you that.'

'I will hardly waste my talent by staying here. The village needs me. Look what has happened already with more genistars.'

'Ah really? This village is already nervous about you, Edeard. You are strong, you are smart. They are neither. Oh, don't get me wrong, this is a pleasant place for someone like me to live out my remaining days. But it is not for you. Ashwell has endured for centuries before you; it will endure for centuries yet. Trust me. A place and people this stubborn and rooted in what they are will not vanish into the black heart of Honious without you. I will write your letter this week. The Barkus caravan is due before the end of the month. I know Barkus of old, he owes me some favours. You can leave with them.'

'This month?' he whispered in astonishment. 'So soon?'

'Yes. There is no benefit in delay. My mind is clear on this matter.'

'The new ge-cats . . .'

'I can manage, Edeard. Please, don't make this any more difficult for me.'

Edeard walked over to the old Master. 'Thank you, sir. This is—' He grinned. 'Beyond imagination.'

'Ha. We'll see how much you thank me in a year's time. The Masters of the Blue Tower are not nearly as lax as I have grown. They will have a fine time beating obedience into you. Your bones will be black and blue before the first day is half-gone.'

'I will endure,' Edeard said. He laid a hand on the man's shoulder, for once allowing the love he felt to shine in his mind. 'I will prove you right to them. Whatever happens I will endure, for you. I will never give them cause to doubt your pupil. And I will make you proud.'

Akeem gripped the hand, squeezing strongly. 'I am already proud. Now come. You are dallying while your friends carouse. Leave now, and I will have yet another fine meal with our three juvenile dunderwits, listening to their profound talk and answering their challenging questions.'

Edeard laughed. 'I am a bad apprentice deserting my Master thus.'

'Indeed you are. Now go, for the Lady's sake. Let me summon up what is left of my courage else I shall flee to the tavern.'

Edeard turned and walked out of the hall. He almost stopped, wanting to ask what Akeem had meant by *they are already nervous about you*. He would enquire tomorrow.

'Edeard,' Akeem called.

'Yes, Master?'

'A word of caution. Stay silent that you are leaving, even to your friends. Envy is not a pretty blossom, and it has a custom of breeding resentment.'

'Yes, Master.'

The sun had dropped to the top of the rampart wall by the time Edeard hurried up a lane off the main street, heading for the granite cliff at the back of the village. Already the glowing colours of the night sky were emerging through the day's blue like trees out of morning mist. Old Buluku was directly overhead. The vulpine serpent manifesting as a violet stream that slithered through the heavens in a fashion which none of Querencia's few astronomers could ever fathom. It certainly didn't shift with the seasons, nor even orbit round the sun. As Edeard watched, a sliver of electric-blue light rippled lazily along its length, a journey which would take several minutes, too weak to cast a shadow across the dry mud of the lane. Odin's Sea was already drifting towards the northern horizon. A roughly oval patch of glowing blue and green mist that visited the summer nights. The Lady's teachings were that it formed the Heart of the Void, where the souls of men and women were carried by the Skylords so they could dream away the rest of existence in quiet bliss. It was only the good and the worthy who were blessed with such a voyage, and the Skylords hadn't been seen in Querencia's skies for so long they were nothing but legend and a faith kept by the Lady's followers. Protruding from the ragged edges of Odin's Sea were the reefs, scarlet promontories upon which Skylords carrying the souls of those less worthy were wrecked and began their long fall into Honious and oblivion.

Edeard often wondered if so many unworthy humans had been carried aloft by the Skylords that there were simply no more of the great creatures left. It would be so typical that humans should bring such casual destruction to this universe. Thankfully, the Lady's teachings said that it was humans who had declined in spirit; that was why the Empyrean Lady had been anointed by the Firstlifes to guide humans back to the path which would once again lead them to the Heart of the Void. It was a sad fact that not many people listened to the Lady's kind words these days.

'Calling to the Skylords?' a voice asked.

Edeard smiled and turned. His farsight had kept watch on her since she stepped out of the church ten minutes ago. One of the reasons he'd chosen this particular route. Salrana emerged from the shadows of the marketplace. Behind the deserted stalls, the church curved up above the rest of the village buildings with quiet purpose. Its crystal roof glimmered in refraction from the altar lanterns.

'They didn't answer,' he said. 'They never do.'

'One day they will. Besides you're not quite ready to sail into the Heart yet.'

'No. I'm not.' Edeard couldn't quite match her humour. He might as well have been travelling into the Heart given the distance to Makkathran. *How will she cope with me leaving?*

He wasn't the only one growing up this summer. Salrana had also put on several inches over the last couple of years; her shoulders were broad as if she was growing into a typical sturdy farmer's girl, but whereas her contemporaries were thickening out ready for their century of toil on the land she remained slim and agile. Her plain blue and white novice robe had grown quite tight, which always made Edeard glance at her in a wholly inappropriate fashion. Not that there was any helping it, she was losing her puppy fat to reveal the sharpest cheekbones he'd ever seen. Everyone could see how beautiful she was going to be. Thankfully, she still suffered from spots and her auburn hair remained wild and girlish, otherwise being in her presence would be intolerable. As it was, he viewed her friendship with delight and dismay in equal measure. She was far too young to be wanting to bed, though he couldn't help wondering how long it would be before she was old enough. Such thoughts made him fearful that the Lady would strike him down with some giant lightning bolt roaring out from Honious itself. Though of course Her priestesses did marry.

Irrelevant now. Even if I do come back, it won't be for years. She'll be with some village oaf and have three children.

'You're in a funny mood,' Salrana said, all innocent and curious. 'Is everything all right?'

'Yeah. Actually it is. I've had some good news. Great news.' He held up a hand. 'And I will tell you later, I promise.'

'Gosh, a secret and in Ashwell. Bet I find out by noon tomorrow.'

'Bet you don't.'

'Bet me what?'

'No. I'm being unfair. It's a private thing.'

'Now you're just being cruel. I'll pray to the Lady for your redemption.'

'That's very kind.'

She stood right up close to him, still smiling sweetly. 'So are you off up to the caves?'

'Er, yeah, one or two of the others said they might go in. I thought I'd see.'

'So when do I get asked?'

'I don't think Mother Lorellan would want you in the caves at night.'

'Pha. There's a lot of things the good Mother doesn't know I do.' She shook her hair defiantly, squaring her shoulders. The aggressive pose lasted a couple of seconds before she started giggling.

'Well I'll pray she doesn't find out,' he told her.

'Thank you, Edeard.' Her hand rubbed playfully along his arm. 'Who'd have thought it just a few years ago. Both of us happy. And you: one of the lads now.'

'I was in a fight before they accepted me.' *I killed people.* Even now he could still see the face of the bandit before the man smashed into the tree, the astonishment and fear.

'Of course you were, that's a typical boy thing. That's why you're going into the caves again tonight. We all have to find a way to live here, Edeard. We're going to be in Ashwell for a long long time.'

He couldn't answer, just gave her a fixed smile.

'And watch out for that Zehar. She's already bragging how she intends to have you. She was very descriptive. For a baker's apprentice.'

'She. Is? She wants . . . ?'

Salrana's face was devilsome. 'Oh yes.' She blew him a kiss, giggling. 'Let me know the details. I'm dying to know if you can really do such wicked things.' Then her back was to him, her skirt held high by both hands, and she went racing off down the slope, giggling all the way.

Edeard let out a long breath. His emotions were as unsteady as his legs. If there was ever a reason to stay in Ashwell, he was looking at it. His farsight followed her long after she'd turned a corner on to main street, making sure she was safe as she ran along on her errand.

There were a number of caves burrowing into the cliffs behind Ashwell. A lot of them had been expanded over the decades, modified into storerooms for the long winter months, where the temperature and moisture hardly varied at all. Several of the larger were used as barns. Edeard wasn't interested in those. Instead, he headed for a small oddly angled fissure in the rock on the western end of the cliff, only thirty yards from where the encircling wall began. He had to scramble up a pile of smoothed boulders to reach it, then grip the upper lip and swing himself into the darkness. Anyone larger than him would have real trouble passing through the gap; he'd only be able to use it for another year or so himself. Once inside, the passage opened up, and the soft background babble of the village's longtalk cut off abruptly. His immediate world contracted to a dank gloomy blackness; even his farsight ability couldn't perceive through such a depth of rock. All he could sense was the open cavity around him. Only after he'd gone round a curve did he see a glint of yellow light ahead.

Seven apprentices were gathered in the narrow cave with its high crevice apex, sitting round a couple of battered old lamps whose wicks were chuffing out a lot of smoke. Their talk stopped as he entered, then their smiles bloomed in welcome. It was a gratifying sensation of belonging. Even Obron raised a cheery hand. Fahin beckoned him over. Edeard was very conscious of Zehar watching him with a near-feline intent, and gave her a nervous grin. Her answering smile was carnivorous.

'Didn't think you were coming,' Fahin said.

'I got delayed slightly,' Edeard explained. He opened his bag and pulled out the large wine bottle, which earned him some appreciative whistles as he held it up.

Fahin leaned in closer. 'Thought you were running scared of Zehar,' he murmured in a knowing whisper.

'Sweet Lady, has she told everyone but me?'

'I overheard it from Marilee. She was trying to get Kelina to take some vinak juice from Seneo's pharmacology store. I assumed you were party to it.'

'No,' Edeard growled.

'Okay. Well should the need arise, and I do mean *rise*, just ask me. I can get you a phial without anyone being any the wiser, especially Seneo.'

'I shall remember it well, thank you.'

Fahin nodded, as if unconcerned. An attitude confirmed by his passive surface thoughts. He unbuckled his ancient physick satchel and took out some dried kestric leaves. The pair of them became the centre of some not very subtle attention from the other apprentices in the cave.

Edeard shifted position and opened the wine. It was dark red, which Akeem always claimed was a sign of quality. Edeard was never certain. All the wine available in Ashwell had a strong taste which lingered well into the next day. He supposed he'd get used to it eventually, but as for actually liking it . . . 'Fahin, where do you see yourself in fifty years?'

The doctor's tall apprentice glanced up from the little slate pestle he was preparing. 'You're very serious tonight, my friend. Mind you, she does have that effect on people.'

For an instant Edeard thought he was talking about Salrana, then Fahin's eyes glanced over at Zehar, a movement amplified by his over-size lenses.

'No,' Edeard said irritably. 'Seriously, come on: fifty years' time. What are you working towards?'

'Why I'll be doctor, of course. Seneo is actually a lot older than most people realize. And she says I am her most promising apprentice in decades.' He began grinding the kestric leaves with smooth easy motions of the mortar.

'That's it? Village doctor?'

'Yes.' Fahin wasn't looking at Edeard any more, his

thoughts took on an edge. 'I'm not like you, Edeard; Honious take me, I'm not even like Obron. I'm sure you're going to build our Eggshaper Guild to greatness over the next century. You'll probably be Mayor inside thirty years. Ashwell's name will spread, people will come, and this land will flourish once again. We all hope that from you. So, given the circumstances, village doctor and your friend in such times is no small goal after all.'

'You truly think I will do that?'

'You *can* do it.' Fahin mashed up the last flakes of leaf into a thin powder. 'Either that or you'll lead a barbarian army to sack Makkathran and overthrow the old order. You have the strength to do either. I saw it. We all did. That sort of strength attracts people.'

'Don't say that,' Edeard said. 'Not even in jest.'

'Who's jesting?' Fahin poured the kestric powder into a small white clay pipe, adding some tobacco.

Edeard stared at his friend in some alarm. *Is this what people think? Is this why I make them nervous?*

'You know the gate guards say they still farsight your fastfoxes at night sometimes,' Fahin said. 'Do you keep them out there?'

'What? No! I sent it away when we got back; you were with me, you saw me do it. And how would the guards know that, the old fools. They're asleep most of the night anyway, and they can't tell one animal from another at any distance.'

'These fastfoxes have collars.'

'They're not mine!' he insisted. 'Wait, there's more than one? You know I only mastered one. When did they see them?' he asked in curiosity.

Fahin struck a match and sucked hard on his pipe stem, pulling the flame down into the bowl. 'I'm not sure,' he puffed out some smoke. 'A couple of months now.'

'Why did nobody tell me? I could find out if they are real.'

'Why indeed?' The match went out, and Fahin took a deep drag. Almost immediately, his eyes lost focus.

Edeard stared at his friend with growing dismay. They all gathered up here for a drink and a smoke and talk, just as apprentices had done since Ashwell was founded. But lately Fahin was smoking on a near-nightly basis. It was a habit which had grown steadily ever since they got back from the Witham caravan.

'Sweet Lady,' Edeard muttered as the other apprentices came over. *Maybe leaving this place is the right thing to do.* Fahin passed the pipe up to Genril. A smiling Zehar held out a hand for Edeard's wine. He deliberately took a huge swig before handing it over.

The first thing Edeard did when he woke up was retch horribly. When he tried to turn over he banged his temple hard on cold floorboards. It took a moment to realize, but he wasn't lying on his nice soft mattress. For some reason he was sprawled on the floor beside the cot, still fully dressed apart from one boot. And he stank!

He groaned again and felt the acid rising in his throat. Gave up all attempts at control and threw up spectacularly. As he did so the fear hit, squeezing cold sweat from every pore. He was shaking as he wiped pitifully at the fluid dribbling from his lips, nearly weeping with the misery. Hangovers he could take, even those from red wine, but this was more than just the payback for overindulgence. He'd felt like this before. The forest. The bandit ambush.

His body was reacting to the alcohol and a couple of puffs on the pipe. While his mind was yelling at some deep instinctive level of the mortal danger closing in out of the surrounding darkness. He forced himself to sit up. A thin pastel light from the night sky washed round the shutters revealing his small room. Nothing was amiss, apart from himself. He whimpered from the sheer intensity of fright pouring through him, expecting something terrible to envelop him at any second. The hangover made his head throb painfully. It was hard to concentrate, but he slowly managed to summon up some farsight and scan round.

The three apprentices were asleep in their dormitory. He forced the ability further, almost crying out from the pain sparking behind his eyes. Akeem, too, was asleep on his bed. Out in the courtyard, the young genistars dozed the night away, shuffling and shaking as was their style. A couple of cats trod delicately along the roofs as they tracked small rodents. By the gate, the ge-wolf in its traditional stone guardkennel lay curled up on its legs, big head swaying slowly as it obediently kept watch on the road outside.

Edeard groaned with the effort of searching so far, and let his farsight wither to nothing. He was still shaking and cold. The front of his shirt was disgustingly sticky, and the smell was getting worse. Nausea threatened to return. He struggled out of the shirt and lurched over to the nightstand where there was a glass of water and took several large gulps. In the drawer at the bottom of the little stand was a pouch of dried jewn petals soaked in an oil which

Fahin had prepared. He opened it, closed his eyes and shoved one of the petals into his mouth. It tasted foul, but he took one final gulp from the glass, forcing it down.

In all his sixteen years he had never felt so wretched. And still the fear wouldn't abate. Tears threatened to clog his eyes as he shivered again, hugging his chest.

What is wrong with me?

He wobbled over to the window and pushed the shutters open. Cool night air flowed in. Odin's Sea had nearly fallen below the horizon, which meant it was no more than a couple of hours past midnight. The low thatched roofs of the village were spread out around him, pale in the wan flickering light of the nebulas. Nothing moved. But for whatever reason the sight of such serenity simply made the fear even worse. For an instant he heard screams, saw flames. His stomach churned and he bent over the window sill.

Lady, why do you do this to me?

When he straightened up he instinctively looked at the village gate with its twin watchtowers. There was no sign of the guards. But then they were nearly half a mile away and it was night. Edeard gathered his breath and gripped the side of the windows in grim determination. His farsight surged out. *If they're all right I'm going straight back to bed.*

The towers were built from smooth-faced stone; recent decades had seen them strengthened inside with thick timber bracing. Even so, there were no holes in the walls, just some alarmingly long cracks zigzagging up and down. Their parapets were large enough to hold ten guards who could fire a number of heavy weapons down on anyone foolish enough to storm the gate. Tonight the eastern tower was empty. A solitary man stood on the western parapet underneath the alarm bell. He was facing inwards, looking across the village. Three bodies lay on the flagstones at his feet.

Edeard lurched in shock, and tried to refocus his farsight. It swept in and out before centring back on the parapet. The lone man's thoughts shone with a hue of satisfaction; Edeard felt a filthy mental smile. 'Greetings,' the man longtalked.

Edeard's throat contracted, snagging his breath. 'Who are you?'

Mental laughter mocked him. 'We know who you are. We know all about you, tough boy. We know what you did to our friends. Because of that you're mine tonight. And I promise you won't die quickly.'

Edeard yelped in horror and dived away from the window. Even so he could still feel the tenuous touch of the other's farsight upon him. He put as much strength as he had behind his longtalk, and cried: 'Akeem! Akeem, wake up. The bandits are here. They're in the village.'

His mental shout was like some kind of signal. The soft glow of minds materialized in the alleyways and lanes that wound through the cottages and Guild compounds. Edeard screamed. They were everywhere!

So many! Every bandit in the wilderness must be here tonight.

'What in the Lady's name,' Akeem's fuzzy thoughts came questioning.

'Bandits,' Edeard called again, with voice and mind. 'Hundreds of them. They're already here.' He jabbed every ge-wolf in the compound with a mental goad, triggering their attack state. Loud, dangerous snarling rose from the courtyard.

Five bandits appeared in the street outside the Guild, strong and confident, making no further attempt at cover. They didn't have the muddy skin and wild hair of the ones in the forest; these wore simple dark tunics and sturdy boots. There were no bows and arrows, either. Strangely they wore two belts apiece, looped round their shoulders so they crossed over their chest. Little metal boxes were clipped on to the leather, along with a variety of knives. Whispers spilled out of the aether as they longtalked. Then Edeard sensed the fastfoxes walking beside them; each had two of the tamed and trained beasts.

'Oh sweet Lady, no,' he gasped. His mind registered Akeem longtalking the other elders, fast and precise thoughts raising the alarm.

It was too late. Flames appeared among Ashwell's rooftops. Torches thick with oil-fire spun through the air, guided by telekinesis to land full square on thatch roofs. The fire spread quickly, encouraged by the dry months of a good summer. A dreadful orange glow began to cover the village.

The ge-wolves were racing across the Guild courtyard. Edeard extended his third hand with furious intent and slammed the gates open for them. That was when he heard the noise for the first time. An awful thunderous roar as if a hundred pistols were all firing at once. White light flashed across his open window, and his mind felt the dirty glee of the bandits' thoughts coming from the street below. Ge-wolves fell in torment, their minds radiating terrible flares of pain as their flesh was shredded. Some of them managed to survive the strange weapons to collide with fastfoxes. The metallic roaring abated as the animals fought, tearing at each other as they writhed and spun and jumped.

That was when Edeard heard a woman scream. There was too much turmoil, too much anguish storming across Ashwell, for his farsight to track her down, but he knew what the sound meant. What it would mean for every woman in the village caught alive. And girl.

He sent a single piercing thought at the church. 'Salrana!'

'Edeard,' her panicked longtalk barked back. 'They're here, they're in the church.'

His mind found her instantly, farsight zooming in as if he was illuminating her with a powerful beam of light. She was cowering in her room in the Mother's house which formed the back of the church. Inside the dome itself, three bandits were advancing along the empty aisles, radiating triumph and contempt as their fastfoxes stalked along beside them. Mother Lorellan was already out of bed and heading for the church to deal with the desecrators. For a devout woman her mind shone with inordinately strong aggression.

The bandits and their fastfoxes would cut her to ribbons, Edeard knew. 'Get out,' he told Salrana. 'Move now. Out of the window and into the garden. Stay ahead of them, keep moving. Head for the market, it's cobbled, there's no fire there. I'll meet you at the corn measure station.'

'Oh Edeard!'

'Do it. Do it now.'

He raced over to the window. It wasn't such a big jump to the street, and the carnage the fastfoxes were wreaking on the surviving ge-wolves was almost over. Whatever victors were left he could take care of them. Flames were racing across the thatch of the terraced cottages opposite. Doors were flung open, and men charged out, shields firm round their bodies, knives held high. The bandits raised their weapons, and the noise began again. Edeard watched numbly as the squat guns spat a blue-purple flame. Somehow they were firing dozens of bullets, reloading themselves impossibly fast. The villagers shook and flailed in agony as the bullets overwhelmed their shields.

'Bastards,' Edeard yelled, and jumped.

'No! Don't.' Akeem's longtalk was strong enough to make half the village pause. Even the guns were temporarily stilled.

Edeard landed, his bare heel shooting pain up his leg. He turned towards the nearest bandit, crouching as if he was about to go for a wrestling hold. Somehow he sensed both Akeem and the bandit in the guardtower both holding their breath. The bandit in front of him lifted the dark gun, snarling with delight. Edeard reached out with his third hand, closing it round the gun. He wasn't sure if even his shield could withstand quite so many bullets striking at him, but like every gun, you first had to pull the trigger. The bandit's eyes widened in surprise as his own shielding was unable to ward off Edeard's power. Then the street was subject to an unnerved screech as the bandit's fingers were snapped in quick succession. Edeard rotated the gun in front of the bandit's numb gaze until the man was staring right into the muzzle, then pulled back hard on the trigger. The discharge was awesome, even though it lasted barely a second before something snarled inside the gun's mechanism. It blew the bandit's head apart. Tatters of gore lashed down on the muddy street.

Three other bandits raised their guns. Edeard exerted himself, gripping their flesh tight with his third hand, preventing the slightest movement. 'Get them,' he told the surviving villagers stumbling out of the blazing cottages.

'Oh, your death will be exquisite,' the bandit in the watchtower sent.

A gun roared behind Edeard. He turned, flinching, to see the fifth bandit falling on his own weapon, borne down by a swarm of ge-chimps which Akeem had instructed.

'I did say "don't",' Akeem's longtalk chided.

'Thank you,' Edeard replied. The villagers were dispatching the bandits with a ferocity that he found disturbing. Edeard let go of the bloody corpses. Then everyone was turning to him, awaiting guidance.

'Get into the Guild compound,' he told them, aware of how it became an eerie echo of Melzar's instructions back in the forest. 'Group together. That will give your shields real strength.'

'You, too, lad,' Akeem said as Edeard picked up one of the bandit's guns. It was a lot heavier than he was expecting. A sweep with his farsight revealed an internal mechanism that was inordinately complicated. He didn't understand anything about it other than the trigger. There didn't seem to be many bullets left in the metal box in front of the stock. 'I have to help Salrana.'

'No. All's lost here. Get out. Live, Edeard, please. Just survive tonight. Don't let them win.'

Edeard started running up the street, wincing every time his boot-less foot touched the ground. 'They won't destroy this village.'

'They already have, lad. Take cover. Get out.'

He sent his farsight flowing out ahead, alert for any bandits. Saw a fastfox loping along an alley. When it emerged Edeard was almost level with it; he pushed his third hand into the creature's skull and ripped its brain apart. It fell in the evil wavering light of burning thatch. The street was a gulley of leaping flame, as bright as any dawn. Screams, shouts and gunfire split the harsh, constant flame-growl.

'You are good, aren't you?' the watchtower bandit taunted.

Edeard pushed his farsight into the tower, but the man was no longer there. A quick scan of the surrounding area revealed nothing except the broken main gates and dead village guards. 'Where did he go?' Edeard asked fretfully. 'Akeem, help, I can't sense half of them.' He actually heard a gun mechanism snick smoothly, and hardened his shield. The blast of bullets came from a cottage he'd just passed. He got lucky, he decided afterwards, not all of the bullets hit him, the bandit's aim was off. That and his mind picked up a quiet longtalked, 'No, not him.' Even so, the force of the shots which did hit was enough to send him sprawling backwards, half dazed. He instinctively lashed out with his third hand to the source of the shots. A bandit went staggering across the road, shaking his head. Edeard reached up to the furnace of thatch above, and tugged hard. Dense waves of flame peeled off the disintegrating roof and splashed down over the bandit, driving him to his knees. His screams were thankfully muffled.

'Are you all right?' Akeem asked.

Edeard groaned as he rolled back to his feet, There were flames everywhere, their ferocity sending huge sparking balls of thatch high into the sky. Windows and doors were belching out twisting orange streamers. The heat was intense on his bare torso, he was sure he could feel his skin starting to crack and blister. 'I'm here,' he replied. 'But I can't sense them, I don't know where they are.' And he knew the watchtower bandit was coming, slipping stealthily through the swirling flames and sagging walls.

'Try this,' Akeem said. His longtalk voice became stretched as if rising to birdsong. It seemed to fill Edeard's skull. A knowledge gift, thoughts and sometimes memories that explained how to perform a specific mental task. Edeard had absorbed hundreds of basic explanations on the art of sculpting but this was far more complex. As the song ended he began to shape his farsight and third hand together into a symbiotic force that wove a darkness through the air around him. It was like standing in the middle of a thick patch of fog.

'Now please,' Akeem pleaded. 'Get out. Do not waste your life, Edeard, don't make some futile gesture. Please. Remember: the Blue Tower in Makkathran. Go there. Be someone.'

'I can't leave you!' he cried into the terrible night.

'The village is already lost. Now go. Go, Edeard. Don't let everything be wasted.'

Edeard wanted to shout out that his Master was wrong, that his valiant apprentice friends and strong Masters like Melzar and Wedard were leading the fight back. But looking at the fiery devastation around him he knew it wasn't true. The screams were still filling the air, along with the snarl of fastfoxes and the deadly clamour of guns. Resistance was contracting to a few Guild compounds and halls. The rest of the village was burning to ruin. There was nothing to be saved. Except Salrana.

Edeard forced himself to his feet and started running towards the market again. Once, a bandit hurried past him along the street, not five yards away. The man never knew how close they were. Edeard could so easily have killed him, extracted some vengeance. But that would have shown the watchtower bandit where he was, and even through his anger and desperation Edeard knew he had neither the skill nor strength to win that confrontation.

He sped past three more bandits before charging into the marketplace. The square was surrounded by a wall of flame, but it was cooler amid the stalls. Two bandits were holding down a woman, laughing while the third of their band raped her. Their fastfoxes prowled round the little group, keeping guard.

Edeard just couldn't ignore it. He even recognized the woman though he didn't know her name; she worked at the tannery, helping prepare the hides.

The first the bandits knew of anything amiss was when their fastfoxes suddenly stopped circling. All six beasts swung their heads round, huge jaws opening to ready fangs the size of human fingers.

'What—' one of the bandits managed to say. He brought his gun up, but it was too late. The fastfoxes leapt. More screams echoed out around the stalls.

'Ah, there you are,' a longtalk voice gloated. 'I was worried you'd run away from me.'

Edeard snarled into the smoke-wreathed sky. Try as he might, he couldn't track where the longtalk was originating.

'Now what are you doing there, apart from slaughtering my comrades? Oh yes, I see.'

Edeard was aware of Salrana hunched up behind the counter in the corn measure stall, glancing upwards with a puzzled expression. He started to sprint towards her.

'He's in the marketplace,' the bandit announced across the whole village. 'Close in.'

Edeard sensed bandits turning to head towards him.

'Oh she is lovely. The very young one from the church, isn't it? Yes, I recognize her. Well congratulations, my tough little friend. Good choice. She's certainly worth risking everything for.'

Edeard reached the corn measure stall, and dropped his concealment. Salrana gasped in astonishment as he appeared in front of her.

'Got you.'

Edeard was only too well aware of the urgent satisfaction in the bandit's longtalk. There was the tiniest flashover of pounding feet, leg muscles straining with effort *to get there, to capture the feared boy.*

'Right at the end I'm going to cut your eyelids off so you have no choice but to watch while I fuck her,' the bandit said, twining his longtalk with a burst of dark pleasure. 'It'll be the last thing you see before you die. But you'll go straight to Honious knowing this; I'll keep her for my own. She's coming with me, tough boy. And I'll put her to work every single night. Your girl is going to spend the next decade bearing my children.'

'Get up,' Edeard yelled, and tugged at Salrana's arm. She was crying, her limbs limp and unresponsive. 'Don't let him get me,' she wept. 'Please, Edeard. Kill me. I couldn't stand that. I couldn't, I'd rather spend eternity in Honious.'

'Never,' he said; his arms went round her and he enfolded her within his concealment.

'Get the fastfoxes in the market,' the bandit ordered. 'Track him. Find his scent.'

'Come on,' Edeard whispered. He started for the main entrance, then stopped. Over ten bandits with their fast-foxes were heading up the street towards him. They ignored the frantic chickens and gibbering ge-chimps that were running away from the swirl of lethal flames consuming the buildings. 'Lady!' He searched round, not daring to use his farsight in case the diabolical bandit could detect that.

'I don't care if the fire's making it hard to track. Find him!'

The bandit's tone was angry, which was the first piece of good news Edeard had encountered all night. Now he glanced round, he saw just how awesome the fire had become. Every building was alight. A foul smoke tower billowed hundreds of feet over the village, blocking the constellations and nebulas. Below its dismal occlusion, walls were collapsing, sending avalanches of burning furniture and broken joists across the lanes. Even the bandits were becoming wary as the smaller alleys were blocked. Of course, the blazing destruction was also closing off Edeard's escape routes. What he needed was a distraction, and fast. His third hand shoved a pile of beer barrels, sending them toppling over. Several burst open. A wave of beer lapped across the cobbles, spreading wide. As the same time he grabbed the minds of as many genistars he could reach, and pulled them into the market, offering them sanctuary. The animals bounded over the stalls, stampeding down the narrow aisles. Flustered fastfoxes charged after them, shaking off their mental restraints to obey more basic hunter instincts.

'Almost clever,' the bandit announced. 'You think that'll cover your smell? Well why don't you avoid this, tough guy?'

The bandits in the market square formed a loose line, and began firing, sweeping their blazing gun muzzles in wide arcs. Genistars howled and whimpered as the bullets chewed through their flesh. They jumped and sprinted for cover as lines of bullets swept after them. Fastfoxes snarled in hatred and distress as they too were hit. Dozens of animals tumbled lifeless on to the cobbles. Blood mingled with beer, washing down the slope.

Edeard and Salrana hunched down as bullets thudded into the stalls around them. Wood splinters whirled through the air. They started to crawl. It wasn't long before the guns stopped. Edeard waited for the next longtalk taunt, but it didn't come. 'Hurry,' he urged her. Holding hands, they ran for the alley which led round the back of the Carpentry Guild compound. Bandits and their fastfoxes were on patrol around the walls. The inside of the compound burned like a brazier as fire consumed the woodworking halls and timber stores, sending vast plumes of flame into the smoke-clotted sky. The slate roof of the main building had already collapsed. Edeard wondered if anyone was still alive inside, maybe sheltering in the cellars. Surely Obron would have found a way. He couldn't imagine a world without Obron.

They came to a crossroads, and Salrana made to turn right.

'Not that way,' he hissed.

'But that's down to the wall,' she whispered back.

'They'll be expecting that. The fastfoxes will scent us if we try to climb over the ramparts.'

'Where are we going then?'

'Up towards the cliff.'

'But . . . won't they search the caves?'

'We're not sheltering in the caves,' he assured her. He found a dozen genistars still alive nearby, mainly dogs, with a couple of chimps and even a foal; and ordered them to walk across and around the track they were leaving to lay false scents. Though he suspected not even fastfoxes would be able to track them with so much smoke and ash in the air.

It took a couple of minutes to reach the site where the new well was being dug. So far Wedard and his team had only excavated five yards down, with barely the top third lined in stone. 'In you go,' Edeard told her. There was a small ladder leading down to the wooden framework at the bottom of the hole where ge-monkeys spent their days digging into the stone and clay.

'They'll look in here,' Salrana said desperately.

'Only if it's open,' Edeard said grimly, and gestured at the big stone cap which would seal the shaft once it was complete.

'You can move that?' she asked incredulously.

'We'll find out in a minute. But I'm pretty sure no one can farsight through it.'

Salrana started down the crude ladder, her mind seething with fright. Edeard followed her, stopping when his head was level with the rim. This was the biggest gamble, the one on which both their lives now depended, but he couldn't think of any way out of the village, not past the fastfoxes and alert bandits. He fired a longtalk query directly at the Eggshaper Guild compound. 'Akeem?' he asked quietly. There was no reply. He still didn't dare use his farsight. With a last furious look at the raging fire-storm which was his home, he reached out with his third hand and lifted the huge slab of stone. It skimmed silently through the air, keeping a couple of inches off the ground before settling on the top of the well shaft with a slow grinding sound. The orange glow of the flames, the sound of collapsing masonry and human anguish cut off abruptly.

Edeard waited for hours. He and Salrana clung to each other on the planking at the bottom of the pit, drawing what comfort they could from each other. Eventually, she fell into a troubled sleep, twitching and moaning. He wouldn't allow himself the luxury.

Is this all my fault? Were they seeking revenge for the ambush in the forest? But they started it. His worst guilt came from a single thought which nagged and nagged at his soul. *Could I have done more?* Now he was sober and the worst of the hangover had abated, he kept thinking about the sensation which had woken him so abruptly. It *was* the same as the alarm he'd felt in the forest, a foresight that something was wrong. Normally the senior priestesses of the Empyrean Lady claimed to have a modest timesense; granted of course by the Lady Herself. So such a thing was possible. *If I hadn't been so stupid. If I hadn't wasted the warning . . .*

He didn't want to open the stone cap. The scene which he knew would greet them was almost too much to contemplate. *My fault. All my fault.*

A few hours after they took refuge, some slices of pale light seeped in round the edge of the cap where the stone rim wasn't quite level. Still Edeard waited. The rise of the sun wasn't going to automatically make the bandits go away. There was nothing left for them to fear for tens of miles. It would be the villages now who would wait for the fall of each night with dread.

'We never suspected they were so well organized,' Edeard said bitterly. 'Me of all people, I should have realized.'

'Don't be silly,' she said. In the dark she reached out for him again, her slim arm going round his waist. 'How could you have known? This is something beyond even the Mother to see.'

'Did Mother Lorellan have a timesense?'

'Not much of one, no. Yesterday evening she was concerned about something, but she couldn't define it.'

'She couldn't see her own murder? What kind of time-sense is that?'

Salrana started sobbing again.

'Oh, Lady, I'm so sorry,' he said, and hugged her tight. 'I didn't think. I'm so stupid.'

'No Edeard. You came to help me. Me, out of everybody in Ashwell; all your friends, your Master. Why? Why me?'

'I . . . All those years, it was like just me and you against the world. You were the only friend I had. I don't think I would have made it without you. The number of times I thought about running off into the wild.'

She shook her head in dismay. 'Then you'd have been a bandit, you would have been one of the invaders last night.'

'Don't say that. Not ever. I hate them. First my parents, now . . .' He couldn't help it, he hung his head and started weeping. 'Everything. Everything's gone. I couldn't help them. Everybody was scared of how strong I am, and when they really needed me I was useless.'

'Not useless,' she said. 'You helped me.'

They spent a long time just pressed together. Edeard's tears dried up after a while. He wiped at his face, feeling stupid and miserable. Salrana's hands came up to cup his face. 'Would you like me?' she whispered.

'Er . . . I. No.' It was a very difficult thing to say.

'No?' Her thoughts, already fragile, fountained a wave of bewildered hurt. 'I thought—'

'Not now,' he said, and gripped her hands. He knew what it was, the shattering grief, the loneliness and fright; all so evident in her thoughts. She needed comfort, and physical intimacy was the strongest comfort of all. Given his own shaky emotional state it would have been heartening for him, too. But he cared too much, and it would have felt too much like taking advantage. 'I really would, but you're young. Too young.'

'Linem had a child last year, she wasn't quite as old as I am today.'

He couldn't help but grin. 'What kind of example is that for a novice to set to her flock?'

'Flock of one.'

Edeard's humour faded. 'Yes: one.'

Salrana looked up at the stone cap. 'Do you think any of them are left?'

'Some, yes. Of course. Ashwell village is stubborn and resilient, that's what Akeem always said. That's how it's resisted change so effectively for the last few centuries.'

'You really wanted to?'

'I—' He found it disconcerting the way she could jump between topics so lightly, especially when *that* was one of the subjects in question. 'Yes,' he admitted cautiously. 'You must know how beautiful you're becoming.'

'Liar! I have to visit Doc Seneo three times a week to get ointment for my face.'

'You are growing up lovely,' he insisted quietly.

'Thank you, Edeard. You're really sweet, you know. I've never thought of any other boy. It's always been you.'

'Um. Right.'

'It would be terrible to die a virgin, wouldn't it?'

'Lady! You are the worst novice in the whole Void.'

'Don't be so silly. The Lady must have enjoyed a good love life. She was Rah's wife. Half of Makkathran claim to be descended from them. That's a lot of children.'

'This has to be blasphemy.'

'No. It's being human. That's why the Lady was anointed by the Firstlifes, to remind us how to discover our true nature again.'

'Well right now we need to think survival.'

'I know. So how old do I have to be? Your age?'

'Um, probably, yes. Yes, that's about right.'

'Can't wait. Did you go with Zehar last night?'

'Not— Hey, that is not your concern.' For some stupid reason, he suddenly wished he had given in to Zehar's advances. *She'll be dead now; quickly if she was lucky.*

'You're going to be my husband. I'm entitled to know all about your old lovers.'

'I'm not your husband.'

'Not yet,' she taunted. 'My timesense says you will be.'

He threw up his hands in defeat.

'How long are we going to stay in here?' she asked.

'I'm not sure. Even if there's nothing left to scare them off, they won't want to stay too long. The other villages will know what's happened by now. The smoke must have reached halfway to Odin's Sea, and the farms would have fled, longshouting all the way. I expect the province will raise the militia and give chase.'

'A militia? Can they do that?'

'Each province has the right to form a militia in times of crisis,' he said, trying to remember the details Akeem had imparted about Querencia's constitutional law. 'And this definitely qualifies. As to the practical details, I expect the bandits will be long gone before any decent force can get here, never mind chase them into the wilderness. And those guns they had.' He held up his trophy, frowning at the outlandish design. No doubting its power, though. 'I've never heard of anything like these before. It's like something humans owned from before the flight into the Void.'

'So that's it? There's no justice.'

'There will be, as long as I remain alive they will curse their boldness of this day. It is their own death they have brought to our village.'

She clutched at him. 'Don't go after them. Please, Edeard. They live out there, it's their wilderness, they know this kind of life, the killing and brutality, they know nothing else. I couldn't stand it if they caught you.'

'I had no notion to do it right away.'

'Thank you.'

'Okay, I think it's the afternoon now. Let's take a look.'

'All right. But if they're still there and they see us . . . I can't be his whore, Edeard.'

'Neither of us will be caught,' he promised, and meant it. For emphasis he patted his gun. 'Now let's see what's out there.' He started to apply his third hand to the cool stone. Lips touched his. His mouth opened in response and the kiss went on for a long time.

'Just in case,' Salrana murmured, pressed up against him. 'I wanted us both to know what it was like.'

'I . . . I'm glad,' he said sheepishly.

This time it was a lot harder to move the huge stone

slab. It was only after he started he realized how exhausted he was, and hungry, and scared. But he shifted the stone a couple of inches until a slim crescent of mundane grey sky was visible. There were no excited shouts or farsight probes down into the pit. He couldn't send his own farsight across much distance given the tiny gap and the fact he was still below ground. Instead, his mind called out to the Guild's sole ge-eagle. His relief when the majestic bird replied was profound. It was perched up on the cliffs, distressed and bewildered. What it showed him when it took flight swiftly brought his mood back down again.

There was nothing left. Nothing. Every cottage was a pile of smouldering rubble; the Guild compounds with their sturdy stone walls had collapsed. He could barely make out the street pattern. A thin layer of grubby smog drifted slowly over the ruins.

When the eagle swooped in lower, he could see the bodies. Charred clothes flapped limply on blackened flesh. Worse still were the parts that stuck out of the debris. Motion caught the eagle's attention, and it pivoted neatly on a wingtip.

Old Fromal was sitting beside the ruins of his house, head in his hands, rocking back and forth, his filthy old face streaked by tears. There was a small boy, naked, running round and round the wrecked market stalls. He was bruised and bleeding, his face drawn into a fierce rictus of determination, not looking at anything in the physical world.

'They're gone,' Edeard said. 'Let's go out.' He dropped the hated gun and shoved the slab aside.

The stench was the worst of it; cloying smell of the smoking wood remnants saturated with burnt meat. Edeard almost vomited at the impact. It wasn't all genistars and domestic animals that were roasting. He tore a strip of cloth from his ragged trousers, damped it in a puddle, and tied it over his face.

They halted the running boy, who was in a shock too deep for reason to reach. Led old man Fromal away from the hot coals that had been his home for a hundred and twenty-two years. Found little Sagat cowering in the upturned barrels beside the working well.

Seven. That was how many they and the eagle found. Seven survivors out of a village numbering over four hundred souls.

They gathered together just outside the broken gates, in the shadow of the useless rampart walls, where the reek of the corpses wasn't so bad. Edeard went back in a couple of times, trying to find some clothes and food, though his heart was never in the search.

That was how the posse from Thorpe-By-Water village found them just before dusk. Over a hundred men riding horses and ge-horses, well armed, with ge-wolves loping along beside them. They could barely believe the sight which awaited them, nor did they want to accept it was organized bandits who were responsible. Instead of giving chase and delivering justice, they turned and rode back to Thorpe-By-Water in case their own loved ones were threatened. The survivors were taken with them. None of them ever returned.

*

Edeard used his longtalk to tell Salrana: 'The caravan is here.'

'Where?' she answered back. 'I can't sense them.'

'They've just reached Molby's farm, they should be at the village bridge in another hour or so.'

'That's a long way to farsee, even for you.'

'The ge-eagle helps,' he admitted.

'Cheat!'

Edeard laughed. 'I'll meet you in the square in half an hour.'

'All right.'

He finished instructing the flock of ge-chimps clearing out the stables and excused himself with Tonri, the senior apprentice. All he got for his courtesy was an indifferent grunt. Thorpe-By-Water's Eggshaper Guild hadn't exactly welcomed him with open arms. There was a huge question about his actual status. The Master hadn't yet confirmed him as a journeyman. Edeard's request that he should be recognized as such had generated a lot of resentment among the other apprentices, who believed he should be the junior. That his talent was so obviously greater than any of them, even the Master, didn't help the situation.

Salrana had been accepted a lot more readily into the Lady's Church by Thorpe-By-Water's Mother. But she wasn't happy, either. 'This will never be our home,' she told Edeard sadly after their first week. Thorpe-By-Water's residents didn't exactly shun the refugees from Ashwell, but they weren't made welcome. Rulan province now lived in fear of the bandits. If they could strike Ashwell, which was three days' ride from the edge of the wilderness, they could strike anywhere in the province. Life had changed irrevocably. There were patrols out in the farmlands and forests constantly now; and craftsmen were having to leave aside all non-urgent tasks to strengthen village walls. Everyone in the Rulan province was going to be poorer this winter.

Edeard walked into the market square to the same averted glances he'd been getting every day for the last three weeks. With its stalls and cobbled floor it was remarkably similar to the one in Ashwell. Larger, of course, Thorpe-By-Water was a bigger village, built in a fork of the River Gwash, providing it with natural protection along two sides. A canal moat had been dug between the two fast-flowing water courses, with a sturdy drawbridge in the middle, completing the defences. Edeard thought that might make them safer than Ashwell. There really was only one real point of entry. Unless the bandits used boats. Where would bandits get enough boats from . . .

His farsight was casually aware of Salrana hurrying towards him. They greeted each other in front of one of the many fish stalls. She was dressed in the blue and white novice robe of the Lady, one which was slightly baggy this time.

'Almost like before,' Edeard said, looking her up and down. He was quietly aware of the glances she was drawing from the other young men in the market.

She wriggled inside it, pulling at the long flared sleeves. 'I'd forgotten how prickly this fabric is when it's new,' she said. 'I only ever had one new one before at Ashwell, for my initiation ceremony; the rest were all second-hand. But the Mother here has had five made for me.' She gave his clothes an assessment. 'Still not found a weaver?'

Edeard rubbed at his ancient shirt with its strange mis-coloured patches. His trousers were too short as well, and the boots were so old the leather was cracked along the top. 'You need money for a weaver to make a shirt. Apprentices are clothed by their Guild. And apprentices without status get the pick of everything the others don't want.'

'He still hasn't confirmed your journeyman status?'

'No. It's all politics. His own journeymen are totally inept, and that's mostly thanks to his poor training. They lose at least six out of every ten eggs. That's just pitiful. Even Akeem's apprentices didn't lose that many. They're also five years older than me, so putting me on their level would be an admission of how rubbish he actually is. I didn't appreciate what I'd got with Akeem.' He fell silent at the painful memory. They should have made time to recover the bodies, to give their village a proper funeral blessed by the Lady.

'You knew,' she said supportively.

'Yes. Thanks.' They wandered through the market, Edeard looking enviously at the various clothes on display. As an apprentice he wasn't allowed to trade any eggs he sculpted, they all belonged to the Guild. Akeem had been decently flexible about it, believing in a quiet rewards system. But now Edeard found himself with no money, no friends, and no respect. It was like being ten years old again.

'One of the patrols came in last night,' Salrana said as they walked. 'The Mother was at the meeting of village elders this morning; the patrol leader told them they'd found no sign of bandits, let alone a large group of them. Apparently there's talk about cutting down the patrols.'

'Idiots,' Edeard grunted. 'What were they expecting to find? We told them the bandits can conceal themselves.'

'I know.' Her expression turned awkward. 'Our word doesn't count for much.'

'What do they think destroyed Ashwell?'

'Give them some grace, Edeard; their whole world is being turned upside down right now. That's never easy.'

'Whereas we've had a cosy ride.'

'That's not nice.'

'Sorry.' He took a long breath. 'I just hate this: after all we went through, and we get treated as if we're the problem. I really should have kept that gun.' He'd left it at the bottom of the well shaft, not wanting any part of a bandit legacy. The gun was pure evil. Ever since, he'd been trying to draw the fidgety little components he'd sensed inside. Thorpe-By-Water's blacksmith had laughed when he'd taken the sketches to him, telling him no such thing could be made. Now people were becoming sceptical about the whole repeat-shooting-gun story.

'You did the right thing,' she said. 'How awful would life be if everyone had a weapon like that.'

'It's pretty awful that the bandits have it and we don't,' he snapped at her. 'What's to stop them sweeping through the whole province? Then further? How about the entire region?'

'That won't happen.'

'No, it won't, because the governor will raise an army. Thankfully, there are more of us than them, so we can win no matter how terrible their weapons are. But that will mean bloodshed on a scale we've never known.' He wanted to beat his fists against the nearest stall. 'How did they get that gun? Do you think they found one of the ships we came in?'

'Maybe they never left the ship they came in,' she said in a small voice.

'Perhaps. I don't know. Why will no one listen to us?'

'Because we're children.'

He turned to snarl at her, then saw the deep worry in her thoughts, her tired face dabbed with greenish ointment. She was so lovely. Somehow he knew Akeem would approve him risking everything to save her. 'I'm sorry. I don't know why I'm taking it out on you.'

'Because I'm the only one who listens,' she told him.

'Lady, it's worse here than at Ashwell in some ways. The elders are so . . . backward. They must inbreed like dogs.'

Salrana grinned. 'Keep your voice down,' she scolded.

'Okay,' he grinned back. 'Not much longer now, I hope.'

People were gathering along the side of the market square to watch the caravan arrive. Edeard counted thirty-two wagons rolling along the road and over the drawbridge. Most had terrestrial beasts tethered to them; horses, donkeys, oxen, cows; some had pens carrying huge pigs. Ge-wolves padded alongside. There were more outriders with pistols than Edeard remembered from before. The wagons were as large and impressive as he recalled, with their metal-rimmed wheels as tall as him. Most of them were covered by curving canopies of dark oiled cloth, though several were clad in tarred wood almost like tiny mobile cottages. Entire families sat on the driver's bench, waving and smiling as they wound their way into the market. Every summer the caravans would tour the district, trading animals, seeds, eggs, tools, food, drink, and fancy cloth from Makkathran itself. They didn't always visit Ashwell, but Edeard could remember the excitement when they did.

Even before the wagons had stopped, villagers were

shouting up at the travelling families, asking what they'd brought. It was a good-natured crowd who had little time for the Mayor's welcoming speech to the caravan leader. Trading was already underway before the formalities were over. Samples of wine and beer were handed down, mostly to apprentices. Edeard chewed on some dried beef that had been flavoured with a spice he'd never tasted before. Salrana picked daintily at trays of fruit and pickled vegetables though she was less restrained when it came to exotic chocolates.

As the evening sky began to darken, Edeard was in considerably better spirits. A lot of the villagers were making for home and supper before returning for the night's traditional festivities. He and Salrana made their way to the lead wagon. The last remaining villagers were leaving, studiously ignoring the Ashwell pair as they did so.

Barkus, the caravan Master, was also as Edeard remembered. A man several decades into his second century, but still hale. He had the largest sideburns Edeard had ever seen, white whiskers bristling round the curve of his jawbone, framing ruddy cheeks. His barrel torso was clad in a red silk shirt and an extravagant blue and gold waistcoat. 'And what can I do for you two?' he chortled as Edeard and Salrana edged in close to his wagon; his large family glanced at them and kept about their work, extending the awning on a frame of martoz wood to form an extensive tent. 'I think we've run out of beer samples.' He winked at Edeard.

'I want to come with you to Makkathran, we both do.'

Barkus let out a booming laugh. Two of his sons sniggered as they pushed the awning pegs into the hard ground. 'Very romantic, I'm sure. I admire your pluck, young sir, and you my Lady's lady. But sadly we have no room for passengers. Now I'm sure that if the two of you are to be ah ... how shall we say, *blessed* by an addition, your parents won't be as fearsome as you expect. Trust me. Go home and tell them what's happened.'

Salrana drew her shoulders back. 'I am not pregnant. I take my vows of devotion very seriously.'

Which blatant lie almost deflated Edeard's indignation. 'I am Edeard and this is Salrana; we're the survivors from Ashwell.' He was very aware of the silence his statement caused. Barkus's family were all looking at them. Several strands of farsight emanating from the other side of the wagon swept across them. 'I believe you knew my Master, Akeem.'

Barkus nodded sagely. 'You'd best come inside. And the rest of you, get back to work.'

The wagon was one of those boasting a wooden cabin. The inside was fitted with beautiful ancient golden wood, intricately carved with a quality which would have eluded Geepalt and his apprentices. Every section of the walls and ceiling were made of doors which came in sizes from some no bigger than Edeard's fist to those taller than he. Barkus opened a pair of horizontal ones, and they folded down into long cushioned benches. Two of the small doors along the apex slid aside to expose misty glass panels. Barkus struck a match and pushed it through a small hole at the end of the glass, lighting a wick. The familiar cosy glow of a jamolar oil flame filled the cabin.

Edeard smiled round, very impressed.

'I remember your Master with great fondness,' Barkus said, waving them on to the bench opposite himself. 'He travelled out here with us a long time ago. I was barely your age at the time. Your Mother, too, novice Salrana, always showed us kindness. Both will be missed and mourned. It was a terrible thing.'

'Thank you,' Edeard said. 'I don't wish to impose, but neither of us can stay in Thorpe-By-Water. We're not very welcome, and in any case it's too close to Ashwell.'

'I understand. The whole province is shaken by what happened, though I've heard a great many different versions already. Including, I have to say, a couple which cast you in a less than favourable light, young man. I held my tongue at the telling of such tales because I remember you from our last visit, four summers ago. I also remember what Akeem said about you. He was impressed with your talent, and old Akeem was not easily swayed, especially by one so young.'

'Edeard risked his life to save me,' Salrana said.

'That also I have heard.'

'Before that night, Akeem said he wanted me to go to Makkathran to study at the Blue Tower of my Guild. I would – no, I *will*, see his wish come true.'

Barkus smiled softly. 'A worthy goal, young man.'

'We will work our passage,' Edeard said forcefully. 'I will not freeload.'

'Nor I,' said Salrana.

'I would expect nothing less,' Barkus said. He seemed troubled. 'However, it is a long way, we will not reach Makkathran until next spring, and that is if all goes well. Many caravans have already cut short their regular journey to leave this province. The stories of Ashwell's fate are many, but they have unnerved all of us. As I remember, Akeem said you have a strong third hand?'

'That's true. But my talent is in sculpting. There are

many wild defaults in the woods and hills of this province. By the time winter falls I can sculpt you a pack of ge-wolves that no bandit gang will ever get past no matter how strong their concealment. I can sculpt them with a stronger sense of smell than any you've used hitherto. I can also sculpt eagles which will circle for miles on every side of the convoy searching out the slightest hint of treachery or ambush.'

'I'm sure you can.' Even now Barkus was unsure.

'I can also teach you and your families this,' Edeard said. He wove his concealment around himself. Barkus gasped, leaning forward blinking. Edeard felt the caravan Master's farsight whipping back and forth across the cabin. He quietly got up and sat next to the startled Barkus, then withdrew his concealment. 'How could the bandits attack you if they can't see you?'

'Dear Lady!' Barkus grunted. 'I never knew such a thing . . .'

'Akeem gifted this to me.'

Barkus regained his composure quickly. 'Did he now. Akeem was right about you, and so I think are half the tales. Very well my dear youngsters, I will accept you both as family tyros. You will come with us as far as Makka-thran. And you will indeed work your passage. Let's see if you think such nobility is worthwhile when we reach the Ulfsen Mountains. However, Edeard, this arrangement is conditional on you not teaching anyone your concealment trick, do you concur?'

'I do, sir. I don't understand why, though.'

'You haven't taught it to anyone in Thorpe-By-Water, have you?'

'No, sir.'

'That's a good political instinct you have there, my boy. Let's just keep it that way, shall we. There's enough trouble infecting our poor old world as it is without everyone sneaking around unseen. Though if you can find a way for farsight to uncover such trickery, I'd be grateful if you would inform me at once.'

'Yes, sir.'

'Good lad. We leave with the dawn light in three days' time. If you're not here that morning, we still leave. Though I don't suppose your Master will object to your exodus.'

'I don't believe he will, sir.'

'Makkathran!' Edeard said as they hurried away from the wagon. Now Barkus had said he'd take them, all his earlier worries and doubts had dried up. He'd thought that he was running away, that he was being a coward for putting all the provinces between himself and the bandits, for allowing them to deal with the problem and endure their blood being spilt to safeguard the land while he lived a safe comfortable life in the city. But now they were going and that was that. 'Imagine it.'

'I can't believe it.' Salrana's smile was wide and carefree. 'Do you think it will be as wonderful as the stories we've heard?'

'If it is only a tenth as fabulous as they say, it will be beyond anything I have dreamed.'

'And we'll be safe,' she sighed.

'Yes.' He put his arm round her shoulder. In a brotherly fashion! 'We'll be safe. And what splendid lives we'll live in the capital of the world.'

4

The glitch had been surprisingly easy to find. But then Troblum supposed Emily Alm didn't have a lot of time to insert it, nor would she suspect he'd come looking, at least not right away. She'd made several modifications to the blueprint; in itself each one was relatively innocuous which made them even harder to spot, but the cumulative effect was enough to throw the binding effect out of kilter. It was less than an hour's work for him to remove them. Then he restarted the production process.

With that underway, his u-shadow established a secure one-time link back to his apartment. Now he knew that Marius was trying to manipulate him, and would go to any lengths to achieve what he wanted, Troblum knew he needed an escape route. There was only one which would put him beyond even the representative's reach: the colonies. After the Starflyer War each of the old Dynasties had been left with a fleet of redundant lifeboats, starships capable of evacuating the entire senior strata of each Dynasty to the other side of the galaxy where they would have been safe had the Prime alien won. Given the phenomenal amount of money poured into their construction, the Dynasty leaders were never going to scrap them simply because the Commonwealth was victorious. Instead, the lifeboats set off to found new worlds and cultures completely independent of the Commonwealth. Over forty ships had launched, though even that figure was ambiguous; the Dynasty leaders were reluctant to admit how much money they'd poured into their own salvation at the expense of everyone else. In the following centuries, more colony ships had set forth. No longer exclusive to Dynasties, they had carried an even broader selection of beliefs, families and ideologies seeking to break free to a degree which even the External Worlds could never offer. The last major departure had been in AD 3000, when Nigel Sheldon himself led a fleet of ten starships, the largest craft ever built, to set up a 'new human experience' elsewhere. It was strongly rumoured at the time that the ships had a transgalactic flight range.

With the ultra-secure link established to his apartment, Troblum used a similarly guarded connection for his u-shadow to trawl the unisphere for the possible destinations of the colony ships within this galaxy. There were over a hundred departures listed, and subsequently thousands of articles presented on each of them. A lot of those articles speculated on why not one colony had got back in touch, even if it was only for a 'so there' message. Certainly there were no records of any Navy starships stumbling across a human world anywhere else in the galaxy, not that they'd ever explored a fraction of a per cent of the available H-congruous stars. Of course, it was the core of Living Dream dogma that most, if not all, such voyages had wound up inside the Void. However, a lot of genuine academic work had gone into estimating probable locations, despite the best efforts of the dwindling Dynasties to suppress such work. Even assuming the studies were correct, the areas that needed to be searched were vast, measuring hundreds of lightyears across. But *Mellanie's Redemption* was a fine ship, she should be able to make the trip out to the Drasix cluster, fifty thousand lightyears away, where the Brandt Dynasty ships were said to have flown.

Troblum knew he wouldn't miss the Commonwealth, there was nobody he had any attachment to, and most of the colony worlds would have a decent level of civilization. If he did find the Brandt world, they would presumably be glad to accept his knowledge of biononics which had been developed long after their ships had departed. That just left the problem of what to do with his Starflyer War artefacts. He couldn't bear to be parted from them, yet if he transported them to the hangar, Marius might notice. He began instructing the apartment net on shipping arrangements, then made a painful call to Stubsy Florac.

The Neumann cybernetics took thirty-two hours to produce a planet-shifting ftl engine. Troblum stood underneath the sparkling cylinder as the terminal extruder finished, marvelling at its elegance. His field functions reported a dense knot of energies and hyperstressed matter all in perfect balance. So much exotic activity was present it almost qualified as a singularity in its own right.

If the colony doesn't want biononics, they'll surely want this.

He watched in perfect contentment as force fields manoeuvred the cylinder into *Mellanie's Redemption*. The modified forward cargo hold closed, and Troblum sent the device into standby mode. Nobody would be able to break the command authority encryption, not even ANA he suspected. The device was his and his alone.

Once it was safe and shielded he went back into the office and restored Emily Alm's glitches to the blueprint, then began adding some of his own, at a much deeper function level. Now the engine really was unique.

Marius called several hours later. 'Have you finished your analysis yet?'

'Just about. I think I'm going to have to initiate a complete redesign of the exotic stress channels.'

'That sounds bad and I don't even know what you're talking about.'

'It's not good, no.'

'I'm sure our funds will cover it. But for now I need a small favour.'

'Yes?'

'I want you to take a colleague to our station.'

'A passenger?' Troblum asked in alarm. If there was someone else on board, he would never be able to fly free. With a growing sense of dismay he realized that was probably the whole idea. Had Marius detected something? He would have sworn nothing could get through his encryption, but then ultimately he was dealing with an ANA Faction.

'Problem? Your ship can accommodate more than one person, and it's a relatively short flight. We're still inside the Commonwealth, after all.'

There was a definite implication in that. 'Not a problem. I'll need to flight prep.'

'That shouldn't take more than an hour. Bon voyage.'

There had been no polite enquiry as to whether he was

ready, in fact it was more like an order. Annoyance warred with a slight curiosity. *What do they need me for so urgently?*

'Troblum?'

'Wha—?' Troblum twisted round as fast as his bulk would allow. There was a man standing in the office, a very tall man whose skeletal skull was frizzed by a stubble of ginger hair. He wore a simple grey suit that emphasized exceptionally long limbs. 'Who the fuck are you?' Troblum's biononics had instantly cloaked him in a defensive force field, now his own weapons enrichment was active and targeting the intruder.

'I'm Lucken. I believe you're expecting me?'

'You're . . .'

'Your passenger, yes. Is the ship ready?'

'How did you get in?'

Lucken's face remained completely impassive. 'Do you require assistance to prepare for flight?'

'Ah, no.'

'Then please begin.'

Troblum adjusted the front of his old toga suit in angry reaction to the arrogant imposition. 'The umbilicals are already attached. We'll leave as soon as the tanks are full. Do you want to go to your cabin?'

'Are you embarking now?'

'No. I have important work here to complete.'

'I will wait. I will accompany you on board.'

'As you wish.' Troblum settled back in his chair, and reactivated the solido projectors. Just to show how indifferent he was.

Lucken didn't move. His eyes never left Troblum.

It was going to be a long flight.

*

The station was a real flight into nostalgia. It had been fifty years since Troblum saw it last, and he never thought he'd be back – in fact he was rather surprised it was still intact. *Mellanie's Redemption* took three days to fly from Arevalo to the unnamed red dwarf star. There were no planets, solid or gas, orbiting the weak speck of ruddy light, just a large disc of mushy hydrocarbon asteroids. There were less now than there had been when he first came to work here. He smiled when he remembered that test sequence. It was the last time he'd been genuinely drunk, and hadn't cared what a fool he was making of himself.

Mellanie's Redemption dropped out of hyperspace ten AUs away from the star and eight thousand kilometres directly above their destination. Troblum accelerated in at seven gees, heading straight for the centre of the dark torroid that measured five kilometres in diameter. A squadron of defence cruisers shed their stealth effect and soared around the starship in fast tight turns. They were over a hundred metres long, like quicksilver droplets frozen in mid-distortion to produce bodies of warped ripples sprouting odd pseudopod crowns. Their flight was so elegant and smooth they resembled a shoal of aquatic creatures cavorting with a newcomer. However, there was nothing playful about the quantum-level probes directed at the *Mellanie's Redemption*. Troblum held his breath as he waited to see if the sophisticated shielding around the forward hold would deflect the scan. It did, but then he'd helped design the cruisers – seventy years ago now. He found it interesting that nothing new had been produced in the intervening decades. Human technology was edging ever closer to its plateau. Emily Alm was probably right about her time in the Navy; given their knowledge base there was nothing new in the universe, just innovative variants on that which already existed.

The cruisers escorted them into the station. *Mellanie's Redemption* fell below the rim of the torroid, and slid along the broad internal tube, which was almost as long as its diameter. Observing the structure through the starship's modest sensor net Troblum could see that vast sections had been reactivated. The titanium-black fuselage was covered in long slender spikes as if a sharp frost had settled across the whole station. The majority of spikes were translucent blue-white; though in among them, seemingly at random, several of the smaller ones were glowing with a low crimson light, as if they'd caged a few of the photons from the nearby sun.

Troblum piloted *Mellanie's Redemption* to the base of a red spike which measured nearly seven hundred metres long. A hangar door was open and waiting for them. When it closed, he couldn't help but think of the door to an antique jail cell slamming shut.

'Thank you for flying Troblum Lines, and have a pleasant day,' he said cheerily.

Lucken opened the airlock and went outside. The man hadn't spoken a single word since they'd embarked. Hadn't slept, either, just sat in the central cabin the whole time. He'd vanished by the time Troblum activated a small case and pulled his emerald cloak on. *Mellanie's Redemption* looked small and inadequate inside the giant shiny-white cavity. White tubes had wormed out of the floor to plug into her umbilical sockets. There was no sign of the external door or indeed a way into the station. As Troblum walked along the curving floor, gravity shifted to accommodate him so he was always standing vertical. The whole effect was quite disorientating on a visual level.

A woman was waiting for him under the starship's nose. She was his height, completely hairless, with large perfectly round eyes that dominated her flat face. Her neck was long, over twenty centimetres, but invisible behind a sheath of slim gold rings, as if it was some kind of segmented metallic limb. All of her skin had the surface shimmer of a toga suit tuned to steel-grey. Troblum assumed her skin had actually been biononically modified, the effect was so tight around her. A lot of Highers close to download chose to experiment with physiological modifications.

'Greetings,' she said in a pleasant, almost girlish voice. 'I've heard a lot about you.'

'Sadly I can't return the compliment,' he said, reading off the protocol behaviour program showing in his exovision.

'I'm Neskia, I run the station. My predecessor was most favourable in his assessment of your abilities. Our Faction would like to thank you for returning.'

As if I had a choice. 'All very well, but why exactly am I here? Is the swarm malfunctioning?'

'Not at all.' She gestured gracefully, her neck curving in a fluidly serpentine motion to keep her face aligned on him as she started walking. Troblum followed her along the curve, his case hovering just behind his head. Up above them, a circular door irised open. The station's internal nature had certainly changed in seventy years.

'Oh.'

'You sound disappointed,' she said and hesitated by the door.

Troblum wasn't sure if the circle had flipped out of the curve to stand upright or if the local gravity manipulation was even weirder than his ordinary senses told him. He refused to verify with a field scan. Disorientation attempts were really very childish. 'Not disappointed. I assume I'm here to inspect and validate the swarm, just in case the worst case Pilgrimage scenario proves true. There have been a few recent advances which could be used to upgrade.'

'The swarm has dispersed to its deployment point. It has been constantly upgraded. We don't anticipate the Void's expansion to pose any problem.'

'Really? So that's why you kept this station going.'

'Among other things.' She stepped through the door and into a corridor that had the old simple grey-blue layout which Troblum recognized. They hadn't changed everything.

'I've assigned you a suite in sector 7-B-5,' Neskia said. 'You can have it modified to your own tastes, just tell the station smartcore what you want.'

'Thank you. And the reason I'm here?'

'We are building twelve ultradrive engines to power the Pilgrimage fleet. Your experience in the assembly techniques we are using is unmatched.'

Troblum stopped abruptly, his case almost banging into the back of his head. 'Ultradrive?'

'Yes.'

'You mean it's real? I always assumed it was just a rumour.'

'It isn't. You'll be working with a small team, fifty or so experts have been recruited. The Neumann cybernetics that built the swarm will handle the actual fabrication.'

'Fascinating.' His bleak mood at being blackmailed and bullied actually began to lift. 'I'll need to see the theory behind the drive.'

'Of course.' Her huge eyes blinked once. 'We'll brief you as soon as you've settled in.'

'I'm settled right now.'

*

Araminta waited in the flat until Shelly arrived to take full legal possession. She didn't have to do it, Cressida's firm was tackling the sale registration – which meant nothing had gone wrong. But supervising the handover in person added that little professional touch; and in business, reputation was a commodity which couldn't be bought.

She watched from the balcony as Shelly's capsule landed on the designated pad outside, followed by a larger cargo capsule which used the public pad. The flat seemed strangely unattractive now Araminta had moved the dressing furniture out, all carefully chosen pieces that emphasized how spacious and contemporary the property was.

'Is everything all right?' Shelly asked as Araminta opened the door.

'Yes. I just wanted to check you were happy.'

'Oh yes. I can't wait to get in.' Shelly was already walking past her, smiling contentedly at the empty rooms. She was a tall, pretty girl who had her own salon business in the district. Araminta was slightly jealous about that, mainly because Shelly was a year younger than her and obviously successful. *But then, she's never made the Laril mistake.*

Shelly caught sight of the big bouquet of flowers resting on the kitchen worktop. 'Oh, thank you, that's so sweet.'

'My pleasure.' Araminta's u-shadow transferred the flat's activation codes over to Shelly. 'Now if there are any problems, please call me.' She had to flatten herself against the wall as she made her way downstairs. A regrav lifter was hauling a big scarlet and black sofa up to the flat. It wasn't quite what Araminta would have chosen, but ... She shrugged and left the house.

Her old carry capsule flew her across Colwyn City to the Bodant district where it settled on a public parking pad. The morning was a dull one, with grubby-ginger clouds darkening towards rain as the wind blew in from the sea. Araminta climbed out and smiled up at the six-storey apartment block. It was a fairly standard layout, ribbed by white balconies that dripped with colourful vines and flowering creepers. The corners were black glass columns alive with purple and blue refraction stipples that swarmed up and down like rodent climbers. At night the effect was sharp and conspicuous, but under a dank daylight sky it lacked any kind of verve. There was a gold crystal dome on the roof, sheltering a communal pool and spa gym. A wide swathe of elegantly maintained gardens along the front were sitting on top of the private underground garage.

Cressida's sleek purple capsule slipped down out of the low clouds to land beside Araminta. 'Well, darling, what a coup.' The lawyer was wrapped in a furry black and white coat that snuggled cosily round her with every move. She glanced up at the front of the building, eyes narrowing as she saw three balconies piled high with junked fittings. 'I have the access codes and the owner certificates. So let's go up, shall we?'

Araminta had bought the entire fourth floor, with all five apartments. The whole apartment block was undergoing redevelopment, presenting an opportunity she couldn't resist when Ikor, one of the original developers, had pulled out. Cressida walked into the first apartment and rolled her eyes. 'I can't believe you've done this.'

'Why not? It's a perfect opportunity for me.' Araminta grinned at her cousin's dismay and walked over to the balcony doors. The glass curtained wide for her and she stepped out. There was a faint sound of buzzing and drilling as the other developers prepared their floors for occupancy. 'It's ninety years old, it needs a makeover. And look at the view.'

Cressida pushed her sapphire-glossed lips together as she looked out across the Bodant district's park to the Cairns beyond. There was a marina along the embankment directly opposite them, its curving deco buildings radiant white, as if they had just been forged in some fusion furnace. 'You got the wrong side of the park, darling. Over there is where the action and the smart money is. Besides, here you're only a few streets from the Helie district. Really!'

'Stop being such a grump. I've proved I can do this, and you know it.'

'I also know how much you paid for these hovels. Honestly darling, a hundred K each. Were you kidnapped and held for ransom?'

'They have three bedrooms each. They need a lot less work than the flat. The two largest have this view. And I cleared a forty K profit on the flat.'

'I still can't believe the bank gave you the money for this.'

'Standard commercial loan. They liked my business model,' Araminta said proudly.

'And Ozzie's coming back to save us all. Go on, you can tell me. You slept with the entire staff of the local office, didn't you?'

'It's very simple economics.'

'Ha! That just proves you don't know what you're talking about. Economics is never simple.'

'I renovate one of them – this one probably – as the show apartment, and sell the rest off-plan based on people seeing the quality of the finish. The deposits will pay off the mortgage while I refurbish them.'

'This is the best one? Oh help me.'

'Yes, this one. And Helie is an up-and-coming area. Don't be so negative. It's annoying.' Her tone was more prickly than she'd intended.

Cressida was instantly apologetic. 'I'm sorry, darling. But my life is without risk now. Honestly, I admire you for taking this gamble. But you have to admit, it is a gamble.'

'Of course it's a gamble. You never get anywhere in life without taking a gamble.'

'Well well, whatever happened to the little farmgirl from Langham?'

'She died. Nobody came to the funeral.'

A perfectly shaped eyebrow rose in surprise. 'What have I unleashed on the world?'

'I thought you'd be happy to see me move forward like this.'

'I am. Are you going to do all the work yourself, again?'

'Most of it, yes. I've got some new bots, and I know where to go for all my supplies and fittings now. This is going to be a prestige development, you'll see, all the apartments will fetch a premium.'

'I'm sure they will. Did you know most of the hotels in town are fully booked?'

'Is that relevant?'

Cressida wiped the balcony rail with a hand then leant on it. 'There's a lot of Living Dream devotees flooding in. Rumour in the gaiafield is that the Second Dreamer is on Viotia.'

'Really, I didn't know that, but then I haven't accessed a news show in weeks. I'm a working gal these days.'

'Keep it quiet, but the government is worried about the pressure that's going to be put on housing, among other things – like public order.'

'Oh, come on!'

'Seriously. We've had over two million of the faithful arrive in the last seven weeks. Do you know how many have left again?'

'No.'

'None. And if they all apply for residency, that's going to shift the political demographic.'

'So we're receiving immigrants again. That's how planets develop. There's going to be a big demand for housing. I come out a winner.'

'All I'm saying is that in times of civil disturbance property values take a dive.'

'It's that serious?' Araminta asked in sudden alarm; after all, Cressida was very well connected.

'You know there's always been an undercurrent of resentment towards Ellezelin. If the Living Dream numbers keep rising at their current rate, then there could be trouble. Who wants to wind up living in a hierocracy?'

'Yes, but there's the Pilgrimage. That'll call them back

to Ellezelin, won't it? And it's not like they're going to find this stupid Second Dreamer, least of all here. The whole thing's a political stunt by the new Cleric Conservator. Isn't it?'

'Who knows. But I'd respectfully suggest, darling, that you find a sucker who you can offload these apartments on to at very short notice.'

Araminta recalled how keen Ikor had been to sell to her. And it was a good deal, or so it seemed at the time. *Am I the sucker?* 'I suppose it wouldn't harm to look for one,' she said.

Mr Bovey let loose a small chorus of swearing as four of him tried to manoeuvre the old-fashioned stone bath along the hallway and through the bathroom door. It was an awkward angle, and the apartment's rear hallway wasn't particularly wide.

'Can I help?' Araminta sang out from the kitchen where she and three bots were making last-minute changes to the new utility connections ready for the units she'd ordered.

'I'm quite capable, thank you,' quadraphonic voices grunted back.

His hurtful insistence made her giggle. 'Okay.' It was another twenty minutes before one of him walked into the kitchen. He was the Bovey she'd first encountered in his macrostore's bathroom aisle, the one with ebony skin and an ageing body. In his biological late-middle-age he may have been, but he didn't shirk from hard work. His wrinkled forehead was smeared with sweat.

'I made some tea,' she said, gesturing at the kettle with its cluster of ancient cups. 'You look like you need a break.'

'I do, my others are younger.' He smiled in admiration at the steaming cups and the packet of tea cubes. 'You really did make it, too, didn't you?'

'Waiting for my culinary unit to arrive,' she said with a martyred sigh.

'It's in the next load, I promise,' he told her, and picked up a cup. His eyes took in the packets of folded food and the hydrator oven. 'Are you actually living here?'

'Yeah. Not renting saves me a bucket load of money. I mean, what's the point? I've got five apartments, and they're not that bad – the roofs don't leak and the rest is just aesthetics. I can stick it out for a few months.'

'You know I really admire your attitude. There's not many your age would take on a project like this.'

She batted her eyes. 'And what's my age?'

'Honestly? I've no idea. But you come across as a first life.'

'I'll own up to that.'

'Can I offer you an alternative to hydrated food tonight? There's a nice restaurant I know.'

She grinned, her hand curling round her own mug of tea. 'That would be lovely. Oh, I don't like curry!'

'That's okay, some mes don't, either.'

'Your tastes are different?'

'Sure. Taste is all down to biochemistry, which is subtly different in every human body. And, face it, I have quite a variety to chose from.'

'Okay,' she said, and dropped her gaze bashfully. 'I have to ask. I've never been on a date with a multiple before. Do you all come and sit at the table with me?'

'Nah, I think that would be a little full on for you,

wouldn't it? Besides, I have the macrostore to run, deliveries to be made, installation, that kind of thing. My life goes on the whole time.'

'Oh. Yes.' It was a strange notion. Not an objectionable one, though.

'Now if you were another multiple, it might be different.'

'How?'

'We'd book the whole restaurant of romantic tables for two and take over the lot. Yous and mes everywhere having fifty different conversations simultaneously and trying out the entire menu and wine list all at once. It's like speed dating in fast forward.'

She laughed. 'Have you ever done that?'

'Tell you tonight.'

'Right. So which one of you do I get sitting at that romantic table for two?'

'You choose. How many mes and which ones.'

'One, and you'll do just fine.'

Araminta took a great deal of thought and care over what to wear and which cosmetic scales to apply. Dressed exactly to plan two hours early. Took one look at herself in the mirror and chucked the whole image. Fifty minutes later all the cases in her bedroom were hanging open. Every outfit she had bought in the last two months was draped over floor and furniture leaving little space to walk. She'd experimented with four different styles of scale membrane. Her hair had been sparkled then damped. Oiled then fluffed. Bejewelled with red scintillators, blue scintillators, green, blue-white . . .

In the end – with eleven minutes to go – she took an

executive decision: go basic. Mr Bovey wasn't the kind to concern himselfs with surface image.

His capsule landed on the pad outside, and she took a lift down to the lobby. The doors opened to a dusty space piled with junk and newly delivered boxes. It was all illuminated by too-bright temporary lighting.

Mr Bovey was dressed in a simple pale-grey toga suit with minimal surface shimmer. He smiled as the doors opened, and said: 'A lady who is on time, now that's – oh, wow.'

She permitted the smallest nod of approval as he stared. In her mind was an image of his customers left unattended, installations stalled, delivery flights landing at the wrong addresses all over town.

'You look,' he swallowed as he tried to regain equilibrium, 'fantastic. Absolutely amazing.'

'Why thank you.' She held her hands behind her back, and presented the side of her face for a formal greeting kiss like some girly ingénue. It was the right choice then. A black sleeveless dress of plain silky fabric with a wide cleft down the front, barely held together by a couple of slim black emerald chains, making it look as if she was about to burst out. Hair glossed pale auburn, and brushed with just a couple of waves to hang below her shoulders. No scales other than lips slightly darker than her natural pigmentation, and emerald eyelash sparkles on low radiance. Most important was the sly half-smile guaranteed to totally befuddle the male brain – all of them.

Mr Bovey recovered. 'Shall we go?'

'Love to.'

The restaurant he'd booked was Richard's. Small but stylish, occupying two floors of an old white stone house in the Udno district. The owner was also the chef; and as Mr Bovey explained he had a small boat which he took out down the estuary a couple of times each week to catch fish for the specials.

'So do you date other multiples?' she asked once they'd ordered.

'Of course,' he told her. 'Not that there are a lot of us on Viotia yet.'

'What about marriage? Is that only with multiples?'

'I was married once. A multiple called Mrs Rion. It was,' he frowned, as if searching for a memory, 'pleasant.'

'That sounds pretty awful.'

'I'm being unfair to her. We had a good time while it lasted. Sex was great.' His smile was shameless. 'Think on it, thirty of her, thirty of me. All of us at it every night. You singles can't get that close to physical paradise even in an orgy.'

'You don't know how good I am in an orgy.' As soon as she said it she could feel her ears burning. But it was the second time she'd startled him this evening, and they weren't even an hour into the date. *Cressida would be proud of me.*

'Anyway . . .' he said. 'We called time on the marriage after seven years. No hostilities, we're still friends. Thankfully, we didn't merge our businesses as well. Always sign a pre-marriage contract, no matter what you are.'

'Yes. I found that out the hard way.'

'You've been married?'

'Yeah. It was a mistake, but you were right, I'm young. My cousin says mistakes are the only way to learn.'

'Your cousin is right.'

'So are you going to try and convert me tonight?'

'Convert you?'

'Sell the whole multiple idea. I thought you believed multiples are inevitable.'

'I do. But I'm not an evangelical. Some of us are,' he admitted.

'And you date – uh . . .'

'Outside the faith? Of course I do. People are interesting no matter what type they are.'

'Highers seem quite boring. If that sounds bigoted, I should explain my ex is currently migrating inwards.'

'Not a wholly balanced opinion, then.'

Araminta raised a glass. 'Ozzie, I hope not.'

'Going Higher is wrong, it's a technocrat route. We're a humanist solution to immortality and evolution.'

'You still rely on technology, though.'

'It's a very small reliance. A few gaiamotes to homologize our thoughts. It's a simple procedure.'

'Ah hah! You *are* trying to convert me.'

He grinned. 'You're paranoid.'

'All divorcees are. So are any of you female?'

'No. Some multiples are multisexual, but that's not for me. Too much like masturbation I'd imagine.'

'I've just thought of something, and you have to answer because it's not fair.'

'What's not fair?'

'Well, you can see that I'm not with anyone else this evening—'

'Ah,' his smile turned devious. 'So in among all the hard work the rest of mes are doing back at the macrostore, is there another of me in a different restaurant chatting to another woman? Right?'

'Yeah,' she admitted.

'Why would it have to be a different restaurant?' he gestured round extravagantly. 'Be honest, how could you tell if one of them is me?'

The idea made her draw a breath and glance round.

Mr Bovey was laughing. 'But I'm not,' he assured her. 'All I'm interested in tonight is you and you alone.' His gaze dropped to the front of her dress. 'How could I not be?'

'That's,' she took another drink of the wine, 'very flattering, thank you.'

Which got the evening back on more or less standard lines.

The mighty creatures fly free amid glorious coloured streamers which glow strongly against the infinite dark of the outer reaches. They loop round the great scarlet promontories which extend for lightyears, curving and swooping above the mottled webbing of faint cold gas. As they fly, the notions of what was brush against their bodies to tingle their minds as if they are travelling through the memories of another entity. Such a notion is not far from the truth, especially this close to the nucleus of their universe.

This one she tenants turns lazily along its major axis, aware of its kindred surrounding it. The flock is spread across millions of kilometres. Over a planetary diameter away, another of its own is also rolling, mountain-sized elongated body throwing its vacuum wings wide, tenuous tissues of molecules as large as atmospheric clouds that shimmer delicately in the thin starlight. Somewhere out across the vast gulf it is aware of the whispers of thought arising once more from a solid world. Once more there are individual minds growing strong again, becoming attuned to the fabric of this universe. As it basks in the gentle radiance pouring out of the nebula, it wonders when the minds will have the strength to truly affect reality. Such a time, it agrees with its kindred, is sure to come. Then the flock will depart the great nebula to search out the new-comers, and carry their completed lives back to the nucleus, where all life eventually culminates.

It was a pleasurable notion which made Araminta sigh contentedly even though the creature was slipping away into the darkness where it dwelled. Misty starlight gave way to a row of flickering candles. The gossamer breath of nebula dust firmed up into strong fingers sliding along her legs; more hands began to stroke her belly, then another pair squeezed her breasts. Sweet oil was massaged into her skin with wicked insistence. Tongues licked with intimate sensuality.

'Time to wake up,' a voice murmured.

On the other side of her another voice encouraged, 'Time to indulge yourself again.'

Amid a delicious drowsiness Araminta bent herself in the way the hands were urging. She blinked lazily, seeing the Mr Bovey she'd had dinner with standing beside the vast bed. He smiled down. As she grinned back up at him she was impaled from behind. She gasped, startled and excited, seeing a look of rapture cross his face. A further set of hands started to explore her buttocks. She opened her mouth to receive the cock of a really young him. Which was extremely bad of her.

She didn't know how many hims she was accommodat-ing this time. She didn't know if it was nearly morning or still the middle of the night. She didn't care. Flesh and pleasure were her here and now, her whole universe.

After the meal at Richard's, his capsule had brought them back to his place, a large house set above the city's south bank with lawns that reached down to the river. It wasn't even midnight. Several hims were in the lounge, a couple were cooking, three were in the swimming pool. More were resting or sleeping upstairs, he told her.

It was like holding court. Her sitting on a broad leather sofa, hims on either side, and more sprawled on cushions at her feet as they chatted away. She took a long time to fight down her instinct that they were all separate people. He enjoyed teasing her, switching speaker mid-sentence, even arguing among himself. But the simultaneous laughter his bodies came out with was endearing. It was a wonderfully languid seduction.

Then the one she'd gone to dinner with leaned over and kissed her. By then the wine and the anticipation were making her heart pound and her skin burn.

'You choose,' he murmured silkily.

'Choose?'

'How many, and which ones.'

She'd glanced round, and seen identical expressions of delight and eagerness on each of him. For that long moment every one of him was completely indistinguishable; he could have been clones. That was when she accepted on a subconscious level that he truly was one.

'You, of course,' she told her dinner companion. 'You did all the hard work getting me back here, after all.' Then she pointed. 'You.' The handsome one. 'You.' Young and very well muscled – she'd seen that when he climbed out of the pool.

The chosen three led her upstairs. Araminta thought that was daring enough, but the night swiftly evolved into a strenuous sexual adventure as Mr Bovey began teaching her acts that could only be performed as a group. 'Trust me,' one of him said as he opened an aerosol in her face. 'It's a booster. It'll amplify your pleasure, sort of even things up between you and mes.' Araminta breathed it down. It was potent.

They gathered round, strong hands supporting her in different positions. She was made to climax with each of him in turn, with the booster increasing the sensation each time as it gradually saturated her bloodstream. After the third one she flopped back on the mattress in a lovely warm fugue. That was when she saw more hims had arrived to wait silent and naked around the bed. She didn't protest as they stared down excitedly. 'Yes,' she told them. In unison the fresh bodies closed in.

More than once that night Araminta swooned from a combination of exhaustion and aerosol-fuelled ecstasy. Each time he allowed her a small rest before rousing her again. Those were the occasions when she dreamed her strange dream.

She didn't wake up until mid-morning. When she did, the details of the night had merged together into a single strand of relentless animal behaviour. She'd surprised herself by yielding to everything he'd demanded from her.

The dinner-date Bovey was lying on the bed beside her. He was the only one left in the bedroom. 'Good morning,' he said with soft politeness.

'Yeah,' Araminta said. She still felt hopelessly tired, as well as unpleasantly sore. The aerosol had worn off, leaving her skin cool and slightly clammy.

'You look beautiful when you're sleeping, did you know that?'

'I . . . No one has told me that before.'

'How do you feel?'

'Uh, okay I suppose.'

'All right,' he said in an understanding tone, and stroked some dishevelled hair from her face. 'Let me put it this way; would you like another night like that?'

'Yes,' she whispered, and knew she was blushing. Despite the frequent outrages he'd committed it had been absolutely the best sex she'd ever had. Exactly the kind of multiple-partner athleticism Cressida always boasted about and she'd been too timid to try. But last night it had technically only been one man; this way she got the thrill without the emotional guilt – almost.

'I hoped you would. Not every single can cope with me like that. You're very special, Araminta.'

'I . . .' She hesitated, unsure how much to confide. *Which is stupid.* 'It was like I was becoming part of you. Is that silly?'

'No. With an experience that acute there's always a merger through the gaiafield with anyone nearby, though you mostly remained closed to me. Was that by choice?'

'I don't have gaiamotes.'

He gave her a curious look. 'Interesting. I was sure . . . nah, skip it. The house is running a bath for you.'

'Thank you. So where do we go from here?'

'There's a play on at the Broadway Empire, some kind of comedy, with real actors. I've booked for tonight.'

Which wasn't quite what she wanted qualifying. 'Lovely. And after?'

'I would like you to come back here, back to this bed. I'd really like that.'

Araminta nodded demurely. 'I will.' She didn't think it

could ever be as exciting as last night had been. First times were always special, but if hes were just as randy tonight it would still be the hottest sex in town. She eased herself off the bed, drawing a sharp breath as she straightened up. 'Um, how many bodies have you got?'

It was his turn to seem reticent. 'Over thirty.'

'How many . . . last night?'

'Six,' he said with a very male grin of satisfaction.

'Ozzie!' *That's it, I'm now officially a complete trollop. Can't wait to see Cressida's face when I tell her that. Six! She'll be as jealous as hell.*

'What do you want for breakfast?' he asked as she opened the door to the en-suite bathroom.

'Orange juice, Bathsamie coffee strong, croissants with strawberry and hijune jam.'

'It'll be ready when you are.'

*

The regrav capsule sped low over the scrub desert. Dead and desiccated bushes virtually the same colour as the crumbling jaundiced mud from which they'd grown merged to a speckled blur as Aaron looked down through the transparent fuselage. Their jumbled smear confused his visual perspective, making it difficult to tell if their altitude was one metre or a thousand. He often found himself searching for the capsule's jet-black shadow slithering fast across the low undulations to provide a clue.

A couple of minutes before they reached the ranch, he saw a fence; posts of bleached wood sticking up in a section of desert which appeared no different to the rest of the wretched expanse. Rusty spikewire sagged between them. More fences flashed past underneath as they drew closer.

The fields they marked out were smaller, closer together. Eventually the clutter of buildings which comprised the ranch itself were visible, nestling at the centre of a vast web of spikewire.

'What does he raise out here?' Corrie-Lyn asked.

'Korrimues,' Aaron said.

'I can't see anything moving.'

'Wrong season, I think.'

She gave the vast desert a disapproving look. 'There are seasons out here?'

'Oh yes. It rains every ten years.'

'Gosh, how do the ranchers stand the excitement?'

The capsule began to circle the ranch. He counted eight large outlying barn sheds, all built from an ancient ginger-coloured composite, while the house in the middle was a white stone structure surrounded by a big emerald garden. An outdoor swimming pool shimmered deep turquoise. Terrestrial horses cantered around a broad paddock.

'Okay, that actually looks rather nice,' Corrie-Lyn said grudgingly.

His field functions reported the capsule was being given a broad-spectrum scan. 'Not quite paradise,' he muttered. His own passive scan was registering some dense power clumps in the ground. They were arranged in an even circle around the perimeter. A defence ring of some kind.

The capsule settled on a designated zone just outside the garden.

'Can you . . .' he started to say to Corrie-Lyn, then saw her disinterested expression. 'Just leave the talking to me, okay?'

'Of course I will. Shall I just stay in here? Or would you

like to gag me? Perhaps you'd prefer me stuffed into a suspension pod?'

'Now there's true tempting,' he told her cheerfully, ignoring the scowl.

Paul Alkoff was leaning on the five-bar gate which led to the paddock, dressed entirely in faded blue denim with a Stetson perched on his head. A tall man who was finally allowing his seven and a half centuries to show. His hair was snow white, worn long at the back but perfectly brushed. His movements were noticeably slow, as if each limb was stiff. With skin that was tanned dark brown his pale-blue eyes seemed to shine out of his thin face. A neatly trimmed goatee added to his palpable air of distinction. Even Aaron recognized he was in the presence of a formidable man; he immediately began to wonder just how much living had been crammed into those seven hundred and fifty years. A great deal, if he was any judge.

'Sir, thank you for agreeing to see me.'

Corrie-Lyn shot him a surprised look at the respectful tone.

Paul gave a small smile then lifted his Stetson an inch off his hair and inclined his head to Corrie-Lyn. 'Ma'am. Welcome.'

'Um, hello,' a thoroughly confused Corrie-Lyn managed.

'Don't normally allow your kind in my home,' Paul said directly to Aaron. 'So you'll understand if I don't ask you in and break bread with you.'

'My biononics are for combat, I'm not Higher.'

'Uh huh. Don't suppose it makes no difference these days, son. That battle was fought a long time ago.'

'Did you win?'

'Planet's still human, so I guess we did some good back then.'

'So you are Protectorate?'

'My old partners asked me to let you land. When I enquired, I heard they got leaned on by people high up in the movement, people we haven't heard from in a long time. You made that happen, son, so I'd appreciate it if you don't go all coy with me now.'

'Of course not.'

'What do you want?'

'Information.'

'Figured as much.' He turned and rested his elbows on the top of the gate. 'You see Georgia out there? She's the one with the dappled mane.'

Aaron and Corrie-Lyn walked over to the gate. 'Yes, sir,' Aaron said.

'Frisky little thing, ain't she? I can trace her blood-line right back to Arabians on Earth from the mid-nineteenth century. She's as pure as they come. Not an artificial sequence in her whole genome; conceived naturally and born from her mother's belly just as every one of her ancestors have been. To me, that is a thing of beauty. Sublime beauty. I do not wish to see that spoiled. No indeed, I don't want to see her foals *improved*. She and her kind have the right to exist in this universe just as she was intended to by the planet that created her.'

Aaron watched the horse as she cantered around, tossing her mane. 'I can understand that.'

'Can you now? And my hat.'

'Sir?'

Paul took his Stetson off, and examined it before returning it to his head. 'This is the real McCoy, I'll have you know. One of the very last to come out of Texas, over two hundred and fifty years ago in a factory that's manufactured them for damn near a millennia, before ANA finally shut down what it regarded as an inconsequential irrelevance. The once-humans who live on that poor ole world these days don't even make them as a hobby any more. I bought a whole batch and keep them in stasis so every time I wear one out I'll have another, a fresh one. I have only two left now. That's a crying shame. But then I don't expect to be around long enough to use that last one. It'll sit right there on top of my coffin.'

'I'm sorry to hear that, sir.'

'So tell me, son, do you see what I am now?'

'Not quite, no.'

Paul fixed Aaron with a perturbingly intense stare. 'If I can get all hot under the collar about the purity of a hat, just think what I'm like when human heritage is threatened with extinction.'

'Ah.'

'Yes. I'm Protectorate, and proud of it. I've played my part in preventing those obscene perversions from spreading their sanctimonious bullshit supremacy across these glorious stars. Higher isn't like some old-fashioned religion or ideology. With them, fellas who hold two different beliefs can argue and cuss about such notions all night long over a bottle of whisky and laugh it off in the morning like gentlemen. But not Higher culture. I regard it as a physical virus to be exterminated. It will contaminate us and take away choice. If you are born with biononics infecting your cells, your choice is taken away from you. You *will* download your thoughts into ANA. That's it. No option, no alternative. Your essence has been stolen from you before you are born. Humans, true humans, have free will. Highers do not. No indeed.'

'And the life they live between birth and download?' Corrie-Lyn asked.

'Irrelevant. They're the same as pets, or more likely cattle, cosseted and protected by machines until the moment they're ready to submit to their metal god in a final sacrifice.'

'So what's the point in that god creating them?'

'Ultimately, there won't be one. Despite the years, this is early days yet. ANA believes it is our replacement. If it is allowed free rein it will see us extinct.'

'A lot of species continue after their post-physical plateau,' Aaron said. 'For most a singularity is a regeneration event, those that don't go post-physical diversify and spread across new stars.'

'Yes. But no longer what they were.' Paul gazed out at Georgia again. 'Unless she is protected, the universe will never see her like again. That is wrong. It cannot be allowed.'

'The radical Higher movement is almost extinct,' Aaron said. 'There are no more infiltrations. ANA saw to that.'

Paul smiled thinly. 'Yeah, and ain't that an irony. Maybe the Good Lord is having a joke on his metal pretender over morals.'

'I need to ask you about your time as an active Protectorate member.'

'Go right ahead, son. I don't know what you are, but I'm pretty sure what you're not, and that's the police or some version of them.'

'No, sir, I am not.'

'Glad to hear it.'

'I'm here about Inigo.'

'Ah. That was high up on my list. You two looking for him?'

'Did you know he was Higher?'

Paul's reaction startled Aaron. The old man slapped his hand on the gate, and produced a beaming smile. 'Son of a *bitch*! I knew it, I goddamn knew it. Hell, he was a wily one. Do you know how long we watched him?'

'So you suspected?'

'Of course we suspected.'

'That means Erik Horovi was Higher?'

'Erik? Hell no. Poor kid. He was used just like the sisters by that bastard angel.'

'Sisters? Are you talking about Inigo's aunt?'

'You don't know so much after all, do you, son?'

'No, sir. But I do need to learn. It is urgent.'

'Ha. Everything is urgent. The whole universe is in a hurry these days. I know it's that way because I'm older, but damn—'

'Erik,' Aaron prompted gently.

'We'll start with the angel. You know what they are?'

'I've heard of them.'

'The radical Highers wanted to convert entire worlds to their culture. They didn't want to give people a choice about it. Like I said, if you're born with biononics you don't have any options in life, in what you become. So back then these angels would land on a planet and do their dirty work; starting the infection which would spread across the entire population. Now the Protectorate watched the spaceports for anyone with biononics, and kept tabs on them while they were visiting. Still do, so I gather. So the angels would land out in the wilds somewhere. They'd jump offship while it was still in low orbit, and their force fields would protect them through aerobraking.' He gave Aaron a long look. 'Could you do that?'

'Yes, I suppose so. It's just a question of formatting. But back then it would have been cutting edge.'

'Oh the bastards were that, for sure. The force fields were what earned them their name. They were shaped like wings, and brought them down to the world amid a fiery splendour. A lot of them got through unnoticed. This time, though, we got lucky; a sympathizer out fishing saw the thermal trail it left over the ocean and called it in. Me and my team tracked the monster to Kuhmo. But we weren't quick enough. By the time we got there it had hooked up with Erik Horovi and Imelda Viatak, who were dating just like normal kids. Now the thing with angels is they're hermaphroditic, and they're beautiful. I mean really beautiful. This one was exceptional even by their standards, either a pretty boy or a real humdinger of a girl depending on your own gender. It was what you wanted it to be. So it made friends with Erik and Imelda and went to bed with both of them. Erik first. Now that's important. Its organs injected his sperm with biononics. Then it lay with Imelda and impregnated her with Erik's altered sperm.'

'Contraception?' Aaron queried.

'No use. Angels can neutralize it faster than any medic. So the kids find they're having a baby, and the DNA test proves it's theirs no question. Biononics are hellishly difficult to detect in an embryo even today. Back then it was near impossible. So, bang, you've got a changeling in the nest without ever knowing it. Biononics don't come active until puberty, so by then it's too late. Plant enough of them in a population, and a few generations later most of the births are Higher. But we intercepted this little love triangle in time.'

'The college art block,' Corrie-Lyn said.

'Yes, ma'am. You might say the angel put up something of a fight. But we got it. All you really need to defeat bion-onics is a heavier level of firepower. The art block got in the way.'

'What about the baby?'

'We took Erik and Imelda back to our field head-quarters. She was pregnant, about two weeks gone as I recall, and it was infected.'

'I thought you couldn't tell.'

Paul looked straight ahead at the horizon. 'There are ways you can find out. You have to test the cells directly.'

'Oh, Ozzie,' Corrie-Lyn breathed, her face had paled.

'We took it out of her and checked. No kind of embryo can survive that kind of test. Fortunately we were right this time, it was one of them.'

'You're not human, no matter what you claim.'

Aaron gave her a furious look. She started to say something then threw her hands up in disgust and walked away.

'Sorry about that,' Aaron said. 'What happened?'

'Standard procedure in cases when the girl knows she's pregnant, which Imelda did. We can't wipe weeks from their memories, that would be detectable. So we took another ovum from her and fertilized it with Erik's contri-bution, and implanted. Then they both got a memory wipe for the evening they spent with us. Next morning they wake up with a bad hangover, and can't remember what they did. Typical teenage morning after.'

'Did it go wrong, then?'

'No, son, everything worked perfectly. Nine months later they had a lovely little girl. A normal one.'

'So how was Inigo conceived?'

'Imelda had a sister.'

'Sabine.'

'Yes. They were twins. Identical twins.'

'Ah. I think this is starting to make sense.'

'I should have realized. It's every teenage boy's ultimate fantasy; plenty of men, too.'

'He slept with both of them.'

'Yes. Him and the angel. You just confirmed that for me. Finally. Part of the Protectorate's whole clean-up procedure is to review the angel's memories, to find out who it has contaminated. Hacking into its brain is a terrible, terrible thing, one of the greatest abuses of medical technology possible. It takes days to break the protection which biononics provide for the neurones. I used to do it for the team, may God forgive me, but it was necessary. There's no other way of discovering what those devil-spawned monsters have been up to. It's not an exact science, now or then. Minds are not tidy little repositories like a memory kube. I had to merge my mind with its and endure its vile slippery thoughts inside my own skull. When I reviewed its recent memories I actually experienced coupling with Imelda.' He closed his eyes, clearly pained by the fraudulent memory. 'Her face was inches from me. She tasted so . . . sweet. But, now, I don't suppose it was all her. Rather, the memories weren't just of her. I couldn't tell the difference between the girls. Dammit, at the time I didn't know there was a difference I should be searching for.'

'So Inigo was born as part of a radical Higher infiltration plan.'

'Yes. We were shocked when we found out Sabine was pregnant, but that was just before she was due. There were a lot of arguments within my team about what we should do.'

'Snatch the baby and test it.'

'That was one option. The mild one.' Paul looked over at Corrie-Lyn, who was sitting on a low concrete wall outside one of the barns. 'But intervention becomes progressively difficult as time winds away, especially once the child is born. We're not ... There's a difference between abortion and infanticide – to me, anyway. And once it was born it has a legal right of residency. Even if we took it away from the mother and shipped it back to the Central Worlds, they'd just send it right back. Legally, it's a mess. Which is why the Protectorate was formed, to stop the whole nightmare scenario before it gets politically complicated.'

'So what did you do?'

'I never really believed the girls having a kid two weeks apart was coincidence. In the event, we settled for observation. If Inigo was infected he'd give himself away eventually, they all do.'

'But he didn't.'

'No. We monitored him off and on for over twenty-five years. He never put a foot wrong. He was a straight down the line normal human. School. University. Girlfriends. Not exceptionally sporting. Got injured when he played football. Had to get a job. Kept out of local politics. Signed up with a rejuve finance company. When he took aerosols he got high. Took a boring academic position in the state university cosmology department. There was nothing to indicate he had biononics. Right up until you arrived today I'd still have said he most probably didn't. I had come to accept that his birth maybe was coincidence after all. Believe me, son, if we'd confirmed it when he reached legal age we would have made a quiet ultimatum.'

'Leave or die.'

'Yes. There's no other way you can treat them.'

'Then he did leave, didn't he? All the way to Centurion Station.'

'Yes. And what a goddamned pitiful mess that's turned into. Half the aliens in the galaxy want to shoot us out of space. Who can blame them?'

'It's only the Ocisen Empire.'

'You mean they're the only ones who have declared themselves. Don't tell me you think the others are just going to sit back and let us wreck the very stars themselves.'

'Who knows? If I can find him maybe we can put a stop to the whole Pilgrimage.'

'I should have killed him in the womb when I had the chance.'

'Whatever he is, he's not Higher.'

'He might not be polluted with their culture, yet, but it will come to him eventually.'

'Apparently not. He found an alternative to a route you believed was set in stone. His destiny is inside the Void, not with ANA.'

Paul shrugged. 'Whichever one it is, it's not a human destiny.'

'Our destiny is what we decide to make it. Free choice, remember.'

'You're wrong, son. I see you believe in yourself, and I wish you well in that. But you're wrong.'

'Okay, we'll just differ on that one. What happened to Erik?'

'Bodyloss.' Paul caught Aaron's expression. 'Not us, it was a genuine accident. He was working hard to support both girls. A decent lad, I guess. The farmer he was helping out didn't do very good maintenance. The agribot chewed him up something bad. This was maybe six months after the kids were born. His insurance was all paid up, but he'd only just had his memorycell fitted. It's always the same in cases like that. The new body only has a few months of memories, which is never enough to install a decent level of personality. In his re-life state he was very childlike, ironically because his entire childhood was what he lacked. There was no real emotional connection with the sisters and his two children. Not immediately. Imelda worked hard at correcting that. She did well. They went off together. Sabine and little Inigo got left behind. It kicked off a huge family row. The sisters never really spoke after that.'

'Which is why Aunt Imelda got written out of his official history.'

'That's pretty much it. Yes.'

'I've never met a more despicable human,' Corrie-Lyn said as the regrav capsule lifted from the ranch. 'And I include our dear Cleric Conservator in that statement.'

'Did you ever meet a Higher angel?'

'No.'

'Well then.'

'That's it?' she shouted angrily. 'That's your justification?'

'I'm not trying to justify anything. All I'm doing is pointing out that for every action there is an equal and opposite reaction. What he used to do was part of the era.'

'He's a psychopath. Fuck knows how many babies he's killed. He belongs in suspension for the rest of eternity.'

'Dead, you mean.'

'Whatever!' she snapped, and slumped down into the cushioning. Her delicate features set in a furious sulk.

'I told you to leave the talking to me.'

'Shut the fuck up.'

'Well at least he helped us.'

'How?'

'There now you see, if you hadn't gone stomping off in a huff . . .'

'Screw you. I bet you were Protectorate before the memory wipe. It certainly fits.'

'No.'

'You can't be certain, though. And how come you have such highly placed contacts in their filthy organization?'

'I simply know who to ask in such circumstances, that's all. Information does not imply compliance; and I don't know where my data originates from.'

'Pah!' She turned to watch the desert skim past.

Aaron waited a minute for her to relent. When she didn't, he smiled quietly and said, 'Inigo bought a rejuvenation policy.'

'So?' She managed to spit it out with more petulance than a tantrumming five-year-old.

'It was part of his attempt to fit in with a normal existence,' Aaron continued passively. 'No one with biononics needs a rejuvenation treatment, that's strictly for Advancers and normals. Biononics maintain human cells at an optimum state; the body doesn't age biologically after you hit twenty-five. He did it to fool the Protectorate. After all, he knew what his heritage was, which means he knew what they would do to him if he made a slip.'

'And that helps us how?'

'It means he had a secure memory store. It probably dates right up to his assignment to Centurion Station.'

'I'm so sorry, I didn't realize you were deaf. *And that helps us how?*'

'Somewhere on Anagaska there's an electronic version of the young Inigo's personality. Alkoff gave me the name of the company he bought the policy from.'

'That's not going to— Oh dear Ozzie! You have got to be kidding.'

Aaron grinned cheerfully at her. 'About time this planet saw a little excitement.'

*

Prior to the Starflyer War, when the Commonwealth was essentially one society comprising predominantly physical citizens, the government created a very senior committee named the ExoProtectorate Council whose brief was to evaluate the threat level presented by each new alien species as it was discovered. After ANA came on line and took over design, manufacture, and operation of the Commonwealth Navy's warships, threat became something of a non-term. If the old Commonwealth could defeat the Primes, ANA with its near post-physical technology was unlikely to be menaced by anything less than a malevolent post-physical. That wasn't to say that the remaining physical sector of the Commonwealth couldn't encounter a whole load of grief out among the stars. So the ExoProtectorate Council lived on in a modified form inside ANA, operating independently from ANA:Governance.

Its meetings were few and infrequent. Therefore, when Admiral Kazimir called for one, every delegate appeared, suspecting the reason. They met in a neutral perceptual reality in a secure location within ANA, comprising an old-fashioned conference room with rather extravagant white and orange furniture and a panoramic window showing them the Mollavian plains with their wall of hydrogen volcanoes. Sheets of ice-pebble meteorites sleeted downwards, burning crimson contrails with lightning forks rippling in their wake.

Kazimir activated the perceptual reality, and materialized in the seat at the head of the table. Gore flicked in a millisecond later, sitting directly to Kazimir's right. He was followed by Justine. Ilanthe was next to appear, a delicate-looking woman dressed in a blue and grey leotard. Her dark hair had been cropped short and coloured with purple streaks. They didn't represent any kind of enrichments, they were just highlights. It was a style which Kazimir thought he recognized, but couldn't quite place without running a check through his enhanced neural structure. Ilanthe wasn't worth the effort; she was the Accelerator Faction's appointment to the Council, and enjoyed making mischief where she could. The trick with her was not to rise to the bait.

Crispin Goldreich arrived in the seat next to Justine. Over a thousand years ago he'd been a Senator sitting on the original ExoProtectorate Council. It was an appointment he'd maintained ever since. Kazimir and

ANA:Governance allowed him to remain because when it came to advising on the political angle of a crisis there were few better short of a full Governance convocation. Unfortunately, his usefulness was limited by a somewhat xenophobic view of aliens; several members of his family had been lost on Nattavaara during the Starflyer War, which had shaped his opinion ever since. As such he was a strong advocate of both the Isolationist and Internalist Factions.

The last two were Creewan and John Thelwell, who respectively put forward Custodian and Darwinist Faction positions.

'Thank you for attending,' Kazimir said. 'I have implemented this Council because the situation with regards to the Ocisen Empire has entered a new stage. The Navy squadron deployed in the Hancher domain have detected a massive Empire fleet now in flight. Its trajectory is aimed directly at the Commonwealth, specifically the sector containing Ellezelin.'

'How many ships?' Justine asked.

'Two thousand eight hundred and seventeen,' Kazimir replied. 'Of which nine hundred are their Starslayer class, the biggest, most expensive warships they've ever built. The Empire's economy has suffered a significant downturn over the last forty years in order to facilitate their production. They are armed with warheads similar to quantumbusters. They think we don't know about them, but we detected the trials they conducted forty-five years ago.'

'They have quantumbusters?' Crispin asked.

'A variant of, yes,' Kazimir said. 'Such a development was inevitable. They make our atom-bomb-era species look like a bunch of pacifists.'

'And the Navy hasn't bothered to share this with us?'

'The Empire believes their advantage is that we don't know. To make it public knowledge that the Empire possesses a device which the External Worlds would regard as a doomsday weapon would be to give away our advantage, not to mention damaging public confidence.'

'They must be insane,' Creewan muttered. 'The Emperor must realize how we'll react to an assault of that nature. They know how strong we are.'

'Actually, they don't,' Kazimir said. 'Nobody outside ANA:Governance and myself knows the exact capability of the deterrence fleet.'

'Please tell me it is strong enough to deal with the Ocisen Empire.'

'Don't concern yourself on that score. They do not pose any sort of threat.'

'Are they alone?' Gore asked. 'The Ambassador was quite adamant that they'd dug up some decent allies.'

'There were no non-Empire ships in the fleet which launched,' Kazimir said.

'We'll make a politician out of you yet, my boy. So do we know for sure that the Starslayer class are only armed with quantumbusters, or have they found some nasty leftovers from someone who went post-physical?'

'We'd have to intercept a Starslayer and scan it to be certain of the precise contents,' Kazimir said. 'I don't advise that. In Ocisen terms that provocation would be a declaration of war. Plus, we'd tip their hand about how powerful we are.'

'Well what the hell do you advise?' Crispin asked. 'They're going to find out eventually.'

'I'd like to avoid that. What I'd like to see applied to the Ocisens is something along the lines of intense diplomatic persuasion so that they turn the fleet round and go home.'

'Won't happen,' Creewan said. 'If the Empire has launched what is essentially their entire Navy at us, it will be politically impossible for them to return until the Pilgrimage has been halted. Asking them nicely just won't hack it. We'll have to use force.'

'What about another more immediate threat to the Empire?' Justine suggested. 'Some unknown ships approaching from another direction? We could deliver that, surely?'

'Yes,' said Kazimir. 'But it simply postpones the inevitable. We can manufacture what appears to be a threat, but if their fleet returns to challenge an intruder then our bluff will be called. I cannot blow up star systems simply to maintain an illusion. No matter the morality, there is a considerable physical problem with radiation. Our Firewall project showed that.'

'How long until they get here?' Ilanthe asked.

'Their flight-time to Ellezelin is seventy-nine days,' Kazimir said. 'A significant figure, because the Pilgrimage fleet will not be completed by then. It is reasonable to assume their aim is to hit the Pilgrimage ships while they're still on the ground. If the Living Dream were to get its ships into space, they would be a lot harder to intercept, especially for the Empire.'

'Then I don't understand your reluctance to create a diversion. Once the Pilgrimage ships are in space, the Empire fleet is effectively neutralized. You don't have to do anything as dramatic as blow up a star on the other side of the Empire. Launch a thousand drones with a phantom signature, so it appears a hostile fleet is heading to the Empire. Buy us some time for Living Dream.'

'They'd know,' Gore said. 'It's the timing again. They launch their fleet. We have to delay it and oh look, here's an unknown threat coming at them from the other side of space. How about that for coincidence? Even the Ocisens aren't that stupid.'

'Don't count on it,' John Thelwell muttered.

'It would have to be a credible threat to divert them,' Kazimir said.

'So skulk around the Empire's borders and wreck a couple of stars, or at least planets.'

'We employ the word *Empire* too glibly,' Justine said. 'The most literal translation of their planets is, *Worlds upon which we nest.* I'm ashamed this committee is prepared to demonize the Ocisens to justify force. We must concentrate on peaceful solutions.'

Ilanthe gave Gore a small victory smile as he glowered at his daughter.

'If they weren't sending a fleet towards us armed with enough quantumbusters to wipe out every Commonwealth planet I might not refer to them as a bunch of psychopathic fuckheads,' Gore snapped. 'As it is, we are here to advise the Navy on how to respond. You met the Ambassador. Exactly what sort of peaceful overture do you think the *Empire* will respond to?'

'We have to provide them with options,' Justine said. 'Preferably ones which allow them to save face.'

'Like pressuring Living Dream not to launch its ridiculous Pilgrimage,' Creewan said.

'Outside this committee's remit,' Ilanthe said swiftly. 'We advise the Navy on its response.' She didn't even turn to look at Creewan. 'You want to push for something like that, bring it up at a political meeting, or even Governance.'

'It is a valid option,' Justine said.

'Not here it isn't. Here we decide on how many of their suns we turn nova in order to convince them to turn back.'

'Nobody is turning Empire suns nova,' Kazimir said. 'As I said, their fleet does not pose a physical threat to any aspect of the Commonwealth. It can be effectively neutralized.'

'That's quite a big claim,' Ilanthe said. 'You sure about that?'

'Providing they do not possess an excess of stolen post-physical technology, yes.'

'Then do just that, neutralize them. Stop them cold in interstellar space. It's not like they have a back-up fleet to send if anything goes wrong.'

Kazimir glanced round the table. 'Is that the recommendation of this committee?'

'It certainly is not,' Justine said.

'And your plan is . . . ?' Ilanthe enquired archly.

'A warning,' John Thelwell said. 'In all likelihood, several warnings, considering who we're dealing with. Followed by a demonstration of our capability and intent.'

'Would that be several demonstrations?' Justine asked acidly. 'Just to get the point over how big and scary we are.'

'Once they see they cannot stop the Pilgrimage they will turn back.'

'That implies a governing factor of logic and reason,' Crispin said. 'This is the Ocisens we're talking about.

They're committed to stopping us. Even if it meant the death of every starship in their fleet, they'll keep coming.'

'The warships will be disabled, not destroyed,' Kazimir said. 'I could not countenance such a loss of life.'

'Then I don't even see what you convened us for,' Crispin said.

'Because Governance and I don't want to reveal our true capability outside a genuine and serious threat, which this is not.'

'Rock and a hard place,' Gore grunted. 'The only way to deal with them without huge loss of life all round is by using ANA's technology, which in turn makes us frightening to all the physical aliens knocking around this section of the galaxy.'

'This is a morals debate?' Ilanthe mocked.

'It might even get the Raiel worried about us,' Justine said.

'Gets my vote,' Gore said. 'Supercilious little turds. It's about time someone gave their pedestal a good kicking.'

'Oh, stop it,' Justine told him.

Gore leaned forward. 'Deliver a warning to the command ship,' he said. 'If it is ignored, disable that ship. If they continue after that, take the lot of 'em down. Use the lowest level of technology we've got that will do the job, but do it.'

'Seconded,' Crispin said.

'I would point out that it will be a nestling of the Emperor in charge of the fleet,' said Creewan. 'The political implications of the ruling nest being defeated are not good. The likelihood of subsequent instability are strong.'

'Which neither harms nor concerns us,' John Thelwell

said. He gave the Custodian a dismissive glance. 'We've given the Empire a beating before; they never learn.'

'Our position gives us an obligation,' Justine said.

'Only according to human morals,' Ilanthe said. 'These are aliens.'

'I wish to remain true to myself, thank you,' Justine said primly.

'Of course you do.'

'I vote against any physical force being used against the Empire fleet, no matter how restrained. We need to seek an alternative.'

'Thank you, Mother,' Kazimir said. 'Anyone else against the motion?'

Creewan raised his hand.

Kazimir looked round the table. 'Then it is the majority vote that the Navy delivers a warning to the command ship, and subsequently disables it if that warning is ignored. I will initiate that immediately.'

'And what if they keep on coming after the command ship is taken out?' Justine asked. 'Which they will, and you all know it.'

'Then I will reconvene this committee,' Kazimir said.

She let out an exasperated hiss of breath, and against all etiquette withdrew instantly. The others stared at the vacated space as the perceptual reality adjusted to her absence.

'That's what being in a real body does for you,' Ilanthe muttered archly.

'I will, of course, provide a secure link to the Navy ship delivering the ultimatum,' Kazimir said. 'All of you will be able to access the event.'

'How long until the demand is made?' John Thelwell asked.

'I'd like to bring in a ship which I know has the ability to disable a Starslayer without loss of life,' Kazimir said. 'We have that capability in the Hancher assistance squadron. Flight time will be within ten days. The warning will allow them one Earth day to turn round.'

'We'll be back here in a fortnight, then,' Gore predicted.

Less than a second after the meeting officially ended, Ilanthe requested access to Gore's personal perceptual reality. He'd been expecting it and permitted her entry as he ambled along the white-sand beach below the headland. She walked up out of the water, wearing a blue and white bikini.

'Very Ursula Andress,' he said appreciatively. Gone was the spiky Cat hairstyle of the meeting, she was shaking droplets out of long honey-coloured tresses.

'Thank you.' Ilanthe squinted up at the noon sun, holding a pale hand across her forehead. 'The governors you have configuring this place are very crude. Am I likely to get sunburn?'

'They're not crude, just strong. Prevents hostiles trojaning in nasty surprises. And no, you won't get sunburn, just increase your skin pigmentation factor.'

'Ah.' She blinked as her skin darkened to a rich bronze. 'It's still a very earthy environment to me. Will you get me drunk and seduce me?'

'Sex is common enough between enemies.'

'Oh, Gore,' she pouted. 'We're not enemies. Besides we both got what we wanted out of the meeting.'

'Did we?'

'We both voted for the same thing. Why? Is dear Justine still sulking?'

He started walking along the shoreline again. 'One word of genuine advice: don't ever underestimate my daughter. I still do occasionally. It's a mistake.'

'Point taken. Do you think Kazimir will delay because of her?'

'Fuck no. He's the most Right Stuff human you'll ever meet. Government gave him a clear order, so he clicks his boot heels, salutes, and presses the button.'

'You are so anachronistic. You really should update your references.'

'What? Haul myself all the way into the twenty-fifth century?'

'Well, one step at a time.'

'That's when you were born, wasn't it?'

She chuckled. 'They're right. You are pure evil.'

'Who's they?'

'Just about everybody.'

'They're probably right then. So what can I do for you?'

'Can we deal?'

'On the Pilgrimage? Sure.'

'Interesting capitulation. Why do I not believe you?'

'It's going to be a cusp event. Every Faction knows it. Hell, even some of the animals outside are waking up to what's going on. The Darwinists are wetting themselves with excitement. And your lot aren't much better, running round, pushing and prodding in places you shouldn't.'

'I don't know what you're talking about.'

'That arsehole Marius is clocking up a lot of lightyears.'

She pretended shock, her hand going to the base of her throat. 'As is your Delivery Man.'

'True Conservatives are paranoid little creatures. They have good cause.'

'You claim you're not one of them?'

'I have an affiliation.'

'Funny, according to our files you're the chairman of the board.'

'You really should update your references.'

She put her hands on her hips. 'Look, do you want to deal or not?'

'You're very hot in that pose, you know that?'

'Gore!'

'All right, what are you offering?'

'Some détente. A little less manipulation from both sides.'

'Let the animals decide, you mean. I don't think I can buy that coming from you. In any case, we've both spent so long moving our pawns into place that they'll just keep on going without us now.' He tilted his head to one side, and smiled. 'Or am I missing something?'

'No.'

'Really? Perhaps some critical event that you need to work smoothly?'

'Moments like that are made up by historians after the event to justify their own dreary existence. There's no one thing which will make or break the Pilgrimage.'

'Really? Have you ever tried telling Ozzie or Nigel that the actions of an individual are historically invalid?'

'Nobody manipulated them. And this is a distraction. We simply want both sides to cool down.'

'So the Accelerator Faction wants to let galactic events be decided by animals. Humm. No wonder you don't like my environment, it doesn't have any flying pigs.'

'Is that your answer?'

'No. But I am mildly curious. Unless either a Faction or ANA:Governance itself intervenes, the Pilgrimage ships will launch. So what the fuck exactly is the Accelerator line on the galaxy being devoured by the Void, exterminating all life including ourselves?'

'It won't happen. This is why I'm here, to tell you we have taken precautions in the event of the worst-case scenario.'

Gore stopped and turned to stare at her, genuinely surprised. 'What the fuck are you talking about?'

'If the Void's boundary sweeps through this sector of space, Earth and ANA will be perfectly safe.'

'You don't know that.'

'Oh yes we do.'

'I really, *really*, hope you're not basing your goals on some chunk of weapons technology you've managed to cobble together with a couple of old replicators. The Raiel can't defeat the boundary. Even ANA:Governance can't work out what will happen if and when the Void's boundary washes across itself.'

'That level of expansion is extremely unlikely, to the point of sheer impossibility. Firstly, the stars of the Wall have tremendous mass; enough to empower the will of every Living Dream pilgrim for centuries. It is an absolute fallacy that every star in the galaxy will be engulfed by the Void. Raiel propaganda shouted in tedious repetition by the Ocisens. The Raiel are an ancient failed race, as changeless as the Void itself, they have no right to dictate to us. Even if the entire galactic core gets devoured it doesn't matter. There's nothing alive in there, the planets are radiation-saturated husks of rock. You even believe it yourself, always accusing us of wanting the devourment. Have I ever said that?'

'No. I know exactly what Accelerators want: fusion. Right? You want to merge ANA with the fabric of the Void continuum. You think that's how we'll achieve post-physical status.'

'You have accessed Inigo's dreams, we know the Conservatives have analysed them as thoroughly as everyone else. Inside the Void, the mind directly affects the fabric of the universe, we can take charge of our own destiny.'

'No, no, no,' Gore shouted. 'The Void is not a fucking universe, it is a microverse, a tiny insignificant little speck of nothing. In cosmological terms, it doesn't even register. You can play God in there, for sure, the Waterwalker does it. But you're only God in there, nowhere else. It is an alien version of ANA, that's all. That's not transcendence, it's being so far up your own ass you can't see what's going on outside.'

'It is a huge opportunity for growth. The Void has stalled, it has been changeless for millions – billions – of years. We can reinvigorate it. Humans have already begun that process; ordinary pitiful animals that now have mental powers even we can only fantasize about. Imagine what will happen when ANA has full access to such a technology, and begins to manipulate it in new directions.'

'Sweet Ozzie, you are pitiful. I'd be contemptuous if I considered you sentient, but you're not even that.'

'We knew you would be opposed to the fusion, this is what our offer concerns.'

'Go on,' Gore said suspiciously.

'We will duplicate ANA. Those who wish to attain

fusion with the Void can stay here, those who do not can transfer over and fly free.'

'That doesn't solve a fucking thing, girlie. The Void can't be allowed to fuse with a post-physical mind, or even ANA – which, face it, isn't there yet.'

Ilanthe's expression hardened. 'Your language betrays you. *Can't be allowed?* You don't have the right to make that judgement. Evolution will occur, either triggered by the Pilgrimage, or a more direct connection. For all you know the Waterwalker himself may bring about expansion.'

'He happened a thousand years ago, ten thousand for all we know.'

'Time is irrelevant in there.'

'Shit! You're not Accelerators, not any more, you've seen the light and converted to Living Dream.'

'We have seen an opportunity to advance ourselves, and taken it. We have never hidden our purpose from anyone.'

'Accelerators didn't start out lusting after the Void.'

'Now you are betraying your age, your own changeless nature.'

'I should just get out of the way then, should I? Maybe simply erase myself? Make it all nice and simple for the New Order.'

'You are responsible for your own destiny.' She shrugged an elegant shoulder. 'Your choice.'

'Okay, granted; and I will make it, believe me. But assuming you're right and the Void doesn't expand like a hyperspace tsunami when the Pilgrimage gets inside, how are you going to fuse ANA with it?'

'We don't have to. Highers will travel with the Pilgrimage ships. They will study the true nature of the Void fabric and the mechanism which generates it.'

'If it can be built once,' Gore said quietly, 'it can be built again.'

Ilanthe smiled. 'Now you understand. We can build a second Void here in this solar system and bring about the fusion right away. ANA will evolve and transcend.'

'Nice science experiment. What happens if it doesn't work? ANA is the core of Higher culture, Earth is the physical centre of the Commonwealth. If you take that away, two cultures will suffer.'

'I never thought I'd hear that: Gore Burnelli, whining liberal. Normal, Higher and Advancer humans will have to make their own way in the universe. That, too, is evolution.'

'In a galaxy that your arrogance will have given a very short future.'

'Our solution is one that will satisfy all Factions. Both of us can carry on almost as before.'

'You weren't even born on Earth. I was. It's my home. And I'm not letting anyone fuck with it.'

'Then you are even less developed that we gave you credit for. Our offer stands. I expect the other Factions will take us up on it when they see the inevitability of what is to come.'

'Are you planning to blow the Empire fleet out of space?'

Ilanthe looked genuinely indignant. 'Of course not. They are an irrelevance. Kazimir will deal with them, one way or another.' She smiled coldly. 'Please consider our offer,

Gore. It is made in the spirit of reconciliation. After all, if anyone can be said to be ANA's father, it is you. Time perhaps to let go and allow your child to make its own way in life.' She trotted back into the waves and dived below the water.

Gore stared at the surf where she disappeared, his mind tracing her withdrawal from his personal reality. 'Fuck me,' he grunted.

When he walked along the dirt track that curved up around the headland he found Nelson already sitting by the pool at the base of the tower. As usual, there was a tall drink on the table beside him.

'Did you get all that?' Gore asked as he sat down.

'I got it all. I just don't think I believe much of it. For a start she's being very glib about the Pilgrimage ships actually getting inside. What are you going to do?'

'I knew they wanted the kind of abilities the Void fabric has, that's a logical development on the way to becoming post-physical, but I'm concerned about their method of acquisition. I don't believe a damn word about some bunch of selfless academics going with the Pilgrimage to study how the thing is put together. We're going to have to root around a little harder to find out what they're really up to out there. Find out what you can about that guy Marius was visiting on Arevalo, that physicist: Troblum.'

'Will do. And what if ANA does finally become capable of ascending to post-physical status?'

'I've always known it would right from the start. That was the whole point of it – well, that and giving ourselves the ability to defend the Commonwealth.'

'Are you going to try and stop it?'

'Of course not. I just don't want the natural process hijacked. And that's what's going to happen if we're not careful.'

*

It was already night when Aaron's regrav capsule landed on the pad of St Mary's Clinic, just outside the reception block. He stepped out and looked round. The clinic was set in four square miles of thick forest, with individual buildings scattered across the landscape. Tall gistrel trees formed a dark wall around the pad, their long feathery branches blocking any view of the villas, medical blocks, spas, and leisure domes he knew were out there. The only light came from the long windows of the reception block, thirty metres away, shining round the black trunks.

Corrie-Lyn stood beside him, straightening her blouse. Her face screwed up. 'Gosh, I love the whole gloomy jungle-with-wild-creatures look they've gone for. Very welcoming.'

'Perhaps we could get your manic depression eradicated while we're here.'

'Screw you.'

'Now remember, *darling*, happy faces.'

He gripped her hand and produced a big bright smile. She almost shook free, then remembered and drew a reluctant breath. 'Okay, but this better be quick.'

The reception doors opened as they walked towards the low building. It was a plush interior, which looked as if it had been carved out of pink and gold marble, with secluded grotto chambers recessed into the wall of the central hall. Most of the chambers had been utilized by exclusive retail outlets as display booths for their inordinately expensive designer clothes and products.

Their personal clinician was waiting to greet them; Ruth Stol, who was clearly designed to promote the clinic's expertise, with a body that resembled a teenage goddess draped in semi-translucent silver and pink fabric. Even Aaron, who was perfectly mission-focused, took a moment to admire and smile at the vision of vitality who extended her flawless hand in greeting. His field functions detected a discreet scan from the building security net, which he deflected easily enough, showing the sensors an image of a moderately overweight man. The additional volume around his torso was actually provided by a bandolier harness carrying an array of weapons.

Ruth Stol was devoid of all enrichments, though she had more macrocellular clusters than the average Advancer, and her nervous system shone with impulses operating at the kind of rate which normal humans could only achieve with a serious dose of accelerants.

'Thank you so much for choosing our clinic, Mr Telfer,' she said. Her hand pressed against Aaron's palm, squeezing flirtatiously. His biononics ran a check for pheromone infiltration. *Paranoid!* But her touch and voice were definitely arousing him, his exovision grid showed his heart rate up, skin temperature rising.

'No infiltration,' his u-shadow reported. So it was all natural, then. *Hardly surprising.* 'You're welcome,' Corrie-Lyn said in a voice so cold it should have produced ice droplets.

'Er, yeah,' Aaron mumbled belatedly. He reluctantly withdrew his hand, enjoying the coy amusement in the clinician's limpid green eyes. 'Thanks for seeing us at such short notice.'

'We're always happy to help couples achieve a more secure relationship,' Ruth Stol said. 'I believe you said you wanted twins?'

'Twins?' Corrie-Lyn repeated blankly.

'That's right.' Aaron put an arm round Corrie-Lyn's shoulders, feeling the muscles locked rigid. 'The best we can have.'

'Of course,' Ruth Stol said. 'Boys or girls?'

'Darling?' Aaron enquired.

'Boys,' Corrie-Lyn said.

'Do you have an idea of their physiological status?'

'At least as good as you,' Aaron told her, which produced another smile. 'And I'd like the pair of us to be advanced to that level, too. It's about time I went cutting edge.' He patted his bulky stomach ruefully. 'Perhaps a little metabolism tweaking to thin me down.'

'I'd be very grateful for that,' Corrie-Lyn said. 'He's so repugnant to look at right now. Never mind sex.'

'Oh, darling, you promised not to mention that,' Aaron said tightly.

She smiled brightly.

'It's a wonderful step to acknowledge any problems right at the start,' Ruth Stol said. 'You'll be an enviable family. We can begin our appraisal tomorrow, and review what we can offer you. Our premium service will fast-track your changes; I don't expect this to take more than a couple of weeks. Were you intending to carry the twins yourself?' she asked Corrie-Lyn. 'Or is it going to be a womb tank?'

'Haven't decided.' Corrie-Lyn smiled back. 'I love him

enough to consider the physical burden, but you'll have to show me what you can do to make pregnancy easier before I commit.'

'How sweet. I'll have a simulated sensory package of the full pregnancy option ready for you to review in the morning, and remember we can always reverse the changes afterwards.'

'Lovely.'

'We've given you villa 163, which has its own pool, and it's not far from block three where you'll receive your treatments.'

'Excellent,' Aaron said. 'I think I'll go and check out the main pool and the restaurants first, especially that Singapore Grill I've heard about. What about you, dear?'

'It's been a long day. I'll go to the villa, and organize that.' Corrie-Lyn eyed the various displays around the hall. 'After some shopping. I really like some of these designs.'

'Don't spend too much.' He gave her a farewell peck on the cheek and headed out of the door. His u-shadow extracted the clinic map from the local net, which would give the appearance of normality for another few minutes. 'Can you get into the vault?' he asked it.

'No. There are no data channels into the vault.'

Aaron took a path away from the landing pad which would lead to the main pool building, a large blue-tinted dome that housed a lush tropical environment, with the pool itself fashioned to resemble a lagoon. The path lit up like a strip of glowing yellow fog under his feet. 'What about the security system?' he asked his u-shadow.

'I can only access the lower levels. All guests are under permanent surveillance of some kind, several are red-tagged.'

'Really? Are we red-tagged?'

'No.'

'Will they know if I leave the path?'

'Yes. Various passive sensors are feeding the smartcore.'

'Start some diversions, please. Trigger alerts and attack the security net in several places, well away from me. Nothing to warrant a police call-out.'

'Initiating.'

Aaron left the path and started to run through the trees. His suit spun a stealth effect around him. After a minute slipping unseen through the forest he arrived at the administration block. There were two storeys above ground, while his research had shown ten floors cut into the bedrock beneath the forest. The secure storage vault was on the bottom. His field function scan revealed a complex array of sensors guarding the walls and surrounding swathe of garden.

He began to sprint past the last trees, accelerating hard with field-reinforced muscles until he was at the edge of the lawn, then jumped, extending his force field wide, shaping it into two long swept-back petals. Suspended between his invisible wings he glided directly at a specific window on the upper floor like a silent missile. He grinned into the air that rushed against his face and rippled his suit. Excitement was starting to build, which his biononics could only suppress so much. Even though he knew what he was going to have to do, he was still enjoying himself; this was what he existed for.

Aaron let out an em pulse from his biononics, targeted to disable the sensors and power supply around the window. When he was five metres from the wall, he triggered a disruptor effect. Glass turned to white powder and blew inwards with the sound of damp cloth being ripped. He cancelled his force-field wings and dropped through the hole, hitting the floor with a roll.

Inside was a long finance department office. Deserted and dark. Door locked. He didn't use the disruptor effect, simply smashed it down with amplified muscle power. The corridor outside ran the length of the building. Orange emergency lighting produced strangely angled shadows across the walls. His scrambler effect knocked out the net across half of the building. He jogged to the emergency stairwell and burst through. Vaulted over the rail and landed with a loud thud on the concrete floor below, integral force field absorbing the impact. He scanned round.

Two security managers were sitting in the control centre, both heavily enriched. They were standing motionless as their u-shadows interfaced them with the clinic's security net and they struggled to make sense of what was happening across the forest.

The door broke apart as Aaron walked through it. Eight energy-dumps flew out from the bandolier straps under his suit, hand-sized black discs that zipped through the air like cybernetic hornets. They struck the security managers before either could fire a shot. Both of them were transformed into silhouettes of searing white light as their personal force fields were relentlessly overloaded; tendrils of electricity lashed out from the incandescent shapes, grounding through the desks and chairs next to them. Ribbons of smoke crept up from the carpet round their feet. They began to thrash about as the discharge of energy soared to an unbearable thunderclap screech. Light panels in the ceiling detonated into splinters of bubbling plastic.

Aaron drew a jelly gun from the bandolier harness as the nimbus of light on the first manager began to fade. The man's force field flickered erratically into a purple and orange shroud. Dark shadows infiltrated the dying luminescence, exposing swathes of smouldering uniform. Aaron fired. The manager disintegrated in a spherical wave of gore that splattered across the room. After that, Aaron simply waited a few seconds until the energy-dumps completed their work on the second manager, and her force field spluttered out. The room was plunged into darkness as she fell to the floor in a sobbing heap, barely conscious.

He knelt beside her and took the surgical cutter from his pocket. The little black and silver gadget extended its eight malmetal arms as he placed it carefully on her head. Unlike Ruth Stol, the clinic hadn't designed any beauty into the security manager. She had a plain round face with dark enriched eyes; the skin on her cheeks was red raw from the crackling electron currents. Tears were leaking across them as she gazed up at Aaron.

'Please,' she croaked.

'Don't worry,' he told her. 'You won't remember this night when you're re-lifed.'

The cutter settled on the crown of her head like some vampiric creature, the arms tightening to obtain a better grip on her singed flesh. Microsurgery energy blades slid out and began to cut. Aaron waited with only the sound of gooey blood droplets drizzling down from the soot-caked ceiling to break the dark silence of the room.

'Procedure complete,' his u-shadow reported.

Aaron reached down, and gently pulled the surgical cutter. It lifted upwards with a slimy sucking sound, taking the top of her skull with it. A small amount of blood welled up around the edges of the severed bone, dribbling down through the matted hair. Her exposed brain glistened a pale grey in the weak emergency lighting shining in from the corridor outside.

He poised his left hand a couple of centimetres above the gory naked flesh. The skin on his palm puckered up in seven little circles. Slender worm-like tendrils began to wriggle out of each apex. He brought the hand down on her brain, and manipulated his force field to bond the two together, preventing his hand from sliding, even fractionally. The tendrils insinuated themselves into her neurone structure, branching again and again like some plant root seeking moisture. These tips were hunting out distinct neural pathways, circumventing conscious control over not just her body but her thoughts.

Synapses were successfully violated and corrupted. His mentallic software began to pull coherent strands out of the chaotic impulses.

Her name was Viertz Accu. A hundred and seventeen years old. Advancer heritage. Currently married to Asher Lel. Two children. The youngest, Harry, was two years old. She was upset that she'd pulled another late shift; little Harry did so like her reading to him before bedtime.

Aaron's software moved the acquisition focus up towards the present.

All earlier emotional content was now superseded by sheer terror. Body's sensory input was minimal, sinking below waves of pain from the force field collapse. One memory rising above all the others, bright and loud: the surgical cutter descending. Starting to repeat. Thoughts becoming incoherent as the memory degenerates into a psychosis loop. Limbs shake as bodyshock commences.

Forget that, Aaron's thoughts instruct the brain he now rules. He has to concentrate, to exert his own thoughts to squash the terror memory. His influence is assisted by the flawless positioning of the neurone override tendrils, making it impossible for her to resist. A different kind of mental pressure is then exerted. Her conscious thoughts wither to insensate status, effectively sinking her into a coma.

Stand, he commands the puppet body.

It straightens up, and Aaron rises beside it. His hand remains locked in place on top of her ruined head by the mucilage force field.

Clinic security system review. Schematics flip up into their mutual exovision, showing alert points. His u-shadow ends its roguish electronic assaults as he accesses the clinic net through Viertz's private secure link. False signals are generated within the administration building to replace the equipment he neutralized during his entry.

Codes. Up from Viertz's own memory and her macrocellular clusters spill file after file of codes for every aspect of the clinic. He deploys them to damp down the security net, reducing it to a level-zero state. Another set of commands reset the smartcore's alertness, convincing it that it was receiving malfunction warnings and the security managers now have everything under control.

Several operatives across the forest are calling in.

It's all right, he mouths and Viertz sends on a secure link. *There's been a spate of glitches, those boogledammed glints have been getting into the cabling again. They were chewing on a node, little bastards.* Boogledammed is a phrase Viertz is fond of. Glints are tiny native rodents infesting the forest and always causing problems to the clinic and its machinery, despite two illegal attempts by the management to exterminate them.

Generally the explanation is accepted. Viertz exchanges a few more in-character comments with colleagues, and signs off.

Vault.

They walk along the ground-floor corridor, side by side, Aaron's hand still firmly in place on her head. Viertz's code opens the lift doors. Aaron extracts additional overrides which will clear him to accompany her down to the bottom.

The vault level poses more of a problem. It is covered in sensors, all of which are linked directly to the clinic smartcore through isolated, protected circuits. There are no overrides he can utilize to smooth his passage. If it sees him it will immediately query his identity.

The mission is now time-critical.

As the lift reaches the vault level, Aaron uses an em pulse to kill all power circuits and unguarded systems. His scrambler field disables the protected security network. The smartcore now knows something is wrong, but cannot detect what. The entire floor is an electronic dead zone.

Aaron slides the lift door open with his free hand. Metal provides considerable resistance. The activators emit a screech as they are buckled by the pressure he exerts. He steps into darkness. Field function scans and infrared imaging reveal the short, empty corridor ahead. He walks along it with the zombie Viertz marching beside him until they reach the large vault door of metabonded malmetal at the end. Both wall and door are guarded by a strong force field, powered independently from within. His free hand strokes across the undefended corridor wall until his fingers are resting over the armoured conduit carrying part of the security net's cabling. He presses down. A small disruptor pulse disintegrates the concrete. Dust pours out, and he pushes his hand deeper into the hole. He has to excavate up to his elbow until he reaches the conduit. There is a brief clash of energy fields and the conduit shatters, exposing the optical cables inside.

The fingertips of this hand extrude slender filaments which penetrate the optical cables, immersing themselves into the blaze of coherent light flashing along the interior. His enrichments are interfaced directly into the smartcore through an unprotected link. A torrent of destructive software is unleashed by his u-shadow, corroding the smartcore's primary routines like acid on skin. In the first eight milliseconds of the assault, the smartcore loses over half of its intellectual processing capacity. Its default preservation routines withdraw its connections to the vault security system, allowing it to retreat and lick its wounds in isolation.

Aaron's u-shadow turns its attention to the connections along the other end of the expropriated optical cable, and examines the security network inside the vault. It takes less than a second to map out the system's nodes and kubes allowing it to remove the smartcore's control and safeguard procedures. The force field switches off, and the thick door opens with a low swish of retracting malmetal.

Aaron removes his hand from the ragged hole. He and Viertz walk forward in tandem, passing through the air/dust shield with a gentle *buzzt*. Independent lighting panels click on, revealing a shiny oblong chamber filled with floor-to-ceiling racks of translucent pink plastic kubes.

The registry is a simple slim pedestal of metal just inside.

Viertz accesses the dormant software within. She is asked for her DNA-based authority certificate.

As he passes the threshold, Aaron's field scans reveal two strange energy signatures emerging from the walls on either side of the vault. It is the final failsafe to protect the priceless half-million secure memorycells within the vault. Not listed anywhere in the security net inventory, and quietly imported from a Central World where such technology is unexceptional. Two guards with heavy weapons enrichments sealed within the temporal suspension zone of exotic matter cages. Their enrichments were already fully powered up when they began their two-year duty period. They do not ask questions as they step back into real-time, they simply open fire.

Aaron's force field is immediately pushed close to overload as it struggles to protect him and Viertz. His disadvantage is terribly obvious as energy beams pummel into him and the woman. Dense waves of scarlet photons ignite with blinding ferocity around his chest and arms. He staggers back half a step.

Send authority certificate.

But the pedestal uses non-military-grade hardware. It cannot receive and acknowledge any information in such a hostile electromagnetic environment.

'Shit!' His bandolier belts launch a flock of electronic countermeasure drones and five niling-sponges. The guards twist away from the threat, ducking behind the racks. Aaron reaches out with his free hand and manages to grip the top of the pedestal as the last of the energy barrage drains away from his force field. The filaments emerge from his fingertips and try to burrow into the nodes and cables underneath the metal.

Both guards spin out from behind the racks and open fire again. The niling-sponges cluster together and activate their absorption horizons. Energy beams from the weapons curve bizarrely through the hot air to sink harmlessly into the black-star blooms now drifting sedately in front of Aaron. Their horizons start to expand significantly. The guards shift to kinetic carbines. Their hypervelocity projectiles are unaffected by the niling-sponges and smash against Aaron and Viertz. The force field flares bright copper, shading up towards carmine. Aaron can feel the strain the impacts are punishing his body with, reinforcement fields are struggling to hold him upright.

On your knees.

Viertz sinks quickly to the shiny floor, presenting a smaller, more stable target. His filaments have penetrated the metal casing of the pedestal, and begin to affiliate themselves with the fine mesh of optical strands beneath.

A couple of energy-dumpers skim towards Aaron. He shoots them with a simple ion shot from an enrichment in his forearm. His force field has to reformat momentarily to allow the ions through. It is a weakness which the guards exploit ruthlessly, concentrating their fire. He feels the kinetic projectiles lance into his shoulder and upper torso. Combat software reports five direct hits. Field scans reveal the nature of the foreign projectiles. Number one is a straight explosive, which is countered by a damping field, turning it to a lump of white hot metal. Two releases a pack of firewire tangles, which expand through his flesh, ripping it apart at a cellular level, incinerating as they go, wrecking bionomic organelles. They can only be staved off by a specific frequency disruptor field to attack their molecular structure, which has a debilitating effect on the biononics still functional in the area. Three dispenses a nerve agent in sufficient quantity to exterminate five hundred humans. Biononics converge quickly to counteract the deadly toxin. Four is another explosive, neutralized along with one. Five is a cluster of microjanglers, microbe-sized generators that jam his nervous system, inhibiting biononic and enrichment operations; a secondary function is to induce pain impulses. They require a scrambler field to kill them.

Blood pumps out from the cratered flesh and torn suit, to be flattened back beneath the reformatted force field. The surrounding fabric of his suit is quickly saturated. Biononics congregate around the edge of the wounds, acting in concert to knit the damage back together, sealing up veins, arteries, and capillaries. Inside his body the firewire tangles halt their expansion as the disruptor sabotages their molecular cohesion. It is too slow, they are causing a massive amount of damage. Damage which is amplified by the microjanglers.

Aaron flings his head back to scream in agony as the microscopic technology war is fought within his muscles and blood vessels. But still he keeps hold of both Viertz and the pedestal.

His biononics shut off a whole series of nerves, eliminating the pain and all sensation in his shoulder and arm. A disconcertingly large section of the medical status display in his exovision is flashing red. Nausea plagues him. Shivers run along his limbs. The field medic sac in his thigh pushes a dose of suppressants into his bloodstream.

Another wave of kinetics pound him. He is in danger of

falling backwards. His biononics and enrichments are reaching maximum capacity. Countermeasure drones do their best to confuse the enemy targeting sensors, but the narrow confines of the vault almost make such systems irrelevant.

His filaments interface with the registry kube in the pedestal.

Send authority certificate.

The registry software acknowledges Viertz's authority. And the u-shadow runs a search for Inigo's secure store. It locates the memorycell. The physical coordinates are loaded into Aaron's combat routines. A volume of eight cubic centimetres to be held inviolate. The rest of the vault's structure is now expendable.

He lets go of the pedestal and Viertz. The woman slumps forward, a motion which jolts her unsecured brain. A fresh upwelling of blood bubbles out around the circle of cut bone. The protective swirl of niling-sponges deactivate, their black horizons folding in upon themselves. Aaron raises his head and smiles an animal snarl through the clear air at the guards. Their barrage has paused as they take stock.

'Payback time,' he growls enthusiastically.

The first disruptor pulse smashes out. Half of the precious racks rupture in a maelstrom of molten plastic. Both guards stagger backwards. Jelly gun shots hammer at their force fields. Energy-dumpers zip about, launched by both sides. Black niling horizons expand and contract like inverse novas. Kinetic projectiles chew into the vault's concrete and marble walls. More racks suffer, shattering like antique glass. The plastic catches fire, molten rivulets streaking across the floor, spitting feeble flames from their leading edges.

Aaron positions himself between the guards and Inigo's memorycell, shielding it from any possible damage. He manages to puncture the force field of one guard's leg and fires the jelly gun into the gap. The leg instantly transforms to a liquid pulp of ruined cells. The guard screams as he topples over. His force field reconfigures over the stump, allowing the blood and gore to splash across the ground where it starts to steam softly. Energy-dumpers attach themselves to him like predatory rodents. He thrashes about helplessly as his force field diminishes.

Now it is just Aaron and the remaining guard. They advance on each other, each trusting in his own weapons enrichments. This is no longer a battle of software or even human wits. It is brute strength only which will prevail now.

At the end they resemble two atomic fireballs colliding. A shockwave of incandescent energy flares out from the impact, vaporizing everything it touches. One fireball is abruptly extinguished.

Aaron stands over the clutter of charcoal which seconds before was his opponent. While still staring down he extends his good arm sideways. An x-ray laser muzzle emerges from his forearm. Its beam slices through the head of the legless guard. Curves up to annihilate the man's memorycell. Aaron lets out a long sigh, then winces at the dull pain throbbing deep in his shoulder. When he glances at it, the bloodstain has spread across most of his chest. The hole torn and burned through the suit fabric reveals nothing but a mangled patch of blackened skin seeping blood. His medical monitors report the firewire tangles have burrowed deep, the damage is extensive. Sharp stabs of pain from his left leg make him gasp. His knee almost gives way. Biononics act in concert to trace and eliminate the microjanglers that are cruising recklessly through his bloodstream. If they infiltrate his brain he will be in serious trouble. The medical sac is still pumping drugs into him to counter shock. Blood loss will become a problem very soon unless he can reach a medical facility. However, he remains functional, though he will have to undergo decontamination for the nerve agent. His biononics are not satisfied they have located all the toxin. The field scan function fine tunes itself, and scans again.

Aaron walks over to the rack containing Inigo's memory-cell. Niling sponges flutter through the air, and return to his bandolier, snuggling back into their pouches. His feet crunch on a scree of fragments before squelching on blood and plastic magma. Then the memorycell is in his hand, and the most difficult stage of the mission is over.

Flames are taking hold across Viertz's uniform as he walks out of the vault. She has not moved from her kneeling position. Aaron shoots her through the head with the x-ray laser, an act of mercy in case her memorycell is still recording impulses. It's not like him, but he can afford to be magnanimous in the face of success.

Three minutes later Aaron made it out on to the roof of the administration block. He walked over to the edge, drawing breath in short gasps. The numb shoulder wound had started to coldburn, radiating out waves of dizziness which his medical enrichments could barely prevent from overwhelming him. A terrible burst of pain from his legs, stomach and spine drilled into him, blinding him as he convulsed. Unseen in his exovision displays, the biononics reported progress in their quest to trace and eliminate the remaining elusive microjanglers still contaminating his blood.

Slowly, stiffly, he straightened up again. Teetering close to a two-storey fall. His u-shadow reconnected to the unisphere as soon as he clambered up out of the lift shaft, and reported that the remnant of the smartcore was yelling for help on just about every link the clinic had with the unisphere.

'Police tactical troops are responding,' the u-shadow informed him. 'Clinic security officers are arming themselves. Perimeter is sealing.'

'We'd better leave then,' Aaron said with bravado. He winced again at a shiver of phantom pain from his collar bone, and called Corrie-Lyn. 'Let's go. I'm at designated position one-A.'

'Oh,' she replied. 'Are you finished already?'

For a moment he thought she was joking. 'What?'

'I didn't realize you'd be that quick.'

Anger swiftly turned him to ice. The schedule he'd given her was utterly clear-cut. Not even the unexpected guards and subsequent fire fight had delayed him more than forty seconds. 'Where are you?' His exovision was showing him a local map with the police cruisers closing on the clinic at mach eight.

'Er . . . I'm still in the reception area. You know they have some really nice clothes here, and Ruth Stol has actually been quite useful with styling. Who'd have thought it? I've already tried on a couple of these lovely wool—'

'Get the fuck into the capsule! Right fucking now!' he

395

screamed. Tactical software assessed the situation, corresponding with his own instinct. The roof was far too exposed. Another involuntary shudder ran up his legs, and he went with it, tumbling over the edge, totally reliant on his combat software. The program formatted his force field to cushion his landing. Even so, the pain seemed to explode directly into his brain as he thudded into the ground. He rolled over and stumbled to his feet. Far too slowly.

'The doors won't open,' Corrie-Lyn said. 'I can't get to the capsule. The alarm is going off. Wait . . . Ruth is telling me not to move.'

Aaron groaned as he staggered erratically across the band of lawn surrounding the administration block. Not that the trees would provide the slightest cover, not against the kind of forces heading for him. Seeking darkness was a simple animal instinct.

'Take the bitch out,' he told Corrie-Lyn.

'What?'

'Hit her. Here's a combat program,' he said, as his u-shadow shunted the appropriate file at her. 'Go for a disabling blow. Don't hesitate.'

'I can't do that.'

'Hit her. And call the capsule over. It can smash through the doors for you.'

'Aaron, can't I just get the capsule to break in? I'm really not comfortable hitting someone without warning.'

Aaron reached the treeline. His legs gave way, sending him sprawling in the dirt and spiky vines. Pain that was nothing to do with the microjanglers pulsed out from his damaged shoulder. 'Help,' he croaked. 'Oh fuck it, Corrie-Lyn, get the capsule here.' He started crawling. His exoimages were a blurred scintillation coursing round his constricting vision.

'Hey, she's grabbed me.'

'Corrie-Lyn—'

'Cow!'

'I can't make it.' He pushed against the damp sandy soil with his good arm, trying to lever himself back on to his feet. Two police capsules flashed silently overhead. A second later their hypersonic boom smashed him back down into the ground. Tree branches splintered from the violence of the sound. Aaron whimpered as he rolled on to his back.

'Oh, Ozzie, there's blood everywhere. I think I've broken her nose. I didn't hit her hard, really.'

'Get me,' he whispered. He sent a single command thought to the niling-sponges in his bandolier harness. The little spheres soared away into the night, arching away over the waving trees. Violet laser beams sliced through the air, as bright as lightning forks. He grinned weakly. 'Wrong,' he told the unseen police capsules.

The niling-sponges sucked down the energy which the capsules pumped into them. Theoretically the niling effect could absorb billions of kilowatt hours before reaching saturation point. Aaron had programmed a limit in. When the police weapons pumped their internal levels to that limit, the absorption effect reversed.

Five huge explosions blossomed high over the forest, sending out massive clashing pressure waves. The police capsules couldn't be damaged by the blast, their force fields were far too strong for that. But the wavefronts sent them tumbling through the night sky, spinning and flailing out beyond the edge of the forest as the regrav drives fought to counter the force. Down below, trees tumbled before the bedlam as if they were no stronger than paper, crashing into each other to create a domino effect radiating out from the five blast centres.

A blizzard of splinters and gravel snatched Aaron off the ground and sent him twirling five metres to bounce badly. Amazingly he was still holding the memorycell as he found himself flat on his back gazing up into a sky beset with an intricate webbing of lambent ion streamers.

'Corrie-Lyn,' he called desperately.

Above him, the pretty sky was dimming to infinite black. There were no stars to be seen as the darkness engulfed him.

Inigo's fourth dream

After breaking camp just after dawn the caravan was on the road for three hours before it finally topped the last ridge and the coastal plain tipped into view. Edeard smiled down on it with an adrenaline burst of enthusiasm. With nearly a year spent travelling he was finally looking at his future. Riding on the ge-horse beside him, Salrana squealed happily and clapped her hands together. Several pigs in the back of O'lrany's cart grunted at the sudden noise.

Edeard ordered his ge-horse to stop. The caravan pushed on inexorably, wagon after wagon rolling down the stony road. Directly ahead of him the foothills of the Donsori Mountains fell away sharply to the awesome Iguru Plain below. It stretched away for mile after long mile. A flat expanse of rich farmland, almost all of which was under cultivation; its surface marked out in huge regular fields filled with verdant crops. A massive grid of ditches fed into wide, shallow rivers delineated by protective earthen embankments. Forests tended to sprawl around the lower slopes of the odd little volcanic cones which broke the plain's uniformity. As far as he could see there was no pattern to the steep knolls. They were dotted purely at random.

It was a strange geography, completely different to the rugged surrounding terrain. He shrugged at the oddity and squinted to the eastern horizon. Part imagination, part horizon-haze, the Lyot Sea was just visible as a grey line.

No need to imagine the city, though. Makkathran bestrode the horizon like a sunwashed pearl. At first he was disappointed by how small it was, then he began to appreciate the distance involved.

'Quite something, isn't it?' Barkus said as he rode his aged ge-horse level with Edeard.

'Yes, sir,' Edeard said. Additional comment seemed superfluous. 'How far away are we?'

'It'll take at least another half a day for us to get down to the plain; this last stretch of road down the mountains is tricky. We'll make camp at Clipsham, the first decent-sized town on the Iguru. Then it'll be near enough another day to reach Makkathran itself.' He nodded pleasantly and urged his ge-horse onward.

Almost two days away. Edeard stared entranced at the capital city. Allegedly, the only true city on Querencia. The caravan had visited some fabulous towns on their route, large conurbations with wealthy populations; several had parks bigger than Ashwell. At the time he'd thought them grand, sure that nothing could actually be larger. *Lady, what a bumpkin I am.*

'Doubts here, of all places?' Salrana asked. 'Those are some very melancholy thoughts you've got growing in your head there.'

'Just humbled,' he told her.

Her thoughts sparkled with amusement, producing a teasing smile. 'Thinking of Franlee?'

'Not for months,' he answered with high dignity.

Salrana laughed wickedly.

He'd met Franlee in Plax, a provincial capital on the other side of the Ulfsen Mountains. A spree of bad luck on the road, including broken wheels and sick animals, as well as unusually early autumn storms meant the caravan was late reaching Plax. As a consequence, they'd been snowed in for over six weeks. That was when he met Franlee, an Eggshaper Guild apprentice and his first real love affair. They'd spent most of the awful cold weather together, either in bed or exploring the town's cheaper taverns. The Eggshaper Guild's Master had recognized his talent, offering him a senior apprenticeship with the promise of journeyman status in a year. He'd been *this* close to staying.

But in the end his last promise to Akeem gave him a stronger direction. Leaving had been so painful he'd been sullen and withdrawn for weeks as the caravan lumbered slowly along the snowy Ulfsen valleys. A misery to live with, the rest of the caravan had grumbled. It took the remainder of winter and putting the Ulfsens between himself and Plax before he'd recovered. That and Roseillin, in one of the mountain villages. And Dalice. And . . . Well, several more girls between there and here.

'Look at it,' he said earnestly. 'We did the right thing.'

Salrana tipped her head back, half-closing her eyes against the bright morning light. 'Forget the city,' she said. 'I've never seen so much sky.'

When he glanced up he understood what she meant. Their high vantage point gave them a view into the azure infinity which roofed the plain. Small bright clouds scudded far overhead, wisps so tenuous they were almost sapphire themselves. They seemed to twist as they traced long arcs above the Iguru before hitting the mountain thermals where they expanded and darkened. *The wind above the city always blows in from the sea*, he remembered Akeem saying, *when it turns round, watch out*. 'What's that smell?' he asked, puzzled. The air was fresh, zingy almost, yet somehow tainted at the same time.

There was laughter from the wagon that rolled past. 'You backward village boy!' Olcus, the driver, mocked. 'That's the smell of the sea.'

Edeard dropped his gaze back down to the horizon. He'd never seen the sea before. In truth, from this distance it didn't look much: a grey-blue smudge line. He supposed it would become more interesting and impressive as they drew nearer.

'Thank you, old man,' he called back, and supplied a fast hand gesture. By now, he was on good terms with just about every family in the caravan. Abandoning them in Makkathran was going to be at least as hard as leaving Plax.

'Come on,' Salrana said. She ordered her ge-horse forward. After a moment, Edeard followed suit.

'I was talking to Magrith at breakfast,' Salrana said. 'She told me this road was the same one which Rah travelled on when he led his shipmates out of the strife which followed their landing on Querencia. He would have seen the city for the first time from this very same spot.'

'Wonder what he made of the Iguru,' Edeard muttered.

'There are times when I really don't understand you, Edeard. We've reached Makkathran, which I only ever half-believed in anyway. Us two, Ashwell villagers no less, are here at the centre of our whole world. And all you do is talk about the stupid farmland outside.'

'I'm sorry. It's . . . this place is odd, that's all. Look

round, the mountains just end, like something cut them off.'

'I'm sure there's a Geography Guild if you're that interested,' she sniffed.

'Now that's an idea,' he said with sudden apparent interest. 'Do you think it would be hard to get into?'

'Oh!' she squealed in exasperation. Her third hand shoved against him, trying to push him off his saddle. He pushed right back, which sent her hunching down, tightening her grip on the reins. 'Edeard! Careful.'

'Sorry.' It was something of a standing joke along the caravan that he didn't know his own strength. He shook his head and concentrated on the phalanx of genistars walking alongside the caravan, making sure the ge-horses were pulling wagons in a straight line, ge-wolves kept close, and the ge-eagles spiralled wide. The surface of the road was excellent, laid with large flat stones, well maintained – it was almost like a town pavement. But then this was the main road through the mountains and led directly to the capital. Both eyes and farsight picked out several wagons and small convoys winding their way up and down the broad switchbacks ahead of them. He also saw a group of men on horseback accompanied by ge-wolves who were picking their way leisurely up the road. They'd reach the head of the caravan by noon, he reckoned.

With his senses open wide he slowly grew aware of the city's emanations. It was a quiet background burble, similar to the aura of any human settlement. Except this time he was too far away to be sensing Makkathran's population, no matter how talented and receptive he was. Besides, this had a different tempo to human minds; slower and so much more content. It was the essence of a lazy summer's afternoon distilled into a single long harmonic. Pleasant and relaxing. He yawned.

'Edeard!' Salrana called.

He blinked, the worry in her mind switching him to full alertness. His ge-horse was meandering close to the edge of the road. Not that it was dangerous, there was no sheer slope until further down the hill where the switchbacks began, here there was just uneven ground and the curving crest. A quick couple of instructions to the ge-horse's mind corrected his direction.

'Let's try and arrive intact,' she said scathingly. 'Lady, but your riding is still terrible.'

He was too disquieted to try and correct her with their usual banter. He could no longer sense the city's lumbering thoughts – too much adrenaline pumping through his veins. Now the city was in sight, he was getting genuinely excited. At last the dreadful past was well and truly behind them.

It was midday when the caravan drew to a gradual halt amid the groaning of wood and metal brakes, the snorting of animals and quiet grumbles of humans. They were strung out over half a mile, curving round one of the longer switchbacks which made it awkward for anyone else trying to use the road. The captain of the militia patrol who made them stop was mildly apologetic, but insistent none the less.

Edeard was only a couple of wagons behind the front as Barkus asked, 'Is there a problem, sir? This is our annual trip, we are well known to all the civic authorities.'

'I know you myself, Barkus,' the captain said as he eyed the caravan's ge-wolves. He was sitting on a midnight-black terrestrial horse, looking very splendid in a ceremonial blue and scarlet tunic with polished brass buttons gleaming down his jacket. Edeard used his farsight to examine the revolver in the man's white leather holster. It was remarkably similar to the one that had belonged to Genril's family. The rest of the militia were similarly armed; they certainly weren't carrying anything like the fast-firing gun of the bandits. Edeard didn't know if that was a good thing or not. If the city did possess such weapons, they probably wouldn't be put out on show with a patrol like this.

'However, I don't remember you having so many ge-wolves before,' the captain said.

'We were in the Rulan province last year; a village was sacked by bandits, farms suffered losses in raids. You can't be too careful.'

'Damned savages,' the captain spat. 'Probably just two tribes fighting over some whore. I don't know why you venture out there, Barkus, they're all bandits and ne'er-do-wells if you ask me.'

Edeard slowly sat up very straight, keeping his gaze fixed on the captain. He strengthened his shield around him.

'Do nothing,' Barkus shot at him with a longtalk whisper.

'Edeard,' Salrana hissed quietly. He could sense the rage in her own thoughts, barely contained. All around him, the minds of his friends were radiating dismay and sympathy.

'But profitable,' Barkus continued smoothly. 'We can buy very cheaply indeed out there.'

The captain laughed, unaware of the emotional storm gathering around him. 'For which my friends in the city will pay greatly, I suppose.'

'That's the essence of trade,' Barkus said. 'After all, we do travel at considerable risk.'

'Well good luck to you, Barkus. But I am responsible for the safety of Makkathran, so I must request that you keep your beasts on a leash within the city walls. They won't be used to civilization. We don't want any unfortunate accidents.'

'Of course.'

'You might want to get them accustomed to the idea as soon as you reach the plain.'

'I'll see to it.'

'Jolly good. And no trading to the denizens of the Sampalok district, eh?'

'Absolutely not.'

The captain and his men turned round and rode off down the road, their pack of ge-wolves chasing along behind.

Barkus saw the caravan start off again, then urged his ge-horse back to Edeard and Salrana. 'I'm sorry you had to hear that,' he said.

'They're not all like that in the city, are they?' Salrana asked anxiously.

'Sweet Lady, no. Officers in the militia are usually the younger sons of an old family; little idiots who know nothing of life. Their birth provides them with a great deal of arrogance, but no money. The militia allows them the illusion of continuing status, while all they actually do is search for a wealthy wife. Thankfully they can do no real harm patrolling out here.'

Edeard was almost shocked by the notion. 'If they need money, why don't they join a Guild and develop their psychic talent, or begin a new business?'

To his surprise, Barkus burst out laughing. 'Oh, Edeard, for all the distance you've travelled with us, you still have so much further to go. A nobleman's son *earn* a living!' He laughed again before ordering his ge-horse back to the next wagon.

After Clipsham, Edeard just wanted to take a horse and gallop across the Iguru until he reached Makkathran. Surely it would take no more than a few hours. However, he managed to keep his impatience in check, and dutifully plodded alongside the wagons helping to soothe the ge-wolves who were unused to being on a leash.

It was warm down on the plain, with the gentle constant wind blowing a sea-humid air which Edeard found strangely invigorating. Winter here was a lot shorter than he was used to in the Rulan province, Barkus explained, though those months could see some very sharp frosts and several snow blizzards. By contrast, summer in the city was very hot and lasted for more than five months. Most of the grand families kept villas in the Donsori Mountains where they spent the height of the hot season.

The Iguru's farmland reflected the climate, with luxuriant growth covering every field. The road was lined with tall slender palm trees cloaked in ribbons of cobalt moss and sprouting tufts of scarlet and emerald leaves right at the top. Crops were different to those Edeard was used to. There were few cereal fields here, but plenty of citrus groves and fruit plantations, with acre after acre of vines and fruiting bushes. Some cane fields were being burnt back, sending black smoke plumes churning up high into the clear sky. It was volcanic soil underfoot, which contributed as much to the healthy verdant hue of the vegetation as did the regular rain and sun-soaked sky. Armies of ge-chimps bustled about over the land, tending to the plants, with supervisors riding among them on horses. The farm-houses were grand white-washed buildings with red clay tile roofs, as big as the Guild compounds back in Ashwell.

For all they spent hours rolling forward that morning, the panorama on both sides of the straight road remained unnervingly similar. Only the volcanic cones offered land-marks by which to measure progress. Edeard could see veins of silver streams running down their slopes before vanishing into the dense skirts of dark-jade trees. But there were no caldera crowns; they rose to simple rounded crests. Many of them had cottages built on narrow ledges, compact yet elaborate constructions which his friends explained were little more than pavilions for the city's wealthy to spend languid days enjoying the fabulous view; more common was to install a favoured mistress in one.

Traffic began to increase as they neared Makkathran. Terrestrial horses were now more common than ge-horses; their riders wearing expensive clothes. Wagons piled high with produce from the farms and estates of the plain lumbered towards the markets and merchant warehouses. Fancy carriages with curtained windows rattled past. Edeard was surprised to find them shielded from casual farsight by a mild variant of his own concealment ability; their footmen radiated sullen anger discouraging anyone from prying further.

The final approach to the city walls was home to an astonishing variety of trees. Ancient black and grey trunks sentried the road on either side, sending gnarled boughs overhead to form twined arches that were centuries old. At first Edeard thought there had been some kind of earthquake recently. All the trees, no matter their age and size, leaned one way, their branches bowing round in the same direction. Then it slowly dawned on him that the constant wind had shaped them, pushing their branches away from the shoreline.

For the last quarter of a mile, the ground was simple flat meadow, home to flocks of sheep. When they left the shelter of the trees, Edeard was awarded his first sight of the city since they'd descended out of the foothills. The crystal wall faced them, rising sheer out of the grass to a height of thirty yards. Although transparent, it possessed a gold hue, distorting the silhouettes of the buildings inside, making it impossible to gather a true impression of what lay within. It formed a perfect circle around the city, the same height all the way round except for the port on the eastern side where it dipped down to allow the sea to wash against the quays. Querencia's gentle tides had no visible effect on it; the stubborn crystal was as immune to erosion forces as it was to all other forms of assault. Neither bullets nor pickaxes could chip it, glue didn't stick to it. As a defensive barrier it was nearly perfect.

Its only known susceptibility was to telekinesis, which could gradually wear down its strength. That was how Rah opened the city to his people; a powerful telekinetic, he systematically cut through the crystal, shaping three gateways. Legend said each one took him two years to carve out. His followers fixed the huge detached segments to giant metal hinges, transforming them into tight-fitting gates. In the two millennia since, they had only ever been shut eight times. For the last seven hundred years they had remained open.

The caravan passed through the north gate. It was seven

yards wide at the base, arching up ten yards above Edeard's head. The gate itself was hinged back flat against the wall on the inside. He found it hard to believe the huge thing could actually still move; the hinges seemed wondrously primitive contraptions, all bulbous iron joints and girders studded with rivets. Yet they hadn't corroded, and the pivots were kept oiled.

Directly inside, to the left of the road, was a broad swathe of paddock land named the High Moat, which followed the wall's curve round to the Upper Tail district next to the port. As horses were prohibited from the main districts many families maintained stables here, simple wooden buildings that had been added to over the centuries; there were also stockades for cattle and traveller pens, even a couple of cheap markets. On the opposite side of the road, the similar crescent of Low Moat led round to the Main Gate. Running along the inner edge of the Moats, was the North Curve Canal, lined with the same whitish material from which the majority of the city was fabricated, resembling icy marble yet stronger than any metal which humans could forge on Querencia.

Edeard stared enchanted at the gondolas as they slid along the canal. He'd seen boats before, Thorpe-By-Water had them in abundance, as did many other towns. Yet those were coarse workaday cousins compared to these elegant black craft. They had shallow keels, with tall prows rising out of the water carved into elegant figures. The cushioned benches of the midsection were covered from the hot sun by white awnings, while the gondolier stood on a platform at the stern, manipulating a long punt pole with easy grace. Each gondola was home to at least a couple of ge-cats. Edeard smiled happily at the traditional genistar forms, which were swarming in and out of the salty water. Unlike the bloated creatures he had shaped back in Ashwell these were streamlined aquatics, with webbed feet and a long sinuous tail. The surface of the canal was alive with ripples as they continually chased after nimble fil-rats and chewed on strands of trilan weed to keep the canal clear.

'Oh my great Lady,' Salrana gasped, gawping out at the city.

'We did the right thing,' Edeard said with finality. 'Yes, we did.' Now he was inside the crystal wall, the true aura of the city was washing against him. He'd never sensed such vitality before, the kind of exhilarating emotional impact that could only come from so many people pursuing their hectic lives in close proximity. Individuality was impossible to distinguish, but the collective sensation was a power-house of animation. He felt uplifted simply by standing and drinking in the sights and sounds.

The caravan turned off the road. Barkus had a quick conversation with a city Travel Master who assigned them three pens on High Moat where they could set up to trade. The wagons rumbled along the narrow track to their final destination.

Edeard and Salrana walked their ge-horses over to Barkus's wagon. An act rich with association to that time back in Thorpe-By-Water when they'd come to the caravan master for help. The old man's family had been setting up the awnings on either side of the ancient wagon. They'd all been strangers back then, curious and suspicious. Now Edeard knew them all, and counted them as friends – which made this so very difficult. Salrana's thoughts were subdued and morose as Barkus turned to face them.

The old caravan master eyed the packs they were both carrying. 'You're really going to stay here, then?'

'Yes, sir.'

He hugged both of them. Salrana had to wipe some tears from her eyes. Edeard was fighting to make sure the same thing didn't happen to him.

'Have you got enough money?'

'Yes, sir, we're fine.' Edeard patted at the pocket inside his trousers. Along the route he'd sold enough ge-spiders to pay for weeks in a lavishly appointed tavern; and he was dressed respectably again.

'If it doesn't work out, we'll be here for a week. You're welcome to come with us. Both of you. You'll always have a home on the road with us.'

'I will never forget your kindness,' Edeard said.

'Nor I,' Salrana added.

'Go on then; be off with you.'

Edeard could see in the old man's agitated thoughts that this was just as painful for him. He gripped Barkus's arm and squeezed tightly before turning away. Salrana threw her hands round the caravan master's neck, and kissed him gratefully.

The road which had brought them into the city ended just short of the North Curve Canal. They walked beside the waterway for a little while until they found a bridge over. It was made from a tough ochre-coloured variety of the ubiquitous city material, a simple low arch to which wooden railings had been added on either side. Edeard had to clutch his shoulder bag tightly there were so many people using it, bustling against him. But no animals, he realized; not even ge-chimps. The bridge took them into the Ilongo district, which was made up of small box-like buildings, two or three storeys high with vaulting lierne roofs, and walls which often leaned away from perpendicular. Windows followed no pattern: there were angled slits, crescents, teardrops, circles, ovals, but never squares; they all had panes of a thick transparent crystal which grew, shaped, and replenished itself in the same slow fashion as the structures themselves. Entrances were simple arched oblongs or ovals cutting through ground-floor walls; it was the humans who'd added the wooden doors, fixing hinges into the structure with nails hammered into place with telekinesis. Over the years the pins would slowly be ejected by the city material as it repaired the puncture holes they'd made, necessitating re-fixing every decade or so. The constant sedate renewal of the city's fabric made the whole place look fresh, as if it had only just been completed.

The gap between the buildings was narrow. Sometimes, beside a canted corner, there was barely a couple of feet left between walls, forcing Edeard to turn sideways to squeeze through; while other passages were broad pavements allowing several people to walk side by side. They came across little squares and courtyards without warning, all of which were provided with fountains of fresh water bubbling up through the top of a thick pillar.

'Does nobody work?' Salrana asked in puzzlement after they'd been thoroughly jostled for ten minutes negotiating the narrow pavements. 'The whole city must be walking about.'

Edeard simply shrugged. The district was a confusing maze. It was also where he discovered the city material was almost opaque to farsight. He could only sense the murkiest of shapes on the other side of the walls; and he certainly couldn't perceive right through a building. He wasn't used to having his perception cut so short, it unnerved him slightly. Eventually he summoned his ge-eagle, and sent it soaring above the roofs, mapping a way for them.

He wanted to get to the Tosella district where the Eggshaper Guild had its Blue Tower. It was the district to the east of Ilongo, separated by the Hidden Canal. Despite it being so close, they took forty minutes to negotiate Ilongo before crossing the thin canal on a small wooden bridge.

Tosella's buildings were on a much larger scale than the ones they'd seen so far. Long rectangular mansions with tall slit windows stacked on top of each other up to six storeys high and topped with concentric ring domes that intersected each other like waves frozen in mid-swirl. The ground directly outside their walls was fenced off with high slender pillars, separating the public pavement from emble-mata mosaics of glittering primary-colour flecks. Their ground floors were arched cloisters enclosing central quads where prim gardens grew in long troughs under the cool tinted light shining through the roof skylights high above. For the first time in the city, he sensed the minds of genistars. A ground floor in one of the mansions had been converted into stables for them. He even glimpsed appren-tices and journeymen scurrying round the quads, their thoughts anxious and subdued as they tried to keep in their Master's good graces. It brought a smile to his face as he recalled some of Akeem's more outrageous stories of an apprentice's life in Makkathran.

'I know everyone asks this,' Salrana said as they tarried beside one of the huge mansions, admiring the subtle rainbow shades refracting off its glittering snow-white frontage. 'But I wonder who built this place?'

'I thought it was the Firstlifes. Isn't that what the Lady said?'

'It doesn't actually say that in any of her teachings. All she says is that the city was left by those who came before.'

'They couldn't have been humans, then.'

'What makes you say that?'

'Oh we can use it well enough, the concept of shelter is universal, I suppose. But nothing here is quite right for us. For a start, there were no gates until Rah arrived.'

'So the builders sailed in and out via the sea; that certainly ties in with all the canals,' she answered with a smile.

'No.' He couldn't match her light humour. His gaze swept along the length of the mansion. The root of architecture was species-based, from the basic functionality to the aesthetic; and Makkathran just didn't fit human sensibilities. He felt out of place here. 'Humans never built this place, we just adapted to it.'

'Aren't you the know-it-all; and we've only been here an hour.'

'Sorry,' he grinned. 'But it is intriguing, you have to admit that.'

'They say Eyrie district is the really weird one. That's where the Pythia has her church, which is the only building ever formed for humans. The city granted it to the Lady so her flock would be close to the towers when the Skylords finally return.'

'Towers?'

'Yes. That's where the Skylords alighted the last time

they were here, the day they took Rah's spirit to its rest in Odin's Sea.'

'Oh. Hey wait, you mean humans designed the Lady's Church?'

She gave a mock sigh. 'See? If you'd ever bothered to turn up to church you'd have known that. It's right there in the Lady's scriptures.'

He gave the mansion another suspicious look. 'That's like shaping genistars but with buildings. I wonder if the city builders brought the defaults to Querencia.'

'If the Geography Guild turn you down you could always apply to the History Guild.'

'Cheeky!' He took a swipe at her.

Salrana danced away laughing, and stuck her tongue out. Several passers-by gave her a curious look, unused to seeing a Lady's novice behave in such a fashion. She pulled a contrite face and held her hands demurely behind her back, eyes and mind still sparkling with amusement.

'Come on,' he said. 'The quicker we get to the Blue Tower the quicker we get you locked up in the novice dormitory where you belong – out of harm's way and not causing any trouble.'

'Remember our promise? I'm going to be Pythia and you're going to be Mayor.'

'Yeah,' he grinned. 'It might take a couple of years, but we'll do it.'

Her smile faded away as her thoughts grew sober. 'Edeard, you won't forget me, will you?'

'Hey – of course not.'

'I mean it, Edeard. Promise. Promise we'll still talk each day, even if it's just a longtalk hello.'

He held up a hand, palm towards her. 'I swear on the Lady, I won't forget you. Such a thing is just not possible.'

'Thank you.' Her impish smile returned. 'Do you want to kiss me again before we both get locked up in separate dormitories each night?'

He groaned in dismay. 'Maybe I should just leave with the caravan.'

It was Salrana's turn to take a swipe at him.

The Blue Tower was in the middle of the Tosella district, standing at least twice the height of the biggest mansion they'd seen so far. For its walls, the city material had shaded down to a dark azure which seemed to soak up the sunlight, as if the facade possessed its own nimbus of shadow. Standing at the base between flying buttresses which resembled ancient tree roots Edeard felt quite intimidated by the heartland of his Guild. Surely such a structure had never been intended to house a profession which existed to lighten the load of people's lives. It was more like a fortress which bandits would dwell in.

'Are you sure you want to do this?' Salrana asked uncertainly. She was just as daunted by the overpowering structure as he was.

'Er. Yes. I'm sure.' He wished the vacillation in his thoughts wasn't quite so blatant.

They walked in through a wide door whose resemblance to a giant mouth was uncomfortably obvious. Inside, the walls and floor changed to the darkest red with a surface sheen to match polished wood. Strong beams of sunlight from the high lancet windows cut through the gloom of the broad entrance hall.

Edeard didn't know where to go, there didn't seem to be any kind of official to direct visitors to the appropriate room. His determination was fading fast, leaving him stalled in the middle of the wide open space.

'I somehow don't think this is where the apprentices have their dormitories,' Salrana said from the side of her mouth. There were several groups of men in the hall, all talking quietly together. They wore fine clothes under flowing fur-lined gowns with the egg-in-a-twisted-circle crest of the Guild embroidered in gold thread on both collars. Disapproving glances were cast at Salrana and Edeard, followed by a surprising number of people focusing their farsight on the youthful pair.

Edeard's own farsight alerted him to three guards armed with revolvers marching across the entrance hall. They wore light drosilk jackets over their immaculate white cotton tunics. The Guild crest was prominent on their helmets.

The sergeant glowered at Edeard, but was marginally less hostile to Salrana when he saw she was in her full novice dress. 'You two,' he grunted, 'what's your business here?'

So much for the warm welcome to a fellow Guild member from far away, Edeard thought dourly. Then he realized he wasn't at all intimidated by the guard. After bandits the sergeant and his little squad seemed faintly ludicrous. 'I am a journeyman of the Guild,' Edeard said, surprising himself by how level and authoritative his voice was. 'I've come from Rulan province to complete my training.'

The sergeant looked as if he'd bitten into a rotten fruit.

'You're very young to be calling yourself a journeyman. Where's your badge?'

'It's been a long journey,' Edeard said, suddenly not wanting to explain what happened to his village to someone who would never understand life beyond the city. 'I lost it.'

'I see. And your letter?'

'Letter?'

The sergeant spoke slowly, contempt colouring his thoughts. 'Your letter of introduction to the Guild from your Master?'

'I have none.'

'Are you trying to take the piss, sonny? Your pardon, miss,' he said grudgingly at Salrana. 'Leave now before we take you to the Courts of Justice for trespass and theft.'

'I have committed no theft,' Edeard protested loudly. 'My Master was Akeem; he died before writing a letter of introduction.'

'The only reason to trespass here is to thieve something from us you little country shite,' the sergeant snapped. 'Now you've gone and fucked me off, and that's not good for you.' He reached for Edeard, then blinked in surprise as his hand slithered off an extremely strong telekinetic shield. 'Oh . . . you asked for this.' His third hand tried to grab.

Edeard warded him off easily, then hoisted the sergeant off the ground. The man yelled in shock as his feet kicked about.

'Take the little shite down,' he cried at his men. Their third hands closed round Edeard, to no avail. They went for their pistols, finding their arms moving slowly through impossibly thick air.

'Edeard!' Salrana squeaked.

Edeard couldn't quite comprehend how things had turned so crazy so fast.

'Enough,' a baritone voice commanded.

Edeard's farsight showed him an old man walking across the hall towards them. Long robes flowed behind him as he strode forwards. He'd taken to weight in his latter years, ochre trousers cut high so his curving belly didn't overhang, a baggy shirt to continue the discreet disguise, but his weight was still obvious from the podgy fingers to the rolling neck and heavy jowls. Yet he carried himself with the vitality of a man half his age. Even without sensing his regimented thoughts he was obviously a man of considerable authority.

'Put him down,' he ordered Edeard.

'Yes, sir,' Edeard said meekly. He just knew this was a Master equal to Akeem. 'I apologize. I was left little cho—'

'Be quiet.' The man turned to the sergeant, who was straightening his clothes, not making eye contact with anyone. 'And you, Sergeant, need to keep your temper in check. I am not prepared to have the Blue Tower guarded by petty-minded paranoia. You will learn a more rational attitude or you'll see your days out guarding a Guild estate on the other side of the Donsori Mountains. Do I make myself clear?'

'Sir.'

'Away with you while I determine how big a threat this boy presents.'

The sergeant led his men away, but not before managing a last look at Edeard which promised dire vengeance.

'Your name, boy?'

'Edeard, sir.'

'And I am Topar, a Master of the Guild Council, and deputy to Grand Master Finitan. That should give you an idea of how deep you just dipped yourself in default crap. My Lady's novice, may I enquire your name?'

'Salrana.'

'I see. And I judge that both of you have only recently arrived in Makkathran. Correct?'

'Yes, sir,' Edeard said. 'I'm really sorry about . . .'

Topar waved an irritated hand. 'I should be annoyed, but the name Akeem hasn't been heard in our august Tower for a considerable time. I am intrigued. Did I hear you say he is dead?'

'Yes, sir. I'm afraid he is.'

For a moment the gusto vanished from Topar's stance. 'A shame. Yes, a very great shame.'

'Did you know him, sir?'

'Not I, no. But I will take you to someone who did. He will want the details, I'm sure. Follow me.'

He led them to an archway at the rear of the hall, and began to climb the broad stairs beyond. As he ascended, Edeard knew he'd been right about whoever created the city not being humans. The stairs were cumbrous, more like a slope of solidified ripples. They curved enough to provide an unsure footing, while their spacing was awkward for human legs. Edeard soon found himself sweating as they continued to climb round and round; his calf muscles weren't used to such strenuous exercise.

At one point, when they must have been four or five storeys above the hall, Topar turned round to smirk at the two youngsters. He grunted as if satisfied by their tribulation. 'Just imagine how much rounder I would be if I didn't have to negotiate these five times a day, eh.' He chuckled and carried on.

Edeard was panting heavily when they finally stopped in some kind of large anteroom. He had no idea how high they'd climbed, but the top of the tower could surely only be a couple of feet above them. That altitude would explain how light-headed he'd become.

'Wait here,' Topar said, and went through a wooden door bound with thick iron filigrees.

The walls of the anteroom were still red, but lighter than those of the lower floors. Overhead, the ceiling glowed a pale amber, turning Edeard's skin an unpleasant shade of grey. He dumped his shoulder bag on the floor and sank into a large chair of curving wooden ribs. Salrana sat on one next to him, looking thoroughly bewildered. 'Are we in trouble or not?' she asked.

'I don't think I care any more. That pig of a sergeant. He knew we were harmless.'

She smiled. 'You're not.'

He was too tired to argue. His farsight was all but blocked by the tower walls; but he could just sense two minds behind the wooden door. There was very little to discern about their emotional composition, but then walking through the districts he'd noticed how adept city people were in guarding their feelings.

Topar opened the door. 'You can come in now, Edeard. Novice Salrana, if you would be so kind as to indulge us for a moment longer. Someone will be here to take care of you momentarily.'

Even before he went into the room, Edeard guessed he was being taken to Grand Master Finitan. As he went in, he nearly faltered as a farsight swept through him like a gust of cold air. The hair on the back of his arms stood up in reaction. A little thought occurred to him that if anyone could see through a psychic concealment, it would be this man.

Grand Master Finitan sat in a high-back chair behind a large oak desk, facing the door. His office must have taken up nearly a quarter of the tower at this level. It was huge, but almost empty; there was no furniture other than the desk and chair. Two of the walls were covered by book-shelves containing hundreds of leather-bound tomes. Behind him, the wall was mostly crystal window with thin lierne ribs, providing a view clear across Makkathran. Edeard's jaw fell open. He only just managed to stop himself running over and gawping like a delighted child. From what he could see at this angle, the undulating rooftops swept away for miles, while the canals cut through them like blue-grey arteries. Looking at it like this, he knew for certain that the city was alive. Here, humans were nothing more than foreign bacteria living in a body they could never fully comprehend.

'Quite a sight, isn't it?' Grand Master Finitan said gently. In many respects he was the physical opposite to Topar. Slim and tall, with thick hair worn down to his shoulders, only just beginning to grey. Yet his age was evident in the lines creasing his face. Despite that, his thoughts were tranquil, he was curious and affable rather than dismissive.

Edeard shifted his gaze back to the Grand Master. 'Yes, sir. Er, I apologize again for what happened downstai—'

The Grand Master raised a finger to his lips, and Edeard fell silent. 'No more of that,' Finitan said. 'You've travelled a long way, yes?'

'From Rulan province, sir.'

Finitan and Topar exchanged a glance, smiling at some private joke. 'A long way,' Finitan said sagely. 'Some tea?' His mind sent out a fast longtalk instruction.

Edeard turned to see a door open at the base of one of the bookshelf walls; it was too small for a man, barely four feet high. Ge-chimps scampered out bringing a pair of chairs and a tray. The chairs were positioned in front of the Grand Master's desk, while the tray with its silver tea service was placed on the desk beside a cradle which held a genistar egg.

'Sit down, my boy,' Finitan said. 'Now, I understand you claim our colleague Akeem is dead. When did this happen?'

'Almost a year ago, sir.'

'Those are some very dark thoughts in your mind accompanying that memory. Please tell me the story in its entirety. I believe I'm old enough to endure the full truth.'

Embarrassed at his mind being so transparent, Edeard took a deep breath and began.

Both the Grand Master and Topar were silent when he finished. Eventually, Finitan rested his chin on steepled forefingers. 'Ah, my poor dear Akeem; for his life to end like that is an unforgivable tragedy. An entire village slaughtered by bandits. I find that extraordinary.'

'It happened,' Edeard said with a flash of anger.

'I'm not questioning your tale, my boy. I find the whole concept deeply disturbing, that there is some kind of society out in the wilds different to our own; and one which is so implacably hostile.'

'They're animals,' Edeard growled.

'No. That's your instinctive reaction; and a healthy one

it is, too. But to organize such a raid is quite an accomplishment.' He sat back and drank some tea. 'Could there really be a rival civilization somewhere out there beyond our maps? They have concealment techniques and fanciful weapons. I'd always believed such things were the provenance of this city alone.'

'You have the repeat-fire guns?' Edeard asked. In all his travels, no one had ever heard of such a thing. A year of constant dismissal had made him doubt his own memories of that terrible night.

Finitan and Topar exchanged another glance. 'No. And that is more worrying than knowing how to conceal yourself. But how lovely that Akeem knew the technique which is supposed to be practised only by Guild Masters.'

'He was a Master, sir.'

'Of course. I mean those of us who sit on the Council. Sadly, Akeem never achieved that. It was politics of course. I'm afraid to say, young Edeard, that you are going to learn life here in the city is all about politics.'

'Yes, sir. Did you know Akeem, sir?'

Finitan smiled. 'Have you not worked it out yet, my boy? Dear me, I thought you quicker. We share a bond, you and I. For he was my Master when I was a lowly young apprentice here.'

'Oh.'

'Which means you present me with a very unpleasant problem.'

'I do?' Edeard said anxiously.

'You have no formal letter of confirmation from your Master. Worse than that, with your village gone, we cannot ever confirm that you were taken in by the Guild.'

Edeard smiled uncertainly. 'But I know how to sculpt

an egg.' His farsight swept through the egg on the Grand Master's desk, revealing the folded shadows of the embryo inside. 'You have sculpted a ge-dog; I don't recognize some of the traits, they're outside the traditional form, but it is a dog. Two days from hatching, I'd guess.'

Topar nodded in appreciation. 'Impressive.'

'Akeem was the best Master,' Edeard said hotly.

Finitan's sigh was heavier than before. 'You have obviously received Guild training, and you clearly have skill as well as strength. And that is the problem.'

'I don't understand, sir.'

'You say Akeem made you a journeyman?'

'Yes, sir.'

'I cannot accept you into the Guild at that level. I know this seems intolerably harsh, Edeard, but there are formalities which even I have to follow.'

Edeard was aware of his cheeks burning. It wasn't quite anger, but all he could think of was the pettiness of the Guild Master back in Thorpe-By-Water. Surely the Grand Master, the leader of the whole Eggshaper Guild, couldn't be so small-minded; what he said was law to the Guild. 'I see.'

'I doubt it, but I do sympathize with the exasperation you must feel. I will be delighted to accept you into the Guild here in Makkathran, Edeard, but it must be as a junior apprentice. I cannot make exceptions, especially not in your case.'

'What do you mean?'

'To acknowledge your journeyman status without a formal letter from your Master will lay me open to a charge of favouritism from others on the Guild Council.'

'Politics,' Topar said.

'I understand,' Edeard whispered. He was frightened he was going to burst into tears in front of them. To get to Makkathran, to be in the presence of the Grand Master, then to be told all he had achieved was worthless because he lacked a piece of paper ... 'Pardon me, but that's stupid, sir,' he said sullenly.

'It's much worse than that. But I appreciate your politeness, my boy.'

Edeard sniffed and wiped his nose. 'How long would it take me to get back to being a journeyman?'

'Here at the Blue Tower, and assuming you have the appropriate talent: seven years. Appointing you a journeyman at your age was ... ambitious, even for Akeem. But at the same time so very typical of him.'

'Seven years,' Edeard repeated numbly. Seven years of repeating every lesson and knowledge gift he'd ever undergone. Seven years of having to hold himself back. Seven years of obedience to journeymen less able than himself. *Seven years!*

'I know what you're thinking, and I'm not even using farsight,' Finitan said gently. 'It is a terrible thing to ask you to undergo.'

'I'm not sure I can,' Edeard said. 'I thought when I came here I wanted nothing more than to be a part of the Guild, but now ... These formalities, Akeem always said I would find them so difficult. I thought he was teasing.'

'Listen to me, Edeard,' Finitan said. 'For I am about to say something which borders on the sacrilegious.'

'Sir?'

'The hierarchy we have in the Guilds, not just ours, but all Guilds, exists for those who seek to further themselves within our political system. Talent in your chosen field plays a part, but always it is down to money and politics. That is the way things are here in the capital. If you are not born into a grand family and have ambition then you join a Guild and fight your way to the top. Now consider that very carefully because this is a choice that will decide the rest of your life for you. Is the Eggshaper Guild what you truly want? It is what I wanted, and I have achieved my goal. I am Grand Master. But look at the battles I have to fight on every level. I am surrounded with so many people seeking the same thing, seeking this seat in this office, that I cannot make an exception for someone as gifted as yourself because a hundred years ago I had a Master that went on to teach you. Is that sanity, Edeard? Is that the life you want for yourself? To have a dozen such considerations every day, to be unable to put a foot wrong, to continue tradition no matter how dry and worthless it is because that is what supports you. To be unable to change, even though change was the one thing above all that used to drive you. That is what I am, Edeard, that is what Topar is. I despair of myself at times, of how helpless I have become, entrapped in the very system I once wanted to alter and improve.'

'But, sir, if you can't make changes, who can?'

'Nobody can, Edeard. Not now, not in these times. Our society is mature. Change is instability. That is why every institution we have resists change. To maintain the status quo is our sole objective in life.'

'That's wrong.'

'Yes, it is. But what do you want to do about it? Do you want to spend seven years working your arse off to become a journeyman, to make that first real step towards receiving Master status, at which point your talent is irrelevant and the politicking begins in earnest. You build allies and make enemies on every council upon which you sit in order to gain greater power and control. But it is only power and control over the councils. Ultimately it amounts to very little.'

'Are you saying I should go back and join the caravan?'

'No. My offer to admit you to the Guild is genuine and remains open while I am Grand Master. Who knows? Maybe you will make a difference if you make it to this office. I should tell you now that nobody under a hundred years old has ever sat here.'

'I don't know,' Edeard said helplessly.

'There is one alternative. You already know how to sculpt eggs, by joining the Guild you would be acknowledging your life is now orientated to a political goal. However, the city constables are always seeking recruits. It is a noble profession. My position on the Upper Council allows me to sponsor you into their ranks. They would delight in accepting someone with such a strong third hand. And this city desperately needs men of good stature to enforce the law. Without that we will all become nothing.'

'A constable?' He wasn't even sure what a constable was.

'Even a city as sophisticated as Makkathran has crime, Edeard. Decent people, especially those in the poorer districts, live in fear from gangs who roam the streets at night. Merchants suffer thefts and increase their prices accordingly, which injures everyone. You would be helping people directly. And immediately. Unlike the other Guilds, constable apprentices are not tucked away out of sight toiling to make their Master's life easy. The hierarchy of the constables is a lot less complex than any normal Guild. The prospect for advancement is good. You're smart and strong. I will not delude you that it is an easy life, for it is not. But you've even been in a real life-or-death fight, which is more than any other recruit. You should do well.'

'I'm not sure.'

'Of course not. I didn't expect you to give me an answer immediately. You need time to think about your future. What you decide now determines the rest of your life. Why don't you escort your friend to her church, then take a good look around. Get a feel for the city before you make your mind up. If you do want to give the constables a try, longtalk Topar here, and we will arrange for your admission.'

'Thank you, sir.'

'You are welcome. And Edeard.'

'Sir?'

'I'm glad Akeem had such a gifted pupil at the end. It wouldn't have been easy for him in Ashwell; you must have helped enrich his life considerably.'

'Thank you.' Edeard rose from the seat, knowing his time was up. 'Sir? Why did Akeem leave the Blue Tower?'

Finitan smiled fondly. 'He was like you, my boy. He wanted to make a difference, to help people. Here, he could do very little. Outside our crystal wall, in Ashwell, I suspect he had a profound effect on the lives of the villagers.'

'Yes, sir; he did.'

'What happened in there?' Salrana demanded when Edeard reappeared in the anteroom. 'You don't seem very happy.'

'I'm not,' he admitted and picked up his shoulder bag. 'Come on, we need to get you to the church before nightfall. I'll tell you what happened on the way.'

*

'You can't give up,' Salrana said as they crossed a bridge over Grove Canal into the Eyrie district. Her voice was pleading. 'Not after so much.'

'Finitan was right, though. What's the point? I can already shape eggs as well as just about anyone. If I join the Guild I'll be doing it to climb up the hierarchy, nothing else. And what's there even if I do become Grand Master? Sitting at the top of a tower organizing the Guild while everyone else on the Council waits for me to make a mistake. I'd have a million enemies and no friends, and nothing will change. I won't be helping anyone. Remember Ashwell, what it was like before people accepted the genistars could improve their life? Well Makkathran is a thousand years along from that. You can't shape better genistars, you can't increase the amount in use here.'

'Then when you become Grand Master you must push genistars out on people next to the wild lands. The Eggshaper Guild can still make a difference to everyone beyond the Iguru Plain. You've seen what life's like in the distant provinces. Make it better for them, Edeard, make their life as easy as it is for everyone here.'

'It's too much,' he said. 'I can't do it, Salrana. Most of all, I can't stand seven years as an apprentice again. I just can't. I've learned the Guild teachings, I've been on the road fending for myself for a year. Any position less than journeyman would be a huge step backwards for me. I'm sorry.' He could just see Akeem shaking his head in that weary way of his. The guilt was terrible.

She stroked his cheek, which brought astonished glances from passers-by. 'I'm not going to give up on you. And I'm certainly not going to let you give up on your own dream. Not after what we've been through.'

'I don't know what I'd do without you.'

'You're welcome,' she said spryly.

He glanced up at the strangely twisted spires that jutted out of the ground like gigantic stalagmites. Even the smallest was higher than the Blue Tower. There were no windows or balconies, just a single entrance at ground level leading to a central spiral stair. Right at the tip, they flared out into broad platforms that looked terribly unstable, as if they would snap off at any second.

After the madcap bustle of the other districts they'd experienced, Eyrie was almost deserted by comparison. With night falling, the devout were making their way to the central church of the Empyrean Lady for the evening service of prayer and thanksgiving. Light was beginning to shine out of crevices in the crinkled towers around them, washing the hard ground in a pale tangerine illumination. Edeard regarded it curiously, realizing it was the same glow that had lit his way up the stairs of the Blue Tower, somehow the city material emitted it without heat.

'Where will you go tonight?' she asked.

'I don't know. Find a cheap tavern with a room, I suppose.'

'Oh Edeard, you'll be so lonely there. Why don't you go back to the caravan? Anyone there will be happy to lend you a cot.'

'No,' he said firmly. 'I won't go back.'

She pressed her teeth together in dismay. 'Your pride will be the end of you.'

He smiled. 'Probably.'

The Lady's central church was impressive. A large cloud-white dome with the top third made of the same crystal as the city wall. Three wings radiated out from the middle, lined with balconies.

'I'm here,' Salrana said in wonder. Tears glinted in her eyes and her mind shone with happiness. 'The Lady herself lived the last years of her life here. Can you feel how sacrosanct this ground is? It's all real, Edeard. The Lady's message to the word is real.'

'I know,' he said.

The main door to the church was wide open, shining a broad fan of rose-gold light across the broad plaza outside. Several Mothers dressed in splendid white and silver robes stood on the threshold to give a personal welcome to their congregation. Salrana straightened her shoulders and walked up to the first. There followed a long conversation which Edeard did his best not to eavesdrop on. It culminated with the Mother embracing Salrana. Another two Mothers hurried over at her longtalk call. They all began chattering excitedly around the suddenly overwhelmed girl.

Salrana turned, holding an arm out to Edeard. 'They'll take me in,' she said, her face suffused with delight.

'That's good,' he said softly.

'Come, child,' said the first Mother, and put her arm protectively around Salrana. 'Young man.'

'Yes, Mother.'

'We commend you for aiding our lost soul. May the Lady bless you for what you have done.'

He didn't know what to say, so he just ducked his head gracelessly.

'Will you stay for the service?'

'I, er, have to get to my lodgings, thank you.' He backed away and turned, walking quickly across the plaza.

'Don't forget,' Salrana's longtalk voice chided him. 'Talk to me first thing tomorrow. I want to know that you're all right.'

'I will.'

Even with the cold orange light shining down from the twisted towers, he was unnerved walking through the empty district. The dark upper sections of the towers formed black silhouettes against the glowing night sky. His mind kept firmly focused on the warm aura of human minds on the other side of the Grove Canal. Before he reached any bridge he came to a decision. His farsight strained to reach the Blue Tower. The sparks of minds were very hard to distinguish through its walls, but he persevered and eventually found one he recognized.

'Excuse me, sir?' he longtalked to Topar.

There was a small burst of surprise from the man, quickly smothered. 'Where are you, Edeard?'

'In Eyrie, sir.'

'And you farsighted me through the walls of the Blue Tower from there?'

'Er, yes, sir.'

'Of course you did. So what can I do for you?'

'I know this probably seems sudden to you, sir, but I have thought over what the Grand Master said to me. I'd like to join the constables. There's nothing else for me here.'

'Yes, we did make that promise to you, didn't we. Very well. Report to the main constable station in the Jeavons district. By the time you get there they will be expecting you. Your letter of sponsorship will be with the captain in the morning.'

'Yes, sir. Please thank the Grand Master for me, sir. I'll not let him down.'

'Somehow, Edeard, I don't think you will. One word of advice from a lifelong citizen of Makkathran.'

'Sir?'

'Don't let your fellow constables realize how strong you are, not at first. It may attract the wrong kind of interest. Politics, remember?'

'I remember, sir.'

*

'Get up, you little turds!'

Edeard groaned, immensely tired, blinking against the orange light flooding down into the dormitory. His thoughts were a confused whirl as reality intruded into the shrinking dream.

'Come on. Up! I haven't got the time to nurse you pathetic tits. If you can't even get up in the morning what use are you? None. Which doesn't surprise me in any respect. I want every one of you dressed and in the small hall in five minutes. Anyone who doesn't make it before I close the doors can piss off right back home to your mummy again. Now move it.'

'Whaa—?' Edeard managed. Someone walked past the end of his bed and whacked his feet with a truncheon. 'Ouch!'

'If you think that hurt, wait till I get to work on your feelings, farm boy.'

Edeard hurriedly pushed the blanket down and rolled out. There were six bed alcoves in the dorm room, only two were empty. He'd met the other constable recruits last night, a quick session before Chae, their squad's training sergeant, marched in and barked at them to shut up and get some sleep. 'Because you've got an early start in the morning.'

As he struggled into his shirt, Edeard suspected it was Chae who'd just woken them. The voice was familiar.

'He's got to be kidding,' said Boyd, a tall lad with lank blond hair and large ears. The fourth son of a baker in the Jeavons district not far from the station, he was in his early twenties and as he saw his elder brother take on more and more of the bakehouse he finally acknowledged he wasn't going to inherit any part of the family business. His sisters were married off, and his other brothers had all left the district to forge their own way forward. He lacked their entrepreneurial streak, so decided the only way out was the Guilds or signing up with either the militia or the constables. He didn't have the money to buy into the militia; and his psychic talents were limited.

'Oh no he's not,' Macsen said as he hurriedly pulled up his own trousers. His story was similar to Boyd's. He was the unrecognized son of a mistress to a grand family's patriarch. Usually such a father would quietly buy such an offspring a minor commission in the militia or smooth the way for entry to a professional Guild such as the lawyers or clerks. Unfortunately, this patriarch chose to travel on one of his trading ships voyaging south along the coast when one of the Lyot Sea's rare storms blew up. The wife and eldest son threw Macsen and his mother out of their estate cottage on the Iguru even before the memorial service had been held.

Edeard shoved his bare feet into his boots. 'We'd better do as he says, at least until we figure out how serious the officers are,' he said. He looked at the locker beside the cot where his shoulder bag was resting, and briefly wondered if it would be safe. Not that there was much of value inside. *And anyway, this is a constable station.*

'Chae's serious all right,' Dinlay said. Their final room mate was also a youngest son, but his father was a constable. As such, Dinlay was the only one to already have a uniform. He was doing up the silver buttons on the front of his dark-blue tunic. The little metal circles had been polished to a sheen, as had his black ankle-high boots. The trousers were pressed, showing a sharp crease down the front. It wasn't a new uniform, but you had to look carefully to see any wear. Dinlay had told them last night it used to belong to his father when he was a probationary constable. Out of the four of them, he seemed to be the only one enthusiastic about their new profession. He used a longtalk whisper to tell them, 'Father said Sergeant Chae is a heavy drinker. He was sent to this station because he's screwed up everywhere else in the city.'

'So they put him in charge of training recruits?' Macsen exclaimed.

Dinlay winced, glancing about uncomfortably. 'Not so loud. He doesn't like being reminded he threw his career away.'

Boyd chuckled. 'Career. In the constables. Aren't you the comedian.'

Dinlay gave him an angry look before putting his wire-rimmed glasses on. There was something about him which reminded Edeard of Fahin, not just his short-sight problem, but the way he was so dedicated to his life choice, yet at the same time so obviously wasn't cut out for it.

Edeard shivered despite pulling on a thick woollen

jumper. He hadn't thought of Fahin in a long time. It was an unfortunate way to start his first morning.

Not that it was morning yet, he noticed, as they scurried down the station's central stair to the small hall where they would spend the next six months learning their new craft. The glowing nebulas of Querencia's night sky were still visible through the feathery curtain of cloud drifting in from the sea. Dawn was at least another hour away.

Edeard still wasn't used to the way Makkathran buildings blocked his farsight. So he was surprised when they arrived in the hall that another probationary constable was already there along with Sergeant Chae. She was about his age, perhaps a little older, with dark hair cut shorter than he'd ever seen on a girl before. Her face was rounded with chubby cheeks and what looked like a permanent scowl. Even by Makkathran standards, her thoughts were heavily veiled, allowing no hint as to her true feelings. Edeard tried not to be too obvious in the way he checked her out, but when his eyes switched from her legs – long but thighs rather too plump – to her chest he suddenly realized she was watching him. She raised an eyebrow in scornful query. His cheeks reddened and he turned away.

Chae was standing at the head of the room, under one of the ceiling's circular light patches. Thankfully, his anger seemed to have vanished. 'Very good, boys and girls, almost on time. Now believe it or not, this early morning is not designed with the sole purpose to make your lives miserable, I'll have plenty of opportunity for that over the next few months. No. Today I want us to get acquainted. That means, we'll be starting with some simple tests to discover the level of your psychic abilities – or the lack of them.

This way we can combine you into a squad which together will perform a great deal better than the sum of its parts. And believe me you will need to work together. There are gangs out there who will happily shred your flesh and feed you to the fil-rats if you try and interrupt their activities.'

Edeard wasn't quite sure he believed that, and hoped his thoughts didn't show his doubt. He concentrated on trying to achieve the same passivity that everyone else was displaying.

'Constable Kanseen, would you begin, please,' Chae said. He gestured at the bench in front of him. There were five metal balls resting on the ancient wood, the smallest was the size of a human fist, while the others were progressively larger. A sixth ball sat on the floor, a good eighteen inches in diameter.

'Which one?' Kanseen asked.

'You just show me what you can do, young lady,' Chae said. There was a strong note of contempt ringing through his voice. 'That way I can assess what duties to assign you. If any.'

Kanseen's face hardened into an even more disapproving scowl. She glared at the fourth ball. It slowly rose into the air.

Macsen whistled approvingly and clapped. The other probationary constables grinned appreciatively. Edeard took a moment, and joined in the acknowledgement. He assumed someone had given her the same advice as him about not revealing her full strength.

'That it?' Chae asked.

'Sir,' Kanseen grunted.

'Okay, thank you. Boyd, let's see what you're made of.'

A grinning Boyd stepped forward. The fourth ball quivered and rose a couple of inches above the wood. Boyd's brow glistened with perspiration.

Macsen managed to lift the fifth ball. Dinlay produced a confident grin and elevated the fifth and second balls, which drew him a heavy round of applause. Even Kanseen joined in.

'All right, Edeard, show them how the countryside is so much better than the city.'

Edeard nodded slowly and moved forward. The others were watching eagerly. He was sorely tempted to fling the sixth ball right at the sergeant, but Topar's caution was still fresh in his mind.

His third hand closed round the fifth ball and sent it bobbing up through the air until it was halfway to the ceiling. The others cheered. He lifted the second ball, then made a show of straining to lift the third, allowing it to hover a few inches above the wood.

The first ball shot off the table and streaked towards Edeard. His shield hardened, deflecting it easily enough. At the same time he dropped the three balls he was holding aloft.

All of the probationary constables fell silent, staring at him and Chae.

'Very good, Edeard,' Chae drawled. 'You almost convinced me. Little too much time between the hit and the drop, though. Work on that.'

Edeard gave the sergeant a sullen stare.

Chae leaned forward, in a stage whisper he said: 'I have friends in the Eggshaper Guild guard, lad.'

Edeard reddened.

'Constables should be honest above all else,' Chae continued. 'Especially with their own squad mates. Ultimately your lives may depend on each other. Now do you want to try again?'

Edeard pulled the sixth ball into the air. He heard Boyd gasp in surprise.

'Thank you, Edeard,' Chae said. 'Now then; farsight. I have placed some markers around the district. Let's see who can find what.'

Edeard let the sixth ball down gently. He wondered what Chae would have said if he'd known how much more he could lift.

The psychic tests went on for another hour, measuring their various talents until Chae declared he'd had enough of them. Edeard was interested in the results. Kanseen had a farsight almost as good as his own, while Dinlay could probably longshout halfway across the Iguru Plain – a capability he was inordinately proud of. Macsen's shield seemed disproportionately stronger than his third hand – nothing Chae threw at him got through. Boyd was all round unexceptional. It left Edeard wondering if he was above average or if his squad mates were distinctly below average. Sergeant Chae's psychic ability was certainly powerful enough.

Chae told them to get some breakfast then report for uniform fitting. 'If any of you have money I'd advise you to spend it on your tunic. Those without money will have the cost taken out of their pay for the next six months, and I assure you it won't leave you with much at the end of the week.'

They trooped along to the station's main hall, a long chamber with an arching ceiling and a big crystal window at the far end. Some of the benches were already occupied.

A sergeant told them the bench at the far end would be theirs for the duration of their probationary period. The rest of the constables ignored them.

Ge-monkeys hurried out of the kitchen bringing crockery. They were adept at receiving orders, Edeard found when he instructed one to bring tea and scrambled eggs. At least the station provided their food. He wondered if he should try to longtalk Salrana. The sun was just starting to rise outside.

'I've never seen anyone lift so much,' Boyd said. 'You've got a lot of talent, Edeard.'

Edeard shrugged.

'I claim first rights to stand behind him when the shit starts flying,' Macsen said. 'And the bullets.'

'You all look like you can handle yourselves if we get pushed into a corner,' Edeard said.

'Don't have a lot of choice, do we?' Macsen said. 'Not enough skill for a Guild, and not rich enough to buy into the militia. So here we are, all of us clinging to the arse end of life and we're only just starting out. One big long fall into the sewage from here on in, my fellow failures.'

'Ignore him,' Dinlay said. 'He's just bitter at the way he got treated by his father's family.'

'Not as bitter as they'll be when I'm through with them,' Macsen said with unexpected heat.

'Plans for revenge?' Kanseen asked.

'Don't have to plan. Those arrogant turds break the law a dozen times a week. One day I'll have the clout to have the whole lot of the bastards locked up and ruined.'

'Now that's what I like to see: ambition.'

'How come you didn't join a Guild, Edeard?' Macsen

asked. 'You have more psychic talent than the rest of us put together.'

'I don't want to be ordered around for the next seven years,' he told them simply.

'Lady bless that,' Dinlay said. 'We just have to grit our teeth for six months and we've made it.'

'That's a curious definition of making it,' Kanseen said in a dismissive voice as a ge-monkey brought her a tray with a bowl of porridge and a tall glass of milk. 'Being allowed out on to the streets by ourselves to be shoved around by gangs and get beaten up trying to stop tavern fights.'

'Then why are you here?' Macsen asked.

She took a long drink of milk. 'Do you see me being a proper little wife to some oaf of a tradesman?'

'Not all tradesmen are oafs,' Boyd said defensively.

Macsen ignored him. 'Good for you,' he told Kanseen.

Her head turned ponderously to stare at him. 'Not interested, thanks.'

Edeard grinned while Dinlay and Boyd both laughed.

'Me neither,' Macsen insisted, but he'd lost the moment and sounded very insincere.

'So is Chae right about buying the uniform?' Edeard asked. He was conscious that he probably had more coinage in his pocket than the others.

'Depends,' Dinlay said. 'If you're definitely going to be a constable then it doesn't matter how you pay. But if you're uncertain then you're best off having them take it from your wages, that way when you leave after a couple of weeks you hand the uniform back and you haven't lost any of your own money.'

'Oh face facts,' Macsen said. 'If we're here, it's not because we're uncertain: we're plain desperate.'

'Speak for yourself,' Dinlay said. 'This is my family profession.'

'Then I apologize. I don't have the nicety of alternatives.'

'You could have joined the gangs,' Kanseen said lightly. 'It probably pays better.'

Macsen showed her a fast hand gesture.

'How bad are they?' Edeard asked. 'The gangs, I mean. I'd never heard of them before I reached town.'

'Lady, you really are from the countryside, aren't you,' Macsen said. 'When did you get here?'

'Yesterday.'

'*Yesterday!*' he said it in a voice so loud that several constables glanced curiously over at their table.

'Yesterday,' Edeard said firmly.

'Okay, well, too late now. The gangs are big in some districts and not in others; the majority are based in Sampalok. If you're rich they're not much of a problem, if you're poor then it's more difficult for you. They specialize in protection. Think of them as an alternative tax system to the Grand Council.'

'But with violence,' Dinlay said. 'They're murderous scum, and they should be wiped out.'

'After first being fairly found guilty in court,' Macsen said with a smile.

'They're a real problem and getting worse,' Boyd said. 'My brother is having to pay them to leave the bakery alone, and he's only ten minutes away from this station; which puts him about as far from Sampalok as you can be. It used to be safe there; my father never used to have such trouble.'

'Why doesn't he report them to the constables?' Edeard said.

Macsen gave a disrespectful snort. 'Take a look around you, Edeard. Would you ask us to protect you from an organized gang who think it's funny to throw your children or your mother into the canal with a rock tied to them? Are you going to stand outside a baker's shop for twenty-four hours a day for ten years just to save them? Do you think Chae would let you? And if he did, what about everyone else in the district? No. They're a fact of life in Makkathran now. The best the constables do is maintain an uneasy truce and stop us from falling into complete anarchy.'

'So young, so cynical,' Kanseen said. 'Ignore them, Edeard, it's nothing like as bad as they say.'

'I hope not,' he said in a subdued voice. Maybe he was still suffering from the shock of city life, but he had an uncomfortable feeling that Grand Master Finitan hadn't been entirely honest with him about life in Makkathran.

5

Investigator, second level, Halran stood in the vault's open door and surveyed the chaos inside. Every surface – walls, floor, ceiling, corpses – had been covered in a thick carpet of blue-grey gossamer fibre, as if a million spiders had spent the night spinning their webs together. The slender strands were actually semi-organic filaments that had taken over three hours to neutralize the nerve toxin leaking from spent kinetic projectiles, and also damp down several other lethal energy surges coming from munitions left over from the firefight. Halran was mildly surprised that the St Mary's Clinic would use nerve agents, but then important people did like reassurance that their secure memory stores were truly *secure*. He'd told the clinic manager that he'd be inspecting their toxic armaments user certificate at noon. A timescale long enough for high-level calls to be placed and the correct licence to be procured. It was that kind of flexible interpretation of procedure which had earned Halran his last two promotions. He figured what the hell, the big boys ran the world anyway, there was little capital to be made from annoying them. That was why the Police Commissioner handed him this assignment. And as soon as he got it, the Mayor's assistant was calling him to explain certain political considerations. Foremost of which was that the complete destruction of half a million memorycells belonging to the wealthiest, most influential people living in the state had not actually happened. If there was a temporary glitch in kube data retrieval due to the unfortunate accident with the clinic's power generator it was regrettable, but not a cause for alarm, nor excessive media interest. Reporters could cover the damage to the forest, they were not to be permitted into the administration block and its sub-levels.

Halran's u-shadow completed its analysis of the gossamer and reported that decontamination was complete. 'All right,' he told the eight-strong forensic team standing behind him in the corridor, 'I want a full scene survey down to a molecular level. No budget limit; this is way way above our usual priority rating. Col, Angelo, you build the event sequence for me. Darval, see if you can get me the name of the memorycell that bastard Telfer was after.'

Darval peered over Halran's shoulder; the emergency lighting projector rigged up in the doorway produced a silver-blue holographic glow throughout the vault, eliminating shadows. It made the gossamer shimmer softly, resembling a rippled moonlit lake as its undulations smothered the congealed splinters of half a million kubes. 'How in Ozzie's name am I going to do that, Chief?'

Halran gave him an evil grin. 'There should be one missing. So all you have to do is reassemble the fragments of those that are still here, and tell me which one was taken.'

'Fuck me.'

'Good point. Plan B: go through the names on the registry and assign them a probability of someone wanting to steal their memories. Start with political, criminal, and financial categories.'

Darval gave a reluctant nod.

'Force fields on at all times, please,' Halran ordered. 'There were some very nasty munitions loose in here, I don't want to take any chances.'

The forensic team moved cautiously into the vault. Examiners scurried in with them, bots like lead cockroaches scuttling along on black electromuscle legs, bristling with sensory antenna that wiggled though the gossamer to stroke the surfaces beneath. Over two thousand were released, streaming over the floor and up the walls to build up a comprehensive molecular map of the vault.

Halran waited until the tiny bots had whirled round the corpse of Viertz Accu before he gave her a more detailed inspection. Her cocooned body was still in a kneeling position, spine curved forward as if she was at prayer. They'd found the top of her skull upstairs while they were waiting for the gossamer to run its decontamination procedure. Halran knew what that implied – this was turning into a bad case from every angle.

His exovision overlaid the results of the examiners, showing him the narrow burn lines on her exposed brain. A lot of energy had been applied in a fashion he recognized. He applied a deep-scan module, tracking the depth of the beam penetration. Her memorycell had been destroyed.

'I hope she backed up recently,' he muttered.

'What do you make of these, Chief?' Angelo asked. He was standing in front of an exotic matter cage.

'Nice idea, I suppose. I haven't seen one before. Telfer obviously didn't know they were here.'

'Much good it did the clinic. Those guards didn't exactly slow him down, did they?'

'No. His enrichments were off the scale.' Halran called up the main case file again. Telfer appeared in his exo-image, a picture taken in the main reception area, showing a possible oriental ethnicity, but with odd grey eyes. Age locked into his thirties, which was unusual, and with a dense stubble shadow. Completely unexceptional. Which Halran knew to be deliberate. Not that visual features meant anything in this day and age; even DNA identification was inconclusive now – and they had enough of that from the blood trail back up to the roof. The picture showed him smiling as he greeted the beautiful young clinician. His accomplice, though, was a different matter, she certainly didn't qualify as unexceptional; a real beauty with a freckled face and thick dark-red hair. Cute nose, too, he thought admiringly. People would remember that face.

Everything about their arrival was perfectly normal, right up to the moment the clinic security net started glitching and Telfer vanished from the smartcore's passive surveillance. The raid, too, was extremely professional. Apart from the exit. The woman had seemed almost surprised, as if she was improvising the whole thing. Which didn't make a lot of sense.

'Chief,' Darval called.

'Yep.'

'The registry was hacked.'

Halran started to walk over to where Darval was stooped over the registry pillar. Several examiners were crawling over its gossamer cloak, prodding the top with their antennae. 'Has there been physical—' he began to say. The sentence was never finished. A woman walked into the vault. Halran gave her a surprised look, about to ask who the hell she was – suspecting another of the Mayor's staffers – because nobody else could get through the police cordon without his permission. Then her face registered and Halran didn't need to ask, he knew all about this living legend; everyone in law enforcement did. 'Oh sweet Ozzie,' he murmured – and an already bad case turned nightmare on him. She was shorter than most of the citizens of today's Commonwealth, but the confidence she exuded was so much greater than average. Harlan had encountered enough Highers in his time to recognize their slightly smug self-belief; she was on a level far above them, with a composure that rated glacial. Her face was enchanting, a combination of pre-Commonwealth Earth's Filipino and European features framed by thick raven hair brushed straight and devoid of any modern cosmetics, a beauty he could only describe as old-fashioned. Which was fair enough given she hadn't changed her appearance once in the last fourteen hundred years.

The whole forensic team had fallen into awed silence, staring at the woman.

Halran stepped forward, hoping he was concealing his nerves. She wore a conservative cream-coloured toga suit over a figure that was as ideal as any created by St Mary's specialists. When he attempted to scan her using the most subtle probes his enrichments could produce they were deflected perfectly. It was as if nothing was there; the only empirical proof he had that she existed was his own eyesight.

'Ma'am, I'm Investigator Halran, in charge of this case. I, er, that is we, are very flattered you're here.'

'Thank you,' said Paula Myo.

'Can I ask what your interest is?'

'It's not my interest; I am only ANA:Governance's representative.'

'In this universe,' Darval whispered to Angelo.

Paula gave him a sweet smile. 'The old jokes are always the best ones. And they don't come much older.'

Darvel's expression turned sickly.

'Okay,' Halran said. 'So what's ANA:Governance's interest?'

'Mr Telfer.'

'Is he Higher?'

'What do you think?'

'His weapons biononics are the most sophisticated we've ever seen on Anagaska. The vault guards were hired purely on the basis of their enrichments, and he took them both out in less than a minute. So if he's not Higher, he has access to the best the Central Worlds have to offer.'

'Very good,' Paula complimented. 'So?'

'He's probably working for one of your Factions.'

'Excellent rationale, Investigator. That's exactly why I'm here, to see if that particular conclusion is correct. Now I'd like first access to all your forensic results, please.'

'Er, I'll see you get copies, of course.'

'Your planetary government has granted ANA:Governance full cooperation on this case. I'm sure you appreciate the politics involved. Please feel free to check with your Commissioner, and even the city's Mayor; but that's not copies. I require first, and unrestricted, access to the raw data, thank you.'

Halran knew when he'd lost a battle. 'Yes, ma'am. First access. I'll set that up right away.'

'Thank you. Now who's analysing the registry?'

'That's me,' Darval said awkwardly.

'Who do you think Telfer was after?'

Darval glanced at Halran, who gave a tiny nod. 'Easy, actually. One of the secure stores belonged to Inigo.'

'Ah,' Paula smiled. She closed her eyes and drew a long breath through her nose. 'When was the last update?'

'3320.'

'The year he left on his Centurion Station mission,' she said. 'And he didn't return to Anagaska until 3415, correct?'

'Yes,' Halran said. 'Living Dream's central fane on Anagaska was built in Kuhmo; he was here to dedicate it.'

'Interesting,' Paula mused.

'You think someone's going to full-clone him?'

'Why else would you steal his mind?' Paula said. 'Thank you for your cooperation, Investigator. And I'd still like those results as they come in.' She turned and started to walk out of the vault.

'That's it?' Halran asked.

Paula halted, tipping her head to fix the investigator with a level stare. 'Unless you have something else to add.'

'What about Telfer?'

'Good luck hunting him down.'

'Are you going to help us?'

'I won't put any obstacles in your way, political or otherwise.' She left the vault, leaving Halran staring at his team in confusion and indignation.

Paula walked out of the administration block and glanced round at the forest. The air blasts had produced superficial damage, most of the clinic's buildings were still intact, and while the larger trees had been toppled there were still enough younger ones to maintain the forest once the dead trunks had been cleared away. A police cordon extended for several hundred yards, with uniformed officers reinforcing the patrolbots. Clinic ground staff were working with contractors and forestrybots to clear the worst of the damage. Little curls of smoke were drifting upward from the blackened ground where fires had burned for a couple of hours during the night before being extinguished.

She didn't pause as her field effect scanned round, but two of the contractor crew were red tagged by her u-shadow. Both of them were shielded, utilizing sophisticated deflection techniques only available to high-grade biononics. Hers, of course, were even more advanced. They were keeping their distance from the cordon, but her eyes managed to zoom in and snatch a facial image. Her u-shadow produced a cross reference for both of them in less than a second. Once upon a time, about a thousand years ago, Paula would have confronted them there and then. These days she liked to think she'd mellowed somewhat, although in truth it was more advantageous to let them think she hadn't spotted them.

Paula had been born on Huxley's Haven, a unique world funded by the Human Structure Foundation, which genetically modified every citizen so they would fit into a simple social structure framed within a low-technology civilization. To the horror and dismay of the rest of the Commonwealth, what they condemned as genetic slavery actually worked, producing a population that was mostly happy with their predetermined lot. The few malcontents were kept in order by police officers who received specific psychoneural profiling. Among other traits was a variant on obsessive compulsive disorder to ensure they never gave up the chase. The Foundation had created Paula to be one of them, but she'd been stolen from a birthing ward by a group of radical liberals intent on liberating the poor slaves. She'd grown up in the Commonwealth at large, first becoming an investigator in the Serious Crimes Directorate, and then for the last seven hundred years acting as an agent for ANA:Governance.

Huxley's Haven still existed, its society chugging quietly along on its ordained course without changing or evolving. The Greater Commonwealth had very little contact with it these days; Paula herself hadn't been back for over three hundred years, and that had essentially been nostalgia tourism. There was no need to keep an eye on it. ANA: Governance was very protective of non-Higher cultures. A policy which, ironically, gave Paula very little opportunity to return; her designated task of preventing the ANA Factions pursuing their illegal interference among the External Worlds kept her incredibly busy.

Her u-shadow established an ultra-secure link to Justine Burnelli. 'I'm at the Anagaska clinic,' she said.

'And?'

'We were right; the raid was organized by a Faction.'

'Any clues which one?'

'Well Marius and the Delivery Man are hanging round outside, which implies they are as interested as we are.'

'Ergo they didn't do it.'

'Don't be so sure. I've never known the Accelerators and the Conservatives to be so blatant before. More likely one of them did it, and the other is trying to expose or counter them. You know what they're like.'

'Whose memorycell were they after?'

'Now that's where it gets interesting: Inigo.'

'Oh my. Really?' Justine said. 'I'm surprised Inigo left himself open to that level of exposure.'

'To be exact, Inigo pre-Living Dream. This is an old store.'

'How does that help anyone?'

'I'm not sure. The Conservatives will benefit if he returns and stops the Cleric Conservator's Pilgrimage project. But there's no way of telling if he will. He might just applaud and join the Pilgrimage himself.'

'If one of the Factions full-clone him they'd be in possession of a puppet messiah. Very useful for endorsing your own agenda.'

'Except this won't be a full-clone,' Paula said. 'This is an early version.'

'I have a theory that might fit.'

'Go.'

'A full-clone early version would presumably be able to receive dreams from the Void just like the original, which would give its controllers a considerable advantage over their opposition.'

'You mean they'd be able to reach the supposed Last Dream?'

'More likely the new Skylord Dreams. Ethan still hasn't found the Second Dreamer, despite a phenomenal amount of effort. Did you know Living Dream is modifying every gaiafield confluence nest it sponsors? And that's about eighty per cent of the Greater Commonwealth. They're getting desperate; the new dreams are increasing. They're not just fragments any more. Whole sequences are seeping into the gaiafield.'

'I don't think Living Dream are behind the raid.'

'They'd benefit enormously,' Justine said.

'Yes, but, my u-shadow has identified the woman assisting Mr Telfer. It's Living Dream's ex-Councillor Corrie-Lyn. Now *persona non grata* to Living Dream, and wanted for several body-loss charges on Ellezelin. The Commonwealth warrants are quite extensive. They also list an accomplice called Aaron, who shares the facial features of Mr Telfer.'

'Now that is interesting. Any idea about Aaron alias Mr Telfer?'

'No. But the pair of them transferred to a starship immediately after the clinic raid. There's only one starship unaccounted for on Anagaska right now, the *Artful Dodger*.'

'What's the history?'

'Standard private yacht, registered on Sholapur.'

'Oh now we're getting somewhere. Sholapur: so in other words we don't know who it belongs to.'

'Indeed. There's no real background available; however, the *Artful Dodger* was on Ellezelin until just after the ruckus at the Riasi fane.'

'Corrie-Lyn used to be Inigo's lover. Could she be pining for him? A full-clone would be one way of getting him back.'

'No. She's a pawn. Telfer is using her to get to Inigo.'

'How does an out-of-date memorycell help them get closer to him? Enough people have tried to find him. He's probably left the Commonwealth entirely. Either he set off to get into the Void by himself, or he's gone and joined Ozzie.'

'He hasn't joined Ozzie. I checked that fifteen years ago.'

'I was always envious of the life you lead,' Justine said. 'All that glamorous danger and travel, there's something intoxicating about it to a sheltered little rich girl like me. How was Ozzie?'

'Like me, essentially unchanged.'

'Who do you think this Aaron character is working for?'

'As you say, there are a lot of Factions and organizations who would benefit by finding Inigo. This raid simply tells us how urgent their pursuit is becoming. Nobody has been careless enough to show their hand until now.'

'So what's your next step?'

'This raid is only one aspect of a much larger process of political events. I think it's important to find the Second Dreamer before Living Dream do. That person will obviously play a huge part in determining the outcome of the Pilgrimage.'

'Wow, you still think big, don't you?'

'I always believed that solving a case is a holistic process. It's one of the few things I have remained true to in the last thousand years.'

'And what about Aaron and Corrie-Lyn?'

'That's the aspect I'll stay visible on. It won't take Investigator Halran long to identify Corrie-Lyn, and things will become quite public after that. If I start enquiring after the Second Dreamer it will create too much interest amid the Factions.'

'Would you like me to start looking for the Second Dreamer?'

'No. You're highly visible to the Factions. Almost as much as myself. I think it would be best if you could keep an eye on the Delivery Man and Marius.'

'I'll do that. Who gets to track down the Second Dreamer, then?'

Paula smiled broadly, knowing how the Faction agents

out in the forest would focus on that and wonder. 'The last person anyone would suspect, of course.'

*

The condition of the utility feed pipes in the third apartment were a lot worse than Araminta had expected. She spent three unscheduled hours that morning tracing them through the walls and floor, supervising the bots as they ripped the corroded tubes out. It all made a great deal of mess, which meant more clean-up, which meant more time not spent on preparing the wall frames for the new fittings, which pushed completion back just that little bit further.

Her u-shadow told her when it was eleven o'clock, which barely gave her enough time for a spore shower in the fourth apartment, where she was living. Two of the old shower's five nozzles weren't working, and one of the remaining jets smelt funny. She just had time to apply some freshener and dress in smart trousers and jacket before the clients were due. The perfumed spray damping her skin gave her an unexpected flashback to the day she found out Laril had left Viotia and her liberal use of travel-clean back in those days. All of which gave her a guilty prod that she hadn't been back to Nik's for ages.

She gritted her teeth against stupid sentiment and went out into the vestibule as the lift brought her new clients up from the lobby. Danal and Mareble were dressed strangely. Her in a long skirt of wide-weave ginger cotton, topped by a suede waistcoat with brass buttons that was worn over a plain white blouse. Sturdy brown boots were just visible below her swirling hem. Her thick raven hair was brushed back, its waves bound in simple elastic cloth bands. He wore leather trousers and boots similar to hers. A yellow jacket was almost hidden beneath a brown overcoat made of some oiled fabric.

Despite their historical appearance, Araminta couldn't help but smile as the lift doors opened. There was something irrepressibly enthusiastic about them. Youthful grins and the eager way they glanced around, the way they held hands the whole time.

'Welcome,' she said. The golden-wood door to the showcase apartment swung open.

She'd dressed the apartment with a simple two-tone colour scheme in each room, and kept the furniture minimalist. The floor of the open-plan living room was an expensive ebony-wood parquet. Artfully positioned tables and chairs and settee were all reproduction Herfal style, with sharp curves and metal-moiré legs – a popular fad three centuries ago. The balcony was open, and it was a warm clear day outside, showing the park off to great effect.

Mareble drew a breath as they walked in. 'It's fabulous,' she exclaimed. 'Just what we're looking for.'

Danal chortled. 'Forgive my wife, she obviously doesn't believe in showing our hand before negotiations.'

'I did the same thing with the original vendor,' Araminta confessed. 'It's easy to become devoted to these apartments very quickly. I'm actually thinking about keeping one for myself.'

Mareble stood in front of the balcony door. 'Would the one we're considering have the same view?'

'Apartment three is on the corner,' Araminta gestured

along the balcony. 'You get one aspect facing the park, as well as a view westward across the city. The suspension bridge is visible that way.'

'How lovely.'

'Can we see it?' Danal asked.

'Not just yet. City health and safety codes won't let me take people into an accredited construction site.' *And it's a complete shambles, which might put you off.*

'Construction site? Are there structural problems?'

'Absolutely not. The structure is perfectly sound. An independent deep-scan survey file is registered at City Hall if you'd like to verify it. I'm just refurbishing and remodelling. Unfortunately, the city chooses to class that as construction because I'm replacing the electrics and utility feeds. It's just more filework for me, that's all.'

Danal gave a sympathetic sigh. 'That sounds just like Ellezelin. Dear Lady, the Waterwalker never had to put in requests to the Orchard Palace if he wanted to get things done. Try telling that to our government.'

'Now, darling,' Mareble squeezed his hand tighter. 'He has a thing about bureaucrats,' she explained.

'We all do,' Araminta assured them.

'Thank you,' Danal said.

'So are you moving here from Ellezelin?' Araminta asked.

'Oh yes,' they chorused happily.

'I'm a confluence nest technician,' Danal said. 'There's a lot of work going on upgrading the whole gaiafield right now. It's especially important on Viotia.'

'Why is that?' Araminta asked.

'The Second Dreamer is here,' Mareble said. 'We're sure

of it. The last few dreams were so much more vivid than those first fragments. Don't you think?'

'I don't have gaiamotes,' Araminta said, keeping it light, as if it was some minor fault with an appliance she was going to get corrected, praying it wouldn't make any difference to the deal. She needed their deposit on apartment three; they hadn't been as easy to sell as she'd envisaged and her suppliers were submitting payment demands.

Mareble and Danal both wore the same compassionate expression, as if they felt sorry for her. A concord which instantly reminded her of Mr Bovey.

'The gaiafield is not something I could live without,' Mareble said quietly. 'I can always sense Danal no matter where we are, even when we're planets apart; that kind of permanent emotional connection is so satisfying and reassuring.'

'And of course we know Inigo's Dreams. Intimately,' Danal said. He smiled with the placid bliss only the truly devout could ever achieve.

Araminta tried to replicate that mien of joy. 'I didn't know you could tell where a dream came from,' she said, hoping that would divert them from her tragic defect. There was nothing the devout of any sect or ideology enjoyed more than making the benefits of their belief obvious to outsiders.

'That's the thing with the gaiafield,' Mareble explained earnestly. 'It's not all clear and precise like the unisphere. Human thoughts are not digital, they're emotion. I had the *feeling* with the last few dreams of the Skylord; they were close to me. Now the nests remember them they've lost that aspect, not that they aren't still wonderful. We're all hoping that we'll experience the Skylord flying to Makkathran to collect the Waterwalker's soul. After everything he's done for the people of Querencia, and us, he deserves to rest within Odin's Sea.'

Something about Mareble's evocation made Araminta pause, as if it connected with some old recollection. Which was stupid. 'I see,' Araminta said. Her knowledge of the whole Waterwalker epic was sketchy at best, she certainly didn't know any details. 'That's why you want to live here?'

Mareble nodded eagerly. 'I'm convinced the Second Dreamer is here. One day soon he'll reveal himself and the Pilgrimage can begin.'

'Will you join it?'

They smiled at each other, and clasped hands again. 'We hope so.'

'Well at the risk of being crass, you won't find anywhere better to wait than here.'

'I think we can consider putting in an offer,' Danal said. 'An uncomfortable number of our fellow followers are looking for property on Viotia. Living in a hotel is pleasant, but we'll be happy to move into a real home.'

'That I can fully appreciate.'

'We're prepared to offer you the full asking price, but we would need a guarantee that the apartment will be completed on time.'

'I can put my certificate on that file, yes.'

'And the virtual model we accessed, it was nice, but . . .'

'I want to make some changes,' Mareble said quickly. 'The technology needs to be de-emphasized, and the décor should be more naturalistic.'

'Naturalistic?'

'Less manufactured products, more wood. As it is on Querencia. We're not against technology, we use it all the time, but it shouldn't be featured. For instance, can you install a proper cooker in the kitchen? One with an oven and hob?'

'I'll check City regulations and get back to you on that one.'

'So can you supply me with a *proper* cooker?' she asked Mr Bovey that night over dinner. She was at his house, sitting at a small table on the balcony which overlooked the lawn. The River Cairns ran along the bottom edge where the mown grass gave way to shaggy reeds and a lengthy clump of coran twister trees that dangled chrome-blue fronds into the water. Bright lights in the buildings along the opposite bank glinted off the smooth black surface. It was a lovely relaxing ambience, with a delicious meal several hims had cooked, and three hims sitting with her. A pleasant end to an exasperating day.

'Actually, yes,' the handsome blond one said.

'You say that with such confidence.'

'Because I've already supplied three in the last ten days,' the shorter one with a dark complexion told her. 'Living Dream fanatics do like their primitive comforts. They prefer water baths to spore showers, too.'

'Dear Ozzie, my cousin was right, they are taking over. I ought to raise the price on the last two apartments.'

'I don't want to throw a damper on the evening, but I actually find that prospect quite disturbing. Mainly because it's rapidly becoming true. There are a lot of them here now, millions.'

'I'd have thought the rush for housing will benefit you as much as me, probably more so.'

'Financially yes,' the blond said, holding up a kebab of spiced torkal and pork, marinated in red honey. 'But multiples don't fit into the Living Dream ethos.' He bit into the meat and started chewing. 'We didn't exist in Makkathran,' the Oriental one explained.

'Surely they're not against your lifestyle, are they?' She had an unpleasant thought of how devoted Mareble and Danal were to their ideology, to the complete exclusion of just about everything else. That didn't make them hostile, just unaccepting.

'Oh never actively, no. Perish the thought. Their precious Waterwalker wanted everyone to live together and get along without conflict. But tell me this, how did your buyers react when they found out you weren't sharing the glory that exists only within the gaiafield?'

'Surprised,' she admitted. 'Then I think they wanted to convert me.'

'I bet they did.'

'It won't last long,' she assured him. 'As soon as the Pilgrimage starts, they'll all flock away to join it. My couple told me that. They're only here because they think this is where the Second Dreamer is hiding.'

'Which is equally disturbing.'

'Why?' she asked as she poured herself some more of the excellent rosé wine.

'If you're the next chosen one, why hide? And more than that, why keep releasing the dreams that let everyone know you exist and are in hiding?'

'I don't understand anything about Living Dream. The whole thing seems stupid to me.'

'The word you're looking for is dangerous,' the short one said. 'Too many impossible promises; too many people believing. Bad combination.'

'You're an old cynic.'

All three hims at the table lifted their wine glasses. 'Guilty and proud of it.'

'You have gaiamotes. Are these second dreams real?'

'Is a dream real?' three mouths grinned in unison. 'The dreams exist. Everything else is down to personal perspective. If you want to believe in them, then the Second Dreamer is somewhere out there receiving dreams from a Skylord somewhere inside the Void. If not . . .'

'I don't know what to believe. I'm almost tempted to get gaiamotes just to find out.'

'Take it from me,' said the blond. 'It's not worth it. The gaiafield is just another fad that got hijacked by a bunch of fanatics.'

'Why did Ozzie invent it?'

'He said so that people could understand each other better. If we had more empathy we would be more peaceful. Nice theory. Haven't seen it having much effect on human nature recently.'

'Yet you wouldn't exist without it. And you think you're the future.'

The Oriental Mr Bovey produced a modest smile. 'True. And I doubt Ozzie envisaged us, either.'

She held her wine glass close to her face, and dropped her gaze demurely. 'I never envisaged you.'

'There's a lot of things we don't know about until we encounter them.' The Oriental Mr Bovey pressed up against her and plucked the glass from her hands. She liked the warmth of him against her. On her other side, the blond one stroked her cheek and turned her unresisting head for a kiss.

She closed her eyes. Hands stroked her spine. Hands stroked her legs. The kiss went on and on.

'Come with me,' one him instructed.

The kiss ended, and she saw all three of him smiling in *that* way, gentle and knowing, not bothering to conceal his anticipation.

The three hims escorted her to a warm second-floor bedroom where the lighting was a cosy candle-flame orange. She stood at the end of the bed while they stripped off in front of her, just the way she liked, making her the centre of attention, the centre of desire. Then it was her turn, removing her clothes slowly, showing herself off, drinking in the admiration from hims, exultant with approval. When she was naked, hes began to explore her flesh with formidable intimacy. 'Yes,' she finally shuddered in delight, and they lifted her on to the bed.

Rushing headlong through space the creature could feel stray molecules kiss its broad vacuum wings as it stretched them wide. Scintillations from the tenuous impact dripped from its trailing edge, leaving a weak contrail of fluorescence through the empty gulf. Ahead, a star gleamed bright against the glorious background of an undulating turquoise nebula, creating a warm pressure of photons which so very slowly assuaged its physical nourishment. The creature spun leisurely in the rich torrent of light as it listened to the thoughts grow stronger on the solid planet that was still lightyears away.

One thought was exceptionally clear. 'You see, you have to rest now; if you were multiple another body could simply carry on. The ecstasy would continue for hours. More bodies could perform at the same time; imagine that pleasure you've just experienced doubled, quadrupled, increased tenfold. Wouldn't you like that? Wouldn't your life be so much better, so much greater . . . ?' The thought dwindled away into the vastness as the solar wind cooled and dimmed.

There were only two hims asleep on the bed when Araminta woke. She checked the time in her exovision and groaned in dismay. Five past seven already. There was so much to do in the third apartment today. The bots should have spent the night stripping out the old tiles in the fifth apartment, but her u-shadow revealed they'd stopped work at three in the morning as they encountered a problem their semisentient software couldn't cope with. She had two prospective buyers for apartment four arriving before noon.

'Great Ozzie,' she complained as she heaved herself out of bed. No time for a shower. She grabbed the clothes she'd worn to dinner last night – which really weren't everyday garments. *Must bring a bag with some decent clothes for morning. Would he object to that?*

She escaped the bedroom without waking the Mr Boveys. Scuttled down the stairs, raking fingers through awful strings of tangled hair. The smell of coffee and toast was permeating out of the big kitchen. Which was sorely tempting given her body's chill. *I must ease off those booster aerosols.* Surely a single minute spent with one cup of tea wouldn't jeopardize the whole day?

She put her head round the archway to smile into the long open-plan kitchen diner. Five hims were sitting round the breakfast bar, with another three lounging in the big old settee. 'Hi—' The smiled faded from her face. A woman was perched on the sixth stool at the breakfast bar wearing a big fluffy towelling robe. One him had his arm round her, hand lovingly massaging the base of her neck. The woman glanced up from a big mug of steaming coffee, and pulled a delinquent face. 'Oh, hi there. I'm Josill. I guess I was being worn out by the half of hims you weren't with last night. Hes' good sex, huh? I managed four.' She grinned round proudly at her entourage of Mr Boveys.

Araminta managed to freeze her expression before she did anything petty like glare or pout or start shouting about what a useless pile of shit he was. 'Right,' she said in a croak. 'Got to go. People I'm honest with coming to see me.' She headed for the front door, as fast as she could without actually running. Even managed to get outside. Her old carry capsule was resting on the gravel pad. Fifteen metres away.

'Just hold on.'

She turned. It was the body she'd had that first dinner date with. He always used that one to talk to her with when it was something serious. Obviously working the whole age equals wisdom angle, with maybe a little trust mixed in. 'Drop dead,' she snapped. 'All of you.'

'You knew I would date other women.'

'I . . .' She spluttered with indignation. 'No! Actually, no I didn't! I thought we—' Some stubborn little part of her was desperately trying not to cry in front of him. What the point was with someone who knew her so completely eluded her – still she wasn't going to give him the satisfaction of seeing how much she cared.

'Listen to me.' He stood in front of her, taking a moment to compose himself. 'You are a lovely, fantastic person. I haven't met someone I was this attracted to in years. And I think you know that.'

'Well this is a—'

'Funny way of showing it? No. No. That's a single person's line, not mine.'

'How ridiculous,' she shouted.

'Maybe you've been trying to hide from this, I don't know. Adjusting to multiple life does take time. It isn't easy, and you're upset.'

'I'm not upset,' she announced haughtily.

'I have a great time with you, every time no matter where we go and what we do, and that's the problem. Think on this. You are a wonderful, healthy, strapping girl with a huge sexual appetite. Every man's dream. And I'm always amazed and excited by how many mes you take on when we go to bed. But not even you can physically satisfy thirty-eight male bodies every night. We've been going out all this time and there are still some mes you haven't met, let alone had sex with yet. You get me all hot and randy, and every time you do that the majority of mes are left frustrated.'

'I ... Oh. Really?' It was kind of obvious when he explained it like that. But he was right, it really wasn't something she wanted to think through.

'I can only take so much. Josill and the others help release the pressure you create.'

Others. Again, something she didn't want to consider. This whole multiple thing was turning out to be one giant complication. She took a breath and stared at the gravel round her feet. 'I'm sorry. You're right, I didn't consider that part of it. It's been so good for me I just assumed it was the same for you. Singles thinking, huh.'

'Yes.' He put a hand on her shoulder. It comforted her – that whole wise and sympathetic thing still. 'But I'm hoping, really hoping we can work through this.'

She gave the door a guilty glance. 'I'm not sure I can get round the idea of you having sex with her as well. Were you . . . no. I don't want to know.'

He raised an eyebrow. Waited patiently.

Araminta sighed. 'Last night, were you having sex with both of us at the same time?'

'Yes.'

A particularly malicious thought crept out of her mind. 'And she could only cope with four?'

'Fraid so.'

'Poor girl.' Her little spike of humour withered away. 'I don't know about this. I'm not sure I can cope. There would need to be so many women. That's not part of a long-term relationship.'

'Listen, I said you were special right at the start, and the more I get to know you the more I know that I don't want to lose you.'

'So what do you do? Get half of you neutered? I really can't . . . not thirty-eight.'

He grinned. 'That's my Araminta, considering it even now. But there's another option, isn't there?'

'What?'

He didn't answer straight away. Instead his hand touched her chin, tipping her head back until she couldn't avoid staring into his eyes. Eventually she gave a defeated little nod. 'I get myself some extra bodies,' she said in a quiet voice.

'I'm not going to browbeat. I couldn't do that to you, it

470

would be wrong. The decision has to be you alone. I just want you to think about it. You've seen all the practical benefits first-hand. And I reminded you about the sexual advantages again last night.'

She fixed him with a firm stare. 'Tell me: if I do this, would you stop dating the other women? Would it be just you and me?'

'Yes, emphatically, just you. Yous in my life, yous in my bed. Cross my hearts. I want this, Araminta, I want this so much. I wish you had gaiamotes so I could show you just how serious I am. We'll just have to settle for registering it at City Hall instead.'

'Ozzie! A marriage proposal and a lifestyle change in one. And it's not even half past seven yet.'

'Sorry you had to run into it like this.'

'Not your fault. You're right, I should have thought about this. So I'll be a big girl and think about it properly now. Don't expect an answer right away. This is a hell of a lot more than I'm used to dealing with in a day.'

His arms went round her, hugging tight as if he was the one seeking reassurance. 'It's momentous. I remember. So take all the time you need.'

*

He rode the gigantic horse for hour after hour, his young legs barely stretching over the saddle. In the distance were real mountains, their snow-capped peaks stabbing high into the glorious sapphire sky. He was leaving them behind, riding away from the forests that covered the foothills. It was wild veldt beneath the hooves now, lush tropical vegetation split by streams and small rivers. Trees from a dozen planets grew across the low slopes, their contrasting evolutions providing a marvellous clash of colour and shape. Hot air gusted against him, heavy with alien pollen.

His friends rode beside him, the six of them shouting encouragement to each other as they wove around the knolls and ridges. None of them yet adult, but now finally old enough to be trusted out on their own. It was days like this which made sense of his life, full of freedom and joy.

Then the cry went up. 'The king eagles, the king eagles are here.'

He scoured the brilliant sky, seeing the black dots above the rumpled horizon. Then he too was yelling in welcome, his heart pounding with excitement. The horse ran faster as the noble lords of this world's sky grew larger and larger.

Red lights flashed across the heavens. The king eagles elongated, black lines curving and twisting to form a grey rectangular shape. His horse had vanished, leaving him lying flat on his back. The red lights turned violet-blue and began to retreat as the top of the medical chamber opened. A face slid into view, peering down. He blinked it into focus. Very pretty and heavily freckled, with a mass of dark red hair tied back.

'You okay?' Corrie-Lyn asked.

'Urrgh,' Aaron told her.

'Here drink this.' A plastic straw was eased into his mouth. He sucked some welcoming cool liquid down his sore throat.

'What?' he mumbled.

'What?'

'What happened?'

'You've been in the ship's medical chamber for a couple of days.'

He winced as he tried to move his arms. His whole left side was stiff, as if the skin had shrunk. 'A moment,' he told her. His u-shadow flipped medical records into his exovision. He skipped the details, concentrating on the major repairs. The damage had been more extensive than he expected. The projectile entry wounds combined with firewire mutilation and toxin contamination meant the medical chamber had to cut and extract a lot of ruined tissue and bone from his chest. Foreign meat had been inserted, neutral-function cells which could have their pre-active DNA switched to mould the cell into whatever organ, bone, or muscle function they were replacing. He spotted a supplementary file, and opened it. The foreign meat stored in the chamber actually wasn't so foreign, the DNA was his; it also had full-complement biononic organelles.

The repairs had been woven into his body by the chamber and his existing biononics. They were still integrating which was why he felt so awful. Estimated time for the biononics to complete the binding and the cells to acclimatize to their new function was a further seventy-two hours.

'Could have been better, could have been worse,' he decided.

'I was worried,' she said. 'Your wound was huge. The blood . . .' Her face paled, even the freckles faded.

Aaron slowly shifted his arms back along the chamber padding, propping himself up. At which point he realized he didn't have any clothes on. 'Thank you.'

She gave him a blank look.

'I should be thanking you, shouldn't I? What happened? The last thing I remember was you hitting Ruth Stol.'

'That little princess bitch.'

'So? What came next?' Aaron swung his feet over the lip of the capsule; his inner ears seemed to take a lot longer to register the movement. Bulkheads spun round him, then twisted back. The starship's cabin was in its lounge mode, with long couches extending out from the bulkhead walls. He hobbled over to the closest one as the medical chamber withdrew into the floor. Sitting down he tentatively poked his chest with a forefinger. Half of his torso was a nasty salmon pink, covered with some glistening protective membrane.

'I did what you suggested,' Corrie-Lyn said. 'The capsule smashed its way into the reception hall. I just got inside when there was this almighty explosion over the forest. It knocked the capsule around quite a bit, but I was caught by the internal safety field. We zipped over to the administration block. You were . . . a mess, but I managed to pull you inside. Then we rendezvoused with the *Artful Dodger* outside the clinic, the way you set it up. The starship put its force field round the capsule while we transferred in. Good job. The police were going apeshit with me. They were shooting every weapon they had at us; there were craters all over the place when we took off. I told the smartcore to get us out of the system, but it followed your preloaded flightplan. We're just sitting in some kind of hyperspace hole a lightyear out from Anagaska. I can't make a unisphere connection. The smartcore won't obey me.'

'I loaded a few options in,' he said. His u-shadow gave the smartcore an instruction, and a storage locker opened. 'Do you think you could get me that robe, please?'

She frowned disapprovingly, but pulled the robe out. 'I

was really worried, I thought I was going to be stuck here for ever if you died. It was horrible. The medical chamber would rejuvenate me every fifty years, and I'd just sit in the lounge plugged into the sensory drama library being drip fed by the culinary unit. That's not how I want to spent eternity, thank you.'

He grinned at her drama queen outrage as he slipped the robe on. 'If the chamber could rejuvenate you, it could certainly re-life me.'

'Oh.'

'In any case, if I die, the smartcore allows you full control.'

'Right.'

'But!' He caught hold of her hand. She jerked round, suddenly apprehensive. 'None of this would have happened if you'd been ready to pick me up when I told you.'

'I haven't seen any decent clothes in weeks,' she protested. 'I just lost track of time, that's all. I didn't *mean* to be late. Besides, I thought you got wounded before the scheduled rendezvous.'

He closed his eyes in despair. 'Corrie-Lyn, if you're on a combat mission, you don't call a fucking time-out to go shopping. Understand?'

'You never said combat. A quick raid sneaking into their vault, you said.'

'For future reference, a covert mission in which all sides are armed is a combat situation.'

She pulled a face. '*Nothing they have will be a match for my biononics.*'

'I never said that.'

'Yes, you did.'

'I . . .' He let out a breath and made an effort to stay calm. *Yoga. She always made us do yoga. It was fucking stupid.*

Corrie-Lyn was frowning at him. 'You okay? You need to get back in the chamber?'

'I'm fine. Look, thank you for picking me up. I know this kind of thing is not what your life is about.'

'You're welcome,' she said gruffly.

'Please tell me we still have the memorycell.'

Corrie-Lyn produced a minx smile and held up the little plastic kube. 'We still have the memorycell.'

'Thank Ozzie for that.' His u-shadow told the smartcore to show him the ship's log; he wanted to check how much effort had been made to try and track them. Since they'd left Anagaska in a hurry, several starships had run sophisticated hysradar scans out to several lightyears – but nobody could spot an ultradrive ship in transdimensional suspension. The log also recorded that Corrie-Lyn had managed to circumvent the lock-out he'd placed on the culinary unit to prevent it making alcoholic drinks. Now really wasn't the time to make an issue of it.

'Okay,' he told her. 'I don't think anyone's spotted us. Though there were some mighty interesting comings and goings just after our raid. Several ships with unusual quantum signatures popped out of hyperspace above Anagaska; the smartcore thinks they might be ultradrives in disguise.'

'Who would they be?'

'Don't know. And don't intend to hang around to ask. Let's get going.'

'Finally.'

He held his hand out, carefully maintaining a neutral expression.

Corrie-Lyn gave the kube a sentimental look, and took a while to drop it into his palm. 'I'm not sure I like the idea of you reading Inigo's mind.'

'I'm not going to. Memory assimilation isn't like accessing a sensory drama off the unisphere, nor accepting experiences through the gaiafield. A genuine memory takes a long time to absorb. You can compress it down from real time, but still this kube contains nearly forty years of his life. That would take months to shunt into a human brain; it's one of the governing factors in creating re-life clones. If we're going to find him before the Pilgrimage, we don't have that much time to spare.'

'So what are you going to do?'

'Take it to someone who can absorb it a lot quicker than I can, and ask nicely.'

'You just said human brains can't absorb stored memories that quickly.'

'So I did. Which is why we're setting course for the *High Angel*.'

Corrie-Lyn looked shocked. 'The Raiel starship?'

'Yes.'

'Why would the Raiel help you?'

He smiled at the kube. 'Let's just say that we now have an excellent bargaining point.'

Corrie-Lyn didn't have the kind of patience for extensive research. Aaron had to fill in the decades and centuries she skipped through when she started to access the files her u-shadow trawled up on the Raiel. Humans discovered the

High Angel back in 2163, he explained, when a wormhole was opened in its star system to search for any H-congruous planets. CST's exploratory division quickly confirmed there were no worlds that humans could live on, but the astronomers did notice a microwave signal coming from the orbit of the gas-giant Icalanise.

'What's that got to do with angels?' she asked. 'Were they all religious?'

'Not astronomers, no.'

When they focused their sensors on the microwave source they saw a moonlet sixty-three kilometres long with what looked like wings of hazy pearl light. The wings of an angel.

'Sounds like they were religious to me, if that's the first thing they think of.'

Aaron groaned. With more sensors urgently brought on line, the true nature of the artefact was revealed. A core of rock sprouting twelve stems which supported vast domes, five of which had transparent cupolas. Cities and parkland were visible inside.

It was a starship; a living creature, or a machine which had evolved into sentience. Origin unknown, and it wasn't telling. Several species lived in the domes. Only the Raiel consented to talk to humanity, and they didn't say very much.

Several of the biggest astroengineering companies negotiated a lease on three of the domes, and the *High Angel* became a dormitory town for an archipelago of microgravity factory stations producing some of the Commonwealth's most advanced, and profitable, technology. The workforce and their families soon grew large enough to declare autonomy (with *High Angel*'s approval), qualifying for a seat in the Senate.

With the outbreak of the Starflyer War, *High Angel* became the Commonwealth's premier Navy base while the astroengineering companies turned their industrial stations over to warship production. More domes were grown, or extruded, or magically manifested into existence to accommodate the Navy personnel. Still nobody understood the *High Angel*'s technology.

'Do we know more about it now?' she asked.

'Not really. ANA might; the Central Worlds can duplicate some functions with biononics; but the External Worlds haven't managed to produce anything like it.'

Humans, he told her, had to wait for two hundred years after the War before the massive alien starship's history became a little clearer. Wilson Kime's epic voyage in the *Endeavour* to circumnavigate the galaxy revealed the existence of the Void to the Commonwealth, complete with Centurion Station and the Raiel defence systems maintaining the Wall stars. Other Navy exploration ships discovered more *High Angel*-class ships; the one species common to each of them was the Raiel.

Confronted with that evidence, the Raiel finally explained that they created the *High Angel* class of ships over a million years ago while their species was at its apex. It was a golden age, when the Raiel civilization spread across thousands of planets; they mixed with hundreds of other sentients, guided and observed as dozens of species transcended to a post-physical state. They even knew the Silfen before their Motherholme dreamed its paths into existence.

Then the Void underwent one of its periodic expansion phases. Nothing the Raiel could do stopped the barrier from engulfing entire star clusters. Gravity shifted around the galactic core as stars were torn down into the event horizon. The effect on civilizations just outside the Wall stars was catastrophic. Stars shifted position as the core gravity field fluctuated; their planets changed orbits. Thousands of unique biospheres were lost before evolution had any real chance to flourish. Whole societies had to be evacuated before stormfronts of ultra-hard radiation that measured thousands of lightyears across came streaming out into the base of the galaxy's spiral arms.

After it was all over, after rescue and salvage operations that went on for millennia, the Raiel declared that the Void could no longer be tolerated. The Firstlife who had created it while the galaxy was still in its infancy clearly didn't recognize the horrendous consequences it would have on those who lived after their era. The Raiel created an armada of ships that could function in any quantum state which theoretically might exist within the Void. And they invaded. A hundred thousand ships surrounded the terrible barrier and flew inside, ready for anything.

None returned.

The Void remained unbroken.

What was left of the once colossal Raiel civilization launched a rearguard action. A defence system to reinforce the Wall stars was built in the small hope it might contain the next macro-expansion. More ships were created to act as arks for emergent species, carrying them away from the doomed galaxy across the greater gulf outside where they could re-establish themselves on new worlds in peaceful star clusters. It was the last act of beneficence from a race that had failed its ultimate challenge. If they couldn't save the galaxy, the Raiel swore they would endure to the bitter end, shepherding entities less capable than themselves to safety.

'That's not a version of history I can believe in,' Corrie-Lyn said softly as the file images shrank to the centre of the cabin and vanished. 'It's very hard for me to accept the Void as something hostile when I know the beauty which lies within.' She took a sip of her hot chocolate and brandy, curling up tighter on the couch.

'That version?' Aaron queried from the other side of the cabin.

'Well it's not as if we can ever verify it, is it?'

'Unless I've got a false memory, you've got nearly six hundred years of human observations from Centurion Station to confirm the very unnatural way in which the barrier consumes star systems. And who was it now that took some of them? Oh yes, that's right: Inigo himself.'

'Yes, but this whole crusading armada claim? Come on. A hundred thousand ships with weapons that can crunch up entire stars. Where are they? None of Inigo's Dreams showed the smallest relic.'

'Dead. Vaporized into component atoms and consumed like every other particle of matter that passes through the barrier.' He paused, slightly troubled. 'Except for the human ship which got through and landed on Querencia.'

'Pretty crappy tactics for a species of self-proclaimed masterminds. Didn't they think of sending a scout or two in first?'

'Maybe they did. You can ask when we get to the *High Angel*.'

She gave him a pitying look. 'If they even let us dock.'

'Oh ye of little faith.'

The *Artful Dodger* fell back into spacetime ten thousand kilometres from the *High Angel*. Icalanise was waxing behind the alien starship, a horned crescent of warring topaz and platinum stormbands. Four small black circles were strung out along the equator, the tip of the umbra cones projected by a conjunction cluster of its thirty-eight moons.

Several sensor sweeps flashed across the starship. *High Angel* still hosted a large Commonwealth Navy presence. The base Admiral took security seriously. A fresh identity complete with official certification was already loaded into the smartcore for examination. Aaron's u-shadow requested docking permission with the New Glasgow dome for the *Alini*. They received almost immediate approach authority.

The archipelago of industrial stations glided lazily along a thousand-kilometre orbit, forming a dense loop of silver specks round the *High Angel*. Service shuttles zipped between them and the human-inhabited domes, collecting advanced technology and materials for forward shipment to the External Worlds where such systems were still prized. 'How about that,' Aaron muttered appreciatively as he accessed the ship's sensor imagery. 'An angel with a halo.'

'You can take religious analogies too far,' Corrie-Lyn chided.

There were seventeen domes rising out of the core's rocky surface now. The six occupied by humans all had crystal cupolas, allowing them to see the cities and park-land inside. Four of the remainder were also transparent to a degree; the spectra of alien suns shone out of them, following their own diurnal cycles. Strange city silhouettes could be seen parked on the landscapes within. At night they would shine with enticing colourful light points. One of those belonged to the Raiel. The remaining domes were closed to external observation, and neither *High Angel* or the Raiel would discuss their residents.

Following Aaron's instruction, the starship's smartcore aimed a communication maser at the Raiel dome. 'I would like permission to dock at the Raiel dome, please,' Aaron said. 'There is a resident I wish to speak to.'

'That is an unusual request for a private individual,' the *High Angel* replied with the voice of a human male. 'I can speak on behalf of the Raiel.'

'Not good enough. You're aware of the nature of this ship?'

'I do recognize it. Very few of ANA's ultradrive vessels have ever come into my proximity; the technology is extremely sophisticated. You must be one of its representatives.'

'Something like that, and I need to speak with a specific Raiel.'

'Very well. I am sending you a new flight path, please follow it.'

'Thank you. The Raiel I'd like to meet is Qatux.'

'Of course.'

The *Artful Dodger* changed course slightly, curving round the massive dark rock of the *High Angel*'s core towards the stem of the Raiel dome. Large dark ovals were positioned at the base, just before the point where the pewter-coloured shaft fused with the rock crust. One of the ovals dematerialized, revealing a featureless white chamber beyond. The *Artful Dodger* nosed inside, and the outer wall rematerialized behind it.

'Please stand by for teleport,' the *High Angel* said.

Corrie-Lyn looked very startled.

'Once again,' Aaron said. 'And yet still without any hope of you paying the slightest attention: let me do the talking.'

Her mouth opened to answer.

The cabin vanished, immediately replaced by a broad circular space with a floor that glowed a pale emerald. If there was a ceiling it was invisible somewhere in the gloom far above. An adult Raiel was standing right in front of them. Corrie-Lyn gasped and almost stumbled. Aaron hurriedly reached out and caught her arm. He didn't have any memory of being on Earth and using the planetary T-sphere, but the abrupt translation was about what he'd expected.

'Dear Ozzie,' Corrie-Lyn grunted.

'I hope you are not too shocked,' the Raiel said in its mellow whisper.

Aaron bowed formally. The Raiel was as big as all the adults of its species, larger than a terrestrial elephant, with a grey-brown skin that bristled with thick hairs. Not that Aaron was an expert, but this one looked like an exceptionally healthy specimen. From the front its bulbous head was surrounded by a collar of tentacle limbs; with a thick pair at the bottom, four metres long and tipped with segmented paddles which were intended for heavy work. The remaining limbs were progressively smaller up to a clump of slender manipulators resembling particularly sinuous serpents. Each side of its head had a cluster of five small hemispherical eyes that swivelled in unison. Below them on the underside of the head, the skin creased up into a number of loose folds to form the mouth zone. When it spoke, Aaron could just glimpse deep wet crevices and even a row of sharp brown fangs.

'No, that's fine,' Corrie-Lyn stammered. She remembered her manners and dipped her head awkwardly.

'I have not met humans in the flesh for some time,' said Qatux in its sad-sounding whisper. 'I was curious. I didn't realize my name was still known to you.'

'I'm afraid I only know your name, nothing more,' said Aaron. 'But I thank you for agreeing to see us.'

'My part in your history was brief. I took part in a human expedition during the Starflyer War. I had friends. Human friends, which is unusual for a Raiel, then as now. Tell me, do you know of Paula Myo?'

Aaron was surprised when his heart did a little jump at the name. *Must be the medical treatment.* 'I've heard of her.'

'I liked Paula Myo,' Qatux said.

'She is an ANA:Governance representative these days.'

'And you are not?'

'Not at her level.' Aaron prayed Corrie-Lyn wouldn't start mouthing off.

'Why are you here?' Qatux asked.

'I have a request.' He held up the kube. 'This is the memorycell of a human. I would like you to receive the memories. There are questions about his personality I need answering.'

Qatux did not respond. Its eyes swivelled from Aaron to Corrie-Lyn, then back again.

'Can you do that?' Aaron asked. He was aware that something was wrong, but didn't know what. His mind kept telling him that Qatux was the Raiel who was most likely to help in this fashion. So far on this mission all that intuitive knowledge loaded into his subconscious had been correct.

'I used to do that,' Qatux whispered. 'At one time I was captivated by human emotional states. I married a human.'

'Married?' Corrie-Lyn blurted.

'A most nice lady by the name of Tiger Pansy. I had never known someone so emotionally reactive. We spent many happy years together on the planet you named Far Away. I shared her every thought, every feeling.'

'What happened?' Aaron asked, knowing this wasn't going to be good.

'She died.'

'I'm sorry.'

'She died most horribly. A woman called the Cat prolonged her death for many days. Deliberately. I shared that time with my wife. I experienced human death.'

'Shit,' Aaron mumbled.

'I have not known human thought or emotion since. At the end, my wife cured me of this strange weakness. It was her last gift, however unwillingly given. I am Raiel again. I now hold high rank among my own kind.'

'We shouldn't have asked you to do this,' Corrie-Lyn said humbly. 'We didn't know. I'm so sorry.'

Aaron wanted to use a stunshot on her. 'It's Inigo,' he said, holding the kube up again. 'The human who dreams the lives of humans inside the Void.'

Once again Qatux was perfectly still. This time its eyes remained focused on Aaron alone.

'Aaron!' Corrie-Lyn hissed through clenched teeth.

He could feel the anger powering out of her through the gaiafield, and completely ignored it. 'I'm looking for him,' he told the huge silent alien, staring straight into its multiple eyes. 'He needs to be found before his Living Dream believers spark off another devourment phase with their Pilgrimage. Will you help?'

'Inigo?' Qatux asked, the whisper had softened to near inaudibility.

'Yes. The kube holds his personality right up until he left for his Centurion Station mission. His formative years. Everyone knows his life since he founded Living Dream, even the Raiel. Or perhaps especially the Raiel. If you combine that knowledge with his formative years, I thought you might be able to understand his motivations, that you could work out where he has gone for me.'

'The Raiel have wanted to know the inside of the Void for so long. It is all we exist for now. We are its nemesis as much as it is ours. For over a million years we were content with the role fate had given us. And then a human comes along, and simply dreams what is in there. None of us are. The strongest of our race fell into that evil place, and no trace remains. Nothing.'

'It's not evil,' Corrie-Lyn said sullenly.

'I would like to believe that. I cannot. We have known the Void from a time before your species achieved sentience. It is the destroyer of life, of hope. Nothing escapes it.'

'Millions of humans live inside the Void. They live lives full of hope and love and laughter, they live lives better than any of us out here.'

'To do so, to achieve their greater life you envy so much,

they are killing you. They are killing this galaxy. And now you wish to join them, to increase the damage to a level you cannot imagine.'

'Will you stop the Pilgrimage?' Aaron asked.

'Not I. Not this arkship. That is not the purpose of this Raiel; we are custodians alone. However, there are other Raiel who serve a different purpose. They are the defenders of this galaxy. I do not know what they will do to your Pilgrimage.'

Aaron glanced at Corrie-Lyn. Her mouth was set into a purposeful line.

'Can you help us with Inigo's memories? If I can find him, talk to him, there may be a chance he'll stop the Pilgrimage.'

Qatux moved towards him. Eight stumpy legs on either side of its underbelly tilting forward to move it in a smooth undulation. Aaron held his ground, though he was aware of Corrie-Lyn taking a small shuffle backwards; her emotions seeping into the gaiafield turning from pride to concern.

'I will do what I can,' Qatux said. It extended a medium-sized tentacle.

Aaron exhaled in relief, and handed the memorycell over. The tentacle tip coiled round it and withdrew, curling backwards. Just behind the collar of tentacles, hanging off the equivalent of a Raiel neck, innumerable small protuberances of flesh dangled down, each one crowned by a small heavy bulb that was technological in origin. The kube sank through the dark surface of a bulb like a pebble falling into water.

A long shudder ran along Qatux's bulk, and the giant alien let out a sigh that seemed close to pain. 'I will tell you when I have finished,' Qatux said.

Aaron and Corrie-Lyn were unceremoniously teleported back into the *Artful Dodger*.

*

The Mars Twins were an unusual turgid red as their upper-atmosphere hurricanes swirled and battled along thousand-kilometre fronts, obliterating the dark shadows which occasionally hinted at surface features. Their dour ambiance matched Cleric Conservator Ethan's mood as he strode through the Liliala Hall. Above him the storms rampaging across the visionary ceiling flashed purple lightning and pummelled away at each other like waves assaulting a beach. They swirled together, veiling the two small planets. The silent, vivid battle made for an impressive entrance as he swept through the arching door into the Mayor's suite.

Rincenso and Falven, two of his staunchest supporters on the Council, were waiting for him in the first anteroom; cautious expressions made more sinister by the amber lighting. All they allowed of themselves into the gaiafield was a polite radiance of expectation. Not even Ethan's easily sensed mood could make them waver.

He beckoned them to follow as he pushed through into the oval sanctum. Strong sunlight shone in through the high Rayonnant-style windows, illuminating the grand wooden desk identical to the one which the Waterwalker had sat behind when he was Mayor of Makkathran. Five simple chairs were arranged before it. Councillor Phelim stood at the side of one, waiting for Ethan to sit himself behind his desk. He wore the simple everyday blue and green robe of a Councillor. It was meant to testify to an open and approachable person who would take time to solve someone's problem. On Phelim it was off-putting, emphasizing his height and severe facial features.

'So the Skylord would seem to be on its way to Querencia,' Ethan said as he sat down.

Falven cleared his throat. 'It is heading for some kind of planet. We have to assume it is Querencia. The prospect of another planet housing humans in the Void would open many complications for us.'

'Not so,' Rincenso said. 'I don't care how many other H-congruous planets there are, nor who lives on them. We are concerned only with Querencia and the Waterwalker. It is his example we wish to follow.'

'Too many unknowns to pronounce on,' Falven said.

'Not that many, surely,' Ethan said. 'We cannot doubt the Second Dreamer is dreaming a Skylord. This creature is aware of the souls and minds of living sentient entities. It and its flock are flying towards a solid planet to collect those souls and carry them to Odin's Sea. This flight fulfils every teaching of the Lady.'

'I wonder what life in Makkathran is like now,' Rincenso mused. 'So much time has passed.'

'You'll find out soon enough,' Ethan said. 'The hulls of our Pilgrimage ships are being fabricated. We will be ready to launch soon. Phelim?'

'We should have the hulls and internal systems finished by September,' Phelim said. 'The cost is colossal, but the Free Market Zone has a considerable manufacturing capacity. Component construction is heavily cybernated: once the templates are loaded in, production is a simple process. And of course, no matter how much criticism we face, External World companies are always eager for our money.'

'September,' Rincenso said. 'Dear Ozzie, so close.'

Ethan did not look at Phelim. No one else had been told of the ultradrive engines Marius had promised to deliver. 'The physical aspect goes well,' he said. 'That just leaves us with our enigmatic Second Dreamer to deal with. We still don't know why he hasn't revealed himself, but it is significant that his dreams have become so much more substantial as the ships are built.'

'Why does he not come forward?' Falven said. The gaiafield revealed the flash of anger in his mind. 'Curse him, are we never to find him?'

'He is on Viotia,' Phelim said.

'Are you sure?'

'Yes. The gaiafield confluence nests on Viotia were the first to receive his last dream. They disseminated it across the Greater Commonwealth gaiafield.'

'Do you know where on Viotia he is?'

'Not yet. But now we have confirmed the planet, our efforts will be concentrated on determining the exact geographical location. Of course, people move about. And if he is actively seeking anonymity he will simply relocate after every dream.'

'Which must be prevented,' Ethan said simply.

'How?' Rincenso asked.

'This is why I have asked you two here today, my dearest friends and allies on the Council. The Second Dreamer is crucial to Pilgrimage. He is the one who must ask the Skylords for guidance through the barrier, and onward to Querencia. In the absence of Inigo, he is the one who will light our way.'

'So what do you want us to do?' Falven asked.

'There are several routes available to us,' Ethan said

quietly. 'I believe the one we will end up travelling along is to bring Viotia into the Free Market Zone.'

The two Councillors gave each other a puzzled look.

'It *is* part of our Free Market Zone,' Falven said.

'By treaty, yes,' Ethan said. 'It is not one of our core planets. Yet. We must be prepared to complete the admission process, culminating with Ellezelin opening a wormhole between our two worlds. Following that, Viotia's government should adopt a more favourable stance towards Living Dream. Ultimately, I would like to welcome them into our hierocracy.'

Falven sat back, looking startled.

Rincenso merely smiled in appreciation. 'There are a great many of our followers there already. Enough to tilt the demographic?'

'Possibly,' Phelim said.

'In which case I would be happy to raise the proposal in the Council.'

'I, too,' Falven said slowly.

'There is a degree of hostility and resentment currently being shown to our followers on Viotia,' Ethan said. 'If a wormhole were to be opened, binding their economy to ours, that resentment will manifest itself in street violence. We would need to guarantee the security of all Living Dream adherents.'

'Do we have that ability?' Falven asked cautiously.

'There are enough national security forces spread across the core planets of the Free Market Zone to enforce the rule of law on Viotia,' Phelim said. 'We have been recruiting additional personnel since Ethan's ascension to Conservator.'

'Enough for this?'

'Yes.'

'Oh. I see.'

'I regret any inconvenience this may cause to Viotia's citizens,' Ethan said. 'But we cannot afford to lose the Second Dreamer.'

'If we just knew why he's refusing to reveal himself...' Rincenso said acrimoniously.

'Because he doesn't yet know,' Ethan said with a weary sadness.

'How can he *not know*?'

'It took several weeks for Inigo to realize what was happening. At first he believed his dreams to be some kind of overspill from a full-sense drama that was leaking into the Centurion Station gaiafield. I believe that confusion is repeating again. To begin with all we had were small fragments, glimpses of the Skylord which we edited together. Now the contact has been established, the length and strength of the dreams are increasing. As they did with Inigo. Soon they will reach a crescendo and the Second Dreamer will realize what he has been chosen to do.'

Falven gave the others in the oval sanctum an uncomfortable look. 'Then why do we need to incorporate Viotia?'

'What if the Second Dreamer isn't an adherent of Living Dream?' Ethan asked mildly.

'But—'

'There's a much worse scenario than that,' Phelim said. 'If one of our opponents were to reach him first and use him to sabotage the Pilgrimage.'

'They'll be looking,' Rincenso said.

'Of course they'll be looking,' Ethan said. 'But we have a huge advantage with our command of the gaiafield. Not even ANA's despicable Factions can intrude upon that. We must reach him first.'

'And if he refuses to help?' Falven enquired.

'Change his mind,' Phelim told them. 'In a very literal sense.'

'I suppose that's necessary,' Rincenso said uneasily.

'I would hope not,' Ethan said. 'But we must be prepared for all eventualities.'

'Yes. I understand.'

'What I would like to do first is make a simple appeal to both the Second Dreamer and the Skylord,' Ethan said.

Falven's thoughts rippled with surprise, which he made no effort to hide. 'A unisphere declaration?'

'No. A direct intervention into the next dream.'

'How?'

'The Second Dreamer is issuing his dream into the confluence nests in real time,' Phelim said. 'Right at the end of the last dream, as it fades away, there is an anomaly, a tiny one. It is extremely hard to spot, we believe it has escaped attention among the majority of our followers. But our Dream Masters have been reviewing those last moments. There is a human emotion intruding into the Skylord's stream of consciousness. A weak sense of pleasure, but one with considerable sexual connotations. In all probability we are witnessing post-coital satisfaction.'

'The Second Dreamer receives the Skylord's dream when he's having sex?' Rincenso asked incredulously.

'The human brain is most receptive when relaxed,' Ethan said. 'The period immediately after sex certainly generates that state.'

'Did this happen to Inigo?' Falven was almost indignant.

Ethan's lips twitched in amusement. 'Not that I'm aware

of. But Inigo never issued his dreams in real time, so I don't suppose we'll ever know. But this anomaly is the strongest indicator we have that this is real-time dreaming. In which case we should be able to intervene, to converse with both the Second Dreamer and the Skylord. If we can successfully perform the latter intervention we may be able to establish a direct connection without the Second Dreamer. In which case our problems will be solved. Viotia becomes an irrelevance, as does our elusive Second Dreamer. And we will be one step closer to the Void.'

'That would be . . . wonderful,' Falven said.

'Our Dream Masters are now monitoring Viotia's confluence nests for the time the Second Dreamer starts to dream. When it happens we will make the attempt.'

'And if that fails?'

'Then you will bring your proposal to Council.'

*

Fourteen hundred years was a long time alive by anyone's standards. However, there were Commonwealth citizens who had remained in their bodies for longer; Paula had even met a few of them. She didn't enjoy their company. Mostly they were Dynasty members who couldn't let go of the old times when their family empires used to run the Commonwealth. After biononics and ANA and Higher culture changed the Central Worlds for ever, they'd grabbed what they could of their ancient wealth and re-established themselves on External Worlds where they set about recreating their personal golden age.

They had the money and influence to be bold and build new experimental societies, something different, something exciting; but for all their extraordinarily long life, they'd never experienced another way to live. And the longer they managed to maintain their own little empire around them the more resistant to change they became. Nothing new was attempted, instead they mined history for stability. On one planet in particular their social engineering reached its nadir. Iaioud, where a ruling Halgarth collective had founded and maintained a society that was even less susceptible to change than Huxley's Haven by the simple expedient of prohibiting conception. At the end of a fifty-year life every citizen was rejuvenated and memory wiped – except the state knew who they were and what job they did best. On emerging fresh from their clinic treatment they would then be appointed to the same profession again, and spend the next fifty years working as they had done for the last fifty – hundred, three hundred years. It was the ultimate feudalism.

Three hundred years ago, Paula had led an undercover team of agents there, infiltrating the clinics which performed the rejuvenation treatment and slowly corrupting them. Over the next few years memory wipes became incomplete, allowing people to remember what had gone before. Thousands of women discovered that their revitalized bodies had a functional uterus again. Underground networks were established; first to help the criminal outcasts who had given birth to children, then assuming a greater role in offering political resistance to the Halgarth régime.

Forty years after Paula and her team finished their mission to sow dissent on Iaioud, a revolution overturned the Halgarth collective using minimal force. It took a further hundred and fifty years for the twisted world to regain its equilibrium and claw its way back up the socioeconomic index to something approaching the average for an External World.

At the time, Paula had worried she still wasn't ready for that kind of mission. Change was a long time coming within herself. It was one thing to realize intellectually that she had to adapt mentally to keep up with the ever-shifting cultures of the Greater Commonwealth. But unlike everyone else, she had to make a conscious decision to alter herself physically in order for that evolution to manifest. Her carefully designed DNA hardwired her neurones into specific personality traits. In order to survive any kind of phrenic progression she had to first destroy what was. An action which came perilously close to individuality suicide. And in her, as in every human, vanity wasn't something bound to DNA; she considered her existing personality to be more than adequate – in short, she liked being herself.

But in slow increments, every time she needed to undergo rejuvenation, she modified a little bit more of her psychoneural profiling. At the end of the three-century process, she was still obsessive about a great many things, but now it was through choice rather than a physically ordained compulsion. One time long ago, when she'd tried to mentally overcome her need to apprehend a criminal in order to achieve a greater goal, the effort had put her body into a severe type of shock. By removing the Foundation's physiological constraints her mind could now flourish in ways her long-departed designers never envisaged. She'd been born with the intention of tracking down individual criminals, the kind that might plague the society of Huxley's Haven; but now she had the freedom to take an overview. Yet none of the liberations she selected for herself ever touched the core of her identity, she always retained her intuitive understanding of what was right and wrong. Her soul was untainted.

Iaioud tested her new, versatile self to the extreme. She accepted that the way in which the Halgarth collective had set up the constitution was intrinsically wrong, oppressing an entire population. In fact she would have probably acknowledged that before. But the whole nature of Iaioud's rigid society was uncomfortably close to that of Huxley's Haven. After a while she decided that the difference was simple enough. On Iaioud, people were being kept in line by a brutally authoritarian regime misusing Commonwealth medical technology. While on Huxley's Haven, strictures and conformity came from within. Possibly there had been a crime, right back at the founding, when the Human Structure Foundation started birthing an entire population with DNA modified to their grand scheme. The old liberal groups might have been right – a thought which would have finally pleased the radicals who had stolen her as a baby. But however great the sin committed at its genesis, the constraints placed on the population of Huxley's Haven were internal. Its people now couldn't be changed without destroying what they were. By far the bigger crime.

So she convinced herself, anyway. These days she wrote it off as an argument between philosophies. Interesting, and completely disconnected from real life. The Commonwealth had enough real problems to keep her fully occupied. Though even she had to admit, the whole Pilgrimage issue was throwing up some unique complications.

For once she couldn't decide if Living Dream had the right to set off on Pilgrimage, and be damned to possible consequences. The dilemma came from the total lack of empirical evidence that the Void would consume the rest of the galaxy. She had to admit that a lot of pro-Pilgrimage Factions and commentators were right to be sceptical. The assumption that Living Dream were courting annihilation was all based on information which came from the Raiel. The immense timescale since the last catastrophic macro-expansion phase would distort any information no matter how well stored; throw in aliens with their own agenda and she simply couldn't accept the claim at face value.

ANA:Governance was also keen to acquire more information on the situation, which gave Paula a useful outlet for her energies, and thankfully little time to brood over the politics involved. Her assignment, as always, was to stop the Factions from engineering the physical citizens of the Commonwealth into actions they wouldn't otherwise have performed.

She'd left St Mary's Clinic and returned to her ship, the *Alexis Denken*, a sleek ultradrive vessel which ANA: Governance had supplied and armed to a degree which would alarm any Navy captain. She left the planet, then hung in transdimensional suspension twenty AUs out from the star. It was a position which allowed her to monitor the ftl traffic within the Anagaska system with astonishing accuracy. Unfortunately, the one thing her ship's sensors couldn't do was locate a cold trail. There was no trace of Aaron's ship. Given the time between the raid on the clinic and her arrival, she suspected he had an ultradrive ship. Marius certainly had one. Her u-shadow monitored him arriving back at the city starport and getting into a private yacht. *Alexis Denken*'s sensors tracked it slipping into hyperspace. For those in the know, the signature was indicative of an ultradrive.

An hour later, the Delivery Man took off in his own ship, which had an equally suspicious drive signature. He flew away in almost exactly the opposite direction to Marius. Ten minutes later another starship dropped out of transdimensional suspension where it had been waiting in the system's cometary halo, and began to fly along the same course as the Delivery Man.

'Good luck,' Paula sent to Justine.

'Thanks.'

Paula opened an ultra-secure link to ANA:Governance. 'It appears your ultradrive technology is completely compromised,' she reported.

'To be expected,' ANA:Governance replied. 'It does not require my full capacity to derive the theory behind it. Most Factions would have the intellectual resources. Once the equations are available, any Higher replicator above level-five could produce the appropriate hardware.'

'I still think you should exert a little more authority. After all, the Factions are all part of you.'

'Factions are how I remain integral. I am plural.'

'The way you say it makes it sound like you have the electronic version of bi-polar disorder.'

'More like multi-billion-polar. But that is what I am. All individuals who join me do so by imprinting their personality routines upon me. I am the collective consciousness of all ANA inhabitants, that is the very basis of my authority. Once that essence is bequeathed they are free to become what they want. I do not take their memories, too, that would be an annexation of individuality.'

'You have to pass through the eye of the needle to live in the playground of the gods.'

'One of Inigo's better quotes,' ANA:Governance said

with a cadence of amusement. 'Shame about the rest of that sermon.'

'You don't help make my job any easier.'

'Any and all of my resources are available to you.'

'But there's only one of me, and I feel like I'm battling the Hydra out here.'

'This lack of self-confidence is unlike you. What is the matter?'

'The Pilgrimage, of course. Should it be allowed?'

'The humans of Living Dream believe it to be both their right and their destiny. They are billions in number. How can that much belief be wrong?'

'Because they might be endangering trillions.'

'True. This is not a question which has an answer. Not in the absolute terms you are demanding.'

'What if they do trigger the Void's final devourment phase, or at least a bad one?'

'Ah, now that is the real question. It's also one which I doubt we can have prior knowledge of. Neither I nor any of the post-physicals I have interacted with are aware of what happens inside the Void.'

'Inigo showed you.'

'Inigo showed us the fate of humans in the Void. Which incidentally isn't too dissimilar to downloading yourself into me; though the Void has the advantage of quasi-mystical overtones to win over the technophobes among humanity. And you get to remain physical. What he did not show us is the nature of the Void itself.'

'So you're prepared to take the risk?'

'At this moment I am prepared to let the players strut the stage.'

'Yes. That's about as un-definitive as it gets.'

'If I were to forbid the Pilgrimage and enforce that decision, it would trigger a split within myself. Pro-Pilgrimage Factions such as the Advancers would likely attempt to create their own version of myself. And kindly remember I am not a virtual environment. I am fully established within the quantum field intersections around Earth.'

'You're scared of a rival?'

'The human race has never been so unified as it is today. It has taken our entire history to reach this congruity. People, all people, lead a good life filled with as much diversity as they wish to undergo. They migrate inwards until they download into me. Within me they are free to transcend in any way imagination and ability can combine. One day, as a whole, I will become post-physical. Humans who do not wish to travel along that path will begin afresh. That is the vision of evolution which awaits us. A "rival" focal point would distort that, possibly even damage or dilute the moment of singularity.'

'There can only be one god, huh?'

'There can be many. I simply wish to avoid engendering hostile ones. No one wants to see a war in heaven. Trust me, it would make a Void devourment seem trivial.'

'I thought diversity was our virtue.'

'It is one of them, and as such flourishes within me.'

'But . . .'

'It is also a danger that can lead to our destruction. Opposing forces have to be balanced. That is my function.'

'And this is one instance where you're going to fail if you're not careful.'

'Undoubtedly.'

'So we have to find other options.'

'As people have sought since civilization began on Earth. That, I think, is a greater virtue.'

'Okay then.' Paula took a moment to marshal her thoughts. 'I'm uncertain who is behind the raid on the clinic. It is puzzling why the Advancers and Conservatives should both have their representatives there after the fact. Do you think a third Faction is involved?'

'Very likely. I do not know which one. Many alliances are being formed and broken. However, you may soon be able to establish the identity. Admiral Kazimir is currently receiving a report from the base Admiral at the *High Angel*. He will probably ask you to tackle it.'

'Ah.'

'If you need anything.'

'I'll let you know.'

The link ended. Paula sat back on the deep curving chair which the starship's cabin had moulded for her. Given her own uncertainty about the mission, she was feeling vaguely troubled by the lack of reassurance ANA:Governance could offer. She supposed she should be grateful it was so honest with her.

Kazimir called less than a minute later. 'How did the Anagaska enquiry go?' he asked.

'Positive result. It was definitely someone with advanced bionomics and possibly an ultradrive ship. The target was Inigo's old memorycell.'

'Interesting. And I've just had a report that the *Alini*, a private starship, docked at *High Angel*.'

'How is that relevant?'

'It docked at the Raiel dome. The Navy sensors detected a drive signature which could indicate an ultradrive.'

Paula was suddenly very interested. 'Did it now? There are very few humans the Raiel will allow into their dome. Who does the *Alini* belong to?'

'Unknown. It's registered to a company on Sholapur.'

'I'm on my way.'

*

The Delivery Man landed at Daroca's main starport, parking his ultradrive ship, the *Jomo*, on a pad connected to the third terminal building, which dealt with private yachts. Then he started walking across the field to the nearby hangar zone. Even knowing all about the diversion bug infiltrated into the ground navigation section of the starport's smartcore didn't help him. All the hangars were identical, the rows regimented. It was mildly confusing. Not that he would lose his way, not with all his enrichments and an instinctive sense of direction. But just to be on the safe side ... His u-shadow snatched real-time images from a sensor satellite and guided him directly.

Eventually, he was standing at the base of a glossy black wall where the small side door was protected by an excellent security shield. Not even his full field function scan could determine what lay inside. He smiled. *This* was more like it.

His biononics began to modify their field function, pushing a variety of energy patterns against the security shield, introducing small instabilities which quickly began to amplify. His u-shadow reached through the fluctuating gaps and launched a flurry of smart trojans into the hangar net.

The door irised open.

Ninety-seven seconds. *Not bad.*

Inside, his field function scanned round looking for possible guard armaments, while his u-shadow rifled through the hangar's electronic systems. Troblum had set up a fairly standard defence network, with concentric shielding around the main section of the hangar. The physicist was clearly more interested in maintaining privacy than physical protection.

His scan didn't reveal any human presence in the hangar. The first office was clearly just a reception area, cover for anyone who did make it past the diversion system. Beyond that was a second office with one of the biggest smartcores the Delivery Man had ever seen. It wasn't connected to the hangar network, or the unisphere. His u-shadow established a link to its peripheral systems and began to probe the available files.

The Delivery Man went on into the main hangar. He whistled softly at the vast array of Neumann cybernetic modules occupying half of the space inside. The machine was powered down, but he was familiar enough with the technology to guess its sophistication probably put it beyond a level-six replicator. That was not something an individual Higher citizen normally possessed. No wonder Troblum needed such a large smartcore, nothing else could operate such a rig.

'Can you access the main memory?' he asked his u-shadow.

'Not possible for me. I will need high-order assistance.'

The Delivery Man cursed, and opened an ultra-secure link to the Conservative Faction. There was a small risk it could be intercepted by another Faction or more likely ANA:Governance itself, but in light of what he'd stumbled across he considered it necessary. 'I need help to gain access to Troblum's smartcore. It should tell us what he's been building with this machine.'

'Very well,' the Conservative Faction replied. With his u-shadow providing a link, the Delivery Man could almost feel the Faction's presence shift into the hangar. It began to infiltrate the smartcore. While it was doing that, he began to look through the mundane files in the hangar's net to try and find delivery schedules. The individual components of the machine had to come from somewhere, and the EMA to obtain them went far beyond an individual's resources. There was no court the Conservatives could use to confront the Accelerators with, even if he established a datatrail back to their representatives; but if he could find the proxy supplying Troblum with additional EMA there was a chance he could find other illicit EMA transfers from the same source. A whole level of Accelerator operations would be uncovered.

'There is only one design stored in the smartcore,' the Conservative Faction announced. 'It would appear to be an ftl engine capable of transporting a planet.'

The Delivery Man swung round to stare at the dark machine looming above him, his gaze drawn to the circular extrusion mechanism in the centre. 'A whole planet?'

'Yes.'

'Would it work?'

'The design is an ingenious reworking of exotic matter theory. It could work if applied correctly.'

'And this built it?' he said, still staring at the machine.

'There have been two attempts at producing the engine. The first was aborted. The second appears to have been successful.'

'Why do they want to fly a planet round at ftl speeds? And which planet?'

'We don't know. Please destroy the machine and the smartcore.'

The Delivery Man put his hands on his hips to give the machine an appalled look. 'What technology level can I go up to here?'

'Unlimited. Nobody must know it ever existed, least of all Highers.'

'Okay. Your call.'

The Conservative Faction ended the link, leaving the Delivery Man feeling unusually alone. Now he knew the purpose of the machine the silent hangar had the feel of some ancient murder scene. It wasn't a pleasant place to be, putting him on edge.

He called the *Jomo*'s smartcore, and told it to fly over. The hangar's main doors were open when it arrived, and it nosed through the security screen to settle on the cradles inside. Its nose almost touched the wall of Neumann cybernetics.

The Delivery Man made sure the hangar security screen was at its highest rating before he stood underneath the *Jomo*'s open airlock to be drawn up by an inverted gravity effect. Once inside he used a tri-certificate authorization to activate the Hawking m-sink stored in one of the forward holds. The little device was contained inside a high-powered regrav sled, which slipped out to hover in front of the Neumann cybernetics. With that in place, the Delivery Man aimed a narrow disrupter effect at the machine, just above the Hawking m-sink. A half-metre section of equipment vaporized, producing a horizontal fountain of hot ionized gas. It bent slightly in mid-air to pour into the Hawking m-sink, which absorbed every molecule. The Delivery Man tracked the disruptor effect along the front of the machine, with the Hawking m-sink following.

It took forty minutes to vaporize the entire machine. When it was over, the quantum black hole at the centre of the Hawking m-sink had absorbed three hundred and twenty-seven tonnes of matter, putting the regrav sled close to its weight lift limit as it edged back into the starship's hold. The Delivery Man requested flight clearance from the starport, and the *Jomo* lifted into Arevalo's warm summer skies.

Justine watched it go from the safety of her own ship, parked on a pad eight hangars down the row.

*

Twilight was bathing Hawksbill Bay with a rich gold hue, mild enough so that strange constellations could twinkle merrily across the cloudless sky. The only sound around the pavilion's swimming pool came from the waves breaking around the rocks of the headland below.

'An ftl engine that shifts planets,' Nelson said. 'Got to admire them. They don't think small.'

'They don't think: period,' Gore grunted. 'ANA is embedded in the local quantum fields. You can't just rip it out and fling it across the galaxy on a blind date with the Void.'

'They obviously believe it. Troblum's EMA came through one of their front committees. He built the engine for the Accelerators.'

'Don't believe it,' Gore said, shaking his head. 'He even made a presentation to the Navy about the Anomine using something like this to haul the Dyson barrier generators into place. Asked Kazimir to fund a fucking search for them for Christ's sake. Why would Ilanthe allow him to go public with the idea? They'd atomize him before he even put in a call for a meeting with the Navy. No, we haven't got enough information yet.'

'Makes sense if it's a diversion,' Nelson said reluctantly. 'They wouldn't build anything so critical to their plans on a Higher world. We don't.'

'And he's taken years to get it built, on a fairly pitiful budget. Wrong priority level. We really need to find Troblum and ask nicely what he's really been doing for the Accelerators.'

'He left Arevalo a while back. Filed a flight plan to Lutain. Never showed up there, or any other Commonwealth World, Central or External.'

'We need to find him,' Gore repeated firmly.

'That's not going to happen. Either the Accelerators have him, or he's hiding, or more likely he's plain and simple dead.'

'Then we find out which one it is.'

*

Justine stood in the middle of the weirdly empty hangar and called Paula.

'There's something seriously wrong here.'

'In what way?' Paula asked.

'I think the Delivery Man just cleared the whole place out.' Justine slowly looked round the big empty space, opening her optical vision to Paula. 'See that? There was something in here. My field scan shows those power cables were cut by a disruption effect, same goes for the support girders. Whatever it was, it was sizeable and used up a great deal of power. But the *Jomo* is no bigger than my ship. Which only leaves one option how he did it.'

'I thought the Hawking m-sink was even more secure than ultradrive technology. It would seem I'm wrong, which is disturbing.'

'Kazimir will have to be told,' Justine said. 'If there are starships flying round the Commonwealth equipped with that kind of weapon the Navy should know about it. The Factions don't use the most principled people as their representatives.'

'I'll leave that to you.'

'Great. Thank you. He's still human enough to blame the messenger.'

'He's a professional. You'll be all right. Do you know where the Delivery Man is heading?'

'His direction indicated Earth when he left my sensor range. I imagine he'll want to dump the mass stored in the Hawking m-sink first, and he'll do that deep in interstellar space. Expelling it will produce a colossal gamma burst.'

'Leave him alone for now. The focus is shifting back to Living Dream.'

'Why?'

'Our sources in the movement are reporting an alarming development,' Paula said. 'Living Dream is readying all the civil security forces on all the core worlds of the Free Market Zone. Leave has been cancelled and they're undergoing martial law enforcement training.'

'Martial law? Where is that applied in the Free Market Zone?'

'It isn't. Yet. But if they were to annex Viotia they would

probably need that many police troopers to keep the populace under control.'

'Jesus! Are they planning that?'

'Ethan is becoming desperate to gain control over the Second Dreamer. He's the one person who could still stop this whole Pilgrimage in its tracks.'

'And everyone believes he's on Viotia,' Justine said, appalled. 'Dear heavens, an interstellar invasion. In this day and age, it's unthinkable, it's left over from the Starflyer War.'

'Start thinking it. I made a mistake not giving this a higher priority. We really need to offer ANA:Governance's protection to the Second Dreamer. That way no one will be able to pressure him into either helping or hindering the Pilgrimage.'

'But first we have to find him. How long before you can get your agent working on this?'

'Very soon now. I'm on my way to see him with one slight detour.'

Justine eyed the hangar's inner office suspiciously. There was an empty space which three communications conduits led into, their ends cut off clean. 'Whatever they were building here was clearly important, and the Delivery Man took quite a risk covering it up. I don't think we have a lot of time left.'

'The Pilgrimage ships won't be ready to fly until September.'

'And the Ocisen Empire fleet will be here in late August, that's less than three months away. I'd like to suggest a lead no one else seems to be following.'

'What's that?'

'Inigo started to dream when he was at Centurion Station. Did anyone else?'

'If they did, we'd know about it.'

'That's the point: would we? Suppose the contact was a weak one that was never fully established. Or the recipient didn't want any part of Inigo's religion. A reluctant person just like the Second Dreamer has turned out to be.'

'I think I see where you're going with this, or rather intend to go.'

'I want to check out the confluence nest on Centurion Station, see if it has any memory of Void dreams, or fragments of them. Maybe the Second Dreamer started his connection with the Skylord when he was there, just like Inigo.'

'You're right, no one else has covered that angle.'

'If I leave now, my ship can get me there in five hundred hours.'

'You're going to fly there? Why not use the Navy's relay link?'

'Too much chance of it being intercepted.'

'If you do find anything it'll take you another five hundred hours to get back. It'll probably all be over by then.'

'If I find anything important, I'll use the relay link to send you the name in the heaviest encryption we have.'

'Okay. Good luck.'

*

Troblum woke up slumped in the chair he'd sat in all day reviewing various schematics. His exovision displays had paused at the point where he'd fallen asleep. Colourful profiles of exotic mass density modulators floated like mechanical ghosts around him, each one beleaguered by shoals of blue and green analytical displays. Supposedly these components would perform their designated function without any trouble; the designers had simply scaled up from existing ultradrives. Except, nobody had ever built them this size before, which left Troblum with a mountain of problems when it came to the kind of precise power control they needed. And they hadn't even got to the fabrication stage yet.

He stretched as best his thick limbs would allow and tried to get out of the chair. After two attempts which made him look like a overturned glagwi struggling to right itself his u-shadow ordered the station to reduce the local gravity field. Now when he pushed with his legs and back he gave his body an impetus which propelled him right out of the clingy cushions. Gravity returned slowly, giving him time to straighten his legs before his feet touched the decking. He let out a wet belch as the falling sensation ended. His stomach was still churning, and his legs felt weak and stiff. He had a headache, too. The medical display in his exovision showed him his sugar levels were all over the place. There was a load of crap about toxins and blood oxygen levels too, which he cancelled just as the nutrition and exercise recommendations came up. *Stupid anachronism in the age of biononics.*

He set off to the saloon which the ultradrive team used as their social and business centre. It also had the best culinary units on the station. When he arrived several of the tables along the curving wall were occupied by groups of people discussing various aspects of the project. He saw Neskia with a couple of technicians he recognized from the team handling the drive's hyperspace fluidity systems. They all stared at him as he sat down in the spare seat, wincing as his knees creaked. Both technicians registered mild disapproval. Neskia's long metallized neck curved sinuously so her flat face was aligned perfectly on him. 'Thank you,' she said to the technicians. 'We'll go with that.'

They nodded thanks and left.

'Was there something you wanted?' she asked Troblum in a level voice.

'I need to change the design for the mass density modulator,' he said. A maidbot slid over with a tray of food his u-shadow had ordered from the culinary units. He started unloading the plates.

Neskia's face tipped down; her large circular eyes regarded the food without any trace of emotion. 'I see. Do you have the proposed new design?'

'No,' he mumbled round a mouthful of spaghetti. 'I want you to okay the change before I waste a week on it.'

'What's wrong with the existing modulator?'

'It's a pile of crap. Doesn't work. Your idiots didn't take the power control requirements into account.'

'Do you have an analysis of the problem?'

Troblum could only nod as he chewed his hot floratts bread with mozzarella and herbs. His u-shadow sent the file over.

'Thank you. The review team will examine this. You will have a reply in an hour. That is the procedure.'

'Sure. Good.' He sighed. Great that the tech problem was sorted, but the spaghetti with its balls of jolmeat and attrato sauce could have done with more black pepper. He reached for his tankard, only to find Neskia's hand on top of his, preventing him from lifting the beer. Her skin shimmered between white and silver. He couldn't sense any temperature from her fingers, hot or cold. 'What?'

Her eyes blinked slowly, turning the irises from black to deep indigo. 'In future. In public. While you are here in my station. Please ensure your social interaction program is running, and that you follow its advice.'

'Oh. Okay.' He dipped his head towards the tankard.

'Thank you, Troblum.' She lifted her hand away. 'Was there anything else? The project seems to be absorbing most of your time.'

'Yeah, it's interesting. I might get some crossover into one of my own projects. Ultradrive is a fascinating re-working of quantum dimensional theory. Who came up with it?'

'I believe it was ANA:Governance. Is it important?'

'No.' He pushed the spaghetti plate aside, and started on the rack of lamb.

Neskia still hadn't stopped looking at him. She was about to speak again when two people came over to stand beside their table. Troblum finished chewing before he glanced up – he knew that was the kind of thing the social program counselled. Marius was looking down at him with his usual rarefied contempt. But it was his companion who turned Troblum immobile. His limbs wouldn't move. Thankfully, neither did his mouth, which stopped him from opening his jaw and grunting in shock. He couldn't breathe either as something like frost ripped down through his lungs.

'I'd introduce you,' Marius said coldly. 'But of all the people on this station, Troblum, you are the one who doesn't need it. Now do you?'

'Really,' the Cat said, and grinned. 'Why's that?'

Troblum's very dark fascination kept his muscles locked up tight. She wasn't easy to recognize, she didn't have that trademark spiked hair out of all her history files. It was still short and dark, but today she wore it in a smooth swept-back style with a pair of slim copper shades perched up above her forehead. She was dressed in a chic modern suit rather than the leather trousers and tight vest she used to favour. But that darkish complexion and wide amused grin veering on the crazy . . . There was no mistake. She was so much smaller than he imagined, it was confusing, she barely came up to his shoulder height, yet he'd always visualized her as an Amazon.

'Troblum has a penchant for history,' Marius said. 'He knows all sorts of odd facts.'

'What's my favourite food?' the Cat asked.

'Lemon risotto with asparagus,' Troblum stammered. 'It was the specialty dish at the restaurant you waitressed in when you were fifteen.'

The Cat's grin sharpened. 'What the fuck is he?' She turned to Marius for an explanation.

'An idiot savant with a fetish about the Starflyer War. He's useful to us.'

'Whatever turns you on.'

'You're in suspension,' Troblum said flatly; he couldn't help the words coming out even though he was afraid of her. 'It was a five-thousand-year sentence.'

'Aww. He's quite sweet, actually,' the Cat told Marius. She gave Troblum a lewd wink. 'I'll finish it one day. Promise.'

'If you have a moment, please,' Marius asked Neskia. 'We need to sort a proper ship out for our guest.'

'Of course.' She stood up.

'Oh yes,' Marius added, as though it were of no consequence. 'Is Troblum behaving himself?'

Neskia looked from Marius to Troblum. 'So far so good. He's been quite helpful.'

'Keep it up,' Marius said. He wasn't smiling.

Troblum bowed his head, unable to look at any of them. Too many people. Too close. Too intrusive. *And one of them is the Cat!* He wasn't prepared for that kind of encounter today. Nor any day. But she was out of suspension – somehow, walking around. *She's in this station!*

His medical display flashed up blue symbols down the side of his exovision, telling him his biononics were engaging, re-animating his chest muscles, calming them into a steady rhythm. It hadn't registered with him the way he'd started to suck his breath down as if his throat was constricted. A small cocktail of drugs were flushed out of macrocellular glands, bringing down his heart rate.

Troblum risked a glance up, his face pulled into a horrendously guilty expression. The three of them were gone, out of sight, out of the saloon. He was gathering an excessive number of curious looks from his colleagues who were still seated. He wanted to tell them, to shout: *It's not me you should be staring at.*

Instead, he felt the trembling start deep in his torso. He stood up fast. Which made his head spin. Biononics reinforced his leg muscles, allowing him to hurry out of the saloon. In the corridor, his u-shadow diverted a trolly-bot for him sit on. It carried him all the way back to his quarters, where he flopped on to the bed. He loaded a nine-level certificate into the lock even though he knew how useless that was.

The Cat!

He lay on the bed with the cabin heating up, feeling the shock slowly ebbing away. Release from the physical symptoms did nothing to alleviate the dread. Of all the megalomaniacs and psychopaths in history, the Accelerators had chosen to bring her back. Troblum lay there in the warm darkness for hours wondering what they were facing which was so terrible they had no choice but to use her. He'd always been behind the whole Accelerator movement because it was such a logical one. They were nurturing an evolutionary lineage which had started with single-cell amoebas and would end with elevation to post-physical status. A necessity that couldn't be disputed. The other Factions were wrong, it was that obvious. To him. Accelerator philosophy appealed to his physicist nature; because that hurtful vicious bastard Marius was right, there was very little else in the way of personality.

Forget that. It's not relevant.

Because anything that has to use the Cat to make it work can't be right. It just can't.

Inigo's fifth dream

'—thus because the city is deemed to be a sole entity in its own right no human can "own" their residence in the traditional legal sense. However, in the fifteenth year after Rah's arrival, the newly formed Upper Council passed the first Act of Registry. Essentially that means that any human can claim a residence within the city wall for their own usage. In order to register you simply have to find a house or maisonette or room which is unoccupied, stay in it for two days and two nights, then register your claim with the Board of Occupancy. This claim once notarized will allow you and your descendants to live there until such time as they choose to relinquish it. As there are no new buildings, and can never be, the most desirable and largest homes were claimed within ten years of Rah opening the first gate. These are now the palaces of our most ancient families, the District Masters, and as such can have up to five generations living in them, all of them first sons waiting to inherit the estate and seat on the Upper Council. The remaining available accommodation in the city today is small and badly configured for human occupation. Although even this is diminishing rapidly. Thus, while districts such as Eyrie are basically uninhabitable—'

Edeard hoped he hadn't just groaned out loud from the terrible boredom. He was now as adept as any Makkathran citizen at veiling his emotions from casual farsight, but if Master Solarin from the Guild of Lawyers used the word *thus* one more time . . . It was a mystery how the old man could talk so long without a break. Rumour at the station was that Master Solarin was over two hundred and fifty years old. Edeard would be surprised if that were true. He certainly didn't look that young. His white hair had receded so far that the top of his skull was now completely bald, something Edeard had never seen before, though the remaining strands were long enough to reach down over his shoulders. And his limbs were horribly thin and frail, while his fingers had swollen to the point where he had trouble flexing them. His vocal cords, however, suffered no such malaise.

Along with his fellow probationary constables, Edeard was sitting on a bench in the small hall of the Jeavons station, listening to their weekly lecture on basic Makkathran law. In another two months they'd be facing a batch of exams on the subject, which they had to pass in order to graduate. Like all of them, he found Solarin a sore test of patience. A quick scan round showed Boyd was almost asleep. Macsen's eyes were unfocused as he longtalked the girls in the dressmaker's shop at the end of the street. Kanseen appeared to be paying polite attention but Edeard knew her well enough now to see she was as bored as him. Dinlay, though, was sitting up with rapt attention and even taking notes. Somehow Edeard couldn't quite laugh at that. Poor old Dinlay had so much to prove to his father and uncles he would undoubtedly pass his exams with high grades. That presented the rest of them with the very real danger that once they graduated, Dinlay would be appointed their squad leader. It would be something he took *very* seriously.

'—thus the precedence was set for the lower ancillary court to hear any application to evict when a civil malfeasance is suspected of taking place within the property itself. In practice a full hearing is unnecessary, and you may request a provisional eviction notice from the duty magistrate who acts as *de facto* high council to the lower court. And that I'm afraid brings this session to its successful conclusion. We will deal with the criteria for such application next week. In the meantime I'd like you all to read *Sampsols Common Law*, Volume Three, chapters thirteen through twenty-seven by the time I return. It covers the main parameters of weapons usage within the city wall. I might even enliven our time together with a small test. How exciting that will be, eh? Until then, I thank you for your interest and bid you farewell.' Solarin gave them a vague smile and removed his gold-rimmed glasses before shutting the big book he'd covered with annotations. His ge-monkey placed it carefully in a leather shoulder bag along with the other books the lawyer used for his lecture.

Dinlay stuck his hand up. 'Sir?'

'Ah, my dear boy; sadly I am in something of a rush today. If you could possibly write your question down and submit it to my senior apprentice at the Guild, I'd be most grateful.'

'Yes, sir.' Dinlay's hand came down and his shoulders slumped with disappointment.

Edeard remained seated as the lawyer walked slowly out of the hall, assisted by two ge-monkeys, wondering what Solarin would actually look like *rushing* somewhere.

'Olovan's Eagle tonight?'

'Huh?' Edeard shook himself out of his absurd day-dream.

Macsen was standing over his desk, a smug expression on his face. 'Clemensa will be going. Evala said she's been asking about you. A lot!'

'Clemensa?'

'The one with the dark hair always tied up in a long tail. Big chest. Big legs, too, sadly, but hey, nobody's perfect.'

Edeard sighed. It was another of the girls from the dress-maker's. Macsen spent most of his time sweet-talking them or trying to set them up with his friends. Once he even tried to match Kanseen with a carpentry apprentice – he wouldn't be doing that again. 'No. No. I can't. I am so far behind on my law texts, and you heard what Solarin said.'

'Remind me.'

'There's going to be a test,' Edeard said wearily.

'Oh right. It's only the exam at the end which counts. Don't worry. Listen, I've got a friend in the Lawyer's Guild. A couple of gold shillings and he'll gift us the whole *Sampsols*.'

'That's cheating,' Dinlay said hotly.

Macsen put on a suitably wounded expression. 'In what respect?'

'In all respects!'

'Dinlay, he's just winding you up,' Kanseen said as she got up to leave.

'I'm being perfectly serious,' Macsen said, his face as innocent as a newborn.

'Ignore him,' she said, and gave Dinlay's shoulder a gentle shove. 'Come on let's find some lunch before we go out.'

Dinlay managed one last scowl before hurrying after Kanseen. He started to ask her something about the residency laws.

'Must be true love,' Macsen warbled cheerfully as they turned out of sight.

'You're evil,' Edeard decided. 'Pure evil.'

'Only thanks to years of practice and dedication.'

'You know he's going to be our squad leader, don't you.'

'Yes. He'll get his appointment the day after the Eggshaper Guild announces its sculpted a ge-pig that can fly.'

'I'm serious. His grades will be way above ours, plus his father and a whole load of family are already constables. Senior ones at that.'

'Chae isn't stupid. He knows that'll never work.'

Edeard wanted to believe Macsen was right.

'Um, Edeard, are you really not interested in Clemensa?' Boyd asked.

'Ho, this is perfect,' Macsen said, rubbing his hands together. 'Why, do you fancy your chances?'

'Actually, yes,' Boyd said with more courage that Edeard had credited him with.

'Good for you. She's a lovely girl. As randy as a drakken in a bloodfrenzy, I just happen to know.'

Boyd frowned. 'How do you know?'

'Evala told me,' Macsen said smoothly. 'Her last boyfriend was dumped for not having enough stamina.'

Boyd gave Macsen a suddenly entranced look. 'I'll come with you tonight. But you have to get Evala to put in a good word for me.'

'Leave it with me, my fine friend. You're as good as shagged senseless already.'

Edeard rolled his eyes and promised the Lady he'd be good for evermore if she'd just stop Macsen from being . . . well, Macsen. 'Come on, let's get something to eat before the constables grab it all again.'

'Oh yes,' Boyd said. 'Our helpful and welcoming colleagues. I hate the way they treat us.'

'Only for another two months, that's all,' Macsen said.

'You really think they'll show us any respect after we qualify. I don't.'

'No they won't,' Macsen agreed. 'But at least we can shovel shit on to the new probationees. I know it'll make me feel better.'

'We're not going to do that,' Edeard said. 'We're going to talk to them, help them with problems, and make them feel appreciated.'

'Why?'

'Because that's what I would have liked to happen with us. That way more people might just be encouraged to join up. Haven't you counted the numbers, not just at this station but citywide? There aren't enough constables in the city. People are starting to organize themselves into street associations to take on the gangs. That's going to undermine the rule of law.'

'Great Lady, you really mean it, don't you?' Macsen said.

'Yes,' Edeard said forcefully, and let them sense his mental tone so they knew he wasn't joking with them. 'I know what happens when civil government means nothing. I've seen the violence that the barbarians use when a society leaves itself open to any bastard who knows how weak it is. And that's not going to happen here. Makkathran can't be allowed to tear itself apart from within.'

'I don't know why you're worried about Dinlay being squad leader,' Macsen said, equally serious. 'You're the one. Sir!'

Edeard was still slightly self-conscious about wearing the constable uniform in public. Only the white epaulettes distinguished probationees from regular constables. The rest of it was *actually real* as Macsen put it. A smart dark-blue tunic with silver buttons up the front; matching trousers with a wide regulation leather belt containing a truncheon, two pepper-gas phials, a pair of iron handcuffs with a fiendishly tricky six-lever lock that was just about impossible to pick with telekinesis, and a small first aid pack. Under the tunic was a white shirt, that Sergeant Chae made very sure was indeed an unblemished white each morning. Boots were up to an individual, but they had to be black and at least ankle-high (but not over the knee); they also had to shine from polishing. The domed helmet was made from an epoxied drosilk mesh, with padding on the inside to protect the wearer's skull from a physical blow. Like the others, Edeard had bought his own drosilk waistcoat, which was supposedly tough enough to resist a bullet. Macsen had gone one further, and bought drosilk shorts.

In theory the cost wasn't too bad. But in practice every constable needed two tunics, and at least three shirts. Then there was a constant supply of flaked soap for the dormitory's ge-chimps to wash everything. Edeard gained considerable kudos when the others found how good he was at instructing the ge-chimps with laundry tasks. After the first week Chae stopped trying to find fault when they turned out in immaculate uniforms each morning.

The daily routine hardly varied. In the morning they would have various physical and telepathic teamwork training sessions, followed by lectures. In the afternoon they would be taken out on patrol under the alarmingly vigilant eye of Chae. Sometimes their division captain, Ronark, would accompany them. Evenings were theoretically all their own. Study was advised at least during the week.

Edeard always hated it when Ronark did come out with them to 'check on progress'. The man was in his eighties, and was never going to rise any higher than his current position. His wife had left him decades ago, his children disowned him. That just left him the constables, which he believed in with a religious fervour. Everything was done according to regulation; variations were not permitted, and such infringements were subject to severe fines, restrictions and demotions. Jeavons station had one of the lowest recruitment rates in the city.

Nobody paid any attention to them when Chae led them out of the station at one o'clock precisely. Ronark was standing at his curving fish-eye window above the big double gate, observing the shift change, clocking the patrols in and out on his ancient pocket watch. Out on the narrow pavement, a squad was double-timing back to the station, its corporal red faced and panting as they tried to minimize their delay. Three ge-dogs scampered along beside them, happy at the run.

Probationary constables were not permitted genistar support. Thankfully, Chae kept a discreet silence about Edeard's ge-eagle, which now lived with two others in the station's rooftop aviary.

Jeavons was a pleasant enough district. It even had a

small park in the centre which a team of city ge-monkeys kept in good horticultural order. There was a big freshwater pond in the middle, with exotic scarlet fish measuring a good two feet long – they always seemed sinister to Edeard, who disliked their fangs and the way they looked up at everyone who stood by the rail watching them. But the park had a football pitch marked out, and he occasionally joined the games at weekends when the local lads ran a small league. He rather enjoyed the fact that Jeavons didn't house many grand families; its buildings were on a rela-tively modest scale, though the mansions along Marble Canal were regal enough. The carpenters, jewel smiths, and physicians all had their Guild headquarters there. It was also the home of the astronomical association, which had been fighting for Guild status for seven centuries, and was always blocked by the Pythia, who claimed the heavens were a supernatural realm, and astronomy verged on the heretical. Boyd, of course, was full of gossipy facts like that as they walked the winding streets; he probably knew the layout better than Chae.

Today Chae led them over Arrival Canal and into the smaller Silvarum district. The buildings here were oddly curved, as if they were once clusters of bubbles that had somehow been compressed. Squeezed-up insect hives, Boyd called them. None of them were large enough to be palaces, but they all belonged to wealthy families – the smaller merchants and senior Masters of professional Guilds. The shops all sold goods far beyond Edeard's dwindling coinage.

As they passed over the ornate wooden bridge Edeard found himself walking with Kanseen.

'So you're not going out tonight?' she enquired.

'Nah. I don't have much money left, and I really need to study.'

'You're serious then, about turning this into a career.'

'Ask me again in a year's time. In the meantime I'm not going to blow it by being stupid. I need to graduate.'

'All of us do,' she said.

'Humm.' Edeard eyed Macsen, who was lingering on the end of the bridge, exchanging some good-natured words with a gondolier passing by underneath. The gondola's benches had been removed, replaced by a simple slatted platform carrying a pile of wooden crates. 'For someone supposedly thrown penniless on the street, Macsen seems to have a lot of coinage.'

'Didn't you hear?' she said with a superior smile.

'What?'

'His mother has been taken up by a notorious Master in the Musician's Guild. She's living in a nice little maisonette in Cobara district. Apparently he's a hundred and ten years older than her.'

'No!' Edeard knew he shouldn't be interested in this gossip, but such talk was Makkathran's second currency. Everybody had some piece of hearsay or rumour about the District Master families that they couldn't wait to share. And scandal was the hugest currency of all.

'Oh yes. He used to be in one of the travelling bands which tour round the Iguru and villages in the Donsori Mountains.' She leant in closer to murmur. 'Apparently he had to stop touring some while ago because there were so many *offspring* in those villages. Now he just tutors apprentices at the Guild building and plays for the families.'

Some little memory surfaced in Edeard's thoughts; late-night talk in a tavern several months ago that he wasn't supposed to hear, and she had said *notorious*. 'You're not talking about Dybal?'

Kanseen's smile was now victorious. 'I couldn't possibly say.'

'But . . . wasn't he caught in bed with two of the Lady's novices?'

'That's part of his myth. If he wasn't so popular with his satire songs they'd have thrown him out of the Guild decades ago. Apparently they're very *upbeat*. The younger members of noble families idolize him, while the older ones want him to wind up in the bottom of a canal.'

'Yeah, but . . . Macsen's mother?'

'Yes.'

Kanseen seemed disturbingly pleased with herself, mainly because of his incredulous reaction. That was the way with her, always coming on just that little bit superior. He didn't buy it, that was just her way of coping with the probationary period, establishing a reasonable barrier around herself. It couldn't be easy being a girl in the constables; there certainly weren't many.

Chae started off heading directly for the plaza where the Chemist Guild headquarters was situated. The pavements between the buildings were a reddish brown in colour, with a central row of thick cones rising to waist height. They were filled with soil and planted with big saffcherry trees whose branches created a verdant roof between the bowed walls on either side. Pink and blue blossom was just starting to fall, forming a delicate carpet of petals. Edeard tried to keep searching the pedestrians for signs of criminal activity the way Chae kept telling them. It was hard. Akeem's memory had remained crystal clear and true on one aspect of city life: the girls. They were beautiful. Especially those of the noble families, who seemed to use districts like Silvarum to hunt in packs. They took a great deal of care about how they appeared in public. Dresses which had plunging necklines, or skirts with surprising slits amid the ruffles; lace fabric which was translucent. Hair styled to look carefree. Makeup skilfully applied to emphasize smiles, cheekbones, huge innocent eyes. Sparkling jewellery.

He passed one gaggle of maidens in their mid-teens who wore more wealth with the rings on one hand than he would earn in a month. They giggled coyly when they caught him staring. Taunted:

'Can we help you, Officer?'

'Is that really your truncheon?'

'It's a long truncheon, isn't it, Gilliaen?'

'Will you use it to subdue bad people with?'

'Emylee is very bad, Officer, use it on her.'

'Hanna! She's indecent, Officer. Arrest her.'

'Does he have a dungeon to throw her in, do you think?'

Third hands performed indecent tweaks and prods on private areas of his body. Edeard jumped in shock before hastily shielding himself, and turning bright red. The girls shrieked in amusement at his behaviour and scuttled off.

'Little trollops,' Kanseen muttered.

'Er, absolutely,' Edeard said. He glanced back – just to make sure they were causing no trouble. Two of them were still checking him out. More wild giggles rang down the street. Edeard shuddered and faced front, hardening his expression.

'You weren't tempted, were you?' Kanseen asked.

'Certainly not.'

'Edeard, you're really a great bloke, and I'm glad to be in the same squad as you. But there's still a lot of the countryside in you. Which is good,' she hastened to add. 'But any family girl would eat you for breakfast and spit out the pips before lunch. They're not nice, Edeard, not really. They have no substance.'

Then how come they look so gorgeous? he thought wistfully.

'Besides,' Kanseen said. 'They all want District Master first sons for husbands, or guildsmen or, if they're desperate, militia officers. Constables don't come close, not in status or money.'

After the plaza they made their way along to the markets. There were three of them just a couple of streets away from the Great Major Canal which bordered Silvarum's northern side. Open areas not quite as big as the plaza, packed full with stalls. The first one concentrated on fresh food. A quilt of canvas awnings formed an undulating ceiling, stitching all the stalls together, whilst providing a strangely warm shade underneath. The still air was heavy with scents. Edeard stared at the piles of fruits and vegetables with mild envy as the stallholders called out their prices and promises of taste and quality. It had been a long time since he'd sat down to a truly decent meal like he used to eat at the Guild compound back in Ashwell. Everything at the station hall came wrapped in pastry; and none of the ge-chimps in the kitchen had ever been instructed in the art of making salad.

'Those are melancholy thoughts,' Kanseen said quietly.

'Sorry,' he said, and made an effort to be alert. Chae said markets were always rife with sneak thieves and pickpockets. He was probably right. Here, as always, the stallholders greeted them warmly, with smiles and the odd gift – apples, pears, a bottle or two; pledges of a good deal if they came back off duty. They liked the constables to be visible. It discouraged pilfering.

Edeard had been dismayed by the reception they received in some districts and streets as Chae led them right across the city. Sullen expressions and intimidating silences, unshielded emotions of enmity. People turning their backs on them. Third hands jostling when they were close to canal banks. Chae, of course, had walked on undaunted, but Edeard had been unnerved. He didn't understand why whole communities would be repelled by law and order.

They moved on to the second market, the one specializing in cloth and clothes. There was a dismaying number of young women strolling along, examining colourful fabrics, chattering happily among themselves. He kept a small shield up, and did his best not to make eye contact. Though there were some truly pretty girls who just begged for a second look. Macsen had no such inhibitions. He chatted happily to any girl who even glanced in his direction.

'You never said which district you come from,' Edeard said.

'I didn't, did I?' Kanseen agreed.

'Sorry.'

'You need to stop saying that, as well,' she said, and smiled.

'Yes. I know. It's just that all of you are used to this.' He gestured round. 'I'm not. There are more people here in this market than ever lived in Ashwell.' For a moment he was struck by real guilt. He thought about his home less and less these days. Some of the faces had faded from memory. Not Akeem, that never would; but Gonat now – did he have red hair or was it dark brown? He frowned from the effort of remembering, but no clear image came.

'Bellis,' Kanseen said. 'My family lives in Bellis.'

'Right,' he said. Bellis was on the eastern side of the city, close to the port, and directly over the Great Major Canal from Sampalok. They hadn't patrolled round there yet. 'You've never been back to see them.'

'No. Mother didn't approve of my becoming a constable.'

'Oh. I'm sor— Shame.'

'I think she would have preferred me to take the Lady's vows.'

'Nothing wrong with that.'

'You really are from the countryside, aren't you?'

'Is that bad?' he said stiffly.

'No. I guess that's where the values this city used to have are kept alive, out there beyond the Donsori Mountains. It just gives me a shock to hear someone with convictions, that's all. You're rare in Makkathran, Edeard. Especially in the constables. That's why you make people uncomfortable.'

'I do?' he asked, genuinely surprised.

'Yeah.'

'But . . . You must believe in values. Why else did you join?'

'Same as half of us. In a few years I'll shift over to bodyguard work for a District Master family. They're always desperate for people with a constable's training and experience. Particularly one like me; female constables are very thin on the ground. And the noble ladies need protection as much as their husbands and sons. I can just about name my own price.'

'Oh.' The notion surprised him, he'd never considered the constables as a route to anything else, let alone something better. 'Who do I make uncomfortable?'

'Well Dinlay for a start. He believes in truth and beauty just like you, and he's a lot noisier about it. But you're stronger and smarter. Chae's going to nominate you as squad leader.'

'You don't know that.'

She smiled. It made him realize how attractive she actually was; something the uniform normally made him overlook. But that smile was a match for any of the silly family girls swanning round the market.

'Put money on it?' she challenged.

'Of course not,' he said with mock indignation. 'That's bound to be illegal.'

They both laughed.

'You two need a room?' Macsen called over his shoulder. 'I know one that'll do cheap rates.'

Kanseen gave him a forceful hand gesture.

He pulled a face. 'Wow, it's true; you can take the girl out of Sampalok, but you can't take Sampalok out of the girl.'

'Arsehole,' she growled.

'We're on patrol,' Chae snapped. 'What does that mean?'

'Professionalism at all times,' the squad muttered dutifully.

'Then kindly remember that, and apply it.'

Macsen, Kanseen, and Edeard grinned at each other as

they moved on to the third market, which featured crafts. Stalls displayed small items of furniture, ornaments, cheap jewellery, and alchemic potions. There was even a section selling rare animals as pets. The awnings here were all a uniform orange-and-white-striped canvas arranged in hexagonal cones with centre poles swamped by eaglevine. It was warm underneath, but the full power of the sun was held back.

Edeard stretched his farsight out across the Great Major Canal that ran the length of the city from the Port district to the Circle canals where the Orchard Palace was situated. Ysidro district was on the other side from Silvarum, wedged between the back of Golden Park and the Low Moat. It was where the Lady's novistery was sited.

'This a good time?' his mind enquired.

'Hello,' Salrana replied with a burst of good cheer. 'Yes, I'm fine. We're in the garden, planting summer herbs. It's so lovely in here.' A gentle image gift came with her happiness. He saw a walled garden with conical yews marking out gravel paths. Vines and climbing roses painted the walls in bright colour. There was a broad lawn in the middle, which was unusual in Makkathran; it was trimmed so neatly Edeard wondered what kind of genistar they used to chew it down. A snow-white statue of the Lady stood at one end, almost as high as the walls. She was smiling down on the novices in their white and blue robes as they skittered about with wicker baskets full of plants.

'Nice. Why don't you use ge-chimps to plant the herbs?'

'Oh, Edeard, you have got to start reading more of the Lady's teachings. The purpose of life is to achieve harmony with your environment. If you use genistars for everything, you establish a barrier between yourself and the world.'

'Okay.' He thought that was stupid, but clamped down tight on the emotion for fear Salrana would sense it. She was developing quite an acute empathy these days.

'Where are you?' she asked.

'I'm patrolling Silvarum's markets.' He let her see the bustle surrounding him, showing the rich stall displays.

'Arrested anybody bad?'

'No. They all run in terror from us.'

'Oh, Edeard, you feel sad.'

'Sorry.' He caught himself and winced. 'I'm not. It's just boring, that's all. You know I'm actually looking forward to my exams. This'll all be over after I take them. I can be a proper constable then.'

'I can't wait to see your graduation ceremony.'

'I don't think it's that grand. The Mayor hands us a pair of dark epaulettes, that's all.'

'Yes, but it's at the Orchard Palace, and all the probationary constables from the city are there, and their families are watching. It's a big event, Edeard, don't knock it.'

'I wasn't really. Do you think you'll manage to get to it?'

'Of course I will. Mother Gallian approves of formal functions like that. I've already told her you're graduating.'

'Hey, those exams aren't easy, you know.'

'You'll pass, Edeard. I'll ask the Lady to give you simple questions.'

'Thanks! Can you get out this weekend?'

'I'm not sure. It's difficult with the main service on—'

Angry shouts up ahead made Edeard look round. His farsight could sense several minds inflamed with fury. Around them were minds blazing with sour determination; they began to move faster and faster.

Shouts reverberated under the awnings.

'Stop them!'

'Thieves. Thieves.'

'Kavine is hurt.'

'Thieves in the market!'

Identical longtalk cries flooded into the aether. Jerky image gifts of faces clashed in Edeard's mind. Too many, and too poor to make any sense.

His farsight swirled round the shifting commotion, contracting on the centre. Men were running, their arms flailing wide as people swarmed round. Hands gripped long metal blades, swiping wide, keeping everyone away. Overtones of fear bubbled into the clamour of longtalk.

'That's us!' Sergeant Chae shouted. 'Come on. Constables! Clear the way! Constables coming through.' His longtalk was directed to warn people sauntering between the stalls at the same time as he shouted. He began to run. Edeard immediately followed, as did Macsen and Kanseen.

'Move! Move aside!'

After a moment of shock, Boyd took off after them. Dinlay had frozen, his mind radiating dismay.

Edeard was running hard now, keeping close to Chae. People were jumping out of the way, pressing themselves against the stalls to open a path. Women were screaming. Children shouted, excited and fearful. The theft ahead was still kicking up a hurly-burly.

'Remember: act together,' Chae told them all with remarkably calm longtalk. 'Minimum of two at all times, don't get separated. Keep your shields up.'

Edeard sent his ge-eagle streaking through the sky, heading towards the edge of the market where the thieves must surely emerge. Every street beyond the rippled roof of canopies had a covering of pleasant saffcherry trees, their pink and blue blossom clotting any view of the pavement and people below. His farsight was still concentrating on the criminals as they sped from the scene of the robbery. There were four of them, three wielding the blades, while the fourth was lugging some kind of box. From what Edeard could sense it was full of metal. And plenty of the stalls around him were displaying jewellery.

Chae drew his truncheon as they burst through a group of people gathered round a couple of overturned stalls. A man lay on the floor groaning and thrashing about, blood pooling beside him.

'Lady!' Chae exclaimed. 'All right, stay back, give him air.' He scrambled for his medical pack and knelt beside the fallen stallholder.

'A doctor?' Chae's longtalk demanded, rising over the general clamour. 'Is there a doctor in the Silvarum craft market? Wounded man.'

Edeard's farsight was still following the criminals. 'Come on,' he yelled at Macsen and Kanseen.

'Where?' Macsen demanded. 'I've lost them.'

'They've just reached the edge of the market. Albaric Street. I can still sense them.' He ploughed on through the clutter of bystanders.

'Edeard, no!' Chae yelled after him.

Edeard almost stopped at the command, but he just couldn't ignore the fleeing thieves. *We can still catch them.* It would be their first real arrest. So far all they'd ever done in their four probationary months was clear drunks off the streets and break up fights. Never any real constable duty. He charged along a narrow passage between rows of stalls. Macsen and Kanseen were racing after him.

'Come back,' Chae bellowed.

Ignoring the sergeant sent a flash of wicked glee along Edeard's nerves.

Stall holders were cheering the three probationary constables as they sped on through the market. Edeard and Macsen were using their longtalk to order people aside. By and large it was working. They were closing the gap on the fleeing thieves.

Edeard's ge-eagle swooped low over the saffcherry trees of Albaric Street, its wings skimming inches above the waving blossom. The four thieves were pounding along the pavement underneath, heading straight for the Great Major Canal. Their blades had been sheathed so as not to draw attention. Even so, the minds of people around them pulsed with curiosity and alarm.

'Where are they going?' Kanseen demanded.

'Got to be the canal,' Macsen replied. There was a lot of exhilaration flooding along his longtalk voice.

Edeard finally saw the end of the market up ahead; the striped canvas roof gave way to the hazy radiance of blossom-filtered sunlight. 'Can you locate any other constables?' he demanded.

'Lady, it's all I can do to watch where I'm going,' Macsen complained.

'What are you planning on doing?' Kanseen asked, all apprehension and doubts.

'Stopping them,' Edeard said. *Wasn't that obvious? What was wrong with her?*

'There's more of them. And they've got blades.'

'I'll take them down,' he growled. Her uncertainty flowed away from him, as if it was another landmark he'd left behind.

They were closing fast now. Albaric Street was almost deserted compared to the busy market, allowing the constables to race onwards, weaving round the occasional recalcitrant pedestrian.

The ge-eagle flashed over the last saffcherry tree. It showed Edeard the street ending abruptly at the edge of the Great Major Canal. The big waterway stretched away on both sides, cutting the city in half. Away to the west was the Birmingham Pool, intersecting the Outer Circle Canal, while eastwards the High Pool formed a junction with Flight Canal and Market Canal. There were only two bridges between Silvarum and the Padua district on the other side, one beside each pool. Like every bridge over the Grand Major Canal they were narrow and steep; most people preferred to use a gondola to cross the hundred-and-fifty-yard width of water. Several were bobbing at a mooring platform where the street ended.

'Got them,' Edeard exclaimed. 'They just ran out of street.' His jubilant mood suddenly dropped as the four criminals sped down the wooden steps to the platform and hopped on to a waiting gondola. It looked scruffy and badly maintained compared to the craft that normally slid along the city's waterways, with dull scratched paint and a drab awning. There were two gondoliers standing on the back, both holding a pole. 'Oh Honious!'

'What?' Kanseen demanded. She was red-faced and breathing heavily, but still keeping up.

'Boat,' he gasped back at her. 'Come on, we can still catch them.' Right in front of him a very grand-looking old lady in a billowing black and white dress and her entourage of younger handmaids were leaving one of

Albaric Street's high-class restaurants. His longtalk demands to move didn't seem to be registering with any of them. He dodged round the old lady, cursing. A third hand swatted at him as one might an annoying insect. He flashed her an exasperated look.

The ge-eagle spiralled up, watching the shabby gondola ease out from the mooring platform and into the multitude of craft flocking along the big canal. Downbeat the gondoliers might have been, but they knew their watercraft. With two punts available, and working in harmony, they were soon moving a lot quicker than anything else on the water. The four thieves flopped down on the benches, and started laughing.

Edeard, Macsen, and Kanseen came hurtling up to the canal bank, coming dangerously close to toppling down into the water as they stopped at the top of the mooring's wooden steps.

'Bastards!' Macsen shouted at them.

One of the gondoliers raised his green and blue ribboned boater in mocking salute. They were already twenty yards downstream. Edeard knew with grim certainty they'd be going all the way down to Sampalok, and the wounded stall owner would be ruined. 'Help us,' he called down to the gondolier who was left moored below. 'Take us after them.' This gondola was a fancy craft, its black paintwork shining in the afternoon sun, the awning embroidered with a scarlet bird crest. Somehow Edeard just knew it belonged to the old woman behind.

'Not a chance, pal,' the gondolier called back. 'This is Mistress Florell's private gondola.'

For a moment Edeard considered shoving him into the

canal, and commandeering the craft to set off in pursuit. Except he didn't have the first idea of how to use a punt pole.

'Somebody help,' he called with his voice and longtalk. It drew a few interested looks from the gondoliers out on the canal. But no one even asked what he wanted.

A chorus of jeering carried over the water. Thirty yards away, the criminals were leaning over the gunnels to wave and gesture. Edeard stared at his tormentors with a rage that chilled his blood. He smiled back savagely. Some hint of his fury must have flashed out. Macsen and Kanseen swayed back. The jeering stopped.

Edeard reached out with his third hand and plucked the box from the man holding it. Hands grasped empty air in futility as he lifted it ten feet above the gondola. The thieves exerted their own third hands, trying to prise it back. 'Is that the best you can do?' Edeard taunted. They never even managed to unsettle his grip.

People on nearby gondolas watched in silence as the box drifted sedately through the air. Edeard's smile turned malicious as it landed softly at his feet. He crossed his arms and gloated. 'Don't come back to our district,' he long-talked to the departing gondola. 'Not ever.'

'You're fucking dead, you little shit,' came the answer.

Edeard pressed his third hand down against the bow of the gondola, causing it to rock alarmingly. But it was too far away now for him to capsize. And the six of them hurriedly erected a strong enough shield to deflect him.

Macsen started laughing. His hand came down hard on Edeard's shoulder. 'Oh Lady, you are the greatest, Edeard, the absolute greatest. Did you see their faces?'

'Yeah,' Edeard admitted with a malign grin.

'They won't forget today,' Kanseen said. 'Heavens, Edeard, you must have frightened the life out of them.'

'Let's hope, eh.' He smiled at his friends, very content with the way they'd bonded that little bit more from the shared event. A frilly parasol hit the side of his arm. 'Ow!'

It belonged to the old woman they'd pushed past. 'In future, young man, you will display the correct courtesy due to your elders and betters,' she snapped at him. 'You could have knocked me over the way you were charging about with complete disregard for anyone else. At my age, too; I would never have got up again.'

'Er, yes, madam. Sorry.'

'Mistress Florell!' she said, her wavery voice rising an octave with indignation. 'Don't you pretend you don't know who I am.'

Edeard could hear Macsen chortling behind him, it was muffled as if a hand was over his mouth. 'Yes, Mistress Florell.'

Her eyes narrowed with suspicion. Edeard thought she looked at least as old as Master Solarin. 'I shall be reporting you to my nephew,' she said. 'There was a time in this city when the constabulary had decent people in its ranks. That time is clearly over. Now get out of my way.'

He wasn't actually *in* her way, but he took a step back anyway. She brushed past with a swirl of her tent-like skirt to descend the steps to the mooring platform. Her entourage followed with immaculately shielded minds. A couple of the handmaids flashed him amused grins. They all settled in the gondola.

'See,' Macsen said, sliding his arm round Edeard's shoulders. 'That's our true reward, the respect of a grateful populace.'

'Who *is* that?' Edeard whined.

Which set Macsen off laughing again.

'You really don't know, do you?' Kanseen said incredulously.

'No.'

'Among other family connections, Mistress Florell is the Mayor's aunt.'

'Oh. I suppose that's not good, then?'

'No. Every Mayor for the last century is some relative or other to her. She basically decides who the Grand Council will elect.'

Edeard shook his head and checked the gondola below. Mistress Florell had vanished under the awning. The gondolier gave him a wink, and cast off.

'Let's get back,' Edeard said.

A cheerful Macsen bent over to pick up the box. He shot Edeard another look as he felt the weight. 'I can sense a whole load of necklace chains in here. Must be gold.'

'I hope he's all right,' Edeard said.

'Chae?' Kanseen asked. She sounded slightly nervous.

'No. The stall holder.'

'Oh yeah. Right.'

High above the Grand Major Canal, the ge-eagle soared lazily on a thermal, keeping the shabby gondola in sight as it hastened towards Sampalok.

Most of the crowd had gone when Edeard and his companions returned to the scene of the crime. Several stall holders in their distinctive dark-green aprons were fussing round the stalls they'd righted, restoring the display of goods. Boyd and Dinlay were helping to fix the awning directly overhead, which had ripped free when the stalls were shoved over.

The wounded stall holder was still on the ground. A woman was tending to him, a doctor's satchel open at her feet as she knelt beside her patient. Two young apprentices were aiding her. Between them they'd bandaged the stall holder's chest, now the doctor was holding herself perfectly still, eyes closed, her hands pressed gently on the bandages as her telekinesis operated on the torn flesh underneath, manipulating blood vessels and tissue. Her distinguished face was puckered with intense concentration. Every now and then she would murmur some instruction to her apprentices, who would apply their telekinesis as she directed.

Edeard watched intently, trying to sense with his farsight as well. Old Doc Seneo had never used her third hand to operate with; though Fahin had always said the technique was in the Doctor's Guild tuition books.

'You three okay?' Boyd's longtalk asked.

'Of course,' Macsen retorted.

Boyd glanced over to where Sergeant Chae was talking to a group of stall holders. 'Careful,' he mouthed.

Chae marched over, his face set in a furious mask. Edeard thought his boots were going to leave imprints in the grey-brown market pavement he was stamping them down so heavily. By some process Edeard didn't quite understand, he was now standing ahead of Macsen and Kanseen.

'I believe I gave you a direct order,' Chae said in a menacingly level tone.

All Edeard's good humour at recovering the box faded

away. He'd never thought Chae would be quite this angry. For once the sergeant was making no attempt to shield his feelings. 'But, Sergeant—'

'Did I or did I not tell you to stop?'

'Well . . . yes. But—'

'So you heard me?'

Edeard hung his head. 'Yes, Sergeant.'

'So you disobeyed me. Not only that but you put the safety of yourself and your colleagues in danger. Those men were gang members, and armed. Suppose they had pistols?'

'We got it,' Macsen announced defiantly.

'What?'

'We got it back from the bastards,' Macsen said loudly. He turned slightly so he was facing the gaggle of stall holders, and held up the box.

The burst of amazement emanating from the market folk surprised Edeard. It also silenced Sergeant Chae, though he continued to glare at the constables. Macsen walked over to the people closest to the wounded man. 'Here,' he said, and proffered the box. One of the younger men in a green apron stepped forward. 'I am Monrol; Kavine is my uncle. This is what they stole from him.' He turned the lock dial with several precise twists, and the lid popped open. 'It's all here,' he said with a smile. He showed the open box to the market. 'All of it. They brought it back. The constables brought it back.'

Someone started clapping. They were soon joined by the onlookers. Whistles of approval split the air, then the three constables were abruptly surrounded by the men and woman in green aprons. Their hands were shaken, their backs were pummelled. A beaming Monrol gave Macsen a hug, then moved on to Kanseen. Edeard, too, was swept up in his embrace. 'Thank you, thank you.'

'Sergeant Chae,' a deep voice boomed.

The stall holders fell quiet as Setersis came forward. Edeard had seen him a couple of times before, normally when he was complaining to Chae about the infrequency of constable patrols through the market. Setersis was the head of the Silvarum stall holders' association, and through that had a seat on the city traders' council; as such he had almost as much political influence as a Guild Council Master.

'Did I hear right?' Setersis asked. 'Did the constables finally come to our aid?'

For once Chae looked uncertain. 'We were able to assist.' He stopped glaring at Edeard, and produced an almost sympathetic expression. 'I was about to ask the more reckless members of my patrol to report what happened on the chase.'

'Reckless members, eh?' Setersis grinned at the three probationary constables. 'Yes, you are young, aren't you? Good for you. If we had more constables with balls we wouldn't be in the sorry state we are. Your pardon, my girl.'

'Granted,' Kanseen said graciously.

'Come then, so tell me what happened on the chase. Did you manage to accidentally drop the scum into the canal?'

'No, sir,' Edeard said. 'I'm afraid they got away on a gondola. They headed down towards the port.' Something made him hold back from mentioning that his ge-eagle was showing him the thieves had already passed through Forest Pool and were approaching Sampalok.

'None of the gondoliers would help us,' Macsen blurted. 'We asked them.'

'Ha! Fil-rats in human guise,' Setersis grunted. 'Still, you did a good job. I can't remember the last time a constable returned stolen goods.' He gave Chae a meaningful glance. The sergeant's lips tightened. 'You have my thanks. I'm sure my fellow stall holders will show their appreciation next time your patrol ventures into the market.'

Edeard knew he was grinning like a fool. It didn't matter, so were Macsen and Kanseen. Then he finally caught sight of Dinlay, who looked like his closest family had just died.

Once the doctor announced Kavine would be all right, Chae declared that the patrol was over and they were going back to Jeavons station. He led them out of the market without another word. Edeard couldn't work out if they were in serious trouble or not; the sergeant's mind was perfectly shielded.

Macsen shot Boyd a direct longtalk query, which he shared with Edeard and Kanseen: 'What did Chae say?'

'Nothing much,' Boyd replied, equally furtive. 'He was yelling for you to stop. When none of you came back, he just concentrated on helping the stall holder. I had to hold the flesh together to slow the bleeding down. Lady! I thought I was going to faint there was so much blood. Monrol said they hacked him a couple of times with those blades to make him let go of the box. I wish I'd gone with you instead, but I just hesitated for that first second. I'm sorry.'

'Don't be,' Edeard said. 'The more I think about it, the more stupid I was. Chae was right.'

'What!' Macsen exclaimed out loud. He glanced at Chae, but the sergeant didn't seem to notice.

'There was four of them, and they had blades; six if you count the gondoliers. We could have been killed, and it would be my fault.'

'We got the box back.'

'Luck. That's all. Pure luck. The Lady smiled on us today. She won't tomorrow. We have to act like proper constables; stay together, work as a team.'

Macsen shook his head in dismay. Edeard gave Kanseen an apologetic shrug.

'I went with you,' she told him quietly. 'I got just as carried away. Don't try to claim this is all your fault.'

He nodded. Up ahead, Chae was still marching on, not looking round, his back rigid. Beside him, Dinlay was avoiding any communication with his friends. When they'd walked back to the market from the Great Major Canal, the three of them had been triumphant; now that whole mood was badly inverted. Right there, Edeard felt like turning round and heading off out of the city. It was going to be awful back at the station, he just knew it.

'That's not the kind of attitude the returning hero is supposed to wear,' Salrana told him, her longtalk conveying a lot of concern.

Edeard tipped his head up to give the sky a sheepish smile. 'I'm sorry. We did it, though, we actually chased off some thugs from a gang.'

'I know! I farsighted you the whole time. You were terrific, Edeard. I wish I'd chosen to be a constable.'

'Our sergeant doesn't share your opinion. And what's worse, he's right. We didn't behave properly.'

'Have you told the stall holder that?'

'That's not the point.'

'Yes it is, Edeard. You did good today. It doesn't matter how you did it. You helped someone. The Lady saw that, and she'll be pleased.'

'Sometimes you have to do the wrong thing—' he mouthed silently. Some good cheer returned as he tried to imagine what Akeem would have to say about all Chae's rules and procedures. It would be short and very succinct, he knew.

'What?' Salrana asked.

'Nothing. But thank you. I'm going to go back to the station now and do whatever it takes to put things right with my sergeant.'

'I'm always so proud of you, Edeard. Talk to me tonight, tell me what happens.'

'I will. Promise.'

When they got back to the station Chae's temper seemed to have vanished. Edeard was expecting to be shouted at as soon as they passed through the big gates. Instead Chae stood there with a genuinely weary expression on his worn face; for once his shielding had slipped enough for Edeard to sense just how tired his thoughts were. 'Small hall,' he told the squad.

The others dutifully trooped into the building. Edeard waited until they were through the doorway.

'It was my fault,' he told Chae. 'I encouraged the others to follow me. I didn't listen to you, and I ignored procedure.'

Chae studied him, his own mind becoming inscrutable again. 'I know. Now would you like to guess what will happen if Setersis hears I gave you all a bollocking?'

'Er, he'd probably take our side?'

'He would. Now grow up fast, lad; learn how things balance in this city. Come on, I need to talk to all of you.'

The other constables rose to their feet when Chae came into the small hall. Dinlay saluted smartly.

'Pack that in,' Chae said. His third hand shut the hall doors. 'Sit down.'

The squad exchanged mildly perplexed looks. Except for Dinlay, who was still keeping himself apart.

'So how do you think we did?' Chae said.

'Wrong procedure,' Kanseen ventured.

'Yeah, wrong procedure. But we saved a stall holder's life. Some gang scum got a nasty surprise. And we recovered the stolen merchandise. Those are all the plus points. The constables will be popular in Silvarum's markets for a couple of weeks. That's good, there's nothing wrong with that. I'd even go so far as to say the rule of law was upheld. Edeard?'

'Sir?'

'Did your eagle follow them back home?'

'Er, yes, sir. I watched them go into Sampalok. It's a building not far from the Grand Major Canal. They haven't come out yet.'

'So we know which building they probably live in. What do we do about that? Do we put together a big squad and go in and arrest them?'

'Probably not.'

'Why? They've broken the law. Shouldn't they be brought before a court?'

'Too much effort for a minor crime,' Macsen said.

'That's right. So bring the eagle back, please.'

'Sir.' He sent a command through the sky above

Makkathran, and felt the eagle soar round, dipping the wing vertically back to the ground. It began to flash back over the big canal.

Chae was giving him an odd smile. 'And you really can longtalk that far, can't you?'

'Sir?'

'All right. Now, I'm not mad at you, any of you. So just relax, and for the Lady's sake try to listen to what I'm about to tell you. What you did today was what you joined up for, preventing criminal activity and protecting the people of this city. That's good, it shows you have a sense of duty, and loyalty to each other. Technically, it's my duty to get you all through the next two months; then you're on your own, and I start with the next batch of hopeless youths. My responsibility to you ends then. But what I have got to try and instil in you before you go out by yourselves is a sense of proportion, and maybe even some political awareness. Let's think about this. Those gang members are going to be a little shaken by Edeard's strength, and furious that they came back empty-handed after taking so much risk. Next time they go out they'll want to make sure their crime produces some results. So they'll go the extra mile to make sure. Boyd, what would you do in their shoes? How would you make certain?'

'Take a pistol?'

'Very likely. So whatever constable patrol tackles them, is going to get shot at.'

'Hold on,' Edeard said. 'We can't let that stop us. If we become so afraid of cracking down on the gangs that we do nothing, they've won.'

'Correct. So?'

'Next time, we chase them out but that's it,' Macsen said.

'Good option. Though actually your response was about right. I didn't behave too well out there, myself – mainly because I was worried about you lot running off like that. There's an old natural law that says for every action there is an equal and opposite reaction. If those gang members come into a market in broad daylight and use a blade on a stall holder, then they must expect a reaction from the constables. They were the ones who overstepped the mark on this occasion. But that still doesn't mean three of you can go chasing off after four of them. With or without blades and pistols, you were outnumbered. That has "tragedy" written all over it. So that was wrong. It was also wrong to leave a member of the public injured and unattended. You didn't stop to assess, which is the most critical thing to do; you also let raw instinct override my orders, which is the greater crime no matter how much you thought yourselves in the right. I'm supposed to be training you to respond to situations in a professional manner, and I clearly haven't drilled it in hard enough. Now I'm quite prepared to write today's lapses off to first-time excitement and the general confusion. You need experience more than you do theory, so nobody's getting disciplined and there'll be no recriminations. But under-stand this, it *must not* happen again. Next time we encounter a criminal act in progress you follow procedure to the letter. Do I make myself clear?'

'Yes, Sergeant,' they choursed.

'Then we understand each other. So take tonight off, get yourselves down to the Olovan's Eagle for a drink or ten, and be back in this hall for another dose of theory first thing tomorrow morning. I'll also go against my own policy to tell you something: unless you completely screw up your graduation exams you will all pass your probation.'

'I was useless,' Dinlay complained. 'I just froze. I was just so useless.' He gulped down more of his beer.

Edeard looked over at Macsen, who simply shrugged. They'd been in the Olovan's Eagle for an hour, and Dinlay had said very little else. It was a small miracle they'd got him to join them in the first place. He hadn't said ten words since Chae dismissed them from the small hall.

'You froze for a couple of seconds, that's all,' Kanseen said. 'That means you were close to Chae when he ordered us all to stop and help the stall keeper. You couldn't do anything else.'

'I should have ignored him like you did. I didn't. I failed.'

'Oh sweet Lady,' Kanseen grumbled and sat back in her own chair. She was wearing a blue and white dress with orange flowers. It wasn't the most stylish garment Edeard had seen in Makkathran, nor the newest, but she looked good in it. Her short hair still set her apart from all the other girls, who wore theirs fashionably long. But he rather liked it this way, it suited her, setting off a flattish nose and thin dark-green eyes. Now he'd known her for a few months she wasn't quite as intimidating as she had been at the start. Not that he thought of her as anything other than a colleague and friend.

'Nobody failed,' Edeard said. 'This afternoon was chaos, that's all. And you helped Chae with the stall holder.'

'I froze,' Dinlay said wretchedly. 'I let you all down. I

let my family down. They expect me to be the station captain within ten years, you know. My father was.'

'Let's have another drink,' Macsen said.

'Oh yes, that'll solve everything,' Kanseen said sourly.

Macsen gave her a wink, then shot a longtalk order to one of the tavern waitresses. Something else must have been said. Edeard caught her flash him a mock-indignant smile.

How does he do that? It's not what he says, it's his whole attitude. And why can't I do it? Edeard sat back to give his friend a critical examination. Macsen was sitting in the middle of a small couch with Evala on one side, and Nicolar on the other. Both girls were leaning in towards him. They laughed at his jokes, and gasped and giggled when he told them what happened in the market, an extravagant tale of thrills and bravery Edeard didn't quite recognize. He supposed Macsen was quite handsome, with his light brown hair and flat jaw. His brown eyes were constantly filled with amusement that bordered on nefarious, which was an additional attraction. It helped that he always dressed well whenever they went out. Tonight he'd pulled on fawn-coloured trousers cut from the softest suede, belted by woven black strands of leather. His sky-blue satin shirt just showed under a dark-emerald frock coat.

See, I'd never have the courage to wear a combination like that, but he carries it off perfectly. The epitome of a grand family's junior son.

In fact the rest of them looked quite drab in comparison. Edeard used to be quietly pleased with his own black jacket, tailored trousers, and knee-high boots. Now he'd been relegated to the poor friend who Macsen's girls felt sorry for and tried to pair up with their own charity case girlfriend. On which note ... Edeard tried not to stare over at Boyd, who was sitting on the opposite side of their table, his face bewitched. Clemensa was next to him, chattering away about her day. She was easily the same height as Boyd, and must have been close in weight, too. Edeard couldn't help the way his eyes always slipped down to the front of her very low-cut dress every time she bent over, which was suspiciously frequent.

The waitress brought over the tray of beer Macsen had ordered. Dinlay immediately reached for his tankard. Edeard fumbled with the money pouch in his pocket.

'Oh no, my round,' Macsen said. His third hand deposited some coins on the empty tray. 'Thank you,' he said sincerely. The waitress smiled. Evala and Nicolar pressed in closer.

Edeard sighed. *He's always so polite, as well. Is that what does it?*

'Boyd,' Macsen called out loudly. 'Close your mouth, man, you're drooling.'

Boyd snapped his jaw shut and glared at Macsen. A bright flush crept up his face.

'You pay him no heed,' Clemensa said. She brought a hand up to Boyd's cheek, turned his head and kissed him. 'A girl likes it when a man pays attention.'

Edeard thought Boyd might faint with happiness.

'Got to go,' Dinlay muttered. 'Back in a minute.' He stood up and swayed unsteadily, then headed for the archway at the back of the saloon where the washrooms were.

The fact that there were toilets on an upper floor was one of the many revelations about city buildings which had taken Edeard a time to get used to. But then a tavern which sprawled over many floors was also a novelty. As was the pale-orange light radiating out of the ceiling that was nearly as bright as daylight. The first night they'd visited the Olovan's Eagle he'd wondered why there was no straw on the floor. Life in the city was so *civilized*. Sitting here in the warmth, with a window showing him the lights outside stretching all the way to the Lyot Sea, good beer, comfortable with his friends, he found it hard to fit this with the crime and gangs who cast such a shadow over the streets outside.

'What are you doing?' Kanseen hissed at Macsen. 'He's had too much to drink, already.'

'Best thing for him. He's not a fighting drunk. Another couple of pints and he'll fall asleep. Next thing he'll know it's tomorrow and we'll be so busy he won't have time to brood. Tonight's what we need to get him through.'

Kanseen looked like she wanted to protest but couldn't think how. She looked at Edeard.

'Makes sense,' he admitted.

Macsen placed another order with the waitress.

'My liver has to sacrifice its life so we can get Dinlay through graduation,' Kanseen complained.

'In the constables we stick together,' Edeard said and raised his tankard. 'To the memory of our livers. Who needs 'em?'

They drank to that.

'Don't worry,' Macsen said. 'I've made arrangements. Our beer is watered. Dinlay's has two shots of vodka in each pint.'

Even Kanseen had to laugh. She tipped her tankard to Macsen. 'You're so . . .'

'Beautifully evil?' Edeard suggested, giving his tankard a mortified stare. *This is watered? I couldn't tell; it tastes the same.*

'Spot on,' she said.

'I thank you.' Macsen put his arms round the shoulders of the girls and pulled them in; kissing Evala first, then Nicolar.

'Not just tonight we've got to worry about,' Boyd said.

'Does our Boyd need to worry about tonight?' Macsen asked Clemensa.

She gave Boyd a hungry look. 'He certainly doesn't. After what you did today, you're all heroes in my book. That needs a lot of rewarding.'

'He's going to want to prove himself,' Boyd said. 'Nothing the sergeant said is going to hold him back. Next time we come across a fight or a robbery, Dinlay will be at the front and aching to take on the bad guy.'

'I figured that too,' Edeard said.

'We'll have to be ready,' Kanseen said. 'We can't hold him back, that would make it worse. But we can be up there with him.'

'Everyone together,' Macsen said. He raised his tankard. 'No matter what.'

'No matter what,' they toasted with a roar.

Edeard still couldn't taste the water.

The four ge-monkeys from Jeavons constable station walked slowly along the street, looking like pallbearers as they carried a comatose Dinlay home to his dormitory bed.

Kanseen kept looking back to check. 'Do you think he'll be all right?'

'Not really,' Edeard said. 'If Macsen was serious about the vodka, he's going to have the hangover from Honious tomorrow morning.' He turned to inspect the ge-monkeys himself. Using them wasn't the ideal solution, but it was better than him and Kanseen hauling Dinlay along. Boyd and Macsen had stayed on at the tavern with the girls. There were private rooms upstairs which they'd no doubt be using that night. Edeard was trying to keep his envy in check.

'Macsen!' she exclaimed.

'He's not so bad. Actually, I'd rather have him by my side than Dinlay.'

'Some choice.'

'And you're preferable to all of them.' All that beer and now the balmy night air were making him light-headed. That must have been why he said it.

Kanseen said nothing for a while as they walked back along the long, nearly deserted street. 'I'm not looking for anyone right now,' she said solemnly. 'I just broke up with a man. We were engaged. It . . . ended badly. He wanted a nice traditional girl, one who knew her place.'

'I'm sorry. But I have to say it's his loss.'

'Thank you, Edeard.'

They walked on a while more, shadows shifting as they passed under the bright orange light patches on the outside of the buildings.

'I don't know what it is about you,' she said quietly. 'I'm not just talking about how strong your third hand is. You stand out. You're what I imagine the sons of noble families are supposed to be like, or were like before they got so rich and fat.'

'Nothing noble about me.'

'Nobility doesn't come from a bloodline, Edeard, it comes from within. Where was your village?'

'Ashwell, in the Rulan province.'

'Doesn't mean anything, I'm afraid. I don't know any geography beyond the Iguru Plain.'

'Ashwell was a long way past there, right on the edge of the wild lands. I'll show you on a map if I can find one. It took a year for us to travel here.'

'Gift me.'

'What? Oh.' Edeard concentrated, trying to find a recollection that would do his home justice. Spring, he decided, when the trees were bursting into life, and the sky was bright, and the winds warm. He and some other children had gone outside the rampart walls and taken the long route round to the top of the cliffs where they looked down on the cosy buildings sheltering below.

He heard a soft pull of breath, and realized how heavily involved in the memory he'd become, lacing it with melancholy.

'Oh, Edeard, it's so beautiful. What happened? Why did you leave?'

'It was attacked by bandits,' he said stiffly. In all the time he'd spent in the station dormitory he'd never told his new friends the truth about Ashwell. All they knew was that he'd lost his family to bandits.

'I'm sorry,' she said. For once she dropped the veil round her thoughts, allowing him to sense the sympathy. 'Was it very bad?'

'Salrana and I survived. And five others.'

'Oh, Lady! Edeard.' Her hand held his arm.

'Don't worry. I've come to terms with it. Except for

losing my Master, Akeem. I still miss him.' The emotional currents welling up in his thoughts were both unexpected and alarmingly strong. He truly thought he'd put all this sentiment and mourning behind him. Now all he'd done was picture his old home, and the feelings were rushing back as strong as the day it had happened.

'You should talk to one of the Lady's Mothers. They give excellent council.'

'Yeah. Maybe.' He made his legs work again. 'Come on, I have a notion Chae isn't going to be too gentle with us tomorrow.'

The ge-monkeys laid Dinlay out on his mattress and pulled a thin blanket over him. He never woke, just groaned and shuffled round a bit. Edeard couldn't be bothered to take his friend's boots off, he was suddenly incredibly tired himself. He barely managed to remove his own boots and trousers. The dormitory's ge-chimps scampered about, collecting his clothes for the laundry.

Of course, now he was actually lying down, his mind was too restless to deliver the sleep his body craved. He sent a thought to the main ceiling's rosette pattern of illumination, and it dimmed to a nebula-glow. That was about the only reaction the city buildings ever did have to human thought. The ge-chimps quietened down. Faint sounds from downstairs whispered through the big empty room, the usual comings and goings of the night shift officers. Edeard had never really got used to the way walls in the city curved. Back in Ashwell, walls were laid out in straight lines; the nine sides of his old Guild courtyard were considered pretty adventurous architecture. Here in the dormitory, the oval bed alcoves were almost rooms in their own right, with arching entrances twice Edeard's height. He liked to imagine the dormitory was actually some kind of aristocratic bedroom, and that maybe the race which created Makkathran had more than two genders. Hence the six beds. That would make the station an important building. He couldn't quite assign a use for the honeycomb warren of little rooms below ground which were used as prisoner cells and store rooms. As he thought about it, he let his farsight drift down through the translucent grey panorama of the station's structure. The image was such that it seemed to surround him, engulf him. Gravity pulled at his mind, and he sank ghost-like through the floor of the basement. There were fissures in the ground beneath, smooth fissures that looped and bent as they wound deeper and deeper. Some were no wider than his fingers, while others were broad enough to walk through. They branched and intersected, forming a convoluted filigree that, to his quixotic thoughts, resembled the veins within a human body. He felt water pulsing through several of them, while strong winds blew along others. Several of the smaller fissures contained threads of violet light which appeared to burn without ever consuming the fissure walls. He tried to touch them with his third hand, only for it to slide through as if he were grasping at a mirage.

His farsight expanded, becoming tenuous. The fissures spread away from the station, burrowing under the street outside, knitting with other extensive hollow filigrees which supported the surrounding buildings. Edeard gasped in wonder as his farsight grew and grew; the more he relaxed the more he could perceive. Slivers of colour shone through his mind, as if this shadow world was growing in texture. He couldn't even sense the dormitory any more. The station was a small glowing jewel embedded in a vast whorl of similar multichromic sparks.

Makkathran.

Edeard experienced the wonder of its thoughts. Immersing himself in a melody where a single beat lasted for years, chords so grand they could shake the very ground apart if they ever gained substance. The city slept the long sleep of all giants; untainted by the pitiful frantic tempo of parasitic humans crawling through its physical extremities.

It was content.

Edeard bathed in its ancient serenity, and slowly fell into a dreamless sleep.

6

'How long?' Corrie-Lyn asked.

Aaron growled again and ignored her. He was inside a gym cage that the starship's cabin had extruded; testing the flexibility and strength of his restored upper torso. Pulling weight, pushing weight, bending, twisting. Working up a sweat as endurance was evaluated, measuring the oxygen consumption of the new flesh, blood flow rate, nerve speed . . .

'You knew Qatux could do it,' she whined. 'So you must know how long it'll take.'

Aaron gritted his teeth as gravity shifted off vertical and increased, forcing him to pull the handle he was gripping while stretching at the same time. Biononics reported the tendons were approaching their tear limit.

His patience was also undergoing a strenuous work-out. They'd been back in the *Artful Dodger* for fifteen hours, a time which Corrie-Lyn had devoted to drinking and moaning. She now considered handing over Inigo's memories to be a terrible betrayal, not to mention a bad idea. A really bad idea. Stupid actually. As she kept saying.

'So it'll have like a mini-Inigo hanging round inside its own brain?'

Aaron took a look at the oxygen usage in his shoulder muscles. The levels were only a couple of points off the original muscle. Not bad for a couple of days. Drugs and biononics had done what they could, the rest of it was down to good old-fashioned exercise. A decent callisthenics program should see the levels equalize over the next week or so. He shut the gym down.

'Something like that,' he said.

Corrie-Lyn blinked at the unexpected answer. She rolled over on the couch and reached for the pitcher of tasimion margarita. 'So you ask the mini-Inigo a question . . .'

'And Qatux answers it for us. Yes.'

'What a load of bullshit.'

'We'll see.' He slipped his T-shirt off, and examined his torso. The membrane was starting to peel off. Underneath, the new skin was tender, but at last the colour was deepening to the same shade as the rest of him. 'I'm going to take a shower,' he said.

'You're shaping up good,' she giggled. 'Need a hand in there?'

Aaron rolled his eyes. 'No thanks.' He now had a strong theory of his own why Inigo had run away from Living Dream, and it wasn't anything to do with Last Dreams or the pressure of being idolized by billions. *Maybe she only turned into this after he left?*

The gym sank into the wall, and there was a moment's pause before the shower cubicle extended out from the same section. He slipped his shorts off and stepped in as Corrie-Lyn let out a wolf-whistle. He must be recuperating, his cock was stirring. But if Qatux did come up with a notion of where the reluctant messiah was hiding out, she'd be more necessary than ever. So he turned the spore temperature down about as low as it would go, and thought of other things. Unfortunately, with a memory that didn't reach back past Ethan's appointment he didn't have much to mull over. Except his odd dreams. That horse ride ... he'd been young. So it must have been his childhood. Seemed pleasant enough.

After he'd showered, they carried on their research into the odd Raiel who'd agreed to help them. Clued in by what it had said they'd sent their u-shadows out into the unisphere to search for files on the history of Far Away during the Starflyer War. The first surprise was to find just over a million files on the period available. It took eight hours for them to filter it down to relevant and useful information. Even then, there was no direct evidence Qatux had been there.

There were endless documents on Bradley Johansson's team of Guardians chasing the Starflyer back to its lair, and how they joined up with an odd security team that Nigel Sheldon assigned to help them. Admiral Kime was one of them, of course; that was a common history text. His audacious hyperglider flight over Mount Herculaneum, and subsequent rescue by Nigel himself. Anna the Judas. Oscar the martyr. Paula Myo and the Navy interdiction squad, Cat's Claws.

'I didn't know it was Nigel who originally sent the Cat to Far Away,' Corrie-Lyn exclaimed. 'What was he thinking of?' She was sober again after a meal and a couple of alcohol-binder aerosols. Aspects of the search seemed to genuinely interest her.

'Be fair, he couldn't see the future.'

There were some appendices that claimed the pursuit was aided by an alien. But the context was strange. The

Bose motile was known to be part of Nigel's secret clique at the time. There were no references to a Raiel. One file said the Barsoomian group helped Johansson because he'd brought their genetic holy grail to Far Away. Again, nothing as to what that grail actually was.

'Let's try another angle,' Aaron said. He told his u-shadow to find all files relating to a Commonwealth citizen called Tiger Pansy around the time of the Starflyer War.

The cabin's portal projected a rather startling image.

'No way,' Corrie-Lyn said.

Aaron stared at the woman in equal disbelief. She was a complete mess. Terrible hair; bad facial reprofiling ruining the symmetry of her eyes, nose, and lips, appalling cosmetics making them appear worse; ridiculous breast enlargements; tight, short clothes that no girl over twenty could ever get away with wearing, let alone this one, who must have been close to rejuvenation time again.

'Signed to the Wayside Production company on Oaktier,' Corrie-Lyn read off her exovision. 'Appeared in a large number of their, aha, *productions*. Left them in the last year of the Starflyer War. No subsequent information. Nothing; no residency listing on any planetary cybersphere, no records of rejuvenation treatment, no bodyloss certificate. She simply dropped out of sight.'

Aaron shook himself and cancelled the projection. 'Easy enough at the time. There was a mass migration from the Lost23 worlds which the Primes had invaded. After that, it got even more chaotic.'

'Coincidence?'

'The Raiel are not known for their lies. Maybe Qatux did marry her. She certainly looks the emotional type.'

'That's not quite how I'd describe her,' Corrie-Lyn

muttered. 'And how did she get to Far Away? The planet was virtually cut off for decades until the starlines started flying there.'

'She must have been with the Johansson team. I don't think it's relevant.'

'No, but it's interesting. Why would a Raiel go there?'

'You want to ask?'

She shook her head. 'Naa, too intimidated.'

'I'll ask for you.'

'No. Let's just drop it.'

'You're right though. It is interesting. I was obviously given the correct information. Qatux helps humans.'

'He said he used to. Until Tiger Pansy was killed.'

'By the Cat, no less. That'd be enough to shock anyone out of their dependency routine, no matter how delightful and ingrained.'

'Yes, well, thank Ozzie, Paula Myo finally caught her.'

'Yeah. And in about another four thousand years we can all share the joy of her coming out of suspension.'

'Urrgh. I won't be around for that no matter what.'

'Qatux knew Paula Myo,' Aaron said. 'I wonder if that's relevant.'

'How could it be?'

He waited for a moment to see if his subconscious produced any clues. It didn't. 'No idea.'

The *Artful Dodger*'s smartcore told them the *High Angel* was calling. 'Please prepare for teleport,' the alien starship told them.

'Oh bollocks,' Corrie-Lyn said as she clambered to her feet. 'I really don't like this—'

The cabin vanished. Once again they were standing in the large circular chamber facing Qatux.

'—part.' She wrinkled her nose in distaste.

Aaron bowed to the Raiel. 'Thank you for obliging us.'

'You are welcome,' the big alien whispered.

'Were you successful?'

'I have lived through Inigo's early life. It was not that distinguished.'

Aaron looked straight at Qatux, avoiding Corrie-Lyn. His gaiamotes revealed the pique which that last remark had triggered in her mind. 'None the less, it must have provided you with an understanding of his behaviour patterns.'

'Guilt drives him.'

'Guilt?'

'He spent his whole life hiding what he was from everyone, his family, those he loved, and his enemies.'

'Are you talking about the Protectorate?'

'Yes. He was aware of their constant surveillance. Towards the end he took perverse enjoyment from maintaining the illusion that he was an ordinary Advancer. But such a lie weighed heavily on him. It was one of the main reasons he volunteered for duty at Centurion Station.'

'All right, I can buy into that scenario. Given the circumstances of his later life, where do you think he might have gone?'

'Hanko.'

Which wasn't the kind of answer Aaron was bracing himself for. Not even close. 'The Second47 world?'

'Yes.'

'I know that was where Anagaska's population originated from, but they were forced off because it became uninhabitable after the Prime attack. There's nothing there, not any more.'

'Inigo was always fascinated by what he considered his true ancestral home,' Qatux said. 'Remember he did not belong in Anagaska's Advancer culture. Hanko gave him a psychological ground point, amplified by an ancestor obsession rooted in his psyche due to the loss of his father so soon after his birth. Such a trauma affects any child, Higher as much as Advancer, especially when the event is regarded with such bitterness by his mother.'

'A wound she kept open, unintentionally or otherwise.'

'Correct. Hanko provided the perfect solution to someone as displaced as Inigo. A real place, yet at the same time unattainable. The illusion which could not be broken. He often contributed to charities which supplemented the official government Restoration teams. A telling point. He was never a wealthy man on Anagaska.'

'And you think he's gone back there?'

'If he abandoned Living Dream due to his own uncertainty on the direction it was taking, I would assign it a very high possibility. He is Higher, the radiation and climate will have little physical effect on him.'

'There are a lot of unknowns in this assumption.'

'If you had certainties you would not be here.'

'I apologize. I was expecting you to say he had fled the Commonwealth, or there was some secret cabal devoted to helping him. But Hanko would certainly explain why no one has found him.'

'Will you go there?'

Aaron looked over at Corrie-Lyn, who looked very puzzled. 'Yes,' he said.

*

'Ambition and good intentions are always an excellent starting point,' Likan said. 'Then before you know it you come right smack up against reality. You either adapt, become realistic and respond in kind, or you flounder along until you sink under the weight of your own capitulations. Now I know those of you in this auditorium aren't quitters. Hell, quitters couldn't afford these ticket prices.' He grinned round at the murmur of dutiful amusement. 'In life, either you get pressured or you apply pressure. Same for business—'

Three rows back from the small podium, Araminta glanced round at her fellow entrepreneurs. It was like the gathering of a clone army. All eager young business people, smartly dressed and sharply styled; hanging on to every word the richest man on the planet had to say about acquiring that same wealth. Each one of them desperate for a tiny hint of which way the market would go, a quip about financial trends, what new law to watch out for, a state project that was worth trying to bandwagon.

If they thought the Sheldonite would give them that, they were in for a big disappointment. Basic research: Likan was a ruthless man. He was here in Colwyn City to give another of his How-I-Made-It lectures for publicity and prestige, not to help fledgling rivals. A high profile helped his business, and in addition he got a buzz out of being adulated. This whole evening exemplified his favourite catchphrase: win-win.

Bovey would hate all this, she knew, and smiled secretively at the knowledge. Sitting amidst the faithful, such thoughts were near-sacrilege. But then Bovey had a little bit of a hang-up about the genuinely rich and powerful.

All politicians were worthless incompetents. All billionaires corrupt criminals. It was one of those quirks she was fond of. It could be quite funny hearing his youngest self, the biological fourteen-year-old, raging on about the cabinet secretary for social affairs. Mr Bovey had the true hatred of every self-employed person for bureaucracy, and the taxes it demanded to keep functioning; and, worse, expanding. In her mind, fourteen-year-olds didn't have adult concerns like that, it was all angst and impossible aspirations at that age. She recalled it well.

Araminta sighed warm-heartedly. Louder than she intended. She saw Likan's gaze flick in her direction, though his speech never faltered. Her lips pressed together in self-censure.

The speech was exactly what she was expecting. Plenty of motivational talk, a few anecdotes, a whole load of financial-services product-placement, and an excess of toothy smiles during the pauses for applause and laughter. Araminta even clapped along with the rest of them. It was all standard stuff, but there were some nuggets among the waffle. She was interested in his early years, how to make the jump from a small operation like hers up to a more corporate level. According to Likan, advancement was all down to risk, and how much of it you were prepared to take. He mentioned self-confidence a lot, along with determination and hard work. Araminta wondered if he'd ever met Laril. Now *that* would be an interesting conversation.

Likan finished, and was provided with a standing ovation. Araminta got to her feet with the rest of them, and applauded half-heartedly. She wished he'd been more specific, maybe given some case-study examples. The chairman of the Colwyn Small Business Association thanked their distinguished guest, and announced refreshments were available in the function room outside.

By the time Araminta made it out of the auditorium, her fellow small business owners were forming tight little groups to chatter away to each other while they gulped down the free drinks and canapés. From the snippets she overheard on her way to the bar the majority ran virtual companies. Talk was about expansion curves and cross-promotional market penetration and share options and when to merge. Men glanced at her as she walked past. There were welcoming smiles, even a few pings to her u-shadow, offering compliments and invitations. Her u-shadow didn't respond – pings were *so* adolescent. *If you want to take me out to dinner have the courage to ask me to my face.* She'd chosen a deep-turquoise dress that comp-lemented her hair colour. Strictly speaking the neckline was low and the hem high for a business occasion; but she now had the confidence to buck convention – at least on a small level. Independence and all that exposure to Cressida had given her that.

'Pear water,' she told the barman.

'Interesting choice.'

She turned to find Likan standing behind her. For someone so rich, his appearance was puzzling. The skin on his face was slightly puffy, with flushed cheeks as if he were permanently out of breath. His biological age was higher than usual, fixed in his late thirties rather than the mid-twenties everyone else favoured. The clothes he wore were always expensive, but never quite gelled, as if he got his dress sense from adverts. His jacket with a shark-skin shimmer was chic, but not with that particular purple shirt and green neck twister. And the brown shoes were best worn when gardening.

'I have to work later tonight,' she said. 'Can't afford lack of judgement from alcohol.'

'Good self-control. I like that.'

'Thank you,' she said levelly.

'I got the impression you weren't impressed tonight.'

People nearby were discreetly looking their way. Likan's voice was as forceful as it had been on the podium. That at least gave the impression of a strong personality.

Araminta sipped her pear water, wondering how to play this. 'I was hoping for more detail,' she told him.

'What kind of detail? Come on, you paid for your ticket, you're entitled.'

'Okay: small company, doing well. Needs to step up a level. Do you re-invest profits and ride a gradual expansion with each project slightly larger than the last, or do you take the bank loan and jump ten levels.'

'How small a company?'

'One-woman band, supported by some bots.'

'Company product?'

'Property development.'

'Good choice for a start up. High profitability relative to scale. There is a ceiling, though, especially with one person. After the first three properties there should be enough profit to take on more staff. With that you move on from one property at a time, and start multiple developments. Timing for that has never been better, property is the hot item here today thanks to Living Dream.'

'Everything is relative. With that demand, a developer has to buy high.'

'Then this developer should buy a whole street that's in

decline. It's a profit multiplier, the individual unit prices rise because you've taken the entire street upmarket and made it desirable.'

'That's a big step.'

'The level of risk you are prepared to undertake is proportional to your growth potential. If you don't take it you are declaring this far and no further. That will define your life. I don't think you want that.'

'Question: would you advise the staff expansion be accomplished by becoming multiple?'

'No.'

'Why not?'

'Going multiple only seems like a solution to a solo act. Ultimately it's a lifestyle choice rather than a business one. Ask yourself what you can accomplish by being multiple that you can't by good aggressive management. As you came to listen to me tonight I know you're already thinking ahead, thinking big. Property is a foundation stone for a corporate empire. A good one, I still have a vast property portfolio, but to achieve real market dominance you must diversify and interlock your interests. That's what Sheldon did. He used his interstellar transport monopoly as a cash source to fund industrial, commercial, and financial enterprises on a hundred worlds. At the time of the Starflyer War he was effectively Emperor of the Commonwealth.'

'Do you want to be our emperor?'

'Yes.'

Araminta was slightly shaken by his bluntness. She thought he was somehow calling her bluff. 'Why?'

'Because it's a position where you can do whatever you want. The ultimate freedom. Isn't that what we all strive for?'

'With power comes responsibility.'

'That's what politicians tell you when they want your vote. There's a difference between political power and financial power, especially out here in the External Worlds. I'd like to demonstrate that to you.'

'How would you do that?'

'Come and stay with me at my home for a weekend. See first hand what I've achieved. Decide if that's what you want for yourself.'

'What about your wives?' It was common knowledge just how staunchly committed he was to replicating his idol's ideology and life, including (or perhaps especially) the harem.

'What about them?'

'Won't they mind my visit?'

'No. They'll be joining us in bed.'

That'll teach me; you can't be more direct to my face than that. She was pleased with the way she kept her reaction in check, no startled expression, no give-away body language – squaring the shoulders, straightening the back. In effect telling him she could hold her own against him any day. 'I accept,' she said as if it was some kind of request to review finance statements.

'I knew I was right about you,' he said.

'In what way?'

'You know yourself, you know what you want. That's always dangerous.'

'To whom?'

'To everyone else. That's what makes you so desirable.'

'Win-win, then,' she mocked.

*

The *Alexis Denken* slid comfortably into the big airlock at the base of the Raiel dome stalk. Behind it, the stars vanished as the wall materialized again. Paula stood up, pulled wrinkles out of her suit jacket self-consciously, and straightened her spine. The *High Angel* teleported her into Qatux's private chamber. Raiel homes were traditionally split into three sections: public, residence, and private. You had to be a very good friend indeed to be invited beyond the public. The circular chamber had a pale-blue floor while, in keeping with tradition, the ceiling was invisible somewhere overhead. Around her, silver and grey walls rippled as if water was flowing down them, yet there was no sound, no dampness in the air. Beyond the cavorting surface, images of planetscapes and strange galaxies writhed insubstantially. However, one image remained firm and clear, a human face that Paula knew only too well.

She inclined her head to the big alien who occupied the centre of the chamber.

'Paula, I rejoice you are here.'

'It's been a long time, Qatux. How are you?'

'I am well. If I were a human, I would be fit.'

'I am glad.'

'I have risen to the *High Angel*'s fifth echelon.'

'How many are there?'

'Five.'

Paula laughed, she'd forgotten Qatux's sly humour. 'So you're the captain, then.'

'I have that honour.'

'Congratulations.'

'And you, Paula, do you continue to prosper?'

'I continue to be very busy. For me that's about the same thing.'

'That is to be expected. There are few of your species who remain in their bodies for as long as you have.'

'It's also why I'm here. I need information.'

'Just like the good old days. How intriguing.'

Paula cocked her head to one side as she regarded the big alien. That phrase was slightly out of kilter. Qatux's eye clusters remained steady on her. Long ago it would never have been so bold as to tease her. But then long ago it had been something of a wreck, until the Far Away mission came along. Of course, she'd been very different then, too. 'The starship *Alini* has just visited the Raiel dome. Can you tell me if these people were on board?' Her u-shadow retrieved image files for Aaron and Corrie-Lyn.

'They were,' Qatux whispered.

'What did they want?'

'I believe their mission was confidential.'

She gave her old friend a shrewd glance, not liking the conclusions she was drawing. 'It was you who saw them, wasn't it?'

'Yes.' The bottom set of tentacle limbs shivered slightly, the Raiel equivalent of a blush.

'Qatux, did you review Inigo's memories?'

'I did.'

'Why?' she asked, genuinely concerned. 'I thought that had stopped centuries ago. Tiger ...' She couldn't finish. Her gaze was drawn to the face suspended behind the wall. Tiger Pansy's silly carefree grin looked hauntingly back at her, obviously captured at a moment when the woman was blissfully happy.

'I know,' the Raiel whispered. 'It is not a return to my

addiction, I assure you. There would be few Raiel indeed who could refuse the opportunity of experiencing Inigo's mind. He dreams the Void, Paula. The Void! That evil enigma bedevils us to a degree which humans will never appreciate.'

'All right,' Paula ran her hand back through her hair, making an effort to ignore the uncomfortable personal side effects which the case was kicking up. 'Inigo's memorycell was stolen from a clinic on Anagaska. Why did you help Aaron?'

'I did not know the memories were stolen. He arrived in an ultradrive starship. It was intimated that he was a representative of ANA:Governance. In truth, he never confirmed that. I am sorry. I believe I was *had*. How stupid, me of all Raiel. The deception was quite simple.'

'Don't beat yourself up over it. Happens to the best of us. So what did he want to know?'

'He asked me to guess where Inigo might be.'

'Clever man. Which is curious in itself. There aren't many humans who knew of your little problem. One of them must have joined up to a Faction. So what did you tell him?'

'I guessed Inigo might be on Hanko.'

'Hanko? But it's just a radioactive ruin.' She stopped, examining the idea. 'But, Earth aside, it is his ethnic birthworld. Still, an odd choice.'

'Are you aware he was born Higher?'

'No I was not! That has never been on any file. Are you sure?'

Qatux's biggest tentacles waved in agitation. 'I am forty years of his early life, Paula. Through me you are talking to the young Inigo.'

'If ANA:Governance and I didn't know, then it's pretty certain very few other people did, either. That changes his whole profile. No wonder nobody could ever find him. As a Higher he has much greater personal resources.'

'Will you go after Aaron and Corrie-Lyn?'

'I'm not sure. I hadn't envisaged Aaron being so close to finding Inigo. But even if he is on Hanko it'll take Aaron a while to actually track him down. I need to consult with ANA: Governance on this. Thank you for helping, Qatux.'

'You are welcome, Paula. Always.'

She was on the verge of asking to be teleported back to her ship when she hesitated. 'What do the Raiel think of the Pilgrimage?'

'That it is incredibly foolish. Opening the Dyson Alpha barrier was one thing, but this takes your obduracy to a whole new level. Why does ANA:Governance allow it?'

Paula sighed. 'I have no idea. Humans always want to test their boundaries, it's an instinctive thing.'

'It is a stupid thing.'

'We're not as old as you. We don't have species-wide wisdom, let alone responsibility.'

'Higher humans do.'

'The tenet of universal responsibility is the root of their culture, but as individuals they have a long way to go. And as for ANA, it's like the intellectual equivalent of primordial ooze in there; who knows what's going to come wiggling out triumphantly at the end of the day? I'm beginning to doubt ANA:Governance's ability to keep order.'

'Are you serious?'

'I don't know,' she admitted. 'This whole event has me badly troubled. There are too many people playing with catastrophic unknowns. Part of me, the old part that worships order, wants to shut down the entire Pilgrimage project. It's obviously a monstrous folly. Yet the liberal side of me agrees that these people have a right to seek happiness, especially when nothing in the Commonwealth appeals to them. It's indicative of our cultural heritage that we cannot provide a home for everyone.'

'But Paula, their "right" to seek the solution of perfection in the Void will endanger the rest of the galaxy. That right cannot be permitted.'

'Quite. And yet, we don't have conclusive proof that the Void will respond the way you claim.'

Qatux was silent, as if startled. 'You doubt us, Paula?'

'Humans need to know things for themselves. It is our nature, Qatux.'

'I understand that. I am sorry for you.'

'We're being too melancholy. I give you my word I'm working to try and sort out this mess.'

'As always you are honourable. I hope you succeed. I would not like to see our two species fall into conflict.'

'We won't.'

The *High Angel* teleported Paula back into the cabin of the *Alexis Denken*. Like all modern starships the cabin could provide her with every physical necessity; like a hotel room with a particularly bad view. She ordered up a plain chair and took her guitar out of the storage locker. Music was something she'd come to late in life. As her genetically ordained compulsions were slowly erased, so she found her cultural horizons expanding. Art was a whole area she could never quite appreciate, she was always looking for rationalist explanation in every work. Literature was a lot more satisfactory, stories had a point, a resolution. Not that there were many books released into the unisphere these days, current writers tended to produce outlines and scripts for sensory dramas. But the classics were enjoyable enough; the only genre she tended to shy away from was crime and thrillers. Poetry she ignored as an absurd irrelevance. Music, though, had something for every mood, every place. She took a great deal of pleasure from it, listening to everything from orchestral arrangements to singer-songwriters, jazz to gaianature tonality, choral to starsphere dance. The *Alexis Denken* would often streak between star systems reverberating to the sounds of Rachmaninoff or Pink Floyd or Deeley KTC.

Paula sat back and started to pluck a few chords at random, then gradually dropped into Johnny Cash's 'The Wanderer'. She didn't try to sing; there were some limits in life you just had to accept. Instead the smartcore projected the Man in Black into the cabin, and he started to croon along to her melody.

The song helped her think.

She knew she should be heading straight for Orakum or even Hanko, but she was feeling a lot more troubled by Qatux's last comment than she ought to have been. It seemed as though this whole Pilgrimage situation was designed to disrupt her judgement and objectivity.

That, or I'm just getting lonely and uncertain in my old age.

Paula finished strumming. The Man in Black gave her a forlorn look, and she waved her hand dismissively. The smartcore cancelled the projection.

Her u-shadow opened a link to Kazimir – someone who did have empathy for her position.

'What can I do for you?' he asked.

'I'm at the *High Angel*. Aaron gave Inigo's memorycell to Qatux. Someone knew about our friend's predilection.'

'Did Qatux review it?'

'Oh yes. Qatux told Aaron that Inigo was probably hiding out on Hanko.'

'Interesting. Presumably that's where the *Artful Dodger* aka the *Alini* is heading?'

'Yes.'

'Another ultradrive ship arrived in the system just before the *Artful Dodger* departed. The Navy commander at *High Angel* said it stood off in the cometary belt, and left in hot pursuit.'

'Does every Faction have ultradrive ships?' she asked indignantly. 'Justine caught the Delivery Man using a Hawking m-sink on Arevalo.'

'So she told me. I consider it significant that the Factions are openly using such technology. This whole Pilgrimage event could well be the trigger for an irreversible culture split within the human race.'

'Whose side will you take?'

'The Navy was created by ANA to protect humans from stronger, hostile aliens. That is what it will continue to do until I am removed from my position. If ANA chooses to leave the physical universe, I will stay behind and ensure that whatever sections of us remain continue to receive that protection. Is that a side, do you think?'

'No. But it's certainly a plan.'

'Are you going after Aaron?'

'Not immediately. Can you provide some protection for Hanko and Inigo, if he's there?'

'I will observe and advise you of developments; but you

know the Navy cannot intervene directly in the internal affairs of Commonwealth citizens. Despite the scale of the problem, that's what this is.'

Paula was thrown by the answer. She was expecting Kazimir to be a lot more helpful. 'A thousand years ago I stuck to the rules, too. No good comes of it. You need to bend a little, Kazimir.'

'You and other representatives exist so I don't have to. You handle the grey areas, while I deal in black and white.'

'There's no such thing.'

'Nonetheless, I operate within a set of rules that I will not break.'

'I understand. Just do what you can, please.'

'Of course.'

*

The *Artful Dodger* dropped out of hyperspace five thousand kilometres above Hanko's equator. Sensors examined the surrounding environment, bringing up several amber warning symbols, and even a couple of red ones. The local star had an abnormally large number of sunspots chasing across its surface, producing a dangerously thick solar wind. Below the starship's metallic purple hull, a global cloud blanket reflected the star's sharp white glow back into space, its uniform glare broken only by the vast aural streamers that lashed across the stratosphere. Above the atmosphere monstrous arches of violet fluorescence soared out far beyond geosynchronous orbit, engorged Van Allen radiation belts that choked the planet with a hurricane of high-energy particles. The *Artful Dodger*'s hull sparked with a corposant discharge as it slid across into a high-inclination orbit.

'Welcome to hell,' Aaron muttered as he monitored the images from outside. The ship began to probe through the clouds with high-resolution hysradar sweeps, standard radar, magnoscan, quantum signature receptors, and electromagnetic sensors; revealing the lay of the frozen land underneath. Several com-beacon signals appeared on the emerging cartography, the only indication of activity on this bygone world. They broadcast the official channels of the Restoration team, asking all arriving ships to make contact.

Corrie-Lyn watched the images in the portal with a mournful face as the starship flew round and round the planet, building up a detailed survey of the surface. Twelve hundred years after the Prime attack, glaciers were still advancing out of the polar regions. 'I can't believe Inigo was ever attracted to this place,' she said.

'You heard Qatux; he enjoyed the *idea* of an ancestral homeworld.'

'Even if he came here, he'd take one look and leave. There's nothing here.'

'There are Restoration teams down there, even today,' Aaron said, waving at the little scarlet lights dotted across the map. The beacons acted as crude relays across continents, the only communication net on the planet.

'That's got to be the biggest lost cause in the galaxy,' she said.

'You're probably right. Seventeen of the Second47 worlds have officially closed their Restoration projects, and the remainder are winding down. Budgets get reduced every year. Nobody kicks up a fuss about it any more, not like the first couple of centuries after the War.'

After ten orbits, the smartcore had mapped all the

exposed land lurking below the eternal cloud. Sensors had located twenty-three centres of dense electromagnetic activity. The largest was a force-field dome in the centre of Kajaani, the old capital city. All the others were little more than clumps of machinery and buildings scattered across the dead tundra of three continents. No thermal sensor could begin to penetrate the cloud, so he had no way of telling if any of the outposts were occupied. There didn't seem to be any capsules in flight. Electrical activity in the air was strong, interfering with several sensor fields.

'No way of telling if he's down there,' Aaron said. 'Not from up here. I can't even see what ships are parked under the force field.'

'What were you expecting?'

'Nothing more than this. I'm just scouting the territory before we go in to make sure there are no surprises.'

Corrie-Lyn rubbed her arms, as if the cold from the planet was seeping into the cabin. 'So what's our cover story this time?'

'No point in one. It's not like the teams are heavily armed.'

'So you just shoot them one at a time until they give him up to us?'

He gave her an annoyed stare. 'We'll tell them that you're searching for a former lover. He changed his name and profile to forget you, but you've tracked him down here. All very romantic.'

'That makes me look like a complete loser.'

'Oh dear,' he sneered, and told the smartcore to call the beacon at Kajaani.

It took several minutes to get a reply from the shielded base. Eventually a very startled Restoration project director called Ansan Purillar came on line to give them landing authority.

The *Artful Dodger* sank deftly through the three kilometres of the upper cloud layer. Two hundred kph winds buffeted the hull with near-solid clumps of grey mist while lightning clawed furiously at the force field. Eventually they cleared the base of the layer into a strata of super-clear air and the outside temperature plummeted. A gloomy panorama opened up beneath them. Black ice-locked land smeared with long dunes of snow. Denuded of vegetation, every geographical feature was shaded in stark monochrome. Long braids of grubby cloud chased across the dead features.

'It must have been terrifying,' Corrie-Lyn said sadly.

'The Primes dropped two flare bombs into the star,' Aaron told her. 'The only way the Navy could knock them out was by using quantumbusters on the corona. Between them, they produced enough radiation to slaughter every living cell a million times over. Hanko's atmosphere absorbed the energy until it reached saturation point, which triggered a superstorm, which in turn threw up enough cloud to cover the planet and kick off an ice age. And the star still hasn't stabilized. Even if it did, it wouldn't matter; the radiation has completely destroyed the biosphere. According to the files, there's some marine life that's still alive in the deepest parts of the oceans, but that's all. The land is as sterile as a surgical chamber. Check out those radiation levels – and we're still five kilometres high.'

'I didn't appreciate what a scale this War was fought on.'

'They were going to genocide us.' The words were almost painful to speak. It had been a fearful time. Aaron

shuddered. *How do I know what the War was like?* A deeper
instinct assured him he wasn't that old.

The *Artful Dodger* continued its descent through the
rampaging lower clouds, blazing with solar brilliance as
it sloughed off whip-like tendrils of electrical energy. At
this altitude the wind speeds had dropped to a hundred
and fifty kilometres per hour, but the air density meant
the ship's ingrav units were straining to hold them stable
against the pressure.

Corrie-Lyn tried not to look alarmed as the starship
began to shake. High-velocity ice crystals shattered against
the force field as an amok cloud braid hurtled around
them. The crunch of disintegrating ice could be heard
inside the cabin.

'Okay then, this is why there aren't any capsules flying
down here,' Aaron muttered. His exovision was showing
him the force field dome below altering its permeability
index to allow them through. The wind speed was now less
than a hundred kph.

Outside the dome, there was very little evidence of the
city remaining. In its time, Kajaani had been home to three
million people. Its force field had warded off the storms
in the days following the Prime attack, protecting the
wormhole station so that the planet's population could
be evacuated to Anagaska. The process had taken over a
month, with government vehicles transporting refugees
from outlying countries on every continent as the storms
grew worse and worse and vegetation withered and died.
Seven weeks and three days after the planet's Premier
Speaker led the way, CST closed the Hanko wormhole. If
there was anybody left on the planet, they were beyond

contact. Every effort had been made, every known habitation and isolated farmstead searched.

With the people gone, the force fields protecting cities and towns failed one by one, allowing the winds to pound against the buildings and floodwater to scour the ground around them. Not even modern superstrong materials could resist such pummelling for ever. The structures began to crumple and collapse. Eventually, with the climate spiralling down into its ice age, the rains chilled to become snow, then ice. Mushy scree piled up against the frozen ruins, obliterating yet more evidence that this had once been an inhabited world.

The *Artful Dodger* passed through the force field and into the calm bubble of warm air that was the Restoration team's main base. It was centred on one of Kajaani's old parks. Under the protective auspice of the force field, the ground had been decontaminated and replanted. Grass grew once again, as did a short avenue of trees. Clusters of airborne polyphoto spheres shone an imitation sunlight on to the lush greenery; irrigation pipes provided clean water; there were even native birds and insects humming about, oblivious to the dark sky with its sub-zero winds outside.

They landed on a small patch of concrete on the edge of the park which held just one other starship, a thirty-year-old commercial combi-freighter with a continuous wormhole drive that could carry a mix of cargo and passengers. The difference between the two ships was patent, with the *Artful Dodger*'s smooth chrome-purple hull seeming almost organic compared to the Restoration team's workhorse with its carbon-bonded titanium fuselage and fading paintwork.

Aaron and Corrie-Lyn floated gently down out of the airlock to touch down between the five bulbous landing legs. Ten people had turned out to greet them, quite a crowd by the base's standards; and all curious to see the unscheduled arrivals. Ansan Purillar stood at the head of the delegation, a slightly rotund man with fair hair cut short, dressed in a simple dark-blue tunic with a Restoration logo on the arm.

'Greetings to both of you,' he said. 'I'd like to know why you're here. We're pleased to see you, of course, don't get me wrong. But we never have visitors. Ever.' His attitude was pleasant, but there was an underlying determination.

Aaron's biononics performed a fast low-level field scan. Director Purillar was an ordinary Advancer human; as were his co-workers, none were Higher. 'It's rather awkward,' he said with a twisted smile. 'Er, Corrie . . .'

'I'm looking for someone,' she said.

It was a low voice, hauntingly mournful. Aaron was quite impressed; she'd backed it up with a soft ache in the base's tiny gaiafield. The team were suddenly all attention and sympathy.

'A man. Yigo. We were in love. Then it went bad. My fault. I was so stupid. I shouldn't have . . . I don't want to say . . .'

Aaron put his arm comfortingly round her shoulder as she sniffed convincingly, head bowed. 'There there,' he assured her. 'They don't want details.'

Corrie-Lyn nodded bravely and continued. 'He left. It took me a long time before I realized what a mistake I'd made. But I'd hurt him, really badly. I've been looking for him for three years. He changed his name and his profile, but his sister let slip he'd come here.'

'Who is it?' Director Purillar asked.

'I don't know. All I know is what his sister said, that he'd joined the Restoration project. I just had to come. If there is *any* chance . . .'

'Um, yes, sure.' Purillar glanced round at his colleagues, who were busy checking each other out to see if any of them was going to own up to being The One. He waved an arm about. 'Anyone look familiar?'

Corrie-Lyn shook her head despondently. 'No. I probably won't recognize him.' She faced her little audience. 'Yigo, please, if it's you, please just tell me. I just want to talk, that's all. Please.'

Now nobody was meeting her gaze.

'You don't have to do it in front of your friends,' she said. 'Come to me later. I really *really* miss you.' That last was accompanied by a burst of sincere desperation into the gaiafield.

'All right then,' a now thoroughly embarrassed Purillar said to his team, 'I'll get this organized. We can meet up again at dinner.'

People broke off, heading back towards the main expanse of grass, keeping their smiles under tight control. As soon as they were a few paces away, couples went into deep intense conversations, heads pressed close together.

Aaron watched them go, keeping his own face impassive. The base would be talking about this for the next twenty years.

Ansan Purillar was left standing in front of his two uninvited guests, one hand scratching at his fuzz of hair in some perplexity. His gaiamotes were leaking an equal amount of disquiet. 'You're welcome to use the accommodation here. There are plenty of rooms spare, a legacy of when the project was conducted on a grander scale. But, quite frankly, I suspect your own ship would be more comfortable.' He eyed the *Artful Dodger* jealously. 'Our living quarters haven't been updated in a century.'

'That's very kind of you, and of course we'll use the ship,' Aaron said. 'We have no intention of imposing.'

'Quite the contrary,' Purillar said sheepishly. 'You are going to be excellent for morale. The only entertainment we get here is sensory dramas, and they tend to pale after a while. Whereas a quest like this ... One of us dull old souls with a romantic past. Well!'

'How long have you been here?' Aaron asked.

'Myself? I will have notched up twenty-five years in the last hundred and thirty.'

Aaron whistled. 'That's devotion. Do you mind telling me why?'

Purillar beckoned to them, and set off across the grass. 'I'm nearly three hundred years old, so in fact it's a small portion of my life. I don't mind donating the time because I can extend my life as long as I want to make up for it.'

'That sounds almost like Higher philosophy.'

'I suppose it does. I'll probably migrate inwards once the Restoration project ends. Higher culture appeals to me.'

'But why that first donation?'

'Simple enough, I met one of the Restored. She died just after the Prime attack, caught outside a force field when the storm struck. Seven hundred years later one of our teams found her corpse and extracted her memorycell.

She was re-lifed in a clone, and lived happily on Anagaska. It was her contentment which affected me; she had such a busy fulfilling life, there was a huge family, her involvement with the local community. I was struck by how much poorer the world, my world, would have been without her. So I signed up for a tour. Then when you're here you get to see first hand the people who you find, follow them from excavation through assessment and DNA extraction, memorycell rehabilitation, right up to re-life. You understand? I meet the living individual after I dig up their corpse. Innocent people who were struck down, people who didn't deserve to die; victims of a hideous war. Maybe it's self-serving, but do you have any idea how *good* that makes me feel?'

'I can't even imagine. I can see I'm going to have to make a financial contribution when I get back to Anagaska.'

They crossed the big grass field to the low buildings on the other side. Housing for the team members consisted of small individual cottages arranged in five neat circles, each with a central clump of community buildings. As they approached, Aaron saw an open-air swimming pool and several barbeque areas, even a sports pitch was marked out. Only two of the circles were in use now. It was impossible to see what the cottages were built out of; they were all covered by thick creepers with long brown leaves that dangled golden flowers from their tips. It was a pleasant arboreal contrast to the icy desolation outside the force field. A deliberate one he suspected; the vines were nicely shaggy, but pruned so as not to obstruct windows.

Behind the cottages were two modern functional blocks.

One containing the project laboratories, Purillar explained, while the other housed their maintenance shops and garaged their equipment.

'We're heavily cybernated,' he told them, 'But even we need a few technicians to repair the bots now and again.'

'Could he be working as a technician?' Aaron asked Corrie-Lyn.

'Who knows?' she said lightly. 'I just know he's here. Probably. It is a long-shot, after all.'

Aaron didn't look at her. *That hell-damned mouth of hers!* He'd managed to get into the starship's culinary unit program, altering her patches on his original blocks so the drinks she ordered only had half the alcohol content she'd designated. Her attitude hadn't made any miraculous changes. 'Can we meet everyone?' Aaron asked.

'Sure. I suppose. This is a civil outpost after all. I'm not exactly a police commissioner, you know. I can't compel anyone who doesn't want to be introduced.' He gave Corrie-Lyn an apologetic shrug.

'Anyone who refuses is pretty likely to be him, don't you think?' said Aaron.

'Sounds about right,' the director said. 'You do realize that everyone on the planet will now know you're here, and especially why. This is a small operation.'

'How many people is that, exactly?'

'Four hundred and twenty-seven of us; of which a hundred and eighty are here in the base. Five hundred years ago, there were six thousand people involved.'

'How many people have you restored?'

'Two point one million in total,' Purillar said proudly.

Aaron whistled appreciatively. 'I had no idea.'

'The bulk of them were in the early years, of course. But our techniques have improved dramatically since then. Thankfully, because, even with the cold helping preservation, entropy is our real enemy. Come on in, I'll show you.' He stepped through the door of the laboratory block.

The assessment room was the first section they looked in. A big clean chamber with ten long medical tables surrounded by plyplastic limbs tipped with instruments and sensors. One of the tables had a recently discovered corpse on it. Aaron wrinkled his nose up at the sight. It was hard to tell the thing had been human. A dark lump wrapped in shrunken cloth and smeared with grime, its limbs were difficult to determine, showing as long ridges. Strings of hair at one end at least showed him where the head was located. After a minute he realized the corpse was curled up in foetal position.

Two of the Recovery team were standing beside the table in sealed white overalls, peering down through their bubble-helmets as they directed the wand-shape sensors sliding along various creases in the body's surface. Their movements dislodged grains of snow, which were carefully vacuumed up from the table top.

'We keep the temperature in there the same as outside,' Purillar said. 'Any sudden change in environment could be catastrophic. As it is we have to keep the assessment room sterile, too.'

'Why?' Corrie-Lyn asked.

'The radiation has killed off Hanko's microbial life. It's another factor which helps the preservation process. If any bugs got in there, they'd have a feast day, and we'd be left with slush.'

'They must be very delicate by now,' Aaron said.

'Yes. This one is almost intact. We normally deal with broken segments.'

'Don't you use a stabilizer field?'

'Not if we can help it. We found the field actually has a detrimental effect on their memorycells. Don't forget, back then the Commonwealth was still using crystal matrices. In some early cases we scrambled ten per cent of the information.'

'Must be hard to remove the memorycell, then.'

'We don't even try. Once we've extracted enough DNA samples to sequence a full genome, we deploy infiltrator filaments into the crystal. Even that can be hazardous. Powering up a memorycell after this long is fatal. It has to be read cold, which is done a molecular layer at a time. Each one takes about nine months.'

'I'd have thought that crystal memorycells would last longer than this.'

'They built them pretty robust, even back then. But consider what they've endured for twelve hundred years. It doesn't help.'

'Who is he?' Corrie-Lyn asked.

'Her, actually. We think she's Aeva Sondlin. We'll know for certain when her genome has been read, but the location was right.'

'Location?'

'She was found four kilometres from her car. In itself that was hard to find. Washed downstream in a flash flood. We know from records that she lived in the house above the valley's flood level. We think she was making a dash for the nearest town during a break in the storm. There was an official evacuation point set up there, and she informed the authorities she was coming. Never arrived. Must have got caught by the winds, or the water. Maybe she'll be able to tell us.'

'You knew she was missing?'

'Yes. The records of the time aren't perfect, naturally, given the circumstances. But we have a full census, and of course everyone who arrived on Anagaska was fully documented. It's our job to try and determine what happened to those who got lost. We have to handle each case separately. In Aeva's case, we've been searching possible locations for seventy years.'

'You're bullshitting me,' Aaron said.

'I assure you I'm not.'

'Sorry, but seventy years?'

'We start with the route she must have taken, pick the obvious danger points, and seed them with sensor bots. They spread out in a circle, trying to find some trace. Like all our equipment, the bots have improved considerably during the centuries we've been here. The majority are tunnellers, burrowing through the snow and surface soil layers. So much topsoil was displaced during the storms that the continent's whole topology shifted, and now it's all locked into place by the permafrost. Ninety-nine per cent of the people we recover these days are buried. It means the bots operate in highly detrimental conditions even for this world. In total, the Restoration project has deployed four hundred and fifty million since it began. There are still eleven million active and searching. They're not fast moving, but they are thorough.'

'How many people are you still looking for?'

'A third of a million. I don't hold out much hope. Most of them will have been washed into the sea.' He gestured at the wrinkled lump on the table. 'Dear Aeva's car was forty-seven kilometres from the road she used, and that was the easy find; she was deep under sediment. Persistence pays off. We still find about twenty or so each year, even now.'

They moved on into DNA sequencing. To Aaron it was just an ordinary office with five large smartcores. Even in ordinary circumstances, human DNA decomposed quickly; after twelve hundred years on Hanko, only the smallest fragments remained. But there were a lot of cells in each body, each with its own fragments. Piecing them together was possible with the right techniques, and a vast amount of computing power. Once the main sequences had been established, the project could use family records to fill the gaps. In a lot of cases, there were full DNA records from clinics available. As soon as the body had been properly identified, a clone was grown for re-life.

'But not here,' Purillar said. 'Clinics back on Anagaska handle that part. After all, who would want to wake up here? People have enough trouble adjusting to the present – their future – as it is. Most need specialist counselling.'

'Is life that different?'

'Essentially no, and most died hoping for rescue in the form of re-life. It is the amount of time involved which shocks them. None of their immediate family and friends remain. They are very much alone when they wake.'

After DNA there was the memory rehabilitation section, which tried to reassemble the information read from memorycells. A process orders of magnitude more complex than DNA sequencing.

The history archive: for recovered people who couldn't be identified. All of Hanko's civic records, and memoirs of families with lost relatives, the logs and recollections of the evacuation teams. Lists of people who may have been visiting Hanko when the attack started. The Intersolar missing persons list of the time.

Laboratories specializing in analysis of molecular structures; identifying baroque, minute clues the bots had discovered as they wormed their way through Hanko's frozen earth. Trying to place flakes of paint with individual car models. Tying scraps of cloth to specific clothes, from that to manufacturer, to retail outlet, to customer lists, to bank statements. Items of jewellery. Even pets. A long register of unknown artefacts, each one potentially leading to another lost corpse.

The case room. With files on everyone still known to be missing.

Operations centre, which monitored the sensor bots and the outpost teams which were excavating in terrible conditions.

After two hours, they'd met everyone in the building. None reacted to Corrie-Lyn, and nobody tried to avoid her. Aaron quietly scanned all of them. No one was enriched with biononics.

'There are a few other people around,' Purillar said. 'You'll probably meet them tonight at the canteen. We tend to eat together.'

'And if he's not there?' Aaron asked.

'Then I'm sorry, but there's not much I can do,' the director said. He gave Corrie-Lyn an uncomfortable glance.

'Can we visit the outposts?' she asked.

'If he is here, he'll know about you by now. He would have used the beacon net to call in. I guess he doesn't want to get back with you.'

'Seeing me in the flesh might be the one thing he can't resist,' Corrie-Lyn said. 'Please.' Her outpouring of grief into the gaiafield was disturbing.

The director looked deeply unhappy. 'If you want to venture outside, there's nothing I can do to stop you, technically this is still a free Commonwealth world. You can go wherever you want. I'd have advise against it, though.'

'Why?' Aaron asked.

'You've got a good ship, but even that would be hard pressed to manoeuvre close to the ground. We can't use capsules here, the winds are too strong, and the atmospheric energy content too high. The two times we tried to use our ship for an emergency rescue nearly ended in disaster. We aborted both, and wound up having to re-life the team members.'

'My ship has an excellent force field.'

'I'm sure it does. But expanding the force field doesn't help, you just give the wind a bigger surface area to push at. Down here it actually makes you more susceptible to the storm. The only stability you have in the air is what your drive units can provide.'

Aaron didn't like it. The *Artful Dodger* was just about the best protection possible. *Under normal circumstances.* He couldn't forget the way the regrav units had approached their limits bringing them down to the base's force field dome, and that was a big target. 'How do your teams get about?' he asked.

'Ground crawlers. They weigh three tons apiece, and move on tracks. They're not fast, but they are dependable.'

'Can we borrow one? There must be some you're not

using. You said there used to be a lot more personnel here at one time. Just an old one will do.'

'Look. Really. He's not here.'

'Whatever release document you want us to certify, we'll do it,' Corrie-Lyn said. 'Please. Give me this last chance.'

'I've got over twenty teams out there. Half of them aren't even on this continent. We use the polar caps as a bridge to get to the other landmasses. It would take you a year to get round them all.'

'At least we can make a start. If Yigo hears we're going round everyone, he'll know he'll have to face me eventually. That might make him get in contact.'

Purillar rubbed agitated fingers across his forehead. 'It will have to be the mother of all legal release claims. I can't have any come-back against the project.'

'I understand. And thank you.'

After dinner, Aaron and Corrie-Lyn made their way over to the second block to inspect the ground crawler Purillar was oh-so-reluctantly allowing them to use. Overhead, the airborne lights were dimming down to a gentle twilight. The effect was spoiled by constant flares of lightning outside the force field.

'He wasn't at the canteen then?' Corrie-Lyn asked.

'No. I've scanned everyone in the base now. None of them have biononics. Though quite a few have some interesting enrichments. It can't be as tame here as the good director claims.'

'You always judge people, don't you?'

'Quite the opposite. I don't care what they do to each other in the privacy of their own cottage. I just need to make a threat-assessment.'

The malmetal door of garage eleven rolled apart to show them the ground crawler. It was a simple wedge-shape of metal on four low caterpillar tracks. With the bodywork painted bright orange, its slit windows made empty black gashes in the sides. Force field projectors were lumpy bulbs on the upper edges, along with crab-like maintenance bots which clung to the surface like marsupial babies. When Aaron queried the vehicle's net he found it had a large self-repair function. A third of the cargo compartments were filled with spares.

'We should be all right in this,' he told her. 'The net will drive it. All we have to do is tell it where we want to go.'

'And that is, exactly? You know, Purillar was right. If Inigo is here, then he knows I'm here looking for him. He would have contacted us. Me, at least.'

'Would he?'

'Oh don't,' she said, her face furrowed in disgust. 'Just don't.'

'He obviously doesn't miss you as much as you miss him. He left, remember.'

'Screw you!' she screamed.

'Don't hide from this. Not now. I need you functional.'

'Functional,' she sneered. 'Well I'm not. And if we find him the first thing I'll tell him is not to help you, you psychofuck misfit.'

'I never expected anything else from you.'

She glowered, but didn't walk away. Aaron smiled behind her back.

'If he's here, the Pilgrimage will be long gone before we find him,' she said sulkily.

'Not quite. Remember we have an advantage that lets us reduce the search field. We know he's Higher.'

'How does that help?' There was distain in her voice still, but warring with curiosity now.

'The field scan effect would be very useful out there, helping to track down bodies buried in the ground. I can use it to detect anomalies several hundred metres away. It's a little more difficult through a solid mass, but the pervasive function is still capable of reaching a reasonable distance.'

'If he's here, he'll have a better success rate than the others,' she said.

'There are other factors, such as getting the location of a lost person reasonably accurate. Which is all down to how well an individual case has been researched. But yes. It's a reasonable assumption to say the team with the best success rate will be Inigo's.'

'Is there one?'

'Yep. My u-shadow didn't even have to hack any files. They're all open to review. The team with the current highest Recovery rate is working up at Olhava province. That's on this continent, nine hundred kilometres south-west. If we start first thing tomorrow morning, we'll be there in forty-eight hours.'

*

Oscar Monroe had fallen in love with the house the first moment he saw it. It was a plain circle, with a high glass wall separating floor and ceiling, standing five metres off the ground on a central pillar that contained a spiral stair. Both the base and the roof were made from some smooth artificial rock similar to white granite, which shone like mountain-top snow in Orakum's blue-tinged sunlight. The sprawling grounds outside resembled some grand historical parkland that had fallen into disuse, with woolly grass overgrowing paths, lines of ornamental trees, and a couple of lakes with a little waterfall between them. There were even some brick Hellenic structures resting in deep nooks, swamped by moss and flowering creepers to add to the image of great age. That image was one which several dozen gardening bots worked hard at achieving.

He had lived there for nineteen years now. It was a wonderful home to return to every time his pilot shift was over, devoid of stress and the kind of bullshit politics that went in tandem with any corporate job. Oscar flew commercial starships for Orakum's thriving national spaceline, which had routes to over twenty External planets. Piloting was the only job he'd sought since he'd been re-lifed.

Waking up in the clinic had been one hell of a surprise. The last thing he remembered was crashing his hyperglider into an identical one piloted by Anna Kime. Saving the Commonwealth – good. Killing the wife of his best friend – not so hot. Without Anna to wreck their flight, Wilson Kime should have managed to fly unimpeded on a mission that was pivotal in the Starflyer War. Oscar could remember the instant before the collision, a moment of complete serenity. He hadn't expected anyone to recover his memory-cell. Not after his confession, that in his youth he'd been involved in an act of politically motivated terrorism that had killed four hundred and eight people, a third of them without memorycells, mostly children too young for the inserts. The fact that he'd never intended it, that the deaths were a mistake, that they'd missed their actual target – that should never have counted in his favour. But it seemed as though his service to the Commonwealth, and ultimate sacrifice, had meant something to the judge. He wanted to think Wilson had maybe paid for a decent lawyer. They'd been good friends.

'I guess this means we won, then,' were his first words. It even sounded like his own voice.

Above him, a youthful doctor's face smiled. 'Welcome back, Mr Yaohui,' he said.

'Call me Oscar. I was that longer than I was ever Yaohui.' His new identity when he went on the run for over forty years.

'As you wish.'

Oscar managed to prop himself up on his elbows. A movement which surprised him; he'd seen re-life clones several times; pitiful things with thin flesh stretched over bones and organs that had been force-grown to adolescence, unable to move for months while they painfully built up muscle mass. This body, though, seemed almost complete. Which meant the technique had improved. There had been a lot of bodyloss in the War – tens of millions at least. He'd probably been shoved down to the bottom of the list. 'How long?'

'Please understand, er, Oscar, you were put on trial for your, uh, previous crime. It set quite a few legal precedents, given your, uh, state at the time.'

'What trial? What do you mean, *state*? I was dead.'

'You suffered bodyloss. Your memorycell survived the crash intact – legally that is recognized by the Commonwealth as being your true self. It was recovered by one Paula Myo.'

'Uh—' Oscar was suddenly getting a very bad feeling about this. 'Paula recovered me?'

'Yes. You and Anna Kime. She brought both of you back to Earth.'

'But Anna was a Starflyer agent.'

'Yes. Under the terms of the Doi amnesty her Starflyer conditioning was edited out of her memories and she was re-lifed as a normal human. Apparently she went on to have a long life and a successful marriage to Wilson Kime. She was certainly on the *Discovery* with him when it flew round the galaxy.'

Oscar's shoulders weren't so strong after all; he sagged back on to the mattress. 'How long?' he repeated; there was an urgency in his growl.

'You were found guilty at the trial. Your Navy service record was a mitigating factor in sentencing of course, but it couldn't compensate for the number of people who were killed at Abadan Station. The judge gave you suspension. But as the Commonwealth clinics were unable to cope with the sheer quantity of, uh, non-criminals requiring re-life at the time, he allowed you to remain as a stored memory rather than be re-lifed before the sentence began.'

'How long?' Oscar whispered.

'You were sentenced to one thousand one hundred years.'

'Fuck me!'

He was all alone. That was probably a worse punishment than suspension. After all, he wasn't aware of time passing during that millennia, he couldn't reflect and repent on his wrongdoing. But in this present, life was different. Everyone he'd known had either died or *migrated inwards* – ridiculous phrase, a politically correct way of saying they'd committed euthanasia with a safety net. Maybe that was the point of suspension after all. It certainly hurt.

So, with no friends, no family, knowledge and skills that even museums wouldn't be interested in, Oscar Monroe had to start afresh.

The Navy, rather understandably, didn't want him. He explained he didn't expect to be part of the deterrence fleet, and offered to retrain as a pilot for their exploration crews. They declined again.

Back before the Starflyer War he'd worked in the exploration division at CST. Opening new planets, giving people a fresh start, was kind of like a self-imposed penance. Except he'd really enjoyed it. So he did train as a starship pilot. Fortunately the modern continuous wormhole drive used principles and theories developed during his first life, and he brought himself up to speed on its current technology applications quite rapidly.

Orakum SolarStar was the third company he'd worked for since his re-life. It wasn't much different to any other External World starline. In fact it was smaller than most. Orakum was on the edge of the Greater Commonwealth, settled for a mere two hundred years. But that location made it a chief candidate from which to mount new exploration flights, opening up yet more worlds. They were rare events. The Navy had charted every star system directly outside the External Worlds. Expansion to new worlds was also at a historical low. The boundary between Central and External Worlds hadn't changed much for centuries. The old assumption that Higher culture would always be extending outwards, and the ordinary humans would be an expanding wave in front of it was proving to be a fallacy. With inward migration, the number of Higher humans remained about constant; and the External Worlds provided just about every kind of society in terms of ethnicity, ideology, technology, and religion. Should any citizen feel disenfranchised on their own planet they just had to take a commercial flight to relocate. There was very little reason to found a new world these days.

In the nineteen years he'd been on Orakum, SolarStar had only launched three planetary survey flights. Two of these had been closer than the company's long-range commercial flights travelled. Hardly breaking through new frontiers. But he had seniority now. If another outward venture came along, he ought to be chosen. Like all pilots, he was an eternal optimist.

There was no hint of that elusive mission in the company offices when he filed his flight report. He'd just got back from a long-haul flight to Troyan, seventy lightyears away. A fifteen-hour trip with nothing to do other than talk to the smartcore and trawl the unisphere for anything interesting. One day soon, he was sure, people would finally chuck the notion that they had to have a fellow human in charge. He was only sitting up in the front of the starship for public relations. In fact there were probably people sitting in the passenger cabin who were better qualified than him if repairs were ever needed. Not that they ever were.

But at least he got to visit new planets. The same ones. Over and over again.

His regrav capsule sank out of the wispy clouds to curve sedately round the house and land on the grass beside the spinney of lofty rancata trees, nearly twenty metres tall with reddish-brown whip-leaves that swayed in the mild breeze. He climbed out and took a deep breath of the warm, plains-scented air. Out beyond the horizon, Orakum's untamed countryside was carpeted by spiky wildflowers that budded most of the year. Another reason to choose Orakum was its benign climate.

Jesaral was walking out from underneath the house. The splendidly handsome youth didn't quite have a welcoming smile on his face, but definitely looked relieved to see Oscar. He was only wearing a pair of knee-length white trousers, showing off a tanned body that always got Oscar's blood pumping a little faster. Jesaral was the youngest of his three life partners, barely twenty. Which, Oscar suspected, probably qualified him as the worst Punk Skunk in the galaxy. A thousand-year-plus age gap: it was delightfully naughty.

The youth opened his arms wide and gave Oscar a big hug to accompany a long sultry kiss. Enthusiasm sprayed out heedlessly into the gaiafield.

'What's the matter?' Oscar asked.

'Them,' Jesaral said, stabbing a thumb dismissively back at the house.

Oscar refused to sigh. He and his other partners Dushiku and Anja had been a stable trio for over a decade. They were both over a hundred, and completely at ease with each other. At their age they understood perfectly the little accommodations necessary to make any relationship work. It was taking everyone longer than expected to accommodate and adjust to their newcomer – who didn't have anything like their experience and sophistication. Which was what made him so exciting in and out of bed.

'What have they done?'

'It's a surprise for you. And I know how you hate surprises.'

'Not always,' Oscar assured him. 'Depends if it's good or bad. What's this one?'

'Oh no. I'm just telling you there is a surprise for you. I don't want you to be upset that it's there, that's all.'

Oscar used a macrocellular cluster to connect to the house's net. Whatever was waiting inside had been skilfully blocked. That would be Anja, who developed commercial neural routines. She was one of the best on the planet.

'You have the strangest logic I've ever known,' Oscar said.

Jesaral smiled broadly. 'Come on! I can't wait.' He tugged at Oscar's arm, his outpouring of enthusiasm shining like sunrise.

They hurried to the base of the pillar and climbed the wide spiral stair. It brought them out into a small vestibule, planted with colourful bushes from several worlds, their flowers reaching for the open sky above. Ten doors opened off it. Jesaral led the way into their main lounge. In contrast to the exterior, the lounge was clad in caranwood, a local variety that was a rich gold-brown. The grain of the planks had been blended so skilfully it looked as if they were inside a giant hollowed-out trunk. Its furniture was scarlet and gold, contributing to the sumptuous feel.

Dushiku was waiting in the middle of the big room, holding out a tumbler of malt whisky, three ice cubes. He had a mischievous smile on his broad face. 'Welcome home.'

'Thanks.' Oscar took the drink wearily.

'I see Jesaral's restraint is as strong as ever.'

'I didn't tell him,' Jesaral protested.

'So?' Oscar enquired.

Dushiku raised an eyebrow, and half turned, indicating the balcony beyond the glass wall at the far end of the lounge. Anja was standing out there, leaning on the rail as she spoke about some aspect of the gardens below. Her laughter-filled voice was just audible through the open door. Oscar knew the tone well, she was playing perfect hostess: marking her territory. Anja was astonishingly beautiful, a beauty which took a full third of her salary to maintain. Two visits to a clinic each year were considered an essential minimum, for beauty was fluid and fashions were treacherous ephemera even on Orakum. She'd returned three weeks ago from her last treatments, showing off her reduced height and dark satin-texture skin. Her face was all gentle curves veiled by a mane of thick chestnut hair swishing down past her shoulders. Huge fawn-coloured eyes peered innocently out of the shadows, projecting a girlish innocence complemented by a perpetual ingénue effervescence into the gaiafield. Her clothes were deceptively simple, a scarlet T-shirt and dark-blue swirling skirt demonstrating her compact figure's expensive femininity.

Yet for once, Anja wasn't impressing the person she was talking to. Oscar watched the other woman leaning on the rail. Easily half-a-head shorter than Anja, wearing a modern white dress with a slight surface shimmer, and a rust-red short-sleeved jacket. Stylish without Anja's feminine overload. She wasn't responding with the kind of attention Anja was used to extracting from everyone she came across. He could tell. After ten years, Anja's body language, the tone of her voice were an open book. And the more she failed to impress, the more huffy she got. He even allowed some of his amusement to trickle out into the gaiafield.

Anja must have sensed it. Her full lips hardened into a rebuke as Oscar walked towards the balcony. 'Oscar, darling, I've been talking to an old friend of yours.'

The other person on the balcony turned round. Smiled shrewdly.

Oscar dropped the tumbler as his hands along with every other part of his body were shocked into loss of sensation. The crystal smashed, sending the ice cubes bouncing across the polished wood.

'Hello, Oscar,' Paula Myo said.

'Holy shit!'

'Long time no see.'

Oscar couldn't even grunt.

Alarm was starting to seep into the gaiafield as his life partners took in the tableau.

'You two . . .' Jesaral said, his finger rising to point accusingly at Paula. 'I thought—'

'It's all right,' Oscar managed to croak.

'What is this?' Jesaral said accusingly to Paula. 'You said you were friends.'

'We used to be. A long time ago.'

'That old excuse. Again! Everything happened before I was born.'

'Everything did,' Oscar said. His u-shadow summoned a maid-bot to clean up the broken tumbler. Only then did he finally manage a weak smile. 'How are you doing, Paula?'

'Same as usual.'

'Yeah.' She hadn't changed. Not physically. Nothing was different, except maybe her straight dark hair was a couple of centimetres longer. Unlike him, who'd been given a great new Advancer body, based on his own DNA then enriched with all the macrocellular clusters, and stronger bones, more efficient organs, and greater longevity. After eighty-six years, he still wasn't anywhere near needing rejuvenation, although his face was now starting to show signs of his newly lived years – as Anja never tired of pointing out. But her ... He guessed she must be Higher now. Somehow he couldn't see her visiting clinics for vanity's sake.

'You do know each other, then?' Dushiku asked uncertainly.

'Yes.' Oscar cleared his throat. 'Could you give us a moment, please?'

His life partners exchanged troubled glances, flooding the gaiafield with concern and considerable irritation. 'We'll be outside,' Anja said, patting his arm as she went past. 'Just yell.'

The maidbot waddled into the lounge and started sucking up the malt. Oscar backed up to a settee and sat down hard. The numbness was dissipating, replaced by a growing anger. He glared at Paula. 'One thousand one hundred years. Thanks for that.'

'I recovered your memorycell.'

'You put it on trial!'

'You're as alive now as the day you flew the hyperglider. That's more than can be said for your victims at Abadan.'

'Jesus fucking wept! Will you stop persecuting me?'

'I can't make you feel guilty. You do that to yourself.'

'Yeah yeah.' He sank deeper into the cushioning. 'What the hell are you doing here?'

'You live well.' She turned her head, studying the lounge. 'Anja was quite proud of the house. I can see why.'

'My CST R&R pension fund was paid over into a trust

the day the trial ended, courtesy of Wilson. You want to know what one thousand one hundred years' interest looks like? You're standing in it. Bloody inflation! I should have been able to buy a planet.'

'And your life partners; they're good people. Jesaral is rather young, isn't he?'

'Yeah,' Oscar growled at her. 'He's also got a very big cock.'

Paula smiled. 'Did you ever get in touch with Wilson when you were re-lifed?'

'He left a message. So did Anna. They both downloaded into ANA long ago. Which frankly I don't admire. Look, this is bullshit; what the fuck do you want?'

'I need you do a job for me.'

Oscar wouldn't have believed it possible. He was in the same room as Paula Myo, and laughing at her. 'Oh boy, did you ever lose it over the centuries. You want *me* to do a job for *you*? You've got to be fucking joking.'

Paula's answering smile veered towards immoral. 'Exactly.'

Oscar's humour vanished abruptly, leaving him with a very queasy sensation heating his stomach. 'Oh shit: you're not joking.'

'Of course not. It's a perfect arrangement. Who would ever suspect such a thing?'

'No. No chance. Go and blackmail someone else. I'd rather go back into suspension.'

'Come on, Oscar, you're not Jesaral so stop acting like him. I'm not here to threaten, I'm here to ask because I know you and I know what you want.'

'You do not know me, lady!'

Paula leaned in towards him, her eyes shining. 'Oh yes I

do, Oscar. We spent the last few days of your life together. I nearly died, and you did. Don't tell me we don't understand each other. You martyred yourself so that the human race could survive. You are an honourable man, Oscar. Screwed up by guilt, but honourable.'

Oscar was doing his best not to be intimidated by her. 'That was a mad situation. It won't ever happen again.'

'Oh really? Who do you think I work for these days?'

'I'll take a wild guess and say ANA. You never change.'

'You're right about ANA, but wrong about change. I am different.'

'Yeah, it looks it. The same job for thirteen hundred years. I barely recognized you. Paula, you can't change, that is you.'

'Far Away altered me. It nearly killed me, but I understood I had to adapt. So I resequenced my DNA to edit out the compulsive-behaviour trait.'

'It shows.'

'Self-determination can overcome artificial nature.'

'I'm sure the old nature versus nurture philosophers will be delighted to hear it. Why don't you call them and let them know? Oh, yes, right. They're all *dead* for two thousand years.'

'You're trying to avoid answering me. Trying to justify your fright to yourself.'

'Wrong, lady. Utterly totally, wrong. The answer is no. No I will not help you. Would you like that clarifying? No.'

'How bad do you think it is, that I'm here to ask you?'

'Don't care. I won't help you.'

'It's the Pilgrimage. Oscar, I'm worried about it. Really worried.'

He stared up at her, not sure if he could take many

more shocks. 'Look, I've followed the story closely enough, who hasn't? The Navy will stop the Ocisen Empire dead in its tracks. ANA will halt the Pilgrimage ships. It's not stupid. The Void will eat up half the galaxy if Inigo's dumb-ass sheep ever get inside.'

'And you think that's all there is to it? Oscar, you and I were there with Nigel before we travelled to Far Away. You know how complex that situation was, how many factors were at play. Well, this is worse, a lot worse. The Void is only a peripheral event, a convenient gadfly; this is the Factions finally marching out to fight. This is a battle for the destiny of humanity. Our *soul* will be decided by the outcome.'

'I can't help,' he said, mortified by the way it was nearly a wail. 'I'm a pilot for Christ's sake.'

'Oh, Oscar.' Her voice was rich with sympathy. She knelt down in front of him and grasped his hands. Her fingers were warm to the touch. 'Enough humility. It's your character I desperately need help from. I know that once you agree I don't have to worry about the problem any more. You won't quit on me, and that's what's important.'

'This is a nostalgia trip for you. I'm just a pilot.'

'You were just a Navy captain, but you saved us from the Starflyer. I'm going to tell you what I'm asking you to do. And then I'm going to tell you why you'll do it. If you want to hate me for making you face reality then that's fine by me, too.'

He shook his hands loose from her grip. 'Say your piece, then go.'

'The Factions know me, they watch me as I watch their

agents. So I can't have them knowing that I am desperate to locate the Second Dreamer.'

Oscar just laughed. It trailed off into a near-whimper. 'Find the Second Dreamer? Me?'

'Yes. And you know why that'll work?'

'Because no one will be expecting it.' He made it sound like a schoolkid reciting a useless fact.

'Correct. And do you know why you'll do it for me – and please don't shoot the messenger.'

He braced himself. Surely there was nothing else in his life she could threaten him with? *Did I erase a memory? My God, was there another Abadan?* 'What?'

'Because you're bored shitless with this dreary monotonous life you sleepwalk through.'

Oscar opened his mouth to shout at her. Tell her she'd finally flipped. That she was so fantastically wrong. That his life was rich. That he had people who loved him. That every day was a joy. That he never wanted to go back to the crazy days of the Starflyer War. That he'd already endured all the terror and wild exhilaration one life could possibly contain. That such things were best left to the new generation. But for some reason his head had fallen into his hands, and he was sighing heavily. He couldn't look at her. And he could certainly never look at his life partners. 'I can't tell them that,' he whispered painfully. 'How can I? They'll believe it's their fault.'

Paula stood up. A hand rested on his shoulder with gentle sympathy. 'You want me to do it?'

'No.' He shook his head. Wiped the back of his hand across his eyes to remove the annoying smears of moisture. 'No. I'm not that much of a coward.'

'Whatever cover story you need, you've got it. I can arrange . . . anything, basically.'

'Uh huh.'

'There's a starship waiting for you at the local space-port.' She smiled mischievously. 'An ultradrive.'

Oscar smiled faintly, feeling the joy stirring deep inside him. 'Ultradrive? Well, at least you don't think I'm a cheap whore.'

*

This wasn't how Araminta expected to be returning to the Suvorov continent, sitting in an ageing carry capsule as it flew across the Great Cloud Ocean, lower and slower than every other capsule on the planet. It didn't exactly smack of style. She'd always promised herself she'd only ever return to her birth continent when she could step out of some swank luxury capsule and smile condescendingly around at Langham and the family's business.

Not there just yet.

Unfortunately, Likan's estate was on Suvorov. Under-standably, as that was where Viotia's capital, Ludor, was situated. Likan wasn't a provinces kind of person, he had to be near the action. So back across the ocean she went. With a baggage hold packed with her best clothes, and a deepening sense of anxiety.

She was genuinely interested in the Sheldonite's abilities. To get to his level in under a hundred and fifty years illustrated a phenomenal achievement. There was a lot she could learn from him, provided she could get him talking.

Then there was the whole Sheldonite culture thing. Thousands of people on hundreds of External Worlds trying to emulate their ancient hyper-capitalist idol. An emulation dangerously close to blind worship, she thought. But she was willing to suspend judgement until she experienced it first-hand. Maybe this was the route she should be taking. Even Bovey couldn't deny Sheldonism was the pinnacle of business culture. Successful Sheldonism, that was. There were enough failed adherents littered across the External Worlds.

And finally the harem. Typical male fantasy; a rich man making his dreams come true. Yet a lot more common than in Sheldon's day; group-life-partner relationships were growing in popularity among the External Worlds. And she was hardly in any position to criticize; what she'd enjoyed with Bovey was essentially the same arrangement. So here she was, technically free and single, and still interested in experimenting sexually to see what suited her. She didn't think this was going to be her, but she'd surprised herself before with Bovey.

A last wild fling, then. So whatever I discover, this weekend will be win-win.

With that delinquent thought warming her, the capsule finally made land and began to fly over Likan's estate. He owned an area of a hundred thousand square miles, taking in a long stretch of coastline – developed with resort complexes. Massive tracts of farmland with square-mile fields, growing every imaginable luxury crop, the kind nobody produced in a culinary unit, tended by over a million agribots; all processed in immaculately hygienic cybernated factories and sold under his own brands.

Then there was Albany, his industrial complex. Set on a flat plain, it was a square eight miles to a side; tall boxy buildings laid out in a perfect grid; every one a factory or processing plant. A spaceport spread out of one side, long rows of landing pads stretching across the green meadows to a nearby river. Ocean barges clotted the water, while fat cargo starships formed near-solid lines stretching up through the sky. No humans actually lived in Albany itself; the technicians who kept it running were all housed in dormitory towns twenty miles away. She flew over one of them, surprised by how nice it looked, with large houses and plenty of green space, ornate civic buildings providing every amenity.

He owns it all. And more: he created it. Now that is real vision.

Her capsule's net was queried by local traffic control. She supplied her identity certificate and received a descent vector.

Likan's home was actually three separate buildings. Two of them were on the shore of a lake ten miles long. One was a giant chateau made of stone which must have had five hundred rooms. Araminta had seen smaller villages. The second, almost opposite the first, was an ultramodern ovoid of shimmering opalescence that seemed to dip down into the water as it lay longside across the ground. The third was small by comparison, just a wooden lodge atop the cliffs of a rugged island.

The capsule landed outside the ovoid. Araminta was quietly grateful. She wanted to see what it was like inside, if there were any design concepts she could use.

Two of the harem were waiting to greet her when she stepped out. Clemance, a slim teenager, dressed in a simple white shirt and blue cotton shorts. She had a fresh face, freckled on her nose and brow, an eager smile, and fair hair that was barely styled. Not quite what Araminta had expected. While the other, Marakata, was tall and classically beautiful, with ebony skin that gleamed in the sunlight. Her scarlet gown probably cost more than every item Araminta had brought put together. *And that's what she wears in the middle of the afternoon?* Subtle cosmetic scales highlighted jade eyes and a wide mouth. She didn't smile, her whole attitude was one of cool amusement.

Clemance bounded forward, her smile growing even wider. She threw her arms around Araminta. 'Likan has told us all about you. It's so great to finally get to meet you.'

A mildly startled Araminta gave the girl a tentative hug back. 'What did he say?'

'To be careful,' Marakata said. She raised an elegant eyebrow, observing Araminta's response.

'He says you're really ambitious, and smart, and attractive, and your own boss—' Clemance seemed to run out of breath. 'Just all-round fabulous.'

Araminta finally managed to disentangle herself from the girl. 'I didn't realize I'd made such an impression.'

'Likan makes very fast assessments,' Marakata said.

'Do you?' Araminta asked, as cool as she could.

It actually drew a small smile from the imposing woman. 'I take my time and get it absolutely right.'

'Good to know.'

Clemance giggled. 'Come on, we'll show you your room.' She grabbed Araminta's hand and pulled like a five-year-old hauling her parent to the Christmas tree.

'The staff will get your bags,' Marakata said airily.

Araminta frowned, then saw she wasn't joking. A couple of women in identical smart grey toga suits were heading for her capsule, followed by a regrav sled. 'You have human staff?'

'Of course.'

'So Nigel Sheldon must have had them.'

'Humm, you are quite quick, aren't you?'

Clemance laughed, and pulled harder. 'Come on! I chose this one for you.'

They were right up against the scintillating surface. Araminta hadn't realized how big the ovoid was. Standing at the base it must have reached ten storeys above her, though the curvature made it hard to tell. There were no discernible features, certainly no door. The entire base was surrounded by a broad marble path, as if it were resting on a plinth. A couple of thin gold lines had materialized underfoot, which Clemance had followed. She slipped through the torrent of multicoloured light. Araminta followed. It was similar to walking through a pressure field, or a spore shower, a slight tingle on the skin, bright flash against the eye, and she was in a bubble-chamber with transparent furniture delineated by glowing emerald lines, like curving laser beams. Closets and drawers were all empty, chairs and couches contained a more diffuse glow inside their cushions, looking like faulty portal projections. The floor and cupola walls were a duller version of the external scintillations. Only the cream and gold sheets on the bed were what she thought of as tangible.

'The house smartnet is offering an operations program,' her u-shadow told her.

'Accept it.' Her exovision showed her the file opening into a storage lacuna.

Clemance was already sitting on the edge of the bed, bouncing up and down. 'Like it?'

'The house's main entrance opens into a guest bedroom?'

'Only when you need it to be,' the girl said sprightly. 'Tell your control program you want to see out.'

Araminta did, and the walls on one side lost their lustre to show the gardens outside, and her capsule with the regrav sled loading up cases.

'Now, if you need the bathroom . . .' Clemance said. The whole room started to slide upwards, following the curvature of the external wall. There must have been excellent gravity compensators hidden somewhere below the floor because Araminta didn't feel any movement. Then they were sliding horizontally into the centre of the ovoid. Other bubble rooms flowed past them.

Araminta imagined this was the perspective which corpuscles had as they raced through a vein. She smiled in delight. 'How brilliant, the whole thing is protean.'

Her bedroom touched a bathroom, and the wall rolled apart to give her access. The design beyond the new door was more conventional, with a huge pool-bath, showers, dryer chambers. It was bigger than the living rooms back in the apartments she was developing.

'You want to see someone, or go to the dining room for dinner, or just change the view – tell the house,' Marakata said.

'I will,' Araminta said positively.

A door opened opposite the bathroom, and Marakata stepped through. Araminta caught a glimpse of an all-white chamber with a long desk, and gym apparatus. 'I'll see you later,' Marakata said, and the door swept shut behind her.

'Was that a threat?' Araminta muttered.

'Oh ignore her,' Clemance said. 'She's always shy around new people. She's a lot more fun in bed, honest.'

'I'm sure.' Araminta turned round, giving the room a

more thorough inspection. The drawers began to fill up with her clothes. The process was like watching water bubble up into a glass. 'Take me to Likan,' she told her u-shadow.

The room closed the door into the bathroom. Curving walls slipped past; horizontally then curving to vertical. 'And opaque the walls.' Gravity might be perfectly stable, but the sight was strangely disorientating.

Likan's room was huge. Araminta suspected it didn't move often. Everything else in the house would be displaced. It was circular with a polished oak floor which appeared to be a single giant segment. Vat grown; she'd read a file on the process in one of her design courses. The walls were pale pink and blue, with a translucent eggshell texture. They slipped into transparency along a third of the length, providing a panorama out across the lake.

Likan was walking towards her, dressed in a simple mauve sweatshirt and long green shorts. Small coloured symbols were shrinking around him, then vanishing. The walls must be portals, she thought, which gave them a vast projection capacity. This was probably his office. He smiled warmly, paused in front of her and gave her a kiss. The kind of kiss that told her what he was expecting from her later.

'Great house,' she said.

'I knew you'd like it. The concept is an old one, but we've just got the manufacturing process down to an affordable level. Not easy without Higher replicators.'

'I'd like to have the Colwyn City franchise.'

He responded with a warm, admiring smile. 'Now see, most developers would have made a crack about me putting them out of business. But you . . . you see how to adapt and move onward. That's what makes you stand out.'

'Thank you.'

Clemance scampered over to a new door. 'Catch you later.'

Likan waved dismissively as he led Araminta over to the transparent wall. 'Drink? Food?' he asked.

'I'm good for a few hours.'

'Good. The Prime Minister and two cabinet ministers are coming for dinner.'

'Are you trying to impress me?'

'They were coming anyway. But hopefully it gives you an idea of the life I lead. To get this big you have to delve into politics.'

'Colwyn City Hall can be a beast issuing permits.'

'Take the development officer for dinner. Loan your local councillor a high-end capsule. They're all in it for what they can get. Wouldn't be feeding from the public trough otherwise.'

'Unless they're in it to clean up the corruption.'

'Yeah. Those ones are a problem. Fortunately, they don't tend to last long.'

'You're a cynic.'

'Pragmatist, if you don't mind. I'm also a lot more experienced than you in every field. So trust me when I say politicians all have their weakness.'

'What's yours?' she teased.

'One, I'm an easy lay. But you already know that. Two, risk. Risk is my weakness. The sensation when a risk pays off is like nothing else. I always take the risk. I enjoy the reward too much not to.'

'So what risk are you taking right now?'

'You're smart, you've researched me. The finance files, at least. Tell me.'

'I accessed some background on my way over. Opinion is you're dangerously overextended.'

'And those loans have grown significantly in the last couple of years. So why do you think that is?'

'You're going to wipe out property companies with houses like this one? Flood the market.'

He grinned. 'Small scale. I think big. Besides, it'll take a decade for something like this to first become fashionable then generally accepted. Think, what's the most pressing problem Viotia has today?'

'Living Dream?'

'Kind of. Ellezelin is always looming over us. Rightly so. The Free Trade Zone is a massive market; it's not going away and it's always growing. Anyone already operating in it has a huge financial and production capacity advantage over some poor little Viotia company. The worry is that when they eventually open a wormhole here all our companies will lose out to cheap imports. Trade will be one way.'

Her mind went back to Albany, the sheer scale of the place. 'You're going to undercut them.'

'Albany is as automated as anyone can be without replicators. I've spent a decade investing in the most advanced cybernated systems we can have to drive production costs down. To do that, to push each unit cost as low as it can physically go, you have to have massive volume production. That's what's killing me at the moment. The factories are barely ticking over. But when that wormhole finally opens . . .'

'It's not going to be the financial massacre they expect.'

'They import. I export. Only the quantity of those exports will be ten times greater than they assume.'

'You'd need a distribution network.'

His smile was triumphant as he turned out to face the lake. 'Certainly would.'

'Wow,' she said. And meant it. Likan's ambition was so great hers wouldn't even register on the same scale. 'Why tell me? You can't be trying to impress me into bed. You've already got that.'

'Although I have an egotistical opinion of my own ability, I can't actually manage every aspect by myself, even with an augmented mentality. Too many details. For an expansion phase on this level, I need people I can trust in senior management positions; especially offworld.'

'That's very flattering.'

'Yes and no. You'd be capable management, I think; you have the right kind of drive and mindset. You don't have the experience to be top rank, but that will come.'

She frowned. 'Why me?'

'How much research did you really do? On Sheldon himself?'

'None,' she admitted. 'Just what I picked up in school.'

'The old Dynasties were just that, family enterprises. The surest way humans have ever come up with to retain loyalty and control. Nigel used his own flesh and blood.'

'Ah.' It was as if the room was suddenly on the move: downwards.

'All the senior positions were held by his own children,' Likan said. 'That's also what I do.'

A memory abruptly rushed to the fore of her mind. 'Debbina?' she said before she could stop it.

Likan actually winced. 'What did I ever do to you? No,

okay, not my beloved little girl. But a lot of my other children are running sections of my company.'

'And how do I fit into this?'

'How do you think?'

'Spell it out for me.'

'You become one of my wives. You have my children. They take their place in the company.'

'You really know how to romance a girl.'

He flashed her a wry smile. 'Come on, we're grown-ups. Every marriage today is half business. We'll have a great time in bed. I can afford any lifestyle you want. Your children grow up being part of the most dynamic company in this section of the Commonwealth. They'll never want for anything, and they'll be presented with virtually unlimited challenges. I know you well enough to know that appeals. Who wants trust-fund brats, right? And the same goes for you. Stick with me for ten, fifteen years, then you can either continue with a post in the company, or you cut loose with a huge chunk of money and enough insider knowledge to run circles around everyone else.'

'Ozzie's mother! Are you serious?'

'Perfectly.'

'It's very flattering, but isn't it a bit sudden?'

'You think Sheldon hesitated when he saw something he wanted? No way. He went out and got it. And this isn't quite that sudden, now is it? We had a connection back at my symposium; you're not going to deny that, now are you?'

'No,' she admitted.

'So. There's physical attraction. Which just leaves your abilities. I did some research.'

'Your fifth assistant's coffee boy did some research.'

'Indeed,' he acknowledged wryly. 'You're the original kid from nowhere. Rejects the cosy family business route. Looking to get out. Failed marriage. Now on the bounce-back curve. You're hungry. And capable. With the experience my organization can provide you'll flourish.' He sidled up close, and put his arm round her, kissing again, more gently this time. 'I don't want an answer this instant. This is why you're here. Experience everything you can and you want, then take you time and decide.'

Wow, second time I've had that proposal in a month.

'Okay,' she said shakily. 'I'll do that.'

'You mean it? You're not just saying that?'

'No. I mean it.'

Araminta didn't wear her own clothes for dinner. That was the first thing she learned about what membership of the harem would be like. A stylist called Helenna was waiting in her bedroom when it collected her from Likan's airy office. A jovial woman, close to rejuvenation, whose age meant she'd piled on a lot of weight in recent years. Genuinely friendly, she was keen to confide household gossip, most of which made no sense to Araminta, although there was a lot of it. She'd been with Likan for fifty years. 'So I know it all, honey, seen even more. I don't judge anyone, and nothing you do here is going to surprise me. You want anything *special* for tonight, you just ask me for it.' Araminta wasn't sure what counted as that *special*. It was tempting to ask what other girls had requested. One thing Helenna was sure of was that, 'Likan likes his women elegant. So we've got to get you spruced up, ready to stand your own ground against the others.'

That took hours. Her bedroom bounded all over the

ovoid house to link up with various other specialist rooms. The sauna to start with, clearing her pores. Massage, by a man called Nifran, who was as brutal as he was skilful; afterwards she just sort of poured herself off the table with loose floppy limbs. The fitting room. *A house that has a fitting room?* Where she was measured up for her evening dress.

Spiralling down to the salon, where Helenna was finally exposed as a sorceress. Layers of cosmetic membrane were applied, yet when Araminta looked in the mirror there was no sign of them. Instead her nineteen-year-old self looked back at her. A nineteen that she'd never known but always wanted, with sharp cheekbones, absolutely no excess flesh, soft long eyelashes, perfectly clear skin, eyes that sparkled. Another hour saw her hair *repaired*, as Helenna disapprovingly termed the first procedure. Then extended, thickened, softened, waved, and styled.

Clemance had the chair next to her as it was being done. Another member of the harem, Alsena, took the other side. They chatted comfortably enough, which was an insight into the kind of sisterhood the women had. She was given a rundown of Likan's genealogy with emphasis on the wayward children, a saga for which she needed to open a new file in a storage lacuna to keep track of.

For all their friendliness, the girls weren't quite *engaged* with the real world. Which was a pretty bitchy observation, but one Araminta felt applied. If Likan wanted women like her, what was he doing with the others? They certainly didn't aspire to run sections of his corporate empire.

'He likes variety,' Helenna told her as the salon rendezvoused back with the fitting room.

The classic *little black dress* had never fallen out of style.

And looking at the one the fitting room's apprentice sorceresses had conjured up for her, Araminta could see why. She felt randy just slipping into it – so Ozzie alone knew what effect it would have on any male that crossed her path. It clung disgracefully, yet allowed her breasts complete freedom of movement. She blushed the first time she walked in it. Somehow the high hem and silk-gloss microfabric sprayed on her legs made her calves and thighs slim down to that same nineteen-year-old ideal Helenna's spell had blessed her face with for the night.

Pre-dinner cocktails were served to the household and Likan's guests in the music room, which had claimed his office's lake view. Araminta walked in with her head held high, knowing just how great she looked. Likan's double-take, and the smiles from the harem, Clemance's little bounce as she clapped her hands excitedly, were all the accolades she was simply due. It all helped buoy her confidence close to levels of arrogance. So when Likan introduced her to the Prime Minister and her husband, she was perfectly civil, and treated them as if they were almost her equal.

All the while as she made small talk and sampled weird-tasting canapés she kept wondering how Bovey would behave if he were here. He enjoyed his culture, and could be as snobbish about food and wine as anyone. But the company she mingled with; the world's powerful and wealthy, and a few merely famous – she just couldn't get away from the idea of how he'd turn his nose up at them.

Yet here I am, holding my own.

The evening did have a downside. The Prime Minister's husband, who she was seated next to at the dinner table, was fantastically boring. Thankfully, Eridal, one of Likan's older sons, sat on her other side. As smart and charming as Likan, he ran a finance house in Ludor; but he lacked that bullish determination which drove his father. She dutifully tried to not spend the whole evening chatting to him.

When it was all over, after the dining hall had descended to ground level so the guests could walk to their capsules, there were just Likan and eight of his harem left. The door contracted and the walls resumed their sparkle; everyone gave a spontaneous laugh of release which Araminta joined in wholeheartedly.

Likan gave her a congratulatory kiss. 'Dammit I'd forgotten how awful that dickhead was,' he told her. 'I wanted to smack him one, and he wasn't even talking to me. Thanks for putting up with him.'

Doors were opening into various bedrooms around the dining hall. The harem were vanishing through them. Out of all the women at the dinner, they were undeniably the most beautiful, most of them astonishingly so. Despite all Helenna's efforts, Araminta couldn't help but feel like the poor relation in their presence.

'Go and get ready,' Likan told her. 'We'll be waiting.'

He turned and left through a door into a small darkened room. Araminta stared after him for a moment, then summoned her own bedroom. That whole alpha male issuing orders thing just didn't do it for her. For one, he didn't have the charisma to pull it off, not with his dress sense and throwback physical appearance. On the other hand to have accomplished so much was darkly compelling. She grinned at her own inner argument. *What the hell, at least Clemance will be fun.*

'Dress me the way he'll enjoy,' she told the waiting

Helenna. A process which turned out to be more elaborate than she anticipated. For a start it involved Nifran again, who chided her about lack of proper exercise, and how he couldn't relax her enough. What he did with her legs was virtually sex in itself.

Helenna applied some fabulously scented oil which acted in conjunction with Nifran's pummelling to make her flesh glow.

'He's not into sadism or anything, is he?' Araminta asked. These preparations were all very detailed. Her usual idea of getting ready for a hot night was wearing something a man could remove quickly.

'Not to worry, sweetie, he enjoys sex the way he enjoys his women; tasteful.'

Pondering that, Araminta allowed Helenna to dress her. The white negligee was mostly straps, yet perversely managed to cover more of her body than the black dress. She checked herself out in the mirror. *So his idea of tasteful is a Slut Princess? How very male.*

Her bedroom whisked her away to Likan's boudoir – no other word for it. Vast bed in the middle, naughty-shaped furniture, low rose-gold lighting. Harem in attendance, and yes, dressed *elegantly* in silk and satin, with open gowns swirling, lounging on couches sipping champagne as they watched two of their number make love on the bed.

Araminta strolled in, trying not to appear too apprehensive. Likan greeted her, wearing a black robe. 'Champagne?' he offered.

'Thank you.' She took a crystal flute from Marakata, who gave her a detailed appraisal. There was something alarmingly erotic about the way the aloof woman seemed able to look right through the negligee.

'You two should kiss,' Likan said.

Araminta pressed herself against the statuesque woman, enjoying the sensual touch. Marakata certainly knew how to kiss.

When they'd finished Araminta took a sip of the champagne as Likan took her hand and led her slowly over to the couch where Alsena was waiting. Araminta knelt down, and began the kiss.

As she went on to kiss all the other women as he instructed, Araminta decided the experience wasn't so much tasteful as formulaic. Likan had ritualized his lovemaking. Finally she kissed him. After that she was taken over to the bed. There was a specific way of kneeling he wanted her to assume, very sex kittenish. One of the harem helped arrange her hair decoratively over her shoulder.

Clemance removed Likan's gown. Araminta stared at his huge erection.

'I have a gift for you.'

'Yes,' she said emphatically. 'I see that.'

'A program.'

'Huh?'

'A melange I've composed myself over several years. It allows you deeper access to your own mind, opening levels that verge on the subconscious in the way the old yogis achieved through meditation.'

'Right,' she said dubiously. Talk about killing the mood.

He smiled fondly, and stroked her cheek. 'I use it myself to focus. It helps to clean your mind of extraneous thought. You can revert to the animal basics which form our core identity.' His face came close to hers. 'There are no inhibitions to be had in such a state. Whatever you pursue is unashamedly pure.'

'No inhibitions?'

'Clarity is a helpful tool for business. But also for lovemaking. You can concentrate on the sensations of your body to the exclusion of anything else. It helps to amplify even the smallest nerve signal.'

'You mean I can make a climax stronger?' It sounded like an electronic version of the sex aerosols she and Bovey used.

'Yes. There are also adapted biofeedback routines which can influence your physical self. Once you determine the origin of your body's pleasure, you can repeat it.' His voice became softer, tempting. 'As many times as you have the physical strength for.'

Her u-shadow told her he was offering the program. Suddenly, she was feeling very hot in the negligee. 'Scan it for infiltrators and trojans,' she told her u-shadow as she held his level gaze.

'It's clean.'

'Load and run.' Through her exovision she watched the program expand into one of her lacunas. It had many similarities with a learning program, which she allowed to mushroom into her grey matter. Instinctive knowledge bubbled away in her mind.

'Don't be afraid,' Likan said softly. 'I'll use it with you. It will make our first time spectacular.'

She nodded, not trusting herself to speak. Now she considered it, clearing her mind was a simple process; following the rising sleep cycles yet never accepting them. Her breathing steadied, and she grew aware of the body's rhythms, the flow of nervous energy. Heartbeat. Peripheral thoughts fell away, allowing her to centre herself in the boudoir, on the bed. Her awareness grew of the light touch of fabric against her skin. Tiny beads of perspiration clung to her. The sound of bubbles fizzing in the crystal flutes. Likan's breathing. She saw his arm move out, a finger beckon.

Marakata answered the summons, sliding sinuously over the mattress. Her fingers stroked Araminta's skin. The sensations her nerves experienced flowed like a tidal wave into her brain. She gasped at the impact, and pulled her attention to the sensations which were most pleasurable. Wallowing in them.

Under Likan's direction, Marakata plucked the negligee straps off Araminta's shoulders. Air flowed over her exposed breasts, followed by warm fingers. Araminta shuddered fiercely at the touch, smiling as she centred her mind on the feeling. Blood was loud and hot as it rushed into her nipples, swelling the buds.

'There,' she told the owner of the fingers.

The caress was repeated, the ecstasy replicated. Then many hands were gliding over her. Warm eager mouths kissed. She wailed with helpless delight at the symphony of sensation which the harem kindled. The negligee was removed completely. Instinctively she arched her back. Likan's cock slid inside her. The experience was close to unbearable, it was all there was. Still her mind remained steadfast on the torrent of physical joy. Araminta promised herself, no matter what, she would not faint away as she had done with Bovey. This time there were no chemicals fugging her mind, this time she was free to experience its incredible conclusion. She laughed and wept simultaneously as Likan started to move in a powerful rhythm. Then the harem recommenced their virtuoso performance.

*

The Skylord glided across the outer atmosphere of the solid planet; its vacuum wings long since retracted. Thick turbulent streams of the ionosphere swept across its forward section, creating lengthy vibrations across its giant bulk. Energy stirred in specific patterns within it, thoughts mingling with its body's elemental power, manipulating the fabric of the universe outside. Its speed began to slow, as it imposed its wishes on reality. Gently it started to lower itself into the atmosphere. Far below, the minds of the sentient entities sang out in welcome.

'Now!' Cleric Conservator Ethan commanded the obedient waiting minds of the Dream Masters.

Their thoughts flared out into the gaiafield in a single stream, pushing at the dream fabric, seeking entry. Tendrils of raw will prodded and poked at the stubbornly resistant image emanating from the Second Dreamer. As the Skylord began to focus its attention on the ancient coastal city beneath, they felt its perception turn outwards, towards them. It felt them! It knew they were there!

'My Lord,' Ethan called with profound respect. 'We need your help.'

The Skylord's descent halted. Those dreaming the Skylord felt the mass of the planet press against the magnificent creature's perception. In that way they *knew* the winds that blew across the Iguru Plain. Experienced the waves rolling lazily over the Lyot Sea towards the coast. And there, right underneath them, so tantalizingly close, the physical form of Makkathran's buildings brushed against their consciousness. Each one exactly as it was in Inigo's dreams.

Adoration and gratitude swelled out into the gaiafield,

buoying Ethan's thoughts along. 'We seek to reach you. Show us the way to you, my Lord. Receive us.'

The dream shattered into a glorious pinnacle of agony. The Skylord's magisterial thoughts were wrenched away by a terrible power.

'NO!' the Second Dreamer commanded amid the ruined bliss. 'I am me.'

An infinite black surface swelled with malignant anger, sealing the gulf between the gaiafield and the Skylord.

Blinding pain seared deep into Ethan's mind as the blackness snapped at him. He screamed, every muscle contorting to fling him out of his chair and fall into merciful unconscious.

Araminta woke with a gasp, shooting upright on the bed; heart racing and breath coming in judders. She instinctively applied the program's knowledge again; settling her racing mind and quelling her body's distress. It worked a treat.

What the fuck is it with that dream?

It had been quite pleasant to start with, drifting gently above a strange planet; warm sun on her back, mysterious continents rolling by underneath. Then something happened, a smothering sensation that triggered an adrenaline rush, and she had to thrash about, trying to wake herself. Push herself clear from that oppressive constriction. It was as if someone was trying to steal her soul. She yelled defiance at the dark force, and finally managed to wake.

Kicking and writhing around as she shouted. Surely? Yet actually all she seemed to have done was shuffle round a bit and sit up.

She looked about her in confusion. Likan's boudoir was still illuminated by the same warm light. Nobody else was awake. Clemance was curled up beside her, one arm draped over her legs. The girl was stirring, blinking in confusion as Araminta moved. Araminta stroked her tangled hair and cheek, soothing her as she would a troubled child. A drowsy Clemance smiled worshipfully then closed her eyes again.

Araminta blew out an exasperated breath, and slowly sank back down. Despite the supple mattress her body was stressed tight – which would no doubt annoy Nifran. As she lay there rigid, she could hear two of the harem whimpering softly in their sleep. So she wasn't the only one suffering a bad dream. She wondered if she should creep across the room to wake them. But eventually they subsided into a deeper sleep. Yet she still couldn't relax and drop off. There was something scrabbling about in her subconscious that was unsettling her, an elusive memory she was trying to connect. Not the dream, something before that.

Once again, the program came to her aid. She cleared her mind and concentrated on her memories of the orgy. Physically, it had been hugely satisfying – no denying that. And the harem had delighted in teaching her a whole range of sensual acts which they and Likan enjoyed. But it was that ritual thing again; true passion had been missing, and with it the heat which came from abandoning herself the way she did with Bovey. This had been a little too much like mechanics, with all of them busy doing as Likan instructed.

Araminta sat up on the bed again, her skin cooling with shock. The memory of Likan and Marakata was perfectly clear in her mind, all thanks to his own wonderful program. *And how's that for irony.* She thought it through again, then reviewed some other suspicious recollections before finally dropping her head into her hands and groaning in dismay. 'Oh shit.'

True to her word, Helenna didn't judge. She made no comment as the house emptied the drawers and closets, the clothes slithering away through the interstices between the rooms to fill her cases in the butler's lodge. Araminta almost wanted to ask how many others she'd seen leave abruptly after a night with Likan. But that would have been unfair on both of them.

Her bedroom wound through the ovoid house, and opened a door on to the path which ran round the outside of the building. Dawn light was shining a murky grey off the placid lake. Two of the household's smartly suited staff were loading her cases back into her carry capsule.

'It's a shame, sweetie,' Helenna said. 'I had you down as one who'd fit in easily here.'

'Me too,' Araminta said. Gave the maid a quick hug. 'Thanks for everything.'

'Hey, it was nice meeting you.'

Araminta turned and walked out of the bedroom. The door unrolled behind her.

'Wait!' Clemance called out. 'You can't leave!' She was hurrying out of another door, ten metres away, trying to pull on a translucent wrap.

Likan walked behind her, considerably more composed in a thick dark-purple robe. 'Not even going to say goodbye?' he asked. There was a nasty frown on his puggish face.

'The house's net is active. You knew I was leaving. If

you wanted to say anything before I left, you could,' Araminta told him. 'And here you are.'

'Yes, here I am. I would like to know why you're running out. I think I'm entitled after the offer I made you. I know you enjoyed yourself last night. So what is this?'

Araminta glanced at the distraught girl who was hovering between them, uncertain who to go to. 'Are you sure?'

Likan took a step forward and put his arm around Clemance's shoulder, helping to pull her wrap on. 'I don't keep anything from my wives.'

'Even that they're psychoneural profiled?'

His face remained impassive. 'It was helpful to begin with.'

'*Helpful?*' she cried. 'You had them bred to be your slaves. Profiling like that is illegal, it always has been. It's a vile, inhuman thing to do. They don't have a choice. They don't have free will. It's obscene! Why, for Ozzie's sake? You don't need to force people into your bed. I would have probably joined you. And I know there are thousands of others who'd love the chance. Why did you do it?'

Likan glanced down at Clemance with an almost paternal expression. 'They were the first,' he said simply.

'First?'

'Of my harem. I had to start it somewhere. It was the bootstrap principle.'

'What are you talking about?'

'To start with, when you have nothing, you begin by pulling yourself up by your own bootstraps. I needed to be him, to be Nigel Sheldon. He had a harem, therefore I had one. You don't understand what that man was. He *ruled*

641

hundreds of worlds, billions of people. I wasn't joking when I called him an emperor. He was the greatest human who ever lived. I need to know how to think like he did.' He almost ground the words out.

'So you created slaves to achieve that?'

'They're not slaves. All of us are predisposed to various personality traits. The way they combine: that's what makes us individuals. I just amplified a few of the behavioural attributes in the girls.'

'Yeah: submissiveness! I watched them last night, Likan. They obeyed you like they were bots.'

'The relationship is a lot more complex than that.'

'That's what it boils down to. Why didn't you profile yourself to think like Sheldon? If you have to wreck somebody, why not yourself?'

'I have incorporated his known neural characteristics into my DNA. But a neural structure is only a vessel for personality. You need the environment as well. As complete as you can make it.'

'Oh, for Ozzie's sake! You have deliberately, maliciously bred slaves. And you think that's an acceptable way to achieve what you are. That makes me sick. I don't want any part of you or your perverted family. You won't even let them go! Why don't you remove their profiling when they go for rejuvenation treatment?'

'I created them because of my belief, wrongly in your opinion; now you think they should be altered because of your belief. Does that strike you as slightly ironic? There's an old saying that two wrongs don't make a right. I take responsibility for my wives, especially the profiled ones – just as Sheldon would have done.'

Araminta glowered at him, then she switched her attention to Clemance, softening her expression to plead. 'Come with me. Come away from here. It's reversible. I can show you what it's like to be free, to be truly human. I know you don't believe me, but just please try. Try, Clemance.'

'You're such a fool,' the girl said. She pressed harder into Likan. 'I'm not profiled. I like this. I like being in the harem. I like the money. I like the life. I like that my children will rule whole planets. Without Likan, what will yours ever be?'

'Themselves,' Araminta said weakly.

Clemance gave her a genuinely pitying look. 'That's not good enough for me.'

Araminta raised an uncertain hand. 'Is she . . . ?'

'There were only ever three,' Likan said. 'Clemance is not one of them. Would you like to guess again?'

Araminta shook her head. She didn't trust herself to speak. *Marakata. Marakata is one, I know. Perhaps if I just . . .*

'Goodbye,' Likan said.

Araminta climbed into the carry capsule, and told it to take her home.

*

Oscar had never thought he'd return to the very place where he died. Of course, he hadn't expected to see Paula Myo again, either.

Just to make matters worse, enterprising Far Away natives had turned his last desperate hyperglide flight into a tourist attraction. Worse still, it was a failing attraction.

Still, at least Oscar had got to name the brand-new starship which ANA had delivered to Orakum for him, and without much thought went and called it the *Elvin's*

Payback. There was a large briefing file sitting in its smartcore, which he zipped through and sent a few queries to Paula, who by then was back in her own starship and en route to somewhere. She wouldn't say where.

After he'd finished the file, one thing became very clear to him. Paula had severely overestimated his abilities. There were a lot of very powerful, very determined groups searching for the Second Dreamer. Now that might not have fazed Paula, but ... 'I'm only a pilot,' he repeated to her when she called him on a secure TD channel and asked him why he was flying to Far Away. She hadn't said she could track the *Elvin's Payback*, but somehow he wasn't surprised.

'I'm going to need help. And as you trust me, so I trust someone else.' He got an evil little buzz out of not telling her who. Though he suspected she would know – it was hardly hyperspace science.

He landed at Armstrong City starport, which was a huge field to the north-east of the city itself with four big terminal buildings handling passenger flights and a grid of warehouses where the freighters came and went. He picked out a parking pad out near the fence, away from any real activity. As the starship descended he swept its visual sensors across the ancient city that spread back from the shore of the North Sea. Inevitably, there was a dense congregation of tall towers and pyramids above the coast; while broad estates of big houses swamped the land behind. It was all a lot more chaotic than the layout of most Commonwealth cities, which he rather enjoyed. He was looking for a glimpse of Highway One, the historic road where his friends had chased the Starflyer to its doom. All that remained now was a long, fat urban strip following the old route as it struck out for miles across the Great Iril Steppes, as if city buildings were seeking to escape from their historical anchor at the centre. Like every Commonwealth world, Far Away's ground traffic was now a shrinking minority. The sky above the city swarmed with regrav capsules.

Oscar floated down out of the airlock underneath the *Elvin's Payback*, and stood once more on the ground of Far Away. For some ridiculous reason he was trembling. He took a long moment, breathing in the air, then moved away from the starship. His feet pushed gently on the short grass, sending his body gliding in a short arc in the low gravity. He'd forgotten how enjoyable that part of this world was, those soar-lope steps were a freedom like having teenage hormones again.

Once he'd cleared the starship he stopped and turned a full circle. There was the city skyline on one side, some distant mountains. Nothing he recognized. Apart from the glorious sapphire sky. Thankfully, that had remained the same, as the planet's biosphere slowly regenerated with the new plants and creatures which humans had brought to this world.

Warm sea air gusted constantly from the passage of starships using the terminals, ruffling his hair. It was all very different to Orakum's main starport which he flew from, and had barely fifty flights a day. But then Far Away was the self-proclaimed capital of the External Worlds; the planet which had refused political and economic integration with the Greater Commonwealth. Even today, it was technically only an affiliate member. Its staunch independence had inspired a whole generation of newly settled worlds after the Starflyer War. The political will, coupled with the end of CST's transport monopoly which the starships brought, allowed the first cultural division to open within Commonwealth society as a whole. As the Sheldon Dynasty made biononics available, starting Higher culture, so Far Away's Barsoomians introduced genetic improvements which took the human body far beyond its natural meridian, developing into the Advancer movement. After that, Far Away with its fierce libertarianist tradition declared itself the ideological counterweight to Earth and ANA. The Commonwealth's Senators might regard the notion with their ancient wise distain, but Far Away's citizens *believed* their own destiny.

Oscar smiled at the busy city as he experienced the emotional tide of the local gaiafield. Even that had a stridency which celebrated the stubbornness of the inhabitants. His u-shadow opened a channel to the planetary cybersphere, and called a one-time address code he'd been given eighty-six years earlier, on the day he emerged from the re-life clinic. To his surprise, it was answered immediately.

'Yes?'

'I need to see you,' Oscar said. 'I have a problem and I need help sorting it out.'

'Who the fuck are you, and how did you steal this code?'

'I am Oscar Monroe, and this code was given to me. Some time ago.'

There was a long pause, though the channel remained open.

'If you are an impostor, you have one chance to walk away, and that chance is now.'

'I know who I am,' Oscar said.

'We'll know if you are.'

'Good.'

'Very well. Be at the Kime Sanctuary on top of Mount Herculaneum in one hour. One of us will meet you.'

The channel went dead. Oscar grinned. He shouldn't be all fired up by this, he really shouldn't.

His u-shadow contacted a local hire company, and he rented a high-performance ingrav capsule. Given who he was going to meet, he didn't want to risk technology leakage by arriving in an ultradrive ship.

The capsule bounced him over to Mount Herculaneum in a semi-ballistic lob that took twenty-eight minutes. The last time he'd seen the colossal volcano was the day he died by crashing into its lower slopes. Today, his arrival was all a lot more comfortable. The capsule shot out of the upper atmosphere, and followed the planet's curvature southwest. He watched through the sensors as the Grand Triad rose up out of the horizon. They were still the biggest mountains to be found on an H-congruous world. On a planet with a standard gravity, they would have collapsed under their own weight, but here they had kept on growing as the magma pushed further and further upwards. Mount Herculaneum, the biggest, stood thirty-two kilometres high, its plateau summit rising high above Far Away's troposphere. Northwards, Mount Zeus topped out at seventeen kilometres. While south of Herculaneum, Mount Titan reached twenty-three kilometres high; it was the only one of the Triad to remain active.

Oscar's capsule rode a tight curve above the sea-like grasslands of the Aldrin Plains before it began to sink back down again. The view was magnificent, with the vast cone of Herculaneum spread out below him. Its plateau of grubby brown regolith was broken by twin calderas.

Around that, naked rock dropped down to the glacier ring far below, before the lower slopes were finally smothered in pine forests and low meadowland. Luckily for him, Titan was semi-active today. He looked down almost vertically into its glowing red crater, watching the slow-motion ripples spreading out across the huge lake of lava. Radiant white boulders spat upwards out of the inferno to traverse lazy arcs through the vacuum, spitting off orange sparks. Some of them were flung far enough to clear the crater wall and begin their long fall to oblivion.

His sight was inevitably drawn to the long funnel canyon between Zeus and Titan which led to the base of Herculaneum. Stakeout canyon, where the storm winds coming off the Hondu Ocean were funnelled into a rampaging blast of air, which the insane thrill seekers of the early Commonwealth used to fly their hypergliders along, allowing them to sail on winds so strong they'd push them out of the atmosphere and over Herculaneum. He'd never got to attempt that last part, because he crashed his hyperglider into Anna, so Wilson might stand a chance to reach the summit.

Even though he'd braced himself for some emotional shockwave at seeing the site of his death, he felt nothing more than a mild curiosity. *That must mean I'm perfectly adjusted to this new life. Right?*

As he looked along the long rocky cleft in the ground, his exovision pulled up meteorological data and a file telling him that the winds now were never as strong as they had been a thousand years ago. Terraforming had successfully calmed Far Away's atmosphere. Hypergliding was just a legend now.

The capsule took him down to a big dome situated right

on the eastern edge of Mount Herculaneum's plateau, where the cliffs of Aphrodite's Seat began their sheer eight-kilometre fall. There was a pressure field over the entrance to the dome's landing chamber, a big metal cave with enough room for twenty passenger capsules. It only had two resting inside, with another five ordinary capsules parked nearby.

Oscar stepped through the airlock pressure curtains into the dome's main arena, and paid his 20 FA$ entrance fee from a credit coin which Paula had given him. There were three low buildings inside, lined up behind Aphrodite's Seat. He went over to the first, which the dome's net labelled 'Crash Site'. A whole bunch of tourists were just exiting it, heading for the café next door, chatting excitedly. They never registered him, which he found amusing. It wasn't as if his face was any different now.

It was dark inside, with one wall open to the side of the dome above the cliffs. A narrow winding walkway was suspended three metres over the ground, with a pressure field below it, maintaining a vacuum over the actual regolith. There was also a stabilizer field generator running to preserve the wreckage of the hyperglider. The once-elegant fuselage was crunched up into the side of a rock outcrop, with the plyplastic wings bent and snapped. Oscar remembered how elegant those wings had been fully extended, and sighed.

He walked slowly along the walkway until he was directly above the antique. His heart had slowed right down as he imagined his friend terrified and frantic as the craft skidded along the dusty plateau, slipping and twisting, completely out of control. The fate of an entire species dependent on the outcome, and the cliffs rushing towards him. Oscar frowned as he looked down. The hyperglider was actually upside down, which meant there had been an almighty flip at one point. He looked along the ground to the rim of Aphrodite's Seat, where someone in an ancient pressure suit was sitting.

It was a solido projection, Oscar realized as he came to the end of the walkway. Wilson Kime, his head visible in a not terribly authentic bubble helmet. Pressure suit rips repaired with some kind of epoxy, leaking blood into the regolith. The solido Wilson stared out over the Dessault Mountain Range to the east, where the snow-capped peaks diminished into the bright haze of the curving horizon. This was exactly what the real Wilson had seen, what so many people had died to give him; those which history knew, and still more unknown. Twelve hundred years ago this glorious panorama had provided the data to steer a giant storm into the Starflyer's ship, slaying the beast and liberating the Commonwealth. Today, here on that same spot, he could sit in the Saviour View café next door and buy doughnuts named after himself.

'Without you, we wouldn't be here.'

Oscar started. There was a man standing behind him on the walkway, wearing a very dark toga suit.

Great secret agent I make; anyone can creep up on me.

'Excuse me?' Oscar said.

The man smiled. He was very handsome, with a square jaw, dimpled chin, and a flattish nose. Brown eyes were surrounded by laughter lines. When he opened his wide mouth, startlingly white teeth smiled out. 'I nearly got blown away by that burst of melancholy disappointment you let loose into the gaiafield,' he said. 'It's understandable.' He waved a hand round the darkened chamber. 'This travesty is all that exists to celebrate what you and Wilson achieved. But I promise you, *we* know and appreciate what you did. It is taught to all of our children.'

'We?'

The man bowed his head formally. 'The Knights Guardian. Welcome back to Far Away, Oscar Monroe. How can we help you?'

His name was Tomansio, he said as they walked back to Oscar's capsule. 'In full, Tomansio McFoster Stewart. It was my father who provided you with our code eighty-six years ago.'

'I barely saw him. The government had a tight little cordon around my room. They were anxious I should have my privacy. Yet he just walked right in. And out again, too.'

'We thought you'd forgotten us,' Tomansio said. 'Or worse.'

'I'm not what I used to be,' Oscar said. 'At least, that's what I thought.'

'And yet here you are. It's an interesting time to come and seek us out again, for both the Greater Commonwealth and the galaxy at large. Not the kind of time a man chooses to indulge in nostalgia.'

'No. This has nothing to do with nostalgia.'

They sat themselves in the capsule. 'Do you mind if I navigate?' Tomansio asked. 'You would find it difficult to reach our lands unaided.'

'Of course,' Oscar said. His curiosity rose as they slid out of the dome's landing chamber. 'Where are your lands?'

'Where they've always been. From the north-east corner of the Dessault Mountains all the way to the Oak Sea.' The capsule began to accelerate, streaking northward over the mountains as it gained altitude. For the first time, Oscar saw the High Desert around which the lofty peaks huddled protectively.

'And I couldn't find you? I think that peak is Mount St Omer, isn't it? The *Marie Celeste* crashed close by.'

'Knowing and reaching are two separate things.'

'I didn't know you all turned Buddhist and spoke in fortune cookies.'

Tomansio tilted his head to one side with avian precision. His attractive smile poised. 'Ah, I see. I'm not being deliberately enigmatic. Though perhaps I am guilty of overdramatizing. But you are very precious to us, Oscar. I'm hoping to impress you.'

Just for a moment, Oscar felt as if he'd lived through every one of those eleven hundred years. *He had to history mine to understand me. Jesus fuck.* He'd been far too sheltered with his life partners. Small wonder he always felt as if the house put up a cosy barrier between his little family and the outside world.

'We protect our lands with a T-sphere,' Tomansio said.

'Really? I thought only Earth had one.'

'We don't advertise. It's actually quite an elegant defence on so many levels, although it does require a colossal amount of energy to maintain. If you walk or drive or fly towards us, as you approach our border you're simply teleported to the other side. You can't knock on a door which you can never face. You have to be invited in.'

'Cool.'

The lands they fell towards seemed particularly lush. Thick greenery split by meandering rivers, forest and meadowland squabbling to dominate valleys and rolling hills.

Away to the east, a glimpse of the Oak Sea. They re-entered the atmosphere. Strands of cloud rushed up past the capsule's transparent hull, thickening fast. Then they were through, and a forest canopy unfolded below them, leaves of every colour, trees of immense size. Far Away had always celebrated its unique genetic diversity. Starting with a near-sterile landscape, the terraforming teams had brought the seeds of a hundred planets with them to create the ultimate contrasting florascape.

'Here we go,' Tomansio said as their altitude approached three miles.

The view outside suddenly switched. Oscar jumped in his seat. They were now floating a hundred yards above the ground at the head of a long valley. Blue-green grass rippled away for miles on every side, lapping against woodlands that spilled out of the dips in the valley walls. There were houses all around them, built from wood and stone, blending nicely with the environment, like some medieval village back on Earth. Except this was on a much grander scale.

'You live here?' Oscar asked.

'Yes.'

'I'm envious.'

'Appearances can be deceiving.'

The capsule touched down outside one of the stone houses, a long building with age-blackened wood beams protruding from beneath a slate roof. A balcony ran along one side. Big windows were open, showing a glimpse of a very modern interior. The grass swept right up to the walls, emphasizing the impression of natural harmony.

Oscar stepped out wearily. The gaiafield was resonating with a warm subtle joy, wrapping him in a daydream of a child being swept up in its mother's arms; the comfort and security of being *home*.

It was a welcome emanating from the people hurrying across the land to greet him. They came out of nearby houses, or simply teleported in, popping into existence to enlarge the crowd. Then the horses appeared, a whole cavalry squad riding up over a nearby ridge, dressed in some dark uniform which trailed gold and scarlet heraldic streamers behind their shoulders. The horses themselves were clad in a metal mesh, with hems of gold tassels brushing the tips of the grass. He stared at the giant, fearsome beasts, with their metal-clad horns and sharp tusks, memories stirring.

'I've seen one of those before,' he exclaimed, excitedly. 'On our drive to the mountains. A Charlemagne. Somebody guided us.'

'Yes,' Tomansio said. 'We still train to fight on them. But we've never actually ridden them into battle since the Planet's Revenge. It's all ceremonial now, part of our skill set. The riders are here to honour your arrival. As do the king eagles.' He gestured upwards.

Oscar just managed not to flinch; he did gasp, though. A flock of giant avian creatures swirled overhead. Resembling the petrosaurs of Earth's dinosaur era, they had been created by the Barsoomians as part of their quest for genetic expansion. Each one had a rider, dressed in long flowing robes that fluttered behind them. They waved as they passed overhead, turning and twisting with amazing finesse. Oscar grinned unashamedly at their acrobatic antics. Surely those riders had to be strapped on?

Tomansio cleared his throat discreetly. 'Perhaps a few words,' he whispered into Oscar's ear.

Oscar had been so entranced by the king eagles he hadn't noticed just how many people were now gathered in front of him. He gazed across them, slightly unnerved by their appearance. It was as if some kind of athletics squad had turned out to see him. Without fail they were tall; the men handsome, the women beautiful; and all of them hugely fit. Even the smiling, eager children were healthy specimens. He couldn't help but think of H. G. Wells's particular vision of the future from *The Time Machine*. Here in their protected edenistic garden, the Knights Guardians were like Eloi, but with muscles, and *attitude*. Heaven help the Morlock who wandered into this valley.

Oscar drew a breath, *really* trying not to think of the media briefings he had to give while he was in the Navy. 'I haven't been to Far Away for a very long time. Too long, actually. You have made it a thrilling world, a world respected across the Commonwealth. For that I thank you, as I do for this welcome.'

The applause was heartfelt enough. Oscar bobbed his head, smiling round the earnest faces. He was hugely relieved when Tomansio ushered him into the house.

The reception room was clad in what looked like translucent white fabric that emitted a mild glow. There were strange deep folds in the walls, which hinted at parallel compartments. Aspects of the T-sphere, Oscar guessed. The furniture was solid enough, as was the little shrine which rested on a broad ancient wood table at the far end. Oscar slowed to a halt as he stared at the black-shrouded holographic portrait with its single candle burning underneath. The Cat's prim face returned her best enigmatic smile.

'For every Yin, a Yang,' Oscar murmured grimly. He should have known. The valley really had been too idyllic.

Tomansio came up to stand beside him. 'You knew her, didn't you? You actually spoke to her as you travelled to Far Away.'

'We spent a day together on the *Carbon Goose* flying across Half Way. I wouldn't say I knew her well.'

'How I envy you that day. Did she frighten you?'

'I was weary of her. We all were. Perhaps you should be?'

'I would not be frightened. I would be honoured.'

'She is evil.'

'Of course she is. But she is also noble. She showed us the way, she gave the Guardians of Selfhood purpose once more. She was the one who brought us together with the Barsoomians. After the Starflyer was destroyed, after you helped kill it, Oscar, there was nothing left for our ancestors. Bradley Johansson originally built us out of the ruin of enslavement. He forged us into warrior tribes to fight the greatest battle humans had ever known. The battle to save our entire species. And when it was over, he was dead, and we were lost, doomed to wither away as a dwindling band of old soldiers without a cause. An anachronistic embarrassment as Far Away was *civilized* by the Commonwealth.'

'Soldiers always have to hang up their weapons in the end.'

'You don't understand. It was our ethos she rescued. She showed us that strength is a virtue, a blessing. It is our evolution and should not be denied the way the liberals of the Commonwealth do, treating it as if it were some ignominious part of us to be always denied. If we had not

656

been strong, if Bradley had not remained steadfast, the Commonwealth would have died on that same day you did, Oscar. If the Barsoomians hadn't maintained their clarity, today's humans would be emaciated short-lived creatures.' He smiled at the portrait. 'One of us had strength, the other, purpose. She saw them both and combined them into a single bold principle, she gave us a vision we can remain forever true to. There is no shame in strength, Oscar.'

'I know,' Oscar said reluctantly. 'That's why I'm here.'

'I had hoped that. You said you needed help.'

'I do.' He paused. 'What if it goes against your ideology?'

Tomansio laughed. 'We don't have one, Oscar. That's the point of the Knights Guardian movement. We follow one creed: strength. That is what we want to impart to humanity as it grows and diversifies. It is the most basic evolutionary tenet. Those sections of humanity who embrace it will survive, it's as simple as that. We are nature as raw as it can get. The fact that we are perceived as nothing other than mercenaries is not our problem. When we are hired to perform a job we do it thoroughly.'

'I need subtlety for this. At least to begin with.'

'We can do subtle, Oscar. Covert operations are one of our specialties. We embrace all forms of human endeavour, apart from the blatantly wicked, or stupid. For instance, we won't perform a heist for you. The Knights Guardians take their oath of honour very seriously. '

Oscar almost started to ask about the Cat and what she used to do. Decided against. 'I have to find someone, and then extend them an offer of protection.'

'That sounds very worthy. Who is it?'

'The Second Dreamer.'

For the first time since they'd met, Oscar witnessed Tomansio lose his reserve. 'No shit?' The Knight Guardian started to laugh. 'Twelve hundred years without you, and now you bring us this. Oscar, you were almost worth the wait. The Second Dreamer himself!' He suddenly sobered. 'I won't ask why. But thank you from the bottom of my simple heart for coming to us.'

'The why is actually very simple. There are too many people who wish to influence him. If he does choose to emerge from the shadows, he should be free to make his own choice.'

'To go to the Void or not, to possibly trigger the end of the Galaxy in pursuit of our race's fate – or not. What a grail to guard, Oscar. What a challenge.'

'I take it that's a yes?'

'My team will be ready to leave in less than an hour.'

'Will you be leading them?'

'What do you think?'

*

'I was *so* sure!' Araminta exclaimed. 'She was this mild scatty little thing. She did everything he told her to, and I do mean everything.'

'Face it, darling, at the time you weren't in any *position* to be the perfect observer,' Cressida said archly.

'But it was the way she did it. You don't understand. She was eager. Obedient. Like the other ones. I think. Shit. Do you think he was chossing me about? Maybe she is profiled and he told her to always give that answer.' Araminta made an effort to calm down. Alcohol was a good suppressant. She tipped the wine bottle over her glass. There was none left. 'Damn!'

Cressida signalled the smart-suited waiter. 'Quite an offer, though.'

'Yeah. What is it about men? Why are they all complete shits? I mean, what kind of mentality does that? Those women are slaves.'

'I know.'

The waiter brought another bottle over and flipped the seal. 'The gentleman over there has asked if he can pay for it.'

Araminta and Cressida looked across towards the giant floor-to-ceiling window, which gave them a stunning view out across the luminous glow of the night-time city. The bar was on the thirty-fifth floor of the Salamartin Hotel tower, and attracted a lot of tourist types who thought nothing of paying the absurd bar prices. Today every room in the hotel was taken by Living Dream followers, which was why the lobby was besieged by protesters. Araminta had forced her way through the angry chanting mob to plead with the doorman to let her in. She'd been frightened; there was a strong threat of violence building up on the street. Cressida of course had the authorization code to land her capsule on the executive rooftop pad.

The man smiling at them from a table in front of the window was dressed in natural fabric clothes styled as only a Makkathran resident would wear.

'No,' Araminta and Cressida chorused.

The waiter smiled understanding, and started pouring.

Araminta watched morosely as her glass was filled. 'Do you think I should go to the police?'

'No,' Cressida said emphatically. 'You do not go down that road, not ever. He sat you next to the Prime Minister at dinner for Ozzie's sake. You know how powerful he is. Besides which, no police force on the planet would investigate him, and even if they did they'd never be able to prove anything. Those girls – if you were right, and I'm not saying you're not – wouldn't ever be found, let alone analysed to see if their brain was wired up illegally. Forget it.'

'How about the Commonwealth Government? Don't they have some kind of crime agency?'

'The Intersolar Serious Crimes Directorate. So you take a trip to their local office, which is probably on Ellezelin, and you walk in and say you think some of his wives might be psychoneural profiled, because of how they behaved while you were all having sex together, an orgy during which incidentally your macrocellular clusters were running a sexual narcotic program.'

'It wasn't a narcotic,' Araminta said automatically.

'Point in your favour, then. That should do it.'

'All right! What if I told them about his commercial plans? The way he's built up Albany's capacity?'

'Tell whom?'

Araminta pouted. For a friend, Cressida wasn't being very helpful. 'I'm not sure. The industrial association of Ellezelin, or whatever it's called.'

'Do you think they don't know? Albany isn't something you can hide. And exactly what has that got to do with psychoneural profiling?'

'I dunno.'

'Sounds more like vengeance than justice to me.'

'He's a shit. He deserves it.'

'Was he good in bed?'

Araminta hoped she wasn't blushing as she concentrated on pouring out some more wine. 'He was adequate.'

'Listen, darling, I'm afraid this is one of those nasty times when you just have to forget him and move on. You learned a valuable lesson: just how ruthless you have to be to get on in this sad old universe of ours.'

Araminta's head collapsed down into her hands, sending her hair tumbling down around her glass. 'Oh, Great Ozzie, I went and had sex with him! How humiliating is that?' She wished she could get rid of the memory, at least the bit about how much she'd enjoyed herself. Actually, there were various commercially available routines and drugs capable of performing neat little memory edits. *Oh, stop being so self-pitying, girl.*

'There there.' Cressida reached over and patted Araminta's hand. 'By now he'll have had half a dozen more girls in his bed, and won't even remember your name. It never meant as much to him as it does to you.'

'And you're telling me this to cheer me up?'

'That was his deal, wasn't it? You would be the second Friday of months with an R in them?'

'Yeah, I know. Hell, I'm a big girl, I knew what I was doing.'

'With hindsight, yes, the view is always clear.'

Araminta brought her head up and grinned. 'Thank you for not judging.'

'You're still a work in progress. And I think you're improving under my tuition. This was a much smaller mistake than Laril.'

'When you want to cheer someone up, you really go for it, don't you?'

Cressida pushed her glass across the table, and *chinked* it to the rim of Araminta's. 'You're starting to understand life. That's good. So what are you going to do about Mr Bovey?'

Araminta grimaced. 'Mr Bovey's proposal, actually.'

'What! He didn't?'

'He did. Marriage with me once I've gone multiple.'

'And you think I'm pushy! Wait a minute, did he ask you this before you had your little visit to Likan?'

'Umm. Yes.'

'You go, my girl. So what was the Likan thing all about?'

'Trying out options while I consider what to do.'

'Wow.'

'Have you ever considered going multiple? Likan said it was purely a lifestyle choice, not a business one. I'm not so sure. Ten pairs of extra hands would be very useful in my line of work.'

'I haven't considered it, no. It's still only one mind, which is all a lawyer needs. But if you're serious about property development then I can see the practical advantages.'

'It's self-limiting, though, isn't it? It's saying I'll always be somebody stuck doing some kind of manual job.'

'Your pride seems to be a very fluid thing.'

'I just want—' She didn't know how to finish that sentence, not at all. 'I don't know. I was just shaken up by what happened at the weekend. And I had this really awful dream, too. I was like this really big creature flying over a planet when someone tried to smother me. Been having a few of those lately. Do you suppose it's stress?'

Cressida gave her a puzzled look. 'Darling, everyone had

that dream. It was the Second Dreamer's dream of the Skylord over Querencia. And that wasn't someone trying to smother you, that was Ethan trying to talk to the Skylord direct. They say he's still in a coma in hospital with his minions trying to repair his burned-out brain.'

'I couldn't have dreamed that.'

'Why not?'

'I don't have gaiamotes. It always seemed a bit silly to me, like a weak version of the unisphere.'

Cressida became very still; she pushed her glass aside and took Araminta's hand. 'Are you being serious?'

'Serious about what?'

'Didn't your mother tell you?'

'Tell me what?' Araminta felt panicky. She wanted another drink, but Cressida's grasp was surprisingly strong.

'About our great-great-great-grandmother.'

'What about her?'

'It was Mellanie Rescorai.'

After all that work-up, Araminta felt badly disappointed. She'd at least been expecting some Dynasty heir – maybe old Earth royalty. Not someone she'd never heard of. 'Oh. Who is she?'

'A friend of the Silfen. She was named their friend. You know what that means?'

'Not really, no.' Araminta's knowledge of the Silfen was a little vague. A weird humanoid race that everyone called elves. They sang gibberish and had a bizarre wormhole network that stretched across half the galaxy allowing them to literally walk between worlds. An ability which a depressing number of humans found incredibly romantic and so they tried to follow them down their twisting interstellar paths. Few returned, but those that did told fanciful tales of adventure on new worlds and the exotic creatures they found there.

'Okay,' Cressida said. 'It goes like this. The Silfen named Ozzie their friend too. They gave him a magic pendant which allowed him to understand their paths, and even join their communal mind, their Motherholme.'

'Ozzie? You mean our Ozzie? The one we—'

'Yes. Now Ozzie being Ozzie, he broke open the pendant and figured out how the magic worked. That it wasn't magic but quantum entanglement. So humans then started to produce gaiamotes. Our gaiafield is basically a poor copy of the Silfen communal mind.'

'Right. So where does our ancestor come into this?'

'Mellanie was also a Silfen friend. Which is actually a little more than just being given the pendant. Their Motherholme accepts your mind and shares its wisdom with you. The pendant only initiates the contact. After a while, the ability becomes natural – well, relatively speaking. And like all magic it's believed to be inherited.' Cressida let go of Araminta's hands and smiled softly.

'You just said it wasn't magic.'

'Of course not. But consider this. Mellanie and her husband, Orion, came back. They had a little girl, Sophie, while they were out there walking across the galaxy. One of very few humans ever born on the paths, and certainly the first of two Silfen friends. She was attuned to the Motherholme right from the start, and passed the magic on to her children. Thanks to her, most of our family can feel the gaiafield, though it's weaker now with our generation. But on a good night, you can sometimes sense the Motherholme itself. I even ventured down one of the Silfen paths myself when I was younger; it's just outside Colwyn City in Francola Wood. I was thirteen, I wanted adventure. Stupid, but . . .'

'There's a Silfen path on Viotia?'

'Yes. They don't use it much. They don't enjoy planets with civilizations like ours on them.'

'Where does it lead?' Araminta asked breathlessly.

'They don't lead to any one place, they join up and twist. Time is different along them as well. That's why humans who aren't Silfen friends are always lost along them. I was lucky, I managed to get back after a couple of days. Mother was furious with me.'

'So . . . my dreams. They're not actually mine?'

'That Skylord one the other night wasn't, no.'

'It felt so real.'

'Didn't it just.' She glanced pointedly round the bar packed with its Living Dream followers. 'Now you see why they're so devout. If you're offered that kind of temptation every time you go to sleep, well who would want to wake up? That's what the Void is to them. Their dreams, for ever.'

'I don't get it. So what if they're real? That city they always go on about: Makkathran, it's medieval isn't it? And their Waterwalker fights all the time. That's awful. Even if you've got telepathic powers, they're not that special. Our technology is just as good. Who wants to live like that?'

'You seriously need to review Inigo's dreams before you make that sort of judgement. The Waterwalker transforms an entire human society.'

'So he's a talented politician?'

'Oh no, darling, he's much more than that. He revealed the true nature of the Void to us. He showed us what it can do. That kind of power scares me shitless. Which is precisely what so many find so attractive.' Cressida waved her elegant hand round at the Living Dream supporters. 'Ozzie help us if these dreadful little prats ever gain the same ability the Waterwalker discovered. Eating up the galaxy would be the least of our worries.'

Inigo's sixth dream

Nearly eighty probationary constables sat together in a block of seats on the ultra-black floor of the Malfit Hall, while the vast arching ceiling above played images of wispy clouds traversing the beautiful gold and pink dawn sky. Edeard had one of the seats on the second row, his head tipped back so he could watch the giant ceiling in astonishment. He was sure it must be the marvel of the world. His fellow squadmates were all amused by his reaction. Not that they'd actually been in the Orchard Palace before – except for Dinlay. But at least they'd known about the moving imagery. And they hadn't thought to warn him.

Edeard gasped as Nikran rose up into the replica sky. The ruddy-brown planet here was a lot larger than it ever appeared in Querencia's skies. He could see tiny features etched on the world's eternal deserts. For some reason it made him think of it as an actual place rather than an element of the celestial panorama.

'Does anyone live there?' he whispered to Kanseen, who was in the chair next to him.

She looked at him, frowning, then glanced up at the image of Nikran, and giggled.

'What?' Macsen hissed.

'Edeard wants to know if anyone lives on Nikran,' Kanseen announced solemnly.

The whole squad snickered; surrounding squads joined in. Edeard felt his face heating up. 'Why not?' he protested. 'Rah's ship fell on to this world, why not another ship to Nikran?'

'Absolutely,' Macsen said. 'Perfectly valid question. In fact, there's a whole other Makkathran up there.'

Edeard ignored them, and simply looked straight ahead in a dignified manner. He resolved to never ever tell his friends of his dreams, and what they showed him.

The block of probationary constables settled down. Edeard started to concentrate on what he was seeing. They were facing the grand curving staircase that dominated one side of the Hall. Owain, the Mayor of Makkathran, had appeared at the top, followed by the Guild Masters and District Masters who made up the Upper Council. They were all wearing their full ceremonial robes, producing a splendid blaze of colour as they filed down to the floor of the Hall.

'Oh, Lady,' Dinlay groaned.

Edeard caught a sensation of queasiness emanating from his friend. 'Ten seconds maximum,' he told Dinlay using a tiny directed longtalk voice. 'Then it's all over. Just hold it together for ten seconds. You can do that.'

Dinlay nodded, whilst appearing completely unconvinced.

Edeard resisted looking round at the much bigger block of seating behind him, where the families and friends of the probationary constables were gathered to watch them receive their bronze epaulettes. Probably an exaggeration, but half of them were Dinlay's family, and all of them were in uniform.

'I bet there's a crime wave going on in every district,' Macsen had muttered while they were all taking their seats earlier. 'There aren't any constables left out there to patrol.'

Owain reached the platform that had been set up at the bottom of the stairs. He smiled round at the attentive audience. 'It is always an honour and a privilege for me to perform this ceremony,' he said. 'In my position I hear so many people complain about the state which not just the city is in, but of the chaos which supposedly reigns in the lands outside our crystal walls. I wish they were standing here now, to see so many young people coming forward to serve their city. I am heartened by the sense of duty you are displaying in taking this commitment to serve your fellow citizens. You give me confidence for the future.'

Now that's a real politician, Edeard thought uncharitably. The Mayor of all people must have known how inadequate the number of constables was. That the eighty of them here today wasn't enough; that at least an equal number of constables had left in the last few months to become private bodyguards or for a better paid and respected job as a sheriff in some provincial town. *Why doesn't he do something about it?*

The Mayor finished his inspirational speech. The probationary constables stood up as one, then the first row trooped up to the platform to be greeted by the Mayor. The Chief Constable read the probationer's name out to the Hall, while an assistant handed a pair of epaulettes to the Mayor to be presented with a handshake and a smile.

Edeard's row started to move forward. He'd thought

this would be boring at the least, that it was stupid, an irritation he could have done without. Especially as the only person in the audience clapping for him was Salrana, who'd been given the day off from her duties. But now he was here, now he was walking up to the Mayor of the entire city, he actually began to feel a sense of occasion. Behind him, the audience was radiant with pride. They believed in the constables. In front, the Upper Council were registering their approval. None of the councillors had to be here, it was a ceremony repeated three times a year, every year. They'd been to dozens, and would have to come to dozens more. If they'd wanted to cry off, they could have done. But no, it was important enough for them to turn out every time.

And here he was himself, coming forward to make a public pledge to the citizens of Makkathran that he would do his best to protect them and implement the rule of law. This was why Rah and those who followed him into office had created this ceremony and others like it, to recognize and honour the commitment the constables made to their city and lives. It was neither silly nor a waste of time, it was a show of respect.

Edeard stood in front of the Mayor, who smiled politely, and shook his hand as the Chief Constable read out his name. A pair of bronze epaulettes were pressed into his hand. 'Thank you, sir,' Edeard said. There was a lump in his throat. 'I won't let you down.' *Ashwell will never happen here.*

If the Mayor was surprised, he didn't show it. Edeard caught sight of Finitan standing on the grand staircase. The Master of the Eggshaper Guild looked rather splendid in a gold and purple gown, with elaborate scarlet symbols embroidered down the front; his silver-tipped hood was arranged over the left shoulder. He caught Edeard's eye and winked. 'Well done, lad,' his longtalk whispered.

Edeard stepped off the platform. There was a burst of applause. He nearly laughed, it was as if the audience was rejoicing he was out of the way. In fact it was Dinlay's considerable family clapping loudly as their relative received his epaulettes. Dinlay managed to not trip, or throw up, or collapse from fright. He followed Edeard back to their seats with a glowing face, grinning back at his kin.

Afterwards there was a formal reception party, with the Mayor and the Upper Council mixing with the new constables and their families, while ge-monkeys circled the Malfit Hall with trays of drinks. It was scheduled to last an hour. Edeard might have warmed to the graduation ceremony itself, but he planned to be out of the party in under ten minutes.

'No you don't,' Salrana decreed. 'Just look at who's here.'

Edeard frowned round at the people babbling away; the families in their finery, the resplendent Upper Council members. 'Who?'

She gave him a withering look. 'The Pythia for a start. And she noticed me. I felt her farsight on me during the ceremony.'

Edeard took another look round. 'Fair enough, you're the only novice here. She probably thinks you ducked out of your assignments to pick up the free booze.'

Salrana drew herself up. It shifted the fabric of her white and blue robe in a way Edeard couldn't help but notice. If he kept doing that, and kept thinking those accompanying thoughts about how she was growing up, the Lady really would blast him out of existence one day.

'Edeard you can still be disappointingly childish at times. We are both citizens of Makkathran now; you especially today. Try and act in an appropriate fashion.'

Edeard's mouth dropped open.

'Now we are going over to thank Grand Master Finitan for sponsoring you, as is the right expression of gratitude, which you *do* feel; and see if we can be introduced to others in the Upper Council as well. If you're to become Chief Constable, you need to start paying attention to the city's political dynamics.'

'Uh. Yes,' Edeard admitted. 'Chief Constable?'

'That's your route on to the Upper Council now you've chosen the constables over a Guild.'

'I've been graduated eight minutes.'

'Those that hesitate, lose. The Lady's book, fifth chapter.'

His lips twitched. 'I knew that.'

'Did you now?' Salrana raised an eyebrow. 'I might have to test you later.'

'I've had quite enough of exams these last few weeks, thank you.'

'Poor Edeard. Come on.' She pulled at his hand, all girlish again.

Grand Master Finitan was talking to a pair of fellow Upper Council members as Edeard and Salrana approached him. He smiled and turned to them. 'Congratulations, my boy. A proud day for you.'

'Yes sir. Thank you again for sponsoring me.'

'Well, it seems to have put me in credit with the Chief

Constable. You graduated third in your class. That's an astonishing result for someone unfamiliar with our city.'

'Thank you, sir.'

'Allow me to introduce Masters Graley of the Geography Guild and Imilan of the Chemistry Guild. This is Constable Edeard from the Rulan province; a friend of my old Master.'

'Masters.' Edeard bowed formally. Then he saw Salrana pluck at her skirt and hold the fabric up daintily on one side as she performed a peculiar little bow which involved bending her knees and keeping her back straight.

'And Novice Salrana,' Finitan said smoothly. 'Also from Rulan.'

'A pleasure,' Imilan said.

Edeard didn't care for the way the Master's eyes lingered on Salrana.

'You're a long way from home, Novice,' the Master said.

'No, sir,' she said in a polite tone. 'Makkathran is my home now.'

'Well said, Novice,' Finitan said. 'I wish all our citizens were as appreciative of their city as you are.'

'Now, Finitan,' Graley chided. 'This is not the day.'

'Apologies.' Finitan inclined his head at the youngsters. 'So, Edeard, have you had a run-in with our criminal element yet?'

'A few, sir, yes.'

'He's being very modest, sir,' Salrana said. 'He led his squad after some thieves in the Silvarum market. He recovered the stolen items, as well.'

Edeard shifted awkwardly under the scrutiny of all three Masters.

'And are these miscreants now labouring away at the Trampello mine to pay for their crime?' Imilan asked.

'No, sir,' Edeard admitted. 'They got away. That time. They won't again.'

'I imagine they won't,' Finitan said with an edge of amusement. 'Come along, Edeard, let me introduce you to the Mayor. It's about time he saw an honourable man again.'

'Sir?'

'Old joke. We often clash in Council.' He signalled them to follow him. 'Not over anything important to the lives of real people, of course.'

The Mayor of Makkathran was talking to the Pythia just beside the little platform where he'd handed out the epaulettes. If he was bored or annoyed to be introduced to a new constable he didn't show it; Edeard had never encountered a mind so perfectly shielded. Not that he paid much attention. He was entranced by the Pythia. He'd been expecting some ancient woman, full of grandmotherly warmth. Instead, he was disconcerted to find the Pythia retained the beauty of a woman still awaiting her half-century. A beauty only emphasized by her gold-trimmed white robe with its flowing hood which she wore forward, casting her face in a slight shadow.

Salrana did her strange bow again to the Pythia.

'The Lady's blessing upon you, my child,' the Pythia said. She sounded bored in that way Makkathran's aristocracy always did when they had to deal with those they considered to be of a lower order. Which wasn't what Edeard expected from a Pythia. Then she turned her attention to him. Startling light-blue eyes fixed on him, surrounded by a mass of thick bronze hair twined with gold and silver leaves. The eyes narrowed in judgement, which Edeard found heartbreaking. He felt like he'd disappointed her, which was a terrible thing. Then she smiled, banishing his worry. 'Now you *are* interesting, Constable,' she said.

'My Lady?' he stammered. He could somehow feel the Pythia's farsight upon him, as if she were picking through his mind. There was something disconcertingly intimate about the contact. And she was very beautiful. Merely a yard away. Her half smile open and inviting.

Salrana made a groaning sound in her throat.

'I'm not quite that exalted,' the Pythia said lightly. 'There is only one true Lady. My usual form of address is Dear Mother.'

'I apologize, Dear Mother.'

'Think nothing of it. You've come a long way to get here, and you still have a long way to travel.'

'I do?'

But the Pythia had turned to face Finitan. 'What a fascinating young friend you have, Grand Master.'

'I'm pleased you think so, Pythia.'

'So young, yet so strong.'

The way she said it sent a shudder of felonious delight down Edeard's spine. He didn't dare glance in her direction; instead he fixed his gaze on the Mayor, who was frowning.

'Do you foresee great things for him?' Finitan asked jovially.

The Pythia turned to stare directly at Edeard, an act he couldn't ignore, not in a group like this, not without appearing extraordinarily rude. He tried to return the look, but found it incredibly difficult.

'Your potential is very strong,' she said. There was an almost teasing quality to her voice. 'Do you follow the Lady's teachings, Constable Edeard?'

'I try my best, Dear Mother.'

'I'm sure you do. May She bless your endeavours in your new duties.'

Edeard almost didn't hear her. A movement behind Finitan had caught his eye. In horror, he watched Mistress Florell heading towards them, all black chiffon and wide veils hanging from a tall hat. His dismay must have leaked out. As one, Finitan, the Mayor, and the Pythia turned to acknowledge the approaching *grande dame*.

'Aunt!' the Mayor exclaimed happily. 'How lovely of you to come.'

'He's the one,' Mistress Florell declared in her scratchy voice. 'The young hooligan who nearly knocked me to the ground.'

'Now, Aunt.'

'Take his epaulettes away,' she snapped imperiously. 'He's not fit to serve this city. Time was we used to have men of good character in the constables, the sons of noblemen.'

The Mayor gave Edeard a half-apologetic look. 'What happened, Constable?'

'I was pursuing some thieves, sir. Mistress Florell came out of a building. I went round . . .'

'Ha! Tried to run over me, more like.'

'Come, come, Aunt. The lad was obviously just doing his job, a conscientious chap like this is just what we need. Suppose the thieves had snatched your bag, wouldn't you want him to give chase?'

'Nobody would steal *my* bag,' she snapped.

676

'I *am* sorry for any distress,' Edeard said desperately. The horrible old woman just wouldn't *listen*.

The Mayor shuffled round to stand between Mistress Florell and Edeard, flicking his fingers in a *go away* motion. Edeard did a kind of half bow and backed away fast, accompanied by Salrana and Finitan.

'Aunt, you know it's bad for you to dwell on such trivia. Now some of these Mindalla estate fortified wines are really quite lovely, you must try—' There was a note of tired desperation in the Mayor's voice.

Finitan smiled broadly as they hurried off. 'Thank you, Edeard: these reception parties are normally quite tedious.'

'Er . . . Yes, sir.'

'Oh come now, this is your graduation day. Don't let that daft old bat spoil it for you. She's embarrassingly well connected, as would you be if you clung to life for so long. Wouldn't surprise me if she did drink the blood of virgins after all. Your pardon, Novice.'

'I've heard of Mistress Florell, sir,' Salrana said.

'Everyone in the city has,' Finitan said. 'That's why she thinks she's so important, instead of just old and obnoxious.' He put his hand on Edeard's shoulder. 'And I say that as her great-great-nephew, myself. Twice removed, thankfully.'

'Thank you, sir,' Edeard said.

'Now off you go and enjoy yourselves. And, Edeard, when the time comes for you to apply for promotion to officer rank, come and see me again. I'll be happy to sign the letter.'

'Sir?' Edeard asked incredulously.

'You heard. Now be off with the pair of you. It's a bold bad city out there. Have fun!'

Edeard didn't need telling again. He and Salrana made for the Hall's big archway which led out to the ante-chambers.

'Hey, Edeard,' Macsen called, hurrying to intercept. 'Where are you off to?'

'Just out,' Edeard said. He didn't even want to glance over his shoulder in case Mistress Florell was looking his way.

Macsen reached them, and skidded to a halt. 'Mother and Dybal are taking me to the Rakas restaurant to celebrate. It's an open invitation to my squadmates as well.' Macsen stopped, and smiled at Salrana. 'Novice, I had no idea Edeard kept such pleasant company.' He gave Edeard an expectant look, ever the injured party.

'This is Novice Salrana, from my home village,' Edeard said sulkily.

'That is one village I am definitely going to have to visit.' Macsen bowed deeply.

'Why is that, Constable?' she asked.

'To see if all the girls there are as beautiful as yourself.'

She laughed. Edeard groaned, glaring in warning at Macsen.

'The invitation to Rakas is of course extended to the friends of my squadmates, Novice.'

'The friends accept with thanks,' she said primly. 'But only if you stop calling me Novice.'

'It will be my delight, Salrana. And I will also beg you to tell of Edeard's early life. It would seem he's been keeping secrets from us. Those who entrust our lives to him, no less.'

'Shocking,' she agreed. 'I will entertain such a request if correctly made.'

'Salrana!' a horrified Edeard exclaimed.

'Excellent,' Macsen said. 'I'll arrange another gondola for our party. Now, Edeard, where is Kanseen?'

Edeard glowered at his so-called friend.

'Edeard?' Salrana prompted with a jab to his ribs.

'Over there.' Edeard said it without having to concentrate; through his farsight he was automatically aware of all his squadmates – a trait Chae was always trying to emphasize. He pointed to where Kanseen was chatting to a heavily pregnant woman and a man in a smart tunic with the crest of the Shipwright's Guild. 'Her sister came to the ceremony. They're catching up.'

'No sign of her mother, then, poor thing,' Macsen said sadly. 'Ah well, I'll go and ask her.'

'Boyd's family are all here,' Edeard said.

'And we'll yet sink under the weight of Dinlay's relatives,' Macsen concluded. 'So it's just us precious few left. See you at the Outer Circle Canal mooring in ten minutes.'

'What did you say that for?' Edeard asked as Macsen walked over to Kanseen.

Salrana cocked her head to one side and gave him a very haughty look. 'It was a gesture of honest friendship. Why should I not accept?'

'He was flirting with you.'

She grinned. 'Wasn't he just.'

'You're a Novice!'

'We are not professional virgins, Edeard. I seem to remember us kissing. And more, wasn't there a discussion about my age and when you would be ready to bed me?'

Edeard turned bright red. His farsight tried to sense sparks of interest in those standing closest – either they could shield too well, or they hadn't overheard. One thing was sure, she wouldn't back down. *She never has.* Her voice would only grow louder if he persisted. 'I don't wish to recall that day too closely if you don't mind. However, if I've offended you I apologize. I still think of you as my charge, especially after all we have been through. Which is why I overreacted with Macsen. Truly, Salrana, he's had more girls than I have socks.'

Her smile was forgiving. 'I've seen your wardrobe. You only have two pairs of socks.'

'I do not!'

'And they have holes in them. So you just concentrate on worrying about yourself, Edeard. I know and understand all about Macsen and boys like him. That's why he's perfectly harmless.'

'He's perfectly charming.'

'It's not a crime, you know. Perhaps if you showed a little more charm, then you could boast more conquests.'

'Charm, eh?' He bent his arm, and extended it towards her. 'May I escort you to the mooring, Novice Salrana?'

'Why thank you, Constable Edeard. You may indeed.' She linked her arm through his, and allowed him to lead her out of the Hall.

The Rakas restaurant was in the Abad district; which meant a gondola ride down the Great Major Canal. It was the first time Edeard had ever been in one of the elegant black boats. He didn't have the coinage to travel in them ordinarily. Money clearly wasn't an issue with Dybal.

The errant musician was everything Edeard had expected. Wild black hair reaching halfway down his back, barely contained by red leather bands which gave it a peculiar ropy appearance. A long face with weather-beaten creases and sunken cheeks above a narrow jaw; but with brown-gold eyes that always seemed to be seeing the funny side of life as they peeped over narrow blue-lens glasses. His whole mental aura was agreeable, akin to that of a carefree adolescent rather than a man well over a hundred. Just being able to say hello and shake hands was enough to banish Edeard's lingering dismay over Mistress Florell. As their little group assembled at the moorings, Dybal made them all feel welcome, even though they'd never met him before. He instinctively knew the right note to take with each of them.

'Come on then,' he said loudly once they were all present, and led them down the steps. His clothes were large, even though he was improbably slender for his age. Edeard imagined they needed to be that big to contain his ebullience, he certainly achieved the whole larger-than-life image effortlessly enough. Strident voice, big arm gestures, fur-lined velvet jacket, paisley-pattern shirt and leather trousers, their colours mimicking those of the Musician's Guild – or, more likely, a deliberate mockery of them. Edeard was only slightly disappointed the musician wasn't carrying his guitar; he wanted to hear the songs of rebellion which stoked up Makkathran's youth.

Dybal took the first gondola along with Macsen, and Bijulee, Macsen's mother. Edeard watched him talk to the gondolier, holding the man's hand between his own two palms, squeezing intently. Both men laughed, the kind of low merriment which usually came from a dirty joke. Dybal took his seat beside Bijulee, while the still-smiling gondolier pushed off.

'*That* is Macsen's mother?' Kanseen asked as they settled on the middle bench in their own gondola.

'Yeah,' Edeard said. And to think, a few minutes earlier he'd believed the Pythia was an attractive older woman. 'Macsen introduced me just before you arrived.' Which had gone a long way to making his world a better place.

'Can't be,' Kanseen declared as their gondola slipped out on to the Great Major Canal. 'That would mean she had him when she was what . . . ten? She looks like she's my age, for the Lady's sake.'

Edeard sat back on the bench, smiling. He was so content he came *this* close to putting his arm round Salrana, who was sitting next to him. 'Do I hear the little voice of envy, there, Constable?'

'You hear the little voice of disbelief,' Kanseen muttered.

'Perhaps it's his sister, and I misheard.'

'How does she keep her skin so fresh? It's got to be some ointment only available to the rich.'

'Maybe she imports it direct from Nikran.'

Kanseen pulled a face.

'You two.' Salrana laughed. 'You're like an old married couple.'

Edeard and Kanseen carefully avoided each other's gaze. The gondola had already reached Birmingham Pool, the big junction at the top of the Grand Central Canal. From Edeard's position, the entire circle of water seemed to be full of gondolas, dodging round each other as they slipped in and out of the various canals emptying into the Pool. He did his best not to flinch. None of the gondoliers were slowing down, they just seemed to instinctively know where to go. Craft slipped past them, close enough to touch if he'd been brave enough to stretch out an arm. Then they arrived at the head of the Grand Central Canal, and their gondolier gave a hard push on his punt.

The first thing Edeard looked at was the mooring on his right where the thieves had escaped. He caught Kanseen looking at it too. She gave a tiny shrug. Then he forgot all about it, and really enjoyed the view. At the top end of the city, along the Silvarum, Haxpen and Padua districts, the canal was lined with some of the grandest buildings in Makkathran; palaces up to ten storeys high, with huge windows, facades a swirl of colour in weird patterns. Turrets, belvederes, and spires produced a serrated skyline. Ge-eagles bigger than any Edeard had ever sculpted flew in lazy circles around the pinnacles, keeping watch on the approaches to each magnificent family seat. Kanseen pointed out some of them: the palace that was home to the Mayor's family, the ziggurat where Rah and the Lady were supposed to have lived – now home to the Culverit family who claimed direct lineage. She whispered about one red-tinged facade where Macsen's father had lived. When Edeard glanced at the gondola in front, both Macsen and Bijulee were looking in the opposite direction.

All of the stately buildings had low water-level archways leading into the warren of cellars underneath, guarded by thick iron gates which the families maintained in excellent order. The walls of the Purdard family palace were at an angle, actually overhanging the water. When Edeard looked up, he saw a glassed-in mirador running the length of the upper storey, with several youngsters standing watching the gondolas. A fabulously rich trading family, Kanseen said, with a fleet of thirty ships.

They passed through the High Pool, which provided a junction with Flight Canal and Market Canal. There was a bridge on either side of the pool; the first one was the city's own, a simple high white arch to which carpenters attached a broad rail along both sides. Famously, the apex was a ten-yard stretch of crystal, providing a view directly past any pedestrian's shoes down on to the water and gondolas thirty yards below. Not everyone could walk across it, the sight was too much for some; as many as one in twenty, the Doctor's Guild claimed. At Chae's insistence, Edeard and the rest of the squad had used it several times on patrol. Edeard had to gird himself to walk those few invisible yards; the vertigo wasn't strong enough to stop him though it was unpleasant. All of the squad had forced themselves across it – surprisingly, Dinlay had been the least affected. The bridge on the other side of High Pool was constructed out of iron and wood, a bulky creaking thing in comparison to its cousin, yet with far more traffic. Past the Pool, the towers of Eyrie stabbed up into the clean azure sky as if ready to impale any passing Skylord. Fiacre district's cliff-like frontage swarmed with vine plants, with long strands of flowers bubbling out of the emerald and russet leaves. Only the windows remained clear of foliage, producing deep-set black holes in the lush living carpet.

The gondolas pulled up at a mooring just beyond Forest Pool, and everyone climbed out. Dybal paid the gondoliers, and they all set off to the round tower which housed the Rakas restaurant on its third floor. Hansalt, the owner and chief chef, had reserved Dybal a table beside a long window overlooking one of the district's colourful plazas.

'An auspicious day for us,' Dybal announced as a waitress brought over a tray of chilled white wine. 'First, a toast to your squad, Macsen. May you rid the city of crime.'

They drank to that. Edeard gave the glass a suspicious

glance, he'd never seen wine with bubbles in it before, but when he sipped the taste was surprisingly light and fruity. He rather liked it.

'Secondly,' Dybal said. 'To Edeard, for being appointed squad leader.'

Edeard blushed.

'Speech!' Macsen demanded.

'Not a chance,' Edeard grunted.

They laughed and drank to that.

'Thirdly,' his voice softened and he looked down at Bijulee, 'I am very proud to announce that my beloved has agreed to marry me.'

The cheer that went up made all the other customers look over at them. Everyone saw it was Dybal, and smiled knowingly. Macsen was hugging his mother. Edeard and Salrana were astonished, but clinked glasses anyway and downed some more of the bubbling wine. Another two chilled bottles arrived and were quickly poured out.

Afterwards, Edeard always thought back to that meal as the first time he'd been truly happy since Ashwell. The food was like nothing he'd ever eaten before. It arrived on big white plates arranged with such artistry he almost didn't want to eat it, but when he did tuck in the combination of tastes was marvellous. And Dybal had gossip on the city's élite that was downright scandalous. That all started because of Salrana, who was answering Macsen's question about what Novices did all day long.

'I mean no disrespect to the Lady,' he said. 'But surely it must be boring just reading Her scriptures and singing in Her church.'

'Hey,' Dybal objected. 'Less mockery about singing if you don't mind.'

'I've been assigned to Millical House,' Salrana said. 'I love looking after the children. They're so sweet.'

'What's Millical House?' Edeard asked. 'A school?'

'You don't know?' Bijulee asked. She was uncertain if Edeard was having a joke.

'I told you, Mother,' Macsen said. 'He really is from a village on the edge of the wilds.'

'Millical is an orphanage,' Salrana said solemnly. 'I cannot understand why any mother would give up her baby, especially the ones as gorgeous as we get in the nursery. But they do. So the Lady takes care of them. It's a fantastic place, Edeard, the children lack for nothing. Makkathran really cares.'

Dybal gave a *certain* cough. 'Actually, that's a rather exceptional orphanage.'

'What do you mean?' Salrana asked.

'You sure you want to hear this?'

Salrana twirled the stem of her wine glass between her fingers, giving Dybal a level gaze. 'We do take in anyone.'

'Yes, I suppose so. But it helps that you're in the Lillylight district. Consider who your neighbours are. You see, Edeard, Millical House is where the noble families deliver those little unwanted embarrassments which happen when the younger sons are out enjoying themselves with the lower-order girls at the more disreputable entertainment theatres that grace our fine city.'

'The kind you play at?' Bijulee asked mildly.

'Yes, my love, the kind I play at.' He eyed the three young constables. 'Been to any, yet?'

'Not yet,' Kanseen said. Macsen kept quiet.

'Just a matter of time. Anyway, the reason Millical is so well funded is the tradition that the family concerned makes a donation – anonymous, of course – each time a babe is left on the house's charity step for the Novices to take in.'

'Any money for children is distributed equally among all the Lady's orphanages,' Salrana said.

'I'm sure a great deal of the bequests filter down to the other orphanage houses. And the Lady performs invaluable work caring for such unfortunates, as I do know. But if you ever get to work in any of the other houses, you'll notice the difference.'

'And how do you know for sure?' Bijulee asked teasingly.

Dybal turned to face her with a sad smile. 'Because I grew up in one.'

'Really?' Macsen asked.

'That's right. Which is why I'm so impressed with you four youngsters. You came from nothing, especially Edeard and Salrana here, and you're all making a life for yourselves. I admire that. I truly do. You're not dependent on anyone, let alone a decadent family. I know I'm the first to complain about the city's hierarchy, the way democracy has been expropriated by the rich, but there are some institutions which are still worthwhile. People need the constables for the security you bring to the streets and canals, and the Lady for hope.'

'I thought that was what your music brought,' Salrana said with a cheeky gleam in her eye.

'It depends which class you belong to. If you're rich, I'm a deliciously wicked rebel, hot and dripping with sarcasm and irony. They have to pay me to perform – which I'm glad to do for them. But for the rest of the city, the people who toil their whole life to make things work,

I'm a focal point for resentment, I articulate their feelings. For them, I sing for free. I don't want their coinage, I want them to spend it on themselves so they don't have to give away their children.'

'So you compete with the Lady?' Salrana said.

'I offer a mild alternative, that's all. Hopefully an enjoyable one.'

'I must try and get to one of your performances.'

'I'll be happy to escort you,' Macsen said.

'I'll hold you to that,' she retorted before Edeard could intervene. He didn't say anything, not there and then, that would spoil the meal.

'Do you know all the Grand Council?' Edeard asked Dybal.

'Oh yes, they think that by associating with me they gain credibility. What they're actually doing by inviting me to their homes is contributing generously to lyrics of irony and hypocrisy. Why do you ask, Edeard? Do you need to know about their mistresses? Their strange shared interest in taxing cotton production in Fondral province? The scandal over funds for the militia? The money wasted on official functions? The disease of corruption which infects the staff of the Orchard Palace who are supposed to be impartial? How our dear Mayor, Owain, is already buying votes for the next election – the one time he needs public support?'

'Actually no, I was wondering about Mistress Florell.'

'Edeard has met her,' Macsen said with a chortle.

'We all did, while we were on duty,' Edeard countered.

'She hit him with her umbrella,' Kanseen added dryly.

Dybal and Bijulee laughed at that.

'The old witch tried to get Edeard thrown out of the constables,' Salrana said, hot-cheeked. 'At the ceremony today, she told the Mayor to take his epaulettes back.'

'How typical,' Dybal said. 'Don't worry Edeard; she has no real power, not any more. She's a figurehead for the noble families, that's all. They like to make out she's a much loved grandmother to the whole city. Total bollocks, of course. She was a scheming little bitch when she was younger. Which admittedly is history to all of us now. But she had three husbands before her fiftieth birthday, all first sons of District Masters, which is just about unheard of even today. She gave each of them two sons – and some say there was witchery in that. And by strange coincidence, all three second children went on to marry noble daughters in families where the male lineage had faltered in favour of the girls. By the next generation she'd spread her brood through eleven District Master families. With that kind of power bloc in the Upper Council, she controlled the vote for decades. Our last so-called Golden Age; which saw the rise of the militia at the expense of all other arms of government. You see, she believes there's an actual physical difference between the nobility and those without their obscene wealth. In other words, her offspring are born to rule and bring order to the uncivilized masses such as thee and me. Needless to say, she doesn't believe that we should have anything to do with the city's government. That sort of thing is best left to those whom destiny has blessed with good blood.'

'No wonder she didn't like you, Edeard,' Macsen grinned. 'You're not even city born. She could probably smell the countryside on you.'

'Not everyone in the Upper Council believes in that, do they?' Edeard asked, thinking of Finitan. A nephew, he'd said.

'Hopefully not, There are still a few decent noblemen around today. And of course, District Masters' seats on the Upper Council are checked by the Guild Masters. And the Lower Council itself is still directly elected, not that you'd know it in some districts. That makes for a lot of genuine debate in the Grand Council. Rah knew what he was doing when he crafted our constitution.'

'But your songs are still popular.'

'They are. Dissatisfaction with those who rule is always attractive to the majority; it's an obsession which humans brought with them on the ships which fell to Querencia. As a species we find it as easy as breathing. And it's never helped by old men like me who reminisce on how things were always better in our lost youth.'

'You're a rabble-rouser, you mean,' Bijulee said fondly as she ran her hand through his ragged braids of hair.

'And proud of it,' Dybal raised his glass again. 'To making our masters lives a misery.'

The whole table drank to that.

'So what's the story with you and Salrana?' Kanseen asked. It was late at night. The celebratory lunch had lasted all afternoon. Edeard hadn't wanted it to end. He was perfectly relaxed, thanks to that lovely wine with bubbles, the company of friends, eating fine food, making happy intelligent conversation. No, today was a day which, if the Lady were kind, should last and last.

But as was the way of all things, they finished the final bottle of wine, ate the last morsel of cheese and bade each other farewell. Dybal winced theatrically when the bill arrived. The sun had set outside, leaving the city's own cold orange lighting to bathe the streets, along with the faint haze of the nebulas overhead. Edeard announced he would walk Salrana back to Millical House in the Lilly-light district. As it was directly between Abad and Jeavons, Kanseen offered to walk with them.

The orphanage house was a nice one, close to the Victoria Canal, with its own garden and play yard. Yet he couldn't help noticing, it was the smallest building on the street. Salrana had given him a light peck on the cheek before scooting off through the imposing doors which filled the entrance arch.

Edeard and Kanseen carried on together, using a bridge over Castoff Canal to put them in Drupe district, where the palaces matched anything along the Great Major Canal. It was quiet on the narrow streets and broad squares. Bodyguards stood imposingly outside the iron gates of the palaces. Edeard tried not to stare as they passed the alert figures in dark uniforms; he was sure that staying a constable was better than such monotonous duty night after night. That disapproval must have escaped his shielding.

'That's not what I'll be doing,' Kanseen said quietly as their footfalls echoed around them in a narrow street high enough to block out all the night sky except for the slim violet thread of Buluku's meandering tail. 'None of them are ex-constables. Estate workers and farm boys who've come to the city in search of a better life. They only last a couple of years before they make their way back home. That or migrate into Sampalok.'

'Could have been me, then,' Edeard said.

'Somehow I doubt that.'

They walked over the third bridge across the Marble Canal, back into the familiar territory of Jeavons. Gondolas slid past quietly underneath them, a small white lantern glowing on the front of each. Their passengers snuggled up under the canopy, enjoying the romance of the ride. By now Edeard could recognize the wind rising from the sea, the moisture it carried. Clouds were scudding overhead, starting to veil the nebulas. It would rain tonight. In another hour, he decided as he smelt the air.

The constables' tenement was two streets away from Jeavons station, a big ugly building from the outside, but wrapped around a central oval courtyard boasting a pool of warmish water large enough to swim in and overlooked by four levels of walkways. It contained the maisonettes reserved for the constables. Those with families had taken over one end, with the bachelors at the other. Not that it was a fixed divide. Edeard along with the rest of the squad had moved in a couple of days ago. Each morning he'd been woken by children shouting outside his door as they raced along the walkway, playing some exciting game of chase.

Now the children were long in bed as he and Kanseen walked up a set of awkward rounded stairs to the third level where they both had maisonettes.

'No real story,' he told her. 'You know Salrana and I travelled here together. I'm sort of like her elder brother.'

'She's in love with you.'

'What?'

'I was watching her this afternoon. It's obvious to anyone with half a brain. Even Macsen fathomed that out.

Didn't you notice he'd stopped trying to flirt with her by the time the fish course arrived? There's no point. She's only interested in you.'

'She's smart enough to realize how shallow he is. That's all. If they don't fall at his feet in the first five minutes, he moves on. You know what he's like.'

'I never thought I'd see you in denial.'

'It's not denial. You asked a question and I answered it.'

They stopped at the top of the stairs, and looked out over the extensive courtyard. The rim of the pool was a thin intense line of pale-orange. It made the water look very inviting. Edeard knew a lot of the constables went for a night-time dip. His stomach was too heavy from a whole afternoon bingeing, he decided reluctantly.

'Actually, you didn't answer,' Kanseen said. 'All you admitted to was knowing her, which doesn't shed any light on your relationship at all.'

'Lady save me, you really did take in all of Master Solarin's lectures, didn't you?'

'My grades were almost as high as yours, yes. So on that long trip through the mountains and across swamps filled with monsters, did you sleep with her?'

'No!'

'Why not? She's very pretty. And slim. I've seen what your eye lingers on when we're out on patrol.'

'She's far too young, for a start. And she's getting pretty. Doctors in Makkathran have better ointments than we had on the caravan.'

'Edeard!' Kanseen gave a small shocked laugh. 'I think that's the most evil thing I've ever heard you say about anyone, let alone your little sister.'

'Lady, you're cruel. I don't answer a question to your satisfaction and you say I'm in denial; then I give an honest answer and you brand me evil.'

She sucked contritely on her lower lip. 'Sorry. But you can understand why.'

'Not really.' Edeard was looking at her profile in the coppery shimmer thrown off by the surface of the pool. In such a light she looked almost aristocratic, with her strong chin and slight nose, skin painted enticingly dark. She turned to face him, cocking her head slightly to one side in that questioning way he enjoyed.

He leant forward and kissed her. She pressed in against him, hands sliding over his back. For once he dropped his mental guard, showing her how much he delighted in the touch of her, the closeness . . . After a long time they ended the kiss. Her nose rubbed against his cheek, and she let him sense how much that meant to her.

'Come to bed with me,' he murmured. His tongue darted out to lick the lobe of her ear. She shivered from the contact. Hot lines of pleasure flickered across her mind. He was delightfully aware of her breasts against his chest, and hugged her closer. *This is going to be the best ever.*

'No,' she said. Her shoulders dropped, and she rested her hands against his shoulders, moving them apart to end the embrace. 'I'm sorry, Edeard. I feel a lot for you I really do, you know that. That's the trouble.'

'What do you mean?'

'We could work, you and me. I really think we could. Lovers, then marriage, children. Everything. I'm not afraid of that. It's just the timing. It's wrong.'

'Timing?'

'I don't think you're ready for a long-term commitment

yet. And I certainly don't need another fling, not with someone I care about.'

'It wouldn't have to be a fling. I'm ready to settle down with someone as important to me as you are.'

'Oh Lady, you're so sweet,' she sighed. 'No, Edeard. I can't compete against the ideal of Salrana. You're closer to her than you know, or will admit. How could you not be after all the two of you shared. I'm not jealous, well, not exactly. But she's always going to be there between us until you sort your feelings out.'

'She's just a kid from the same village, that's all.'

'Open your feelings to me, show me your naked mind and say you don't want to bed her, that you don't want to know the feel of her against you.'

'I ... No, this is stupid. You're accusing me of ... I don't know: having dreams. This world is full of opportunities. Some we grasp, others we pass by. It's not me who's scared of what might be. You need to look at your own feelings.'

They were standing apart now, voices not raised, but firm.

'I know my own feelings,' she said. 'And I want yours to match mine. That means I can wait. You're worth waiting for, Edeard, however long it takes. You mean that much to me.'

'Well that's got to be the craziest way of showing it. Ever,' he said, trying not to let the hurt affect his voice. His mind hardened against releasing any emotion, which was difficult given the turmoil she'd kindled.

'Tell her,' Kanseen said simply. She reached out to stroke his cheek, but he dodged back. 'Be true to yourself, Edeard. That's the you I want.'

'Goodnight,' he said stiffly.

Kanseen nodded then turned away. Edeard was sure he saw a tear on her cheek. He refused to use his farsight to check. Instead he went into his own maisonette, and threw himself on the too-high bed. Anger warred with frustration in his mind. He imagined Salrana and Kanseen fighting, an image which quickly took on a life outside his control. His fist thumped the pillow. He turned over. Sent his farsight swirling out across the city, observing the vast clutter of minds as they wrestled with their own demons. It felt good not to be suffering alone.

He took a long time to fall asleep.

*

'Rumour has it, the Pythia uses her concealment ability to twist her features. She is over a hundred and fifty, after all; she could give Mistress Florell a run for her money in the withered crone stakes. There has to be some kind of devilment involved to make her look the way she does.' Boyd put a lot of emphasis on that last sentence, dipping his head knowingly.

'Can you do that?' a startled Edeard asked.

'I don't know.' Boyd lowered his voice. 'They say the Grand Masters can completely conceal themselves from view. I've never seen it myself.'

Edeard paused on the threshold of pointing out the slight logical flaw in that admission. 'Right.' They were on patrol in Jeavons, walking alongside the Brotherhood Canal, which bordered the southern side of the district. Beyond the water was Tycho, not strictly a district, but a wide strip of meadow between the canal and the crystal wall. Wooden stables used by the militia squatted on the grass, the only buildings permitted on the common land. He could see stable boys cantering horses and ge-horses along sandy tracks, the morning exercise which they and their predecessors had performed for centuries. Several horses had ge-wolves running alongside.

It was their sixth patrol since graduation. Six days during which he and Kanseen had barely exchanged a word. They'd been perfectly civil to each other, but that was all. He didn't want that, he wanted them at least to go back to how it was before that messed-up evening. How they might arrive back at that comfortable old association was a complete mystery. One he was definitely not going to consult the others on. He got the impression they already guessed something had happened. Knowing them, they'd royally screw up that speculation.

For some reason he'd also held off saying anything to Salrana. Grudgingly, he acknowledged that Kanseen did have a small point there. He really was going to have to face up to the whole 'friends become lovers' issue simmering away between him and Salrana. It wasn't fair on her. She was growing up into a beautiful adolescent, so much more vivacious than any of the city girls he encountered. All he had to do was get over his notion of protectiveness. That was stupid too. She was old enough to look out for herself, and make her own choices. The only person who'd appointed him her guardian was himself. Something he'd done out of obligation, and friendship. To do anything different, especially now, could be considered as taking advantage.

Sometimes you have to do what's wrong to do what's right.

And physically he knew they would be fantastic together.

That body, and as for those legs ... Altogether too much time of late was spent thinking about how her legs would feel wrapped round him, long athletic muscles flexing relentlessly. It would end with them both screaming in pleasure. *We wouldn't even get out of bed for the first year.*

Then after that, after the passion, they'd still enjoy each other's company. Salrana was the only person he could ever really talk to. They understood each other. Two hick kids against the city. Future Mayor. Future Pythia.

He smiled warmly.

'—of course, I could just talk to myself instead,' an irritated Macsen said.

'Sorry, what?' Edeard asked, banishing the smile.

Macsen glanced over at Kanseen, who was standing beside Dinlay, the pair of them looking down on a gondola full of crates, calling something to the gondolier. 'Boy, she really worked you over, didn't she?'

'Who? Oh, no. There's nothing wrong. Kanseen and I are fine.'

'I'd hate to see you un-fine.'

'Really, I'm good. What did you want?'

'The shopkeepers in Boltan Street keep saying strangers are walking along, checking out the buildings with a strong farsight. They're obviously a gang taking a scouting trip. So if we pitch up there in these uniforms we'll scare them off and they'll just come back in a week or a month – whenever we move on. But if we were to loiter around in ordinary clothes they wouldn't know we were there, and we could catch them at it red-handed.'

'I don't know. You know what Ronark is like about wearing the uniform on duty.' As they were starting their third patrol, the captain had unexpectedly appeared and performed a snap inspection. Edeard had almost been demoted for the 'disgraceful lack of standards'. Since then, he'd made sure his squadmates were properly dressed before leaving the station.

'Exactly,' Macsen said. 'If you're a constable in Jeavons you have to be in a uniform, everyone knows that. So they won't be expecting us out of uniform.'

'Humm, maybe. Let me talk to Chae first, see what he thinks.'

'He'll say no,' Boyd told them. 'You know procedure. If a crime is suspected, then you use ge-eagles to observe the area while the squad waits out of farsight range.'

'We don't know how long we'll have to wait,' Macsen said. 'And Edeard only has one ge-eagle.'

'You can sculpt more, can't you?' Boyd said. 'You told us you used to be an Eggshaper apprentice.'

'He can't sculpt without a Guild licence, not in Makka-thran,' Macsen said. 'It's the law; we'd wind up having to arrest him. You know how keen they are on maintaining their monopoly. In any case, this is going to happen soon. We don't have time to sculpt ge-eagles. That's why we have to go patrolling in disguise.'

'Ordinary clothes aren't a disguise,' Boyd protested.

'It doesn't matter what clothes we wear, as long as it's not the uniform,' Macsen said, his temper rising. 'Dress how you want. Maybe in a dress – you're certainly acting like an old woman.'

'Good one, smartarse. If this gang's as clever as you say, they'll know all our faces anyway.'

'Enough,' Edeard said, holding up his hands. 'I will

speak to Chae as soon as we get in. Until then I'll keep my ge-eagle close to Boltan Street. I can't do anything more in the middle of a patrol, so drop it for now, please.'

'Just a suggestion,' Macsen grumbled as he started to walk away.

'Are you deliberately winding him up?' Edeard asked Boyd.

The lanky boy gave a sly grin. 'I don't have to answer that, I'm not under oath.'

Edeard laughed. The Boyd of six months ago would never have dared any mischief at another's expense, let alone a friend.

The squad set off along the canal again, following the gentle curve northwards. Edeard's plan was to stay on the side path until they reached its junction with the Outer Circle Canal, then turn back in to Jeavons. He sent his ge-eagle swooping low over the roofs and towers of the district, guiding it towards Boltan Street. It was a damp grey morning, with the last of the night's rain clouds still clotting the sky as they slid slowly westwards. Every surface was slick with rain. However, the indomitable citizens of Makkathran were out in force as usual, thronging the streets and narrow alleyways.

Edeard's ge-eagle flashed silently above them, ignored by most. Then he caught a movement that was out of kilter. Halfway along Sonral Street, someone in a hooded jacket turned away from the eagle and adjusted their hood, pulling it fully over their head.

It could have been nothing, the ge-eagle was still over fifty yards away. And it was damp, the air chill. Perfectly legitimate for someone to pull their hood up in such circumstances. A lot of people in the same zigzagging street were sporting hats this morning. The man wasn't even alone in wearing a hooded jacket.

It's wrong though, I know it.

'Wait,' he told the squad. He swept the street with his farsight, searching for the one suspicious figure. The man's mind was shielded, though the tinge of uncertainty seeped out. Again, perfectly legitimate, he could be worrying about anything, from a bad quarrel with his wife to debts.

Edeard observed the direction he was taking and ordered the ge-eagle round in a long curve. It settled on the eaves of a three-storey house at the end of Sonral Street out of sight from its target. As he waited, Edeard realized the man in the hooded jacket wasn't alone; he was walking with two others. Then the ge-eagle caught sight of him on the street as he came round one of the shallow turns. By now, the hood had slipped back slightly.

'Oh yes, Lady, thank you,' Edeard said.

'What's happening?' Dinlay demanded.

'He's back,' Edeard growled. 'The thief from Silvarum market, the one who was holding the box.'

'Where!' Kanseen demanded.

'Sonral Street. Top third.'

The squad registered annoyance. 'We can't farsight that far,' Boyd complained.

'Okay, here you go,' Edeard gifted them the ge-eagle's sight.

'Are you sure?' Macsen asked.

'He's right,' Kanseen said. 'It is him, the bastard. I can just farsight him.'

'There are two others with him,' Edeard told them. 'And he's nervous about the ge-eagle, so they're not here for anything legitimate. Let's spread out and surround them.

Keep a street between yourself and them the whole time. I'll track them with farsight, I don't want to risk him seeing the ge-eagle again, that'll scare them off.'

They all smiled at each other, edgy with nerves and excitement.

'Go!' Macsen cried.

After five minutes' steady jogging Edeard wished he paid more attention to keeping fit. As before, Makkathran's citizens were reluctant to give ground to anyone in a hurry, least of all a red-faced, sweating, panting young constable. He dodged and shoved and wiggled his way along streets and through alleys, ignoring the whingers, and glaring down anyone who voiced a complaint. His uniform made it worse with its hot, heavy fabric restricting his movements.

Eventually he got himself into position a street to the west of the trio. His farsight showed him his squadmates taking up positions all around. 'Got them,' Dinlay's long-talk announced as he slowed to a walk.

'Me too,' Boyd reported.

'What do you think they're here to steal?' Macsen asked.

'Small enough to carry easily, valuable enough to be worth the risk,' Dinlay replied.

'Another one who's been paying attention during our lectures. But unfortunately that covers about ninety per cent of the shops around here.'

'Could be something in one of the storerooms, too,' Boyd suggested.

'Or a house,' Kanseen added.

'Let's just keep watch on them,' Edeard told them. 'When they go into a building, we close in. Remember to wait until the crime has been committed before arresting them.'

'Hey, never thought of that,' Macsen said.

Edeard let his farsight sweep through the buildings around the trio, trying to guess what they might be interested in. Hopeless task.

The suspects turned off Sonral Street into an alley so narrow one person could barely fit. Edeard hesitated, they were heading towards his street, but it was a blind alley, blocked by a house wall twenty feet high. His farsight probed around, revealing a series of underground storerooms beneath one of the jewellery shops on Sonral Street. There was a passage leading up to a thick metal door in the alley.

'At least they're consistent,' he remarked. 'That's a jeweller's shop on top.'

'On top of what?' Boyd asked.

'There's some kind of passage leading off the alley,' Kanseen told him. 'It leads downwards somewhere. Edeard, can you actually sense what's there?'

'A little bit,' he admitted reluctantly. 'Just some kind of open chamber. I think.' For a moment he wished everyone had his ability – life would be a lot easier.

'So now what do we do?' Macsen asked. 'We can't rush them, not down that alley.'

'Wait at the end,' Dinlay said. 'They can hardly escape.'

Edeard's farsight was showing him a whole network of interconnecting passages and rooms running under the row of shops. The passages all had locked doors, but once the thieves were inside, there was a chance they could elude his squad within the little underground maze.

'The rest of you get into Sonral Street,' he ordered. 'I'm going round the back to see if I can find another way down there.'

'You're not going in alone?' Kanseen asked. 'Edeard, there's three of them, and we know they carry blades.'

'I'm just going to make sure they don't have an escape route, that's all. Come on, move.'

He was faintly aware of his squadmates hurrying to the broad street beyond the alley. One of the thieves had bent down beside the small door, doing something to the first of its five locks. From what he could sense of the locks, Edeard knew he wouldn't like to try and pick them open. He concentrated hard, pushing his farsight through the city's fabric to map out the buried labyrinth of rooms and passages. In truth there were only three exits in addition to the one the trio were currently trying to break through.

Below that level, though, Edeard sensed the web of fissures which wove the city structures together. Several twisted their way up past the storerooms, branching into smaller clefts that laced the walls of the buildings above. He tracked back, finding a convoluted route that led to the street he was standing in. His third hand reached out, probing the fabric of the wall at the back of a tapering alcove between two shops. Nothing, it was as solid as granite.

Please, his longtalk whispered to the mind of the slumbering city. *Let me in.*

Something intangible stirred beneath him. A flock of ruugulls took flight from the roofs above.

Here, his mind pressed into the rear of the alcove. Something pushed back. Colourful shapes rose into his thoughts, swirling so much faster than the birds overhead.

In his dazed state he thought they resembled numbers and mathematical symbols, but so much larger and more complex than any of the arithmetic Akeem had ever taught him. With these equations the universe could surely be explained away. They danced like sprites, rearranging themselves into a new order before twirling away.

Edeard gasped, struggling to stand up as his legs shook weakly. His heart was pounding far harder than it had been from his earlier run through the streets. He felt the structure of the wall change. When he peered forward it looked exactly the same as before, a dark-purple surface with flecks of grey stretching all the way up to where the curving roofs intersected three storeys above him. But it *gave* when his third hand touched it.

There were people on the street around him, strolling along. Edeard waited until a relatively clear moment, and stepped into the little alcove. Nobody could see him now. His hand touched the section of wall at the back, and slipped right through. The skin tingled round his fingers, as if he were immersing them in fine sand. He walked into the wall. It was a sensation his brain interpreted as a wave of dry water washing across him. Then he was inside. He opened his eyes to complete darkness. His farsight cast around, and showed him he was suspended in a vertical tube. Even without visual sight, Edeard instinctively looked down. Farsight confirmed his feet were standing on nothing.

'Oh, Lady!'

He started to descend. It was as though a very powerful third hand was gently lowering him to the bottom of the fissure which snaked away horizontally under the buildings. Yet he was convinced it wasn't a telekinetic hold. He couldn't sense anything like that; some other force was manipulating him. Oddly, his stomach felt as though he was plummeting even though he was moving relatively slowly.

His feet touched the ground. That was when whatever force had gripped him withdrew, leaving him free to sink into a crouch. When he touched the wall of the fissure, he felt a slick of water coating it. A rivulet was trickling over the toe of his boots – he could hear it gurgling softly.

'It's a drain,' he said out loud, astonished that anything so fantastical could actually exist to serve such a mundane purpose.

Despite perfectly clear farsight, he patted round with his hands. The drain fissure was slightly too small for him to walk along it upright. Its side walls were about five feet apart. He took a breath, none too happy at the claustrophobic feeling niggling the back of his mind, and started to move forwards at a stoop.

The thieves had got through the locked door at the top of the passage. An impressive feat in such a short space of time. Two of them were descending the curving stairs to the door which sealed off the bottom, while the third stood guard outside. Edeard moved faster, navigating several forks along the drain fissure. He observed the thieves manipulate the locks on the second door, and go through. Then he was directly underneath the storeroom they were ransacking. The layout was distinct, the wooden racks laid out in parallel. Small boxes piled up on the shelves. A large iron box in one corner, with a very complicated locking mechanism. They were ignoring that.

Edeard looked up as his farsight pervaded the city's substance above him, a solid mass of rock-like material five yards thick. He concentrated. Closed his eyes – stupid but, well ... And applied his mind. Again the equations rose from nowhere to pirouette breezily around his thoughts. He began to rise up, slipping though the once-solid substance like some piece of cork bobbing to the surface of the sea. Once again his stomach was convinced he was falling, to a degree which brought on a lot of queasiness. He had almost reached the floor, when he realized the thieves would sense him the second he popped up. Quickly, he threw a concealment around himself. Then he was emerging into the storeroom, with a weak orange light shining all around. The floor hardened beneath his boots.

'What was that?' a voice asked.

Edeard was standing behind the rack at the back of the storeroom, out of direct sight. He held his breath.

'Nothing. Fucking stop panicking will you. There are only two doors, and the other one is locked. Now help me find the crap we came here for before someone senses us down here.'

Edeard slowly walked round the end of the rack. He could see the pair of them, moving along a rack, taking boxes off the shelf and prising them open with some kind of tool. A quick look inside, and the box would be tossed aside. Most of them seemed to contain little bottles. Dozens of them were clinking as they rolled about on the floor.

'Here we go,' the one in the hooded jacket announced. He'd just forced open a box full of tiny packets. One was opened to reveal a coil of metal thread. Edeard wasn't sure in the storeroom's low orange light, but it might be gold.

'I'll check out the rest,' the other one said.

The one with the hooded jacked began stuffing the packets into an inside pocket.

Edeard dropped his concealment.

'What the fuck—' Both thieves swung round to face him.

'Hello again,' Edeard said. 'Remember me?'

'Edeard!' Kanseen's panicky longtalk reverberated in his skull. 'Sweet Lady, where've you been? We've been going frantic. How did you get in there?'

'It's the little shit from the market,' the thief in the hooded jacket spat. 'I fucking knew that ge-eagle was on the prowl.' He reached inside his jacket and pulled out a long blade. At the same time his third hand tried to push into Edeard's chest for a heartsqueeze.

Edeard laughed as he deflected the attack. Then his own third hand slipped out and crushed the blade the thief was holding. The metal rippled, then warped into a slim bent spike. Edeard twisted the tip round into a U-shape. 'You're under arrest for theft and the attempted assault on a constable.'

'Fuck!' the other one yelled, and raced for the door.

'One coming out,' Edeard's longtalk told his squad-mates.

'Are you all right?' Dinlay demanded.

'Never better.' He hadn't taken his eyes off the hooded thief. The man held up the ruined knife, and gave an admiring grin. 'Tough guy, huh. Are you smart with it? There's enough precious metal in here to make everyone happy.'

'You want attempted bribery added to the charges?'

'Idiot.' The thief turned his back on Edeard, and walked casually towards the doorway out to the passage.

'Stop right there,' Edeard ordered.

The thief's third hand lifted one of the small bottles into

the air behind him. Edeard frowned uncertainly. Another bottle rose, accelerating to crash into the first. Glass shattered.

A fireball spewed out, dazzling white in the gloomy storeroom. Edeard twisted away instinctively, his shield hardening. Flaming globules splattered against it.

'Edeard!' the squad longtalked in unison.

'I'm all right.' He was blinking his eyes furiously, trying to get rid of the long purple glare-blotches. An acrid smell was growing strong, yet his farsight revealed just a few flickers of flame on the racks closest to the fireball. His third hand swatted them, snuffing the flames before they posed any real danger. Then he noticed the black holes in the boxes scattered across the floor, as if flames had burned through very quickly. The raw edges were still smouldering. When he looked closer, he saw they were coated in some kind of tar which was bubbling away. He shook his head in bewilderment.

'Got them,' Macsen announced victoriously. 'Lady, that last one's an arrogant bastard. You sure you're okay, Edeard?'

'Yeah, I'm fine.' He started to walk out of the storeroom. Some deep instinct made him tread carefully round the patches of hot liquid glistening on the floor. Thin wisps of vapour were layering the air close to the ceiling, producing a stench which made his eyes water. When he passed the bulky metal door he trod on some of the packets containing metal thread. The thief had thrown them all away. Edeard picked one up, frowning.

Why did he do that?

Mystified, he hurried up the passage and out into the alley where his squad was waiting with the subdued prisoners. Now he had time to think about what he'd done, and what the squad had achieved, his elation was rising with the potency of a dawn sun.

*

The court was convened in Makkathran's Parliament House, which dominated the Majate district. Technically one building, its component structures had amalgamated into a village of huge halls, assembly rooms, auditoriums, and offices, with cloisters instead of streets. Right at the centre was the elaborate Democracy Chamber where the Grand Council met to debate policy and laws. Wrapped protectively around that were tiers of offices for the Guild of Clerks who worked to administer the city's regulations and collect taxes. A whole wing contained well-appointed offices for each district representative, where they could be lobbied by their constituents about every perceived and actual injustice. Somewhere inside (underground it was rumoured) were the Treasury vaults, containing mountains of gold and silver, where the coins were minted. The Chief Constable was also based in one of the five conical towers, along with a modest staff. For centuries, the outermost tower, closest to the City Gate, used to house the militia barracks; but they had long departed, the serving soldiers to several barracks within the city, while their General and senior officers had taken up residence in the Orchard Palace next door. The vacated barracks had been eagerly taken over by the ever-expanding Guild of Lawyers.

Although democratically open to anyone, it was the interconnecting domes which ran alongside the Centre Circle Canal which the average Makkathran citizen was most likely to be familiar with. They housed the Courts of

Justice as well as the constabulary's main holding cells. Edeard and the rest of the squad had been shown round by Master Solarin, who explained the history of every corridor and room at inordinate and boring length. Part of their training was to attend trials so they could accustom themselves to the procedures, and listen to the verbal sparring of the lawyers. Edeard had been looking forward to that part, but in all the trials they watched the lawyers had confined themselves to simple questions to those in the witness stand. Though there had been an obscure argument about interpreting a precedent established four hundred years ago to settle a dispute between two fishmongers and their supplier about who got priority on the catch based on the length of the contract. Edeard barely understood the words they used, let alone followed the logic involved. The only criminal trial they'd seen was one where the constables had arrested a bunch of minor family sons during an altercation in a theatre late one night. The young men had all been sheepish, never challenged the senior squad sergeant's account, pleaded guilty to all charges, and accepted the fine without question.

As preparation and experience went, Edeard was beginning to realize how useless it had all been.

Two middle court judges and a Mayor's Counsel judge had been appointed to preside over the case against the trio of thieves they'd arrested. They sat together behind a raised wooden podium which ran along the back of the oval courtroom, clad in flowing scarlet and black robes, with fur-lined hoods hanging over their right shoulders. The Mayor's Counsel also wore a golden chain, signifying his high-ranking status.

Arrayed in the dock on their left the thieves stood with

two court constables in dress uniform standing guard. They had finally given their names. Arminel, the hooded leader called himself. No more than forty, with a drawn pale face and thick sandy hair that he wore long to cover large ears. At no time did he ever look worried. If anything his expression indicated ennui. His accomplices were Omasis and Harri. Harri was still in his teens, the one they'd told to stand guard in the alley. He'd only been charged with complicity to steal. Arminel and Omasis were both charged with theft and aggravated trespass. While Arminel had to face the additional charge of assaulting a constable. The jewellery shop owner had swiftly identified the contents of the two bottles Arminel had smashed together as a highly volatile spirit-based cleaning fluid and acid. Edeard had shivered at the thought of what could have happened if his shield had not been strong enough to ward off the fireball. He'd wanted Arminel to be charged with the attack on Kavine in the Silvarum market, but Master Vosbol, the lawyer that Captain Ronark had retained to prosecute the case, had said no. It was too long ago for witnesses to be considered reliable. 'But I recognized him immediately,' Edeard had cried.

'You saw someone behaving suspiciously,' Master Vosbol said. 'You believed him to be the participant in the previous crime.'

'Kavine will identify him.'

'Kavine was stabbed, quite badly. The defence will argue that makes him unreliable. Let's just go with these charges, shall we?'

Edeard sighed and shook his head.

It really should have served a warning as to the methodology of Makkathran's legal affairs. Instead, the first inkling that their case wasn't as watertight as they imagined came when the defendants all entered a plea of not guilty.

'They can't be serious,' Edeard hissed as Master Cherix, the defence lawyer, stood before the judges and entered the plea. The squad was sitting along the rear wall, all in their dress uniforms, waiting to be called by the prosecution. Captain Ronark sat on one side of them, with Sergeant Chae on the other.

Just about all of the seating was empty. Edeard didn't know if he was pleased about that or not. He wanted the city's citizens to see his squad had helped bring a small part of their troubles to justice. Show them that the law hadn't deserted them.

Master Cherix raised a surprised eyebrow at the exclamation, and turned to look at the squad. Master Vosbol shot them a furious look. 'Be silent,' his longtalk ordered.

It was, Master Cherix explained, a terrible misunderstanding. His clients were honest citizens going about their business when they perceived the blast in the alley. It had blown open a small door, and full of concern for human life they had ventured into the storeroom filled with smoke and flames – at great personal risk – to make sure there were no injured inside. At which point the constables had stumbled upon them, and received a totally false impression.

One by one the three accused took the stand and swore under oath that they had been acting selflessly. As they did so their unshielded minds radiated sincerity, along with a modicum of injured innocence that their good deed had been so misinterpreted. Master Cherix shook his head in sympathy, woebegone that the constables had acted so wrongly. 'A sign of the times,' he told the judges. 'These constables are well-meaning young folk, rushed through their training by a city desperate to make up staffing targets for the sake of politics. But in truth they were far out of their depth on that sad day. They too need to make arrests to prove themselves to their notoriously harsh station captain. In such circumstances it is only understandable why they chose to interpret events in the way they did.'

Edeard met Arminel's stare. *He tried to kill me, and his lawyer's making out it was all a misunderstanding? That we're in the wrong.* It was so outrageous he almost laughed. Then Arminel's expression twitched, just for an instant. That condescending sneer burned itself into Edeard's memory. He knew then that this was not the end. Nowhere near.

After two hours of listening to the defendants, Edeard was finally called to the stand. *About time, I can soon set this straight.*

'Constable Edeard,' Cherix smiled warmly. He was nothing like Master Solarin. He was a young man who dressed like the son of a trading family. 'You're not from the city, are you?'

'What's that got to do with this?'

Master Cherix put on a pained expression, and turned to the judges. 'My Lords?'

'Answer the questions directly,' the Mayor's Counsel instructed.

'Sir,' Edeard reddened. 'No. I was born in the Rulan province.'

'And you've been here for what? Half a year?'

'A little over that, yes.'

'So it would be fair to say that you're not entirely familiar with the city.'

'I know my way around.'

'I was thinking more in terms of the way our citizens behave. So why don't you tell me what you believe happened?'

Edeard launched into his rehearsed explanation. How Arminel tried to avoid the ge-eagle. The squad tracking them along Sonral Street. Arranging themselves in an encircling formation, whilst standing back and observing through farsight. Sensing Arminel picking the locks.

'At which point we closed in, and I witnessed the accused stealing gold wire from the storeroom.'

'I'm curious about this aspect,' Master Cherix said. 'You told your squad to wait in Sonral Street by the entrance to the alley. Yet you went down into the storeroom. But I thought you said Harri had been left "on guard duty" in the alley. How did you get past him?'

'I was lucky, I found another entrance through the shop which backed on to the jewellers.'

Master Cherix nodded in admiration. 'So it was hardly a secure storeroom then? If you could just walk in.'

'It was difficult,' Edeard admitted, praying to the Lady to help him rein in his guilt. But this wasn't a lie, just a slight rearrangement of his true route into the storeroom. 'I just managed to get there in time.'

'In time for what?'

'To see Arminel stealing the gold wire. He was doing that before he flung flaming acid at me.'

'Indeed. I'd like you to clarify another point, Constable. When you emerged after this alleged event to join up with your squad, did Arminel have any of this supposed "gold wire" on him.'

'Well, no, he dumped it when I challenged him.'

'I see. And your squadmates can confirm that, can they?'

'They know . . . yes.'

'Yes, what? Constable.'

'We caught them doing it. I saw him!'

'By your own statement, you were deep underground in the poorly illuminated storeroom at the time of the alleged theft. Which of your squadmates can farsight through fifteen yards of solid city fabric?'

'Kanseen. She knew I was there.'

'Thank you, Constable. Defence would like to call Constable Kanseen.'

Kanseen passed Edeard on her way to the stand. They both had meticulously blank expressions, but he could tell how worried she was. When he sat down next to Dinlay the others all smiled sympathetically. 'Good job,' Chae whispered. Edeard wasn't convinced.

'You have a farsight almost as good as your squad leader?' Master Cherix asked.

'We came out about equal in our tests.'

'So you could sense what went on in the storeroom from your position in Sonral Street?'

'Yes.'

Edeard winced, she sounded so uncertain.

'How much gold wire was in there?'

'I . . . er, I'm not sure.'

'An ounce? A ton?'

'A few boxes.'

'Constable Kanseen,' Master Cherix smiled winningly. 'Was that a guess?'

'Not enough gold to be obvious to a casual farsight sweep.'

'I'll let that go for the moment. Constable Edeard claims you perceived him in there.'

'I did,' she replied confidently. 'I sensed him appear in the back. We'd been worried when we lost track of him.'

'You sensed his mind. There's a big difference between a radiant source of thoughts and inert material, is there not?'

'Yes, of course.'

Master Cherix patted the jacket he wore under his black robe. 'In one pocket I have a length of gold wire. In another pocket I have an equal length of steel wire. Which is which, Constable?'

Edeard concentrated his farsight on the lawyer. Sure enough, there was some kind of dense line of matter in his pockets, but there was no way to tell the nature of either.

Kanseen looked straight ahead. 'I don't know.'

'You don't know. Yet there is only five feet of clear air between us. So can you really say with certainty you perceived my client picking up gold wire when he was on the other side of fifteen yards of solid mass?'

'No.'

'Thank you, Constable, no more questions.'

It came down to an argument between two lawyers. Edeard found himself grinding his teeth together as it was presented as his word against Arminel's.

'Acting suspiciously,' Master Vosbol ticked off on his fingers. 'Gaining entry to a storeroom behind two locked doors. Seen by a constable of impeccable character stealing gold wire. Attacking that same constable. My Lords, the evidence is overwhelming. They came to the storeroom with the express intent of theft. A theft which was valiantly thwarted by these fine constables at great personal danger to themselves.'

'Circumstantial evidence only,' Master Cherix pronounced. 'Facts twisted by the prosecution to support a speculated sequence of events. A country boy alone in an underground city storeroom full of smoke and flame. Confused by the strange environment and regrettably unreliable; his claims unsupported by his own squadmates and friends. My clients do not deny being in the storeroom, responding to the fire as any responsible citizen would. The prosecution has offered no proof whatsoever that they ever touched the gold wire. I would draw my Lords' attention to the precedent of Makkathran versus Leaney, hearsay is inadmissible.'

'Objection,' Master Vosbol barked. 'This is testimony by a city official, not hearsay.'

'Unsubstantiated testimony,' Master Cherix countered. 'Must be accepted as having equal weight to my clients' account of events.'

The judges deliberated for eight minutes. 'Insufficient evidence,' the Mayor's Counsel announced. 'Case dismissed.' He banged his gavel on the bench.

Edeard's head dropped into his hands. He absolutely could not believe what he'd just heard. 'Lady, no,' he gasped.

The defendants were cheering, slapping each other jubilantly. Edeard was disgusted to see Masters Vosbol and Cherix shake hands.

'It happens,' Captain Ronark said gravely. 'You did a perfect job, nobody could do better. I'm proud of you. But this is the way it is in Makkathran these days.'

'Thank you sir,' Dinlay and Macsen murmured sullenly.

Ronark flashed them all an anxious expression, debating with himself if he should say more. 'This will be useful to you,' he said. 'I can imagine what you think of that right now, but next time you'll know what to do, how to be extra careful gathering evidence, and we'll nail that little bastard good and proper.' He nodded at Chae, and walked down to talk with Master Vosbol.

'Buy you all a drink,' Chae said. 'I know how bad this hurts, believe me. I've had smartarse lawyers get scum off on worse charges than this.'

'A double of something illegally strong,' Macsen said. The others nodded in grudging agreement. They looked at Edeard.

'Sure,' he said.

Arminel saluted him with two fingers to his forehead. His smile was gloating.

Edeard quashed his impulse to dive across the court and smash his fist into the man's face. Instead he winked back. 'Be seeing you,' he whispered.

7

The unisphere had never been a homogenous system, nor was it designed along logical principles, which was quite an irony considering the purely digital medium it dealt with. Instead it had grown and expanded in irregular spurts to accommodate the commercial and civil demands placed on it by a proliferating interstellar civilization. By definition the unisphere was nothing more than the interface protocols between every planetary cybersphere, and they were incredibly diverse. Just about every hardware technology the human race had developed was still in operation across the Greater Commonwealth Worlds, from old-fashioned macro-arrays running RI programs, to semi-organic cubes, quantum wire blocks, smartneural webs, and photonic crystals, all the way up to ANA, which technically was just another routing junction. The interstellar linkages were equally varied, with the Central Commonwealth Worlds still using their original zero-width wormholes, while the External Worlds used a combination of zero-width and hyperspace modulation. Transdimensional channels were becoming more common especially among the latest generation of External Worlds. Starships were also able to link in provided they were in range of a star system's spacewatch network. The massive gulf between technologies and capacities within the unisphere meant the management software had swollen over the centuries to accommodate every new advance and application. With effectively infinite storage capacity, the upgrades, adaptors, retrocryptors, and interpreters had accumulated like binary onion layers around each node. They had the ability to communicate with every other chunk of hardware to come on line since the end of the twenty-first century; but with such a complex procedure dealing with every interface, the problem of security increased proportionally. It was relatively easy for a specialist e-head to quietly incorporate siphoning and echoclone routines amid centuries' worth of augmentation files. The problem was one which every user got round by using their own encryption. However, in order to decrypt a secure message, the receiver had to be in possession of the appropriate key. Ultra-secure keys were never sent via the unisphere, they were physically exchanged in advance, a common method for financial transactions. A less secure method was for a user's u-shadow to dispatch a key using one route, then call on another. Given the phenomenal number of (randomly designated) routes available within the unisphere, most people (who even considered it) regarded that as sufficient. It would, after all, require a colossal amount of computing power to monitor every route established to a specific address code for a key, then follow up by intercepting the message.

Of course, that assumption had been made in the early centuries, prior to ANA. For any individual downloaded into ANA, access to that quantity of processing capacity was an everyday occurrence. The Advancer Faction routinely ran a scan of all messages to ANA:Governance to check if any of its own activities had been noticed and reported.

When the Faction's monitor routine detected a starship TD connection established to Wohlen's spacewatch network downloading a key fragment to ANA:Governance's security division an alert was flagged. Over the next two point three seconds, the remaining seven key fragments arrived via routes from seven different planets, and the monitor acknowledged that someone was trying to establish a very secure link. Nothing too out of the ordinary in that, it was the security division after all. However, all eight planets were within twenty-five lightyears of the Advancer Faction's secret manufacturing station. That bumped the alert up to grade one.

Three seconds later, Ilanthe's elevated mentality was observing the secure call itself, placed through the ninth planet, Loznica, seventeen lightyears from the station.

'Yes, Troblum?' ANA:Governance asked.

'I need to see someone. Someone special.'

'I will be happy to facilitate any request in relation to Commonwealth security. Could you please be more specific?'

'I work for the Advancer Faction. Make that "worked". I have information, very important information concerning their activities.'

'I will be happy to receive your data.'

'No. I don't trust you. Not any more. Parts of you are bad. I don't know how far the contamination has spread.'

'I can assure you, ANA:Governance retains its integrity, both in structural essence and morally.'

'Like you'd say different. I can't even be sure if I'm talking to ANA:Governance.'

'Scepticism is healthy provided it does not escalate into paranoia. So given you don't trust me, what can I do for you?'

'I'm entitled to be paranoid after what I've seen.'

'What have you seen?'

'Not you. I'll tell Paula Myo. She's the only person left that I trust. Route this call to her.'

'I will ask if she will be willing to listen to you.'

Fifteen seconds later, Paula Myo came on line. 'What do you want?' she asked.

'There's something you need to know. Something you'll understand.'

'Then tell me.'

'I need to be certain it's you. Where are you?'

'In space.'

'Can you get to Sholapur?'

'Why would I want to?'

'I'll tell you everything I know about their plans for fusion, all the hardware they've built, all the people involved. All that, if you'll just listen to me. You have to listen, you're the only person left who'll deal with it.'

'With what?'

'Come to Sholapur.'

'Very well. I can be there in five days.'

'Don't stealth your starship. I'll contact you.'

The connection ended.

As ANA and its abilities were to the unisphere, so there were hierarchal levels within ANA. Discreet levels of ability surreptitiously established by a few of the humans who had founded ANA. Abilities only they could utilize. They couldn't corrupt ANA:Governance, or use the Navy warships for their own ends. That magnitude of intervention would be easily detectable. But there was a backdoor into several of ANA's communication sections, allowing them to watch the watchers without the kind of effort which the Advancers had to make for the same intelligence. And as they were there first, they had also observed the Advancers and other Factions spread their monitors into the unisphere nodes as their campaigns and reach grew. They knew which messages the Advancers intercepted.

'Ilanthe is going to go apeshit over that kind of betrayal,' Gore said.

'At least we know Troblum is still alive,' Nelson replied.

'Yeah, for the next five seconds.'

'Until he gets to Sholapur at the very least. And never ever underestimate Paula.'

'I don't. If anyone can collect him in once piece, she can.'

'So we might just be able to sit back and relax if Paula does bring back information on what the Advancers are up to. Hardware, Troblum said. That has to be the planet-shifting ftl engine.'

'Maybe so,' Gore said. 'But he was offering that as a bribe to make sure Paula listened to something else, something big and scary enough to get him really worried. Now what the fuck could that be?'

Marius sprinted down the corridor. It wasn't something the universe got to see very often. With his Higher field functions reinforcing his body, the speed was phenomenal. Malmetal doors had to roll aside very quickly or face complete disintegration. His dark toga suit flapped about in the slipstream, for once ruining the eerie gliding effect he always portrayed. Marius didn't care about appearance right now. He was *furious*.

Ilanthe's brief call had been very unsettling. He'd never failed her before. The implications were terrible, as she managed to explain in remarkably few words. He only wished he had time to make Troblum *suffer* for his crime.

He streaked through the three-way junction which put him into sector 7-B-5. Some idiot technician was walking down the middle of the corridor, going back to her suite after a long shift. Marius charged past her, clipping her arm, which broke instantly from the impact. She was spun round, slamming into the wall. She screamed as she crumpled to the floor.

The door to Troblum's suite was dead ahead, locked as of two minutes ago with Marius's own nine-level certificate to prevent the little shit from leaving. The suite's internal sensors showed Troblum sitting at a table slurping his way disgustingly through a late-night 'snack'.

Marius began to slow as his u-shadow unlocked the door. It expanded as he arrived, and he coasted through. Troblum's head lifted, crumbs of burger bap dropping from the corner of his mouth. Despite bulging cheeks he still managed a startled expression.

A disruptor pulse slammed into him, producing a ghost-green phosphorescent flare in the suite's air. Marius followed it up immediately with a jelly gun shot. He would obliterate the memorycell in a few seconds, then that would just leave Troblum's secure store back on Arevalo.

Instead of disintegrating into a collapsing globule of gore, Troblum simply popped like a soap bubble. A rivulet of metal dust spewed out from the wall behind the table where the jelly gun shot hit. Marius froze in shock, his field-scan functions sweeping round. It hadn't been Troblum. No biological matter was in the room. His eyes found a half-melted electronic module on the seat, ruined by the disruptor blast.

A solido projector.

Marius was perfectly still as he stared at it.

'What happened?' Neskia asked as she strode into the suite. Her long neck curved so her head could see round Marius.

'It would appear Troblum isn't quite the fat fool I'd taken him for.'

'We'll find him. It won't take long. This station isn't that big.'

Marius whipped round, the wide irises in his green eyes narrowing to minute intimidating slits. 'Where's his ship?' he demanded.

'Sitting in the airlock,' she replied calmly. 'Nobody enters or leaves without my authorization.'

'It better be,' Marius spat.

'Every centimetre of this station is covered by some sensor or other. We'll find him.'

Marius's u-shadow ordered the smartcore to show him the airlock. The *Mellanie's Redemption* was sitting passively at the centre of the large white chamber. Visually it was there, the airlock radar produced a return from the hull. The umbilical management programs reported a steady drain of housekeeping power through the cables plugged into its base. He queried the ship's smartcore. There was no response.

Marius and Neskia stared at each other. 'Shit!'

Four minutes later they walked into the airlock. Marius glowered at the long cone-shaped ship with its stupid curving tailfins. His field scan swept out. It was an illusion, produced by a small module on the airlock floor. He smashed a disruptor pulse into the solido projector, and the starship image shivered, shrinking down to a beautiful, naked young girl with blonde hair that hung halfway down her back. 'Oh, Howard,' she moaned sensually, running her hands up her body, 'do that again.'

Marius let out an incoherent cry, and shot the projector again. It burst into smouldering fragments, and the girl vanished.

'How in Ozzie's name did he do that?' Neskia said. There was a hint of admiration in her voice. 'He must have flown right past the defence cruisers as well. They never even saw him.'

Marius took a moment to compose himself. 'Troblum helped design and build the defence cruisers. Either he infiltrated their smartcores back then, or he knows a method of circumventing their sensor systems.'

'He compromised the station smartcore, too. It should never have let the *Mellanie's Redemption* out.'

'Indeed,' Marius said. 'You will find the corruption and purge it. This operation must not suffer any further compromise.'

'It was not me who compromised this station,' she said with equal chill. 'You brought him here.'

'You had twenty years to discover the bugs he planted. That you failed is unforgivable.'

'Don't try to play the blame game with me. This is your foul-up. And I will make that very clear to Ilanthe.'

Marius turned on a heel, and walked back to the airlock chamber's entrance. His dark toga suit adjusted itself around him, once more giving off a narrow black shimmer that concealed his feet. He glided with serpentine poise down the corridor towards the airlock chamber which contained his own starship.

His u-shadow opened a secure link to the Cat's ship.

'It's so nice to be popular again,' she said.

'We have a problem. I want you to find Troblum. Eliminate that shit from this universe. In fact, I want him erased from all of history.'

'That sounds personal, Marius dear. Always a bad thing. Messes with your judgement.'

'He's heading for Sholapur. In five days' time he will meet with an ANA representative there, and explain what we have been doing. His ship has some kind of advanced stealth ability we didn't know about.'

'Gave you the slip, huh?'

'I'm sure you'll be more than capable of rectifying our mistake.'

'What do you want me to do about Aaron? He's still down on the planet's surface.'

'Is there any sign of Inigo?'

'Darling, the sensors can barely make out continents. I've no idea what's going on down there.'

'Do as you see fit.'

'I thought this was all critical to your plans.'

'If Troblum exposes us to ANA there will be no plans, there probably won't be an Advancer Faction any more.'

'The strong always survive. That's evolution.'

'Paula Myo is the representative ANA is sending to collect Troblum.'

'Oh, Marius, you're too kind to me. Really.'

*

It should have been tempting. Alone in a small starship with three amazingly fit men, who would probably have been *honoured* to got to bed with him. Oscar had been delighted when Tomansio had introduced his team. Liatris McPeierl was his lieutenant, a lot quieter than Tomansio, with a broad mouth that could flash a smile that was wickedly attractive. He would handle the technical aspects of the mission, Tomansio said, including their armaments. Gazing at the pile of big cases on the regrav sled which followed Liatris about, Oscar had his first moment of doubt; he didn't want to resort to violence, though he was realistic enough to know that wasn't his decision. Cheriton McOnna had been brought in to help because of his experience with the gaiafield. There was nothing about confluence nest operations which he didn't know, Tomansio claimed. Oscar was slightly surprised by Cheriton's characteristics, they were almost Higher; he'd altered his ears to simple circle craters, his nose was wide and flat, while his eyes were sparkling purple globes, like multifaceted insect lenses. His bald skull had two low ridges reaching back from his eyebrows over his cranium to merge together at the nape of his neck.

'Multi-macrocellular enrichment,' he explained. 'And a hell of a lot of customized gaiamotes.' To prove it he spun out a vision of some concert. For a moment Oscar was transported to a natural amphitheatre, lost in a sea of people under a wild starry sky. On the stage far away, a pianist performed by himself, his soulful tune making Oscar sway in sympathy.

'Wow,' Oscar blinked, taking a half step back as the vision cleared. He'd almost been about to sing along, the song was familiar somehow – just not quite right.

'I composed it in your honour,' Cheriton said. 'I remember you told Wilson Kime you liked old movies.'

Now Oscar remembered. 'That's right. "Somewhere Over the Rainbow", yeah?' He took care to reduce his gaiamotes' reception level. Cheriton had produced a very strong emission. It made Oscar wonder if the gaiafield could actually be used in a harmful way.

'Yes.'

The last member of the team was Beckia McKratz, whose gaiafield give-away made it very clear she'd like to bed him. An equal to Anja in the beauty stakes, and minus all the neurotic hang-ups. Oscar wasn't interested. Not even that first morning when he stumbled out of his tiny sleep cabin to find all four of them in the main lounge stripped to the waist and performing some strenuous ni-tng exercise. They moved in perfect synchronization, arms and legs rising gracefully to stick out in odd directions, limbs flexing. Eyes closed, breathing deeply. From their gaiafield emanations, their minds seemed to be hibernating.

Aliens teleported into human bodies, and carefully examining what they could do.

It was all very different to Oscar's wake-up routine, which normally involved a lot of coffee and accessing the most trashy unisphere gossip shows he could find. And that was the whole non-attraction problem. All this devotion to perfection and strength didn't seem to leave them much time to actually be human. It was a big turn-off.

So he crept round the edge of the lounge to the culinary unit, snagged a large cup of coffee and a plate of buttered croissants, and sat quietly in a corner munching away as he watched the strange slow-motion ballet.

They came to rest position, and took one last breath in unison before opening their eyes and smiling.

'Good morning, Oscar,' Tomansio said.

Oscar slurped some more coffee down. That morning routine also included no conversation until his third cup. The culinary unit was suddenly busy churning out plates with large portions of bacon and eggs, with toast.

'Something wrong?' Liatris asked.

Oscar realized he was staring at the man eat. 'Sorry. I assumed you'd all be vegetarians.'

They all exchanged an amused glance. 'Why?'

'When we were flying the *Carbon Goose* across Half Way I remember the Cat kicking up a big fuss about the on-board food. She refused to eat anything produced and processed on a Big15 planet.' His companions' amusement evaporated. To Oscar it was as though he'd been trans-formed into some kind of guru, steeped in wisdom.

'You did talk to her, then?' Beckia asked.

'Not much. It was almost as if she was bored with us. And I still don't get why you idolize her the way you do.'

'We're realistic about her,' Cheriton said. 'But she accomplished so much.'

'She killed a lot of people.'

'As did you, Oscar,' Tomansio chided.

'Not deliberately. Not for enjoyment.'

'The whole Starflyer War happened because humanity was weak. Our strength had been sapped away by cen-turies of liberalism. Not any more. The External Worlds have the self-belief to strike out for themselves against the Central Worlds. That's thanks to Far Away's leadership by example. And the Knights Guardians are the political force behind Far Away. Politicians don't ignore strength any more. It is celebrated on hundreds of worlds in a myriad of forms.'

That was the trouble with history, Oscar thought. Once the distance has grown long enough any event can be seen favourably. The true horror fades with time, and ignorance replaces it. 'I lived through those times. The Commonwealth was strong enough to prevail. Without the strength we showed then, you wouldn't be alive today to complain about us and debate what might have been.'

'We don't want to offend, Oscar.'

Oscar downed the last of his coffee, and told the culinary unit to produce another. 'So sensibilities aren't a weakness, then?'

Liatris laughed. 'No. Respect and civility are highpoints of civilization. As much as personal independence and kindness. Strength comes in many guises. Including laying down your life to give the human race its chance to survive. If the Knights Guardians have one regret, it is that your name is not as famous and revered as the others from your era.'

'Holy crap,' Oscar muttered and collected his coffee. He knew his face was red. *My era!* 'All right,' he said as he sank back on to the chair which the lounge extruded for him. 'I can see we're going to have fun times debating history and politics for the rest of the mission. In the meantime, we do have a very clear objective. My plan is quite a simple one, and I'd like some input from you as we shake it down into something workable. You guys are the experts in this field, and this *era*. So, for what it's worth: there are several ANA Factions extremely keen to find this poor old Second Dreamer, not to mention Living Dream, which has a very clear-cut agenda for him. Between them they have colossal resources which we can't hope to equal, so what I propose is to jump on their bandwagon, and let them do the hard work. We should position ourselves to snatch him as soon as they locate him.'

'I like it,' Tomansio said. 'The simpler it is, the better.'

'Which just leaves us with mere details,' Oscar said. 'Everyone seems to think the Second Dreamer is on Viotia. We'll be there in another seven hours.'

'Impressive flight time,' Cheriton said dryly. 'I've never been in an ultradrive ship before.'

Oscar ignored the jibe. Tomansio had never asked who was employing Oscar, but the ship was a huge giveaway. 'Tomansio, how do we go about infiltrating the Living Dream operation there?'

'Direct insertion. We'll hack their smartcore's personnel files and assign Cheriton into the search operation. He's savvy enough to pass as a Dream Master, right?'

'No problem,' Cheriton said. He sighed. 'Reprofiling for me, then.' He ran a hand along one of his skull ridges.

'I'll make you look almost human,' Beckia assured him.

Cheriton blew her a kiss. 'Living Dream have been altering confluence nests all across the General Commonwealth to try and get a fix on his location,' he said. 'It must be costing them a fortune, which is a good indicator of how desperate they are. It's not a terribly accurate method, but once they narrow it down to a single nest, they'll know the district at least.'

'How does that help?' Beckia asked. 'A nest's gaiafield can cover a big area. If it's in a city it can include millions.'

'If it were me, I'd surround the area with specialist nests and Dream Masters, and try and triangulate the dream's origin.'

'So we can be in the general area just like them,' Oscar said. 'Then it's all down to speed.'

'The Factions will be running similar snatch operations,' Tomansio said. 'We'll be up against their agents as well as Living Dream.'

Oscar picked up on how enthused the Knights Guardians were by that prospect. 'The Faction agents will have biononics weapon enrichments, won't they?'

'I hope so,' Tomansio said.

'You can match that?' Oscar asked nervously.

'Only one way to find out.'

*

It was a gentle valley carpeted by long dark grass which rippled in giant waves as the breeze from the mountains gusted down. There was a house nestled in a shallow dip in the ground; a lovely old place whose walls were all crumbling stone quarried out of the nearby hills. An overhanging thatch roof gave it a delightful unity with nature. Its interior was a technology completely at odds with its outward appearance, with replicators providing him with any physical requirement. T-sphere interstices provided his family with an interesting internal topology, and any extra space they might want.

He stood facing it, holding his bamboo staff vertically in front of him. Torso bare to the air; legs clad in simple black cotton *dirukku* pants. Shutting down bionomic field functions, attuning his perception to sight, sound, and sensation alone. Feeling his surroundings. Nesting cobra: the foundation of self. He moved into sharp eagle. Then twisted fast, assuming jumping cheetah. A breath. Opponent moving behind. Bring the bamboo down and sweep, the tiger's claw. Spin jump as a coiled dragon. One arm bent into spartan shield. Lunge: striking angel. Drop the staff and pull both curving daggers from their sheaths. Bend at the knees into woken phoenix.

A vibration in the air. Heavy feet crushing tender stalks of grass. He raised his head to see a line of black armoured figures marching towards him. Long flames billowed from vents in their helmets as they roared their battle call. His breathing quickened as he tightened his grip on the daggers. The smell of charred meat rolled across the grassland. Aaron gagged on the terrible stench. Coughing violently, he sat up on the couch in the ground crawler's cabin.

'Shit,' he spluttered, then coughed again, fighting for breath. Doubling up. Exovision medical displays showed him his biononics assuming command of his lungs and airway, overriding his body's struggling autonomic functions. He wheezed down a long breath and shook his head as the artificial organelles stabilized him.

Corrie-Lyn was gazing at him from her couch on the other side of the cabin. She'd drawn her knees up under her chin, a blanket wrapped round her shoulders. For some reason she made him feel guilty. 'What?' he snapped, all caffeine-deprived bad temper.

'I don't know,' she said. 'Those warriors represent being trapped, I think. But they came to you outside your home. You were unable to escape what you are, what you had grown into.'

'Oh give me a break,' he growled, and tried to swing his feet off the couch. His blanket was wrapped round his legs. He pulled it off in an angry jerk.

Corrie-Lyn responded with a hurt scowl. 'They could also be a representation of paranoia,' she said with brittle dignity.

'Fuck off.' He told the culinary unit to brew some herbal tea. *To purge the soul.* 'Look,' he said with a sigh. 'Someone has seriously screwed with my brain. I'm bound to have nightmares. Just leave it, okay.'

'Doesn't that bother you?'

'I am what I am. And I like it.'

'But you don't know who you are.'

'I told you: drop this.' He settled into one of the two forward seats, and stared out of the thick windscreen slit. The ground crawler was lumbering forward, rocking about as if they were riding an ocean swell. Outside, the weather hadn't changed for the whole trip, a thin drizzle of ice particles blown along at high speed. High overhead, the dark underbelly of the cloud blanket seethed relentlessly, flickering with sheet lightning. They were traversing a drab landscape, where flood streams had gouged out deep sharp gullies. Broad headlight beams slithered over the dunes of filthy snow which migrated across the permafrost. Occasionally the surface of iron-hard soil was distended by some ruins, or stumps. Otherwise there was nothing to break the monotony.

Corrie-Lyn climbed off the couch without a word and went back to the little washroom compartment at the rear of the oblong cabin. She managed to slam the worn aluminium door.

Aaron rubbed his face, dismayed by how he'd handled the situation. Something in his dreams was eating away at his composure. He hated to think she was right, that his subconscious had somehow squirrelled away a few precious true memories. The personality he had now was simple and straightforward, uncluttered by extraneous attachments or sentimentality. He didn't want to lose that, not ever.

By way of apology, he started entering a whole load of instructions into the culinary unit. Thirty minutes later, when Corrie-Lyn emerged her breakfast was waiting for her on a small table. She pouted at it.

'The crawler's net reckons we're about ninety minutes from the camp,' he said. 'I thought you'd want to fortify yourself before we reached them.'

Corrie-Lyn was silent for a moment, then nodded in acknowledgement at the peace offering, and sat at the table. 'Has anyone been in contact?'

'From the camp? No.' They'd talked to someone called Ericilla last night, telling her their estimated arrival time. She'd seemed interested, though she laughed at the idea of any of her colleagues being an abandoned lover. 'If you knew any of my team mates you'd know you're wasting your time. Romantic they're not.'

'We're still connected to the beacon network,' Aaron said sipping another herbal tea. 'Nobody is owning up, yet.'

'What do we do if he's not there?'

Aaron resisted the impulse to look her up and down again. When she came out of the washroom she'd changed into a pair of black trousers and a light-green sweater with a V-neck. Her hair was washed and springy. No cosmetic scales on her face, but her complexion glowed. Clearly she was ready for her chance to reignite some of the old passion should *he* be there. She'd kept her gaiamotes closed up fairly tight since leaving Kajaani, but the occasional lapse had allowed Aaron to sense a lot of anticipation fermenting in her mind.

'I'm not sure,' he admitted. 'Time isn't in our favour.'

'And if he is there? What if he doesn't want to be hauled back to Ellezelin?'

Just for an instant something stirred Aaron's mind. Certainty. He did know what was going to happen afterwards. The knowledge was all there waiting for him. Ready for the moment. 'I'll just tell him what I have to. After that, it'll be up to him.'

Corrie-Lyn gave him a mildly doubtful stare before tucking in to her first bacon sandwich.

Camp, Aaron decided, was a rather grand description for the place where the team working in the Olhava province had set themselves up. A couple of ground crawlers were parked next to each other in the lee of some rugged foothills. Malmetal shelters had expanded out of their rear sections to provide the team with larger accommodation. But that was all.

Aaron parked a few metres away, and they both pulled on their bulky surface suits. Once his bubble helmet had sealed, Aaron went into the tiny airlock, and waited for the outside door to slide aside. He was immediately hit by the wind. Ice fragments swirled round him. He walked carefully down the ramp, holding the handrail tightly. The wind was squally, but he could stand upright. There were enhancer systems built in to the suit for when the storms really hit. Its main purpose was to protect him from the radiation.

Although there wasn't too much physical effort involved, he wished he'd nudged their ground crawler closer to those of the team. He took nearly three minutes to cover the small gap and clamber into a decontamination airlock on the side of one of the shelters. Corrie-Lyn was grunting and cursing her way along behind him.

Ericilla was waiting for them in the closet-sized suit room. A short woman with a frizz of brown hair flecked with grey. She smirked as Corrie-Lyn wriggled out of her surface suit, licking her lips in merriment. 'No man is worth this,' she announced.

'He is,' Corrie-Lyn assured her.

Aaron had already extended his field-scan function, probing the whole camp. He'd detected four people including Ericilla. None of them were Higher.

Ericilla beckoned. 'Come and meet the boys.'

Vilitar and Cytus were waiting for them, standing in the middle of the shelter's cluttered lounge like an army of two on detention parade. Nerina, Vilitar's husband, gave Corrie-Lyn a weary look.

'Oh shit,' Corrie-Lyn said despondently.

Nerina poked Vilitar in the chest. 'Well that lets you off.'

The two men relaxed, grinning sheepishly. Aaron sensed the tension drain away. Suddenly everyone was smiling and happy to see them.

'I thought there were five in your team,' Aaron said.

'Earl is down in the dig,' Ericilla said. 'The sensor bots picked up a promising signal last night. He said that was more important than, well—' The way she left it hanging told them she was on Earl's side.

'I'd like to see him, please,' Corrie-Lyn said.

'Why not?' Ericilla said. 'You've come this far.'

It was another trip outside. The entrance to the dig was

on the other side of the shelters. A simple metal cube housing a small fusion generator and several power cells. An angled force field protected it from Hanko's venomous elements. There was a decontamination airlock to keep the radioactive air out so the team's equipment could work without suffering contamination and degradation. Big filter units filled the rest of the entrance cube, maintaining the clean atmosphere. The temperature inside was still cold enough to keep the permafrost frozen. Aaron and Corrie-Lyn kept their helmets on inside.

Excavation bots had dug a passage down at forty-five degrees, hacking crude steps into the rocky ground. Thick blue air hoses were strung along the roof, clustered round a half-metre extraction tube that buzzed as it propelled grains of frozen mud along to be dumped on a pile half a kilometre away. Polyphoto strips hanging off the cables cast a slightly greenish glow. Aaron trod carefully as they went down. The solid ground around him blocked any detailed field scan.

The bottom of the crude stairs must have been seven metres below ground level. Ericilla explained they'd cut into a lakebed which had filled with sediment during the post-attack monsoons. There were several people from the surrounding area who had never made it to Anagaska.

The passage opened out into a chamber ten metres wide and three high, supported by force fields. Discarded arm-length bots were strewn over the floor with power cables snaking round them. A couple of hologram projectors filled it with a pervasive sparkly monochrome light. Ice crystals glinted in the sediment contained behind the force field.

There was an opening on the far side. Aaron's field scan

showed him another cavern, with a great deal of electronic activity inside. Someone was in there. Someone who could shield his body from the scan.

'Holy Ozzie,' Aaron breathed.

Corrie-Lyn gave him a curious look and strode into the second chamber. It was larger than the first, a third of its wall surface was covered with excavator bots. They looked like a mass of giant maggots slowly wiggling their way forward into the gelid sediment. A huge lacework of tiny pipes emerging from their tails led back to the start of the extraction tube. Silver sensor discs floated through the air, bobbing about to take readings. Silhouetted by the retinue of cybernetic activity was a lone figure wearing a dark-green surface suit. Corrie-Lyn took a couple of hesitant steps forward.

The man turned, lifting his bubble helmet off. His face had a Latin shading rather than Inigo's North European pallor, and the hair was dark brown rather than ginger. But apart from that, the features hadn't been altered much. Aaron thought it a particularly inferior disguise, as if he was just wearing make up and a bad wig.

'Inigo!' Corrie-Lyn whispered.

'Of all the Restoration projects on all the dead worlds in the galaxy, you had to walk into mine.'

Corrie-Lyn sank to her knees, sobbing helplessly.

'Hey, girl,' Inigo said sympathetically. He knelt down beside her, and flipped the outer seals on her helmet.

'Where've you been, you bastard!' she screamed. Her fist smacked into her chest. 'Why did you leave me? Why did you leave us?'

He wiped some of the tears from her cheeks, then leant forward and kissed her. Corrie-Lyn almost fought against it, then suddenly she was wrapping her arms around him, kissing furiously. The fabric of their suits made scratching noises as they rubbed together.

Aaron waited a diplomatic minute, then unsealed his own helmet. The air was bitingly cold, and held the strangest smell of rancid mint. His breath emerged in grey streamers. 'You're a hard man to find.'

Inigo and Corrie-Lyn broke apart.

'Don't listen to him,' Corrie-Lyn said urgently. 'Whatever he wants, refuse. He's insane. He's killed hundreds of people to find you.'

'Slight exaggeration,' Aaron said. 'No more than twenty, surely.'

Inigo's steel-grey eyes narrowed. 'I can sense what you are. Who do you represent?'

'Ah.' Aaron gave a weak smile. 'I'm not sure.' *But we're about to find out.* He could feel the knowledge stirring in his mind again. He was about to know what to do next.

'I won't go back,' Inigo said simply.

'What happened?' Corrie-Lyn pleaded.

Aaron's u-shadow reported a call was coming in from Director Ansan Purillar. Transferred across the hundreds of desolate kilometres from Kajaani by the small sturdy beacons to enter the camp where it finally trickled down into the excavation through a single strand of fibre-optic cable.

'Yes, Director?' Aaron said.

Inigo and Corrie-Lyn gave each other a puzzled glance, then looked at Aaron.

'Do you have some colleagues following you?' Ansan Purillar asked.

'No.'

'Well there's a ship coming through the atmosphere above us, and it won't respond to any of our signals.'

Aaron felt his blood chill. His combat routines came on line as he instinctively shielded himself with the strongest force field his biononics could produce. 'Get out.'

'What?'

'Get out of the base. Everyone out. Now!'

'I think you'd better explain just exactly what is going on.'

'Shit!' His u-shadow used the tenuous link to the base to establish a tiny channel to the *Artful Dodger*'s smartcore. 'Tell them,' he yelled at Corrie-Lyn.

She flinched. 'Director, please leave. We haven't been honest with you.' She turned to Inigo. 'Please?' she hissed.

He gave a reluctant sigh. 'Ansan, this is Earl. Do as Aaron says. Get as many as you can into the starship. Everyone else will have to use the ground cruisers.'

'But—'

The *Artful Dodger*'s smartcore scanned the sky above Kajaani. Its sweep was hampered considerably by the protective force field over the base. But it showed Aaron a small mass thirty kilometres high, holding position above the thick outer cloud blanket. 'Come and get us,' he told the smartcore. 'Fast.' His exovision showed him the starship powering up. Flight systems took barely a second to come on line. Its force field hardened. Directly overhead, an enormously powerful gamma-ray laser struck the base's force field. A scarlet corona flared around the puncture point, and the beam sliced into the generator building.

Complete force-field failure was an emergency situation which had been incorporated into the base's design. Secondary force fields snapped on over the cottages and science blocks, almost in time to protect them from the first awesome pressure surge. Several sheets of ice crystals hammered against the walls, drilling holes in the grass. Staff caught outside screamed and flung themselves down as the impacts battered them. It was over in seconds as the re-trapped air stilled. When they looked up they could see the parkland being scoured of grass and bushes by the victorious wind. Their starship had been cut in two by the gamma-laser strike, uneven sections lying twisted on the pad as the cold storm buffeted it about.

Beside it, the *Artful Dodger* rose into the maelstrom of radioactive destruction which cascaded across the base the instant the main force field vanished. Sensors showed it a pinprick of dazzling white light searing its way downward, accelerating at fifty gees. The ship's smartcore blasted away at the weapon with neutron lasers and quantum distortion pulses. Nothing happened. The smartcore started to change course. It wasn't fast enough. The lightpoint struck the *Artful Dodger* amidships, unaffected by the force field. Enormous tidal forces tore at the ship's structure, destroying its integrity. Even spars reinforced by bonding fields were ripped out of alignment. Ordinary components were mangled beyond recognition. The entire hull buckled and imploded to a third of its original size. Then the Hawking m-sink punched through the other side of the ship and streaked onwards into the ground. Its intense spark of light vanished. The surrounding ground heaved as if Kajaani had been hit by a massive earthquake, annihilating the remaining buildings and structures. All the secondary force fields died, leaving the collapsing cottages and science blocks exposed to the planet's malignant atmosphere.

The wreckage of the *Artful Dodger* tumbled out of the hurricane to smash into the ruins of the base.

Aaron's contact with the starship was lost as soon as the Hawking m-sink penetrated the hull, when every micro-circuit and kube physically distorted and ruptured.

A couple of Kajaani's sensors had caught the last moments of the star which had bolted out of the churning naked sky. Its speed was such that human eyes registered it as a single line of light, like a perfectly straight lightning bolt. Radiation monitor records showed a swift peak which went off the scale.

'What the hell just happened?' Corrie-Lyn demanded.

Aaron was too stunned to reply immediately. His u-shadow confirmed the beacon relay now ended two kilo-metres short of the base's perimeter.

'They fired on the base,' Inigo said quietly. 'Lady, they were completely unarmed.' He glared at Aaron. 'Was that one of the Factions?'

'Could be. It might even have been the Cleric Conser-vator making sure of his tenure.'

'There's a place in the depths of Honious reserved for your kind. I hope you reach it quickly.'

'Where?' Aaron asked.

Inigo and Corrie-Lyn gave him an identical snort of disgust.

'We'd better get back up to the shelter,' Inigo said. 'I expect they'll want to get to Kajaani right away. We are one of the closest camps.'

As soon as they came through the cramped suit room, Ericilla pointed an accusing finger at Aaron. 'That was you,' she yelled in fury. 'You're responsible. You told them to get clear. You knew who that was. You brought them here.'

'I didn't bring them *here*. Those people were going to catch up with us eventually. The location was … unfortunate.'

'Un-fucking-fortunate?' Vilitar spat. 'There were nearly two hundred people there. We don't know how many of them are still alive, but even if some of them survived the attack they'll be dying from the radiation. My friends. Slaughtered.'

'They'll be re-lifed,' Aaron said impassively.

'You bastard,' Cytus stepped forwards, his fist raised.

'Enough,' Inigo said. 'This won't help.'

Cytus paused for a moment, then turned away, his face contorted with disgust and anger.

'You knew, Earl,' Nerina said. 'You warned Ansan as well. What the hell is going on? Do you know these people?'

'I'm the one they're looking for. I didn't know about the attack.'

The rest of the team stared at each other in mute bewilderment. 'We're going to Kajaani,' Ericilla said. 'We can help recover the bodies before the winds blow them too far.'

'How long before your organization sends another ship?' Aaron asked.

'Like you care!'

'How long? Please.'

'Too long,' Nerina said. 'Hanko isn't part of the unisphere. We can't just yell for help. Our only link to the Commonwealth was the hyperspace link in the starship, which was connected to our headquarters back on Anagaska. Without that we're completely cut off. Anagaska will assume there was some kind of equipment failure; then after we haven't repaired it in a week, they'll probably investigate. If I remember right, we're due a scheduled flight in a fortnight anyway. They'll probably wait until then. Budget considerations.' She snapped it out in contempt.

'By which time radiation poisoning will have killed everyone exposed to the atmosphere,' Vilitar said. 'We don't have enough medical facilities to help them all. Congratulations.' He stared challengingly at Aaron.

'We need to get moving,' Ericilla said. 'The medical systems on our ground crawlers can help a couple of them, maybe more. She pushed her way past Aaron, not looking at him. Cytus managed to knock Aaron's elbow as he went into the suit room.

'You coming, Earl?' Nerina asked.

'Yeah.'

'You've done enough already,' Vilitar said. 'Whoever the fuck you really are. I thought—' He snarled incoherently and hurried into the suit room.

'We'll come with you,' Corrie-Lyn said. 'We can help.'

'The Asiatic glacier is half a day from here,' Nerina said. 'The far end has mile-high cliffs. Why don't you *help* us by driving off them.' She went into the suit room and closed the door.

'Then there were three,' Aaron said.

'We'd better get going,' Inigo said. He faced Aaron. 'You know they'll probably close the Restoration project down because of this.'

'Do you think the next galaxy along will mount a Restoration project for all the species which the Void devourment phase exterminates?'

For a moment Aaron thought Inigo might actually activate his biononics in an aggressor mode. 'You know nothing,' the lost messiah whispered.

'I hope something, though.'

'What?'

'That you have a starship stashed away. Preferably close by.'

'I don't.'

'Really? I find that mighty curious. You took all this trouble to stay lost. Yet you have no escape route if someone came along to expose you.'

'Obviously not, otherwise I wouldn't have been here waiting for you.'

'You wouldn't have been waiting around here if it had just been me,' Aaron said. He gestured at Corrie-Lyn. 'But her? That's different. Seventy years is a long time to be alone. She stayed in love for that long. Did you?'

Corrie-Lyn moved up close to Inigo. 'Did you?' she asked in a quiet voice.

A mournful smile flickered over his lips. 'I'm glad it was you. Is that enough?'

'Yeah,' she rested her head on his shoulder.

'No ship,' Inigo told Aaron. 'And the only way I go anywhere with you, is in a bag as small lumps of charcoal.'

'That's a shame, because I know what weapon they used to take out my starship and the base.'

'Is that supposed to impress me? I expect you know a great deal about weapons and violence. Men like you always do.'

'It was a Hawking m-sink,' Aaron said. 'Do you know what that is? No? They're new and highly dangerous. Even ANA gets nervous around them. Basically, it's a very small black hole, but cranked up with an outsize event horizon to help absorption. It starts off as a little core of neutronium about the size of an atomic nucleus.'

Corrie-Lyn caught the emphasis. 'Starts off?'

'Yes. Its gravity field is strong enough to pull in any atoms it comes into contact with. They're then also compressed into neutronium and merge with its core. With each atom, it gets a little bit bigger. Not by much admittedly, not to begin with. But the larger the surface area, the more matter it can absorb. And after it tore through the *Artful Dodger* it hit the planet. Right now it is sinking through the mantle, eating every atom it encounters. It'll stop at the centre of the planet. Then it just sits there and grows.'

'How big will it get?' she asked anxiously.

Aaron shot Inigo a look. 'Black holes have no theoretical size limit. We used to think that was what the Void was.'

'But . . . Hanko?'

'It'll take about a fortnight to devour the entire mass of an H-congruous world. Except we'll be dead long before that. Hanko will start to disintegrate as it's consumed from within. The continents will collapse in three or four days' time. So, once more, with a awful lot of feeling, do you have a starship hidden nearby?'

*

Araminta kissed three hims as they sat at a table under a gazebo of flowering yisanthal in his garden. 'I missed that,' she told the rugged oriental one.

Mr Bovey smiled in unison. Hes raised his glasses. 'Cheers.'

'Cheers.' She sipped her white wine.

'So?' asked the one she'd had their first dinner with.

Araminta steeled herself. 'If your offer is still open, I'd like to accept.'

She even heard cheering coming from the big house as well as the racket which the three under the gazebo made.

'You've made some old men very happy.'

'Us young ones, too.'

Araminta laughed. 'And I have absolutely no idea how to go about this. The first three apartments will be ready in another week. I've accepted a deposit on the fourth.'

'Congratulations.'

'But until I've completed and the tenants are in, I won't see a profit. I need money to buy bodies.'

'Not as expensive as you might think. A friend, one of us, runs a clinic expressly for that purpose. She always gives discount to a first-expander.'

'Okay.' She took another drink to calm her shudders. It was momentous, sort of like accepting two proposals at once.

The young Celtic one squeezed her arm. 'You all right?' he asked, all full of sympathy.

'I guess so.' She knew she was smiling like an idiot. *But this does feel right.*

Two hims came hurrying out of the house. One of them who seemed about seventeen went down on his knee beside her. A slim athletic build, she saw, with a wild stock of blond hair. He proffered a small box which opened to show her an antique diamond engagement ring.

'I bought it just in case,' he told her.

Araminta slipped it on to her finger, then dashed away the tears.

'Oh, come here,' the youngster exclaimed.

His arms went round her, hugging tight; and she was laughing through the tears. 'I haven't seen you before.'

'I'm a slavedriver to me.'

She put her palms on his cheeks and kissed him thoroughly. 'I would like you to be one of tonight's.'

'My considerable pleasure.'

'I believe you said I still have several yous to get to know.'

'Oh trust me, you'll know all of mes before our wedding day.'

'And I don't mind, and won't complain about other women until I have enough bodies to cope. Just . . . I don't want to meet them.'

'I'll try and keep it to a minimum, I promise.'

'Thanks,' she whispered gratefully.

'Now what sort of bodies are you going to go for?'

'Gosh, I hadn't thought about that,' she admitted. 'What do you like?'

'Got to be a tall blonde Amazon type. Always popular.'

'Oh, and very black as well. Let's cover all the old ethnicities, I have – almost.'

'And one of you has to have huge breasts.'

'More than one!'

She slapped at him, feigning shocked dismay. 'You're appalling. I'm not doing anything like that.'

'That's not what you usually say in bed.'

Araminta laughed. She really had missed this. *I made the right decision.*

Araminta lay on the big bed, listening to three hims sleeping. Two on the bed with her, and one on the couch, curled up in a quilt, all breathing softly, not quite in synch. Tonight she'd refused any aerosols, wanting to try out Likan's program, to make sure it worked with other people, that he hadn't loaded in a hidden expiry key.

It worked.

And how.

Mr Bovey had been surprised, then very appreciative, at how much more responsive her body had become. As she'd suspected, a night in bed with hims had been a lot better than it had with Likan and the harem. *Always nice to have confirmation.*

Now she couldn't sleep. Not that she wasn't tired, she grinned to herself, but she couldn't stop thinking about the engagement, and embracing a multiple lifestyle. It was such an upheaval. Everything was going to change for her. So much so, she was more than a little apprehensive. Her mind was churning over the same questions again and again. Unable to find answers, because she didn't actually *know* about being multiple. The only way to truly find out was to become one.

She turned her head to look at the young red-haired him who was nestled up cosily beside her. He'd help her through the transition, she knew. Mr Bovey loved her. That was enough to take her through the next few months. They hadn't set a date. He'd said he'd like at least two hers to register the marriage with him. Which was fair enough. She *really* needed to finish the apartments. Today had made that even more urgent.

Araminta settled back on to the soft mattress and closed her eyes. She used the program to still her whirling thoughts, emptying her mind. Her body started to calm as she found and slowed its natural rhythms, cycling down. Instead of sleep, the emptiness opening within made her aware of the images which lurked just below conscious thought. Not just one, but a whole range, all tasting and feeling very different. They twisted out of the infinite distance, a connection she now finally understood belonged to herself. Instinctively, she knew how to focus on whichever she wanted. Some were Mr Bovey's dreams, she was familiar enough with him to recognize his mental scent. She sighed fondly as she experienced his presence; part of his mind was so wound up, the poor man, while she also felt his happiness – her own face slithered in and out of his thoughts. One of the connections was completely alien, yet comfortably warm in that way a parent was with a child. Her lips lifted in a serene smile. The Silfen Motherholme. So Cressida had been telling the truth. In which case that oh-so-busy chorus of multicoloured shadows must be the gaiafield.

Araminta embraced the quiet one; the most tenuous connection of all. And found herself gliding through space far from any star. The Void's nebulas glimmered lush and glorious behind her as she rose to the darkness of the outer regions.

'Hello,' she said.

And the Skylord answered.

*

Justine had expected to feel a lot of excitement as her starship, the *Silverbird*, descended towards Centurion Station. Five hundred hours alone in a small cabin with no unisphere connection had left her unexpectedly strung out.

Intellectually, she knew it was a nonsense, a quirk of her primitive body's biochemistry and neurological weakness. But it was still real.

Now here she was, at her destination, and all she could think about was the identical, boring trip back. *I must have been crazy to do this.*

The *Silverbird* touched down on the lava field which acted as a spaceport for the human section of the Centurion Station. Five other starships were sitting there, all of them bigger than hers. The smartcore reported several discreet sensor scans probing at the ship. The tall Ethox tower was the worst offender, using quite aggressive quantum signature detectors. More subtle scans came from the dour domes of the Forleene. There was even one quick burst of investigative activity from the observatory facilities in the human section. She smiled at that as her thin spacesuit squeezed up against her body, expelling all the air pockets to form an outer protective skin. She locked the helmet on.

It was a short walk over the sandy lava to the main airlock. Justine needed it for the sense of space and normality it gave her. She couldn't believe how much she felt reassured by the sight of a planetary horizon, even one as drab as this. When she stopped to look up, angry ion storms fluoresced the sky for lightyears in every direction. Pale mockeries of the nebulas inside the Void.

Director Lehr Trachtenberg was waiting for her in the reception hall beyond the airlock. A formidably sized man who reminded her of Ramon, one of her old husbands. Standing in front of him, shaking his hand in greeting, and tipping her head back just to see his face was another reminder of how negligible her physical body was. Of course, that Ramon connection did shunt her mind back to the possibility of sex.

'This is a considerable honour,' Lehr Trachtenberg was saying. 'ANA has never sent a representative here before.'

'Given the political circumstances back in the Commonwealth, it was deemed appropriate to examine the data from the Void first-hand.'

The director licked his lips slowly. 'Distance makes no difference to data, Justine. We do send the entire range of our findings directly back to the Navy's exploration division, and the Raiel.'

'Nonetheless, I'd like the opportunity to review your operation.'

'I wasn't about to refuse you anything. Especially not after the trip you've just made. To my knowledge no one has ever travelled so far by themselves. How did you stand the isolation?'

She suspected that he suspected the *Silverbird* had an ultradrive, but chose to gloss over the actual journey time. 'With difficulty and a lot of sensory dramas.'

'I can imagine.' He gestured at the five-seater cab which was waiting at the end of the reception hall. 'I've assigned you a suite in the Mexico accommodation block.'

'Thank you.'

'I'm also throwing a welcome party for you in three hours. Everyone is very keen to meet you.'

'I suppose they are,' she said. 'Fine, I'll be there. I could do with some company after that trip.'

They climbed into the little cab together, which immediately shot into the transport tunnel. 'I should warn you that nearly a third of our observation staff are Living Dream followers,' the director said.

'I reviewed personnel files before I came.'

'As long as you know.'

'Is it a problem?'

'Hopefully not. But, as you implied, it's a volatile situation right now.'

'Don't worry, I can do diplomatic when I have to.'

Her suite was equal to any luxury hotel she'd stayed in. The only thing missing was human staff, but the number of modern bots more than made up for it. The Navy had clearly spared no effort in making the station as cosy as possible for the scientists. The main room even had a long window looking out over the alien sections of the station. Justine stared at them for a while, then opaqued the glass. Her u-shadow established itself in the room's net. 'No visitors or calls,' she told it.

Justine settled back on the bed, and opened her mind to the local gaiafield. The darkened room filled with phantoms, colours glinted amid the deeper shadows. Voices whispered. There was laughter. She felt drawn to various emotional states which promised to immerse her in their enticing soulful sensations.

Resisting temptation, she focused her attention on the nucleus of the whimsy, the confluence nest itself. A quasi-biological neural module which simultaneously stored and emitted every thought released into its field. It had memories like a human brain, only with a much, much larger capacity. Justine formed her own images, offering them up to the nest. It responded with association. Naturally, it contained every one of Inigo's dreams; Living Dream had made sure of that. She ignored the vivid spectacle of the Waterwalker's life, brushing those memories aside as she refined her own fancy for a different recollection of life inside the Void. The nest was full of enigmas, the mental poetry left behind by observers baffled by the terrible dark heart of the galaxy. There were compositions of how a life might be lived for anyone fortunate to pass inside; wish fulfilment, easily discernible from the real thing. The promise-prayers which Living Dream's followers made every night to their mystic goal. All were imprinted on the nest. But nothing else. No other glimpse into another life lived on Querencia. No grand mellow thoughts originating from a Skylord.

The garden dome at the middle of the human section boasted trees over two hundred and fifty years old. Oaks with thick trunks sent out thick crinkled boughs, acting as lush canopies above the tables where the station staff were gathering. Up on a rustic tree-house platform, an enthusiastic amateur band were playing songs from different eras stretching back across several centuries, and were keen for requests. It was dusk inside, allowing the sharp violet light of the Wall stars to dominate the sky overhead.

Justine admired the broad patch of eye-searing scintillations with the kind of weariness she reserved for dangerous animals. Her arrival in the garden dome had created quite a ripple of interest. She liked to think that was at least partly due to the little black cocktail dress she'd chosen. It certainly seemed to have the required effect on Director Trachtenberg, who was becoming quite flirtatious as he fussed round, offering her various drinks and selections of the finger food.

Everyone she was introduced to was keen to know

exactly what ANA's interest was in them at this time. She repeated the official line a dozen times that she was just visiting to ascertain the current status of the observation.

'Unchanged,' complained Graffal Ehasz, the observation department chief. 'We don't learn anything these days apart from ion storm patterns in the Gulf on the other side of the Wall stars. That tells us nothing about the nature of the beast. We should be trying to send probes inside.'

'I thought nothing could get through the barrier,' she said.

'Which is why we need a much more detailed study. You can't do that with remote probes fifty lightyears away.'

'The Raiel don't like us getting closer,' Trachtenberg said.

'When you get home, you might like to ask ANA why we still need their *permission* just to fart around here,' Ehasz said. 'It's fucking insulting.'

'I'll remember,' Justine said. The party was only twenty minutes old; she wondered how many aerosols Ehasz had already inhaled.

The director took her by the arm and politely guided her away.

'Sorry about that,' he said. 'There's not a lot of opportunity to blow off steam around here. I run a pretty tight schedule. This is an expensive installation, and phenomenally important. We need to extract the best information we can with what we've got.'

'I understand.'

'It's Ehasz's third stint out here. He tends to get frustrated by the lack of progress. I've seen it before. First time, you're all swept along by the wonder of it all. Then when that fades away you begin to realize how passive the observation actually is.'

'How many times have you been here?'

He grinned. 'This is my seventh. But then I'm a lot older and wiser than Ehasz.'

'So would you like to join the Pilgrimage?'

'Not really. As far as three hundred years of direct observation has shown us, you touch the barrier, you die. Actually, you die a long time before you reach the barrier. I just don't see how they hope to get through.'

'Somebody did, once.'

'Yeah, that's the really annoying part.'

'So what do—' Justine stopped as the ground heaved, almost knocking her feet out from under her. She tensed, dropping to a crouch like just about everyone else. Her integral force field came on. The local net was shrieking out all sorts of alarms. The huge oak boughs creaked dangerously; their leaves rustling as if tickled by a gust of wind.

'Hoshit,' Trachtenberg yelped.

Justine's u-shadow established a link to the *Silverbird*'s smartcore. 'Stand by,' she told it. 'Keep a fix on my position.' When she scanned round the dome it was still intact. Then she looked at the horizon, which appeared to be perfectly level. She'd been expecting big cracks to be splitting the lava plain open at the very least. The ground tilted again. *Nothing moved!* 'What is happening?' she demanded. Some kind of quake? But this planet was a dead husk, completely inactive in any respect.

'I'm not sure.' The director waved an annoyed hand to shush her.

The band were clambering down out of the tree-house as fast as they could go, jumping the last metre off the wooden steps. They'd abandoned their instruments. Justine stared at the drink in her hand as the ground shifted again. The wine sloshed from one side of the glass to the other, yet she was holding it perfectly still.

'Holy Ozzie,' Trachtenberg exclaimed. 'It's gravity.'

'What?'

'Gravity waves. Fucking colossal ones.'

Ehasz hurried over to them, swaying badly as the ground seemed to tilt again. 'Are you accessing the long-range sensors?' he yelled at Trachtenberg.

'What have they got?'

'The boundary! There are distortion ripples lightyears long moving across it. And the damn thing is growing. The sensors in the Gulf can actually see it move. Do you realize what that means? The expansion is superluminal. This is an Ozziefucking devourment phase.'

The ground quivered badly. Water running along the little streams sloshed about, shooting up small jets of spray. For a moment, Justine actually felt her weight reduce. Then it came back, and the neat stacks of crockery and glasses on the tables crashed on to the grass. She stumbled away from the oak tree as it emitted a nasty splintering sound. Emergency force fields were coming on, reinforcing the dome. Around the rim, safety bunker doors rippled open.

'I want everyone to move to evacuation stage one,' Trachtenberg announced. 'Navy personnel report direct to your ships. Observation team, I need a precise picture of what is happening out there. We probably don't have much time, so we must do as much as we can before we're forced off.' He flinched as another gravity wave crossed the station. This time the upward force was so strong Justine felt as though she was going to lift off.

'Is that gravity coming from the Void?' she asked. The prospect was terrifying, they were hundreds of lightyears away.

'No,' Ehasz cried. 'This is something local.' He looked upwards, studying the intricate luminescent sky above the dome. 'There!'

Justine watched two azure moons traverse the sparkling smear of Wall stars. They were in very strange orbits. And moving impossibly fast – actually accelerating. 'Oh my God,' she gasped. The Raiel's planet-sized DF machines were flying into new positions.

'The Raiel are getting ready for the last fight,' Ehasz said numbly. 'If they lose, that monster will consume the whole galaxy.'

This can't be happening, Justine thought. *Living Dream hasn't even begun their Pilgrimage yet.* 'You can't!' she shouted up at the ancient invisible enemy as human hormones and feelings took complete control of her body and mind. 'This isn't fair. It's not *fair!*'

*

A mere five hours after the new dream had flooded into the gaiafield, over fifty thousand of the devout had already gathered in Golden Park, seeking guidance from the Cleric Conservator. They exerted their wish through their gaia-motes. The unanimous desire of fifty thousand people was an astonishing force.

Ethan was only too aware of it as Councillor Phelim supported him on the long painful walk out of the Mayor's offices where the doctors had set up an intensive care bay.

He limped across the floor of Liliala Hall while the ceiling displayed surges of thick cumulus arrayed in mares' tails and clad in shimmering strands of lightning. Even though he'd closed himself to the gaiafield, the power of the crowd's craving was leaking into his bruised brain.

Phelim continued to support him as they crossed the smaller Toral Hall. Its midnight ceiling showed the Ku nebula with its twinkling gold sparks swimming within fat undulating jade and sapphire nimbi.

'You should have called them to your bed,' Phelim said.

'No,' Ethan grunted. For this occasion he would not, could not, show weakness.

They went through the carved doors to the Orchard Palace's Upper Council chamber. Its cross-vault ceiling was supported by broad fan pillars. Dominating the apex of the central segment a fuzzy copper star shone brightly, its light shimmering off a slowly rotating accretion disc. Moon-sized fireball comets circled the outer band in high-inclination orbits. None of Makkathran's enthusiastic astronomers had ever spied its location in the Void.

The Cleric Council waited for him in their scarlet and black robes, standing silently at the long table which ran across the middle of the chamber. Phelim stayed by Ethan's side until they reached the dais, then Ethan insisted on walking to his gold-embossed throne by himself. He eased himself on to the thin cushions with a grimace. The pain in his head nearly made him cry out as he sank down. He took a moment to recover as his body shuddered. Ever since he'd regained consciousness any sudden movement was agony.

The Councillors sat, trying to avert their eyes from the

liver-like semi-organic nodules affixed to his skull, only half-hidden by his white robe's voluminous hood.

'Thank you for attending,' Ethan said to them.

'We are relieved to see you recovered, Cleric Conservator,' Rincenso said formally.

Ethan knew the contempt of the other Councillors towards his supporter without needing the gaiafield. He felt it himself. 'Not quite recovered yet,' he said, and tapped one of the glistening nodules. 'But my neural structure should be fully re-established in another week. Until then the auxiliaries will suffice.'

'How could such a thing happen?' Councillor DeLouis asked. 'Gaiamotes have been perfectly safe for centuries.'

'It wasn't the gaiamotes,' Phelim said. 'The Dream Masters who set up the interception believe the Second Dreamer's panic triggered a neural spasm within the Cleric Conservator's brain. They were attuned to a degree rarely achieved outside a couple's most intimate dreamsharing. The circumstances will not arise again.'

'The gaiafield and the unisphere are rife with rumours that the Second Dreamer is a genuine telepath, that he can kill with a single thought.'

'Rubbish,' Phelim said. His skeletal face turned to DeLouis. For an instant a dangerous anger could be glimpsed in his mind.

DeLouis couldn't meet his stare.

'In any case it is irrelevant,' Ethan said. 'The Dream Masters assure me that such a backlash can be nullified now they understand its nature. Any future contact with the Second Dreamer will be conducted with,' he smiled grimly, 'a safety cut-out, as they call it.'

'You're going to talk to him again?' Councillor Falven asked.

'I believe the situation requires it,' Ethan said. 'Don't you?'

'Well, yes, but . . .'

'I received his latest dream along with the rest of you. It was strong, at least as clear as those of the Dreamer Inigo himself. However, the crucial change within this dream was the conversation the Second Dreamer had with the Sky-lord.' The communication had shocked Ethan more than the pristine clarity of the new dream.

'I come to find you,' the Skylord had replied to the Second Dreamer's greetings.

'We are far beyond the edge of your universe.'

'Yet I felt your longing. You wish to join with us.'

'Not I. But other do, yes.'

'All are welcome.'

'We can't get in. It's very dangerous.'

'I can greet you. I can guide you. It is my purpose.'

'No.'

And with that finality the dream had ended. Before it faded completely, there was a hint of agitation from the Skylord's mind. It clearly hadn't expected rejection.

And it's hardly alone in that.

'The Skylord believes it can bring us to Querencia,' Ethan said. 'That is the final testimony we have been waiting and praying for. Our Pilgrimage will be blessed with success.'

'Not without the Second Dreamer,' Councillor Tosyne said. 'Your pardon, Conservator, but he is not willing to lead us into the Void. Without him there can be no Pilgrimage.'

'He is distressed,' Ethan replied. 'Until now he didn't even know he was the Second Dreamer. To discover you are the hope of billions is not an easy thing. Ultimately, Inigo himself found it too great to bear. So we can forgive the Second Dreamer his frailty, and offer support and guidance.'

'He might realize who and what he is now,' Councillor Tosyne said. 'But we don't even know where he is.'

'Actually, we do,' Phelim announced. 'Colwyn City on Viotia.'

'Excellent news,' Ethan said in a predatory fashion. He watched in amusement as the protest in Tosyne's mind withered away. 'We should welcome him, and thank Viotia for the gift it has brought us.' His gaze turned expectantly on Rincenso.

'I would like to propose bringing Viotia fully into the Free Trade Zone,' Rincenso said. 'And promote it to core planet status.'

'Seconded,' Falven said.

The rest of the Cleric Council responded with bemusement.

'You can't do that,' Tosyne said. 'They'll resist, the Commonwealth Senate will move to censure us. We'll lose every diplomatic advantage we have.' He glanced round the table, seeking support.

'It's not just our ambition,' Phelim said. He gestured at the empty end of the table, opposite Ethan's dais. His u-shadow established the ultra-secure link, and a portal projected an image of Likan standing just beyond the table.

Likan bowed politely. 'Conservator, I am honoured.'

'Thank you,' Ethan said. 'I believe you are acting as an unofficial emissary for your government.'

'Yes, sir. I have just finished talking with our Prime Minister. It is her wish to accept Ellezelin's generous offer to elevate us to core world status within the Free Trade Zone.'

'That's wonderful news. I will inform Ellezelin's cabinet of your decision.'

'The acceptance comes with the understanding that a zero tariff régime will be part of the accord,' Likan said.

'Of course. Full trade will commence as soon as the Second Dreamer joins us here in Makkathran2.'

'Understood. The Prime Minister will award the treaty her certificate of office as soon as it is sent.' Likan's image vanished.

'I believe,' Ethan said into the startled silence, 'that we were about to take a vote. Those in favour?' He watched the hands being raised. It was unanimous. In moments such as this he almost missed Corrie-Lyn's presence on the Council; she would never have left such a Soviet outcome go unchallenged. 'Thank you. I find your support of my policies to be humbling. There is no further business.'

Phelim remained seating as the others filed out. Flecks of light slid across his expressionless face as the comets orbited ceaselessly overhead.

'That was easy,' Ethan remarked.

'They don't know what to do,' Phelim said. 'They're just the same as the devout gathering outside: bewildered and hurt that the Second Dreamer would reject the Skylord. They're in need of strong, positive leadership. You provide that. You have the solution. Naturally they turn to you.'

'When can we open the wormhole?'

'I'll have your government office send the treaty to Viotia's Prime Minister immediately. If Likan doesn't let us down, it'll come straight back. The wormhole can be opened within two hours. We'd prepared a number of sites for it to emerge.'

'I hope Colwyn City was one of them.'

'Yes. It has a dock complex that will serve us very nicely.'

'And our police forces?'

'Forty thousand ready for immediate dispatch, along with transport and riot suppression equipment. We can push them through within six hours of opening the wormhole. Another quarter of a million will follow over the next four days.'

'Excellent.'

'I hoped you'd approve.' Phelim hesitated. 'We never planned on the Second Dreamer becoming aware of his ability in quite this fashion. It'll take us a day to get our Dream Masters into position across Colwyn.'

'But you can shut down all capsule and starship traffic before then?'

'Yes. That's our highest priority. We want to confine him within the city boundary.' Again the uncharacteristic hesitation. 'But in order to locate him, he has to dream again. After tonight, he might not.'

Ethan closed his eyes and sank down into the throne, enervated by his exertion. 'He will. He doesn't know what he's done yet.'

'What do you mean?'

'An hour ago I received a call from Director Trachtenberg at the Centurion Station. He considered it important enough to reveal his affiliation to us and use the Navy's relay posts. Just after the Second Dreamer ended his contact with the Skylord, the Void began a devourment phase. That is not coincidence. It would seem the Skylord doesn't take rejection lightly. Our reclusive friend will have to placate it, or we'll all wind up being consumed by the boundary. Quite an incentive, really.'

Inigo's seventh dream

Edeard woke with a mild hangover. Again. Last night was the third in a row he'd been out with Macsen and Boyd.

He sat up in bed and ordered the light on. The high curving ceiling started to shine with a low cream radiance. One of his three ge-chimps hurried over with a glass of water and a small compaction of powder he'd got from Doctor Murusa's apprentice. Edeard popped the little pellet on to his tongue, and took a drink to swallow. His mind drifted back to that morning years ago in Witham where Fahin had mixed his awful concoction of a hangover cure. It was still the most effective he'd ever had. Edeard was sure the pellets were little more than placebos, providing the apprentice with a small regular source of income. He finished the water quickly. Fahin had always said water helped flush away the toxins.

The circular bath pool in the maisonette's bathroom now had a series of small steps at one end so Edeard could walk down into it. He immersed himself up to his neck, settling into the seat shelf, and sighed in gratification. A ge-chimp poured in a soap liquid which produced a lot of bubbles. He closed his eyes again, waiting for the hangover to ebb away. The water temperature was perfect, exactly body warmth. It had taken him a couple of weeks experimenting to get that right; the bathing water in Makkathran was normally quite chilly for humans. He'd also remodelled the hole in the floor which served as a toilet. Now the ubiquitous wooden box employed by every Makkathran household had gone, replaced by a simple hollow pedestal which the room had grown for him. So much easier to sit on.

Various other little modifications had turned the maisonette into quite a cosy home. The standard too-high cube-shaped bed was now a lot lower, its spongy upper surface softer and more accommodating. Alcoves had shelves in them. One deep nook in the kitchen area was permanently chilly, allowing him to keep food fresh for days just like the larger city palaces did.

That was the greatest blessing of being in the constables' tenement rather than the station dormitory. Edeard could finally choose what he ate again. Half of his first monthly pay had gone on a new iron stove to cook on. He'd installed it himself, adapting the hole the previous tenant had hacked into the wall for the flue. It had pride of place in the kitchen, along with a growing collection of pans. There was even a small basin which could be used for washing up, rather than dumping everything into the bath pool as most people did. He liked that innovation enough to consider sculpting another one in the bathroom just for his hands and face. Although that really would let everyone know he had the ability to rearrange the city's fabric, sculpting it as easily as he once had genistar eggs.

Everyone who visited the maisonette.

So, no one, then.

Macsen had brought a girl back from the theatre last night. One of the dancers! As pretty as any of the grand family girls, but with an incredibly strong, supple body. He knew that because of the revealing clothes she wore when she danced on stage. Edeard gritted his teeth and tried not to be jealous. He and Boyd had struck out again. Though overall it had been a pleasant evening. Edeard enjoyed the theatres a lot more than just sitting round in taverns getting drunk. There were often several musicians up on the stage. Always Guild apprentices. Young and with passion. Just listening to some of their songs, so full of contempt for the city authorities, made him feel wickedly disloyal to the Grand Council. But he knew the words to many of the popular ones, of which several were Dybal's compositions. It was loud in the theatres, some of which were no more than underground storerooms. He'd been startled the first time he heard drums being played, it was as if the musicians had somehow tamed thunder.

One day they'd go and see Dybal playing, so Macsen promised. Edeard hoped it would be soon.

The bubbles started to disappear from the pool as the water cycled through the narrow slits around the bottom. Edeard groaned and climbed out. A ge-chimp had a robe waiting for him. He pulled it on as he walked though into the kitchen area and sat at the small table. It was right next to a cinquefoil window, giving him a view over the rooftops towards the centre of the city.

A ge-chimp placed a glass of apple and mango juice on the table, along with a bowl of mixed oats, nuts, and dried fruit. The juice was nicely chilled; the ge-chimps knew to leave it in the cold nook for an hour before serving it. He poured milk (also cold) into the bowl and started to eat, looking out across the city as it came to life under the rising sun.

It would have been a fine life indeed if he could just stop brooding about all the lawlessness haunting the streets and canals he could see. The squad had finally managed to get some convictions in the court over the last few weeks. But nothing important; some shop thieves in their early teens, a mugger who was drunk most of the time; once the Guild of Clerks sent them out to arrest a landlord defaulting on taxes. They had no impact whatsoever on the gangs who were at the heart of Makkathran's problems.

'You ready?' Kanseen longtalked as Edeard buttoned up his tunic.

He pulled his boots on. New, costing over three days' pay – but well worth it. 'Coming.'

She was waiting on the walkway outside, an oilskin cloak slung over her arm. 'Going to rain today,' she announced.

He eyed the wide clear sky. 'If you say so.'

She grinned as they started down the awkward stairs. Every morning he was *so* tempted to sculpt them into something less dangerous – write the miracle off to the Lady.

'This'll be your first winter in the city, won't it?' she asked.

'Yes.' Edeard couldn't quite imagine Makkathran being cold and icebound, the long summer had been gloriously hot. He'd become a good football player (he considered), with his team finishing third in Jeavons' little park league. Most taverns had seats and tables outside, where many pleasant evenings had been spent. There had even been a few days when he'd started sketching again, not that he showed anyone the results. After saving up some coinage, he and Salrana had finally taken a gondola ride around the city.

'It'll be fun,' Kanseen said. 'There's loads of parties leading up to New Year. Then the Mayor throws a huge free ox-roast in Golden Park for lunch on New Year's Day – except everyone is normally so hung-over they're late. And the parks and plazas all look so clean and fresh when they're covered in snow.'

'Sounds good.'

'You'll need a thick coat. And a hat.'

'On our pay?'

'I know some shops that sell quality for reasonable prices.'

'Thanks.'

'And don't forget to get in an early supply of coal for your stove; the buildings are never quite warm enough in midwinter and the price always go through the roof after the first snowfall. The Lady will damn those merchants, it's criminal what they get away with charging.'

'You're happy this morning.'

'My sister's having her boy's naming ceremony this Saturday. She's asked me to be a nominee for the Lady.'

'Nice. What's she going to call him?'

'Dium, after the third Mayor.'

'Ah, right.'

'And you haven't got a clue who that is, have you?'

He grinned broadly. 'Nope!'

She laughed.

That was the way it was between them these days. Best friends. Any discomfiture left over from that night after the graduation had long faded. Which he was sort of pleased about. He didn't want them to be awkward round each other, but on the other hand he couldn't quite forget about that kiss, nor the way both of them had felt. He'd never quite had the courage to bring up what they'd said. Neither had she.

Which had left him wrestling with his thoughts about Salrana, who was always so sunny and generally lovely. It was now incredibly hard to ignore how feminine she'd become. And he suspected she knew that. Of late her teasing had taken on quite an edge.

The rest of the squad were waiting in the main hall at Jeavons constable station, sitting around a table finishing off their breakfast. Unlike Edeard, few of them cooked for themselves. Macsen had on a pair of glasses with very dark lenses, not too dissimilar to those Dybal wore. Kanseen took one look at him and burst out laughing. 'Were you boys out in the theatres again last night?'

Macsen grunted, and scowled at her over his cup of strong black coffee.

Edeard desperately wanted to ask him what Nanitte, the dancer, was like. It must have been a fantastic night to leave him so wrecked. But friends though they were, Kanseen didn't have much tolerance for that kind of all-boys-together talk.

'Some news for you,' Boyd hissed, checking round the rest of the hall's bench tables to make sure no one was paying attention.

'Go on,' Edeard said as he drew up a chair. There was something almost comical about Boyd's behaviour.

'My brother Isoix is being leaned on again. They came

round the shop yesterday evening as he was shutting up, and said they wanted twenty pounds to "put out the fire". They're coming back this morning to collect.'

Edeard didn't like it. Three times in the last few months Boyd had told them about gang members harassing his brother at the family bakery. There'd never been any specific threat, just warnings about falling into line. *Softening him up.* Well, now the demand had been made. 'That's very stupid of them,' he said slowly.

'What do you mean?' Dinlay asked.

'They must know Isoix's brother is a constable. Why would they risk it? There are hundreds of shops in Jeavons without that kind of connection.'

'They're gang members,' Dinlay said. 'Greedy and stupid. This time, too greedy and too stupid.'

'The ones that turn up won't be important,' Kanseen said. 'Thugs who're affiliated, that's all.'

'Are you saying we shouldn't help him?' Boyd asked hotly.

'No,' Edeard said. 'Of course not. We'll be there to make the arrest, you know that. What Kanseen is saying is that this arrest alone won't stop the problem.'

Macsen hooked a finger over his glasses and pulled them down to look out over the top of the rims. 'We've got to start somewhere,' he croaked.

'You make it sound like we're the ones who are going to break the gangs,' Kanseen said.

'Somebody has to. I don't see the Mayor or the Chief Constable doing it.'

'Oh, come on!'

He shrugged, and pushed his glasses back up. They all looked at Edeard.

'Let's go,' he said. 'And make sure you're all wearing your drosilk waistcoats. I don't want to have to explain casualties to Captain Ronark.'

Boyd's family bakery was at the northern end of Macoun Street, not far from the Outer Circle Canal. The street was narrow and twisty with baroque buildings lined up on either side, making direct observation difficult. At ground level, the sharp turns limited the squad's farsight. The three-storey bakery itself had a central square tower with a soft-ridged mansard-style roof. Tall crescent dormer windows protruded above a mid-storey balcony, while beneath that the lower floor was reached by several flowing steps from the street leading to a wide entrance arch between two curving bay windows. Each one was filled with racks of loafs and cakes. Three ugly metal chimney stacks from the coal-fired ovens rose out of holes hacked into the tower eves, blowing thin smoke into the dampening air.

Edeard positioned his squad carefully. The gang would want a fast exit route, so Macsen and Dinlay were in a shop between the bakery and the canal. Kanseen was covering the other end of Macoun Street, wandering round the stalls of a small arcade, her cloak covering her uniform; while Edeard himself settled down in the first-floor living room opposite. It belonged to a family who ran a clothing shop on the ground floor, and were close friends with Isoix. Boyd himself had returned home for the day, and was helping out in the bakery, dressing for the part in white apron and green cap. Edeard was uncertain if he should use the ge-eagle. In the end he settled for having it perch in a deep guttering furrow on the bakery's tower, almost invisible from ground level. It scared the ruugulls away, but no one else noticed it.

'At least we won't have to escort them far to the Courts of Injustice,' Macsen pointed out as they started their vigil. Edeard could actually see one of the conical towers of Parliament House through the living-room's balcony window.

They waited for two hours. Between them, they raised the alarm five times, only to be proved wrong on each occasion. 'So many citizens look so disreputable,' Kanseen declared after a couple of adolescents ran down the street after their third hands snatched up oranges from a grocery shop display. 'And act it.'

'We're all paranoid today, that's all,' Macsen longtalked back. 'We see the bad in everyone.'

'Is that a song title?' Dinlay asked.

Edeard smiled at the banter. There was a lot to be said for being squad leader. He was sitting in a comfortable arm chair, drinking tea which the wife of the shop owner kept bringing up for him. She brought a rather nice plate of biscuits each time, too. His good humour faded as the young hooligans turned a corner out of sight. Foreboding rose into his mind, strong enough to make his skin tingle. He knew that awful sensation from before. 'Oh, shit,' he whimpered.

'Edeard?' Kanseen queried.

'It's happening.'

'What is?' Macsen asked.

'They're here. It's about to start.'

'Where are they?' Boyd asked. 'Which ones?'

'I don't know,' Edeard said. 'Look, just trust me, please

be careful. I *know* we have to be.' He could sense the uncertainty in their minds, they weren't used to him saying such things. It was difficult to get to his feet, his body was reacting so badly. When he did press up against the balcony window he found it hard to concentrate on the street below.

'I think I see them,' Boyd said.

Two youngish men were walking up the steps into the shop, while a third stood outside. Through Boyd's eyes, Edeard and the rest of the squad watched them swagger into the shop. Isoix straightened up from behind the counter. 'I told you before,' he said. 'I don't have that kind of money.'

'Yes, you do,' the first man said. His gaze kept darting nervously to Boyd, who was standing at the other end of the counter from Isoix.

Wrong, Edeard knew. Why would a gang member be worried about a shop assistant?

'Boyd, he knows what you are,' Edeard sent in the most direct longtalk he could manage, praying the gang members wouldn't pick it out of the general background of Makkathran's telepathic babble.

'Huh?' Boyd grunted.

The gang member glanced at him again, then turned back to Isoix. 'Give me twenty pounds, or we'll torch this place,' he said loudly.

'No,' Edeard said. The hairs on his neck were standing proud. 'No no no.' *Wrong!*

'You,' Boyd said. He pulled his apron aside to reveal a constable's badge pinned on his waistcoat. The two gang members turned to face him.

'I am a city constable, and I am placing you under arrest for threatening behaviour with intent to extort.'

'How do you like that, you bastards?' a gloating Isoix shouted.

'Everyone, close in,' Edeard ordered. He pushed through the narrow door on to the balcony. The gang member left on the street glanced up. And smiled.

'Oh shit,' Edeard growled.

'It's him,' the gang member declared in a powerful longtalk. Then he started running.

Inside the bakery, the first gang member pulled out a small knife. He flung it at Boyd, who swayed backwards. His third hand just managed to push the blade aside. Isoix snatched up a much larger knife, and threw it at the gang members as they fled through the doorway. It whirled out into the street, narrowly missing a woman who was walking by. She screamed.

Edeard vaulted over the balcony rail and dropped to the street below. Landed badly, rolling as his ankle gave way. His shoulder smacked into one of the steps leading up to the clothing shop door. He yelled at the bright pulse of pain, tears squeezing out of his eyes.

His farsight caught Boyd leaping over the bakery counter. Kanseen was sprinting up Macoun Street, her cloak abandoned on the ground by the stalls. Macsen and Dinlay were moving out of their shop, confident and eager. Their shields combined as they stood in the middle of the street, blocking the way. All three gang members were racing towards them.

'Let them go,' Edeard ordered.

Macsen's face registered bewilderment that came close to anger. 'What?'

Edeard had regained his feet, he started to totter down the street. 'Leave them.'

'You can't be serious.' The three gang members were barely twenty yards from Macsen and Dinlay.

'It's a set-up. They knew we were here.'

'Crap,' Dinlay sent. 'I can scan them completely, they've got a couple of small blades between them. That's all.'

'There'll be more, somewhere, waiting for us. Please, just let them go, I'll track them with the ge-eagle.'

Macsen hesitated. He took a step towards the side of the street.

'No!' Dinlay hissed fiercely. He opened his arms wide as the three gang members charged towards them.

'Dinlay, stop it,' Edeard yelled. He was running now, ignoring the pain in his ankle. Kanseen wasn't far behind, charging along like a warhorse, her teeth gritted in determination. Boyd came skidding down the steps from the bakery, and took off after them.

'Stop,' Dinlay proclaimed loudly, holding out a hand as if that alone would bring the whole city to a halt. 'You are under arrest.'

'Oh crap,' Macsen growled under his breath, and instinctively started to move back towards Dinlay. They came together as the three gang members ran into them. Fists swung, legs kicked out. Third hands scrabbled and pushed. Macsen went down with one of the gang members sprawling on top of him, his head cracked against the pavement. Dinlay was shoved hard against the wall of a hat shop, flailing wildly to regain balance. Then the gang member on top of Macsen was scrabbling to his feet, and fled with his companions. Dinlay started to chase after them.

'Come back!' Edeard howled in frustration. He reached Macsen, who was struggling upright, hand clamped on the back of his head. A trickle of blood was running down his fingers.

'What do we do?' Macsen demanded, wincing against the pain.

Edeard's farsight could follow Dinlay easily enough as he ran towards the northern end of Macoun Street. The three gang members were ten yards ahead of him. 'Save him,' he growled out, furious with Dinlay. He sent a single clear thought to his ge-eagle, who immediately took flight.

Kanseen was slowing as she approached Edeard and Macsen. Her face red. Boyd was charging up behind. 'Come on,' Edeard said, and took off again. Kanseen flashed a look of exasperation, and hurried along.

'You okay?' Boyd shouted as he ran past Macsen.

'Yeah.' Macsen took a breath, and started running.

The ge-eagle streaked along Macoun Street, swiftly overtaking Edeard and Kanseen. It shot forward, rising high above the roofs, looking down to see Dinlay racing on, his glasses askew. The three gang members had almost reached the end of the street. It came out just below Birmingham Pool, where a silver-blue bridge connected Jeavons with the lower point of Golden Park. As always, Birmingham Pool was thick with gondolas. A half-dozen moorings lined the edge beside the junction with the Outer Circle Canal all host to several waiting gondolas. The ge-eagle dipped down to the moorings as Edeard tried to work out which of the glossy black craft belonged to the gang. If this was a trap, they'd have their escape well planned.

Just before it happened, the ge-eagle was aware of two other birds, close and closing. It pivoted on a wing, looking up in time to see its attacker plummeting down towards it. Another ge-eagle, bigger, with talons clad in sharpened iron spikes. The impact punched it savagely. Gold and emerald feathers burst out of the collision point. Spikes sank into its front wing shoulder, slicing through skin and muscle, severing veins. Then the bigger ge-eagle twisted to try and snap the central wing bone. Edeard's ge-eagle fought back, writhing round to clamp its jaw on its attacker's rear wing. The two of them tumbled, falling fast. Then the second attacker hit, iron-blade talons ripping into flesh. Edeard and his ge-eagle screamed as one as its wing broke. Edeard saw talons rake towards his face, and ducked. His ge-eagle's mind abruptly vanished from perception, all that was left was a falling mass. The other two ge-eagles hurtled away over Birmingham pool. Edeard was sure he heard the splash as his bird's body hit the water.

'What happened?' Kanseen cried.

'Dear Lady, they *are* waiting for us.' Edeard pulled his perception down to find Dinlay emerging from the end of Macoun Street. 'Stop! Dinlay, for the Lady's sake, I'm begging you.' He pushed his tired legs harder, sprinting for the end of the street. Thirty yards.

'I see them,' Dinlay replied gleefully. He gifted the squad, who saw the three gang members clustering above one of the moorings. They grinned barbarously. For the first time, there was a pulse of uncertainty in Dinlay's mind. He slowed to a halt, ten yards away, on the edge of the pool. Still the gang members did nothing but wait. 'Stay there,' Dinlay told them, taking big gulps of air after his helter-skelter dash, and waving a finger like an ancient schoolmaster dealing with a naughty class. They laughed at him.

Edeard burst out of Macoun Street. Directly to his left was the Outer Circle Canal, with the silver-blue bridge ahead, arching over the side of the pool directly into Golden Park. On his right, the buildings ended to provide a curving *alameda* round the side of Birmingham Pool. Neat stacks of crates were piled up above the various moorings, with shopkeepers and ge-monkeys sorting out their goods with the gondoliers. Tall weeping hasfol trees formed a long line between the edge of the pool and the *alameda*'s crescent facade, their blue and yellow tiger-stripe leaves starting to crisp with the end of summer. A lot of pedestrians were strolling around.

'Dinlay,' Edeard shouted as he ran as fast as he could towards his isolated squadmate.

Dinlay glanced round, a hand adjusting his glasses.

Arminel stepped out from behind one of the hasfol trees, fifteen yards from Dinlay. He had a revolver in his right hand. Edeard watched helplessly as Dinlay finally realized the danger, and began to turn. Arminel brought the pistol up.

'*No!*' Edeard bellowed at his adversary. 'It's me you want.'

Dinlay opened his mouth to cry out in horror.

Arminel fired. He was smiling as he pulled the trigger.

Dinlay's shield wasn't strong enough to ward off a pistol shot. Arminel's aim was excellent. The bullet struck Dinlay in the hip, just below his drosilk waistcoat. Half of the pedestrians around Birmingham Pool yelped at the blast of pain flooding out from Dinlay. Then the vile heat of the bullet's penetration faded rapidly. Dinlay looked down disbelievingly at the blood pumping out of the wound. He collapsed.

Edeard was with him in seconds, falling to his knees, skidding into his limp friend. Dinlay's eyes were wide, he was panting in short gulps, one hand clasped over the bullet hole, skin covered in blood. 'I'm sorry,' he whimpered.

A mass of screaming had broken out along the *alameda*. People were racing for cover. Families hugged each other, cowering away from the gunman.

Right in the centre of all the commotion, Edeard heard the revolver's mechanism *snick*. He widened his shield to encompass Dinlay. The bullet smacked into his side, shunting them over the rough ground. But his shield held. He snapped his head round to snarl at a disconcerted Arminel. 'Not so fucking easy, is it?' he yelled defiantly. Arminel fired again. Edeard groaned in effort as the bullet hit his neck. The shield held. *Just.* Then someone else fired a shot.

Bastards. I knew this was an ambush.

Amazingly, his shield held. If anything it was easier to maintain now. His heart was pounding hard. Anger had washed every other sensation away, making it simple to concentrate on the shield, to see his mind's power, to channel it correctly.

Two more revolver shots thudded into his shield as he lay there, arms hugging Dinlay protectively. They shunted the pair of them a few inches over the ground, but that was all.

'Die, you little shit,' Arminel shouted.

Edeard felt the man's third hand shove against him. He wasn't nearly powerful enough to get through Edeard's shielding. Edeard laughed. Then another third hand was pushing, a third. The three gang members they'd chased joined in. Edeard gasped as he and Dinlay started to slither over the ground.

'Edeard,' Kanseen cried.

'Stay back,' he commanded.

The gang members gave a final push. Edeard and Dinlay were propelled over the edge of the pool, and dropped three yards into the water. The impact broke Edeard's grip on Dinlay. He thrashed about just under the surface, trying to catch his friend again. Water occluded his farsight, making it difficult to perceive. He just made out Dinlay's wretched thoughts drifting down below him, close to extinction. His own clothes were saturated, weighing him down. It was relatively easy to swim downwards, following Dinlay's slow descent to the bottom of the pool.

'Edeard.' Dinlay's thoughts were weakening.

It was dark. Cold. Edeard could make out a shadowy mass, or maybe he was perceiving it. He pushed himself further down, kicking with boots as heavy as lead. His lungs were burning now, making every stroke painful. He would have called the city to help, but he knew it could do nothing. Water was pushing into his nostrils, scaring him.

His hand snagged something. Through the gloom he could see faint dots of light. Dinlay's polished tunic buttons! His fingers groped frantically and he got a grip on some fabric.

Now all I've got to do is get to the surface.

When he tilted his head up, he could see the silver-mirror surface. It seemed a long way above him. And his lungs didn't hurt quite so much any more. His vision was surrounded by red speckling, pulsing in time with his heart. When he kicked his legs they barely moved. His boots were pulling him down.

Oh, Lady, help.

Something knocked into his shoulder. His farsight perceived it as a slim black line.

'Edeard,' the combined longtalk of Kanseen, Macsen and Boyd shouted at him. 'Edeard, grab the pole.' They were a long way off.

The end of the punt pole thumped into his shoulder again. Edeard seized it. Abruptly he was moving upwards. It was a huge effort not to let go of Dinlay. Then the water was growing brighter.

He broke surface with an almighty gasp of air. Someone jumped in beside him, and held on to Dinlay. They were right beside a mooring platform. Hands clutched at his uniform, and he was hauled on to the planks, coughing and spluttering.

Kanseen's incredibly anxious face loomed large over him. 'Oh Lady. Edeard, are you okay?'

He nodded, which set off another bout of coughing. Hands slapped hard on his back as he rolled over on to his side, and vomited up a thin disgusting liquid.

Macsen and a couple of gondoliers were dragging Dinlay on to the platform, blood still pumping out of his hip wound. Boyd was in the water, his face pale.

'Dinlay,' Edeard called weakly.

'We've longshouted for a doctor,' Kanseen assured him. 'You just lie back.'

Edeard didn't. He watched Macsen start giving Dinlay the kiss of life. This was the third time his life had been struck by the force of anarchy and destruction. First the ambush in the forest on the way back from Witham. Then the death of Ashwell. Now this. And that was too many.

'No,' he spat. *Not again. I will not allow this to happen. People cannot live like this.*

'Edeard, sit back,' Kanseen ordered sternly.

'Where is he? Where's Arminel?'

'Stop it.'

He clambered to his feet, swaying slightly as he looked round, taking deep breaths. The edge of the pool was crowded with people, all looking down at the mooring platform. He turned towards Birmingham Pool itself. Most of the gondolas had come to a halt as the drama played out.

One was moving. Fast.

Edeard blinked the salty pool water from his eyes, sending his farsight lashing out.

Arminel was standing on the gondola's middle bench. He gave Edeard a rueful shrug, his thoughts glowing with a cheery regret. It was as if he'd lost a football game. Nothing more. Certainly nothing important. They'd play another game one day, and that time the result might be different.

Edeard's rage left him, dropping away like the water dripping off his soaking clothes. He felt eerily calm.

One of the gondoliers looking over Macsen's shoulder took a frightened step backwards.

'Edeard?' Kanseen said in a subdued voice.

He hadn't known such a thing was possible, he simply did it. There was no choice. As before, Arminel's gondola was moving too quickly. They'd never catch him, never bring him to justice. Edeard's third hand reached out to the water beside the mooring platform and steadied it.

'I'm finishing this,' he declared forcefully. 'One way or another.'

Edeard stepped on the patch of water he was controlling. An astonished gasp went up from the spectators around the edge of Birmingham Pool. Edeard grinned viciously, and took another step. Another. He moved his third hand's grip smoothly, always keeping the leading edge of the stabilized patch just ahead of himself.

Arminel's humour shattered. At the rear of the gondola, the two gondoliers stopped manoeuvring their punts and stared fearfully as Edeard walked across the pool towards them. There was absolute silence as he strode purposefully towards the craft. Every gondola in Birmingham Pool was now stationary. Gondoliers and passengers stared in awe and trepidation as Edeard walked past.

'Move!' Arminel yelled furiously at the gondoliers. 'Get us out of here.'

They didn't respond. The two gang members sitting on the bench with Arminel slowly put their hands up. They edged away from Arminel.

Edeard was ten yards away when Arminel dropped a hand to his waist where the revolver was tucked into his belt. He could sense the man's uncertainty, his fright. The animal backed into a corner. Nobody had any choices left now.

As he covered the last few yards to the gondola, Edeard opened his mind and longtalked with all his might. 'SO THAT EVERYBODY KNOWS. SO THAT NO JUDGE OR LAWYER IS IN ANY DOUBT OF THIS DAY.' And he gifted them his sight.

Makkathran, from the Mayor in his Orchard Palace down to the sailors in the port district, saw a gondola with four men cowering, hands clamped over their ears. The fifth man stood straight, loathing on his face as his hand gripped the revolver sticking out of his belt. They felt Edeard's mouth move. 'Okay gang man, your time in this city is now over. If you think different, give it your best shot.'

Arminel brought the revolver up. Makkathran en masse flinched as the muzzle steadied not two feet from Edeard's eyes.

'Fuck you,' Arminel snarled. He pulled the trigger.

The single unified scream which rang out from the city was later said to be heard halfway across the Iguru Plain. When everyone gathered their breath, and realized they were still alive, they saw the bullet. It floated motionless six inches in front of Edeard's face.

Edeard's mouth moved again, this time into a thin smile. Arminel's expression was frozen in shock.

The last of the gifting allowed Makkathran's citizens to experience Edeard shaping his third hand into a fist. He slammed it forward into Arminel's face. Bone went *crunch* as the man's nose broke. Blood spurted out. His feet left the bench as he was thrown backwards. He landed with an almighty splash in the water, which closed over him.

'You're all under arrest,' Edeard announced.

It was pandemonium on the side of Birmingham Pool as the gondola made its steady way to the mooring platform where Kanseen, Boyd and Macsen waited. On the Jeavons side they were crammed fifteen deep around the edge. Frenzied kids were running over the blue and silver bridge from Golden Park, hanging over the railings, cheering and waving. Over a hundred constables stood behind the mooring platform waiting; half of them were Dinlay's family. People were still pouring out of the surrounding districts on to the *alameda* to see history as it unfolded. Bolder lads were shinning to the top of the hasfol trees to get a better view.

Edeard walked slowly behind the gondola, praying to

the Lady that he wouldn't screw up now, that his telekinetic strength would hold out, and he didn't fall ignominiously back into the water. Out there in the crowd surrounding the pool he saw Setersis and Kavine standing in front of a big contingent of Silvarum market stall holders, leading the applause. A huge array of well-groomed family girls greeted him with shrill saucy laughter as they flashed their petticoats and bloomers. Isoix and his family were there. Evala, Nicolar, and all the girls from the dressmaker's, waving frantically and screaming to attract his attention. He even thought he saw Dybal and Bijulee laughing excitedly among the crowd, but by then he was definitely feeling tired.

The gondola's prow touched the mooring platform. Constables steadied it. Captain Ronark quickly took charge. Chae and several of the largest constables from Jeavons station handcuffed Arminel and his accomplices. A path was cleared across the *alameda*, and the prisoners marched back to the station.

Edeard finally stepped up on to the platform. His legs nearly gave out. He was trembling from exertion. Captain Ronark snapped to attention, and saluted him. Kanseen gave him a huge kiss to the delight of the crowd. 'You Lady-damned idiot,' she whispered into his ear. 'I'm so proud of you.' Macsen pounded his back. Boyd gave him a fierce hug.

'Dinlay?' Edeard asked.

'The doctors have him,' Macsen yelled about the thunderous sound of the crowd. 'He'll be okay. The bullet didn't hit anything vital. Not that he's got anything vital in that area.'

'You scared the living crap out of us,' Boyd said, wiping the tears from his eyes. 'What a stunt, you madman.'

'Look around you, Edeard,' Kanseen said. 'Make sure you see it all. This will be the day you tell your great-great-grandchildren about.'

'Wave to them, you dick,' Macsen ordered. He grabbed Edeard's hand, and held it high, waving and shouting wordlessly.

The cheer that erupted as Edeard grinned sheepishly up at the worshipful horde was scary in its power. The mental strength of so many people united in veneration was overwhelming, verging on a physical force. His grin broadened as Macsen swung him round so the other side of the *alameda* could see him.

'If there was an election today you'd be Mayor,' Boyd said.

'Listen to them,' Macsen said. 'They love you. They want you. You!' He laughed uproariously.

Edeard stared over at the blue and silver bridge, convinced the kids hanging over the railing would fall they were leaning out so far. They were chanting something. At each call, their fists punched the air in unison.

'What's that?' Edeard asked. 'What are they saying?'

'You,' Kanseen shouted back. 'They're calling for you.'

Then Edeard heard the cry in full, and laughed.

'Waterwalker,' the crowd chanted in adoration. 'Waterwalker. Waterwalker. Waterwalker.'

Timeline

1500 years between the Commonwealth Saga and the Void Trilogy

2384 First 'lifeboat' (a Brant Dynasty starship) leaves to found human colony outside Commonwealth

2384 Firewall project concluded, no further outposts of Prime aliens detected

2385 Barsoomians advocate Advancer genetic concept, declare Far Away politically independent from Commonwealth

2413 Last (23rd) original Dynasty lifeboat departs on colony-founding flight

2403 Paula Myo wins final appeal in Senate Supreme Court to have Gene Yaohui serve a 1,100-year suspension sentence

2518 End of post-Starflyer War economic recession as new47 worlds approach completion, resettlement taxes reduced

2520 CST forms starship exploration division to scout new H-congruous worlds

2520–2532	Second47 populations emerge onto their new worlds
2545 onward	Use of large starships to establish Commonwealth 'External' worlds in phase 3–5 space, extending approximately 500 ly out from Earth
2547	The Cat establishes her Knights Guardian movement on Far Away
2550	Commonwealth Navy Exploration fleet founded to explore the galaxy beyond phase 5 space
2552–3450	Contact made with 47 sentient (physical stage) species across the galaxy
2560	Commonwealth Navy ship *Endeavour* circumnavigates galaxy, captained by Wilson Kime, discovery of the Void
2603	Navy discovers 7th High Angel-type ship
2620	Raiel confirm their status as ancient galactic race who lost a war against the Void, builders of High Angel ships, which are trans-galactic arks
2652	Paula Myo arrests the Cat, riots on Far Away
2653	The Cat sentenced to 5,000 years in suspension
2833	Completion of ANA first stage on Earth. Grand Family members begin memory download into ANA rather than to SI
2856	ANA begins to contact other post-physical entities in the galaxy
2867	Sheldon Dynasty gigalife project partially successful, first human body bionomic supplements for regeneration and general iatrics

2872   Start of Higher humans, biononic supplements allowing a culture of slow-paced long life, rejection of commercial economics and old political ideologies

2880   Development of weapons biononics

2913   Earth begins absorption of 'mature' humans into ANA, the inward migration begins

2934   Knights Guardian adopt Higher biononic technology

2955   Phase one worlds now predominately Higher culture

2958   Contact with Hancher homeworld (Tochee-species) 8,640 light years away, on the other side of the Eagle Nebula (7,000 ly)

2967   First neoGuardian downloads memory into ANA

2973–3060   Commonwealth Navy helps defend Hancher homeworld against the Ocisen Empire expansion waves

2984   Formation of radical Highers who wish to convert the human race to Higher culture

2991   Establishment of the Protectorate, an anti-Higher movement, on External worlds

3001   Ozzie produces uniform neural entanglement effect, known as the gaiafield

3040   Commonwealth Navy Exploration Fleet joins Centurion Station, the Void observation project supervised by Raiel, a joint enterprise between over 30 alien species

3084 Non-incursion treaty agreed between Hancher homeworld and the Ocisen Empire

3088 Military assistance agreement inaugurated between Hancher homeworld and Commonwealth Navy, enforcing non-incursion

3120 ANA officially becomes Earth's government, planetary population fifty million (activated bodies) and falling

3150 Ellezelin settled, 420 ly from Earth, pro-cybernetic capitalist Advancer culture

3255 Radical Angel arrives on Anagaska, Inigo's conception

3290 Ellezelin opens wormhole to Tari, 15 ly away, start of Ellezelin Free Market Zone

3320 Inigo goes to Centurion star system, his first dream

3324 Inigo settles on Ellezelin, founds Living Dream movement, begins construction of Makkathran2

3338 Ellezelin opens wormhole to Idlib

3340 Ellezelin opens wormhole to Lirno

3378 Ellezelin opens wormhole to Quhood

3407 Ozzie departs Commonwealth for The Spike to build a 'galactic dream'

3456 Living Dream movement has over 5 billion followers amid the External worlds, very strong across Ellezelin Free Market Zone.

3466 Ellezelin opens wormhole to Agra (last planet to be joined to the Core of the Free Market Zone)

3478 Living Dream becomes majority party in Ellezelin parliament (72 per cent), converts planet to theocracy, Makkathran2 becomes the planetary capital

3503 Gene Yaohui comes out of suspension, re-lifed in new Advancer/Higher body, settles on Tourakom at the boundary of External space, 520 ly from Earth

3520 Inigo 'rests' from public life, Cleric Council assumes guidance of Living Dream

3587 Fragments of Second Dream appear in the gaianet

3589 Ethan elected as Cleric Conservator, announces Pilgrimage